THE INTERLAND SERIES

BOOKS #1, #2, AND #3

GARY CLARK

THE GIVEN

INTERLAND SERIES BOOK #1

For Jude

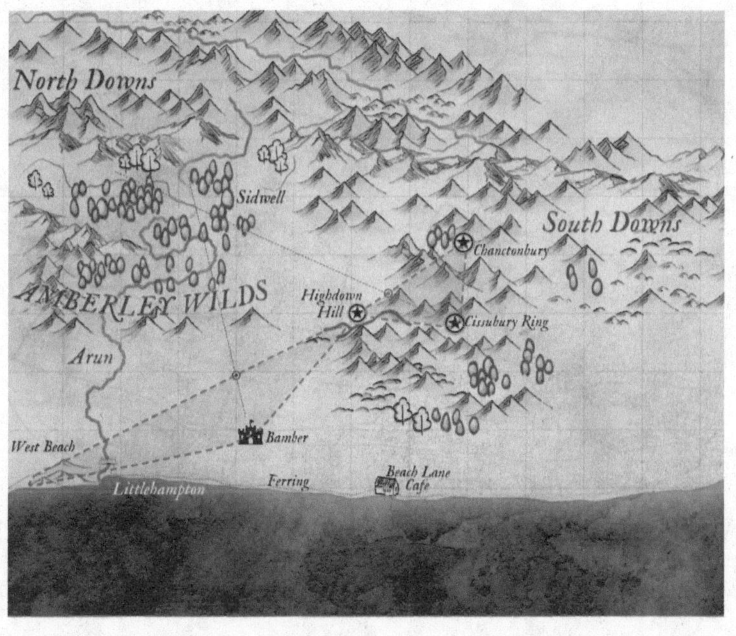

North Downs
South Downs
Sidwell
Chanctonbury
AMBERLEY WILDS
Highdown Hill
Cissubury Ring
Arun
West Beach
Bamber
Littlehampton
Ferring
Beach Lane Cafe

PROLOGUE

Listen. I'll tell you a story. When I was a boy, a young and handsome adventurer, I embarked on a quest through the Amberley Wilds. I was drawn to uncover the myth of the Interland. I was chasing a dream, a vision of a place in legend that had lodged in my mind. It took hold of me and wouldn't let go.

The Wilds are so thick that they're impossible to navigate in any meaningful sense – you have to just feel your way. My grandmother used to say that the only way to get through the Wilds is to connect with the energy of Nature, and then flow with it – push in the same direction, don't resist it.

So I pressed bravely through the thick undergrowth, seeking my connection. Brambles tore my skin and mosquitos raised welts in my neck. Doubt crept in as I grew cold, hungry, and scared. But something pushed me on and sometime before dusk I stumbled into a clearing on the bankside where the river widened onto a flood plain.

I felt a charge in the air. Dusk drew in, and a thin mist hung over the river. The smooth surface of the water stood black and still like a painting. Poppies in the fields waved in the breeze, scenting *the air. A wooden raft, its logs tied with vine, stuck lodged against the bank like an invitation. I climbed aboard.*

After a few minutes drifting through fog, the river narrowed, and I picked up speed. With the wind in my face, the current took me straight to a sheer face of rock, where the river disappeared into a cave.

The gateway to the Interland is where the three rivers of the Wilds meet, converging at a magical pool, an oasis of energy at the heart of the wilderness. The charge was electric as I passed through the hill, a tunnel of rock, and into the pool - the Gateway - where an intricate beehive of caves stretched deep into the earth. I was mesmerised. I felt the energy in the ground, the stone walls, and the Wilds. But more than that, I was a part of it - that delicate interdependence between us and our environment. I was at one with Nature. For the first time in my life, I was free.

PART I

RESISTANCE

1

Jay sat cross-legged on the roof where the sloping tiles connected with the house next door. She gazed across the fields towards the hills of Devil's Dyke. The wind off the sea gave a vicious whip as it rose over the sand and through the Beach Lane housing estate, and Jay sensed frustration in the air. Something was coming. She closed her book, stifling the wind-ruffled pages.

'Jay!' Her dad's voice from downstairs. He called again, his tone more urgent. She climbed through the Velux window to her room. Over her shoulder she glimpsed the flickering light of a fire up on Highdown Hill and she paused for a moment to watch. Her dad called again, and she turned to head downstairs.

Jay avoided the kitchen and made straight for the dining room where her brother Sammy was laying the table. He rolled his eyes at the noise coming through the wall. Jay took four place mats from the cupboard and arranged them on the table. 'What now?'

'Same as always,' said Sammy.

'Anything and everything?'

'Exactly.'

Their mum, Sonia, was *challenged*, to use the words of Jay's best friend, Stitch. She struggled to exist in the world. She was bitter, jealous of everyone. She made Jay feel like she and her brother had done her a terrible injustice just by existing in the world; it was a powerless feeling. Sonia used to drink, not much, but it only took a single glass of wine to bring on her aggression. It wasn't that she threw fists or anything. She would stalk around the house seeking out someone to find fault with. Jay and Sammy learned to stay out of sight, tiptoe, avoid attention.

'Here we are,' Jay's dad, Ben, said as he entered the dining room, placing two bowls of spaghetti bolognese on the table.

Sonia flicked on the television on the sideboard and waved her hand for Ben to shift up so that she could take her favourite seat. Ben shuffled up next to Jay, giving her a wink. Back when she and Sammy were small, when her powers were beginning to surface and life was confusing enough, their parents' arguments scared and confused her. Not so much now. She'd turned 18 last month, and that magic number made her suddenly feel immune to the conflict in the house.

Their arguments took Jay back to one day in particular. She was nine years old, and Sammy was seven. Her parents were arguing, her dad trying to keep his voice down, unaware that kids hear everything no matter how quietly parents speak. They wanted to watch the TV, but the signal was intermittent, so Jay sat next to it and wiggled the aerial to get the picture to settle. That was when she heard her dad's muttering and turned to ask him to be quiet, only to see that his lips were sealed. Yet his words continued. *I won't rise to it. Not this time. I won't let her wind me up. It's not my fault you're like this.*

Then she heard her mum, swearing, bristling with anger, the words pinging around her head like angry bees. Jay screamed and clamped her hands to her ears. She ran upstairs to her loft bedroom where she leaned out of the big Velux window and gulped the fresh sea air. She tried to focus, to read her dad's thoughts again, but couldn't figure the mechanism. She even tried a metal coat hanger from her wardrobe and held it in the air, twisting it around. When her dad came to her room a moment later, she looked him in the eye, trying to read him.

A picture formed in Jay's mind, a simple image of feeling – a sense of warmth and concern. Oranges and greens, swirls, curves and waves of colour. Her dad stood in her room frowning at her, but before he said any words the colours changed and she saw that he knew about the power. He had it too.

'Keep it to yourself,' he whispered.

'It's beautiful!' Jay said.

'Yes, it is. It's a gift. But you have to be careful.' He put a finger to his lips.

Sonia's raised voice dragged Jay from her memory. 'Give it a bash,' her mum shouted at Ben, frustrated at the quality of the picture on the television.

'It doesn't help by hitting it,' Ben replied as he tried to keep from raising his voice. Sammy stiffened and Jay caught his eye and tried to reassure him with a stiff smile.

'Then use your powers, see if they'll fix the TV, if they're good for anything useful,' Sonia said, forking spaghetti into her mouth. Ben stopped and looked at her. Then at Sammy. He'd not spoken to Sammy about the powers, only Jay. Sammy knew of course, it just wasn't something that anyone brought up in conversation. 'What?' Sonia asked, mocking innocence.

'Don't,' said Ben.

'I just can't see the point if you don't use them for the benefit of the family,' she said. 'They're pathetic. Can they pay the mortgage? Fix the car? The TV? No. What a waste. Thank god no one else in this family has been blessed with this "power".' She flashed air quotes as she said the word 'power', drawing out the word with a sneer.

Ben lowered his head, staring into his dinner. Sammy stood to fiddle with the aerial on the TV, turning it until the picture improved. Sonia laughed, 'There you go, Ben. That's *power*. Thanks Sammy, love.'

The room was cold, and though filled with people it felt hollow and empty.

Jay looked at the television as she swallowed her dinner as fast as possible. On the screen, a news reporter, on location, shouted to be heard above a chanting crowd. Sonia mumbled something about the unnecessary protest developing. The BBC News programme was following an escalating crisis outside Downing Street.

'That's a lot of people,' said Jay, a slight shiver at the thought of being stuck in the middle of such a crowd, unable to move.

'Thousands,' said Ben. 'They've been gathering all day. They marched through St James's Park and now they're massing all along Whitehall by the looks of it.'

'What are they protesting?' asked Sammy.

'Nothing better to do,' Sonia said, without looking up, but Jay could see that this was no ordinary protest. A tiny spark of static passed between Jay and her dad – his anticipation meeting with her own.

The police had gathered in numbers behind the gates that sealed off the approach to the Prime Minister's residence. On the other side of the gate was a crowd of angry looking protesters. Jay leaned closer to the television. The aggression in the faces of the protesters unsettled her. A group of police on horseback moved up Whitehall.

'Who's that?' said Jay, motioning towards a striking-looking woman caught on camera at the front of the crowd. The way the crowd moved around her it was clear she was important. She punched the air and then pointed and shouted at the police on the front line at the other side of the gates. 'She's angry.'

'That's Zadie Lawrence,' said Ben, almost a whisper. Jay had heard Zadie's name before. She was a defender of the rights of the gifted. The BBC camera remained focused on Zadie Lawrence as she railed at the police, barring the way through to Downing Street. Jay saw the energy flow from her, shooting from her body like flares. Her passion caught Jay's breath. It sparked something inside of her. She put a hand on her dad's arm, 'We're on her side, right?'

'No,' snapped Sonia.

'Why not?' Ben said. 'She speaks for the oppressed. All kinds of oppressed, not just the Given.'

'She's an extremist,' said Sonia. Jay sensed her dad's pulse quicken, then ease as he took a deep breath. His colours were mixed.

The cameras scanned the protesters. A woman in a red dress with long dreadlocks blew a whistle as she bounced up and down in the crowd. A man held a sign that said *Diversity is Power*. Four young men pushed a police officer who held up his plastic riot shield. Amongst the chaos stood Zadie Lawrence, her arms folded, her eyes nearly closed. Her face was still, an image of peace. While the BBC journalist estimated crowd size, the camera stayed on Zadie.

Suddenly, the line of police guarding Downing Street dropped their shields and began to step backwards. Their arms hung slack, their heads drooped forward. They shuffled until they had revealed the entrance to Downing Street, unguarded. The commentator fell silent as the crowd surged, pouring through the gate and on towards Number Ten. There were more police on horseback, and teams in riot gear with shields and batons. They manoeuvred around the protestors, their shields forming a wall.

Jay sensed the atmosphere as if she were there in person. Aggression hung in the air like a flammable gas cloud waiting for a spark. Ben stood to get closer to the television, leaving his food at the table.

Two police officers at the fringe of the main protest beat a man with their batons as he tried to get away. A police horse barged another into the side of a building, before collapsing on the floor. The camera returned to Zadie Lawrence as she was approached by a line of police.

Jay saw Zadie's colours turn black. 'Dad?' Jay said, her voice trembling. Ben reached across the table and took her hand.

The riot police led a tall man dressed all in black towards Zadie. 'What's happening?' said Jay. 'I don't like this.'

As the police reached Zadie, two of them launched at her with their batons. She went down after the first blow but they continued to beat her. Jay wanted to avert her eyes but couldn't. When the police stopped hitting Zadie, the plain-clothed man approached, crouched and seemed to whisper something in her ear before drawing back. He was doing something to Zadie Lawrence; a dark terrible energy passed from him through her, reducing her in front of the cameras on national television.

Ben looked at Jay, his mouth open and disbelief in his eyes, then back to the screen as Zadie writhed on the floor, her hands clasped to the sides of her head. The man in black stood and nodded to the police officers who reached and pulled Zadie up, dragging her away by her arms, her legs dragging lifelessly along the floor behind her.

Jay glanced at her dad, his eyes fixed on the television, anguish in his expression like she'd never seen before. She turned back to the television as Zadie Lawrence was pushed towards the back of a police van. She'd regained consciousness but was unable to stand.

Just before they pushed her into the van, Zadie Lawrence turned, blood pouring down the side of her face, and looked squarely into the television camera. Jay's world stopped. She felt a bolt of energy and resolve course through her. It was like Zadie Lawrence had looked directly into Jay's mind.

2

It was the last day of term. Exams had finished and Jay sat in her classroom observing her classmates as though they were primates in a zoo enclosure. Tick by slow tick the clock wound down the seconds until the end of the day. She glanced at the door. Mr Sparks was late. Any minute now people would begin walking out. She turned to Cassie. 'We could leave?'

Cassie flicked her beaded braids out of her eyes. 'What about *him*?' she said. She nodded at Stitch, exchanging banter with the football gang. Every once in a while Stitch would forget that he wasn't the same species as those boys.

Jay shrugged. 'Take him with us?'

Two of the boys from the football team, Jason and Gavin, were becoming agitated with Stitch. They were edgy, hacked off at being inside, nowhere to run around and get rid of their pent up energy.

Jay checked her wrist for the tenth time that day. Nothing. Not even a smudge of a mark. She'd turned eighteen over a week ago and still, no mark.

'Nothing?' said Cassie.

Jay shook her head. 'Nope. You?'

'Nah,' Cassie shrugged but neither of them were surprised about that. Neither Stitch nor Cassie expected anything since they'd not sensed any power. In fact, no one they knew in their class had a mark. Stitch would have loved to have some level of power, even just a level *one* appearing on his wrist would make his year.

Still no sign of Mr Sparks, and now Jason and Gavin looked like they were about to get more serious. Jay eyed them nervously and packed her books into her bag. 'We should go.'

'Might be too late.' Cassie stood. Two of the other football boys had joined in, heckling Stitch and tossing his notebook back and forth over his head. Stitch turned and gave Jay and Cassie a look that clearly said *help me out here, OK?*

Cassie took a step towards Stitch, but Jay put a hand on her arm. Cassie had a brown belt; Jay knew she was more than capable of dealing with a handful of boys. 'Wait a minute. There's something I want to try.'

Jay leaned back in her chair. She closed her eyes, tuning in to Stitch. Focusing had been coming much more naturally to her, but she still had to work at it. With a deep breath she entered her friend's mind. She saw that his outward calm betrayed an inner fear. His pulse raced. She sensed the heat on the surface of his skin, the invisible tears forming in the corners of his eyes, his pain. He wanted to walk away but couldn't find the courage to move.

Jay opened her eyes and looked to Cassie. 'He needs a little help,' she said. Cassie made to stand again but Jay shook her head. 'Let me do it.'

Jason was the most aggressive of the four boys circling Stitch. He kept bouncing up on his toes, puffing his chest out. Jay glanced around the room to make sure no one was looking, then closed her eyes once more to focus in on Jason. His mind was a wide-open and empty space, the colours barely visible before his thoughts streamed through without resistance. He felt excitement mixed with anxiety. As he laughed with his friends at Stitch's expense he felt fear and doubt. Jay left his conscious mind, pushing and prodding a channel into Jason's subconscious, diving into his instincts, his reflexes.

As Jay crept around the edge of Jason's unconscious mind, he kicked out at Stitch's foot like he was warming himself up, testing the water. Cassie twitched in her seat, itching to jump up and defend her friend. But she waited. Jason's aggression came through stronger to Jay, sweeping over her as a mix of excitement and fear. He was preparing to impress his friends. The layers of emotion in Jason revealed a vulnerability and opened a door for Jay. She pierced the outer shell of his consciousness and felt a flash of pride. This was the first time she'd managed this with such clarity. The colours and words came like a burst dam, too much for Jay at first as she rocked back in her chair with the force of it. The stream settled to a steady flow, and the colours merged to a thick, sludgy brown.

She filtered and guided Jason's energy, pushing her own influence into his mind, eventually finding what she was searching for, what she thought might be possible but had never before achieved. Then she squeezed and pushed.

Jay opened her eyes and saw Jason step back from Stitch, almost as if fearing him. He looked down at himself to see a dark patch appear at the front of his trousers. His jaw dropped as the patch spread and stretched down his leg. Jay stared, disbelieving. Cassie gave Jay a sideways look, wide-eyed. Jason's friends backed away from him, their mouths open. A smattering of laughter rose from the class as more people noticed. Then the entire class erupted. People stood and pointed before Jason ran from the room.

Jay and Cassie joined Stitch at the doorway.

'Was that you?' asked Stitch, his face beaming with unfailing devotion.

'I wasn't sure I'd be able to do that,' Jay said. She searched Stitch's reaction for any hint of shame, of disappointment in her for taking it too far. She got nothing. Just usual Stitch, adoring. 'Bit of a moment for me, that was,' she said with a smile.

'Couldn't have happened to a nicer bloke,' said Stitch.

'I didn't know that was possible,' said Cassie.

Jay shrugged. 'Nor me.'

Out front, Jay stopped for a moment and stood at the gates with her back to the college building. On the chalk Downs in the distance, the ring of trees on the ancient hill at Chanctonbury was visible and she could sense the energy. It came in pulses, like a heartbeat. With a little focus, the energy was visible, flowing in waves of colour over the hills towards them and spinning off into the trees and the sky.

'Can you feel it?' said Cassie, standing tall at Jay's side.

'What?' said Stitch.

'Freedom,' said Cassie, grinning. 'No more college.'

She skipped ahead. Jay and Stitch followed and the three friends headed towards Jay's house, away from college for the last time. Stitch reached into the inside pocket of his trademark Oxfam suit jacket and pulled out a packet of tailormade cigarettes, not his usual rolling tobacco.

'Special occasion?' said Jay.

Stitch grinned and planted a cigarette between his teeth. 'After that performance with Jason.'

'I've been feeling it,' said Jay, 'especially since my eighteenth. The power is growing, you know?'

'Nope,' said Stitch, catching her eye as he lit his cigarette. He could read her. As far as Jay could tell, he had no power, except that he had an intuition with her. Most would see it as nothing more than expected between two people who'd been friends for years, but Jay sensed he had something more.

'What's up?' asked Stitch. 'You seem... unsettled.'

Since she'd woken that morning, the air smelled acidic. The wind in the trees sounded ragged. Jay pulled back her sleeve to look for a sign – a smudge, a smear of darkness, anything. Stitch smiled and pulled back his own sleeve to expose bare skin. Jay threw an arm around Stitch's shoulder and took a last look up at the view of Chanctonbury before they turned the corner and into South Street.

3
***

Jay led her friends to the little bookshop on the corner. Cassie and Stitch both groaned as she made for the door. 'Five minutes,' she said with pleading eyes as she backed in through the door, the bell ringing to alert Alf Harvey to their arrival.

Stitch headed straight to the back room, to sci-fi and fantasy, Cassie following. Jay pulled a book from her bag to return. Alf looked at her over his glasses, a half smile that left creases around his eyes. He picked up the book, read its title, then slipped it beneath the counter.

The bookshop was formed of two town houses knocked together, the top floor a long loft room dedicated to non-fiction. Jay found a table in her favourite quiet corner with the window overlooking the high street. She dumped her bag and jumper and made her way to the rows of shelves allocated to the Given, breathing in the comforting musty smell of the older books as she slipped through the aisles.

The books and records may have been selective, but they were at least free of the sometimes-twisted perspective that came through the television. Books on the Given weren't normally available for loans, and people had to sign in just to read some of them, but Alf never bothered with Jay. He barely even spoke to her. She sensed he might have power, but it was weak, or he was good at shielding. She figured it was best if she kept her distance from him, and he seemed to be content to allow Jay access to the books she wanted without bothering her. He sometimes even let her take books home.

She made straight for the big encyclopaedias on the bottom shelf. These were the oldest reference books on the Given and not available for open access. She carried two volumes back to her table, then returned to the shelves to pick up an autobiography she'd been dipping into on recent visits.

Sasha Colden was the first Given with significant abilities publicly recognised. Her power had been strong. She had more than the ability to *read* minds, she could also influence and control actions by planting thoughts and suggestions. It was Colden's book that seeded the idea in Jay to dig into the subconscious. Sasha had died before she reached her 40th birthday. Jay couldn't find out how she died, but she wasn't surprised. People with power sometimes simply disappeared.

There was a subtext to Sasha's book that Jay was tuning into. On the surface, the pages depicted a life of discovery, of the dangers and opportunities inherent in power, of a life in the public eye, as the first celebrity Given. Sasha was a woman with two lives. Her private family life was not in the pages of her book. Even her actual name was unknown, only her public persona as Colden.

Sasha's openness had encouraged others to self-declare, to join in the growing excitement around the possibilities of life with powers. But in between the lines of her story, another story was hidden.

There was a creak on the stairs. Jay glanced up to catch Alf Harvey staring at her. They held eye contact for a moment before he looked away, then mounted the final stair before turning to flick through records in the filing cabinet next to the stairwell. Alf often came up to the top floor when Jay was there, and more than once Jay felt that he was keeping an eye on her. Jay picked a couple of books at random from the nearest shelf, the authorised books, and placed them over the encyclopaedias.

She closed the Sasha Colden book and pulled one of the old encyclopaedias towards her, careful to position the other books so Alf Harvey wouldn't see what she was reading. She opened the encyclopaedia at a page she'd bookmarked before, on the modern history of the powers. This was the period before she was born, before the world turned against the Given. Powers had been suspected for centuries, but only verified through tests for the first time less than fifty years ago. People with powers had been treated like royalty back then, holding positions of influence all over the world.

Jay felt the bookseller's presence before he spoke. 'Up here again?' he said.

Jay flinched. They'd never made chit chat before. She looked up at him. Colours seeped from the man like visible gas leaking from the crevices in a rock face. His tones were smooth, his colours neutral, revealing nothing of his intentions. Jay could spot danger in the darkness of people's colours, or openness in the yellows and greens. With Alf Harvey, the colours were a mixture, almost as if he were consciously concealing. And there was something more. The wisps of colour were constrained like she'd not seen before. Most people's colours presented to Jay without ambiguity, but Alfred's flowed for a moment and then disappeared as if sucked up with a powerful vacuum cleaner. The colours were gone before any words could come that Jay could read.

He was an effective shielder. She'd never seen anyone hide

so completely. He left no cracks, nothing but a smooth deflection. Her attempts to read him revealed nothing, and he knew it. She locked eyes with him again and he gave a satisfied, crooked smile that sent a shiver through her bones.

Alf Harvey glanced over his shoulder towards the stairs. 'You need to be careful. Especially in here,' he said.

The muscles in Jay's body tightened, 'Sorry, Mr Harvey,' she said, her voice weak. She gathered her things, closing the encyclopaedia and concealing it with another book. She stood to leave. He knew too much. She had done everything her dad had taught her not to do – she'd been careless.

He took the seat opposite her. 'Hold on, dear. It's OK. And call me Alf.' The soft tone of his voice dispersed some tension in Jay. She stopped packing her things and looked around the room. They were alone.

'It's easy enough to tell by your reading what your interests are,' he said.

Jay shrugged.

'How long have you known?'

'Known what?' Jay said. Alf smiled, and they were silent for a minute.

'OK,' Jay said, 'so what if I have it?' The tightness in her muscles returned. But she wanted to talk, wanted *him* to talk. With a mix of fear and excitement she ached to speak about the powers with someone who understood. She'd talked to Stitch, of course, her best friend since they were small, and to Cassie. Stitch knew all about the Given, the legend and the powers, but not from the inside, not from feeling it, only from studying it.

Alf settled in his seat. 'You need to be careful. We have Scanners who come in here most days, trying to weed out the resistance.'

'What resistance?' Jay asked. She'd heard of the Scanners

before, a word used for people with power who worked for the State, scanning to detect other people illegally using their abilities.

Alf smiled. 'Just keep your head down. Things are a little hotter than usual at the moment, since the protest.'

He turned at the sound of footsteps to see Cassie and Stitch emerge from the stairwell. He stood. 'I'd better head back down, remember what I said.'

4

———

Into the Beach Lane estate, Stitch lagged behind as Cassie quizzed Jay on why she'd been speaking to Alf.

'You know he's senile, right?' Cassie said.

'He's not, he's OK,' said Jay.

'He talks in riddles,' said Cassie.

They crossed the road and almost bumped into a group of boys walking in the opposite direction. Cassie turned and ran after them.

'Cassie...' said Jay. But she'd already caught up with the tallest of the three boys and spun him around. The boy turned and stared at her.

'Sorry.' Cassie dropped her head and ran back to Jay and Stitch.

For a moment no one spoke. Then Stitch asked quietly, 'You thought it was Reuben?'

Cassie sighed.

'You still think about him a lot, huh?' Jay said, gently.

Cassie shrugged. 'That bloke just looked so...' She trailed off.

Jay linked her arm in Cassie's. 'Still gets to you?' she said.

Cassie nodded. 'Just when I think I've got him out of my system, something like that happens.'

'Where did he go? You never told us.'

Cassie looked down at Jay, smiling. 'All I know is what my grandad said, that his family moved away, up north. He knew Reuben's parents. Then we lost Grandad too, so I never had time to ask him about it. But moving away is not a reason to go completely dark. Not a word. No letter, nothing.'

* * *

JAY PUSHED OPEN her front door. When Stitch saw Sammy he held up a hand for a high five. Jay's little brother was just sixteen and already stood a good six inches taller than Jay. He'd always been tall, came out of the womb all gangly and awkward.

Sammy's cheeks flushed as Cassie enveloped him in a hug. Jay wasn't sure if there was a chemistry between them or if it was just Cassie's sheer beauty that knocked her little brother off kilter. Cassie gave him a wink as she pulled away and ruffled his hair.

Jay looked up at her brother. 'We're going up, come if you want?'

Sammy glanced at Cassie and hesitated a moment before he said, 'I'm out, meeting the others, last day and all that. We have some celebrating to do.' He grinned. Jay figured they'd be marking the end of school by working their way through a few cans down on the beach.

The presence of her friends filled Jay's small loft bedroom. Posters on the walls overlapped where she'd bought new ones and not bothered to remove the old. Her dad's old hi-fi separates had made their way into her room, topped by his turntable now in pride of place. Stitch sat in his favourite spot on the floor under the big Velux window and took out his cigarettes. Cassie picked out a few records and passed them to Stitch.

Stitch said, 'So what did Alf have to say?'

'He has power, did you know that?'

Cassie snorted. 'Crazy old man.'

Stitch looked up at Jay. 'He always shows a weird interest in you. He didn't sense your power?'

Jay's head told her to be careful around Alf, like her dad would say, but her heart told her that he was OK, and curiosity said that she'd need to see him again. 'No, I think my secret is safe for now.'

The three friends listened to records and talked about summer plans – debating if they could afford to take the summer without having to find work. Stitch wanted to camp out, live cheap in the hills and woods of the Downs. 'We don't need money,' he said.

'Why camping?' said Cassie. 'We need to *do* something, no point in sitting around on a hill waiting for something to happen.' Stitch opened his mouth to argue then seemed to think better of it.

'We've only just got out of college, what's the rush?' Jay said. Her first thoughts were for exploring her developing power, but in a way that didn't draw attention. Her dad would not be impressed if he sensed her power dispersing into the environment, but she yearned to let it loose. She wondered how long she could even contain it. She looked again at her wrist.

Stitch noticed. 'You need to cut down on wrist inspections. It'll drive you mad. Give it time.'

Cassie stood. 'If you two are getting into spiritual talk again, I'll be off.'

'Tomorrow then?' said Jay. 'We can hang at the beach?'

Cassie nodded and slipped out through the Velux window and onto the roof, from where she'd jump down the side, onto the wall by the tree and into the alleyway that led around to her house.

* * *

IT WAS DARK. Spent record sleeves scattered the bed and floor. Stitch made himself comfortable on the bed next to Jay, their backs up against the wall. He was still wearing his suit jacket. He huffed to himself, 'She always bails out when we talk about the powers.'

Jay knew it too. Cassie would switch off if Stitch talked about the energy of the land – the ley lines and the hill forts.

Stitch smiled at Jay and said, 'What's on your mind?'

'Can't you read?'

'Not today. Can't see anything in there, reckon you're hiding something.'

'You remember the legend that my dad used to talk about?'

Stitch nodded. 'The Interland? I loved those stories. My favourite bit of sleepovers.'

Jay remembered how Stitch's eyes would widen and he'd grow silent as soon as her dad began talking. 'We always thought that they were just his stories. Now I'm not so sure. I think there's more to it.'

'What are you getting at?' said Stitch.

'I don't know. This place. It's all connected. The Downs, the ley lines, the hill forts. And maybe the Interland.'

'Probably, but why are you thinking about all this now?'

'Last night. When I got back. I sat out on the roof with Sammy for a while. When he went to bed I opened up a bit.'

'What did you see?'

Jay couldn't remember much. There was something, some

activity, more than the usual whispers that she would often hear at night. There was a human connection, something dark, and it left a bitter taste. She must have dropped off to sleep then, her head resting on the roof tiles, because a while later she woke to whispers from the south, from the sea. She'd opened to the sea before, many times. It was like lowering a microphone beneath its surface and eavesdropping on the millions of tiny interactions. Not words. Not even thoughts, but communication, meaning, and feeling. Whispers turned to white noise at first. Then she would try to filter, collect the patterns and tune in to the different threads. But they evaded her, like trying to catch fish with her hands.

'Did you know that fish feel love?' said Jay.

Stitch snorted. 'What?'

'Fish.'

'I thought their brains were so small that their memory span was, like, a few seconds.'

'That's crap. They love deeper than we do.'

'Good to know,' said Stitch.

Back when they were sixteen, on a night much like this one, Jay and Stitch slept together. They'd been friends since they were babies – he was like family. They talked about everything together and this evening they got onto the subject of sex. Neither of them had been with anyone yet. One minute they were laughing and joking about it and the next they were kissing and undressing each other. He stayed over that night. Not like his usual sleepovers when they slept in their clothes, top to tail. On that night they slept with their heads on the same pillow. The first time was supposed to be rubbish, but this first time didn't follow that rule. Jay had connected with Stitch. Deeply. The next day they both kind of agreed, without words, that they'd keep the night to themselves.

'So it's worms *and* fish now?' said Stitch, nodding towards the glass-fronted worm farm that took up a quarter of the far wall. It looked like a grand tropical fish tank except filled with layers of composting material and hundreds of worms.

'Worms are far more callous,' said Jay, smiling. 'Very single-minded, determined little buggers. Not as romantic as fish.'

Stitch laughed and leaned in to Jay so that his head rested on her shoulder. She leaned back into him, resting her own head on top of his. She could smell his hair wax, a fresh, herby scent that was so familiar to her it was like it was her own.

'Sammy ate one once,' said Jay.

'What?' said Stitch.

'A worm. He was about three years old. I was five or six. I came in here and he had one hanging out of his mouth. I pulled the end but the other end was lodged down his throat and it broke in half.'

Stitch laughed. 'My dad would've taken me to hospital for a stomach pump.'

Jay leaned over to lie back on her bed. 'How is your dad?' she asked. Since Stitch's mum had died, back when Stitch was eleven or twelve, his dad had been a little off-piste. He'd thrown himself into his faith and seemed intent on blocking out Stitch.

'No change in his condition, as they say in the ICU.'

'Not sure religion is a condition.'

'Depends on your perspective.' Stitch yawned and squeezed himself under Jay's covers, fully clothed, so they were top-to-tail.

'Tomorrow,' said Jay. 'What do you think we should do?'

Stitch's breathing deepened and slowed. 'Night then, Stitch.'

Jay cleared away the record sleeves. She found her dad's *Neil Young* LP, pulled it from its sleeve and lowered it onto the turntable before squeezing back under her covers. Beyond her window a light blinked on the horizon, a bonfire up at High-down. She turned the volume dial on her stereo until Neil Young's voice was low enough not to keep her awake, but loud enough to distract her from her racing thoughts. She lay back on her bed and closed her eyes.

5

A week into summer and still no decisions made. Stitch hadn't been around, saying that he was trying to spend some time at home with his dad. Cassie was fickle as ever, turning up in the middle of the night once, then disappearing for days.

In the lounge, Sammy flicked at the buttons to cycle through the four available channels on the television while Jay read her book, or at least trained her eyes on the words. Ben rested on the sofa, his newspaper balanced on his knee. Sammy's channel-hopping grated on Jay's nerves and her mind wandered. The newspapers said Zadie Lawrence had been imprisoned, but her dad said that he'd heard she'd been killed, along with many others. Jay felt waves of despair and anger that she didn't fully understand, that pulled at her insides.

Sammy gave up flicking through channels. The News programme reported on the success of the government's "home-fires" initiative, their drive to "get back to the roots of British society". Jay watched as Ben's colours darkened. She could feel him worrying that the rising tension and crusade against the Given meant more scrutiny, more chance Jay would be detected.

Jay stood. The room felt too close. The thoughts banging around in her head were too loud. She made for the kitchen and put the kettle on. Ben followed. 'Hey,' he said, 'can you see what's happening?'

'They won't find us,' Jay said.

'They're turning everyone against us, we can't stop it. You heard what they were saying about the Given taking positions of influence, jumping the queues, taking people's jobs. That's the kind of thing that makes people angry.' Ben paced, tapping his fingers along the counter in agitation. 'It's time you understood this.'

'But none of it is true,' Jay said as the kettle boiled.

'It doesn't matter what's true. Jay. Listen. You need to bury it deeper. I've sensed you out on that roof, and if I can see your power, others can too.'

Jay lowered her gaze, unable to maintain eye contact. 'It's not right,' she said, 'the Given have the same rights...'

'The Given don't exist anymore. They've been...'

'*They*?' Jay shouted. 'You mean *us*.'

Jay's dad spoke slowly and deliberately, 'Like I was saying, *they* don't exist. The Given are consigned to history. Imprisoned. Killed. On the run. It's different now; it's not just frowned upon, the powers are illegal. And it's not just here, it's the same in Europe. There have been televised executions in America.'

The kettle clicked off and the bubbling subsided. The room filled with silence. Jay wouldn't allow herself to cry. Nothing useful could come from crying. Yet, tears prickled in the corners of her eyes. 'It's not right...' was all she could say.

Her dad continued, 'They're not stopping at people who

use their power. They're taking anyone that *has* power, whether they're using it or not.'

'Why?'

Ben pulled back his sleeve to show the number two on the inside of his wrist – one of the few times Jay had seen it. 'It's not like we can hide these if someone wants to look. If you give them a reason to come, it's over.' He held her shoulders, 'Do you understand, Jay?'

For the first time in her life, Jay wanted to slap her dad across the face. She was sure that if he referred to the Given as "they" one more time then she wouldn't be able to help herself. Jay wondered again what level she would be, what number would appear on her wrist.

Ben looked over at her wrist. 'Anything showing yet?'

Jay pulled up her left sleeve and shook her head.

'Soon,' he said, sadness passing across his face.

'This crackdown doesn't make sense,' said Jay.

Ben sighed. 'Jake down the club told me that they're recruiting for Readers.' He glanced at Jay. She raised her eyebrows at him and he continued, 'Not the recruitment you might imagine. More of a forced enrolment where the alternative...' He paused. 'Rehab. The *Sub Levels*.'

'So they want high-level recruits? Not like you, and me?'

'Maybe,' Ben said, seeming to sink further into himself. 'There aren't many at the top end though, I imagine they'd take anyone, whatever the level.'

'How many are there at the top levels?' asked Jay.

'Other than Zadie Lawrence, only one other has scored at level eight.'

'Who?' said Jay, thinking about Sasha Colden.

'We're not sure.'

'*We*?'

'I have some friends. Some like us I speak to sometimes...'

'You hypocrite. Who are they?' Jay stiffened, bristling. He *still* treated her as if she were twelve years old, keeping her in the dark, only releasing snippets of information that *he* judged her to be able to deal with. 'Are you a part of the resistance Alf was talking about?'

Ben shook his head. 'Don't listen to that old man. What's he been saying?' Jay shook her head and remained silent. 'It's not a resistance,' Ben said. 'It's just like-minded people. We keep our heads down, attract no attention. It's more like a research group than a resistance these days.'

'Research into what?' She turned away from him and poured water from the kettle into two mugs.

Ben looked at her. 'OK, sit down. You want to know? I'll tell you.' He pushed the kitchen door closed. He picked the milk from the fridge and handed it to her. 'Some of the Given recruited by the authorities went through a transformation process as they became Readers. Their power scaled up. These Readers are dedicated to the purges, using their senses to root out people like us.'

'Scaled up?'

'A level three or four Given is coming out at a six or seven Reader. And they're a nasty bunch, revelling in the State sanctioned power they have. Some of them they call "Scanners", and the more powerful ones are the Readers.'

'So they want to turn us, the Given, into Readers?'

'Maybe. Some of us. But it seems most never re-emerge, so it's only the select few who come out as Readers. The rest of us...' He trailed off. 'They all share one thing – the Scanners and the Readers – they've all accepted the transformation, a one-way ticket. They are no longer part of the Given.'

Jay took a step towards the fridge to scrutinise the arrangement of the magnetic pieces on the fridge chess board. 'Whose move is it?' The kitchen chess match had lasted a month this time, both Jay and her dad taking their time, sometimes a week between moves.

'Your move.'

Jay slid her black bishop into a better attacking position. Her dad watched as she released her finger from the bishop.

'Bold,' he said.

They were silent for a while. Jay stirred sugar into her tea, her mind racing with thoughts about the Readers, their scaled-up power. She wondered whether Zadie Lawrence was dead, or if she'd become a Reader. She would be one who the State would have loved to see on their side, hunting down the rest of the Given.

Ben gazed out of the kitchen window. 'I suppose you remember the legend?' he said.

Jay knew her dad's stories well, from the years of bedtime narrations transfixing her and Sammy, and sometimes Stitch too, for hours. His fiction depicted a far off land, a magical oasis and a source of power. He made a connection between his stories and the words of a myth, an ancient legend.

'You remember, right?' Ben said.

'Kind of.' Jay handed him a mug of tea and waited. He reached for the fridge and moved his magnetic pawn to block the attack from Jay's bishop. He pulled himself up to sit on the kitchen worktop, legs hanging over the side. Jay stood on the opposite side of the narrow galley kitchen and cradled her tea as her dad began his interpretation of the legend.

6

The legend has no fixed point in history. It simply always was, and was handed down through generations. Most people who relayed the story did so by placing it in the context of their own culture, their own country. Even its written versions differed, from tales of hidden islands in the middle of the ocean, to magical portals atop mountains leading to other lands.

Ben insisted that the original source of the story was written into the myths and folklore. 'The parallels are too much to ignore,' he said, 'between the words in the written folklore of the South Downs and what we know of the legend.'

'No one else seems to think so, Dad,' Jay said, smiling with affection, remembering the enthusiasm and joy he would take in embellishing the story a little more every night at bedtime.

'Have you read the folklore?'

Jay nodded. 'Some of it. Compared to your bedtime stories it's about as exciting as reading an instruction manual.'

Ben laughed. 'Well that's fair. There are clues in the folklore, but there are missing pieces.' He lowered his voice. 'Pieces only visible to some people, not everyone.'

Jay snorted. 'Come on, Dad. Seriously?'

'I know it sounds odd. And I'm not saying that I have all the answers, but from what we can tell, the pieces fall into place only for those who need it.'

'Need it for what?' Jay asked.

Ben looked up at Jay. He held out his hand.

'What?' said Jay.

'Let me touch your hand, I want to try something.'

Jay gave a nervous smile, wondering if her dad was going crazy. She held out her hand and Ben placed his on top. He closed his eyes and Jay felt something. It was nothing unusual to connect with her dad, even without touching, but this was different; it came from inside her. A flash of light behind her eyes. Another, brighter this time. Images floated through her mind and she too closed her eyes. The images were just beyond her reach, too distant to grasp, to interpret or to understand. Another flash, a clearer picture this time – an oasis of light, a pool and a cave with water flowing. Then darkness.

Jay withdrew her hand. Ben opened his eyes and shook his head. 'Sorry. I can't get it.'

'What was that?' said Jay, breathless, jumping up to pace the room.

'I think there's a way we can transmit information faster through touch. I had hoped I might impart what I know, all of it, not simply what I'm able to articulate. I don't think I have the information in any decipherable form in my mind. And my power is not strong enough to transmit properly, anyway.'

'I got something. But how did you...'

'Someone did it to me. A long time ago.'

'Who?' Jay continued to pace the kitchen, her mind turning and twisting over what she'd seen through her dad's touch. 'And why?' she said.

'I don't even know if it's possible to transmit information like that. It's just a feeling. It was so long ago it's like it was a dream.'

Jay shook her head as if trying to dislodge something. The image of a pool and interconnected caves swam through her mind. Her eyes wide, she said, 'Tell me what else you've figured out about the legend?' Jay had thought she knew as much as her dad, but now she wasn't so sure, and she'd had enough of his selective truth.

Ben pulled a notebook from the back pocket of his jeans and flicked through pages of hand-written words and pencil sketches. He closed it again. 'If this place is the source, then the Readers would be keen to find it. Even if just to destroy it. Without the source, the Given are powerless and the job of the Readers is done.' Jay nodded.

Ben lowered his gaze. 'As much as we might want to find this place, we wouldn't want to be the ones to lead the Readers there.'

Jay waited. Her dad looked at her. 'And the state is aware of our group. They're actively looking for us, might even be watching.'

'Your *resistance* group?'

Ben smiled. 'You might call it that.' He jumped down off the kitchen surface and moved his magnetic queen to take Jay's bishop, ending her attack.

7

Inside the circle of trees atop Chanctonbury Hill, Marcus gritted his teeth and whittled a stick to within a millimetre of its life, the blade of his knife glinting in the glow of embers from the fire. Smoke rose and dissolved into the night above his head.

He sucked air between his clenched teeth. In the time before he had become a Reader, back when he was one of the Given, Chanctonbury would have been a source of power – up there he would have been like a battery placed on a charger. Not anymore. Now, Marcus felt nothing. His power came from a different place, somewhere controlled not by the energy of the land, but by the State.

He stopped with his knife and kicked a log into the fire. Flames illuminated his face. His skin was weathered, the dark rings around his eyes accentuated by the shadows, and the scar on his face silvery in the light of the flames. A black mark on the inside of his left wrist displayed the number eight.

The hill at Chanctonbury was steeped in layers of history, layers that had each charged the ground with energy. Myth said that the Devil himself created the Hill as he dug the ground for the valley that formed Devil's Dyke, discarding a clump of earth from his spade onto the Downs. The ring of trees at Chanctonbury, like those at nearby Cissbury and Highdown, were visible from as far as the coast in the south, and from the top of the Downs to the north.

A grey squirrel scampered up a tree to a vantage point halfway up, scanning the clearing, an eye on the man with the knife who seemed to shimmer in the light of the fire. Marcus pulled back his sleeve with his knife, tracing the curves of the figure eight, a mark that, before his transformation, had been a figure six.

As if coming in on a breeze, a flash of an image crossed his mind. He was alert, scanning. It was an unknown power signature. Someone new. Someone with power who had so far evaded the authorities, perhaps someone who had now come of age, and come up for air. Their signal was intense, but disturbed, intermittent. The image came again, smeared into his consciousness, a smudge of light and colour. A figure. A silhouette. A voice. All of it fleeting, too momentary to absorb. But something familiar... something from his past.

'Who...' Marcus said aloud, a rising anger in his chest. This new energy was a personal attack. Someone had evaded him, he who was convinced that the world of the powers belonged only to him. He had earned his place. It had been that way since he accepted the mandate handed to him by the State. In the so-called *choice* – the option of life as a Reader over that of a slow diminution of power – he chose life. He had the facial scar to show for it, a mark inflicted by the channelling of substantial power into him, turning him, releasing him.

He dropped his stick into the fire, stood, and looked over his shoulder to the south, his mind open. Another image, a piercing flash this time, crashed into his head like an angry scream.

'Who *is* this?' He wandered towards the edge of the ring of trees, pain piercing his temples, eyes watering. He tilted his head as if to hear more clearly and looked out over the trees towards the coast.

He smiled. Someone with power had strayed into his zone of perception. They were in him now. He had their scent.

8

Sammy scattered the chess pieces over the carpet. 'Black or white?' he said.

'White,' said his dad.

Sammy smiled. 'I'll be white. White goes first.'

Sonia was on the sofa, her head in a magazine. She looked towards the front door, then at her watch as if waiting for something. Jay had been upstairs for most of the morning, her loft room becoming more like her own separate residence, with her own front door via the roof and the Velux window.

'Your go.' Sammy had made his signature opening move, his classic queen's knight offensive. 'Prepare to defend,' he said.

Ben smiled, pleased things seemed to have returned to something like normal. They had reached an equilibrium. There was less coverage of the Given on the television and in the news. Occasionally, there would be whispers of an incident, someone causing a problem for the authorities, but these incidents became rarer, and talk of them less animated, less credible even.

Sammy brought out his second knight. As Ben considered

his defence a sudden wave of nausea hit him. It was as if the wind had been knocked out of him. He looked up at Sonia. 'What?' she said. 'Seen a ghost?'

Ben tuned back to Sammy but he couldn't concentrate. Another pang of nausea shot through him and he jerked his hand to his mouth. 'Sorry, Sammy. I'll be back in a minute.'

'I'll take your go,' said Sammy.

Ben lurched to the downstairs toilet where he leaned over the basin, sweat beading on his forehead. The nausea subsided a little, and he splashed cold water on his face. 'There's a Reader coming,' he said to himself as he dried his face. 'They've found me.'

He threw the towel onto the floor and opened the toilet door in a single move then bounded up the stairs three at a time. 'Jay?' he shouted, stepping towards the open Velux window.

'Hey, Dad.' She poked her head through. 'What's up?'

'Did you feel it?'

'What?' Jay thought for a moment. 'I did sense something. Was that you?'

'Someone's coming,' Ben said.

'Who?'

'One of the government's Readers. A nasty one.'

'It's OK. We can shield. Just close-up. He won't find us.'

'He already has.' As Ben said these words, there was an urgent banging on their front door. They stared at each other, neither moving. 'Stay there, close the window behind you and shield.'

'I'll come…'

'Stay! Please. Stay. We don't know how strong this one is.'

Ben's heart thumped and his skin prickled as he headed back to the stairs, pausing on the top step. He heard Sammy talking to a man at the front door. He summoned all his strength to create as much confusion in the energy as he could, hoping it might shield Jay. His shielding skills were not great, not as good as his ability to sense others with power. The best he could hope for was creating enough confusion for the Reader to think that he was the only one in the house with power. What wasn't clear was whether it was Jay that the Reader had come for, or if it was him. He cursed himself at how stupid he'd been. His resistance work. Careless.

A wave of energy swept through the house, up the stairs and through his body. He almost fell back onto the stairs. This one was scanning with a force he'd not experienced before. His heart raced and his face flushed with the effort of maintaining his shield. He took a moment to compose himself before continuing down the stairs.

'Can I help you?' Ben asked.

The unshaven man looked up.

'This is Mr Jimmy. For you,' Sammy said, and turned to head back to the lounge. 'Don't be long, it's your move.'

'Mr Jimmy?' He was a good ten inches shorter than Ben but he was stocky, almost as wide as he was tall. His three-quarter length jacket looked more like a trench coat.

'Just call me Jimmy,' the man said, looking into Ben's eyes. He held out his identification. Ben glanced at it but he already knew who this man was, *what* he was. As he put his ID badge away, Ben caught sight of the number six on the inside of his wrist. He tried not to think about it, not to leave thoughts in his head that the man could read – he wouldn't stand a chance facing up to a level six.

'And if I have it right,' the man said, 'you must be Ben?'

'What can I do for you?' said Ben. 'We're just in the middle of something.'

'Chess, your boy said. Lovely.' His self-satisfied smile revealed nicotine-stained teeth. 'I've been looking for you.'

'What for?'

'You've been leaking signals for a while now but we couldn't triangulate. Something was blocking. Marcus reckoned it was probably all the bloody ley lines in these parts. It's crazy around here.'

'Marcus?'

'Oh, sorry. Marcus is the boss.'

Ben glanced over Jimmy's shoulder to see if there was a second Reader outside. Ben had heard the name Marcus before, in connection with the fabled level eight, the strongest government reader.

'He's not here, just me,' said Jimmy. 'So what level are you?'

'Level?' Ben was twitchy, like a caged bird.

'Stay with me, Ben. What level are you? Let me see your wrist.'

Ben hiked his sleeve to show his mark.

'Two?' said Jimmy, sounding disappointed. 'I'm surprised.'

'About what?'

'Marcus said you'd be a four or five and that I should bring someone else with me.'

Ben breathed a sigh of resignation. 'So, what now?'

'Perhaps I can come in and we can have a talk? I'd like to hear about your little group. I hear it's growing by the day and there must be a long list of names you're dying to give me?'

'No. If you want to talk, we can do it here.'

A flash of annoyance shot from Jimmy. 'You need to pack a little bag, not too much, and then you need to say your goodbyes. Bring your membership lists or we will just have to come back again and rip everything apart until we find it for ourselves. Come out to the vehicle. You've got five minutes. Don't think about it, just do it. If you try to run, I'll cause you pain. If you take longer than five minutes, I'll cause your wife pain too. If you do anything stupid, like try to take me on, then I'll cause pain to all three of you, and I'll pay particular attention to the boy.'

All three of us. Ben took a deep breath and reinforced his shield. 'Five minutes,' Ben said. He knew that Jimmy meant business, and he knew about the ability of the higher level readers to cause pain through the concentration of thoughts, pain that could debilitate, and, at its worst, cause lasting damage.

The man turned and made his way back to his Land Rover. Ben closed the door then called out for Sammy to come upstairs. He turned and ran up to Jay's room. The longer the Reader was out there, the more likely he'd sense something of Jay.

As Ben climbed awkwardly through Jay's Velux window, she had her eyes closed. 'Hey,' said Ben.

She breathed out. 'Has he gone?'

'Keep shielding.'

'He's still out there?'

'Yes. Can you shield us both?'

'But we're OK, right?'

Sammy appeared at the window. 'What is it?'

'Come out here. I want to talk to you both, I don't have long.' He smiled as Sammy scrambled out of the window and settled next to him. He put an arm around each of his children.

'What do you mean you don't have long?' said Jay.

Ben didn't answer, turned to Sammy. 'You've heard of the Given, right?'

'I know about your powers, Dad, and Jay's.'

'You what?' Ben started.

'I told him,' said Jay, impatient. 'Tell us, Dad. What is it?'

'That man at the door,' said Ben, looking at Sammy and

sensing a rising tide of emotion in his son that was about to spill out. Sammy was a special boy. He had no power that Ben could tell, but he had *something*. He was sensitive, that was true, probably too sensitive. He experienced people's emotions and their troubles as if they were his own. He was intuitive, and he was kind.

'Jimmy?' asked Sammy.

'Yes. He's a Reader. You know what that is?'

Sammy nodded and Jay lowered her head into her hands. 'He detected you.' she said.

Ben put a hand on Jay's arm. 'Listen. We don't have much time. He wants a list of people in my group. I've got five minutes to bring it out front. If I don't, then...' He looked up at the view of the hills. He took a deep breath, taking in as much as he could, not knowing when he'd next be able to feel the energy of the Downs. 'If I don't, then he won't hold back. And he won't stop at me. If he returns, he'll detect you too, Jay. I can't let that happen.'

'Just give him the list. He might let you stay?'

'I don't have a list. There is no such list. But either way, they want me too, not just the list.'

Jay was wide-eyed, pleading, searching for a solution. 'I might be stronger than him. We can try...'

'No, Jay. He's a level six.' Ben looked away, wanting to hold Jay tight and not let go, but he needed to be strong so that *she* could be strong, for Sammy. They would have to survive without him.

'Where will they take you, Dad?' said Sammy.

'A holding camp I expect.'

'Prison,' Jay said. 'Don't dress it up. They'll put you in prison, or *rehabilitation* as they call it.' A realisation showed in Jay's eyes. 'Will they try to transform you?'

Ben shook his head. 'They won't bother with me.' He tried

to pull her closer, but Jay resisted, pushing herself away from him. She shoved her hand hard against his chest. He didn't try to stop her.

'I'm sorry,' he said, then opened out his arm and pulled in Sammy.

'Look, we knew this was always a possibility.'

'Then *do* something. Fight. Do *anything*,' Jay screamed, her face a mass of tears and anger.

Ben pulled her close, using his strength to force her to settle, smothering her screams so the Reader wouldn't hear them. 'Shush,' he said in a stern tone, no time for patience. 'You need to grow up. This could be you. This is serious.'

Jay's struggles gradually subsided. 'What now?'

'We need to think about this as a step on the journey. It might not be the one we'd planned, but we can deal with it.'

'What journey?' said Sammy.

'Our journey. The journey through life. There are always challenges; it's how we deal with them that determines who we are.'

Sammy rubbed his eyes, holding back tears. Jay leaned in closer to Ben. 'They'll come for me too?' she said.

'Not if you're careful. Right now, he doesn't know you're here. More than ever you need to bury it. Shield. Never let your guard down.' Ben took Jay by the shoulders and gently shook her until she met his eyes. 'Give them nothing to go on.'

Jay wanted to be brave but the shudder of a sob passed through her as she looked into her father's eyes. 'We'll never be properly free,' she said.

PART II

POWERS

9

Jay's lungs burned as she pushed herself to keep running. She couldn't shake the feeling that if she slowed, a Reader would be behind her, getting closer. Her father was gone, and it was all her fault. All Jay could think to do was to head to the bookshop and talk to Alf.

She slammed into the door and fell into the shop. 'Alf,' she said, leaning on the counter to keep herself from collapsing onto the floor.

'Jay?' Alf raised an eyebrow, exhibiting no real sense of urgency. 'Back so soon, my girl.'

'They took my dad,' she spluttered, snapping Alf from his serenity.

He said nothing but nodded towards the stairs, his expression neutral and demeanour calm. Colours drifted from him as he looked at Jay – soothing greens and yellows. He made for the stairs. Jay followed.

'Why did they take him? He's just a level two,' Jay said as they sat at her favourite table.

'They might have sensed you.'

'But I have nothing,' said Jay, motioning towards her wrist.

'Not yet.'

She stood and paced the room, looking out through the windows. She saw a Reader in every person that walked the high street.

Alf leaned back in his chair. 'They'll take everyone eventually, but I agree it's odd that they would take a level two.' He paused, thinking. 'They must have sensed something more powerful.' He held Jay's eye for a moment.

'You really think I'm the reason they took him?'

'I'm not saying anything for sure. I know no more than you, but it's possible. Even I can tell that your power is stronger than almost any I've felt.' He leaned and pulled a book from the shelf behind him, the Sasha Colden biography. He slapped it down on the table. 'Like this woman here.'

Jay nodded. 'She had proper power.'

Alf looked towards the stairs. 'Sasha had more than that.' He touched the book cover. 'She was...'

'What about my dad?' Jay interrupted. 'Where are they taking him?'

Alf nodded for Jay to sit. 'I know it's hard, but there's nothing you can do about it now. What you can do is look after number one, or you will be next. It's important the Readers don't find you.'

Jay felt a tingle travel from her neck down her left arm and settle in her wrist. She shivered. She picked at her sleeve, slowly pulling it back. As her sleeve edged back further she saw the marking, its deep blackness like a hole in her wrist. The curve of the lower section revealed, she looked up at Alf whose eyes remained fixed on her arm. She dragged her sleeve back the rest of the way and the figure of eight was clear. Her heart pounded.

Alf nodded. 'Do you have anywhere you can go?'

'No.' Jay laughed without humour. 'I'm not going

anywhere. I can't. I've just finished college. I can't leave my brother.'

'Wait there a minute.' He stood and moved around to the back of the room where he unlocked a cupboard. He returned with a bunch of papers, opening an old, yellowing map on the table in front of Jay. 'This came in a while back. I've not logged it so the Readers don't know about it yet, but I can't leave it too long. They'll suspect something.'

'Where is this place?' said Jay, leaning over the map.

'That's the thing. There are no landmarks. Nothing to locate it. The detail is so generic it could be a thousand places, but look.' He drew Jay's attention to a corner of the map where the topography had been annotated with hand-drawn lines.

'Bows and arrows,' Jay whispered.

Alf looked at her and nodded. 'Like it says in the legend.'

The lines on the map formed the shape of two sets of bow and arrow, with intersecting trajectories, like Ben had described to her. 'But,' Jay stuttered, 'there's nothing here to anchor it. This could be anywhere.' There was no distinguishable coastline, no rivers. 'Anyone could have drawn this, it's just a picture.'

Alf leaned back in his seat. 'Maybe. But it's old for sure. And see here.' He pointed to what looked like clumps of trees. 'This might be Chanctonbury.'

Jay looked closer, 'Or Highdown? Or Cissbury?'

'One of the hill forts,' said Alf.

'Can I take it with me?' said Jay.

Alf shook his head. 'Too dangerous. You take something like this from here, they'll know. Eventually they'll know.' He turned then, looking across to the stairway as a tall man dressed in black stepped up from the stairs and moved towards the window. Alf's face turned grey and Jay sensed his shield begin to show cracks. A shiver crept up her spine, and she saw his fear in colours – a diffusion of dark crimson, almost black it was so deep, expanding into the room like a noxious gas.

'Go,' Alf said.

'Where?'

'Use the back stairs.' He pointed towards a fire escape. Jay held the bookseller's eyes for a moment, deciding whether he was to be trusted, whether those stairs would lead to safety. Through the cracks of his mind, she saw his fear and urgency for her safety, streams of crimson now flowing into a spectrum of yellows.

She grabbed her bag and lunged for the door. A wave of energy shoved at her back. She pushed through to the spiral staircase, looking over her shoulder to catch the eye of the man in black. The door closed behind her, breaking her line of sight to the man. She'd seen enough. She'd seen his darkness, his urgency, almost desperation to get to her. He'd seen her face, her mind.

10

Sammy was up in Jay's face before she'd even closed the front door behind her. 'Where have you been? Mum's going mental.'

'I needed to get out.'

'Well, thanks for leaving me...'

Jay interrupted her brother by pulling him into a hug. His body stiff at first, he relaxed and put his arms around Jay, returning her embrace. 'Sorry,' she said.

They pulled apart, and Sammy let out a sigh. He nodded towards the back room. 'She really has lost it.'

'Like, banging her head on a wall lost it, or gun in the mouth?'

Sammy shrugged. His chest fell. 'More a gentle rocking and incoherent blabbering.'

A shout came out from the lounge. 'Sammy? Is that Jay?'

Jay nodded towards the stairs. 'Can't deal with her right now, you coming?'

Sammy nodded. 'Give me a minute, I'll come up.'

Sammy headed back to the lounge as Jay crept up the stairs. Now more than ever she understood the danger she could be in, and the danger that those around her might be in for being near her. Her power was changing, bubbling below the surface, pushing to be released.

Up on the roof, Jay leaned back against the tiles and took a deep breath of the air flowing over the house from the Downs. She checked over her shoulder into her room then looked again at her wrist. The figure eight was clear.

To the north, the hills slumbered in the warmth of early afternoon while the bristling sea whispered, scratched and scraped for attention. Jay steadied her breathing, relaxing into the natural rhythm of the waves of energy as they washed over her.

The house was positioned at the boundary where the rhythmic low frequency from the hills met the spiky high energy from the sea, each leaving its mark. Jay connected. It wasn't like the colours people projected as their thoughts coalesced, and not like the words that came from those swirling colours. This was different, a mutual connection, more like a joining within the light. For a moment, Jay was part of it, and it a part of her.

'Hey.' Sammy's voice.

Jay snapped back to herself. 'What is it?' She held her fingers to her temples as if to stop her head spinning. 'Where are we?'

'On the roof. You scared me,' said Sammy, sliding down to sit on the tiles next to his sister. 'You were out of it, I couldn't wake you. It was like you were asleep with your eyes open. Weird. If you go mental like *her*, I don't think I can deal with it.'

Jay looked at her brother but said nothing, wondering if, like her, he could see the colours and hear the thoughts of others.

'You were zoned out. Were you reading someone?'

Jay frowned. 'No, that was something else. I'm still working that one out.' She sensed a disappointment in Sammy. 'Have you not felt anything yourself?' she said.

Sammy shook his head. 'I'm as normal as they come,' he said. Jay said nothing but studied her brother's profile as he looked up at the hills. She reckoned that normal would be pretty desirable right now.

11

Ben rubbed his wrist as if trying to erase the artless black marking as he looked out over the prison yard.

Scanners checked every visitor. He'd been just two weeks inside, and had twice written to Jay and Sammy, telling them to stay away. He slumped down on the concrete step next to Matchstick, his ally, who put a hand on Ben's shoulder, the black number three visible on his wrist. 'We need to get out of here,' Matchstick said.

'Not too loud,' Ben said.

'They can't read me,' said Matchstick. 'Most of the Scanners in here are weak.'

'They seem to read me well enough,' said Ben.

'You've spent too long pushing your powers away. You need to focus.'

'So how do we get out of here?'

'It's not the getting out that's the hard bit. It's staying out. As soon as you're out there, higher level Readers will be on you before you can buy your first pint.'

Ben looked at the floor, picturing that pint, sat in the pub garden at the Black Rabbit by the river. He thought of the

Interland. 'What if I knew somewhere we could go? Somewhere they wouldn't be able to get to us?'

Matchstick looked at Ben, trying to read him. 'You're serious?'

Ben had been just a teenager when a Runner's touch transported him on a journey, by river, to the Interland. A safe place. The images, as real to him as if he were there, had lodged into his consciousness over the years. He could smell the rapeseed in the air, the water, the chalk. It was those images that Ben had used to craft his bedtime stories for Jay and Sammy. It was a way for him to get them out from deep inside his mind, to make them real. Unforgettable.

'I need to get out of here. We haven't much time.'

'We have nothing but time.' Matchstick raised his hands to motion around himself.

'If they take us through to rehab, there's no way back.' He locked eyes with Matchstick, daring him to contradict him. He relaxed. 'And I'm worried about Jay, I've been feeling something.'

'What?'

'She's getting stronger.'

'You can feel her from here?'

Ben nodded. 'About a hundred miles away,' he said, pride creeping into his voice.

'Shit. That's strong. You know what that means?'

Ben nodded. 'Of course. That's why we don't have much time. We have to go.'

'If you can get us somewhere safe, before they pick us up, then... yes, I can get us out of here.'

'Leave the safe place to me,' Ben said. His friend put a finger to his lips and nodded towards a guard making his way over to them. Ben stood as the guard reached the concrete steps.

'MacFarlane?'
Ben nodded.
'Visitor.'

* * *

JAY DIDN'T NEED the directions she'd noted down to get to the prison from the bus station, she just headed towards the great towers of its castle-like entrance that dominated the skyline.

Earlier that morning, Jay had woken to the sound of birds outside her window. She turned over in bed and watched as a starling skipped along the ridge-tiles of the house next door. It paused for a moment, looking in her direction, then took off into the tree above. Jay stepped out of bed. She needed to see her dad, whether he liked it or not.

Turning the last corner, she looked up at the prison through its perimeter fence topped with razor-wire. The yellow brick building seemed to go on forever, floor upon floor with countless rows of barred windows. A window for each little cell, and one of those little cells for her dad. The prison receptionist had given her strict instructions: no scarves, no big jewellery, no sandals, no flip-flops.

After signing in, Jay was directed to a waiting area, like a doctor's surgery with a few added extras: a vending machine with chocolate and drinks, another with sandwiches. She emptied her pockets into one of the lockers for visitors' belongings and took a seat. A dog scampered into the waiting area, a spaniel, sweeping through like a hoover with its nose just above the floor. Its harness displayed the prison logo in dark blue with white lettering, and a name: *Sally*. She reached Jay and sniffed at her shoes. Jay's heart raced. She calmed herself with a deep breath. Sally looked up into Jay's face for a moment, and then moved on.

A single chime of a bell signalled the visiting area was ready. Everyone filed into a room with bare, white walls. Jay's dad sat at a table in the middle of the room, sporting a patchy looking beard. He was wringing his hands.

'Hey, Dad.'

Ben stood. 'Jay.'

'Are we allowed to hug?' said Jay.

He opened his arms and held her tight.

'Stand clear!' came a shout from a guard.

As Ben released, he raised a hand to his forehead as if taking his own temperature. 'So good to see you,' he said, 'but you shouldn't have come. Shield, Jay. Please. There are people here that scan. There will be a Reader here somewhere.' He looked around the room, as if trying to identify which of the guards was a Reader.

They sat down and Ben took a deep breath.

'I went to see Alf,' said Jay. Ben frowned and was about to speak when Jay continued, 'He has a map.'

'What kind of map?'

'It has the bows and arrows you told me about. But it's old, and it could be anywhere.'

'Listen to me, Jay.' Ben lowered his voice. 'Your power is strong, I can feel it. You must be a higher level than I thought.'

Jay checked in the direction of the guards and then, back to her dad, she pulled back her sleeve.

Ben stopped mid-sentence. He thrust his hand to cover her wrist, looking around the room for signs that anyone might have seen.

'Shield,' said Ben. 'You need to get away.' He looked around the room. 'Quickly, pay attention.' He opened up to her for long enough to show her his plan of escape.

Jay read the Interland on his mind; his thoughts sent anxiety flowing through her veins. The thought that her home was so unsafe that she'd have to leave too in the hope of finding truth in a myth scared her more than the idea of the Readers. Ben sensed her fear. 'Try and stay calm. I won't be in this section forever before they take me over to *education*, then *rehabilitation* – and the *Sub Levels*. The Interland could be the place where we can breathe again.'

'I'm afraid,' said Jay.

'I know. Find my notebook,' he said.

'What notebook?'

'Black cover, the one I had in the kitchen. You know the one?' Jay nodded. 'Find it and use it to figure out how to get to the gateway. There are notes in there that I have collected. Then use what *you* know.'

'I don't know anything,' Jay said.

Ben shook his head, 'You know more than anyone. It might need some piecing together.'

'This is crazy.' Jay felt a deep sadness run through her, the sense of an ending. Ben looked up and Jay followed his eyes towards the Guard. The Guard, a Reader, focused on the two of them. A chime sounded, visiting time was over. Inmates were to move to the back of the room and visitors to the front.

'Go now. Today. As soon as you get back. And take Sammy. Tell Sammy to take that little fishing book I bought for him. Don't hang about. I'll know when you've gone, I'll feel it. I have a plan.'

'You know where the Interland is?' said Jay.

He shook his head. 'I'm relying on you for that. You need to work it out. When you figure it out, I'll know, then I'll not be far behind. Just remember the stories.'

'Seriously?'

'Find the notebook,' Ben whispered, stepping backwards towards the wall of the visiting room. Jay merged into the stream of visitors as people shuffled from the room.

In the lobby, she collected her belongings from the locker. The Reader had joined two of the security personnel. To get to the exit, Jay would have to walk directly past. She stuffed her coins and watch into her pocket as she walked, not taking her eyes off the Reader. As she reached the exit, the Reader snapped his head up and looked directly at her. She'd been seen.

The Reader pushed across the room. Jay got to the door, but the Reader caught her by the arm, spinning her around. They locked eyes. He rocked back on his heels but tightened his grip like he'd grasped an electric cable and was unable to let go. Jay's fear turned to determination. She pulled herself free, passed through the security gate and on to the exit.

Halfway across the carpark, Jay didn't need to look over her shoulder to know she was clear. She darted around the corner, and made sure her shield was up before dissolving into the maze of side streets.

12

Jay rose early, tiptoed onto the landing and leaned over the banister to see into the old crow's room on the first floor. The door was open, Mum had probably slept on the sofa and not made it to bed. She focused on the notebook then she crept down the stairs, the carpet soft under her bare feet.

Her mum's room was empty, the curtains still open from the day before. She hurried to her dad's side of the bed and riffled through his bedside cupboard. Nothing but junk, trinkets and papers. She knelt to see under the bed. Dust, cobwebs, bags of old clothes, a cardboard box. She pulled the box clear of the bed, opened it, and picked out her father's worn black notebook. Dust diffused into the air as she flicked through the pages. It was full of handwritten notes, sketches and pencil drawings. It smelled of him, of the joy he took in his writing and sketching. She smiled, losing herself for a moment as she browsed through her dad's doodles – his thoughts and feelings.

'Jay?'

Jay started. She slid the box back under the bed and made her way from her mum's room.

Sonia appeared on the landing as Jay stepped onto the stairs to the loft. 'What are you doing?' Sonia asked, her tone less confrontational than Jay was used to.

She turned, keeping the notebook concealed behind her back. 'Hey, Mum.'

Sonia leaned up against the wall and studied Jay. 'You saw him then?' Jay nodded. 'How was he?'

Jay sat on the stair, lodging the notebook behind her. 'He was OK.'

Sonia lowered her head. 'He brought it on himself, you know? Messing around with the resistance. What was he expecting to achieve? I just thank the Lord that you kids don't have to hide and lie like he has.'

Jay edged her sleeve down, making sure her wrist was covered. 'It's not his fault. It's not like he's done anything illegal. He never asked to have power.'

'Power?' Sonia croaked a laugh. 'He never had any power.' She shook her head, her eyes distant. 'Power brings influence. Your dad couldn't influence...' Jay stood. 'Wait,' said her mum. 'I'm sorry. I'm angry with him. What are we supposed to do now?'

'You could get work?' Jay turned to head up the stairs, ending the conversation. She clutched the notebook to her chest. Her west-facing bedroom was cool and dingy in the morning's shade. The walls closed in on her, squeezing the air from her lungs.

Concealing the notebook in her backpack, Jay crept down to the first floor landing. She made sure there was no sign of her mum then poked her head around Sammy's door. Light snoring radiated from under his duvet. She sat on the edge of his bed and peeled back the covers. 'Hey,' she whispered. Sammy jerked awake, wide-eyed, then settled back down, grumbled and closed his eyes again.

She flicked his ear, and he pulled away. 'What? Go away.'

'I found Dad's notebook.'

Sammy turned over and squinted at her. 'You found it? Already?'

'Under Mum's bed. I won't read it here, I'm heading out.'

'You want me to come?'

'No, you sleep,' Jay said, but she needn't have bothered. Sammy's eyes were already closed.

* * *

JAY HEADED to the disused pier. Under the old timbers of the deck, she ducked below the safety fence that kept the tourists out, and sat on the stones where she could lean back on one of the wooden deck supports. On the post in front of her she could see her a carving of her name, faded over the years since she'd scratched it into the wood with a piece of flint. Stitch's name was there too, but not Cassie's. Their friendship with Cassie had come later.

The sound of the sea was hypnotic – the crash of the waves breaking over the sand then the suck and sweep as the sea pulled back the pebbles. Sandflies buzzed around the drying seaweed wrapped to the pier's wooden posts. Jay settled herself into the stones, opened the notebook and started at the beginning.

* * *

HER DAD'S notes were simple in places, cryptic in others. His pencil drawings were intricate. The images drifted through her mind as she walked from the beach to the bookshop on the corner, choosing the longer route along the seafront.

The visit to the prison and her time spent with his notebook reminded Jay of their shared sense of adventure, the excitement they had in solving a puzzle, the connection between minds they'd once made when she was little. She felt a pang of longing. What she wouldn't give to have him here, solving this impossible puzzle with her. She needed help.

The bell rang above Alf's door. A woman Jay had never seen sat behind the bookshop's desk. He was always there, never anyone but him. 'Where's Alf?'

'Who?' the woman said.

'Alfred, the bookseller. It's his shop.'

'If you mean the previous *manager*, he's moved on.' The woman returned her attention to the papers on the checkout and Jay sensed her power. The scrawny, gripey woman was attempting to read Jay so she put up her shield. Her heart thumped. The woman's power was weak. She wouldn't be able to read Jay, but she might sense her power.

Jay stepped back, turned and headed for the stairs, continuing to shield. At the foot of the stairs, she slowed, refocused. She saw that Alf had been taken for questioning by the Readers. In the woman's mind, she saw the Reader, a tall man with a scar from temple to chin. The Reader was strong, Alfred no match for him. Jay stopped, attempting to get her breath.

'Can I help you?' the woman asked.

Jay shook her head and climbed the stairs. She'd been exposed for sure. The woman at the desk would bring the Readers in for Jay. She picked up speed, taking the stairs two at a time, knowing she ought to head in the opposite direction – away from the shop.

The top floor had been closed off with strips of yellow

warning tape. A handwritten sign said 'closed for maintenance'. Jay ducked under the barricade. The top stair gave a familiar creak. She made her way to the shelves at the back.

Someone had removed all literature on the Given. The entire bottom shelf had been cleared, along with sections of the next two shelves up. Jay's heart raced as she searched for the Sasha Colden book. Nothing. Everything was gone.

Her fear rising, Jay moved quickly. She jumped up and covered the distance to the cabinet by the stairs in two strides. It was locked, but the lock was flimsy and three hard pulls burst it open. The lock breaking sounded like a gunshot in the quiet store and now Jay knew she was in deep. Inside the cabinet, the Colden book stared back at her. She slid it into her backpack and turned towards the stairs.

A wave of energy buffeted her. A Reader was close. She backtracked, ducking behind a set of shelves. Two men in black clothes emerged from the stairs. Jay stood rooted to the floor as the men poured into the room, their energy expanding into every corner. They separated, circling the room and blocking both exits. Jay's skin prickled with fear. She shielded, considering making a run for the stairs. The taller of the two men slowed and turned towards Jay as if sensing her. She couldn't see his face. He turned again and continued.

After a circuit the two men regrouped, leaving Jay a glimpse of a path to the back exit. She stumbled out from the cover of the shelves of books and sensed them turn. She felt the tall one spy her and a piercing blackness burrowed into her.

Jay pushed through the fire escape door and onto the stairs, launching herself down the steps, losing her footing in her desperation to flee. She half-ran, half-fell to ground level before the fire escape door above opened. Jay looked up, frozen. The men began their descent, taking their time, unhurried. Jay could see the scar on the tall man's face from two floors down. Her legs trembled. Terror spread through her body. As the men reached the first floor, adrenaline pumped life into her body and Jay turned and ran.

13
____

Jay got home as the sun dipped behind the hill. She slammed the front door then leaned against it, steadying her breath. She was glad to put a barrier between her and the Readers even if it wasn't likely to stop them.

With no sign of Sammy or her mum, she made straight for her room. She paused at the top of the stairs, hearing music.

At the sound of the door opening, Cassie glanced up from flipping through records, her tight beaded braids swishing back and forth. Stitch jumped, threw his cigarette out of the window and held his breath. He coughed, relieved to see Jay. 'Thought you were the old crow.' He gathered himself and scrambled up to lean out of the window and pick his half-smoked cigarette from the roof tiles. 'Where have you been?'

'Beach,' she said, standing in the middle of the room. 'Then the bookshop.'

Cassie looked up from the stack of records. 'Sammy's out there,' she said, nodding towards the window.

Jay climbed out to sit on the roof with her brother who was

looking out over the hills towards the sunset on the horizon. 'Hey. Did you read the notebook?'

Jay nodded. 'Yep.'

'What do you reckon then?'

'Bumped into a couple of Readers in the bookshop. And Alf's gone.'

Sammy's mouth dropped open.

'They clocked me, but I gave them the slip.'

'Wha...' Sammy stuttered, 'did they sense you? Were they looking for you?'

'Maybe. The top floor was cordoned off and a lot of the old books were gone. They came up looking for me.'

'They won't follow you here?'

Cassie and Stitch joined them on the roof, looking at Jay with concern as she answered her brother, 'No. I don't think so,' Jay said, pulling her dad's notebook and the Sasha Colden biography from her bag. As well as her own bookmark poking out, there were other papers crammed into the back of the book. Jay opened it and pulled out the old map that she and Alf had been looking at. Sammy watched as Jay unfolded it, revealing the drawing of the bows and arrows. At the top of the map was a post-it note with handwriting that Jay recognised. 'This is from Alf.'

Sammy read it aloud: *Leave. It's not safe.* He leaned back against the tiles.

'He knew I'd come for the book,' said Jay.

They looked out into the darkness, over the tops of the trees and on to the Downs. Jay could smell the salt in the breeze coming off the beach.

'I reckon we could find it, if it exists,' Jay said. She nodded towards the horizon where the moonlit grey sky touched the black that marked the tops of the trees. 'You see that light flickering over there?'

Sammy sat up straight. 'Yeah?'

'That's Highdown. You know, where we used to take the go-kart with Dad. Every night this time of year there's someone up there lighting a bonfire, summoning the spirits or some other shit.'

Stitch piped up, 'Ley lines, it's not shit.'

'I've been trying to figure something out,' said Jay. 'In the notebook, and Alf's map, the sketches...'

Cassie let out a sigh, interrupting Jay's flow for a moment. 'We've talked about this before. For *years*. If it exists, what makes you think you can find it when no one else ever has?'

Cassie's grandad had disappeared just after they moved to the area. She blamed him for his absence, couldn't talk about him. Losing her grandad came not long after losing her childhood soul mate. Stitch piped up again. 'Of course it exists. You should know, Cassie. Your grandad talked about it all the time.'

'We don't know it's the same place. And don't talk about my grandad. You don't know what he said.'

'I know what you told us.'

'Leave it, you two,' Jay intervened.

'My grandad talked about a place he called "the caverns", but he said nothing about any Interland, and he let nothing useful slip about where the caverns were. There's no reason to think it's the same place, and there's nothing to say that either place is real.'

'Except what Jay's dad said, and his notebook.'

The four of them fell silent. Jay rested her head and searched the sky for the plough, but the stars were dim in the grey-black sky. The only sound was Sammy flicking through the pages of the notebook. She looked at Cassie, then to Stitch. 'Anything?' she said, motioning to her wrist. They both shook their heads as Jay pulled back her sleeve.

She watched as Stitch's eyes widened and he slapped his hand down on the roof tiles. 'I knew it,' he said, pulling Jay's hand closer so that he could study the marking. Jay caught Sammy's eye and he smiled, giving a little nod before turning back to the notebook. Cassie's smile was more strained. She looked away, into the distance.

Sammy looked at Jay. 'This is serious. That marking settles things. We have no choice.'

'Sammy's right,' said Stitch, still holding on to Jay's wrist. 'This is big. This is, like, a magnet. It will draw the Readers in sooner or later.'

Sammy continued to turn the pages of the notebook. 'I reckon he's put enough in here for us to figure out where this place is. If anyone can understand Dad, and make the link between this stuff and his stories, then it's you, right?'

'I think the hill forts are the link,' said Jay.

'How?' said Sammy.

'You remember what Dad said about the Interland? His story about trekking downstream along the River Arun?'

Sammy shrugged. 'I remember bits of it.'

'The maps show the Arun running through the Downs to the estuary on the coast, and, according to Dad's stories, the gateway is at the intersect of ley lines bounded by the ancient hill forts. Like in that map from Alf. The Arun runs right through the Downs, through the area of three hill forts.'

'So it could be right out there?' said Stitch, motioning to the hills in the distance.

'That's one of them.' Jay pointed towards the light winking on the horizon. 'Highdown. Then there's one at Cissbury, and one at Chanctonbury.'

Stitch looked at Jay. 'So, we follow the lines through the three hill forts and find the gateway?'

'Something like that, but they're not on a line, and there's no obvious standout confluence of rivers. There are various tributaries of the Arun that cross with the Rother and the Wey, but no obvious point within the zone of the hill forts. So, I don't know.' Jay leaned over towards her brother to point him at a page in the notebook, a sketch of what looked like a map.

'What's that?' said Stitch.

'It's the closest thing to a map that's in the whole notebook,' said Jay. 'But it doesn't tie up with Alf's map.'

Sammy looked at her. 'You know that book Dad gave me, the fishing book?'

'The engrossing *Fishing With Spinners*,' Jay smiled. 'Dad mentioned that. He wanted you to bring it.'

'You know about the drawings in the back?'

'What drawings?'

'It has a hand-drawn sketch in the back.'

'A map?'

'No. It's more of a sketch of points, like a constellation or something. I always assumed it was just one of Dad's doodles.'

'Go and get it.'

Sammy disappeared through the window, returning a minute later with the little hardback book. He flicked to the back page before handing it to Jay, who studied it.

'Enlightenment?' said Cassie.

'The link between the rivers and the hill forts. The bows and arrows. It might be something.'

Sammy studied the sketches for a minute then looked up. 'So we start there.' He pointed towards Highdown.

'How are we supposed to get there? It's more than a day's walk to Highdown from here. Got to be twenty miles.' What Jay didn't put word to were her misgivings about involving her little brother and friends in what was likely a dangerous mission.

Sammy smiled. 'We can take Dad's car. The Beast. You can drive.'

Jay shook her head, 'It hasn't moved for years,' she said.

'So? It still runs,' said Sammy. 'I started it the other day.'

'I'm in,' said Stitch. 'Let's do it. We can chuck a couple of the tents in the boot. How long till we get to the gateway?'

'Depends where it is, Stitch. We don't know yet,' Jay said.

Sammy thought for a moment then said, 'If we drive, we can get to the car park at the foot of Highdown and trek up to the summit. Maybe a couple of hours. Then we see how we go from there. We should plan to be sleeping under the stars for a few nights at least.'

'Or in the car,' said Cassie.

Stitch shook his head. 'No way I'm sleeping in a car. Tried that. Worst night's sleep ever.'

'Let's not go mad,' said Jay, 'let's think about this. We can't just up and go chasing...'

'Dad needs us to go. He said so,' said Sammy.

'What if he's wrong?' said Jay.

Sammy and Stitch looked at Jay. 'What if he's right?' they said at the same time.

14

Long after Stitch and Cassie had gone home, Jay and Sammy stayed on the roof, making plans. Stitch was going home to pack his rucksack. Cassie was non-committal but Stitch insisted she be ready in the morning.

Jay sighed, worried for Sammy, anxious that as soon as they left home, came out in the open, the Readers would track them. It was one thing shielding within the safety of home, behind brick walls, but out in the open it was more difficult. Her energy would be easier for Readers to detect.

'Is Dad out yet?' asked Sammy.

'I don't know.'

'Can't you look?'

'Where Dad is concerned I have a block. I can't seem to get through to him from a distance.'

'I thought he said he could hear you, sense you?'

'But I can't hear him. I don't know why.'

Sammy yawned. 'Look, Jay, get some sleep. We leave early.' Sammy smiled and disappeared through the window.

Jay looked at her watch: almost 1 am. She reached in through her window and plucked the hipflask of her dad's whiskey from the drawer in her bedside table. She'd lifted it from her dad's coat after he was taken. She unscrewed the cap and sniffed at the top, the smell reminding her of him. She took a swig and winced at the taste, then coughed as it hit her chest. It warmed her. She forced another swig and the night chill didn't feel so harsh. She lay back against the tiles. The flickering light up at Highdown had disappeared. She turned on her side, looked out towards the sea and closed her eyes.

All was quiet at first. Nothing but a gentle ebb and flow of whispers from the depths. 'Tell me what to do,' Jay said into the night. The noise grew as Jay attuned, the whispers becoming a consistent white-noise. She sifted the sounds, filtered, collected and grouped them. But the noise was so desperate, chaotic. 'Slow down,' Jay said aloud, feeling as though she were being cajoled into something. 'What is it?' she whispered back to the sea, and the sounds seemed to sink back into the wind and the waves, allowing Jay to drift off to sleep.

* * *

SHE WOKE SENSING A PRESENCE, shivering in the cold coming from the roof tiles, and pulled herself into a tight ball.

A noise. She strained to hear, then lifted her head to see through the window into her room. Nothing. She struggled for her eyes to adjust to the darkness inside. 'Is someone there?' she said.

The figure of a man emerged from the shadows and into the light of the half-moon, scruffily dressed in dark clothes. In a short-sleeved shirt he made no attempt to hide the mark on his wrist, labelling him as a level six. Jay opened her mouth but no sound came. Before she could move, the man reached and dragged Jay by her top and her hair, back through the window.

She closed her eyes with the pain and screamed aloud. The man clamped his hand over her mouth and Jay silently screamed Stitch's name into her head. He threw her down on her bed and pulled back his fist before putting a finger to his lips.

'Who's Stitch?' the man asked.

Jay's breathing was shallow and rapid, her hands shaking. She told herself to calm down. He came closer. 'You have power. Like your dad.' Jay edged back against the wall. 'I came for the notebook,' the man said, 'but what a bonus. How have we not seen you before?' Jay recoiled further as he leaned forward and pulled her sleeve. 'Level eight,' he said, leaning away from her. The man gathered himself and stared into her. 'You are something quite different.'

* * *

STITCH SAT bolt upright in bed. 'Jay!' he shouted.

He scratched his head, eyes half-closed and looking around his room as if trying to figure out where he was. 'Jay?' he said aloud.

He laid back down and pulled his duvet over his head. A bad dream. Something about Jay. A man threatening her.

'Jay!' Stitch shouted again, once more sitting bolt upright. He checked his watch: 3 am. He flung himself out of bed and scrabbled around for the clothes he'd dumped on the floor.

He grabbed his rucksack, packed the night before, his tent strapped to its base. He made his way downstairs, bumping and scraping with his rucksack against the wall, pictures knocked squint, not bothering to be quiet – it would take an earthquake before his dad would even stir. Reaching the telephone in the hallway, Stitch punched in 999 and waited for the emergency services operator.

'Police, please.'

The voice on the other end was slow and calm, insisting on Stitch giving his name and location before she would listen to the nature of the emergency. Stitch relayed the details of Jay's situation, that there was an intruder in her house, skipping the bit about how Jay had contacted him. The operator dispatched a response team to Jay's address and asked him to stay on the line. Stitch hung up and dialled the number for Cassie's house.

Cassie's brother Charlie answered the phone. 'Hello?'

'Charlie, it's Stitch. Get Cassie for me, it's urgent.'

'She's asleep, Stitch.'

'How weird,' Stitch said. 'I know she's asleep, it's 3 am. Please get her, Charlie, tell her to hurry.'

A long minute passed before Cassie came on the line. 'What's up?'

'It's Jay. She's in trouble. I've called the police and they're on their way round there. We need to go.'

'Go where?'

'To Jay's, meet me in the car park at the One Stop outside your place. Two minutes.' Stitch hung up the phone before Cassie could argue. He took one last look back into his house, the sound of his dad's snoring echoing down the stairs, before turning and leaving by the front door.

* * *

CASSIE WAS ALREADY in the car park as Stitch emerged from the alleyway and into the light of the streetlamps.

'You were quick,' said Stitch.

'You said two minutes,' said Cassie, her arms hugging herself for warmth. 'It's been nearly three minutes.'

They set off towards Jay's house. 'Where's your stuff?' said Stitch.

'What stuff?'

'In case we need to hit the road.'

'I'm sorry, what...?'

'Cassie, come on...'

'Stitch!' Cassie stopped dead.

'OK, walk and I'll talk.' Stitch filled Cassie in on the message he'd heard from Jay. It then took all of Stitch's persuasive powers to stop Cassie turning around and going straight home. Then they saw two men standing outside Jay's house.

'Get back!' Stitch pulled Cassie back into the darkness of the bushes before she could step out into the lamplight.

'Who is it?'

'I don't know, but they don't look like police.' As Stitch said this, a police car emerged, crawling around the corner without its blue lights flashing. It pulled up outside Jay's house.

'They're in no hurry,' said Cassie. Two officers emerged from the vehicle and approached the men. They shook hands. 'Those guys must be Scanners.'

'Readers,' corrected Cassie, edging back further. 'This isn't good.'

After a few moments, the uniformed officers returned to their car.

'We need to get in there,' said Stitch. 'If they figure out who Jay is, they'll take her away. She won't stand a chance.'

'And we will?' said Cassie.

'We can try. Round the back.' Stitch took off running, bent over double, around the houses to the back of Jay's garden. Cassie followed.

Stitch dropped his rucksack at the foot of the tree and they shinned up and onto the roof. Stitch peeked in through the open Velux. Jay was on the floor, face down and motionless. A dark shadow of a man rooted through the drawers beneath her desk. As Stitch watched, he emptied each drawer onto the floor and sifted through the debris with gloved hands. Stitch and Cassie looked at each other, unsure what to do.

Jay's bedroom door opened. Sammy walked in and stopped when he saw his sister lying prone on the floor. Before Stitch or Cassie could call a warning, the man stepped from the shadows and held a cloth to Sammy's face. Sammy struggled, but not for long. After he'd been laid face down beside his sister, the man resumed his chaotic searching.

Cassie pressed her mouth against Stitch's ear and whispered, 'I'll create a diversion. You get them out.'

Before Stitch could answer, Cassie stood and threw open the window with a single, purposeful move and shouted, 'Come on Jay,' in a slurred voice. 'Come out and play.'

Cassie wobbled and teetered on the roof, walking the ridge tiles. The man came to the window and watched her for a moment before pulling himself out onto the roof. 'You should get down from there,' he said.

Cassie stopped and made as if she were squinting to see who he was. 'Well,' she slurred, 'she never told me she had a fancy man.'

'No? Well, I'm offended.'

Cassie wobbled. 'I'm just surprised,' she said, then faked a hiccup.

'Surprised?'

'She would never normally go for someone like…'

'Like what?' the man said, looking around for his best route up the roof slope to get to Cassie.

'Like, short and a little soft around the middle,' Cassie laughed and then made as if she'd tripped, scuttling down the slope of the roof towards the man. He caught her, and they spun around, leaving Stitch a clear path to climb unseen through the window.

Inside, Sammy had woken and was bent over Jay, trying to wake her.

'What's going on?' Sammy asked.

'Readers, we need to go, like right now. There are two more outside.'

'They've come for me,' Jay croaked.

Stitch said to Sammy, 'Grab your stuff. We're leaving now. Be quick!' Sammy ducked out of the room.

Noises from the roof told Stitch that Cassie's drunken charade continued. 'Jay, can you get up? We need to go.' Jay nodded and struggled to her feet. Stitch helped as Jay threw some bits into her bag – the notebook from under her mattress, along with Sammy's fishing book. Spare clothes. A sleeping bag and torch. Sammy arrived back in the room, a rucksack on his back. He nodded at Stitch and the three of them turned to the window.

Cassie had collapsed against the Reader, forcing him to hold her up as they teetered near the edge of the roof. Their backs were turned. Stitch climbed out of the window first, followed by Sammy. As Jay's feet met the tiles, the Reader pushed Cassie aside and turned. He brought his fingers up to his temple. Jay said, 'The others are coming.'

Cassie took her opportunity, brought her shoulder down and, taking him by surprise, sent the Reader over the edge of the roof and into the neighbouring garden.

They peered over the edge at the man tangled in the hedgerow. 'We need to go right now,' Jay said, then glanced back at her room.

Stitch followed her gaze. He could hear that the other two Readers had arrived.

Sammy slammed the Velux window closed. 'Let's go.'

The four of them scrambled down the tree. Stitch hiked his rucksack onto his back and lurched into the alleyway that led to the lockup, where the car was parked. Sammy opened the up-and-over garage door and threw the keys to Jay. She climbed into the front seat of the old Ford and froze.

'What is it?' said Stitch from the back seat.

'Smells of Dad, that manky Drum rolling tobacco he used to smoke.'

'Can we reminisce later maybe?' said Stitch.

Sammy put a hand on her shoulder. 'We really need to move.' Jay turned the key in the ignition. The starter motor whirred and turned over, but the engine didn't fire. Sammy screamed. Two men had turned the corner of the garage. Jay fumbled for the keys in the ignition. Stitch and Cassie joined Sammy in screaming for Jay to move. On the second try the Beast did not disappoint. It sparked into life, rumbling and spluttering. Jay released the clutch and stamped on the accelerator. The car slammed both men into the sides of the garage as it squeezed past at speed, swept away through the gravel car park and into the warren of back streets.

PART III

INTO THE WOODS

15

Cassie had insisted on picking up a few supplies before they headed into the middle of nowhere and as far as Stitch could tell she had no sense of urgency. While they waited, Sammy fiddled with the dial on the car's radio, receiving little but static. Sammy would never see fault in anything that Cassie did. He'd wait a year if that's what she asked of him.

Only Jay seemed to know how much danger they were in. She could feel the Readers.

They were coming.

The streetlamp next to the car flickered and died and Stitch wondered if it was a sign. The rest of the lights in the street blinked out one by one, taking the orange sheen off the morning and revealing its grey reality.

Stitch turned to Jay. 'Did you say anything to your mum about leaving?'

'No time.'

'I wrote my dad a note last night,' said Stitch. 'A long note. More of an essay, actually.'

'Seriously?'

'If he won't talk to me...'

'What did you say?'

'Everything. Laid it all out there.'

'Did it help?' asked Jay.

'I think so. I guess we'll see when all this is over.' He turned to the window. 'Finally,' he said, as Cassie appeared from the alleyway, rucksack on her back. He looked up at Jay, willing her to start the engine, put the beast into gear and hold the clutch. Sammy turned and watched, a weak smile on his face as Cassie sauntered towards the car.

'Oh, seriously, *come on*,' said Stitch.

'Ready?' said Jay, as Cassie closed the boot and climbed in next to Stitch.

'I guess,' said Cassie.

'What did you say to your parents?' Sammy asked.

Cassie shrugged. 'They won't notice I'm gone.' Stitch knew that Cassie was exaggerating her parents' disinterest. Her brother might not register her absence, but her parents would flip.

'But you left them a note or something?' said Jay.

Cassie nodded. 'Said we were going camping.'

* * *

JAY PULLED the old Ford into the car park. They had a steady hour or so climb ahead of them, then through the valley and up to the ring of trees at the Highdown summit.

Stitch opened the boot. Sammy pulled his rucksack from the car. 'It'll be warm tonight. Perfect for a night under the stars.' They tightened the straps of their rucksacks and headed into the trees.

Under the cover of trees, Stitch relaxed a little, feeling at last hidden from the Readers who would be sure to be tracking them. He glanced at Jay. He sensed her worry for her little brother and best friends, her guilt at dragging them all into danger. She would have to dig deep to develop her strength, her power, but she still seemed reluctant to let go and embrace it.

The four stayed close to the edge of the woods, wading through bracken out of sight of the road. Jay led the way to higher ground, navigating on instinct. Within an hour, they had made it onto the chalk ridge and stepped out from the trees. The countryside opened up in widescreen, the sun now directly overhead.

Chest-high rapeseed ran away down the vast slope, thickening to a homogenous sunflower yellow at the bottom of the valley. To the northwest, nearer now, was Highdown.

'Let's rest. Up there.' Jay motioned to a high point on the chalk ridge.

They sat on the hard ground and ate biscuits. Sammy fashioned a small fire to test out his camping kettle, excited when they heard the whistle. Stitch noticed Jay rubbing her temples. 'What happened back there?' Jay said, almost to herself.

'I'm guessing he used some kind of tranquilizer, maybe ether,' said Stitch. 'You were out when we got there.' He looked over at Sammy, 'Hey, Sammy, how's the head?'

Sammy rubbed his forehead. 'Still throbbing.'

'Impressive performance from Cassie though,' said Stitch.

She smiled. 'Enjoyed seeing him plant head first into a hedge.'

Jay looked up into the distance. 'I don't think that will be the last we see of them.'

Stitch gazed over the patchwork landscape. The hill at Highdown was clear, a few miles west of their location. To the northeast was the ring of trees at Cissbury, another high point on the chalk Downs. Like Highdown, Cissbury was a hilltop peppered with trees and falling steeply on all sides. Perfect for sledging in winter. From the top you can see past Brighton to the chalk cliffs in the east, and back towards Highdown. Chanctonbury was out of sight, four or five miles to the north. From above, the three hill forts formed a triangle with each side between five and ten miles long.

'See Cissbury Ring,' Stitch said, pointing.

'Listen a minute.' Jay raised her left arm in the direction of Highdown and her right towards Cissbury. 'The connection of the three hill forts makes a triangle. Like a bow. Imagine it with an arrow pointing towards a fourth location.'

'To the gateway?'

'Maybe, but I don't know which direction the arrow points. I'm hoping we will see when we get to Highdown. But even if we do, there must be another line, a trajectory that intersects this one.'

'How do we find the second line?' said Stitch.

'I'm hoping for divine inspiration,' she said. 'We need to get up to Highdown.'

16

Stitch led the way into the valley. The four of them strung out as they crossed a wooden bridge over a stream, then over a stile and back into the trees before beginning the climb. The shade of the trees brought relief from the glare and heat of the sun. Stitch rested a moment to allow the group to collect before pressing on.

Stitch knew Highdown Hill as well as Jay did. When Jay's dad made a makeshift go-kart from an old pram, they spent Sunday afternoons racing and rattling down the steep chalk slopes. Its wheels were the size of a car's wheels, with thin white rubber strips for tyres. They bounced around on a chipboard base for hours, scraping through narrow gaps and over bumps and humps, screaming and laughing while narrowly avoiding injury. Stitch's arms would get covered in scratches from the hawthorn bushes, their only means of braking, his legs battered and bruised from nicks and bumps on trees and branches.

At the top of Highdown, Stitch turned full circle to look over the fields, and then across to the copse of trees at the summit. He strained his eyes to see if Chanctonbury or Cissbury were visible from where he stood but it was too dark and murky to see. The sea was invisible through the clouds but present in the salty breeze coming over the hill.

'Hey,' said Jay, interrupting Stitch from his thoughts. 'I know where we can set up camp.' She led the way towards the ring of trees at the top of the hill. When Jay entered the copse, she looked as though she'd come up against an invisible barrier. Stitch watched as she doubled back, saying nothing, and found another way to enter the trees.

'What's up?' said Stitch.

'This is the way in,' said Jay. All the hill-fort settlements had distinct entrance points, but these were no longer visible above ground, long buried under layers of history.

Jay chose a quiet spot, within the outer circle of trees but away from the main paths, the central point, and the inner circle. Stitch recognised the terrain from his time up there with Jay and her dad. On the eastern slope, the chalk outcrop dove to a trough that was difficult to negotiate if you were unfamiliar with it. 'Watch your step through there,' he said to Sammy as they side-stepped down to the lower ridge. The view to the north was vast and sheltered from the south wind.

Cassie dumped her bag and turned to Sammy. 'We're gonna need a good fire.'

'On it,' said Sammy.

'You OK?' Stitch asked.

She nodded, forcing a smile. 'They'll be tracking us.'

'You'll know if they get close,' said Stitch.

Jay sighed. 'I hope so,' she said.

'Why don't we set up camp and see if we can see Cissbury and Chanctonbury from here. There might be fires tonight.'

* * *

STITCH'S EYELIDS GREW HEAVY. Sammy flicked through his little hardback book on spin fishing as Cassie and Jay stood looking north over the ridge, Ben's notebook open in Jay's hands.

Stitch shook away his fatigue and stood to join them. 'Chanctonbury?' he said, squinting to see a flicker of orange light in the distance.

Jay nodded. 'And that's Cissbury.' She pointed towards a larger orange glow further east. 'That's the first bow-shape from the legend. The line from here to Chanctonbury is the long edge, the handle of the bow. Then from here to Cissbury, and from Cissbury to Chanctonbury, is the string of the bow, held taut at Cissbury.'

Stitch said, 'That's what you drew on your map?'

'Yes, but the thing you can't see on the map is there.' Jay pointed.

Stitch squinted. 'What?'

'See the line of trees that runs from Cissbury? Thin line of poplars. They run directly from Cissbury to that village.'

'What is it?' Sammy said, joining them.

'I get it. That's the arrow,' said Stitch. 'The trajectory.'

'Exactly. But it doesn't tell us the distance,' said Jay.

* * *

SAT BY THE FIRE, Stitch studied Jay's map, marking out the line of the trees that projected from Cissbury. He and Jay had figured the precise angles from the location of Findon Village in the distance, visible by the streetlights. From this, they marked a line on the map that extended through the Downs, hoping that it would cross a location with a mapped confluence of rivers, but there was none.

'Nothing?' said Cassie, unable to hide her irritation.

'Nothing where two rivers meet. There are a bunch of rivers, tributaries, lakes, all sorts,' said Stitch.

'That's what I found before,' said Jay. 'We need the other trajectory so we can find the intersect.'

'Where's the other bow and bloody arrow then?' said Cassie. Stitch and Jay were silent. Sammy stood and looked out towards the glow at Cissbury.

Stitch closed his eyes and took a breath. He'd read a lot about the hill forts, and their supposed power. He believed in Jay, and her powers, and he sensed her strength growing, fuelled by the energy of the land.

'Stitch?' Jay interrupted his thoughts. 'Remind me what the legend says about the second set of lines, the second bow and arrow?'

Stitch flicked through Ben's notebook, then spoke slowly, dictating the transcription of the legend. 'From the second bow came a second arrow, in a wave of mutilation...'

'Charming,' said Sammy.

'Are there any sea-forts down on the coast?' said Cassie.

'Why?' said Sammy.

'Cassie's right. The wave,' said Jay. 'Could be the wave as in the sea.'

'Exactly,' said Cassie.

'Why *mutilation*?' said Sammy. 'I don't like the sound of that.'

The four of them crowded around Jay's map, tilting it towards the fire for light. Stitch searched the nearby coast on the map for a sign of a fort.

'What about Bamber?' said Stitch, pointing to the castle on the map.

'That's nowhere near the coast, and probably a few hundred years after the time of the legend,' said Jay.

Stitch thought hard, trying to find a link. 'Down at Beach Lane, the café there, you remember? We've been there loads.'

'The grannie café?' said Cassie.

'On the wall in there,' said Stitch. 'They have all those old pictures.'

'You actually looked at those?' said Cassie.

'They talk about Bamber Castle, which used to be on the coast, before the coast moved. Bamber was built as a fortification of existing points of defence on the coast.'

'How do you even know this stuff?' said Cassie.

'I can read,' Stitch said without looking at Cassie. He stared at Jay, willing his enthusiasm to break the surface and give him an ally.

'That's it,' said Jay. 'We need to go for a coffee and cake session.'

'What?' said Sammy.

'Beach Lane Café, we need to get down there.' Jay stood as if to head off.

'Rest first,' said Stitch. 'We have the first bow, and the trajectory. We can go at first light, head back to the car, then get there for that breakfast you wanted, Sammy.'

Jay nodded, took the notebook from Stitch, and settled by the fire. Stitch watched her turning the pages of her dad's notebook and thought of his dad, wondered if he'd be worried.

In his note, he explained how he'd felt frozen out of his dad's life since his mum's death. He looked over at Jay, the light of the fire giving her an unearthly glow. He tried to understand what it would take for his friend to delve deeper into her power, to use the inner strength that Stitch knew was there.

She turned to him and spoke. 'We need to be careful. If I open up too much, I'll end up leading those Readers straight to us, and to the gateway.'

'You need to see what those powers can do if we are to stand any chance of fending them off. We don't know how many of them there are. Or how close they are. If your power is growing like your dad said, then you are our best chance.'

Jay lowered her gaze again. Stitch watched as Jay slipped into sleep, the flicker of light from the fire dancing across her face, lighting the curve of her cheek and accentuating her lips.

Stitch couldn't sleep. Sammy and Cassie huddled for warmth, both asleep. Jay had turned over and was facing away from him, her shoulder rising and falling with her steady breathing. The fire was reduced to embers, but up in the trees behind them an intermittent orange glow flickered. He pulled up the hood of his jacket and climbed to the edge of the inner circle.

Around a small fire in the middle of the clearing were six or seven figures sat on logs. Stitch watched from behind a tree. Outside their circle of log seats they had candles on spikes, embedded in the ground. He caught the occasional scent of incense.

Stitch had read about the pagan rituals up at the hill forts on the Downs. As he watched, one of the figures rose and walked around the circle of candles and back to his seat, like a child's game. There was no music, no rhythmic drumming, no chanting. It was peaceful. He counted the revolutions made by the next figure. 'Six,' he said aloud.

'Seven.' A voice from behind him.

Stitch jumped. An adrenaline spike fizzed across his skin.

He turned to see a tall man, caped and hooded like Obi-Wan. 'Seven,' the man repeated. 'Those in the inner circle each make seven revolutions in the time it takes the seventh member, me, to make seven revolutions of this circle.' He nodded at the tree that Stitch leaned against, a tree that formed part of the inner circle.

'You scared me,' Stitch said, his heart still pounding.

'Join us if you like? Where are your friends?'

'Asleep,' Stitch said.

'Come,' the man said, heading around the circle for a distance before turning in to cross the treeline. Despite himself, Stitch stepped forward. 'No,' the man said, clear and firm. 'Here, come through here.' He pointed between two trees.

The figures watched as they approached. Obi-Wan pointed to a log for Stitch. They each pushed down their hoods so that Stitch could see their faces. Of the seven, three were women. All were middle-aged, all were smiling like they were happy for the new company.

'Why seven?' said Stitch.

Obi-Wan introduced himself then. 'Dave. I'm from London.'

'My friends call me Stitch.'

The others did the same and Stitch took in some of their names – Sally, Joe... all from London.

'Why seven revolutions?' Stitch repeated.

The woman named Sally spoke. 'It's a protection ritual,' she smiled. 'We put back what those of ignorance have opened up. One of the myths says that if you complete seven circuits of the inner circle of trees in the time it takes for the clock to strike twelve times, then the devil will appear. So people try it. They don't realise they're unwinding the coils. The Devil won't appear of course, but they inflict damage, nonetheless. So we come and make the necessary repairs. Seven inner circuits by seven people in the time it takes for seven circuits of the outer circle of trees. Once a month is enough.'

'Wow,' said Stitch.

'You think we're crazy, don't you,' another of the figures said, passing a bottle around for Stitch.

'No thanks.' Stitch waved away the bottle, thinking of the blood-drinking scene in the *Lost Boys*. 'So are you done for the month? Was that it, Devil's access route all closed up?'

They laughed and another bottle of wine was retrieved from a bag. The man next to Sally whispered something in her ear and she looked over, catching Stitch's eye for a moment before he had to look away.

'Joe thinks you have power,' she said.

Stitch looked at Joe and back to Sally, shaking his head. Joe spoke. 'Not in the traditional sense, I don't think.' He looked towards Stitch's wrist. 'I think you have something a little different.' Stitch remained speechless, with a strong sense that he should get away before it was too late, but at the same time a curiosity that glued his feet to the floor. Joe continued. 'Do you have a marking?'

Stitch pulled up his sleeve to show nothing but a pale wrist. Joe stood, examining his wrist and then taking a seat next to him. 'I'm getting a sense of a power in you.'

Stitch smiled and leaned away from Joe. 'Well, that's where you're wrong, my friend.'

'Do you know anything about spiritual healing?'

Stitch shrugged, looking at Joe. 'It's all about the transfer of energy,' Joe said. 'It's not religious.'

Stitch glanced at Sally for reassurance. She smiled back at him and then shook her head. 'Joe, leave him be.'

Joe continued to look at Stitch as if he were peering *into* him. 'It's more about the promotion of natural self-healing by bringing a state of balance, connecting things.'

'Why are you telling me this?'

Joe laughed, then stood to return to his seat. 'I'm saying that you have something of the healer in you. Like me. You bring the energy together, connect it. I bet you're a middle child?'

Stitch shook his head. 'Only child,' he said. He sat and talked with them for some time, sharing in their stories. As he began to yawn more frequently, thinking about getting back before he passed the point of sleep, the pagans rose one by one to leave. 'You're not driving back to London now?' Stitch said, thinking of the volume of wine that they all seemed to have drunk.

'Dave's driving. Tee-total. And he has a minibus licence.' They laughed and began to file towards the south edge of the circle.

'Good to meet you. Good luck on your journey.'

Joe hung back a moment, reached into his bag and pulled out a book, handing it to Stitch. 'You have this. I can get hold of another copy,' he said. Stitch scanned the covers. There was nothing to indicate its title, or contents. 'It's a kind of background and guide to the healing elements of the power,' Joe said. 'It's a bit abstract in places but if you stick with it, then you'll get something out of it I'm sure.'

Stitch stammered, 'Err... sure. Thanks.'

Joe smiled. 'No pressure. Take it or leave it. I might be wrong.'

He turned to leave, and a shiver ran through Stitch as he held onto the book with both hands. He turned his attention back to the fire, the smouldering embers mesmerising as they blurred at the edges through his tired eyes.

*** * ***

JAY WOKE, shivering. It was light enough to see, but the sun had not yet risen above the treeline. She turned over to see Sammy and Cassie draped over each other. She smiled to herself and looked over to the empty sleeping bag where she expected Stitch. She scanned the ridge for a sign of him but all was quiet.

She struggled to her feet and stretched, aching from a restless night on a chalk mattress. She clambered up the bank, slipping and catching her elbow on a flint and crying out. She tried again and made it to the top.

She rubbed her elbow. At the edge of the trees, Jay could see that Stitch was asleep on the ground next to a still smoking fire. She walked around the inner circle, still unable to cross the treeline. Since reaching the top of Highdown the night before, her powers had been confusing. They were tangled, indecisive. Her natural inclination was to bury them as deep as she could. To prevent them from creating that unsettling feeling, the glimmer of anxiety, and the risk of detection.

She stopped at a point along the treeline that her body told her was the entrance – an almost imperceptible communication, a fluctuation in the energy. As she crossed, the wind was taken out of her. She struggled to catch her breath, doubled over, her throat constricting. She couldn't contain the tangled thoughts, the bubbling powers. Visions came, and she shut them down one by one. Through the mind of sleeping Stitch, she saw the seven hooded figures with whom he'd spent the night. The energy of the inner circle was strong, coming in pulses from the floor. The solid earth, the stretching roots of the beech trees reinforcing the very foundation of Highdown, the teeming masses of life below the surface, in the trees, in the sky above them and out to the sea – all were connected.

It took a minute for Jay to compose herself, to steady her breathing. She pushed the tangles down and pressed on through the clearing to where Stitch lay. 'Hey.' She kicked gently at his foot. He groaned and shielded his eyes from the light, squinting. 'What are you doing sleeping up here?'

Stitch looked around himself as if trying to remember. He grunted, 'Pagan sacrifice.'

'Come on, let's go see if we can see the sea.' She headed towards the outer circle of trees. Stitch scrambled to his feet, brushed himself down and followed, limping like he had a dead leg. Jay stood gazing out to sea when Stitch stopped alongside her. She glanced at him. 'You look worse for wear.'

'What are we looking at?' he said.

'There it is,' Jay said, pointing.

'What?'

'Beach Lane Café.' The outline of the café was visible against the white of the sky, standing above the level of the sea front houses like a lifeboat station, on wooden stilts over the sand. Jay turned to head back to the others. 'Let's move,' she said to Stitch, who scampered after her.

18

Just a few hours after Jay and the others had left Highdown Hill, the Reader stood beside the remains of the fire inside the ring of trees, kicking at the charred lumps of wood.

At the summit of Highdown, the Reader, Marcus, stood confused by what he sensed. He felt Jay, her power familiar to him now. But there was more. Others. More than just her friends. He felt an energy interacting with his, distorting what he could see. But something else too, a boy, someone in Jay's group with whom he connected. He felt frustrated; he wasn't used to feeling confused. He kicked hard at a piece of smoking wood, sending it fizzing across the clearing.

Two other Readers stood at the edge of the trees, allowing Marcus his space, although he could hear their every word as clearly as if he were standing right next to them. Jimmy, the Reader responsible for taking Ben away, and for failing to retrieve the notebook, turned to the man next to him. 'You think he smells something, Drake?'

Drake nodded. 'It stinks of her up here. Would have

thought you'd connect better than any of us, since it was you she gave the slip.' Drake stepped away toward Marcus.

Jimmy followed. 'They caught me by surprise. It wasn't just the girl who had power. They were shielding.'

'You need to focus on finding her,' Marcus said as they reached him. Marcus turned towards the coast, sensing that Jay had gone south, away from the Downs and the hill forts. Drake and Jimmy sat beside the remains of the fire and Drake lit a cigarette from a half-burnt stick. Marcus looked out over the fields to the south, towards the sea. He clenched his fists and tried to suppress his growing frustration. Where was that girl?

A parade of soldier ants veered around his boot, repelled by him. The sun reflected off their shiny black bodies as more emerged from the grass, scuttling and bumping into each other.

Marcus remembered Jay as a baby in the pram at the bottom of the garden. He had little experience but she seemed a fussy baby, always interrupting as he and Sonia lay together. Those were lazy days, a different time, the summer just after his transformation. The affair ended less than a year after Jay was born. If he had known back then that the squawking little baby would grow to such strength, to such a threat... he could have ended it before it started. He shook his head to clear it. It didn't matter. Regrets were futile. Now was his time.

Marcus was the strongest Reader on the force. He knew of no one stronger and took pride in this fact. The only threat to his remaining the most powerful was the State's ability to reduce, and the possibility of reduction by a level eight Given. Jay would not be the one to threaten him. He would get to her long before she grew into her powers.

Marcus looked over his shoulder at his two colleagues by

the fire, arguing between themselves. His attention was drawn back to the sea, towards where he could see the Beach Lane Café in the distance. He looked down, kicked out at the ants at his feet and turned to walk south, back towards the car park.

19

As Cassie pulled the Ford out of the Highdown car park, Jay turned to where she'd transcribed the words of the legend.

'Read it aloud, let's hear,' called Stitch from the back.

'It talks about a village at the confluence of rivers. That's the bit we've been getting to. It says the village was damned, cursed, and fated to die –

"In the rainy season, the rivers would swell and burst their banks, destroying houses and businesses. Many villagers left to settle in the surrounding areas. A sink-hole opened up to form a deep lake at the point of confluence of two rivers."

'Two? I thought it was three?' said Sammy.

'Hang on,' said Jay, 'it's coming –

"The sink-hole formed a reservoir, containing the flow from the rivers. Whilst only twenty metres across, the hole was said to stretch deep into the earth's core. At the pit, the villagers saw that a third, previously uncharted, underground river also flowed into the sink-hole. It was this unnamed river of unknown source that was said to bring luck and to lift the curse on the village."

'That's convenient,' said Cassie, turning onto the main road towards the coast.

Jay rolled her eyes and continued. 'It says –

"Some years later, there were three children, sisters, the youngest of whom was persecuted for her witchery. She was protected only by the guile and cunning of her two sisters who kept her safe, hidden from the church elders who pursued her, and would surely have put her on trial. On the warm afternoons of the summer, when the winds dropped, and the sun dipped in the sky, the sisters would break free of the village to explore the land to the north, where the rivers flowed so full of fish you could reach in and take them in your hands."'

'That's Dad's story,' said Sammy.

Jay nodded acknowledgement to her brother then continued –

' *"The youngest loved nothing more than to explore the rivers and flood plains with her sisters, and, truth be told, she was at one with that world. She had the feel of the waters, a sense of its inhabitants, its multitude of living things. The fish would come to her, and she would take them in her hands, whisper to them and return them to the water."'*

'The fish whisperer,' said Cassie.

' *"Not long after the sisters passed their eighteenth birthdays, they came across an unmapped river. A river that disappeared underground. Deducing that it must be the third source that fed their village lake, they built a log raft on which they navigated the river, emerging as they had suspected at the sink-hole lake, plunging beneath the water.*

As the sisters floated to the surface, only two figures appeared, soaked to the skin as they clambered up the side of the pool. The third sister was forever lost."'

'What happened to her?' asked Sammy.

'It doesn't say,' said Jay.

'"After a time, with the flow from the three rivers, the entire area sank deeper into the earth and the village became uninhabitable. It disappeared and was remembered as the Interland."'

Jay finished reading, and the four were quiet for a moment.

'What's up, Jay?' said Sammy.

She looked up from the notebook. 'I feel manic. Since Highdown. I can't seem to stop my powers from bubbling. And there's a Reader on to us and getting closer.'

'Is it the one who was at the house?' said Cassie.

'Someone stronger, and more than one of them.'

Stitch leaned between the front seats. 'We need to keep going. We won't be able to hide. The only thing we can do is stay ahead of them.'

'We need to *lose* them,' said Jay. 'If the Interland exists, we can't risk leading the Readers there.'

* * *

CASSIE PULLED INTO A PETROL STATION. Jay put unleaded in the car as the other three headed inside. Sammy picked a steak pie from the fridge and a bottle of water from the shelf. Stitch and Cassie argued over the merits of Dr Pepper versus Coke.

Sammy joined the queue behind a musty smelling man in a hi-vis jacket. He gave the man some room and looked out over the forecourt to where Jay was still filling the car. A van pulled into the space beside her, the driver getting out to fill the tank. The other man in the front of the van wound down his window to get a look at Jay. Sammy could see that he was speaking to Jay but that she was ignoring him, avoiding his eye.

Sammy smiled at his sister as she entered the shop. 'Making friends, sis?'

'Tossers.'

'What did they say?'

'Usual crap,' said Jay as Stitch joined them in the queue, his arms loaded with food. Cassie had almost as much, including a two-litre bottle of Dr Pepper.

'You two have enough sugar?' said Sammy.

Stitch displayed his goods. 'Enough for all of us,' he said.

'There she is,' said a man entering the store – the driver of the van.

'What's his problem?' Cassie said to Jay.

'Ignore him,' said Jay. Sammy's heart raced. The two men had joined the queue. In Sammy's experience, it was him and Stitch that people usually picked on when the four of them were together. For some reason, men thought that two males accompanying women were fair game for fighting. Winner takes the females. It was always Cassie that got them out of it. Sammy hadn't yet met any guys that Cassie couldn't see off.

The two men continued to make snide comments, smirking and eyeing Cassie who couldn't help but react. 'What you staring at?' she said through gritted teeth. The two men laughed and Cassie turned away from them. At the tills, the men finished paying while the cashier was still working through Stitch and Cassie's mountain of food. As they left, the bigger one brushed past Cassie and said, 'You want to see what I've got in my van, love?' before pushing out through the door. Cassie swung around and headed after him.

'Cassie,' called Jay. 'Leave it, we need to get going.'

Cassie ignored her friend and pushed through the door and after the two men. Sammy watched through the window. Cassie caught up with them as they reached their van. Sammy stared, a mix of admiration and fear for Cassie. 'Shit, Jay. What's she going to do? Those guys are big.'

'Don't worry about Cassie,' said Jay, helping Stitch to bag all their food. 'It's those men you want to be concerned for.'

As the three of them left the shop, Cassie was squaring up to the men, taking a fighting stance. One of the men laughed and turned to head back to his van as the other moved to shove Cassie. She dodged him and kicked out at his leg. He stumbled and turned to Cassie, shouting.

Sammy and Jay got in the car, Jay taking the driver's seat and starting the engine. As Cassie goaded the two men, Stitch disappeared around the back of their van. After a minute, Cassie left the men, shouting, and climbed into the car.

'Finished playing?' said Jay.

'They're not putting up much of a fight,' said Cassie.

'Let's go,' said Stitch, climbing into the back seat next to Cassie.

Jay pulled away as one of the men made as if he would try to get to them, changing his mind as Jay sped away. Through the rear windscreen, Sammy watched with a grin as they ran to the van and jumped in to make chase. 'They're following.'

'No they're not,' said Stitch, smiling. 'I let three of their tyres down. Would have done all four if we hadn't rushed off.'

Sammy and Jay laughed as Jay pulled into the flow of traffic and they continued towards Beach Lane Café.

20

The Café was a tired, glass-fronted building too far from the centre of town to attract tourists, but, nestled in the retirement centre of the south coast, made enough in afternoon teas to pay the rent. It sat on wooden columns, like stilts, over the stones. To get in you had to walk across the pebbles and up a flight of steps to the main doors. Windows stretched the full length of the building, providing every table a view of the beach.

Jay and Stitch walked straight to the back which displayed the local history. Cassie and Sammy ordered tea and chose a table at the window, far enough away from two elderly women sharing a pot of tea.

Jay and Stitch stopped at an old map tacked to the wall, studied it for a moment and then looked at each other. Jay pulled out her notebook, her fingers trembling with anticipation. There was a clear resemblance between her dad's sketch and what they were looking at on the wall.

'The second bow,' said Stitch, moving to the wall and tracing his finger along a line on the map to form a triangle from Highdown Hill, to the Castle at Bamber, and then on to a third location further along the coast. 'Where's this?'

'West Beach, Littlehampton,' said Jay, triumphant. 'That's our next stop. We need to get there and look across to see the trajectory... from here.' Jay pointed to the map. 'That's how we find the intersect.' Jay restrained herself from squealing and hugging Stitch.

'And that's how we find the gateway,' smiled Stitch.

Jay looked back to the map on the wall. 'If we're right. If there's a confluence of rivers at the intersection.'

'There will be. There has to be.' Stitch couldn't stop grinning.

A woman edged towards them with a tray holding two pots of tea and four cups, spilling tea onto the tray as she approached. Sammy went to help, taking the two teapots. The woman left the tray and returned to serve another customer.

'Who uses saucers these days?' said Sammy. 'What's wrong with mugs?' He slid the cups onto the table and mopped up the mess with a paper towel. Jay looked out at the sea, waves folding over each other and breaking where the pebbles turned to sand. She was glad to be inside, protected from the wind and the spray, the chapped lips and the earache.

Sammy sipped his tea and winced. 'Earl Grey. I asked for builder's.'

'Oh, just drink it anyway.' Jay smiled. She sipped her own drink, relieved that it was normal tea. A man came in with his Labrador and ordered a coffee. The woman spooned a measure of instant into a cup and topped it up with boiling water from the urn. Stitch and Cassie continued to explore the information boards.

'You think we've found it?' said Sammy. The woman came back with slices of cake and Sammy tucked in with a plastic fork.

'There must be something more. Dad said it was the source of the power, and a gateway to somewhere we could be safe from the Readers.'

'What stops the Readers passing through the gateway?' said Sammy.

'Their power is drawn from a different source. So they can't enter. Only the Given, or people with no power, can enter. The Readers don't generate energy in the same way.' Sammy finished his cake and eyed Jay's. She pushed it towards him and he tucked in as she poured more tea. She took a sip, burning her top lip. Jay thought for a minute, looking back out of the window, over the pebbles to the retreating tide. Clouds gathered, and spits of rain on the window obscured the view. She thought of her mum. 'Reckon the old crow's going nuts?'

'Only when she realises there's no one to get her tea,' Sammy said. 'Jabba the Hutt without the slaves.' Jay felt an uncharacteristic pang of sympathy for her mother, picturing her as she realised she was all alone.

'You reckon we've picked up any of her genetic traits?' Jay said.

'Let's hope you've got the Jabba, and I've got the...' Sammy trailed off.

'Her drive,' Jay said. 'You've got her tenacity. When she gets the bit between the teeth, she won't let go. You have that, but you've turned it into a positive. You have a determination in you.'

Sammy sat back, puffing out his cheeks. He pulled back his sleeve a little. Nothing. He shrugged. 'You've definitely got some Dad in you,' he said. 'You two and your puzzle-powers.' He paused, thinking.

'What was it like, seeing him at the prison?' said Sammy.

'Bit weird to be honest, like we didn't know each other. All he really wanted to talk about were his plans.'

Stitch bumbled over to the table, knocking into it so that Jay's tea spilled. 'How far to West Beach?' he said as he and Cassie sat down.

'Half hour drive,' said Jay. 'I've walked it before. Nothing like walking the beach at dawn.'

'I'll take your word for it,' said Cassie.

Stitch took the teapot from Cassie and as he lifted it to pour, Jay felt a jolt in her chest as if her heart had stopped, as if the air had been sucked from her lungs.

The tea hung in the air between the spout and the tea cup. The bustle in the café died and her friends sat, frozen in time. Jay experienced a moment of deep clarity. She felt the heartbeat of the Reader as if it were beating in her own chest. She knew it was Marcus, the level eight. He was near, and he was coming. Jay glanced around the café. A wasp caught her eye, frozen in mid-flight near the window. As she stared, its wings came into focus, shimmering in the light. They twitched, then flapped, stopped, then flapped again like an old engine sparking into life. It hit the window, bouncing off and going again, trying to get through to the outside.

The world turned. The tea sloshed into the cup and the noise, chatter and rattling of crockery, returned. Jay stood, pushing her chair back so that it toppled onto the floor. She looked around the room, out through the window to the beach and behind her to the carpark. Nothing.

But he was close, she could feel him.

'What?' said Sammy.

'They're here.'

'Who?' said Cassie.

'Where?' said Stitch.

'Close. I don't know. But they're really close. We need to go right now.'

They scrambled to collect their belongings. Out of the café

and onto the stones, they headed for the car park. Almost to the car, it happened again.

It was as if a blanket had been thrown over her world, silencing the seagulls, the wind and the waves. Her friends and brother stood motionless, in mid-stride, and mid-sentence. She stopped, stepped back towards Sammy and touched his face. His eyes were alive, but fixed and sightless. She turned back towards the car park. A man in black, some fifty yards from them, moved through the frozen time just as Jay did.

Jay recognised the shorter of the frozen men. Jimmy. The Reader. She knew that the man in motion was Marcus. The third figure was presumably another Reader.

As Jay sensed the world begin to turn once more, she spun around to face her friends and opened her arms to stop them in their tracks. Cassie and Sammy bundled into her, squawking their displeasure.

'This way, go, now,' Jay said, ushering them around the back of the café. 'They're coming across the car park.'

They turned to run. Cassie and Sammy led Jay and Stitch to a hiding place under the floor of the café, between the thick wooden stilts.

'We can't stay here,' said Stitch. 'They'll sense us. They'll sense Jay.'

Jay poked her head out around a wooden column to see that the three figures were moving towards the café. 'Too late,' she said. 'I'll shield. We can't move now.'

'They'll come after us,' said Stitch

'Cassie, you take Sammy and Stitch, go by road. Sammy knows how to get to West Beach. But, Sammy, take an indirect route.'

'What about you?' said Sammy.

'I'll go the beach route. I'll have to divert up through the scrubland around Ferring but I know it well enough. They'll not be able to follow easily. And splitting up might confuse them.'

Sammy looked concerned. 'Are you sure? Why can't we all just...'

'No time, Sammy. Get to the car and move off east before doubling back to get to West Beach.'

The three men were climbing the wooden steps to the café door.

'They're in, let's go, around the back way.' Sammy, Cassie and Stitch made towards the car.

'Sammy,' called Jay in a loud whisper, then threw him the car keys. With this, Jay turned and ran towards the sea, not looking back, not wanting to allow Marcus to sense her. She ran until she was onto the sand, around the corner past the first breakwater and hidden amongst the hills of stones.

Someone was running towards her.

'Stitch!'

'I'm coming with you.'

'Why?'

'I'm coming, don't argue. Let's go.' He pushed past her and continued along the beach.

Jay was relieved to have Stitch with her, not for any reason she could make sense of, she just knew it was important for them to be together, in the same place. The tide was out past the sandbank and the beach was deserted. Jay decided they should walk along the wide stretch of wet sand between the stones and the sea. She felt safe closer to the water.

Whispers came over the breeze off the sea, whispers that were now familiar to Jay, and comforted her. The sand under her feet moved as she walked, squirming and squeezing as if helping her along. She imagined the lug-worms buried there, leaving their little pyramid-like casts on the surface, the worms that she and her dad used to dig for to fill the bait box when they went fishing. Now they held her, supported her as she and Stitch made their escape from the Readers. For now, they were safe.

Breaking waves frothed over the beds of mussels in the distant shallows. The wind had dropped and after a few minutes walking, it was already warm enough to shed her hoodie. Stitch sparked up conversation from time to time but Jay couldn't formulate words, her mind scrambled by the events at the café. After a while Stitch gave up and they walked in silence.

21
___

The three men stood in the doorway to the café and looked around. The only people inside were two elderly women and a man with his dog. 'She was here,' Marcus said.

'Well she's not anymore. Which way?' said Jimmy, impatient.

Without a word, Marcus turned and descended the wooden steps. Back on the stones he made his way to the Land Rover, his mind distracted. A time freeze had happened to him just once before, on the day he was asked to read one of the prisoners no one else could break. She had been in custody for weeks, but was too powerful for the other Readers to contain. Marcus had been told to manipulate her to make her more agreeable. As he had approached the holding cells, the world around him had frozen, much like it had outside the café. The episode had made Marcus feel sick. It was as if his mind couldn't grasp what was happening and he shut down for a few minutes. When he had gathered himself, everything around him had returned to normal. But he couldn't carry on. He had to leave.

He'd always put the episode down to a psychological anomaly. A one-off. But now...

'What's wrong?' asked Jimmy.

'I can't talk about it,' said Marcus.

'Which way?' said Drake.

'I'm not sure,' said Marcus.

Jimmy sat forward in the back seat. 'What do you mean you're not sure? Which way? Tell me you know which way?'

Marcus couldn't get a fix on them. The signal was confused. 'They've split up.'

'Then we follow the girl,' said Drake. 'Which way?'

Marcus closed his eyes for a moment and then got out of the car. Jimmy and Drake looked at each other and then followed. Marcus led them back towards the café and onto the stones, heading for the sea. At the water's edge he stopped, looking along the line of the breaking waves towards the west.

'She's walking?' asked Jimmy.

'Two of them.'

'Let's go, they can't be far,' said Drake, starting along the sand but getting bogged down in the soft surface. The sand glooped and moved around his feet. As Jimmy made to step towards his friend, he too found his feet getting stuck.

Marcus took in a deep breath, drinking in the power of the girl, sensing its influence. 'Her power is growing,' he said.

Drake made his way out of the sand. 'You can feel it?'

'And something else. There's something in one of the others.'

'Power?'

'No.' Marcus tapped his own forehead with frustration. 'He's in here.'

'Then you can use him?' said Drake.

Marcus nodded, then closed his eyes. He focused on the connection. It took him just a few seconds to enter Sammy's mind but the connection was weak. Sammy had reached a safe distance, too far away for Marcus to use the full power of control and influence. 'I can't stop them.'

'Then let's go,' said Drake.

'Wait.' Marcus closed his eyes again. He focused again, entering Sammy's mind with force, digging through the consciousness and into the core. He squeezed as hard as he could before Sammy slipped out of range. 'Something at least,' he said.

'Good,' said Drake.

'We need to call in the others,' Marcus said.

Drake looked surprised. 'We don't need more Readers, surely. It's one girl.'

Marcus turned away from Drake. 'I told you. She's more than that, don't underestimate her power.' Marcus turned to see Jimmy still battling with the sinking sand. 'Not this way,' he shouted, 'we go by road.' With this he turned and made back up the beach towards the car park.

22

They stuck to the beach all the way through to Ferring, where the public roads veered north and the sea rolled up against private gardens. 'How can someone lay claim to the sand and the sea?' said Jay. 'Just how far out to sea does it belong to them?' Jay jumped the fence easily enough, daring anyone to try to stop her. Stitch remained quiet, twice looking over his shoulder then following close behind.

Across a stretch of scrubland, over a stile and into the eastern boundary of the tired and grey seaside resort of Little-hampton. Every August, the focus of the town was on cashing in on the seasonal rush. Harvest time. The arcades and the fairground rides pinned between the estuary of the Arun and the sea front hotels buzzed with life and creaked at the seams.

Jay watched Stitch as they walked. He was as close as family to her as you could get. Their sleeping together felt unresolved. There had been times when she wished they could be together, had those kinds of feelings for him, but it was too scary to think of killing what they had.

They stepped onto the wooden decking of the pier, into

the footsteps of Jay's former self as a child, with her dad, and Sammy on a fishing trip. Little about the place had changed. Even the pastel blue paint on the wooden railings was the same, re-painted every spring in anticipation of the coming tourist trade. A group of kids fished off the end of the pier in her dad's old spot. Others dangled their orange crab lines over the sides, their buckets alive with pincers and claws.

'It's big, Dad, it's big,' said a little girl hauling up an impressively large crab. She pushed her dad away as he tried to help her guide it towards her bucket. 'I can do it, I can do it.'

From the end of the pier, Jay could see over the mouth of the river to the West Beach dunes rising above the river wall.

* * *

CASSIE DROVE IN SILENCE. Sammy searched his mind for something intelligent or funny to say. But neither felt appropriate, so he leaned his head against the glass and kept quiet, watching the hedges and trees flicker past.

'This whole thing's bullshit, don't you think?' Cassie said after a while.

'Huh?'

'These men in black, the legend...'

Sammy was surprised that Cassie continued to deny it, despite having her own connections to the place through her grandad. She had such fight and determination, but it came with a bitterness that hung over everything. 'Those men didn't look like bullshit to me.'

Cassie remained silent for a moment, her eyes on the road. 'You know, when we moved over this way from Amberley, me and Grandad wanted to stay. Last thing I wanted was to move. I spent my entire life in that area. It's where Grandad settled when he came over from Jamaica, and it's where he took me and Charlie trekking through the thicket.'

'To find the Interland? The Caverns?'

'It was all about exploring the thicket, the Amberley Wilds and all its life – the trees, birds.' She paused. 'I always hoped he'd take us to the Caverns.'

'Your grandad moved with you?'

Cassie nodded. 'He lasted less than a month before he went AWOL. I think the move broke him. He'd never lived anywhere but Amberley.'

They hit a T-junction and Cassie turned towards the coast. 'I remember Grandad talking about that woman, the one who got involved in the big protest. What was her name?'

'Zadie Lawrence,' said Sammy, remembering the unspoken information passing between his dad and Jay the day of the protest, a communication he now better understood.

'My grandad seemed to think she was the answer to everything, way before the protest.' Cassie laughed. 'She changed things alright. Didn't exactly get the freedom she fought for.'

'Maybe she hasn't finished yet,' said Sammy.

Cassie gave him a sideways glance then slammed the brakes. They jolted to a standstill and Cassie apologised as Sammy got his breath back, thankful to his seatbelt. Cassie let the engine idle a moment as she looked out and up towards the hills in the distance. 'Highdown looks a picture from this angle.'

Sammy looked up towards the peak. 'These hills always get me.' Cassie pulled away and an inexplicable lump formed in Sammy's throat. He swallowed and turned away from Cassie towards the window. As he did so, he felt a wave of nausea. His head spun and he let out an involuntary groan.

'You OK?' Cassie said as Sammy's head lolled and he tried

to stop the horizon spinning in front of his eyes. It was like something was burrowing into his consciousness, digging and unbalancing his sense of reality.

'Spinning out,' said Sammy, unable to keep his eyes open. He leaned back in his seat. 'I need to close my eyes for a bit.' He fought to keep his thoughts from racing, struggling to hold on to his sense of reality. His mind raced in search of an explanation – he was ill, food poisoning, drugged, dying. A cold sweat came over him as a darkness descended, cloaking him in an oppressive, bitter depression.

* * *

THEY WAITED in the car in the gravel car park on West Beach. Sammy watched with his head up against the window as cars gradually left at the end of the day, crammed full of beach gear, kids with sunburned noses.

'They must be close,' Sammy said. His head had settled, but the nausea remained. He felt as if he'd had his mind spooned out – listless, and exhausted, no closer to understanding what happened, what was wrong with him. Cassie was slumped back in her seat, arms crossed.

'Not been here for years,' said Sammy. 'See the pier over the other side? We used to go fishing there with Dad. Don't think I ever caught anything except seaweed.'

'Are you alright now?' Cassie said, concern in her voice.

'I think so.'

'That River looks crazy,' Cassie said, peering through the darkness at the swirling expanse of the Arun as it thrust out to sea.

'It's more dangerous than it looks. Not one to mess with.'

'Challenge accepted,' said Cassie. She opened the door and stripped off her jeans and top. Sammy stared open mouthed as Cassie threw her clothes into the back seat and scampered over the sand to the river wall where she leaned over the railing to see down to the river below. By the time he'd gathered himself to get out of the car, Cassie was already bounding along the river wall towards the sea, 'Bring the stuff,' she called over her shoulder.

23

———

The sea breeze was gentler on the west side of the river. Darkness approached as Jay and Stitch walked alongside the river wall, Jay fending off vertigo as she looked over the railings into the swirl below. The eddies around the posts of the river wall twisted and turned, nudging their way out to sea. The undercurrents along that section were strong, where the river became estuary and pushed towards France. She kicked a stone over the edge and watched as it disappeared without sound into the froth, an ingredient delivered to a witch's cauldron.

Up ahead, Jay heard familiar voices. Sammy shouted at Cassie to get down off the river wall, Cassie laughing back at him.

'Is that...?' said Stitch.

'Yep. God knows what she's doing.' Cassie strode along the river wall, stripped to her underwear. She was tall and stringy, her dark skin shimmering, braids swinging loose around her shoulders.

'What is she doing?' said Stitch. They heard Sammy call for her not to be stupid and to get down.

'Don't worry,' Cassie called back to Sammy, striding and picking up speed so that she was jogging along a wall no more than a foot wide, twenty feet above the river on one side and six feet above the sand on the other. It made Jay dizzy just watching. Sammy ran along the sand to keep up with her. Jay stopped atop the wall, watching Cassie's ballet-like gracefulness as she strode further out to sea. When she got to the point of the estuary opposite the pier on the east beach, Cassie slung a leg over the railing, then the other, to stand facing the river, her back to Sammy.

'Cassie, come on, it's too dangerous,' Sammy shouted.

'It's perfect,' Cassie shouted back. 'I'll catch up with you in the dunes. Go find Jay and Stitch.'

'Cassie!' Stitch shouted, but the wind threw his words back in his face and neither Cassie nor Sammy appeared to hear.

Sammy shouted, his voice carrying to Jay and Stitch on the wind, 'Come on, please...' but his words tailed off as Cassie threw herself forward, her sleek body bending into an elegant dive. Stitch's mouth dropped open. An onlooker screamed. Cassie was invisible as she flew through the air, against the charcoal canvas of the river, and Jay didn't see her hit the water through the gloom and turbulence of its surface.

'Crazy,' said Stitch.

Jay leaned over the river wall to catch a glimpse of Cassie. A seagull swooped across the surface as if searching for leftovers. Nothing but whirlpools and eddies. Panic rose in Jay's chest. She allowed her mind to open to the energy of the river as it pushed and jostled its way towards the sea, expanding in all directions. She sensed little but passing waves of whispers and silence. She pushed and prodded with her mind, drawing power from the water, refusing to accept its silence. A burst of energy sent a jolt through Jay's bones. The whispers grew. She turned to Stitch, half expecting to see him knocked off his feet by the energy she felt flowing from the river. He stood firm, his eyes fixed on Jay. He'd felt something too. Jay turned back to the river, the streamlines becoming more visible in her mind's eye. Discernible and defined they wrapped themselves around the whispers, and around Cassie. Through the gloom, the water seemed to open to Jay, and Cassie became visible, her body wrapped in layers of the river like a baby swaddled.

The whispers came, growing to a wall of white noise. Jay filtered, ordered and arranged until the connection became firm, and it was she, Jay, who held the power of the water. She was in control. Mischievous currents nipped at Cassie, tugged at her limbs and dragged her down, but Jay guided her through the channel of the estuary and clear of the undercurrents. The white noise dampened to whispers, coming and going on the breeze. Cassie was safe.

'Come on,' said Jay. 'Let's help Sammy with those rucksacks.'

Stitch shook his head and tore his eyes away from the gloom of the river to catch up with Jay who was already calling after her brother as he battled to carry two rucksacks. 'What about Cassie?' he said.

'She's fine now, she's safe,' said Jay. They took the back path up past the drinks kiosk, and into the section of dunes between the sea and the golf course. Jay and Sammy took off their shoes and socks, Jay wanting to feel the cold wet sand between her toes. Jay figured that they could get to the high point in the dunes and see all the way back towards Highdown and Bamber.

Sammy was quiet as they walked. He looked tired. His face was pale with dark rings around his eyes. 'Are you OK?' Jay asked, trying to get a better look at him.

'I'll be fine. It's been a weird day. Something took the wind out of me back there but I feel better now.'

Jay could hear music and laughing and was pulled towards its source. West Beach was where people gathered, the kind of people that spent the summer sleeping under the stars, or in little one-man tents, some of them with surf boards, though the surf was rarely any good. As they got closer, Jay could see the orange flicker of a fire and people, in groups of three or four. They parked themselves in the sand, on the periphery but close enough to feel the warmth from the fire, and offloaded their bags. Stitch and Sammy flopped down on the sand, Stitch starting to roll a cigarette.

As Jay pinpointed the highest section of dunes for a vantage point, Cassie emerged from the darkness. The rest of the party goers stopped and stared.

'Took your time,' Sammy said.

'Worried?'

'No,' Sammy said, lying back in the sand.

Jay stood, handing Cassie a towel. 'That river can be lethal,' she said, emphasising her serious tone.

Cassie held Jay's eye. 'I had it covered,' she said.

'I'm heading up there.' Jay pointed. 'To check on this second bow.' She picked the notebook from her rucksack and Sammy stood to join her. Together they climbed the dunes to the high point.

'That's Bamber Castle.' Sammy pointed. In the distance, they could see the light from the castle illuminating its turrets, some six miles east of their location.

'And there's Highdown.' Jay pointed towards the Downs.

'Where?'

'The glimmer up on the hill, a fire. And...' Jay continued, 'yes! There is the trajectory, the arrow.'

'Don't see it,' said Sammy.

'The line of streetlamps from the castle, with the trees.

That's the boulevard that runs north from the castle, down to where your old school is. See it?'

'Is that the trajectory of the arrow?'

'Reckon so.'

'Then it's easy to plot, I know that road.'

* * *

MOST OF THE beach partiers were drinking from bottles and cans. A guy with a beard down to his chest was setting up a barbecue. He squirted lighter fluid over the charcoal to kick things off, leaning back to keep his beard away from the flames. An older man in a tattered anorak and beaten shoes, largely ignored by everyone else, wandered from group to group to scab a smoke or a drink. He settled next to the fire, cross-legged on someone's rug, gazing into the flames.

'Look,' said Stitch. 'See what you've done.' In the distance, the flashing lights of a coastguard boat patrolling the estuary reflected off the surface of the water. Cassie shrugged and continued to pull on her clothes before settling down on the sand. She riffled through her rucksack and took out her sleeping bag, rolling it out to sit on after pulling two bottles of red wine from inside.

A boy with blonde dreadlocks approached. 'Where are you guys from?' he said, though clearly was speaking only to Cassie.

Cassie looked away, disinterested, until the boy handed her the remains of a joint. She stared at it a moment, smiled, and took it.

'From around here.' Cassie nodded in the general direction of the river. 'We're on a quest,' she said, coughing as she exhaled. Sammy turned to Jay and rolled his eyes. They laid out their sleeping bags.

Stitch squeezed in next to Jay. 'Tell me then. What could you see from up on the dunes?'

'We got it, Stitch,' said Sammy. 'Home and dry. Just need to plot it out on the map.' As Sammy spoke, his head lolled and he had to put out a hand to steady himself.

'You OK?' said Stitch.

Sammy shook his head clear, blinking. 'Dizzy spells. Not feeling too special. I'll be OK. I probably need to eat something.'

Jay looked over at her brother. 'Grab something from the rucksack, and have some water. Then rest, OK?'

'Yes, boss.' He smiled.

Stitch turned to Jay. 'So you think you know where it is?'

'We'll see, tomorrow,' said Jay. 'As long as we stay ahead of the Readers.'

Stitch grabbed one of Cassie's bottles of wine, took a swig and handed it to Jay.

'I used to know people down here,' Jay said, glancing at the faces around the fire. 'Not anymore. Did you know that this is a nudist beach by day?' Jay smiled at Stitch.

'No.' Stitch laughed.

'Seriously. If you come down here in the day, you'll see people in the dunes, naked blokes standing with their hands on their hips like mannequins. We used to bring the dog down here sometimes when I was a kid. Scared the crap out of me when I walked straight into a bloke standing stark naked.'

Stitch laughed.

It grew darker, and when the lights from the fairground finally died, the stars emerged with distinction. Cassie had crashed out and dreadlock-boy had moseyed off elsewhere. Sammy was already asleep. Jay and Stitch lay back in the sand, spotting the different constellations and giggling, the effects of the wine loosening their mood.

'So tomorrow's the day?' Stitch said.

'Could be,' said Jay.

The sound of deep breathing came from Sammy's direction. 'You think he's OK? Seems a bit off.'

'Been a bit of a day. I'm sure he'll be fine,' said Stitch.

Cassie let out a snort followed by steady snoring. Stitch laughed. 'Sammy and Cassie have been pretty tight,' he said.

'They have a connection,' Jay smiled. 'Cassie seems more chilled with Sammy than with anyone else.'

'She's bailed us out of a few scrapes.' Stitch lay back on his sleeping bag, turning onto his side towards Jay so that they were close enough for her to feel his warmth. He pulled out a book.

'What are you reading?' asked Jay.

'Too tired to read,' Stitch said, pushing the book into his sleeping bag and yawning again. He closed his eyes.

Jay took a final swig of the wine, emptying the bottle, then pulled her rucksack towards her and picked out the Sasha Colden book.

Jay picked up the story where she'd left off at the bookshop. By the flicker of the fire, her eyes flowed over the words with ease, and she became drawn deep into the story, to a place beyond the pages. With each paragraph, each page, her sense of connectedness with the earth, and the sea, strengthened. The sand shifted beneath her body, cradling her. The whispers from the sea whirled and looped through the dunes on the wind. Alf came into her mind, then disappeared with the whispers.

Feeling protected, she lay back on the sand and closed her eyes for what felt like the first time in days.

24

S omething woke Jay less than an hour later. She'd not been asleep for long, the party still going strong around them. As she turned to check on the others, she saw a man crouching over Cassie, one knee resting in the sand. Her heart punched at her chest, her senses heightened, face tingling with anxiety. She froze, holding her breath. The man was not much older than her. He was tall, solidly built, with dark skin. His expression was one of sorrow, or pity. He gazed at Cassie as she slept.

Jay calmed herself, forced a steady breath. This man didn't look or feel like a threat. 'Hey,' said Jay, keeping her voice low. The man snapped his head up. He held a finger to his lips as he stood, taking a step towards Jay and then veering off towards the sea. He nodded for Jay to follow.

She pushed herself off the sand, careful not to nudge Stitch or Sammy. She hurried after the man, stumbling as she tried to gain traction on the dry sand. As she reached the edge of the pebbles, she looked up to see his silhouette as he stood at the water's edge, his back to her so that his athletic frame was in sharp contrast to the surface of the water, shimmering in the light of the moon. She stopped short, taking a moment to read whatever she could in quick bursts to avoid detection.

The man was a Given. He opened up long enough to show Jay that he was on her side. He had brought a message of support, encouragement, if nothing more. He came to see Cassie too. To see her, but not for her to see him.

'Hi,' said Jay, standing alongside him.

'Reuben,' he said. 'Nice to finally meet you, Jay.'

'Finally?' said Jay, turning to him as he continued to stare out to sea.

'I've missed this.' He nodded towards the water. 'It's the sounds and the smells as much as what you see, don't you think?'

'I guess,' said Jay, trying her best to relax and not scream the many questions swirling in her mind. She knew he meant no harm, and she knew that he came to offer support, not resistance.

'Sorry. I just needed a minute there. The last time I saw the sea was about a year ago. Well, *exactly* a year ago as it happens.' He turned to Jay with a broad smile.

Before he could speak again, Jay twigged. 'You're the Reuben who Cassie grew up with.'

He looked surprised. 'You read that from me?'

'Not everything I figure out is by snooping in people's heads. Some knowledge can be gained the old fashioned way.' Jay returned her own gaze to the sea, a breeze picking up and churning the surface as the waves broke in front of them. 'Cassie told me about her lifelong friend since she was a baby. Her soul mate. The boy who moved away and never stayed in touch. Her best friend.'

Reuben hung his head, shifting the sand with the toe of his boot. 'That's a long story. I hope to be able to explain it to Cassie myself one day.'

'She's just over there.'

'Not today. Not now. I can't. I'm here because I've been tasked with bringing you a message. I can speak only to you. I am forbidden to talk to any without powers. Only to the Given.'

Jay snorted a laugh. She couldn't help but feel cynical, couldn't help the frustration she felt in the face of half-truths, cryptic messages and the uncertainty that seemed to surround everything associated with the Interland. 'Forgive me for not jumping for joy. I don't even know what I'm doing here.'

'There's a good reason, and I think you know that. I don't see that you have a choice.'

'There are always choices.'

'Not for you.' Reuben's tone was firm. 'And especially not with Readers. If they get to you, then that will be it for you and your friends. You don't think they'll simply put you in a nice holding camp and give the rest of them a slap on the wrists?'

'Well then? What message, who from?'

'They said I can't fill your head with too many facts about where you are trying to get to, for obvious reasons.'

'Not that obvious.' Jay frowned.

'Because of the Readers. They are powerful. If you have details, then they can take them. Marcus is a level eight, he could take information from any one of you and you wouldn't even sense it happening.'

Jay pictured the man in the car park. His two colleagues frozen in time but him still moving. 'I've seen him,' she said.

'Where?'

'Back that way.' She nodded down the beach. Reuben shifted on his feet and seemed to flinch a little. 'It's OK, we lost him. He's still on us but he's not close.'

'Can you tell when the Readers are close?'

'Sometimes.'

'That's something. Look, I've been asked to say nothing more than to give you confidence that you are on the right track.'

'So it's at the intersect?'

'I can't say any more. It could put you in more danger and hinder not help. And it could expose the rest of us to great danger.'

'Rest of us?'

'I've missed Cassie.' For a moment Reuben was silent, staring out to sea. Then, 'You can tell her I was here.'

'What do I say? "Hey, Cass, your old mate Reuben was here last night, popped in on his broomstick but I can't tell you why". You know Cassie, do you think that'll go well?'

'I want you to tell her about her grandad.'

'He's alive? He's in this place, the Interland?'

'He's the one who found it. He was custodian of the gateway. He never went through to the Interland, always remained on the outside, watching over it. Cassie's grandad was the one who brought me to the Interland when I turned 18. That's why I was never able to contact Cassie. I didn't abandon her. I didn't know about my power back then, not until the marking showed itself.' He pulled back his sleeve to reveal the number seven.

'But Cassie's grandad knew. He helped me. Introduced me to the underground.'

'Why not Cassie too?'

'She was young. And there was no power in Cassie that her grandad could see. Has she developed any marking since she turned eighteen?'

'Not that I know of,' Jay said. 'What about her grandad? Has he got abilities? Where is he?'

'He's a level four. But he didn't know until he was much older. The mark never came through for him until he passed

60. So now he's gone underground. He's moved from front of house to back of house if you see what I mean.'

Even Cassie's parents assumed that her grandad was dead. How would she ever explain this to Cassie? 'Why are you here, Reuben?'

'To bring a message, like I said. To give you confidence. You can do this. You are close.'

'And to give me a message that will both give my friend Cassie hope and break her heart?'

'There was no other way.'

Jay's frustration grew but she covered it with questions. 'So what happens when we get to the gateway? Will the others be able to pass through to the Interland?'

'Everything's changed. The Interland has grown. The surface world has moved so far in the wrong direction. We must get as many of the Given to a safe place as we can.'

'But I can't just leave my family, my friends.'

'You know that all of you have some level of power? Not just you.'

'What?'

Reuben smiled. 'We think so. Look, you don't have time to waste. You have to remain a good distance ahead of the Readers. Get to the Interland.'

'Where is it?'

'You know where it is.' He turned and started for the dunes.

'Hey,' said Jay. 'We will see you then?'

'I think it's inevitable. We've been waiting for you for a long time.' As Jay watched, he broke into a jog, picking up speed and disappearing into the dunes.

25

In a northern suburb of London, on the outskirts of a residential area that stretched into affluent districts close to the city, the prison towered high above a surrounding patch of industrial land. In the exercise yard out the back, Ben and Matchstick sat apart from the other prisoners, or *customers*, as the authorities referred to them. It was important the institution retain some pretence of what it pretended to offer—rehabilitation and education—not what it truly offered, incarceration.

'We go out with a delivery vehicle,' Matchstick said, nodding towards the security gate where a truck idled. Two guards inspected the vehicle, the back doors of the truck open and its insides under scrutiny.

'I think those Readers would have something to say about that,' said Ben, not yet buying into Matchstick's confidence. He sensed that Jay had already left home and begun making her way through the hills, pursued by Readers. If Ben was to be true to his word, he needed to get out, and soon.

'That delivery bay marks the line between this bit,' Matchstick motioned around himself, 'and the *education* section.'

'And *rehabilitation* beyond that. We need to move. We've been here long enough.' Every one of the 'customers' knew *rehabilitation* was where they sucked the last bit of resistance out of the Given, in a windowless room in the third and final wing of the prison.

'The *Sub Levels*. A small step from release,' Matchstick mused. 'Once educated, rehabilitated and released, we are no longer a disbenefit to society.' He paused, looking at Ben. 'For most, that might be a goal worth pursuing. True freedom from *rehabilitation*.'

Ben sighed. 'I used to think that freedom came from keeping under the radar.'

'A friend of mine, Luke, tried getting out in one of those vans,' Matchstick said. 'We were planning to go together, but I bottled it.' Matchstick thought for a moment, then said, 'We'd been planning it for a while but I got a bad feeling and tried to persuade him to wait a bit. He insisted. He wouldn't stay another night. So he went for it on his own.'

'How do you know he didn't make it?'

'Saw them take him. One of the Readers sensed he was there I reckon, by the way they searched the truck. It was a laundry truck. They had almost everything out on the road before they eventually found him hidden in the back.'

'What happened to him?'

'No idea. He never came back. There were rumours he'd moved on to *education*, which made no sense. The only people that move to *education* are the ones that are toeing the line, meeting their objectives. Not Luke. He was the opposite.'

'So they moved him to another prison?'

'If he was lucky.'

Ben watched the delivery truck at the gate. The guards closed the back doors and banged on the side to signal the all clear. The barrier rose, and the truck pulled out onto the perimeter road. 'I'm not feeling fully confident in your escape plan,' said Ben.

Matchstick laughed. 'My point is, I have developed an upgrade that might work, if we learn from where Luke went wrong.' Matchstick ambled towards the perimeter fence.

'I'm listening,' Ben said.

'To help shield from Readers, we need to put as much dense material as possible between them and us, yes?'

'Yes,' said Ben.

'I used to drive a delivery truck. There's no point in hiding in the back, we need more metal between us. I know the underside of those trucks like the back of my hand.'

* * *

BEN JOINED the queue in the dining room, a few people behind Matchstick. They found an empty table and sat, neither of them touching their food.

'We should eat,' said Matchstick, forking some spaghetti. Ben nodded and tucked in, forcing down the food down despite his nerves. He'd brought his belongings from his cell – a book, and a picture of Jay and Sammy.

'There are three trucks in the delivery bay,' said Matchstick. 'One of them is the type I used to drive. We need to get to that one before it moves out.'

Ben made to stand and Matchstick put a hand on his arm. 'Give it ten minutes.' Ben finished as much of his food as he could stomach and pushed away his tray. He drank the remains of his water and shifted in his seat. The minutes ticked by. Matchstick nodded.

Outside the dining hall they passed a guard and nodded a greeting as they made towards the exercise yard. There were no delivery drivers or guards in the loading bay as Matchstick had predicted. They crouched and made their way around the back of the loading bay to the truck. The back doors were open and Ben took a look inside. 'It's full of laundry,' he said.

'We won't be shielded in there.' Matchstick ducked down to inspect the underside of the truck. 'Follow me.'

Ben pushed himself along on his back as if he were preparing to service the truck. Matchstick had already folded himself up into the small cavity next to the fuel tank. 'There's no room!' Voices approached. Matchstick motioned for Ben to climb into the space between the exhaust pipe and the engine block, pushing himself up from the floor.

The truck rocked as its driver climbed into the front. Matchstick urged Ben on, reaching an arm out for support. As Ben squeezed himself into the impossible gap, breathing in Matchstick's stale odour as he pushed up against his bony body, the truck's engine started and the voices were drowned as the driver put the truck in gear and released the clutch. The only way Ben could keep from falling to the ground was to rest both feet on the vibrating exhaust pipe, bending it precariously.

With a thick waft of noxious fumes, the truck moved towards the exit and Matchstick shifted against Ben's knee. Ben's foot slipped, his leg dislodged and dragged against the rough gravel road, twisting, his trousers tearing, his skin shredding against the stones. Stifling a cry, he kicked up to rest his foot back on the exhaust pipe as the truck came to a stop at the exit gate. The engine died.

Footsteps. 'Something smells weird back there.' Ben could tell it was the voice of a Reader. It exuded arrogance. His words came slowly and deliberately. He paced around the vehicle and opened the back,

'Dirty washing,' said the driver. 'That's your smell.'

'It's not the truck. Something else. Wait here.' The Reader

stepped away and into the security hut. A minute later he came back and asked the driver to step out of the cab. Ben held his breath.

The Reader climbed up into the cab of the truck, sounding like he was rifling around in the passenger seat and searching through the glove box before he stepped back onto the tarmac. 'OK?' asked the driver. The Reader gave no response but instead paced the full perimeter of the truck, arriving back at the driver's door. He crouched, looking under the vehicle.

Ben held tight. Seconds ticked by. The engine of the truck sparked into life, and with a double-tap on the side of the vehicle, the driver edged the truck forward. Ben sensed the power of the Reader as they passed the security hut. He kept still, closing his eyes, shielding, and breathing through the pain in his arms. His feet began to warm on the exhaust pipe. Matchstick lowered his head below the level of the fuel tank to see the road ahead. He nodded at Ben and shouted in his ear above the noise of the engine and the tyres on the road, 'Ready?'

The truck's brakes squealed as they pulled up at a T-junction, the prison still visible in the distance behind them. Darkness closed in, red lights reflected in puddles on the road. The truck slowed, Ben dropped, slipped onto his front and rolled towards the pavement. Without looking back he launched himself across the path and into the darkness of an alleyway just as the traffic light turned green. No sign of Matchstick. He crouched to look under the truck. Matchstick was trying to untangle his sleeve from around the fuel tank mounting. He glanced at Ben just as the truck's engine raced and its wheels began to turn. Matchstick fell, was dragged, his shirt ripped, leaving him on his back in the middle of the road as the truck pulled away. He stood, grinning widely as the truck disappeared out of sight, then he strolled over to the alleyway to join Ben as if nothing had happened.

The street was quiet. A car passed, its windscreen wipers clearing the fresh rain that had started to fall, the sound of its tyres in the wet reminding Ben of home.

26

'Y'ou take the corners like you're driving a go-kart, and stop signs are not supposed to be optional.' The Ford crunched at every gear change, only increasing Jay's moaning, reminding Cassie of her grandad teaching her to drive, warning her how she'd strip her gears if she didn't soften the transition with the right revs.

Cassie's grandad was her last surviving grandparent before he disappeared two years ago. Cassie's brother Charlie had complained they shouldn't be having a funeral when he might be alive. But he must have died. Cassie could consider no reason he'd be alive and not have made contact. Before that, the boy she had thought of as a friend for life had moved away and vanished. The person she had planned to marry, in all the seriousness and depth of a love that began at six years old.

'Grandad never called it the Interland,' Cassie said to Jay as they rounded a corner at speed.

'It's a loaded word,' said Jay. 'Links to the legend and all the myth that surrounds it.'

'I guess,' Cassie said. The events of the past two days had started to convince Cassie that her grandad's old stories, his descriptions of the magic of the caverns, had to be connected with Jay's Interland. The big confusion in Cassie's mind was where truth crossed into fantasy and wishful thinking.

'You used to live in this area?' said Jay.

'I did,' Cassie said. If her grandad had known the whereabouts of the caverns, the Interland, he never spilled. 'We used to go walking a lot. I always thought he was taking me to the Caverns, but he never did.' They would walk for miles, sometimes for hours at a time. Her grandad was always in control of the route, and the timing, always knew where they were, never lost.

'Did you ask him to?' Jay said, as Cassie took a roundabout like it wasn't there, causing Stitch and Sammy to pile up against Sammy's door.

'He said his memory wasn't all that. After a while I stopped asking. But I never gave up hoping, expecting that one day on one of our walks we'd just arrive there.'

'What about Reuben, did he walk with you?'

Cassie gave Jay a sideways glance. 'He came sometimes, why?'

Jay shrugged. Cassie took her eyes off the road to give her a look. 'I thought my grandad might be testing me, waiting until I was ready for something.'

'Waiting for you to come of age?'

'He waited too long, silly old bugger.'

They were quiet for a minute, Cassie concentrating on the winding road. Fields of green and yellow separated by low hedges and fences. They stopped at a T-junction.

'I miss him,' said Cassie.

'I know,' said Jay.

'Left,' came a shout from Stitch in the back, the road map open on his lap. Cassie pulled out, tightened her grip on the steering wheel and jammed her foot to the floor.

* * *

THEY PULLED into the Barley Mow so they could rest, have a drink and study the maps. Stitch opened the car door and sloped towards the entrance of the pub, stretching back his shoulders as he walked.

'Shall we?' Cassie nodded towards the dark red door where a sign indicated the saloon bar. Stitch pushed through and the others followed.

They found a quiet spot in the pub garden overlooking a stream. Cassie spread the map on the table. 'Right, wonder woman,' she said. 'Where is this place?' Jay looked at Cassie and thought of Reuben. She flattened down the map, taking her time to get her bearings, looking from the map to their surroundings and judging their orientation by positioning the stream they were sat next to, the pub, and the road.

'This stream,' Jay said, 'connects into the Rother, just here...' She pointed at the map, Cassie and Stitch squinting to see. 'Then if you follow the Rother to here... it joins with the Arun.'

'Is that it?' Cassie looked up.

'Just south of there is where our two lines intersect.'

'The Gateway?'

'It's our best bet,' said Jay.

'But there's nothing there. That is the definition of the middle of nowhere. There are no roads, or tracks, paths or anything. That is right in the middle of the Amberley Thicket, do you know what that stuff is like?'

Jay shook her head. Cassie took a drink of her cider. 'The woods through there are thick and unmanaged. If you try to walk through there, you quickly get tangled in the overgrown brambles, bracken and everything else. There's a reason it's called "The Wilds". You'd need a JCB.'

'There must be some way,' Jay said. 'Dad said...'

'Your dad never actually went there,' Cassie interrupted. She sighed. 'There are infinite points that you *could* start from, but all of them are a good few miles out from that point.' She slumped back down onto the seat of the rickety picnic table. 'Can't you zone in or something, Jay? We could be walking out there for days and find nothing.'

'Where's your sense of adventure, Cassie,' said Sammy. 'Just because it won't be easy, doesn't mean we can't do it, right Jay?'

Jay looked again at the map and leaned in closer. 'Dad talked about a route along the Arun.' She pointed to a section of the Arun further upstream that ran down from the Black Rabbit pub. 'He described this place, further up, where the Arun widened alongside cattle fields, and poppy fields.'

'Poppies?' Cassie huffed.

'Maybe,' said Jay, uncertain. She continued moving her finger along the map, working her way down-river from the north, along the Arun. 'Like... here.' She pointed to a spot just east of where they had pinpointed the gateway, a place that was labelled *Sidwell*.

'That's not where the rivers meet,' said Sammy. 'And it's not at the intersection.'

Cassie said, 'It could be a starting point.'

'Worth a try,' said Jay, running her finger along an imaginary line between Sidwell and the intersection.

* * *

THE VILLAGE of Sidwell offered nothing but a string of disused farm buildings and a dilapidated church. The road petered out. Cassie squeezed the car up a track for a mile before it reduced to a narrow path. She reversed into a field, hiding the car behind a high hedge. They packed up their rucksacks, attached the two tents and continued on foot.

There were no footpaths or bridleways on the Ordnance Survey map so they walked blind, following their noses and taking the route that looked most plausible. Stitch and Sammy led the way through the trees, Cassie preferring to hang back with Jay. According to the map, they were less than two miles from the point of intersection, and Cassie was surprised that the going was so good – no distinct pathways, but the under-growth between the trees was passable and they moved at a good pace.

Sammy and Stitch stamped down the stinging nettles, allowing Cassie and Jay an easy route in their slipstream. Cassie stole a glance at Jay. 'You OK?' she said, pulling Jay from her thoughts.

'Sorry. Miles away. I'm worried, what are we doing here?'

Cassie linked arms with her friend. 'The only thing we *can* do. Get somewhere safe, away from your stalkers.'

'I've dragged you all into this dangerous world.'

'Whether you like it or not, your world is our world. You think we should have stayed back home and carried on as if nothing was happening? This has been coming for some time.'

'It's not you they want, Cassie.'

'Not yet. Now it's the Given, it's you, your dad, others. But who's next? Another go at immigration? I remember my parents hopelessly trying to defend the rights of my grandad to stay in this country. It was like arguing with a wall. No sense of logic, or compassion, or even law.'

'They succeeded though?'

'Only after he got ill from all the stress and worry. Reckon that was the last straw for him. Wasn't long after that he went walkabout, died in the woods somewhere, probably. Then the letter came that he was given right to remain. Too little too late for Grandad. Stupid old bastard.' Cassie smiled. 'Anyway, I was thinking it's surprising to see you so far from your comfort zone. I was expecting a spaz-out before now?'

'I know. The anxiety is right up there, but there's something holding it back.'

'Thought you were on edge. You getting those things... what is it you used to call them? The thoughts that come into your head?'

'Pop ups,' Jay said.

'Yeah, that's it. Are they coming back?' Jay would become distressed in class, or when they were out somewhere. She'd get anxious and wind herself up so tight that there was nowhere for the tension to go but to explode into some kind of panic attack. And it always started with a simple thought that she couldn't close down.

'Not like before. They're in my head sometimes, but I can ride it. I'm better at it than I was back then.'

Jay reached to push a light branch out of her way and ducked under a more substantial one. 'To be honest,' Jay said, 'I don't think I ever really figured that stuff out. I just got better at managing it.'

The undergrowth thickened. Sammy used a stick to hack at thorny brambles and Cassie and Jay stamped through. Stitch and Sammy stopped and turned to Jay, Cassie a step behind her. 'Let's rest,' said Stitch, nodding towards a clearing by a fallen tree.

'How far away you think we are?' Cassie said.

'Difficult to tell. Maybe a mile,' Jay said as she sat back on the log next to Cassie. 'Might not sound like far, but at this rate it's a good couple of hours hacking through.'

A small bird flitted from a branch and settled on the log next to Sammy. It was no bigger than a mouse, tilting its head to the side and regarding him. On its head, a red-brown streak flowed from its eyes and merged into shades of brown and beige in the feathers that formed its wings.

'What is it?' Stitch said.

Cassie put a finger to her lips. 'Shh, it's a bird.'

'A sparrow,' Sammy whispered. The bird hopped closer along the log and Sammy held out a hand. The bird twitched its head to check the location of the other three people, then back to Sammy. It hopped onto the back of his hand.

Cassie sucked in a gasp, leaning closer to Sammy and the little bird. Sammy didn't seem surprised, then he glanced up as a flutter of sparrows streamed through the trees to rest on the log beside him, on his arm, his shoulder. One landed on Cassie's shoulder, though it lifted off when she let out a muffled scream. The sparrows fussed around Sammy in a cloud before, as quickly as they'd arrived, they streaked away into the sky with squeaks and flapping wings.

'Tell me I didn't just imagine that?' said Stitch, righting himself on the log then standing to look up into the trees after the birds. Jay stood to join him. 'That was a bit strange,' she said.

'Strange?' said Cassie, standing. 'It looked like Sammy and those birds were having a moment.'

'Sparrows,' Jay said.

Stitch nudged Sammy. 'Did that bird... like... say something?'

Cassie laughed. 'Come on, Stitch. Seriously.' She looked at Sammy. 'Tell me you're not talking to the birds, Sammy?'

Sammy smiled. 'Not *talking* to them, exactly.'

'Let's move,' Cassie said, 'before this gets any more Hitchcock.'

* * *

Sammy and Stitch led the way again. Jay put a hand on Cassie's arm to slow her down.

'What?' said Cassie.

'I need to tell you something.'

Cassie waited for Jay to continue. 'Someone came to give us a message last night, on the beach when you guys were asleep. Someone from the Interland.'

'Seriously? What message?'

'It was Reuben. He's a Runner. He's been on the other side, in the underground, ever since he disappeared. He's a level seven.'

Cassie's expression froze as the information sunk in. She smiled, then frowned. 'This is a joke, right?'

Jay shook her head. 'There's more.'

Cassie raised her eyebrows and Jay told her about what Reuben said about her grandad, carefully talking through every detail as Reuben had relayed it to her. Cassie listened in silence and eventually her legs gave way and she sat cross-legged on the floor of the woods. Sammy and Stitch pressed on, their chattering voices still audible in the distance.

Jay sat on the floor with Cassie and took her hands.

'Why didn't they contact me?'

'Reuben said it wasn't an option, or they would have been in touch sooner. It's only now, with the changes that are happening, and with you turning 18, that they have been able to reach out. He said that they're looking forward to you coming in.'

'You kept it from me all day? You know what they meant to me. How could you...'

'I didn't know how to tell you, how to explain.'

'So it exists. For real. It's not just you and your dad gone all magical. This place is for real?'

'Seems that way.' As Jay said these words, there came a

scream from the direction of Sammy and Stitch. Cassie and Jay looked at each other, then shot to their feet, careering through the woods after the others.

* * *

STITCH AND SAMMY hung on to the edge of a hole in the woodland floor, like they'd fallen into a hidden animal trap, the ground a deep hole beneath them.

Jay lurched for Sammy's hand. For a moment, Cassie and Jay struggled to pull the boys out of the hole but they were too heavy. They clung with all their strength. Jay's right foot slipped. Stinging nettles ravaged her arm. Sammy's wrist slipped through her hand, sweat lubricating. Jay's muscles could take no more. Sammy fell, Stitch with him. They screamed in harmony as they crashed through the branches and into free fall. Jay could see nothing but the parted undergrowth and the white of a cliff face.

The girls heard a distant splash, then another. Then nothing. Jay looked at Cassie then to the hole in the floor of the forest. Cassie nodded. They held hands and took a deep breath before stepping into the hole.

PART IV

CONNECTED

Jay hit water a moment after Cassie. Turbulence, bubbles. Jay couldn't tell which way was up. Her skin screamed with pain from the impact and from the cold. Her lungs burned, aching for air. Exhausted from trekking, she was confused, unable to figure how to right herself. Her blood pressure rose, lungs ached, and her mind swam with confusion.

No longer able to hold her breath, Jay opened her mouth and water flooded her lungs. Her vision blurred. The grey-blue of her surroundings faded to black.

* * *

WHISPERS. They snaked their way into Jay's subconscious, connecting with her life force, drawing her up through the water. Jay's head burst through the surface of the water, her lungs emptying with a violent cough as she sucked in air.

She saw Cassie power towards the edge of the pool where Stitch had already pulled himself up onto a rock. She kicked at the water to follow her friends, feeling the rucksack dragging at her back. Cassie reached out from the edge, pulling her up onto the rocks.

'Where's Sammy?' spluttered Jay.

'I take it he can swim?' Cassie said as she looked around the pool then up into the trees atop the white cliffs.

'He can swim.' Something caught Jay's eye on the opposite side of the plunge pool. The grey flint surfaces were darkened, wet, like someone had just climbed out. 'He must be OK.' She pointed. 'In that alcove over there.'

Jay surveyed the water's edge. The water was already still. Above, a clear hole in the undergrowth showed distant sky. The cliff at the top cantilevered a good metre or two out from the edge all the way around, like it had been worn away underneath, scoured by high water levels into the circular, concave neck of a vase. The spots in front of Jay's eyes faded, and she took in the arresting beauty of her surroundings. The ripples through the turquoise blue pool settled so that its surface became static, frozen, reflecting the afternoon sun at its edge. She looked at Stitch. His open-mouthed awe as he looked around. She caught his eye and he shook his head, unable to formulate words.

Cassie called out Sammy's name again, then edged towards the lip of rock to dive in and swim across. Jay held her arm. 'Let's work our way around,' she said, slinging her dripping rucksack back over her shoulders. Stitch brushed his wet hair back and wiped his glasses on his wet top.

The three friends edged around the pool. The water's turquoise sheen lightened further where the sun's rays caught it. Half the pool was in shadow and she guessed there would only be a few hours a day when the sun was high enough for its rays to find their way through the narrow space between the trees at the surface. Birds flapped and fluttered around the chalk cliffs, in homes resting on protruding roots and gathered branches.

From a cave that stretched deep into the cliff, water flowed into the pool, its current visible underwater, some water pouring in from a crevice in the rocks creating a shallow waterfall. The cave's ceiling was too low to walk upright. 'The unnamed river,' Jay said. Cassie looked back at her and then to the mouth of the cave. She dipped her hand into the water, cupping it, allowing it to spill from her fingers. It sparkled as it ran through her hands, as if she were holding diamonds. The scent in the breeze was sweet and fresh. Behind Jay, Stitch stepped over the little waterfall and they pressed on towards the next opening.

The dark patches on the rocks were as Jay had thought, wet from someone dragging themselves from the pool. The alcove that she'd seen from the opposite bank was in fact another cave. That one too was a conduit for water entering the pool. The cave had a narrow opening but then opened out to a wider space, perhaps three metres in height with a river's worth of water flowing in a trough beside a raised section, almost like a canal and towpath. The roar of water echoed around the tunnel, bouncing off the walls and creating a whirling wall of sound.

'Sammy.' Cassie lurched towards the prone figure of Sammy, on the rocks next to the river. Jay hurried after her, a hole in the pit of her stomach.

'He's OK,' said Cassie. 'He's breathing fine. Probably the temperature of the water shocked him more than anything else. Can't see any broken bones or any other obvious damage. He'll come around.'

'How did he get out?' said Stitch.

Sammy stirred. He groaned and moved to sit up, insisting that he was OK but wincing as he moved his left foot. He held his ankle, pulling up his trouser leg to reveal a deep, bleeding gash and swelling. He looked groggy and confused.

Deeper into the cave the thundering river powered past them and into the pool. Jay inspected her brother's ankle. He insisted it was just a sprain. Cassie helped Jay to lift Sammy to a standing position, careful to support his weight. 'How do you break an ankle landing in water?' Cassie said, gently.

'It's not broken,' Sammy said, wincing once more as he tried to put weight on it.

'Let us take your weight,' said Jay. Cassie dragged Sammy's arm around her neck and between her and Jay they helped Sammy further into the tunnel. 'There,' said Jay, nodding towards an opening in the side wall through which they could see light.

They entered a vast cavern, perhaps twenty feet across, with a number of smaller caves leading away from a central atrium. In the roof of the main cavern a shaft rose to the surface, the twilight leaking down to where they stood in the bowels of the hill.

'The Caverns,' said Cassie, her jaw dropping open and a smile forming on her lips.

'The gateway,' said Jay as they lowered Sammy onto a rock.

Before them stood a makeshift kitchen with an open fire pit beneath the shaft that served as a chimney for smoke. It was topped with wood with a grate over as if ready for cooking. To the side were a range of pots and pans of different sizes, all well-used, blackened on the bases and scratched and dented on their sides.

'Someone lives here,' said Stitch.

'Not recently,' said Cassie, lifting the pans one at a time. She scraped a layer of dust and debris from a saucepan. She picked up and shook an old box of matches, then took one out, striking it against the side of the box. It sparked to life, and she shook it to extinguish the flame.

Jay helped Sammy change his clothes for a dry set he'd stored in a bag in his rucksack. He was in pain, woozy, almost sleepy. 'You OK?' she asked. Sammy nodded, then leaned back against the wall of the cave and motioned his permission for Jay to go and explore.

Stitch was sifting through dust-covered notebooks and papers on a makeshift set of shelves on the opposite wall. He flicked through the pages like they were valuable artefacts, his eyes wide at the wonder of what they had found.

Cassie cleaned up a pan and filled it with water from a source that came through from the rocks.

'It's a solution feature,' Stitch said, looking around the cavern. 'They are quite common, but this one is something else.' Jay frowned at Stitch, not entirely sure what he was talking about. 'Limestone and chalk,' Stitch said, 'It weathers, dissolves in the ground water, sometimes opening up these kinds of underground spaces. You'd normally expect them to collapse in on themselves but this one's intact. I guess there's not much up above, so the ground loads are relatively small.'

Jay's gaze lingered on her friend for a moment, sharing in his wonder. She looked around at the crypt-like structure, with natural arches leading to five or six different underground rooms off the central space. The main cavern itself was like an architectural marvel, a grand design created by the natural world.

'Come by the fire, dry off,' said Cassie as the flames grew around the pan of water, the crackling firewood tinder dry and eager to burn. Jay helped Sammy over to a rock by the fire and the four of them sat and offloaded their bags. Jay took a breath, unable to shake the sensation of being in a dream.

Cassie and Stitch each rifled through their bags, salvaging

what they could of the food. Jay opened out the map to dry and pulled out her dad's notebook, protected from the water in its plastic bag. Cassie retrieved the keys to the car and was visibly relieved.

Everything Jay could see looked like it had been made from natural materials, or salvaged. It was clear to her that this was Cassie's grandad's "front of house" as Reuben had called it.

'Bears more than just a resemblance to Dad's stories, eh Sammy?'

Sammy nodded, then grimaced as he lifted his leg to rest his foot up on a rock. Cassie sighed. 'Can you believe it?' she said. 'All this time and it was here.' She looked at Jay. 'My grandad was here?'

Jay nodded. 'You think this is his stuff?'

'Maybe. But it's not been used for years so if he came here like you said, when he disappeared, then he didn't stop for long.'

'Must have gone through,' said Jay.

'You want tea, Sammy?' Cassie said, pulling the pan of boiling water off the fire and onto the side where she'd lined up tin mugs from her backpack.

Jay brought a wad of papers and a notebook from the shelves of the cave and sat next to Sammy. She gave the notebook to her brother and opened out the map on the floor. It was hand-drawn, showing the three rivers converging at a point, and one river flowing out to the south. It was a carefully, intricately detailed map of their location. There were different colours to represent different features. Even trees were carefully positioned and detailed. The map only extended to a hundred metres or so from the pool, with no details of what lay beyond in any direction, and no indication of an entrance to any kind of underground world beyond the pool.

Sammy closed the notebook and leaned back, closing his eyes. He breathed uncomfortably through the pain in his ankle. Jay looked again at the swelling and the cut. She stood and retrieved a pan, filled it with cold water from the spring and returned to Sammy. She placed the pan under his foot and scooped the cool water on to his ankle from her hands. He sucked in air, straightening and tensing with the pain at first, then relaxing.

'I counted two river connections out there,' said Jay. 'Both incoming. Don't know where the outgoing one is, must be under the surface.'

'Three,' said Stitch. 'The third incoming was that opening a little way up the cliff. About ten feet up.'

'I saw that,' said Jay. 'You think that's the Rother? It was only a trickle of water.'

'I know. It's blocked up somewhere by the looks of it.'

'Did you see the unnamed river?' said Sammy. Jay nodded as she continued to scoop water onto his ankle. 'And?' said Sammy.

Jay paused. 'It was just like Dad described it. Magical.' The cut on Sammy's ankle looked deep and the swelling had grown. They'd never be able to get him out of the pool if he couldn't walk.

'Real enough then,' said Sammy, his gaze drifting around the cavern. 'You think dad's hobbits lived down here?'

She looked around. 'Someone certainly did.'

'What about the gateway?' he said.

'That's what we need to find.' Jay filled her brother in about the visit from Reuben, his encouragement, and the information about Cassie's grandad. Sammy seemed a little shell-shocked. She smiled at him. 'Hey, it's a good thing, it means that Dad was right, there really is something down here.'

Stitch reached out for the notebook that Jay had taken from the shelf. 'Can I see?'

'Look,' Jay said, drawing his attention to the hand-drawn map. 'I think we are in here.' She pointed to the map at a point where a series of connected caverns were sketched. 'That river out there, with the towpaths, that's the Arun like we thought. And the one over on the west side, the cave opening up the cliff, that's the Rother, like you said. The third one, on the east side, is the unnamed one, comes down from the north.'

Jay felt a shadow of fear pass across her as she thought of Dad on his own on the run, trying to find his way to the gateway. 'He talked so much about this place but we just thought it was all in his head. The fact that he'd made it all up was part of the magic.'

'But we aren't safe yet. I don't think *this* place is protected. This is not the Interland.'

Cassie called them over from across the other side of the cavern. Stitch and Jay joined her at the shelves. She pointed at one of the maps with hand-written annotations. 'This is my grandad's writing, I'd recognise it anywhere.' The three of them read the words for a minute, seeing that Cassie's grandad had made notes about the various caves and caverns as if he had been systematically exploring and mapping.

'You think he was looking for the gateway?' said Stitch.

Cassie looked at Jay. 'Jay had a visitor last night, a Runner from the Interland.' She turned back to the shelves, leaving Jay to explain it to Stitch.

Stitch became agitated. 'We don't have time to wait. If the Readers are on their way here, we need to keep going.'

'It's been hidden for a reason, we aren't likely to find it easily. We should rest, then work carefully through the clues they've left for us.'

Sammy looked up. 'And Dad's on his way, can you feel him?'

Jay shook her head. Stitch settled by the fire with one of the notebooks that Cassie had identified as one of her grandad's diaries. Jay put a hand on Cassie's arm.

'I'm OK,' she said, pulling away and avoiding Jay's eye. Jay walked away, taking a seat with Sammy and Stitch.

Stitch pulled a book from his bag, checking it had remained dry. He flicked through the pages.

'What is it?' asked Jay.

'Something I got from the pagans up on Highdown,' said Stitch, squinting through his glasses in the dim light.

'You never said...'

Stitch looked up and smiled at Jay. 'They reckon I might have some power.'

Jay laughed, then felt bad for belittling the possibility of power in her friend. She too sensed that Stitch had something, and Reuben had implied the same. 'Sorry, didn't mean to laugh,' she said. 'What's the book?'

'Healing,' said Stitch. 'It's about the theories of connection, the healing potential of the powers.'

'You think there's something in it?'

'Probably not,' said Stitch.

Jay reached for the Sasha Colden book and opened it at her bookmark. The light from above had faded, so she leaned in to the light from the fire. The words flowed into her and she opened her mind. It was if she were reading from within the book, from the inside out. She allowed herself to be drawn into the story, the feel of it and the depth beneath the words. She had a sense of connectedness with her surroundings – the air, the rivers, and the energy in all that was living. It was as if her understanding was crystallising despite having no means to articulate it – it was undeniable.

'I get a sense that this gateway needs to be uncovered in some way, activated. It can't simply be stumbled upon and walked through.'

'How do we open it?' Stitch asked.

'I don't know yet, but I suspect that it's in the legend. Must be something to do with the unnamed river.'

'Can we wade upstream?' said Cassie.

Jay shook her head. 'No chance. Too strong to walk against. Perhaps we need to navigate *down*stream, *into* the pool, somehow.'

* * *

STITCH LOADED THE FIRE, its smoke rising up through the shaft to the surface. It grew dark and Sammy slept, his body recovering from the trauma of his injury. Cassie had devoured three of her grandad's diaries. They passed around the bottle of Dr Pepper and ate the remains of the food they'd picked up at the petrol station. Cassie closed a diary and placed it on the floor in front of her. 'Well, you live and learn,' she said.

'What?' said Stitch.

'These diaries go back to when my grandad was in his twenties. His *twenties*. That's like, more than forty years ago. He'd been coming here since before that, since he was a kid. He used to fish down here with his mate. They found this place, kept it secret.'

'You are kidding,' said Stitch. 'Why didn't he ever bring you?'

Cassie shrugged. 'His parents, my great grandparents, were working at Amberley House. His mum managed the laundry and his dad was one of the grounds staff. He'd told me that before. I'd visited the place with him. They came to England from the Caribbean, after the war. He came over with his mum, a few years after his dad travelled here to find work. Why did he never tell me he knew where this place was?'

'I reckon he was going to,' said Jay. 'But this was his place, he was essentially its custodian, protecting the gateway. It was probably his solace. For him and his friend. Does it say what his friend's name was?'

'Pete,' said Cassie.

Jay laughed. 'That's the name of one of the hobbits in Dad's stories, and the other one was Jack.'

'My grandad.' Cassie grinned. 'My grandad's name is Jack.'

'Reuben said your grandad has power,' said Jay.

'It doesn't surprise me. It's Reuben's power that surprises me most. Level seven is serious. I'd have noticed something.' Cassie drew back her own sleeve and quickly pulled it back down, no sign of any mark. 'What did he look like?'

'Tall,' said Jay.

'He always was tall.'

'Chunky. Athletic I mean. Big hair,' said Jay.

'He still have dreads?'

'More like an afro.'

'According to these diaries, there's a way in and out that they used,' Cassie said. 'An easier route than the one we took.'

'Where?' said Jay.

'They used to come in via the Arun, on a raft. The way out is under the water in the pool.' Jay looked over at Stitch and he nodded.

'Everything's connected,' said Jay.

Cassie said, 'The last diary entry is from around the time he went missing, when he went through, like Reuben said.'

28

The Readers drove as deep into the woods as their Land Rover would take them, before ditching it to continue on foot. Marcus worked on intuition, pulling himself towards the girl by the trail of crumbs she'd left behind, and with his sense of connection with the boy. They remained some distance away, he knew that, but they were heading in the right direction, and they were getting closer with every step.

The girl and her friends had stopped. They were no longer moving away from him and he figured they'd reached their destination. More than the girl's magnetic power, the boy drew his attention. He felt something he couldn't yet untangle. It was the boy who sent him the strongest signal.

'Why do we have to walk through this shit, we have the Land Rover, we can go around,' said Jimmy, sharpening a length of willow to spike and smoke the fish Marcus had pulled from the water.

'This is the only way,' Marcus said.

On his last check-in with the authorities he'd been informed of Ben's escape from prison. Marcus was the one who had located Ben, for Jimmy to bring him in, so he took the escape as a personal slight.

'He's out, isn't he,' said Drake, a nervous wobble in his voice which Marcus took to be an apology for reading him without asking.

Marcus nodded. 'If I'm reading it right, he's on his way to the girl, so we should be reunited with him before long, and Jimmy can have another go at him, eh Jimmy?'

'Who?'

'The girl's father. He's out, and he's with another one of them, a level two or three.'

'They'll be no bother,' said Drake. Marcus figured that the other Readers would be heading in from different routes to converge at the location of the gateway. They'd not be far behind, but it was possible they'd arrive after Ben. The girl and her friends would stand no chance of escape against the full force of the State. She might put up a resistance against Marcus, but it would be nothing in the face of multiple Readers. If they responded as he'd instructed, there could be six Readers, most at level six or seven. He couldn't afford to be careless. He'd do it right this time.

29

Jay's mind raced. She opened her eyes to focus on something static to stop the cavern spinning.

Shivering in the cool, damp air, she stood and pulled up the hood of her top. She collected logs from a small store next to the fire pit, fed them into the embers, and soaked up the warmth as orange light flickered and danced across her face.

The fall into the pool brought home the sharp reality of the danger she had put herself and her friends in, not to mention her little brother Sammy. Their arrival at the pool had both raised the stakes and cleared away the mist of uncertainty. She had a goal, and it was clearer to Jay what she needed to do.

She sat by the fire, the heat from the flames on her back. She sucked air deep into her lungs and closed her eyes. There was life and energy in the caverns. Surrounded by the earth on all sides, in the heart of a hill fed by three rivers, Jay could feel the power. She let it come, opening to its whispers.

With the force of the environment flowing through her, she sensed its urgency, its desire for a connection, not just with her, but with all people. She let herself open and flow with the power all around her. Jay breathed deeply, her eyes closed but seeing more than ever before, feeling more than she was able to understand.

The roar of the river Arun just outside the cave was deafening, louder, rumbling – then nothing. The flames of the fire froze in mid-flicker. Out in the tunnel, the surface of the river was still, like the rough surface of a solidified stream of lava. The whispers buffeting her mind became more subdued. They had her attention now.

Jay felt the substance of her surroundings as if it were in her hands, its texture, the strands of its energy taking an almost physical form. Jay assumed the control. She released the time-freeze, allowing the river to explode into action, the flicker of the fire once more illuminating the entrance to the cave. She breathed in once more and the river slowed to a halt, the surface of the water taking a new shape, the juts and spikes like rough icing on a cake. She released the tension in her body and allowed the water to flow, the fire to burn, and the environment to breathe once more.

She sensed that the power and the energy were with her, there to support her. But there was something else. There was a quid pro quo, a need of the environment in return. She sensed that the answers lay beyond the portal, in the Interland, and the path was becoming clearer.

30

Jay woke, the Sasha Colden book on the floor next to her. She looked over to see that Stitch wasn't there. A flicker of candlelight from an adjacent cave caught her eye.

Chalky gravel stuck to her bare feet as she picked her way over to the entrance to the cave. Stitch saw her as soon as she poked her head around the corner. 'Can't sleep?' he said, returning his attention to a bunch of papers on the grey-white floor. 'Come, sit here.' Stitch motioned to the space next to him. 'See what you can make of these maps, there's something here I just can't piece together.'

He had an old OS map open in front of him, much older than any she'd seen before. He nudged it towards her and she turned it over to see if it had a date, or an edition number. Its front cover was missing. She ran her finger across its pages. Its yellowing surface was smooth to the touch, its text and labels in an unusual font compared to modern maps, and its features less complete, like there were layers of information missing, only the essential elements plotted.

'Looks old,' Jay said.

'There are things here that aren't on our map.' Jay strained her eyes in the gloom of the candlelight to see if she could recognise any landmarks. Stitch switched on his head-torch and passed it to Jay.

'Trace the path of the Arun, up from the coast.'

Jay found Littlehampton, from the shape of the coast, although it was labelled as *Hampton*. The river was labelled as the Arun.

'We have a better map than this,' Jay said.

'From what I read in that old notebook,' said Stitch, 'if it's after nineteen forty, it won't show the truth. Have you found the Arun?'

'Yes.'

'Follow it north. Through Arundel, and into Amberley. See where it crosses the Rother?'

'Yes, just north of Amberley. Roughly where we are.'

Stitch leaned over the map with Jay. 'See there,' he pointed, 'there's a third river to the east. That's the continuation of the Arun. The rivers converge here, and run south together, towards the coast.'

'So where's the third incoming river?' asked Jay.

'There are *three* flows coming into the pool, right, like we saw, and one going out, which we reckon is below the surface. So that's what we see here on this map, except that the third incoming river is not so obvious.'

'Tell me something I don't know,' said Jay.

'See the dotted line stretching to the north?'

'That's a footpath, surely?'

'What colour is it?'

'Grey, same as everything on this map.'

'Look closer, what other features match that colour?'

Jay strained to discern the different shades in the lines on the map. It took a while to tune her vision, but it was clear that the dotted line to the north was intended to represent the same feature as the rivers marked to the south, west and east. 'It's the same shade as the rivers, but...'

'But it's dotted?' Stitch finished her sentence.

'Yes.'

'So what do you think that means?'

'That it's underground?' Jay said. 'But so are the others and they're not dotted on the map.'

'I think the others are only underground in the immediate vicinity of the pool, they are above ground as soon as they escape this hill – the other one, the unnamed one, is underground, according to that map, for several miles.'

Jay followed the dotted river north on the map until it disappeared. 'It heads up towards the River Wey, according to this map, but the line stops somewhere in the North Downs.' Jay leaned in to see where it disappeared but the map features were so basic there was nothing much to see.

'Remind me what else your dad said about the unnamed river?'

'It's the one you have to navigate into the pool to unlock the magic,' Jay said.

'So, maybe that's why there's nothing obvious here. No portal, no gateway. We need to travel the unnamed river towards the pool, which flows through this hill. Maybe there's something inside the hill, on the path of that river?'

'Or maybe it's a magic spell that gets cast when the stars align and the hobbits do a dance,' Cassie said with a snort. She sat down with a huff, cross-legged on the floor, her long legs nudging up against Jay's.

'Yes, very funny,' Jay said.

'But seriously, why didn't someone else do it? Like my grandad?' Cassie said.

'He could have,' said Stitch. 'Was there anything in his

notes about looking for the connection of the unnamed river with the real world rivers?'

Cassie shook her head and Stitch sighed.

'What?' said Jay.

'Something in the legend I keep thinking about,' Stitch said. 'The magic is formed through a connection between the unnamed river and the Given. The sister from the legend. She had powers, right?' Jay nodded. 'So it's *you* that needs to navigate the unnamed river, Jay.'

Jay knew this before Stitch said the words. And she knew that it was to do with the Sasha Colden book. Something in that book was connecting Jay with the power in a way that was unique to her, and Sasha. Jay pulled back her sleeve to look at the number on her wrist. If she had such power, she'd surely be sensing the gateway. She frowned and leaned over the map again. 'The location of the connection is not on this map. And that stretch of underground river, down to the pool, is not on any contemporary maps, nor is it listed in any literature I found in the bookshop.'

Jay bit her bottom lip. 'If we can find that connection we can travel the unnamed river down to the pool.'

'You think it's possible?' Cassie said.

'We can try.' Jay arranged the map on the floor and then leaned back against the wall with Stitch, who had his eyes closed, breathing steadily.

Jay stood, and headed into the main cavern to retrieve the OS map, drying by the fire. Jay could hear the trickle of fresh water through the rocks battling against the roar of the Arun out front. Sammy was motionless, breathing out sleep noises. Jay put a couple more logs on the fire and retraced her steps to the side cave where Cassie continued to study the map and Stitch was fast asleep up against the wall. She motioned at Cassie to follow her back into the main cavern where they spread the two maps alongside each other by the fire.

Together, the girls studied the terrain between the River Wey and the pool. The old map showed most of the underground river as it meandered north from the pool, but not the connection with the Wey. The more detailed map showed the topography of the area as well as geographic features. They could see the peaks and troughs of the Downs, the valleys and the hills.

'Maybe we can predict the path of the underground river all the way through to where it connects with the River Wey. We can compare the river as it was shown on the old map, against the terrain shown on the new map, and maybe get a sense of how it reacted to the topography, how it meandered and how it passed through the land. Then we project that route onto the OS map. What do you think?' Jay said.

'I like it!' Cassie said and they high-fived.

* * *

'STILL CAN'T SLEEP?' Stitch asked, joining Jay a few hours later in the main cavern. Jay smiled at him and continued with her pencil, plotting the last sections of the path of the underground river onto the map.

Jay and Cassie had worked out that there were two possible locations where the connection could be. After Cassie fell asleep, Jay studied the possibilities. The one out east was not likely, given that its path was so tortuous, and the connection with the Wey was in a town centre so not likely to be easily hidden and undiscovered for all this time. The western connection was most likely. It followed the trajectory of the marked section of the river, with a logical path through the valleys of the Downs. It connected with the Wey where it passed through woodland that, like the pool, had no obvious paths or access ways. It looked as if it were only accessible from the river itself. The point of connection was just a few miles west of a place where Jay and Sammy used to go fishing with their dad.

Stitch gave Jay a look, like he was impressed, and squinted to see where she'd predicted the connection to be with the River Wey. 'That's where we need to go,' he said, 'and soon. The Readers must be close.'

31

Ben woke with a chill in his bones, wet from the rain and a night of fitful rest. Matchstick had been snoring from the moment they set down. Even still, he slept.

Ben crawled out of their makeshift camp under the bridge by a canal. He stretched and scrambled down the slope from the bridge abutment and onto the path. He still wore his prison-issue clothes, the left knee of his trousers soaked in blood. A dog-walker on the opposite towpath glanced over and Ben turned to shield the man's view from his face. For all he knew, their faces were already on the day's front pages.

He brushed himself down and took a moment to breathe in the freedom and tranquillity of the forest. Over the fence and across a car park was a superstore, raising a pang of hunger in his belly. He scrambled over the fence and made his way through the car park towards the store.

He headed first for the toilets, washing his face and rinsing his hair before taking the time to pick the gravel from his knee and rinse it clean. He pulled off his prison top and tied it around his waist, looking less conspicuous in his tee-shirt.

The shop had more staff than customers, packing shelves and organising tills. He picked a trolley and worked through the store, avoiding shop assistants. He started in the clothing section, choosing a couple of backpacks and then picking out some clothes for himself. He guessed Matchstick's size, erring on the large side. In the pharmacy section, he collected plasters and antiseptic spray. He completed his shop with packets of cheese, cold chicken, two loaves of bread and bottled water, which he put straight into the rucksacks in his trolley.

Ben loitered behind a clothes display, noting the position of the security cameras. He dumped the prison outfit and pulled on the fresh new clothes. He crammed the rest of the gear into the rucksacks and, slinging one over each shoulder, walked calmly to the exit, not stopping until he'd reached the other side of the car park. He jumped over the fence with more vigour than earlier and jogged along the path back towards the bridge.

Matchstick was standing on the path with two men. He caught Ben's eye and shook his head. Ben turned, passed along a stretch of path before ducking behind a bush so that he could watch from safety.

The men had uniforms but weren't police. Ben couldn't sense any powers. Matchstick looked as if he were deep in a negotiation when suddenly the two men laughed, patted Matchstick and turned to leave.

'What the fuck?' Ben said as Matchstick reached him, checking over his shoulder to be sure the two men had gone.

'Security guards from the industrial estate. They wanted to take me in to the shelter.'

'Here, get rid of those prison overalls. I hope these fit.'

'Stylish,' Matchstick said, holding out the top.

Ben turned to the other rucksack and opened a loaf of bread, handing a slice to Matchstick.

When Matchstick had dressed himself and discarded the old clothes in the bush, the men ate, drank and tended their wounds, saying little about the previous night and how close they had come to not making it out. Matchstick's graze on his back was worse than Ben had thought, a scrape from his shoulder bones down to his coccyx. He helped Matchstick clean it up.

'You gonna contact the old lady?' said Matchstick as Ben tended his wound.

Ben shrugged. 'She'd as likely hand us in as help us out. What about you? Anyone to contact?'

'Nope.'

Ben looked into the sky, noting the location of the sun to get his bearings. He could see that the canal ran east-west as he'd hoped, which meant that it was the Wey & Arun Canal that he'd intended they find and head west. On foot, it could be three days' walking before they needed to diverge from the river and head into open country. If they could find themselves a boat, they would be there in less than twenty-four hours.

'That way?' asked Matchstick, pulling on his top and looking west, reading Ben's mind.

Ben nodded and stood, stretching. 'Could do with a boat.'

Matchstick motioned downstream where Ben could see narrowboats moored along the canal's edge. 'You know how to drive one of those?' asked Ben.

'Born and bred on the London waterways, my friend. Lead the way.'

32

The sun was high in the sky, its rays penetrating deep into the surface of the pool. With a bird's-eye view, you might easily miss the opening through the trees to the pool below, a mere glimmer of cobalt in an otherwise emerald carpet, the rivers converging on the hill like pulmonary routes to a heart.

Sammy's ankle was no better in the morning. Jay strapped it up, then, with Cassie, helped him outside the cavern to sit by the edge of the water in the pool, at the base of the chalk well that had been their entrance the previous day. Jay was anxious to get moving but couldn't consider leaving Sammy.

They picked their way across the rocks, edging towards the unnamed river connection where the green-blue water quietly pushed its way into the pool, creating streamlines and eddies in the darker blue-grey of the pool. The water forced its way through the connection with a power that was too great to battle against, confirming Jay's thought that they'd not be able to work their way upstream.

Jay sat next to Sammy on a smooth rock and leaned back against the vertical white face of the cliff that stretched up and into the greenery. The trees soared, making way for a circular patch of cloudless blue sky. Cassie snorted a laugh. 'Look at that cliff. Our fall could have been nasty. *Should* have been nasty. Good chance of smacking into the rocks on the way down.'

'Best not think about it.' Jay grimaced. It was like being at the bottom of a well, twenty metres across at its base and rising fifty metres in white chalk, then a further fifty in the trunks and branches of the trees. She dipped her hand in the flow of the unnamed river, icy cold on her fingers and clear as tap water as it escaped her grasp and continued into the pool. A sweet smell of nettles came in with a breeze and filled the cave.

'You need to leave,' said Sammy.

Stitch emerged from the main cavern with a notebook in his hand and made his way around the pool to take a place on the rock next to Sammy. He shifted around, looking over towards the river connection in the cliff-side.

'What's up, Stitch?' said Jay.

'Not sure yet,' he said, opening the notebook. 'You know that opening up there, the Rother connection that we were talking about?' He nodded up to the cave opening that they had figured was where the River Rother connected to the pool, only a trickle of water coming through.

'What about it?' said Jay.

'There's a reason it's just a trickle.' Jay, Sammy and Cassie waited for Stitch to elaborate. 'There's a natural blockage, according to these notes. Your grandad's notes I guess, Cassie?'

Cassie leaned over to look at the handwriting. 'Looks like it. Old notes though.'

'It takes exactly twenty-four hours for a pressure to build up. It seems that it's partly due to the natural rising water levels in the ground behind the rock face, with time, and then there's a tidal element.'

'Tidal? Here?' said Jay.

'Yes, the location of the moon and all that, pulling and dragging the ground water. The combination of the tidal cycles and the pressure build-up creates a periodic release.'

'What kind of release?' said Jay, looking up at the hole in the side of the cliff.

'A big one,' said Stitch. 'These notes say that after a release, the rocks, chalk and sandy deposits re-form within the opening, a few tens of metres back into the cliff face, blocking it up again.'

'How did they know that?' said Sammy.

'Because it all comes out in a massive blow out. Then the ground fills back in and it starts all over again. And, because, according to the notes here, it happens every twenty-four hours. Like clockwork.'

'When?' said Jay.

'Some time in the afternoon. So let's watch.' Cassie and Jay looked at each other and then to Stitch, who looked up at the gentle trickle of water from the Rother. Stitch gave Jay a half smile before resting his head back on the white cliff, looking up into the trees. 'See there, about halfway up the cliff?'

'Uh huh,' Jay said, squinting to see a bird resting on a protruding tree root, looking down on them. 'The Phoenix,' Jay said under her breath.

'Like your dad said.'

'My grandad talked about a bird,' said Cassie. 'Said that it used to come to him. What is it?'

'It's a falcon,' said Stitch, 'see the yellow colouring around the eyes and beak, and the claws. It's a female.' He turned to Jay. 'Have you tried to see where your dad is? He could be here?'

'He's not here,' Jay said. 'We need to get back to the car.'

'We know the way out,' said Cassie, standing and looking into the pool for signs of the underwater connection. She looked up towards the falcon. It was restless, moving along the branch and back again.

'What's up with her?' said Stitch.

'She wants to come,' said Sammy. 'Cassie, hold your arm out, she wants to come to you.'

'No way,' said Cassie, but at the same time raising her right arm in front of her. 'She'll never come.' The falcon watched, gave a squawk. Cassie lowered her arm and turned back to the others. 'Look at her. She thinks I'm an idiot, she's laughing at me.' The falcon continued to jiggle on the branch, flapping and nudging along. She squawked again and seemed to topple from the branch. She pumped her wings and soared up towards the trees.

'If she would go to Grandad...' Cassie stretched out her arm. The bird disappeared into the trees. Suddenly, she appeared in the middle of the circle of blue, diving like an arrow towards them. Stitch squeaked in alarm but Cassie stood firm, her arm outstretched. The falcon swooped and opened its wings, slowing almost to a stop in mid-air just above Cassie, then gracefully landing on Cassie's shoulder, ignoring the outstretched arm. Cassie had to bite her lip not to scream out as the falcon's talons gripped the skin of her shoulder.

Jay's mouth hung open with surprise.

Cassie's grin filled her face as the stunning creature settled on her shoulder, her friends aghast. The falcon seemed to be looking right into Cassie's eyes.

With no warning, the falcon took off again, back towards the perch. The force as the bird launched was enough to push

Cassie back into the cliff face, but not enough to wipe the grin from her face as she sat back down next to Jay.

'Wow,' said Jay. Cassie rubbed her shoulder, leaning back and squinting up at the sky through the circular gap in the trees.

'When are we getting out of here?' said Stitch.

Cassie again looked into the pool. 'If the notebook is right, this leads down into the village.'

'So we have to go down there?' said Stitch.

'Definitely,' Cassie said. She stripped off her top and shorts and slipped into the water, bobbing up to the surface and squealing with the cold. She took a deep breath and disappeared. Jay looked at Sammy and Stitch who both stared as Cassie broke the surface and gulped in some air.

'It's there,' she said. 'Less than three feet down, an opening that slopes down through the rocks.' She pulled herself out of the water and Jay noticed Sammy averting his eyes. 'If the notebook is right, at the end of that tunnel, you get to a shallow waterfall...'

'Waterfall?' blurted Jay.

'A little one, a gentle hump that you pass over. Then it's a leisurely drift down for a mile or so and you're in the village.'

'With our rucksacks?' said Jay.

'We could leave them here, we're coming back, remember?'

Stitch stood up next to Cassie, handing her a top to drape over her shoulders. 'We can take a few bits in the small rucksacks, in plastic bags to keep it dry,' he said.

'This is the only way out.' As Cassie spoke, Jay felt the ground begin to vibrate, a low rumble passing up through her body. She looked at Stitch, then over to the cave connection.

'We need to move,' said Stitch, reaching out a hand for

Sammy. The rumbling increased in volume and the four moved with more urgency.

Jay and Cassie reached the cover of the opening to the main cavern. They looked back to see a burst of debris shoot across the pit and hammer into the opposite white cliff face like bullets from a gun. Debris rained down on Stitch as he shoved Sammy to safety, stumbling and almost losing his footing on his bad ankle as Jay caught his arm. Stitch followed, soaked and battered. The stream of water that followed the debris must have been more than two metres in diameter, exploding from the entrance of the cave. It powered across the pool like a jet-washer, dislodging chunks of chalk from the cliff as they watched.

After less than a minute, the jet abated, and the flow reduced back to that of a gentle waterfall into the pool.

33

I don't think I'll be coming with you for this bit,' Sammy said.

'Rubbish. You'll be fine. We can help you,' Jay said as she and Stitch organised the rucksack they'd take underwater.

'The water might be OK but what then? I can't walk on this. You'll be hours with me in tow.'

Jay looked out over the pool, a ripple on the surface as a fish came up for a gulp of air, or an attempt to take one of the pond skaters that skimmed the surface. Her mind returned to her efforts with her powers in the night, the control she felt over time, her environment, the power of the river. 'You know I told you about that weird time freeze thing that happened back at the café?'

'Has it happened again?'

'I might be able to show you.' She closed her eyes and the whispers came –urgent, rushed, more desperate than before. Within a few seconds, Jay had control. She opened her eyes, exhaled and maintained the freeze. She looked up into the sky, a bird frozen in flight. She turned to Sammy – frozen. Closing her eyes once more, she took a breath and put a hand on Sammy's arm, releasing him. He sucked in a breath and coughed as if coming up for air. He jerked his head to look at Jay. 'What the...'

'It's OK,' said Jay.

'What happened? Why has it gone so quiet?'

'Look at that bird,' she said, nodding into the sky.

'What the...' Sammy said again.

'And look at the surface of the water, the insects and the pond skaters.'

'It's frozen,' he said.

'Exactly.'

'Is *everything* frozen?'

'I think so.'

Sammy grinned, then rubbed his eyes, 'Shit, Jay. This is big. You can do anything. We can just walk into a bank and...'

'Sammy,' Jay interrupted. They laughed. 'This is bigger than bank robbery. I feel in complete control, and it doesn't hurt, doesn't wear me down, just feels natural. I wasn't sure if I could bring you in.'

Sammy struggled to his feet and limped over to the edge of the water. He touched his foot on the surface and felt that it was solid, then stepped out onto the flat, silvery surface. Tentatively, as if walking on ice, he moved away from the edge. He laughed, then called for Cassie and Stitch.

'They're not with us,' said Jay.

'Can you unfreeze them?'

'I don't know, I think so. Not now though, we need to go.'

Feeling confident, Jay focused energy on the area of the pool beneath Sammy's feet. It swirled around him as if it were about to become a whirlpool. Sammy squealed, his body turning with the water – once, twice, three revolutions, his scream rising in pitch. She stopped. The surface of the pool steadied and returned Sammy to rest, facing towards Jay.

'This is crazy,' he said.

'Come off the water so I can release it,' said Jay. Sammy edged towards her and she held out a hand. 'There's something in the whispers...'

'Whispers?' Sammy asked as he limped back onto the rocks.

'I get whispers when I connect with the environment. Not intelligible whispers, in terms of their language, but messages that are clear enough to me in a sense.'

'Saying what?'

'Nothing coherent, something about reciprocity,' said Jay. 'What does that word mean to you?'

'Give and take,' said Sammy. 'But what's that supposed to mean?'

Jay released the freeze and the noise of the world returning was deafening. 'I'm not sure yet, but I get a sense that they need help.'

'They?'

'I mean the environment, the eco-systems. They need something. And, for some reason, they see me as part of it.'

'Wow,' said Sammy under his breath.

'It's got something to do with whatever's on the other side of this gateway we are looking for.' Jay looked at her brother. 'That Runner the other night, on the beach.'

'Reuben?'

'They are paranoid and scared to death about the Readers finding the gateway.'

Jay felt a cool wind and shivered. A wave of energy washed over the place and unsettled her for a moment. She helped her brother to stand, then took his weight as they made back to the main cavern to join the others.

It was time to go.

34

Marcus pushed through the undergrowth and out into a clearing by the river. The landscape was flat, and the river seemed to have spread, widening into a lake across a flood plain.

They were close. He'd been searching for the Gateway for years and now he had himself a little homing device, something to draw him in. In all of his previous attempts to complete his mission to weed out the remaining Given, he had failed. It was like trying to find a needle in a haystack. Not this time. This time the needle was calling out to him and he was drawing himself to it like a magnet.

He stepped close to the edge of the water, peering downstream through the mist. In the distance, in the path of the meandering river, a hill peppered with trees rose out of the ground like a monolith. 'That's it,' he said as Drake and Jimmy pushed themselves through the bushes and into the clearing.

'That mountain?' said Drake, moving to join his leader. 'Couple of hours' walk then.'

'Less, if you two move a bit quicker,' Marcus said without humour. Jimmy reached down to the edge of the river and took some water into his hands, drinking greedily, then filled his water bottle. Marcus spat into the river.

Jimmy stood. 'What do we do when we get there?' he said.

Marcus looked at him. 'We do what you weren't able to do before. We take her in.'

'What about the Interland?' said Drake. 'If there's a gateway then we need to find it.'

Jimmy snorted. 'The myth? That place was invented by *them* to give them something to fight for. The only place that has a load of the Given all in one place is rehab,' he said.

'It's a good job no one is asking you,' said Marcus. 'If it's there, then we'll find it.' As Marcus spoke, he felt a now familiar slowing of the world around them. Not the complete time freeze he had experienced at the café; this was something different. He turned to observe his two colleagues, both moving as if in slow motion – their words still audible. The river flowed but at a fraction of its previous rate, edging over the shallow weir just downstream in a way that appeared non-physical.

'What was that?' Drake said, shaking his head as if trying to empty his ears of water.

'Did you feel something?' said Marcus.

'No,' said Jimmy at the same time as Drake nodded. 'No,' repeated Jimmy. 'What's going on?'

'Something hit me,' Drake said. 'Then you went all weird,' he said to Marcus.

Marcus looked downstream, the river behaving normally again. He had no idea what these time freezes were, but he knew it was to do with the girl. 'Let's move,' he said. 'We don't have much time left.'

35

Sammy sat with Jay as she chose a few necessary supplies and transferred them to the smaller rucksack. She included her change of clothes and sealed everything inside a plastic bag before squeezing it into the rucksack.

Cassie and Stitch were going through the same process using the other small rucksack. She could see that they were arguing over what to take, Cassie wanting to travel light but Stitch choosing to squeeze in as much as they could carry.

'When you get through,' said Sammy, 'open the plastic bag and let it fill with air. Then you can seal it again and use it as a float.'

'I will. Don't worry. I just need you to worry about you. Make sure you keep a lookout for anything unusual. If anything happens, get in the pool and go.'

Jay sensed something. She couldn't pin it down as a Reader. It felt more like a weak Scanner, but she couldn't be sure, what with the waves of power coming through from all around. Either way, if there were any Readers or Scanners close by, that was bad news. 'Sammy, why don't you rest out by the pool where you can get a view of all the connections, just to be safe?'

'I will, Jay. Until that Rother connection goes again.'

'Yeah, you might want to avoid that.'

Jay called over to Cassie, 'How far down is the opening?'

'A few feet, you'll be fine. We'll be in the village before you know it.' Jay liked to think that she wasn't worried about going through an underwater tunnel with no certainty of its length or whether it led to the open air or hit a dead-end in the side of the hill, but she was struggling to convince herself.

'Just follow me, Jay, keep close,' said Cassie.

'Why don't I go first, then you can push me along if I get stuck,' Jay said.

'You sure you don't want me to rig up a rope for you to follow?'

'Would you?' Jay said. 'Have you got a rope?'

Cassie laughed. 'I was joking, Jay. It's a couple of feet down to the opening, we'll be out the other side in one breath.'

* * *

THE READERS ENTERED the cave in the side of the hill, their raft bumping up against the rocks at the sides as they edged closer to the pool. Marcus pulled the raft to a stop as they reached the mid-point. Light penetrated only from one end and Jimmy was eager to get back out in the open. It was the noise that was most disturbing, the echo of the sound of the running water reverberating off the rock tunnel walls, like an aeroplane taking off.

Jimmy glanced at Marcus, standing at the helm like a ship's captain. He was miles away, focused on something they couldn't see. Jimmy looked at Drake who shrugged, as if to say that they just needed to let him do what he had to do, whatever that was.

Jimmy looked into the distance as they edged downstream. He could see the turquoise glow of the surface of the river as it emerged into the pool and into sunshine. He was reminded of the lake near his childhood home where he and his brother would go swimming on the weekends. He was drawn to it, impatient to get there.

* * *

JAY HAD JUST DRAGGED the rucksack over her shoulders and tightened the straps when she felt it – a force like a power-drill piercing her temples. This was different to the power she'd experienced when Marcus was close. This was energy targeted directly at her.

Her hands at her temples, Jay squeezed her head to push out whatever was infiltrating her mind. Through blurred vision she saw that Sammy was holding her wrists, speaking to her, terror on his face. She could hear nothing but muffled voices. Cassie was there too, holding her and guiding her to sit. Jay couldn't let go of her head for fear of it exploding with the pressure and pain. Stitch rushed over to her with some water that he poured into his hands and splashed onto her face in a desperate attempt to help.

Jay's dad had told her how the powerful Readers could cause pain and lasting damage. She knew who was responsible for the attack on her mind. Marcus had the power to get inside her head. He was near. He was stamping around in her head. He was relentless. Jay sucked in a breath and screamed as she released it. She took another breath. She concentrated, trying to resist him. Push him away. 'Get out,' she screamed, causing Sammy to release her wrists and Stitch to take a step back. Jay screamed once more, 'Get out!'

Cassie caught Jay as her legs gave way and she slumped onto the floor, conscious but no longer in control of her body. Her mind was becoming the property of another. Her final thought as the fog descended was that they would come now. And there would be nothing to stop them. Jay wouldn't be able to protect her friends or Sammy. She had put them in danger. She had failed.

* * *

'Be patient,' said Drake, reading Jimmy. 'Let him do his thing.'

Jimmy looked quizzically at Drake. 'What's he doing?'

'Digging,' said Drake. Jimmy's frown deepened. Drake elaborated, 'He's digging into her mind, debilitating her. Now that we are close enough.'

'She's mine, remember. I'm the one she gave the slip. I need to bring her in.'

Drake rolled his eyes. 'This isn't about you, Jimmy. Stick to the plan. Marcus does his thing, then we walk in there and take her away.'

Marcus seemed to come around. 'She should be a bit more manageable now.' They picked up speed, shooting towards the mouth of the cave where the River Arun met the magical pool.

* * *

Sammy took a deep breath, trying to calm himself, thinking he'd be no use to Jay if he couldn't keep calm. He leaned over her. She was still breathing. He lifted one of her eyelids to see that her eyes had rolled back in her head. 'We need to get her to a hospital.'

'That's not going to happen,' said Cassie. 'There's no way we are getting her through that underwater tunnel if she's unconscious.'

'Then the hospital needs to come here,' Sammy said, eyes wide, panic surfacing. He forced himself to take slow and steady breaths. 'How about you go, Cassie? Get to the village and call for help.'

'Where do we tell them to come to? Where does the ambulance go?'

'They can get a chopper in here,' said Stitch. Sammy put his arms under Jay and pulled her up to a sitting position. She stirred and Sammy's heart leaped with hope, relief. 'Jay? Talk to me.'

'They're coming,' she mumbled as she battled to hold herself upright. She flopped to the side and Sammy pushed her back up again. 'Readers.'

Cassie jumped into action. 'We need to leave.' Sammy heard a noise behind them, someone approaching from the direction of the Arun. He looked up at Stitch, then turned to see three men enter the cavern.

'Here we are,' the tallest one said. Sammy could tell by their distinctive outlines that these were the three men from the car park at the café: the short and wide one, the tall and skinny, and the tall and bulky. All were in black. He remained crouched next to Jay. Her eyelids fluttered and opened. She put a hand on Sammy's arm. He looked at Stitch again and then over to where Cassie had been. She'd gone. Melted away into the adjoining caves and Sammy was glad that she was out of reach of the Readers. Stitch stood, taking a position in front of Sammy, a protective stance. He stepped towards the three men.

'What do you want?'

'Her.' The tall and bulky one nodded at Jay as she pushed herself up from the floor, rejecting Sammy's attempt to help her.

Sammy looked to the tall man, their leader, a long scar on the side of his face. Their eyes locked and Sammy knew he was Marcus, the level eight that Jay had talked about. Marcus continued to look Sammy in the eye. Sammy felt the connection strengthen, as if it were more than simply this Reader's need to take them in. Marcus dragged his eyes from Sammy and made towards Jay. Stitch stepped to intervene but Marcus did something to cause him to cry out in pain, his hands squeezing the sides of his head.

'Leave him,' said Sammy.

Marcus looked at Sammy. 'You're the brother,' he said. Sammy nodded and looked sideways at Jay, seeing her straighten and focus on Marcus.

Marcus stopped mid-sentence as Jay raised her hands to the side of her head and Marcus rocked back on his heels before recovering.

'I like your spirit, Jay. Not many would have survived that degree of digging. But you...'

'Leave us alone,' Jay said as Sammy and Stitch stood, both unsteady on their feet. For a moment, a flicker of compassion for Marcus had stirred in Sammy, but it was short-lived. Whatever his connection to this man, his connection to Jay was far more powerful.

'We can't leave you alone. You know that. But I'm sure we can come to an arrangement. We want to know about the gateway.'

'What gateway?' said Jay.

Marcus turned to Drake and smiled. 'The gateway that your old man is on his way here to find. The gateway that you kids came here for. The Interland. We all want the same thing.'

'There is no gateway,' said Jay, and she seemed to push again at Marcus with her mind so that he stumbled back once more, this time clutching his head in the same way that Jay and Stitch had done a few minutes before.

Jay screamed and doubled over, her hands on her head. Marcus stepped up next to Drake, and then Jimmy stepped forward. The three of them focused on Jay and she crumpled, sliding to the floor. Stitch shouted for Marcus to stop but the shorter of the Readers pushed him away, knocking his head on the limestone wall of the cave.

Sammy went to his sister. She showed no sign of understanding that he was there, nothing in her eyes but pain. He turned and rushed at Marcus, stumbling on his damaged ankle and slamming into him with no effect, like hitting a wall.

Everything stopped. Sammy fell on his face in the dust. Stitch struggled to his knees and then slumped back down in the dirt on his front. Sammy turned his head to see Jay. She lay motionless, her eyelids flickering and then opening. She looked at Sammy. Her eyes full of sorrow, pain and fear, not for herself, but for him, and Stitch, and Cassie.

'They don't know,' Marcus said.

'There is no gateway,' said Drake.

'If there is,' Marcus said, crouching down to Jay, 'then these idiots don't know about it. Take those two outside,' he said to Drake. He and Jimmy grabbed Sammy and Stitch and dragged them outside to the pool. Sammy caught Marcus's eye as he was dragged away. Nothing. No compassion. No mercy. A minute later, Marcus appeared outside the cave carrying Jay.

'What is it?' Marcus barked at Stitch, who was gazing intently at the Rother.

'Yeah, what are you looking at? Is that the gateway?' said Jimmy, shifting from foot to foot. He made Sammy nervous, he was skittish and unpredictable.

Marcus looked towards the opening of the cave above them, the connection with the Rother. 'What's with this cave?' he said. Sammy and Stitch kept quiet. Drake began to climb up to the opening but Marcus stopped him. 'That's not it,' he called to his friend. 'They're scared of that opening. It's not the gateway.'

He turned to Sammy. 'What is it?' he said. Sammy said nothing, using his full concentration to keep his mind clear and empty. Marcus looked down at his ankle. 'Put these two up there,' he said, nodding towards the cave. 'Tie them together, we might still need them.'

'Aren't we taking them in?' said Jimmy.

Marcus shook his head. 'I don't think so.' As he turned his back, Sammy launched himself at him, trying to force him into the water. Marcus moved quickly, more than one step ahead of Sammy. He turned, reaching out to Sammy, holding him on the edge of the pool, then flinging him around and into the chalk rock-face. Sammy hit his head and slid to the floor. Marcus frowned at him for a long moment, then turned away. 'Tie them together,' he said again.

'With what?' complained Jimmy.

Marcus said nothing. He walked away, towards the main cavern.

'What about the girl?' called Jimmy.

'Leave her, she's no danger to anyone now,' said Marcus. The words pushed their way into Sammy's head, through his pain and into his consciousness. He felt far away. He tried to open his eyes but couldn't draw the strength.

The pounding in Stitch's head subsided and he gathered his thoughts. His hands were tied to Sammy's with a leather belt and they were sat back-to back in the cave opening by the Rother. In a matter of hours, a force of water and rock would launch them, and anything else in its way, at the opposite cliff face.

Jay hadn't moved from where Marcus left her when he dumped her body next to the pool. He watched her chest to see if she was breathing, but he couldn't tell. As he straightened, leaning back into Sammy, he felt Sammy list to the side. 'Sammy? What's wrong?'

Sammy's eyes were closed, and he was leaning heavily, pulling Stitch over with him. 'Sammy,' Stitch repeated, louder this time. Sammy's eyes flickered open, and he righted himself, taking the pressure off Stitch. 'Sammy, are you OK?'

'I think so,' Sammy said, and the slur in his voice sent a shiver of worry through Stitch.

'Sammy, you feel hot.'

Silence.

'Talk to me.'

'Huh?' Sammy grunted.

Stitch shook himself to jolt Sammy from his slumber, pushing back into him. 'Sammy!'

'I'm OK,' Sammy said, sounding a little more lucid. 'I think I have a fever.'

'You're like a hot water bottle back there.' Stitch turned to see Sammy edge up his trouser leg with his other foot. The entire lower leg was swollen, red and purple with bruising. But more than that, the ankle joint was a deep purple-black colour with yellow pushing through. 'Looks infected,' Stitch said.

'I'll live,' said Sammy.

'You better.'

'Where are Cassie and Jay?' said Sammy.

Stitch hesitated. He nodded in the direction of the pool. 'Jay's down there, she's not looking good.'

Sammy stretched to see his sister, lying next to the edge of the pool. 'I need to get to her.'

'You're not going anywhere,' said Stitch. 'Cassie ducked into the caves when those Readers turned up. She's our best chance.' Stitch looked down at Jay, her face turned towards the water, chalk from the floor in her hair and on her cheek. He pleaded for her to come to, sending messages to her, messages that she'd ordinarily hear without effort. She made no move, no flicker of an eyelid or twitch of a limb.

'Where are the Readers?' asked Sammy.

'In the cavern. They're trying to figure out where the gateway is,' Stitch said, wondering what might happen if Cassie took them on. If there were no powers involved, she'd take all three of them without breaking a sweat, but the odds were against her. Marcus had shown what he could do, even to Jay.

* * *

Jimmy threw a wad of papers and maps onto the floor, losing his cool. 'This is all shit, nothing useful here.'

Marcus continued flicking through a notebook, occasionally checking something on the map to his side. 'Pick that up, Jimmy.'

Jimmy started to complain but a mere glance from Marcus focused his mind and he re-stacked the maps and papers. 'Where's Drake?'

'Checking through those caves.'

'I thought you said there was nothing down there?'

'We need to be sure,' Marcus snapped. 'There may just be three of them but you talked of a fourth at the house. Another girl?'

Jimmy nodded. 'She's not here.'

Marcus couldn't shake a sense that she *was* there but had slipped away unnoticed.

The notebooks gave him very little. From what he could see, there were no references to a gateway, and he was beginning to think he'd been right, that there was no such gateway, merely a myth to keep up the morale of the Given.

'Hey, Marcus,' Jimmy said. 'What about the father? Is he close?'

'He's on his way. We'll be ready.'

Marcus had gone too far with Jay. He'd been afraid. The girl had power of a sort he'd not seen before, so he had pushed far enough to neutralise the threat. It was reasonable force, he assured himself. He would be questioned back at base. Jay was valuable, someone whose head the authorities would like to get inside. He could get in a lot of trouble for what he'd done to her.

Marcus shook off the thought, re-directing his energy

towards his primary goal. The mere presence of the Given threatened his existence. Those with the original power, especially where the power was strong, like in Jay, had the key to neutralising the Readers. Marcus knew that with enough focus, and enough of a coalition of the Given, he could be reduced to less than he was even before his own transformation to Reader. And that was not something he could afford to let happen, not something that this girl would make happen. He would not be stopped from wiping away all traces of the Given, wherever they came from.

'Come with me,' Marcus said to Jimmy, replacing the notebook on the shelf and making his way back outside to the pool. Jimmy followed.

Outside, Stitch and Sammy watched from their elevated position in the cave as Marcus and Jimmy approached. Marcus could sense how unwell Sammy had become. The boy filled him with self-loathing for his own weakness, which turned to anger. He approached the prone body of Jay and looked up at Stitch and Sammy. 'Has she moved?' Stitch shook his head. Jimmy tapped at Jay's body with his foot as if she were a dead animal. He trod on her hand, pushing down so that her fingers squashed into the rock. She made no sound.

'Leave her,' shouted Stitch.

Marcus laughed. 'What's the matter, little Stitch?' With his foot, Marcus pushed Jay over onto her front, her arms twisted beneath her at grotesque angles. Stitch looked away. Sammy's head lolled like it was too heavy for him to keep it up.

Marcus dug the toe of his boot into Jay's side and flipped her once more. She slipped over the edge of the rocks and into the water. Stitch howled, the sound primal like an animal in pain. Sammy was silent, slumped on his side. Jay made no sound as her head bounced against a rock and she disappeared beneath the surface of the water.

PART V

THE GATEWAY

37

Unconscious, Jay drew a breath, water filling her lungs. Her body shut down, as if giving up the effort to survive. Her lungs made no attempt to eject the water, her temperature plummeted and her organs began to fail.

Her body sank to ten metres below the surface, into a darker, cooler zone. Her body temperature continued to drop until it equalised with the water, dropping from its normal thirty-two degrees to just over nine Celsius, her skin grey like flint.

She took a breath.

Her lungs ejected water and then re-filled as she took another breath. Inside Jay's lungs, something strange was happening. The alveoli became engorged. Her body's reaction to its surroundings was to force the blood flow through her lungs to maximise the oxygen exchange from the water. With this, much like a fish does as it draws water into its mouth, through its body and out through its gills, Jay was able to retain enough oxygen for her reduced body temperature and reduced heart rate to feed her vital organs.

Four minutes after entering the water, Jay had reached a depth of fifteen metres. The temperature of the water had decreased to less than eight degrees. Fish came. They nudged at Jay's body, exploring.

The whispers came again, pulsing like the pumping of a heart, swirling like eddies in the water, or the rush of wind above the surface. They penetrated her mind with ease, sparking the connections inside. Without opening her eyes, Jay came to awareness. With the water in her lungs, the fish at her side, Jay became closer to the power than ever before.

At six minutes, Jay had risen once more to within a few feet of the surface of the pool, a school of fish nudging and encouraging her body into an upward trajectory, towards the opening of the subaqueous tunnel.

Head first, Jay slipped into the suck of the River Arun, pulled into its irresistible force. Plunging steeply, she was cushioned from the rocks by the swirling energy of the water, the streamlines forcing her through to the outside, away from the confines of the pool. Her head bobbed above the water and she coughed. Her lungs emptied, and she drew a breath of fresh air as she slipped onto her back and floated with the current.

Her body temperature continued to rise, her heart rate returned to normal and her skin regained its colour. She blinked away the fresh river water so that the blue of the sky and white of the clouds came into focus. She shivered, moistened her stiff lips with her tongue and breathed deeply. The fresh scent of the river, the sound of the wind in the branches of the sycamore and beech along the banks, was invigorating.

Tentatively, she kicked her legs, then moved her arms, feeling the ache in muscles not yet pumped with blood. She turned and kicked at the water, taking herself in towards the shore, heading for the shallows beneath the bridge. Jay lay in the water and rested. She remained still for some time before dragging herself up and onto the riverbank.

She stood, shaky and dripping. She walked towards the trees, away from the little parade of shops on the other side of the village green and into cover. She walked through landscape that hardly changed, for beyond the trees were more trees.

At a crossroads in the paths through the woods, Jay slumped onto the floor, drained. Her eyes were closed before she reached the ground.

38

Cassie circled back through the caverns, to the tunnel that carried the River Arun through the hill, a few hundred metres upstream of the pool and her friends.

She slowed as she approached the opening to the main cavern. She could hear two of the Readers arguing amongst themselves. At the opening she stopped, then stepped across the cave's entrance and down the final few metres into the area of the pool where streaks of sunlight penetrated from above.

She stood in an alcove in the cliff wall, out of sight, resting her head against the wall and looking up to the sky as if for inspiration. A loud call filled the air with sound.

The falcon launched. Cassie flinched, shook her head, and at the last moment the bird changed course, flapping its wings to take it into the elevated cave entrance to the Rother.

She saw them then. Sammy and Stitch were slumped on their sides as if shot, back to back and wrists bound. The bird took off again, back to its perch. With a last check towards the opening to the Arun, Cassie ran around the pool to her friends. She jumped to get a hand-hold on the ledge that supported Sammy and Stitch, and pulled herself up. From the darkness of the cave she called, 'Sammy? Stitch?'

Stitch stirred. 'Is that you, Cassie?'

Cassie reached out to him, helping him to sit upright, then turned to Sammy. 'Is he OK?' she asked Stitch.

'Infection in his foot. Check him, is he breathing?'

Cassie reached into her backpack and pulled out a bottle of fresh water, pouring a little into her hands and holding it to Sammy's lips. He remained still, no sign of consciousness. 'He's warm,' said Cassie, running her cool hands across his brow. She dabbed his head and neck with water and moved him into what she hoped was a more comfortable position. 'He's breathing, but we need to get him help.'

'Jay's gone,' said Stitch.

'Gone where?'

'She never came around... and... he pushed her in there.' Stitch nodded towards the pool, unable to speak. Cassie, face grey, stammered, unable to release any coherent words. Stitch continued, 'But she's not dead. I can feel her.'

'So you have powers too now?'

'No, she's sending me messages, it's her power, not mine. Nothing clear, but I know she's alive. She went through the exit, under the water, and down to the village.'

'Do you think she's going to the connection?' said Cassie.

'She must be,' said Stitch. 'But that's miles away, and she's stopped. She's alive, but she's not moving. I think I know where. You need to go there.'

Stitch was worn down to his limits. Cassie reached behind him and started to untie his hands but he stopped her. 'No. There's no point. We won't make it through the exit. I'm not leaving Sammy here. If you untie us, they'll know you've been here.'

Cassie nodded but continued to loosen the knots, easing the pressure on their hands.

'There's a pathway in the village. It leads from the bridge by the river into the woods. She's there, but I don't know how far along. The last signal I got from her was about twenty minutes ago and weak. Fading.' He paused. 'I just hope she's still OK. I don't know what her state of mind is after Marcus's attack. She may be damaged.'

'I'll find her,' Cassie said. She peeked her head around the edge of the cave. 'What are they doing in there?'

'Still trying to find the gateway?' said Stitch.

'I've been all through those caves.' Cassie pulled off her rucksack and checked that her gear was safely contained inside the plastic bag before slinging it back over her shoulders. She dabbed some more water onto Sammy's lips, fed some to Stitch and placed the bottle into his hand. 'You can pull your hands free now. It's loose enough. I'm going before one of them figures out I'm here.'

'Do you know where the connection is?' said Stitch.

'If Jay was right, it's at that little boathouse on the Wey. I'll find it if I can get to Jay.'

'Impossible for anyone but you, Cassie.' Stitch smiled.

'What about Sammy?'

'I've got him,' said Stitch. 'You need to go.'

Cassie considered the option of taking Stitch and Sammy with her. She'd never be able to get all three of them through the opening before the Readers got to them. Stitch guessed her thoughts. 'It's not worth it,' he said. 'Go before it's too late, just hurry.'

Cassie checked Sammy one more time, kissed his forehead

to gauge his temperature. 'He's warm, but not hot.' She touched Stitch on the arm, then lowered herself back down to the edge of the pool. Wasting no time, she slipped into the water and almost without creating a ripple, ducked under and swam from sight.

39

Jay felt nothing physical, no touch on her skin, no pain, no physical sensations except for her sense of smell – the trees, the damp leaves that were her mattress, and the sweet scent of the woodland floor.

Her strangled thoughts broke free, one by one. Whispers floated, goaded, coaxed her out from herself to a greater consciousness. The resistance she held to the inevitable weakened. Control, burying, hiding, all gone. The desire for obscurity and safety in concealment evaporated.

Jay allowed the whispers room to manoeuvre and explore. She opened to the energy, the power within the ground, the trees, the water – the energy that resides in everything. Images coalesced from the feelings, like the colours she saw in her dad's thoughts, combined with a raw energy that gave them life. Her mind began to piece itself back together, but in a new form, a more robust and resilient form, a form that whilst open to the power and possibility within her connected world, one which was protected and strong.

As Jay's mind mended, and her consciousness returned, an

image came to her. Zadie Lawrence. She was smiling, laughing. She was surrounded by tall trees that reached high into
the sky, protective and powerful, elegant and beautiful.

40

As Cassie hovered weightless in the space between the pool and whatever would come next, her cheeks puffed and lungs aching to breathe, a picture of her grandad came to her. His face was clear – the deep laughter lines, the soft brown eyes mottled with amber.

She burst the water's surface. Darkness transformed to light. She twisted herself around as she breached, sucking in a breath as she was swept over a cascading weir and downstream, drifting to where the water flowed clear and still.

The banks grew high with reeds, grasses and trees tall and thin. The slopes were scrappy and muddy, holes for otters, river voles and cray fish. Slipping onto her back, Cassie allowed herself to drift downstream, keeping her nose above the surface.

She pulled herself up onto all fours in the shallows under the bridge, the shiny orange stones digging into her hands and knees, and heaved her water-logged body out of the water to lean up against the bridge pier. Pushing away the urge to sit and rest, she pulled off her rucksack, relieved to see that her plastic bag had done its job. She changed quickly, dragging a pair of jeans up her legs and then stuffing her wet things back into the plastic bag. She clambered up the river bank and onto the green, a well-tended stretch of grass with a cricket square fenced off at its centre.

Across the green at a café where out front were a row of old Vespa mopeds, personalised with motifs and flags. She stepped inside. The café buzzed. A group of bikers had occupied the back half of the place leaving the locals to the front. She looked out again at the row of Vespas, which reminded her of her dad's old moped. She knew that if she picked the right bike, there'd be no need for keys.

She left the café, her rucksack on her back, and went to work on the bike furthest from the door. Within a minute, she had forced the ignition barrel and kick-started its engine. She stepped through to sit and push it off its stand, marvelling at how she'd managed to pick the loudest bike in moped history. With a glance over her shoulder she saw that two of the bikers were already out of the café door and running at her.

She let rip. The Vespa shot forward so fast that she lost control, bumping up the kerb and onto the green. The bike shot from under her and spiralled into a heap on the grass. Cassie sat, stunned for a moment. The bike stalled. She dragged herself off the floor and pulled the bike upright, jumping hard on the kick-start as the two bikers crossed the road. The engine fired and she wheel-spun away. She powered full throttle over the green and towards the path that would lead her into the woods, her bike squealing with the effort, the men's shouts growing distant.

With Stitch's instructions in her head, Cassie guided the bike with its Union Jack paintwork through the opening to the woods, the back wheel sliding out with every turn. She bumped along the uneven surface, raising herself off the seat to keep balance. After a few minutes, the path reached a crossroads where it widened to a clearing with a river running alongside, a tributary of the River Wey. Cassie hid the bike behind a log pile twice her height and dragged off her crash helmet, smoothing down her braided hair and rubbing her forehead where the crash helmet had left a mark. She stepped off, her legs aching, wobbly and numb from the vibration of the little two-stroke engine.

'Where are you?' she said aloud, scanning the perimeter of the clearing. She left the crash helmet on the handlebar of the bike and moved towards where the two paths crossed, as Stitch had directed.

'Here,' Jay's voice from behind her.

Cassie let out a sharp scream before covering her mouth to muffle as Jay pulled Cassie into a hug. 'We were worried about you. How'd you manage to get out of the pool?'

Jay shrugged. 'Not even sure myself. How was Sammy when you left? I'm getting bad feelings from him.'

'Not so good. We need to move, find the connection and get back into the pool. Do you know where your dad is?'

'I think I do,' Jay said, a look of understanding on her face, like she'd discovered something at last. 'He was heading towards the pool but I've set him straight. Set him on a course for the boathouse. We can meet him there.' Jay looked at the Vespa and raised her eyebrows at Cassie.

'Jump on,' said Cassie, collecting the other crash helmet and handing it to Jay. Cassie took the front and Jay slung her leg over the back, holding on to Cassie's waist. She kicked it into action and released the clutch. The bike struggled as Cassie manoeuvred it back onto the path. 'Which way?' Jay nodded for Cassie to take the right-hand arm of the crossroads.

As they bumped out of the woods and onto tarmac, Jay pointed the way, shouting to Cassie to be heard above the noise of the engine, 'Follow the river upstream. It's about ten miles to the boathouse.'

Cassie squinted as she rode, the wind dragging tears from her eyes. The River Wey alongside the road was wide and slow moving between the north and south Downs. Algae had formed on its surface, giving it the appearance of smooth Astroturf in places, with scum forming in the stagnant patches as it meandered.

They emerged from under the trees just south of where Cassie figured the boathouse must be. The road diverged from the path of the river and the bike laboured as the hill steepened. From the top of the ridge they could see down over the valleys on both sides, the river pushing north and west below them. They rested in a layby at a fork in the road for a minute and Cassie checked off the landmarks – Chanctonbury visible to the east, the Cathedral spire in the city centre to the north. She looked out over the ridge. 'Which way?' she said, turning back to look at Jay.

Jay nodded to the left. 'That way. Dad's on his way to the boathouse. He's with someone. Let's go.' Cassie pulled away and down the hill to their left, towards the river.

41

Ben pushed forward on the throttle of the old narrowboat, the engine revving hard as it pushed through warm air coming over the flood plain. He could only hope the Readers had lost their scent, at least for the moment.

Matchstick was below deck. The deep thrum of the boat's diesel engine sent vibrations through Ben's feet. It felt good to breathe the scent of engine fumes and fresh pollen off the fields. But he couldn't relax. Jay and Sammy needed him. They were in trouble, he could feel it.

They scraped their way down river, lurching between the banks of the canal. The boat shed flakes of black paint and spewed clouds of oil-blue exhaust smoke as it slewed and squeezed past the private jetties, punching through the trees.

Matchstick stepped up from below deck, eyes scanning the horizon. He sucked on two roll-ups at the same time, exhaling and handing one to Ben. 'Looks like you've got the hang of it?' Matchstick said.

When they'd taken the boat from its mooring, Matchstick had to work his magic to get it going, twisting wires together as Ben controlled the throttle. When it kicked into life, Matchstick took over and steered the old narrowboat downstream. He showed Ben how to throttle and steer before sinking below deck to rest.

Ben was too wired for sleep. His messages from Jay were sporadic, like messages filtered through static, but he knew she was now north of the pool, at an old boathouse, so he set a new course.

Jay and Sammy were in trouble, this he knew. Not for the first time, he wished he had stronger powers. He checked the dials on the instrument panel: oil pressure looked good, engine temperature high but not in the red. No fuel gauge but there were three, full, diesel containers below deck. He leaned up against the old wood of the cabin and ran his hand over its mottled surface, worn smooth over the decades, almost like soap to the touch. With one hand on the tiller, he guided the narrowboat through a canopy of leaves that dipped to anoint them as they passed. Matchstick, the imprint of a pillow lining on his face, shuffled up to the front of the boat and dangled his legs over the edge.

42

Jay saw the boathouse just at the point the little engine in the Vespa chugged and died. 'We can coast in,' she shouted. She felt a warmth that told her she was close to her dad. He was at the boathouse. The hill took them all the way to the car park.

As they rounded the corner of the old boathouse, a neglected wooden-slatted building in need of paint, Jay's dad stood facing them, his back to the river. His friend, Matchstick, sat on the front of a tatty looking old narrowboat. He skimmed a stone across the surface of the river and then jumped onto the bank to face Jay and Cassie as they descended the slope to the river's edge.

Jay and her dad embraced as Cassie held out a hand to Matchstick. 'Cassie,' she said.

'Pleased to meet you. And you're Jay.' He turned to Jay and seemed to take a little step back as if shocked.

'What?' Jay's dad said to Matchstick.

'The power took me by surprise a little.'

Jay smiled at her dad, felt the usual deep fondness for him that had evaded her when she had visited him in prison. He emitted a different sense to that from before. Escape from prison brings more than physical freedom. It was as if he'd remembered who he was. Jay reached out to him again, and they hugged a second time. 'I missed you.'

'Good to have you back, Jay.'

'We won't get that thing down the unnamed river,' said Cassie, pointing at the narrowboat. Then, motioning to a rowboat tied up alongside the boathouse, said, 'That's more like it.'

Jay looked at her dad. 'We need to move. Sammy's in trouble.'

'How bad is he?'

Cassie spoke up. 'He's got a fever and an infection. He's unconscious.'

'What's the plan, Jay? Why are we here?' said her dad.

While Cassie prepared the boat, Jay told her dad and Matchstick about the connection with the unnamed river, what they'd found in the notebooks and maps at the pool.

'What's it like? The gateway?' he asked.

'Just like you told it, Dad. Just as sparkly, just as magic.' Ben looked down, still thinking about Sammy. 'We met the Phoenix,' she said.

'Seriously?'

'She's a beauty.'

Jay told her dad about Cassie's grandad, his journey to the gateway. About how he'd been going to the pool since he was a kid.

'Where is he now?'

'We think he's on the other side,' said Jay.

Cassie looked up. 'You really think so?' she said, and Jay nodded.

'A chance of keeping some of this freedom,' Matchstick said, throwing their gear into the back of the rowing boat. Jay stood to help Cassie and Matchstick push the boat into deeper water. Cassie insisted on taking the oars at the back, always in the driving seat. Matchstick took the second set of oars at the front. Jay and her dad paddled through the shallows and climbed into the central section, taking seats alongside each other.

'Let's find this connection,' said Ben.

43

Smoke rose and escaped through the shaft above Marcus's head as he fed reams of papers onto the fire.

Drake returned from his detailed search of the interconnecting caves, looking for an exit. He stepped up to the fire pit. 'What are you doing?' he asked.

'We can't leave this stuff here. There are years of notes, maps and sketches.' He threw another armful onto the fire and the heat warmed his face.

'There might be something in there about the gateway,' said Drake.

Exactly, thought Marcus without saying so. 'There is no gateway,' he said.

Drake frowned. 'Where's Jimmy?' he asked.

Marcus nodded out towards the pool. 'Watching the two boys, and keeping an eye out for anyone coming in via the river connections.' Marcus felt very little energy coming from Sammy and Stitch. Their life forces were weak. Sammy had been unconscious for some time and Marcus wondered how long until he died. Marcus resolved not to allow the boy to leave the gateway. If he were to pull through, Marcus would finish him off. It was the only way to quash the conflict inside him, the confusion that could cause him to lose focus. He couldn't afford to fail. The other one, Stitch, had been weakened by Marcus's infiltration of his mind. He was no longer a threat.

Jimmy entered the cavern. 'Pretty sure those two are dead, neither of them has moved for the best part of an hour.'

'They're not dead,' said Marcus. 'They're weak, but I can feel them.'

'What do we do?' said Drake.

Marcus looked at him, frowned, and returned to feeding papers into the fire.

Drake continued, 'We need to take them in. Alive.'

'Forget them. The father is our target now.'

'But...' Drake started.

'But nothing. Our job is to bring in the Given.' He paused. 'Jimmy, get back out there and watch the connections. You can't afford to lose another one.'

Jimmy and Drake both filed back outside. Marcus looked after them, then threw the last of the papers onto the fire. He could feel the approach of the other Readers, their signal was strong – they were close. But so too was the father, and his signal had strengthened, making Marcus uneasy. There was an uncertainty in the air that he couldn't shift, or make sense of.

44

Jay stood in the boat to get a better view up ahead as Cassie and Matchstick edged the boat forward. The undergrowth was thick, trees and bushes overhanging the river on both sides and touching in the middle. The wide river had narrowed to little more than a stream.

'The connection is hidden,' said Jay. 'Keep looking, it will be on the left-hand side, heading south.'

The boat nudged along the narrow gap between the branches of trees, Jay having to duck under from time to time. 'Stop rowing a minute,' she said, listening. 'You hear that?' she whispered.

'No,' came the reply from Cassie and Matchstick.

'Something,' said Ben.

Jay moved over to the side of the boat and strained her eyes to see into the bushes. 'Row back a bit,' she said.

Cassie and Matchstick dug in their oars, splashing water up and into the boat as they pushed against current to reverse. They dragged three deep strokes and then let the boat drift, coming to a halt and then relenting, to drift with the flow of the river again.

'There.' Jay's voice rose with excitement. Matchstick draped his oars over the foliage to stop them drifting. Jay pointed through the branches to a cave, a small opening into darkness, where the water from the River Wey diverged.

'That can't be it,' said Cassie. 'We won't even get the boat in there.'

'It's bigger than it looks, push back those bushes,' Jay pointed. 'This is it, pull us around, hurry.'

Jay's dad reached out and grabbed hold of a branch, helping Cassie and Matchstick manoeuvre the boat towards the entrance to the cave. Once they had pulled into the streamline of the cave, the boat obeyed their wishes and slipped into the pathway they needed, dipped over a shallow weir and into the cave.

'Heads down,' Matchstick shouted. The boat entered the cave and total darkness. Everyone ducked, unsure where the cave ceiling began as the boat picked up speed, bumping the sides of the cave as it shot through the channel. Jay held her breath, hoping jagged rocks wouldn't punch a hole in their boat and leave them upended in the water, unable to see.

'Jay!' her dad called, reaching out for her. 'Hold on to me.' Jay leaned into her dad and they huddled together, holding on to each other as well as to the seat.

Jay could just about make out that Matchstick was doing the same, holding tight and keeping down. 'Cassie,' Jay shouted, 'are you OK?'

Cassie shouted back that she was OK and the four of them could do nothing but keep down and hope.

After what seemed like forever, Jay felt the boat begin to slow. The noise abated a little and Jay sensed space, as if the cave had opened up above their heads. Light penetrated the darkness. The cave walls were nothing but black shapes, moving, distorting and fooling her. After another minute, the boat slipped down into a steep curve and out into a spectacular underground cavern, like a lost, subsurface lake.

The boat slowed almost to a stop. The four of them said nothing, all gazing at the spectacle that surrounded them. It was like being in the grand atrium of the London St Pancras Station but with trees and vines growing up the sides and to the roof. The roof itself was closed but for a series of gaps where light streamed through, illuminating the cavern. Water flowed from cracks in the rocks and dripped from the openings in the roof. All along the sides of the cave, birds nested among the tree roots. A fish broke the surface of the water and rolled over in the sunlight.

Jay's dad couldn't help his grin taking over his face as he looked at Jay, then back to where the fish slipped back beneath the surface. 'Rainbow trout,' he said.

'If only we had the spinners.'

Matchstick dipped his oars back into the water as the boat drifted, dragging them back on course for the point where the river continued downstream.

'Keep us moving, Matchstick,' said Jay. 'Sammy needs us.'

Cassie pulled hard on her oars, Matchstick following her lead.

'This place is unreal,' said Cassie as they left the tranquillity of the lake cavern and back into a tunnel, darkness enveloping them once more. Now the river widened and the roof was higher. The flow was slower and there was a little light leaking in from both ends. In the distance they could see daylight, and Jay knew that they were looking at the pool.

Jay's senses were electric. She could feel the power of the earth surrounding them, the energy of the water beneath them. It was as if the vastness of the lake-cavern had followed them into the cave. The whispers came, stronger than before.

She looked back over her shoulder towards the cavern. There was nothing but a bright, blinding light.

The round circle of turquoise light in the distance grew, and with it, the power and the intensity of the energy that flowed through Jay in waves. She felt Sammy, his waning life force, the infection flowing through his veins. He was hot, his pulse was weak, his breathing laboured. But he was fighting. And Stitch was there too, fighting with him.

'What's that?' said Cassie, as they passed an opening in the rock, at a joint where it looked like two rock masses had been displaced. Before they could register its significance, they had moved past, picking up speed as they drew nearer to the opening to the cave.

Jay felt the pressure of the Rother, building behind the blockage just feet from where Sammy and Stitch lay semi-conscious. It was about to blow, pushing rock and debris at bone-shattering force.

And she felt Marcus. Waiting. He was ready for them.

45

As the little rowing boat squeezed through the opening and into the pool, the pressure in Jay's head, the whispers, the energy, reached a crescendo.

The water from the unnamed river carried the four of them, in their boat, into the pool and followed with a thrust of water that flowed full-bore through the cave entrance, the light behind piercing the clear spray.

The flow from the river met a swelling from the depths of the pool The pool's surface rose, and together they shot into the air, up through the shaft and the chalk well, where they were met by a third stream of water and debris from the Rother. The jet from the Rother pushed through, taking Sammy and Stitch into the pool with Jay, her dad, Cassie and Matchstick.

Through the third and final connection, the Arun, the water bubbled and boiled, rising above the level of the main central cavern where Marcus and the other Readers stood, transfixed by the shaking beneath their feet, the deafening sound of the water shooting through from the connecting rivers. As Marcus turned towards the entrance to the cavern, the River Arun powered in and washed the three of them off their feet and out into the connecting caves.

In the pool, the Arun joined the Rother and the unnamed river to create a true convergence of the three rivers at the rising surface of the water in the pool. Inside, the swirl of energy and power from the earth, the water, the eco-systems, caught Jay and the others, suspending them in the eye of the storm.

* * *

THE EXPLOSION SUBSIDED, depositing Jay at the side of the pool. The water from each of the connections returned to their normal flows, the birds to their perches.

Jay's heart thumped and her fingers trembled. Ben pulled himself to stand next to Matchstick, over the other side of the pool. Stitch leaned down over the prone body of Sammy, his head bowed. No sign of Cassie. And no evidence of Marcus or the other Readers – though she could feel their presence.

She ran around the perimeter of the pool and joined Stitch. Sammy's eyes were closed. 'He's breathing,' said Stitch. 'I thought he was dead.' Jay held Sammy's head in her hand, cushioning it from the rocks. Stitch said, 'I really thought he was dead. When we were up there. I couldn't hear his breathing and couldn't feel any pulse.'

'Shh, Stitch,' said Jay. 'It's OK. We're going to get out of here.'

'I think I connected with him,' said Stitch.

'Really?'

Stitch nodded. 'I think so.'

Ben and Matchstick joined them, Ben leaning down to see Sammy. 'He OK?'

'Still out, but he's alive,' said Jay.

Her dad felt Sammy's head with the back of his hand and then leaned in to kiss his forehead. 'Bit of a temperature.'

'Where's Cassie?' said Stitch. Jay stood, looking around the pool. No sign of her. She called out but no response. She called out again, this time someone responding.

'Who's Cassie?' came the voice of Marcus as he emerged from the connection to the Arun, Jimmy and Drake close behind.

46

Stitch dragged Sammy back into an alcove in the side of the cliff to give him some protection from the bomb Jay sensed was about to go off.

Ben and Matchstick stood alongside Jay, facing Marcus and the other two Readers positioned the other side of the pool. 'They have more power than us,' said Ben.

'We have more to lose,' said Matchstick. Jay felt the power bubbling beneath her skin, the energy flowing up through the floor and into her body. She felt her own power connecting with that of her dad and Matchstick. She looked over at Marcus, standing tall. She felt his arrogance. As she studied him a time fracture passed over them, like a glitch. She could see that Marcus felt it too, and it shook his confidence.

Sammy still lay slumped in the corner, skin pale. 'Passed, has he?' Marcus said, and Jay sensed something lurking – a sadness, a vulnerability in Marcus's eyes. She looked again at her brother, then over to the Reader. Pieces slotted into place in her mind.

'You're his biological father,' Jay said, barely a whisper.

Marcus shook his head, as if trying to shake away Jay's

words. 'We told you that this wasn't a game,' he said. 'Told you the easiest way for all of us was for you to come back with us.'

Jay looked at Ben and read the sadness in her dad. He'd known all along. He may not have admitted it to himself or anyone else, but Jay could see that he knew. 'He's my boy,' Ben said. 'In every way that matters, he's *my* boy.' Jay nodded and turned back to face the Readers.

'Here we are,' said Marcus. 'All together again.'

Jay felt Matchstick bristling with anger and determination. 'Wait,' said Jay, but Matchstick was already moving. He was in a trance, determination etched into his face. Jay and Ben followed, catching up with Matchstick as he stood less than three feet from Drake. Marcus and Jimmy a step behind, both smiling.

'That's better,' said Marcus.

Matchstick threw himself at Drake who put up his hands to hold him back. They connected, and sparks passed between them, their hands glowing as they wrestled and channelled their powers through their fingers. The sleeves of Drake's top caught fire and the two men stumbled to the floor, locked in a fiery battle.

Ben took the opportunity and lurched for Jimmy, taking him by surprise and knocking him to the floor, opting for a more traditional fist fight than Matchstick's use of powers. Jimmy was chunky and strong but no match for Ben's athleticism. He was younger and fitter, and with a series of punches, Jimmy landed on the floor with a thump.

Jay felt Marcus's power surround the man like a protective barrier. She took a step back, wavered, stepped forward again. He continued to exude arrogance.

He reached for her. She tried to lift her arms to protect herself but they did not respond. He closed his hand around her neck and stepped closer, looking into her eyes and beyond. 'What level?' he said, to himself more than to Jay.

When Jay looked into Marcus she saw nothing. An abyss. His fear of the State was total; he would stop at nothing to destroy anyone he deemed a threat. Someone had something on him, some means to control him through fear. More than anything, his focus was that no one with power levels approaching that of his own survive. He tightened his grip on Jay's neck.

Matchstick pulled himself back to his feet by Jay's side, his hair still smoking from Drake having got the better of him. Her dad lay at her feet, knocked over by Jimmy who had reverted to his superior powers when Ben had gained the upper hand in their fist fight.

Marcus squeezed his hand tighter around Jay's neck.

Drake knocked Matchstick to the floor and knelt over him, his hand on Matchstick's forehead as if he were penetrating his mind.

Ben called out in pain as Jimmy focused in on him. He reached out for Jay but she was unable to break free of Marcus's grip.

Jay closed herself to the surrounding chaos. Her eyes shut tight. Then she opened to the whispers, the sounds and the power of her environment. The energy rose through her feet and the world stopped – ground to a crunching halt like a spanner had been lodged inside the cogs of the machine.

arcus looked around the pool, wide-eyed, and Jay pulled herself from his grip. She stepped forward, shoving him back against the face of the cliff. She looked brave but coursed with fear. Would she would be able to prevent the Readers from taking them all away?

Marcus continued to gaze around the pool, mesmerised by the silence, the stillness, unconcerned by Jay having broken free of him. She focused in on him but he deflected her, brushing her off with his own power like she was nothing.

Jimmy and Drake began to stir, releasing themselves from the freeze, but Matchstick and Ben were still frozen in time.

As Drake and Jimmy stood, three further figures appeared at the cave entrance to the Arun. More Readers. Marcus turned and waved for them to join him. 'It's over, Jay,' said Marcus, now flanked by five powerful Readers. Jay knew that she could never overpower this many Readers, but she couldn't put the others at risk. Frozen, they were safe from danger.

Her time had run out, she'd not been able to connect

completely, to harness the power well enough. Her legs trembled, she propped herself up on the chalk wall and looked around her, up into the sky.

Stitch's voice came through into Jay's head, calling her name. She turned to see that he remained frozen in time, leaning over the prone body of Sammy. As she looked at his statue, his scream came through once more. *Jay! Believe in yourself! You got this!*

She needed to be *surrounded* on all sides by the energy. In the water, or in the caverns. She needed to get the Readers into her own space, where the power would be with her. Without releasing time, Ben and Matchstick still frozen like rock, Jay turned to Marcus. 'What about the gateway?' she said. The Readers all looked at her and she put up the strongest shield that she could muster to prevent her thoughts leaking through.

'You know where it is?' Marcus said.

'If you let them go, I'll show you.'

'She doesn't know,' said Jimmy. 'She's lying.'

Marcus put up his hand to silence Jimmy, and Jay knew that he wouldn't be able to ignore the possibility. If he could locate the entrance to the gateway, and confirm that it existed, then he and the State would be able to take the ultimate control. They would contain the Given, cut off their entry to the source and diminish their power to worthless levels. The Readers may not be able to enter the depths of the Interland, for the energy of the source, but they could reduce it to all but dust.

'Show us,' Marcus said.

Jay walked through the middle of the group of Readers, feeling their power aching for release. She led the way through to the main cavern, drawing the Readers away from the others, pausing just once to check that all six were following. The cavern smelled of bonfire, the remains of the notebooks and maps still smoking in the fire pit. She made her way towards the far wall of the cavern, the Readers filing in behind.

She turned to face Marcus as he stood at the front of the formation of Readers.

'Where is it?' said Marcus, looking towards each exit from the main cavern in turn.

Stitch's voice came to Jay again. Energy flowed through her, building her strength from the inside out. Whispers came. They guided her. Tingles travelled from the tips of her fingers through to her arms. This was the place. She could channel the power. Stitch was with her.

She had something that Marcus didn't have, the Readers didn't have. Their energy didn't come from nature as hers did.

She looked at Marcus as he cast his gaze around the room, still looking for the gateway. He was self-centred, too introspective to connect in any meaningful way with anyone else, or any other system. Jay was at one with the earth, the power of the water, and all living things that formed the walls, the floor, the ceiling.

'What is this,' Marcus said, stepping forward as Jay let her sleeve fall back into place. Jay felt the power pulsing through her body from below her feet. She no longer feared her power, she embraced it, welcomed it.

Marcus stepped closer. 'Whatever it is, it won't help you. I'm stronger. *We* are stronger.' He motioned towards the other Readers. 'You know there's nothing you can do about it. But you still have one option. Come in to *rehabilitation*.'

'Never.'

'Come with us. We could even save the boy, Sammy.' Jay saw through Marcus's words. He had no intention of allowing her and Sammy to return with him.

Her arms at her sides and fingers pointing to the floor, the power gathered strength. Her vision faded and Marcus whirled around in her head, his voice, his thoughts. She felt his hand close around her neck once more, and then the other hand. He squeezed. She closed her eyes, and the whispers intensified. He squeezed harder and air stopped passing into her lungs. He squeezed harder again, and pushed her up against the wall of the cavern, her feet leaving the floor.

Jay remained calm.

The five Readers were sucked towards the walls like magnets, the air forced from their lungs at impact. The walls of the cave behind Jay softened and shaped around her body, cradling her. The vines that penetrated the rocks twisted around her, supporting her weight, curling around Marcus's wrists. The water from the crevices in the rocks, the sun that penetrated through the shaft above their heads, poured down on them, covering them in clear, fresh water and powerful light.

Jimmy was the first to be pulled into the wall by the vines, screaming as his body amalgamated with the rock and then silent as he was crushed, his body now part of the undulating face of the cave wall. Drake and the others fought, but the vines remained strong, taking the Readers one by one into the stone.

Marcus pulled away, releasing Jay. 'What is this?'

'This is more than you, Marcus,' said Jay, her eyes sparkling with power, her feet barely touching the ground, her body tingling. She stepped towards him and he held his position. He reached out, not for her neck this time but to push her away. The force of his blow was re-directed back through his arm. 'Reciprocity,' said Jay through gritted teeth.

'Stop,' said Marcus, gathering himself once more.

'Every action has an equal but opposite reaction, Marcus.

With every pain you inflict, there is a consequence. Reciprocity.' With this, Jay released the environment. The noise of the Arun pounded into the cavern. Marcus stiffened and used all of his power to try to penetrate Jay's mind. She felt it. Felt him digging at her defences. If he got in, he'd do damage this time, he aimed to destroy her. 'You're not strong enough, Marcus,' she said, re-directing his attack back on himself. With a rush of energy from all around her, Jay channelled her power to enter Marcus's mind, and she started to dig.

Marcus hit the floor just as the water from the River Arun crashed into the cavern, throwing both Jay and Marcus into a tornado of currents. As quickly as the water arrived, it drained back into the Arun and out through to the pool. Marcus dragged himself to his knees at Jay's feet, looking up into her eyes. Jay saw that his power had diminished. He had been reduced. He lifted a hand to the side of his face to feel the fresh scar, parallel to the old one, from temple to just below the chin. He shook his head in disbelief, stammering, 'No... n... no.'

PART VI

INTERLAND

48

Jay splashed through the water on the floor of the cavern towards the pool, the only sound the noise of the thundering river. She sensed the others, outside, her friends, her dad, and Sammy. As she reached the pool, she saw Cassie pulling herself from the water. She stood as Jay approached. 'Is it done?'

Jay nodded and Cassie wrapped her arms around her. 'What happened to you?' asked Jay.

'I don't know,' said Cassie. 'We shot through into the pool and then the world went crazy. I was up in the air, but under water at the same time. Where are the Readers?'

'Gone,' said Jay with confidence. 'Marcus is the only one left, but he's no threat. He has no power.'

'What about...?' said Cassie.

Sammy was lying on his back on the rocks, his dad crouching beside him.

'Is he OK? Is he hot?'

Her dad put his hand to Sammy's head. 'He's cold,' he said.

Jay pushed to get to Sammy. 'Is he breathing?' She leaned

down and put her ear to his mouth, then put a finger to his neck to feel for a pulse, her hands trembling.

His eyelids flickered and Jay breathed out with relief. She knew, sensed, that he was OK. She could feel him coming back to her. He had shaken off the infection and was growing in strength.

Cassie pushed past Jay, panic in her eyes. Sammy blew gently into her ear. She pulled away, rubbing her ear. 'What the...' Then she returned to listen again. This time, as she listened for his breathing, Sammy leaned forward and kissed Cassie on the side of her head. She drew away slowly this time, a grin forming as she sat up, not looking at Sammy, as Jay, Ben and Stitch laughed.

'You... Sammy,' said Cassie, still grinning. She kicked him lightly on the leg and he recoiled, wincing.

'Hey, not the ankle,' he said, pulling himself up to a sitting position. He dragged back his trouser leg to reveal much reduced swelling in his ankle. Cassie kicked him again, then leaned down and cuffed him on the back of the head before taking his face in her hands and landing a smacker of a kiss on his lips.

49

With their backs up against the chalk cliff, they gazed up through the opening in the trees to the clear sky above.

Jay had checked back in the main cavern but Marcus had gone, disappeared. It was possible he'd slipped into the pool and away through the exit when they'd been seeing to Sammy. Either that or he'd tried to head back upstream alongside the Arun. Whichever way he'd gone, Jay was sure he would be no threat to them. Even if he had anything left in him to fight with, there was nothing for him to come back to. No gateway that he'd ever be able to find.

Jay sat between Ben and Sammy, Matchstick on the other side of Ben. Sammy stretched out his leg and dipped his foot into the pool. Cassie stripped off her jeans and top and dived in, beckoning the others to join her. Sammy motioned towards his foot. Stitch shuffled up next to Sammy, leaving Cassie to it.

'How is it?' said Stitch.

'Better.'

'You had us worried.'

Sammy smiled at Stitch. 'Something of the healing hands you have there.'

Stitch shrugged. Jay smiled at her brother. 'We did it. Marcus is done.'

'*You* did it,' said Ben, leaning back and closing his eyes. 'I don't know what went on in that cavern between you and those Readers, but something big happened.'

'I realised something... from Sasha Colden.'

Matchstick leaned forward. 'Sasha Colden?'

Jay nodded. 'She had something to do with this place I think, she was more than just a level eight.'

'She's mythical. What they called *Connected*,' said Matchstick.

Ben huffed, 'I thought you didn't believe in this place?'

'She had a connection with the universe that no one else had.'

'What about Zadie Lawrence?' said Jay.

'She was strong. Tough woman. Level eight from what I heard, but not *Connected*.'

'So what's Jay then?' said Sammy.

'Connected,' said Matchstick, leaning back against the chalk cliff.

Cassie jumped out of the pool and Sammy threw her a top. She slipped her wet body back into her clothes and squeezed herself in between Sammy and Stitch. Jay looked up at the cliff face to see the falcon edging out onto its branch, as if to join them.

'Phoenix is back,' Sammy said.

Jay's dad looked up and grinned. 'Told you kids there was a phoenix down here. You should listen to your old dad.'

'Watch this,' Cassie said, jumping up and beckoning to the bird. With no further prompting, the falcon rocked off the branch and soared up into the sky, diving like it had before and pulling up in a graceful swoop to land this time on Cassie's outstretched arm.

Cassie let out a squeak of excitement and pain as it clenched onto her arm. Sammy stood, hobbled over to Cassie. He held out his arm, his hand touching Cassie's hand. The falcon edged along Cassie's arm like it was a tree branch and onto Sammy's arm. It remained still for a moment then turned to take in the others sitting on the floor, mouths half open, before launching into the air and back to its branch.

'Wow,' said Jay's dad. 'How'd' you do that, Sammy?'

'I have a thing for the birds, it seems,' said Sammy, hobbling back to sit down, with Cassie's help.

'What now?' said Cassie. 'If there's no gateway, what now?'

'Who said there's no gateway?' said Jay, matter-of-fact.

They all turned to look at her. Ben spoke. 'You know where it is? It's here?'

'Of course.' Jay smiled. 'It's here, I can feel it as clearly as I can feel gravity.'

'You can't *feel* gravity,' said Cassie.

'Where is it?' said Stitch, looking up and around himself.

'Me and Cassie passed the opening on the way in here, with Dad and Matchstick. On the unnamed river.'

'The cavern we passed through?' said Cassie.

'No,' said Jay, standing. 'Closer to here, there's a connection, an opening in the roof of the tunnel. I felt it more than saw it. Did you not feel the pressure change as we passed under it before emerging into here?'

Cassie shook her head, then Ben said, 'I felt something. But we can't get upstream, not against that flow. Are you sure there's something there?'

'There's something there for sure. Where it leads, I can only guess.' She walked towards the connection of the unnamed river as the others stood and brushed themselves down. 'As for working against the flow, that's less of a problem if you can *stop* the flow, freeze it for a little while.'

* * *

IT CAME EASIER THAN BEFORE. Jay had only to focus for a moment to stop the world on its axis before releasing her friends, her dad, and Sammy. As they joined in her static world, they each struggled in turn to take in this frozen, silent landscape. Jay ducked and stepped through the mouth of the cave, the opening to the unnamed river.

She led the way for a hundred metres upstream, the light fading with distance from the pool so that it was near pitch black by the time Jay stopped. She looked up to what looked like a darker section of the roof which could be an opening. 'Help me up,' she said to her dad. Matchstick and Ben formed a human frame for Jay to climb, with a steadying hand from Cassie. She managed to poke her head into the opening but could see nothing in the darkness. She jumped back down.

'We need more height.'

Stitch stepped forward as if he had a plan. 'If we can form a stronger base, with three of us, and we can get Cassie on the top, it might work. Cassie's the tallest and probably the lightest.'

With Ben and Matchstick at the base, and with Jay and Stitch creating a second level, they hauled Cassie up and onto Jay and Stitch's shoulders. She pushed herself up into the hole. 'I'm in,' she said.

'What's there?' said Matchstick.

There was no answer.

'Cassie?'

Jay moved beneath the hole to see Cassie's face lit with excitement as she pulled herself further into the hole.

Cassie turned and held a hand out for Jay to follow her up and then Stitch. Soon they were all inside except Ben.

'You'll have to jump,' said Jay. 'Jump with your hands outstretched and we'll get hold of you.' She called for Matchstick to help so that there were four of them leaning through the hole to catch Ben. On his second attempt, Matchstick and Cassie caught his hands, with Jay and Stitch grabbing on to help lift him through the hole.

'Thought I'd have to stay behind for a minute there,' said Ben as he pulled himself over the ledge and stood to join Jay.

'No chance,' said Jay. 'Not letting you go so easily this time.'

50

A s Jay stepped into the connecting tunnel, her dad close behind, the other four stood facing a waterfall that poured from the roof and drained away below their feet into the cracks and crevices of the rocks.

'Through there?' said Stitch.

Jay nodded. 'That's it.'

Jay led the way through the waterfall and into a wider tunnel that opened out into a cavern. As she passed through the water, she saw three figures standing in the tunnel some twenty metres ahead.

Jay immediately recognised Reuben, but not the other two – a woman in her forties, and an older man. Cassie came through the waterfall and then broke into a run. 'Grandad!' she called, launching herself at the man and throwing her arms around him. He rocked backwards and laughed, embracing his grandaughter. She pulled away then, and pushed out at him, scolding him.

'I'm sorry, Cassie. It was the only way.' Cassie hugged him again, holding on tight. As Cassie withdrew from his embrace, her grandad nodded towards Reuben. Cassie stared. When it clicked, she stepped back a pace.

'Cassie,' he said. 'Now you're here, I can explain. *We* can explain.' Cassie looked unsteady on her feet and Sammy stepped forward to hold on to her arm.

'You must be Reuben,' Sammy said.

Reuben nodded. 'Old friend of Cassie's. I came down here to train as a Runner. I couldn't say anything, Cassie. I'm sorry.' He stepped towards her but Cassie retreated.

'We can explain everything,' the woman said.

'Who are you?' Stitch asked the woman.

Jay spoke. 'Zadie Lawrence.'

Zadie smiled at Jay. 'I've waited a long time to meet you, Jay. It's a pleasure. And we will be forever grateful for what you did down there. Marcus was the biggest threat to the sanctuary of our world.'

'He might still be down there,' said Stitch.

Jay and Zadie both shook their heads and spoke at the same time. 'His power has gone.'

Zadie indicated for Jay to follow them into the caves.

'Where are we going?' asked Jay.

'To the place you've been looking for. You've found it. This is where you can rebuild your strength, amongst friends. The community here has been waiting for this day, waiting for a reason to believe that we can make a change. We have some work to do, but this is the beginning of a process to take back our world.'

Ben stepped forward. 'Look, Zadie, we came here to escape from the fighting, the Readers. We didn't come to join an army, if we wanted a war we'd have...'

'Dad, it's OK,' Sammy said. 'How many people are down here?'

'Nearly a hundred,' said Zadie. 'About half with powers.'

'How many level eights?' asked Stitch.

'There is only one,' said Reuben, looking at Zadie.

The five from above ground fell into step, following the others into a new world.

Jay looked back as they walked through a warren of tunnels, not convinced she'd be able to find her way back to the entrance if she needed to. As they approached a large opening, the sound of talking, laughter and the chinking of crockery leaked with the light into the tunnel ahead.

Cassie looked deflated, as if they'd failed when she should be elated that they'd won, they'd found what they were looking for. As they followed Zadie into the great cavern, Stitch propped Sammy up with an arm around his waist.

The bustle of activity faded and all faces turned to observe the new arrivals. Jay reckoned on there being about fifty or sixty people in the room, and still it looked big. Light filtered down from the roof where Jay guessed there must have been an opening into the trees, much like at the outside pool. The smell of food made Jay's mouth water and she realised she'd not eaten properly for days. In the middle of the room, three large pots of stew bubbled away, the smoke and fumes rising through a chimney-like construction and into the roof. She scanned the faces, old and young, some with smiles and others with curiosity but all with a semblance of hope, as if in expectation of something from their visitors.

Zadie Lawrence called for attention. The room quieted. She introduced Jay and the others as *new members* and the room gave a smattering of applause. 'Please make them welcome, we have some special abilities with our new members, powers that we hope will help us to re-invigorate our community and bring back some of the magic that left us when Sasha passed.'

As Zadie stepped down, a young boy of no more than twelve or thirteen handed her two bowls of steaming stew. She passed a bowl to Jay and motioned for her to sit. More children came, handing bowls of food to Sammy and the others, each of them finding seats where they were accompanied by others introducing themselves. Sammy sat with Jay and Zadie.

'Who's that?' Jay nodded at a photograph on the wall behind where they sat.

'I'd have thought you would know?' said Zadie.

'Sasha Colden,' said Jay, now recognising the face of the woman whose autobiography she had in her backpack. She was older in the photograph than in her picture in the book. Her features were more distinct, the lines and creases in her face hinting at her great knowledge and power.

'She founded this community. She is the Godmother of the Given.' Zadie looked at the picture with affection and, Jay sensed, sorrow, and even a little guilt. 'She passed before I joined. Despite the Runners' attempts to bring me in to work with her, I resisted. I thought I knew how to stand up to the State, and their attempts to wipe us off the face of the earth. Direct action. Of course the authorities knew better. They had their own weapons. People like Marcus, who you dealt with out there. It was Marcus's superior who reduced me after the protest.' She pointed to the scar down the side of her face, much like the one Marcus had, and like the second scar that Jay had given Marcus when she reduced him. 'I never thought I'd recover from this.'

'His superior?' said Jay. She had assumed that Marcus was at the top of the food chain of the Readers. The thought of him having a superior sent shivers up her spine. Zadie nodded. 'How did you get away, to get here?' Jay asked.

Zadie looked towards Reuben, who was deep in conversation with Stitch. 'He brought me in. I was his first apparently. He'd only recently become a Runner. Saved my life. My power had been drained when he found me. It took me a good few weeks to recover down here. It was almost like learning my powers from the start. It came back eventually.' She turned her head to the side to show Jay the scar. It had a silvery sheen like Marcus's, and ran from her temple to under her chin, just like his. 'Battle scar,' Zadie said.

'I've seen one like that. On Marcus.'

'I heard,' said Zadie. 'He was made a Reader in the early days. We don't know if it was voluntary or by force. Someone went to work on him and by the time he came out the other side he was a fully signed up agent of the State.'

Jay exchanged a look with Sammy, who gave a slight shrug. 'When did Sasha die?' he asked Zadie.

Zadie turned to him. 'A few years before Reuben brought me in.' Zadie explained that Sasha Colden spent years alone in the underground at first. She had been drawn to the place and abandoned her normal life to re-imagine herself. She became a recluse. 'Story says that she was forced to leave her family and her son.' She looked at Ben.

Ben's mother had died before Jay had been born. Jay had never known her grandmother. Old Alf Harvey had talked about her, but... She turned back to Zadie as she continued. 'She spent years without seeing or speaking to another human. The world assumed she'd died. Then Pete and Jack found her.' She nodded towards Cassie's grandad. 'They found the pool at the gateway to the Interland when they were kids, and they were still visiting the place when Sasha connected with them. Cassie's grandad is older than Sasha would be if she were still alive.' Zadie smiled. 'It was Pete and Jack who helped her find her purpose again.'

Ben came over, moving closer to the portrait on the wall, studying Sasha Colden's picture.

'What happened then?' asked Sammy.

'Sasha reached out and brought in a small group with high-level powers. We think at levels six and seven. She established some protocols to protect what she'd built. They made the level sevens Runners, people who would leave the underground just once a year to bring in others who were at risk. But *only* once a year, to ensure the security of the Interland.'

'Any other level eights?' asked Jay.

'No,' Zadie said, and went on to explain how the community continued to grow around Sasha Colden, with Jack and Pete remaining the custodians of the pool, the link between the outside and the underground. 'Before Sasha died, she said to those that were here that there would be another like her. Another level eight.'

'That was you?' said Sammy.

'No,' Zadie replied. 'I am a level eight for sure.' She showed her wrist, the crisp and distinct figure eight undeniable. 'But Sasha meant more than just a level eight. We think she was referring to someone who would be *connected*, like her. The connected power comes only through genes, through blood relations.' Zadie looked at Jay, who averted her gaze. Zadie turned to Sammy. 'Do you have a level, Sammy?'

Sammy shook his head, pulling back his sleeve to show that there was nothing there, not even a smudge.

'I sense you have something. How old are you?'

'Sixteen,' said Sammy.

'Then you have a little while to go.'

Zadie looked up as a boy around Jay's age came over to relay a message. 'All three Runners are back in, Zadie.'

'Thank you, David. Can you let them know that we will need to get all the Runners together later, including Reuben?' The boy nodded and turned on his heels.

'How many Runners are there?' asked Sammy.

'Just four, including Reuben. There are only four in here at level seven. How about you, Jay? Anything on your wrist yet?' asked Zadie.

Jay pulled back her own sleeve, the figure eight clear. Zadie reached out for Jay's hand, pulling her closer so that she could inspect her wrist. 'Definitely an eight. Question is whether there's anything else coming.'

'You mean a "C"?' said Jay.

Zadie nodded. 'There's something I need to show you when you're ready, after you've rested.'

52

'We held a *funeral*,' Cassie shouted at her grandad, drawing looks from around the room. 'I cried for you, for weeks.'

A young girl brought them some food and Jack motioned for Cassie to sit. He explained the circumstances of his entry to the pool, and how he and his childhood friend, Pete, had looked after the entrance caverns for so many years. He was Sasha Colden's closest confidant. He had a duty to the Given. He pulled back his sleeve to reveal a number four.

'You...' Cassie stuttered, 'you have power. You never told me.'

'I was an unusual case. My mark was never clear. Even into my sixties, there was nothing but a smudge. After I brought Reuben in...'

'*You* brought Reuben in?'

He looked down at his bowl of stew, lifting a spoon to his lips. He took a deep breath. 'Reuben has something special, something different. Like your friend, Jay, but with a different calling. He was born to be a Runner. Sasha Colden had her eye on him from when he was just a boy, and my job was to keep him safe until the time was right for him to come in. When he turned eighteen and his mark started to appear, I had to bring him in. He wouldn't have lasted a month outside.'

'No one said anything to me. No message. Nothing.'

'It was forbidden. And for good reason. If just one of those things, those Readers, found their way to the gateway then all this would be at risk.' He looked around the cavern. 'And without this, the Given would be hunted to extinction.'

Cassie finished her food. Her body felt heavy, as if saturated, no longer able to support itself. Her grandad put a hand on her arm and she looked him in the eye. She smiled at him, the beginning of an uneasy forgiveness.

Sammy had been taken away for medical treatment. Matchstick and Ben were talking to a group over by the cooking pots. Jay was with Zadie Lawrence. As she took in her surroundings, Cassie's gaze settled on Stitch and Reuben, talking together, Stitch being introduced to two men who seemed very excited to meet him. Reuben looked over and caught Cassie's eye. He excused himself from Stitch and made his way over to Cassie and her grandad. Cassie looked away.

'Hey,' said Reuben.

Cassie's grandad stood, shaking Reuben's hand. 'You've done well today I hear?'

'It's been a good week, what with these new arrivals, and some positive movement with the level seven I saw today. Our strength is growing.'

'What level seven?' said Cassie.

Reuben smiled. 'One we've been tracking for some time. He's from the north. Just turned eighteen, little older than you, Cassie.'

'You track all of them?'

'Not all. The ones we know about. Little by little. The more we bring in, the more Runners we can train and the more we can track. We need level sevens to become Runners.'

'Why?'

'Because it's only level sevens and higher that can resist the Readers. We can, with training, prevent the divulgence of information. Readers can't get in our heads, as long as we know how to block.'

'So no one else leaves?' Cassie said, an indignant tone in her voice.

Her grandad spoke. 'No. That's why we have to be sure, we have to wait for people to choose their own path, come when they are ready.'

Cassie's head reeled. The thought of being trapped in this place, the supposed sanctuary turned prison. A tomb. 'You can't stop people leaving!'

'Cassie.' Reuben put a patronising hand on her arm and she pulled it away. 'The point is, the *plan* is, that we all leave, once we are ready, and the time is right for us to make the changes for the better above ground. We hope you and your friends will be part of that.'

Cassie put her head in her hands, still unable to accept the situation as her fate, as the only option. For something purporting to be freedom, she felt trapped.

'Let me show you around,' Reuben said, holding out a hand to help Cassie up. Her grandad sat back down, nodding at Cassie to go with Reuben.

She ignored his hand but stood. 'OK,' she sighed. 'Let's have a look around this dungeon.' She looked over at Jay, laughing with Zadie Lawrence. 'Where's Sammy?' she said.

'Receiving treatment, I'll show you.'

Reuben led the way from the main cavern into one of the connecting tunnels. The sounds of voices faded. They walked in silence for a while, passing several other tunnel connections that branched off from the main pathway. After a minute or so, having walked maybe a hundred yards, they entered another, smaller cavern, a kind of lobby to an adjacent room that was different to the other rooms. This one looked as though it had been constructed by hand, rather than naturally formed. It had vertical walls and an arched roof, mined so that records could be efficiently stored from floor to ceiling in spaces protected from water that might penetrate through cracks and holes, yet illuminated by the light from the light-well above. There were some six or seven people in the room, all working at their own makeshift desks, poring over the records and notes.

'This is where we store records,' said Reuben. 'Intelligence from the Runners, and from other sources we have on the outside that pass information to the Runners when we go out.'

'What's it for?' said Cassie, turning to see a man working in the room approach.

The man smiled the broadest of grins. 'Cassie?' he said. It was old Alf Harvey, the bookseller. Before Cassie could argue, Alf embraced her, a tear edging from the corner of his eye. 'Is Jay here?'

Cassie nodded, Alf drew her in to another hug and then turned to leave. Reuben smiled. 'He's been looking forward to you guys coming in.'

'Jay thought he'd been taken,' said Cassie.

Reuben continued his tour. 'Intelligence on the Given. Our aim is twofold: one, to contact people who need an escape from persecution; and two, to predict where the powers will be, with whom they are concentrated, so we can get to them before the authorities do, offer them an alternative to incarceration.' Cassie thought again how the difference between incarceration above ground and entrapment underground might not be so great. 'There's a whole world of difference, Cassie. Like you wouldn't believe.'

Cassie pulled back her sleeve again to take another look at her smudge. Reuben took a step towards her. 'I didn't know...'

'You wouldn't know, you weren't there,' Cassie said, then felt stupid for sounding so bitter. *Childish*, she thought to herself.

'It's OK,' said Reuben.

'Will you *please* stop reading me without asking,' Cassie shouted at Reuben so that he stepped back from her. 'Just because you can read me, doesn't mean you have permission. Is that what you lot do in here? Read whatever you like, don't bother asking?'

'Sorry.'

'Just don't.' Cassie turned away from him.

'Your friend Stitch has a level too.'

Cassie turned. 'Stitch? What level?'

'It's not clear yet, it's a strange one. He showed me his wrist, and it doesn't look like a number. I've never seen anything like it and I've seen a lot of people's markings.'

'What is it then?'

'It looks like the beginnings of the letter "C". Like Sasha Colden, but without the number, just the letter. In Sasha, we thought that the "C" depicted her *connection* with all things. But with Stitch, I don't know. He's gone to see Zadie.'

Cassie thought about Stitch, how he seemed to be so connected with Jay. He knew better than anyone what she was thinking, what she needed. He was the one who heard her call for help the night the Readers came.

'You have a level then?' said Reuben.

Cassie shrugged. 'Nothing distinct. But there's something coming.'

'Can I see?'

Cassie turned back to Reuben and lifted her sleeve. He took her hand in his and she could feel his presence, his energy. She tried to remain calm. She had loved this boy for as long as she could remember. But she'd got over him. He disappeared, and she had moved on. She was not about to allow him back inside her head.

'Probably a level one or something so nothing to get excited about,' she said.

Reuben stepped closer to Cassie, leaning towards her so she could feel his warmth. 'Now even a level one is...'

'Thought you were showing me around?' Cassie interrupted, pulling away and turning back to the entrance. Reuben followed her out of the records room and led her away to another set of tunnels and another cave.

'Sammy!' Cassie called, seeing him prone on a bed with someone leaned over examining his ankle. He had his hands behind his head. He turned to Cassie with a grin.

'How is it?' she asked.

The man tending to Sammy's ankle mumbled, 'Nasty. Not broken but possibly a cracked bone and certainly a deep gash. It looks like it's had some attention but Sammy's memory is shot, do you know who treated it?'

'No one,' said Cassie. 'Strangely enough there aren't many doctors down there.'

'He'll have to keep off it for a while, we don't have the means for a plaster cast down here right now but I'll strap it up.' He looked up and smiled at Cassie. 'I'm Tommy.'

Sammy retained his grin. 'Hear that? Smashed it. Been on it for hours, days, and it's smashed to pieces. Scale of one to ten on the pain: eleven. Scale of one to ten on the courage and bravery: eleven. Isn't that right, Tommy?'

Tommy smiled as he kept his concentration on the strapping he was applying to Sammy's ankle. 'Right, Sammy. Brave warrior.'

Reuben laughed. 'Good to see your spirits are up, Sammy,' he said. 'I'll show you the rest of the network, Cassie? The residential area is through the back there...'

'I think I'll stay here with Sammy for a bit.'

Reuben nodded and turned to leave. 'Another time,' he said. 'We've got time. It's good to see you again, Cassie.'

Cassie turned her attention back to Sammy, taking a seat next to his bed and reaching for his hand.

53

Jay noticed that the air was cooler at the lower levels, and the walls were damp with a constant trickle from above. The only light came from a candle Zadie held before them as they walked.

'Mind your step,' Zadie said over her shoulder.

After their welcome meal, and having had some time to rest and store her things in the residential section of the underground, Zadie had come to find Jay. They talked on their way down to the lower levels. Zadie said that Stitch had come to see her, displaying signs of a mark that no one had seen before.

'I've heard of such a marking,' Zadie said to Jay.

'Someone else down here?' asked Jay.

'No. Just rumours. The only verified marking with a "C" is Sasha Colden's, but hers with the number eight as you know. But I heard rumours of another with a "C" and no number. Someone connected closely to Sasha Colden. Someone with whom Sasha had a special connection. A direct connection.'

They reached the bottom of the rock steps and Jay watched as Zadie walked the perimeter of the room, lighting a series of candles set into alcoves in the walls. The room revealed itself with a central pillar where water trickled down from above and disappeared into the ground.

'Look here,' said Zadie.

Jay peered around the pillar at where Zadie was motioning. Three separate streams of water trickled in at a rate no greater than that from a tap, each a different hue. They combined at the centre of the pillar and disappeared in a single flow into an opening in the rock below. Jay recognised it as like a mini version of the confluence of the rivers above ground.

'This is the Rother.' Zadie pointed to the gentlest trickle of water. 'This is the Arun, and this one is the unnamed river.'

Jay could see the sparkle in the emerald-green of the unnamed river water. At their convergence, the water bubbled and boiled, pushing back up in a geyser-like spray before discharging through a hole in the rock and away through the floor.

'Who built this?' said Jay, mesmerised by its beauty, its intricate functionality.

'No one. It's natural. I am told that it's been here from long before any of us arrived, even before Sasha Colden was here.'

'What does it mean?' Jay asked, unable to take her eyes off the continually changing shapes created by the water which, in turn, cast shadows across the walls from the candles around the perimeter.

'This is what we hoped you might be able to help us with. We don't know for sure because there's no one here that was around when Sasha Colden was here. Only Jack, Cassie's grandad, but he was never inside the hill, in the underground.'

'How should I know?' asked Jay, a half-hearted question given that deep inside she sensed there was something connecting her with this place, this room, and with Sasha Colden.

'Show me your wrist again,' said Zadie, stepping towards Jay and drawing back her sleeve. Jay tore her eyes away from the confluence and looked down at her wrist. The number eight had sharpened, its edges defined and black as night against her pale arm. With it, the letter "C" had started to form. It remained blurry at its edges but distinguishable as a letter "C".

'Eight-C,' said Zadie. 'Like we thought.'

'I can feel something,' said Jay, her eyes returning to the confluence, the joining of the three streams of water at six levels below the pool at the surface. An energy rose in her chest, a pulsating vibration beneath her feet. Zadie spoke but her words became lost in the whispers that came from all sides – from the walls, the floor, and from the streams of water flowing through the pillar before her. The whispers grew louder, clearer. The message was more transparent than before, translated to a language that had become like Jay's native tongue. She absorbed the energy, the knowledge, the needs and the desperation of her surroundings. She understood. And, they understood.

* * *

JAY WOKE on the floor of the cave, Zadie and Stitch both in her face, calling her name.

'What? Is that you, Stitch?'

Zadie and Stitch helped Jay to a sitting position. 'She's OK,' said Stitch.

'How did you know?' Zadie said to Stitch.

'I heard her calling, inside. I just knew.'

Jay groaned, 'Look at your wrist, Stitch.'

Stitch turned his hand to show his wrist. No number but a crystal-clear letter "C". He put his wrist up alongside Jay's, where her "8C" had also crystallised in contrast.

'You're Jay's connection,' said Zadie. 'Sasha Colden had one too. Someone who connected and completed the power, the connection with the environment. Everything.'

Stitch smiled. 'I always knew I'd be the chosen one.'

Jay laughed, pulling herself up to stand. 'So what does this mean?'

Zadie smiled, taking Jay's arm on one side, Stitch taking the other. 'It means that you two are the next generation of power. You will help us finish what Sasha Colden started.'

'And what was that?' said Stitch.

'Taking back what belongs to us, and to everyone else. Re-connecting the people, and the environment.'

Jay felt strength returning to her body as she climbed the steps, the force of energy that was the Interland supporting her from the inside, and the arm of Zadie and the shoulder of Stitch helping her up from the outside.

Jay and Stitch entered the central cavern. Ben sat on a rock with a notebook. He stood and opened out an arm to pull Jay into a side-by-side hug.

'What's the notebook?' said Jay.

Her dad nodded towards the portrait of Sasha Colden. 'One of Mum's diaries, it seems,' he smiled. 'Your grandmother's notes.'

'Thought so,' Jay said. She pulled back her sleeve to show her dad the "8-C" on her wrist.

* * *

CASSIE ENTERED the cavern with Sammy, propping him up on his strapped-up leg as they shuffled over to join them. Jay's dad helped Cassie get Sammy sat down on a rock. 'How is it?'

Sammy smiled. 'It's good, Dad, I'm on the mend.'

Cassie nudged Jay and turned her arm to show the inside of her wrist. The beginnings of a number seven were clearly visible. Jay had known that Cassie had power growing, but a level seven surprised all of them, most of all Cassie.

Jay took a breath, looked up into the vast ceiling of the cavern, shards of light penetrating from the sky above. Energy pulsed through her body and she relaxed into it. For the first time, she allowed her power to flow without fear of detection.

At last, she was free. Her new environment, the Interland, was a place to savour and to protect. It was a place that would provide a foundation, and spark the beginning of a new journey – one that would take the fight back to the world above.

End of Book #1

INTERLAND

INTERLAND SERIES BOOK #2

For Evan

JAY
Toyah
Sammy
Cassie
Pinto
STITCH
INTERLAND

PART I

1

The sea made a white streak across the horizon where rolling waves broke on the sandbanks. From the crest of Highdown Hill, one of the three highest points in the county, Cassie stood facing the ocean and kicking at the dirt, sending shards of flint spinning over the ledge. Darkness had drawn in. She hugged her arms to her body and shivered.

Her eyes rested on the Beach Lane Café, visible in silhouette against the light grey sea, its stilts holding it gracefully aloft above the stones. To the north, the dip, slope and soar of hill upon hill felt intimidating, sheer power trapped in land.

Cassie absently scratched at her arm. She glanced at the dark tattoo-like number, seven, distinct against the pale skin of her inner wrist. She couldn't hide her sense of pride. Never would she have believed she could be a level seven. Her power gave her freedom. She was a *Runner*.

The ring of trees decorating the top of Highdown was a distinctive feature of all the hill forts in the south – sacred places for some, popular locations to congregate for others. A small campfire gathered momentum in the centre of the inner ring. Around the fire was a familiar scene: figures huddled for warmth, some sitting, some moving in the night air. Waves of energy flowed from the land. All three of the hill forts in the area attracted their fair share of visitors, including the spiritualists, chanting incantations to ward off the Devil, drinking wine to ward off the cold.

As she watched, Reuben's athletic figure came into view, skirting the ring of trees. He strode with a confidence that both impressed and annoyed Cassie in equal measure. The world seemed to make way for Reuben, to accommodate him. He was born lucky. He was a Runner, like her, but more experienced. He'd been making trips out of the Interland for over three years, whereas this was Cassie's first proper mission, not counting the training excursions with Zadie Lawrence. Those early trips out of the Interland were simply to familiarise Cassie with the requirements of the Runners – the dangers and the importance of keeping out of sight and moving quickly. *Get out, get the mission done, get home.* The Interland was safety.

She noticed Reuben do a double take at the sight of the hooded figures around the fire, heads down as if in prayer. He had a smirk on his face as he approached Cassie. 'Something odd going on over there,' he said.

'Someone has to keep the Devil out,' Cassie said, returning Reuben's smile. Out towards the sea, total darkness approached and Cassie was glad of Reuben's presence. He stood alongside her so that their arms touched, the shiver that moved over her skin reminding Cassie of the strength of feeling that had once existed between them.

Reuben pointed to the west, to the estuary of the River Arun. 'West Beach,' he said. It was the place where Reuben first reached out to Cassie and her close friend, Jay, before they came to the Interland.

'You never stopped to talk,' Cassie said, a bitterness coming through in her tone that she hadn't intended. However much she told herself that she forgave Reuben for leaving when they were young, she'd not forgotten. The Interland had drawn both Reuben and her grandad away from her without warning, and now her grandad was gone. Forever. He died just a few months after their reunion at the Interland. It was as if he'd reached the end of his journey and was happy to leave. She had to relive being abandoned by him all over again. Their reunion had not been long enough for Cassie to get to know him again, but long enough for his loss to hit hard once more.

She had loved Reuben when they were younger. As deeply as she could have imagined back then in her early teens. Now? It was complicated. They'd been apart for too long. So much had passed. She'd changed – turned twenty. Then there was Sammy, Jay's brother. At nearly eighteen, he'd moved from being her best friend's kid brother to something more. Their connection was undeniable. Even thinking of him now made a small heat blossom in her chest, followed quickly by a pang of guilt.

She turned to Reuben. 'So have you figured out the route?' her tone a little warmer than before.

'We can train-hop most of the way. If we hit trouble, we get off and go cross-country on foot.'

Over the past year, the excursions of the Runners had become more dangerous. Rundown districts had enveloped entire towns. Frequent power cuts and empty supermarket shelves meant desperate, fearful people. Then there was the Given. Back before Cassie found the sanctuary of the Interland, before the Zadie Lawrence protest that fuelled the crackdown by the State, the Given walked freely among the public. They enjoyed similar rights and were respected. Now, the

Given had been pushed into extinction. The few that remained outside the Interland were in hiding, scared for their lives.

'How far?'

'We'll be there by lunchtime tomorrow. We can bed down here tonight, head off at first light.' Reuben turned, motioning for Cassie to follow back to their camp.

Cassie touched his arm. 'Hey, sorry,' she said.

'What for?' Reuben stopped.

'Just now. Didn't mean to snap.'

'Didn't notice,' Reuben said, turning away.

Cassie watched as he scuffed through the long grass towards the ring of trees, the fire now raging so that the tree trunks flickered orange. She followed in his path. They'd set up camp over the north ledge, out of sight and sheltered from the southerly wind. She caught up with him and linked arms as they passed through the ring of trees, avoiding the inner circle so as not to disturb the pagans. He glanced at her, but something over Cassie's shoulder caught his eye. He stopped. Cassie turned to see the group of pagans stand and push down their hoods as they looked towards the two Runners. Cassie took a step back. 'Can you feel it?' she said.

'Power,' Reuben said. 'Lots of it.'

'They must have been shielding. These aren't pagans,' said Cassie. 'We need to leave.' Before they'd moved more than a few metres, more figures appeared at the outer circle of trees.

'Readers,' said Reuben.

Cassie's heart raced, her mind spinning with questions. 'How did they know we'd be here?' she said as Reuben held tight to her arm.

Two of the figures stepped aside to allow someone through. A man emerged, a silhouette in the shadow of the moon as he approached Cassie and Reuben.

2

———

At just past noon in the main cavern, the dining hall, beams of light from above reflected off the rocks, bouncing around the cavern as if they were alive. Trailing branches, bracken and ivy snaked through the opening towards the inner sanctum. Birdsong echoed above Jay's head, distracting her from her book. A cool stream of air flowed over her face and she closed her eyes, taking a deep breath. The air was fresh, scented by the woodland above.

'Hey,' said Pinto, approaching and taking a seat next to Jay. Pinto was eight years old. He arrived at the Interland with his sister, Toyah, nearly two years before Jay arrived with friends Cassie and Stitch, and her brother, Sammy.

'Hi you,' said Jay, gazing at her little friend with his smooth complexion, hair down at his shoulders and his deep brown eyes. 'Where have you been, beautiful boy? Health Centre?' As part of his study, Pinto shadowed the doctors.

Pinto ignored Jay's question. 'You seen Toyah?' he asked.

His sister was nearly ten years older, her mark well defined on the inside of her arm – a level six. They came to the Interland alone, no parents, no explanation. They chose not to tell of their past, and Jay never asked. Most people in the Inter-land had a difficult story – people they left behind, or people they ran from. Jay shook her head. 'You looked in her room?'

Pinto nodded, then slumped his shoulders. He looked up into the roof of the cavern. 'What were you looking at?'

Jay returned her gaze to the roof. 'Breathing in some of the freedom.'

'The outside?' asked Pinto. 'Toyah says that *inside* is free-dom. Where there aren't any Readers. But I'm not sure.'

Jay slung an arm around him and smiled. His face flushed a little. 'Toyah's right,' Jay said. 'The world out there's got worse since I arrived here, and a lot worse since the last time you were out there. You're in the safest place you can be right now.'

'Readers are no bother for you, with your power,' Pinto said.

Jay lowered her gaze. 'It's not always that easy. Can't say I've managed to get a hold on the power yet. And there are some powerful Readers out there.'

Pinto looked Jay in the eye. 'More powerful than you?'

Jay shrugged. 'Who knows? Best we don't find out if you ask me.'

'How do you know how bad it is out there?' Pinto craned his neck to see as high as he could.

'Intelligence from the Runners. Hey, you could be a Runner one day?'

Pinto shrugged. 'Might not have power.'

'You will.' Jay felt Pinto's power already. He'd be strong. Alfred, the bookseller who had helped Jay find the Interland, was convinced Pinto had something special. Not a level eight but something far rarer, a level five in the making. Alfred always had a strong intuition for people's level of power. There were no level five Given inside the Interland or anywhere else as far as Alfred knew. He said that a level five was the only one to have the power over inanimate objects – a telekinetic ability. But they could be unpredictable. Alfred described it as being like an unstable element, its electrons spinning around a central nucleus with an imbalance, liable to break up with great force. So they needed to work hard at controlling their power, harder than most.

Jay sensed Pinto already felt the beginnings of his power. When Jay was his age, she too had felt her power fizzing just below her ability to control it. 'Show me,' she said, reaching for his wrist.

'I'm only eight,' Pinto said.

Jay grabbed for him, tickling him until he squealed. 'Show me,' she said, pulling back his sleeve. 'Oh my word, a level nine,' Jay shouted out. 'Someone come quick, we have a level nine here, help, the power is too much...' Pinto giggled and tried to pull away from Jay. She held him tight, and they laughed.

'Hey,' Jay said. 'Have you looked for Toyah at the Free Cave?' Jay's brother Sammy discovered the Free Cave not long after they'd arrived at the Interland. It was a place they'd kept to themselves. Other than Sammy, Jay and Stitch, only Pinto and Toyah knew of it. To get there, you had to pass through the residential wing and up into an opening in the roof of the passage near Sammy's room. Sammy often explored the tunnels and caves on his own, discovering openings and connections between the different bits of the Interland, including a hidden passage through to the Interland stores he used to sneak food back to his room. One route he followed, eventually wound its way to a spectacular cavern that they all named the *Free Cave*.

'She wouldn't go there on her own,' said Pinto.

'She might be with Sammy?'

Pinto shrugged. Jay nudged into him and jumped up off their rock seat. 'Let's go look.'

* * *

JAY AND PINTO checked Sammy's room on their way to the connection. It was empty. The opening in the cave roof just past Sammy's room, in the dead-end section of tunnel, was virtually invisible in the darkness.

'Come on,' said Pinto, nodding up at the ceiling.

Jay looked back down the tunnel, then to Pinto. 'You sure you're up for this?'

Pinto rolled his eyes and gestured for Jay to help him up. She linked her hands together to form a foothold for Pinto and he launched himself towards the opening, holding Jay's shoulders and squeezing through the hole. Jay jumped and edged her elbows over the ledge, pulling herself up with help from Pinto. Pinto twisted the end of his torch, focusing it to a wide angle. He scurried ahead, crouching below the low ceiling. Even in the light of the torch, the walls were black as coal.

'Slow down,' called Jay. 'Remember the drop.'

After just a few minutes, as Jay's back began to ache from bending over, they approached the first drop. Sammy had reached this point three times and headed back before his fourth visit, when he decided to lower himself over the edge. The shaft curves, so a torch only illuminates about halfway down the fifty-foot drop. But it's not far before the shaft levels out to a steeply sloping tunnel and then to horizontal again. It's easy when you know this, but Jay wondered sometimes about her brother, and how he took that leap of faith the first time.

Pinto didn't hesitate. He turned around and grinned at Jay as he lowered himself backwards into the hole, his torch clutched between his teeth. Jay let him get some distance and then followed, catching him up as he paused for breath at the bottom of the shaft. 'This is the best bit.' He nodded ahead.

The passageway opened out so they could easily stand. They picked up speed, Pinto breaking into a run as light entered the tunnel through cracks in the rocks. Through the smaller cracks, water seeped into their pathway, like a series of little waterfalls that Pinto dashed through, laughing and skipping at every one. The combination of the light through the rocks and the water gave a sense of the unreal. Jay felt that in this place was the true magic and wonder of the Interland.

They reached the junction. Sammy called it the *fifty-fifty* place, joking that if you took the wrong branch, then that would be the last you would see of the world. He said the wrong branch led deep into the earth where light could not penetrate, and where all life was sucked into the walls of the tunnels and nothing could survive. Jay smiled at the thought of Sammy's embellishments, much like their dad used to do when he read them stories as kids.

'Left,' said Pinto.

Jay laughed, 'Sure, you go left and see who gets there first.'

Pinto grinned and bolted through the opening to the right branch. Jay thought about her friend, Stitch. He hated the tunnels. Any hole narrower than he was tall would be too much of a psychological barrier for Stitch. He'd only been to the Free Cave once and spent the entire time fretting that he wouldn't be able to get back and that he'd have to live out his days trapped in the irony of the Free Cave.

Jay and Stitch had drifted apart since being inside the Interland, despite the strength of the connection of their power. The closer the energy connected them, the further apart Jay felt. Stitch was preoccupied with the technicalities of the power, how it worked, and how they should channel it. Jay could become absorbed in the feelings, the sense of the energy, but not so much in the physics of what was going on, as was Stitch's distraction. Jay missed him.

In the tunnels, Cassie was the opposite of Stitch. Jay was certain that Cassie had been to the Free Cave more than any of the rest of them, even Sammy, and probably she'd been further. If there was somewhere difficult to reach, Cassie would be the one to give it a go.

'What are you frowning at?' said Pinto, interrupting Jay's thoughts.

Jay smiled. 'Just thinking about Cassie.'

'She's the best Runner. The toughest,' said Pinto.

'She is,' Jay said as they reached their next and penultimate obstacle before the Free Cave. She stopped at the edge of a drop that reminded her of the water slide at the pool back home. Except this one had no guarantees of a soft landing. Jay hesitated, peering down the steep slope.

'Scared?' Pinto smiled. To answer her little challenger, Jay stepped over the edge, crouching and using her feet to slide down the water-smoothed slope and into the darkness. Just past the first bend, the slope steepened and Jay knew she'd have to lean back and slide on her backside if she was to avoid tipping forward and launching herself head-first. Her heart raced. Even after a dozen times, her stomach floated through her chest to her throat and she let out a scream. Pinto laughed as he piled into her from behind and they both rolled down the final few feet towards the cave.

* * *

JAY AND PINTO stepped into the Free Cave at a ledge around ten feet from the ground. Light pushed in through the roof where tree roots had grown through the rock, opening up the ceiling in great sections and proving the strength of flora over rock. Boulders the size of London black cabs had fallen from the roof and nestled in the ground below them, carpeted in a deep green moss. The nearest boulder was close enough for Jay to jump to, then the next led her and Pinto to the floor of the cavern. They stopped, and Pinto pointed. 'There,' he said. Sammy and Toyah had climbed the east rock face and reached the high ledge. Sammy always said that the high ledge was a potential alternative route out of the Free Cave, and would be the next stage of his exploration. Cassie declared that she would be first to get up there and see where it led, but it seemed Sammy and Toyah had beaten her to it.

Sammy reached for Toyah's hand and Jay glanced at Pinto, but his attention was on the ground – searching for interesting stones. Sammy and Toyah held hands as they moved forward into the cave together.

'Toyah,' called Pinto as he reached the base of the cliff, looking for a place to climb.

Toyah and Sammy emerged from the cave once more, and Toyah called for her brother to stay put. 'We will come back down.'

Jay found a rock to rest on as Pinto scurried around, occasionally leaning down to pick up a stone, examining it for a moment before putting it in his pocket or throwing it into a pool of water. Jay closed her eyes, enjoying the deep connection she felt with the earth. A warm glow seeped into the back of her eyes and the sounds of the cavern were drowned by the whispers – soft at first, then more urgent, merging to a white noise. The white glow intensified, and she was dizzy, her head swimming with the force of the power.

'Jay.' Her brother's voice, his hands on her shoulders, gently shaking her. The whispers dissipated, the glow subsided, and she opened her eyes. 'You having one of your moments?' he smiled.

'I'm OK,' said Jay.

She looked up to see Pinto jostling with Toyah. Toyah said: 'You know you're not supposed to come down here without me.'

'But...'

'But, nothing. With me or not at all. OK?'

Jay turned back to Sammy. 'Hey,' she said. 'You made it up there.' She nodded towards the high ledge.

'Piece of cake.'

'Does it lead anywhere?'

'Somewhere. But we didn't get far. Just into the entrance there, then it tightens up, too small to walk through.'

Jay looked over at Toyah, then back to Sammy with a smile. He shrugged, non-committal, and Jay decided not to ask.

'Cassie back yet?' Sammy asked.

'Not yet.' Jay sensed something was wrong but couldn't get the feeling into focus. She looked at Sammy for confirmation of her gut feeling. 'Do you sense anything?'

Sammy shook his head. 'I'm sure she'll be fine.'

* * *

JAY WOKE FROM A RECURRING NIGHTMARE, her body covered in sweat. She blindly scrabbled in the dark to get a hold on something. The clutter on her bedside shelf clattered to the floor. She tried to slow her racing thoughts – to understand where she was. That space between dream and reality terrified Jay – that moment in which it was impossible to be sure whether the images imprinted on her mind were real, or if they were part of a dream.

The nightmares were always the same. She was in the cavern. Marcus was there, the leader and most powerful of the State's Readers. She re-lived the moment he and the Readers closed in. The events of that day merged and twisted together in her nightmares. The pain that he caused when he infiltrated her mind was amplified in her dreams, and she couldn't shake him out of her head. Sammy's injuries were so bad, and she couldn't reach him. Stitch was gone. She called for him, but he never responded.

Every time, she woke with tears streaming down her face, sweat pouring off her body, and hyperventilating so much that she would see stars.

She stood, straining to catch a glimpse of light from the rocks above but getting nothing but darkness. She felt around the floor of her room for her torch. Her hand closed around its cold metal and she breathed a sigh of relief as the light bounced around her room, bringing her back to her real world, the one in which Marcus was no longer a threat.

The man stood in the shadow of a tree so that Cassie couldn't see his face. She looked him up and down. He was no taller than her. No power that she could sense. It was true that, unless the shielding was expert, she'd be able to sense power in someone this close. 'Who are you? What do you want?'

'Call me Hinton,' he said, his voice calm and measured, then flicked his head to signal for the Readers to back off. They melted into the background, just a handful remaining within earshot.

The uneasy feeling in Cassie's stomach radiated to her skin. 'We'll be off then,' she said, stepping back.

'Stay. Show me your mark,' Hinton said, quiet but firm. A Reader approached Cassie and before she registered his movement had taken her by her left hand and roughly pulled back her sleeve. Hinton glanced at her number—seven.

Reuben stepped forward, raising a hand, but before he made contact with the Reader, he doubled over in pain, clutching the sides of his head, screaming like a trapped animal. Three more Readers approached and focused on

Reuben, Hinton remaining in the shadows. Cassie could feel their energy piling into her friend. Instinctively, she stood between Reuben and the Readers, trying to deflect their attack.

Hinton raised a hand, and his soldiers stopped their digging. Reuben collapsed onto the floor. Cassie knelt next to him and witnessed a scar form on the right side of his face, a scar characteristic of the effects of Reader attacks on the mind – a scar like the one displayed by Zadie Lawrence back at the Interland. Reuben's eyes swam with a mist of confusion as he slumped onto his side, curling tighter into a ball with every laboured breath.

'What do you want?' Cassie snarled at Hinton. 'Show me your face.'

'You're Cassie,' the man said.

'Congratulations,' said Cassie, trying not to reveal her uneasiness about him knowing her name. Hinton laughed without humour, then gave an almost imperceptible flick of his head to his Readers. Cassie felt a sharp pain enter both sides of her head at her temples, a pain so intense that her legs almost buckled. She swayed, her hands to her head, eyes streaming. As suddenly as it had begun, the pain seeped away, leaving her reeling.

The man waved back his Readers once more. So he had no direct power of his own. He was not one of the Given. But he had something more powerful – he had control. The Readers moved quickly, responded to his signals as if it were the man himself inflicting the attacks. And, more than that, he had a resistance. Cassie could not read him.

Reuben's eyes remained closed, his breathing shallow. The scar on the side of his face had taken the shape of a long curve from temple to chin and he was trembling, barely conscious.

'Let's go,' said Hinton, turning, instructing Cassie to follow.

She stood firm, glancing down at her friend and back to Hinton. 'Oh, the boy? You don't think we should leave him here?' Cassie remained silent, trying again to read the man but getting nothing. A flicker of annoyance emanated from Hinton's dark outline, coming through in his voice. 'Come with me. Now, or you join your friend.'

Cassie knelt next to Reuben, stroked his head. The scar had reddened, almost glowing in the darkness. She took a deep breath, held it. Tensed her muscles and sprang.

Hinton barely had to move to avoid the impact of Cassie. Once more, pain coursed through Cassie's head, her neck and shoulders. Through blurred vision, she saw Hinton's face emerge from shadow as he watched her suffer the pain. She hit the ground, a face full of the woodland floor at the man's feet. She shrivelled like a burning leaf, tightening. She screamed but heard nothing. Flopped further to the floor, the pain receding, Cassie prised her eyes open a crack. Three men in dark clothes stood over her. Hinton walked away. The Readers leaned close to Reuben, and he writhed in pain once more, but he made no attempt to get away, or even to lift his hands to his head.

'Reuben?' Cassie whispered into the cool, damp air. His body twitched under the focus of the Readers. She tried again to move, but her limbs would not respond, her head like a rock. Hinton glanced at her, then back to Reuben, who had flopped over onto his side so that he faced Cassie, eyes half open with nothing behind. Nothing left. The scar on the side of his face had opened, a crack from which his life seeped.

She looked into his vacant eyes and knew. Reuben was dead.

4

T he dining hall cavern bustled with activity. The children laid plates, bowls and cutlery as the day's cooks brought out serving bowls of steaming soup. A well of light penetrated from above, where interconnected caves and channels meandered to the outside world.

Jay scanned the seats around the table for Stitch. He was sat alone, in a world of his own, studying the inside of his wrist. His lop-sided hair had grown so that his fringe covered one eye. She tapped him on the shoulder and slumped down on the bench next to him, making him jump. Jay laughed, 'Looking for something new?' He motioned to his wrist where the letter "C" was displayed in pitch black.

He pulled his sleeve back further. 'I'm the only one in this place without a number,' he said, flicking his hair out of his eyes.

'You're special, like you always said.' Jay nudged into him, then reached to tear some bread from the homemade loaf in the middle of the table.

'Show me yours again,' said Stitch. Jay sighed and pulled

her own sleeve back to show Stitch the "8C" on her wrist. He leaned in to study it. 'My letter is bigger than yours.'

Jay returned to her food. 'Size isn't everything.' Stitch went back to studying his own wrist. 'What's the problem, Stitch? We've been through this. You have something different to the others, and so do I. You and I are connected. We come as a pair. The same as Sasha Colden.'

'What for?' said Stitch. 'What's the point?'

'Why does there always need to be a point?' Jay knew Stitch felt the intensity of the power they had together. She could feel it herself, even if she didn't always understand it. When she was with him, her inner power took on a different form, something deeper. She felt part of him, like they could be one person. And there was something more: a connection between them and everything around them, from the ground beneath their feet, the air around them, and the water flowing between the rocks.

Stitch shrugged and reached for the bread. 'It scares me. It's big. And it doesn't always add up.'

'I know, but we're safe here. No Reader can get to us here, with the protection of the energy in this place. You feel that?'

A boy ran into the dining hall, panting and stuttering, visibly distressed. Zadie Lawrence crouched next to the boy and held his hands. He took a breath and could eventually get his words out: 'The Runners. Two of them haven't returned. Something must have happened.'

Runners never returned late unless something had happened to stop them returning to the Interland. Jay stood. She knew it was Cassie and Reuben. Even before the boy had spoken, she had a sense something was wrong, that Cassie was either too far away for her to feel her presence, or that something had happened. Stitch looked up at Jay. 'Cassie?'

Jay nodded. She could sense Cassie from a distance.

Reuben was not so easy. The strength of connection over distance was as much to do with how well people were connected personally, as it was a product of the strength of their power – their marking. She moved around the table to join Zadie. 'It's Cassie,' Jay said, 'and Reuben.'

'I feel it too,' said Zadie, her expression grave.

Stitch joined them. 'We don't know for sure,' he said.

'It's Cassie. I can feel it,' said Jay.

Stitch shook his head. 'She'll be alright, she's badass. No one messes with Cassie.'

But Zadie looked troubled. There had been more incidents between Runners and Readers recently. The Readers had been increasing their activity, like they were building up to something. Cassie was a high value target. She and Reuben had great power, like all the Runners.

Stitch scratched his head, his frown deepening. 'We need to find them.'

Jay shook her head. 'We can't go out there. Away from the source, we won't have the same strength of power. It's too dangerous.'

'How do you know?' said Stitch, frustration in his voice. 'We've never been out, not since the day we found this place, and our powers were revealed.' He pulled his sleeve back again to display his marking.

'I just know,' Jay said.

'I think Stitch is right, Jay,' said Zadie. 'Someone needs to go after Cassie and it makes sense for it to be you. We can send someone with you.'

'I'll go,' said Stitch.

'No,' said Zadie. 'We need you here to keep a line of communication open with Jay. We can send a Runner.'

'But we're stronger together,' Stitch said.

Zadie ignored him.

Jay sat down on a stool. She tried to push her fears to the back of her mind, the prospect of once more being alone and open to attack from Readers, away from her dad and from Sammy. 'I can't go,' she said, looking up at Stitch, her eyes blurring with the tears forming. 'I'm sorry.'

Stitch nodded.

Zadie sighed, 'We'll work something out.'

5

Hinton woke to the sound of screams.

Downstairs, his three-year-old daughter, Megan, squealed with laughter as she was tickled by Sarah, his wife. He smiled and turned onto his side to check the clock. Seven-thirty. If he got up now, he'd have time for a lazy breakfast with his two favourite girls. He slung his legs out of bed and rubbed his eyes in the glare of the light coming through a gap in the curtains. He must fix those curtains. They hung off the end of the runner, several curtain hooks missing.

Megan ran past the foot of the stairs, hysterical with delight. She was closely pursued by Sarah, who caught sight of Hinton as he descended the double-width wooden staircase, dressed ready for work, his tie loose around his neck and his collar up. 'Morning lazy bones,' she said, her smile as bright as the open-plan ground floor where morning sun poured in through a wall of glass.

'Daddy...' came Megan's voice as she hurtled back towards the stairs. Hinton leaned down and whisked her into his arms. He planted a stubbly kiss on her cheek and she recoiled.

'Shave your beard, it's prickly,' she said as she stroked his chin, trying to pull at the hairs.

Sarah headed back towards the kitchen. 'What's today got in store for you?' she asked as she poured coffee for Hinton and topped up her own mug.

Hinton set Megan down and she scuttled off calling for the dog, Misty. 'It'll be busy, some new inmates. I might be late.'

'Can't the others deal with it? Does it always have to be you?'

Hinton gave his wife a look that told her he had no choice. She dropped the subject and handed him his coffee. 'You want eggs?'

'Thanks.' Hinton joined his daughter at the breakfast table, collecting his briefcase on the way and pulling out a file he'd brought home from work.

'What's that,' Megan asked, not taking her eyes off the Lego tower she was constructing on the table.

'Work,' he said.

'Criminmals... crinimals?' Megan asked, struggling with the word.

Hinton laughed, 'I guess.'

'Are all your work friends bad people?'

'No.' Hinton smiled, watching for a moment as Megan carefully placed another Lego brick on the top of her precarious looking tower. 'My work friends are good people. It's the people that we keep there that need guidance.'

'You keep bad people?'

'We look after them, try to help them make good choices.'

'Mummy said I make good choices. Mummy said you help people. I want to help people too.'

'You will, one day.' Hinton closed his file as Sarah placed two plates of eggs on toast on the table. 'Come on you two,' she said as Megan's Lego tower finally toppled. She giggled as the pieces scattered across the table and onto the floor. Then she crossed her arms and sat back in her seat with her arms folded, a broad grin on her face.

'Butter wouldn't melt,' Hinton said, smiling at his wife.

* * *

CASSIE WOKE, the side of her body numb against the cold floor. The room was mostly shadows, lit only by a single lightbulb recessed into the ceiling. The floor was a solid, smooth metal, and the walls a heavy steel. She raised herself onto her elbows and looked towards the heavy-set metal door. No handle on the inside. No window, nothing.

Her head was a symphony of pain, a dull ache punctuated by crescendos of agony. She struggled to stand, one hand holding her forehead, moving slowly towards the door. She tried to prise it open from the inside. It wouldn't budge. She banged on the wall with her fist, but the steel structure resisted her blows, soaked up the sound as if they were six feet thick.

She thought of Reuben, the blankness in his eyes as the life withdrew from his body. She had watched him slip away, had felt his heartbeat slow, weaken, and then stop. Her own heart ached with the thought. She couldn't believe that he was gone, so soon after they'd got to know each other again. She never told him how much he meant to her.

The door gave a deep clunk and swung inward like the opening to a vault. A man entered and Cassie recognised him from the darkness up on Highdown. She stepped back to put as much distance between them as the cell would allow. His expression was neutral – no hint of interest in her, no urgency. She tried to read behind the expression but got nothing. The door closed with a thump. He stared at Cassie for a moment as he leaned back against the opposite wall, licked his finger and rubbed at an invisible mark on the sleeve of his jacket. He cleared his throat.

'Do you know where you are?'

Cassie shook her head.

Hinton leaned down and brushed at his trouser leg, then stood, pushing himself off the wall and stepping a little closer to Cassie. 'We call it *Education*. The second step in the process, before our customers move on to the final stage of true rehabilitation, where the powers no longer cause them any problems.'

'What *customers*? Prisoners?'

'We don't look at it like that. We think of it more as customers who don't yet know what they are shopping for until they've been through the programme.'

'Well, I can see how that thinking might help you sleep better at night,' Cassie said, her pulse quickening. She was in the prison. She thought of Ben, Jay's dad. Ben had been interned here, a prison for the Given, before escaping to the Interland. He had told her about the place, its three stages: Incarceration, Education and Rehabilitation. No one was ever seen again after moving into *Education* or *Rehabilitation*.

She looked to the door, then to Hinton, a smirk on his face as he returned her gaze. He had no power. There were no Readers in the room. Cassie focused in on the man, his mind, channelling her energy into him, digging.

A sharp pain pierced Cassie's head, and she reeled, slamming back against the solid steel wall before her legs weakened and she couldn't stop herself slumping to a crouch position. She looked around. The man had not moved, but for a widening grin. She stood, refocussed, and dug deeper this time. She could overcome this man; he had no power she could sense. This time the pain took away all the strength in her legs and she collapsed to the floor, panting.

'That won't work in here, Cassie. Look around you.' Hinton motioned around the oppressive, grey cell. 'Nothing living. No natural materials, no windows, no natural light...'

Pain radiated from inside the middle of Cassie's skull. She held her head in her hands as though it might split into pieces. He stepped towards her and crouched. 'You may be having trouble thinking right now, so let me speak clearly: In here, you're mine.' Cassie could feel his breath, fresh with the smell of toothpaste. His clothes exuded a scent of clean washing. He was immaculate.

'Why?' Cassie managed to mumble.

'You'll find out. For now, I'm happy we've managed to do this little experiment with the power of a Runner. That's what they call you, isn't it? A big old level seven like you?' Hinton leaned in and edged back Cassie's sleeve to reveal her number. 'A Runner,' he said, standing to leave. 'You must be so proud. Your pal, Jay, must be really worried about you.'

Cassie startled at his mention of Jay, at the thought that Jay could be a target.

He smiled. 'Oh yes, I know all about your little Interland gang. And you're going to help me find them. They're destined to be my most satisfied customers yet!'

6

In Jay's room, Sammy and Stitch sat on the bed, Jay on the chair at her little desk fashioned out of the rock. On the chessboard between the two boys, Sammy moved his bishop three squares. 'Check,' he said, then turned back to his sister. 'Anything? Any clues?'

Jay continued to study the map; Sammy shifted between sitting on the bed and standing next to Jay, unable to keep still. 'Chill out, Sammy, let me think.'

Stitch frowned. 'I thought those moved sideways?'

Sammy snorted, 'The rook moves sideways, the bishop diagonally.' Stitch let out a sigh of frustration.

Jay kept bent over the map. 'Highdown,' she said under her breath.

'What about it?' Sammy said as Stitch studied the chessboard.

'If there's somewhere Cassie and Reuben could have run into a Reader, it would be up on one of the hill forts,' said Jay.

'A Reader wouldn't be any bother for Cassie and Reuben. Even for Cassie on her own,' said Sammy.

'Well, something's happened, we know that.'

'We won't know what, unless we head out there and find them,' said Stitch. Zadie wanted Jay to go with another Runner, Davey, to look for Cassie, and for Stitch to stay behind, but Jay had no intention of leaving the safety of the Interland without Stitch.

Sammy paced the room. He nudged Stitch to hurry up with his move. 'Come on. Use your mighty level-C power to get in my head,' Sammy teased.

'Better a level C than nothing,' Stitch said.

Jay looked up at her little brother. 'Anything coming through yet, Sammy?'

Sammy pulled back his sleeve. 'Something, but it could be anything. Probably a level eight.'

'Level zero more like,' said Stitch.

At that moment, Jay's dad came into the room with his friend, Matchstick, and Zadie just behind. Sammy stood. 'Any news?'

'Nothing yet,' said Zadie. 'We've come to speak with Jay.'

Jay looked up from the map. 'They could have run into trouble at Highdown, send the Runners there,' she said.

Zadie looked to Sammy. 'Can you boys leave us for a moment?'

'They can stay,' said Jay. Matchstick sat with Sammy and Stitch.

Zadie gave a shrug and stood next to Jay. 'I want you to reconsider.'

'I'm not going out there,' Jay said, looking to her dad for support.

Ben crouched next to her. 'Jay, we think it's the only way. You're the only one who can track them. No one else here will have the sensitivity, the power.'

'What about her?' Jay nodded at Zadie. 'Or the Runners? Davey can track.'

'I need to stay here,' said Zadie. 'You know that. The people here are my responsibility. But you're right about Davey. He will accompany you. Davey is one of the most experienced Runners. He'll be there to help protect you, and to track Cassie and Reuben.'

'I'll go,' said Sammy.

'No,' Ben said without hesitation. 'You're staying here.'

Jay scowled at her dad. 'So he stays and I go. Why am I the expendable one?'

'Jay,' Ben said. 'That's not it. There's no point in Sammy being exposed again, you know what happened last time. We nearly lost him.'

'I can go,' said Matchstick.

Ben raised his eyebrows at his friend. 'If it needed an old man, then I'd go.'

Jay said, 'Sasha Colden barely left this place once she'd settled here. There was a reason for that. *You* might not get it but I can feel it. If I leave here, especially without my connection, then I'm vulnerable. She was your mum,' Jay said, looking at her dad. 'She was our blood. She knew. Can't you sense it?'

Zadie turned to leave. 'This conversation is over. I'll ask Davey to collect you first thing in the morning, get yourself ready.'

With Zadie gone, Ben stood. He briefly touched Jay's shoulder, then turned to leave. 'It's the only way,' he said, then he and Matchstick left the room.

Jay's mind raced; she took short, shallow breaths. The Readers all around her. She gasped to get a lungful. *It's not real. It's a memory. See the memory. Notice the memory. Sit with the feeling. Feelings can't hurt you.* The Readers closed in. Her breaths shortened as she struggled to squeeze air into her lungs. *Deep breath. In for three... out for four.*

'Easy...' said Stitch, holding out a hand to comfort Jay.

'I've got a bad feeling,' said Jay, brushing him off. 'Something's wrong about all this. We don't know what it's like out there. It's a different place. I'm not a Runner, I don't have what Cassie has. I can't face those Readers again, not like before...' She broke off, sat on her bed with her head in her hands.

Sammy went to her. 'You've changed too, Sis. You're stronger, more powerful than before, and you know more about the power. There's no Reader more powerful than you.'

'What about Marcus?'

'He's dead,' said Sammy.

Jay wasn't so sure. There was never a body, no evidence that he'd gone. It was true that Jay felt nothing of him, but she couldn't be sure.

'Look, Jay. Cassie's up against it right now,' said Sammy. 'You're our best hope to find her and bring her back safely.'

'She means a lot to you, doesn't she?'

'Well, I mean I guess...'

'More than me?'

'Of course not! You're my sister. But maybe I believe in your powers more than you do.'

Stitch sat on the other side of Jay and put a hand on her arm, quickly removing it when Jay flinched. She moved to get away from them, their sympathy and their infuriating encouragement. 'Leave me alone for a bit,' she said. Sammy began to say something but Jay cut him off. 'Now, Sammy. Please.'

The boys filed from Jay's room, Stitch turning as he reached the door. 'I'll come back later,' he said, then stepped out into the passageway.

Alone, Jay allowed her tears to come, silently forming in the corners of her eyes and running down her face. She rubbed at her cheeks as if trying to scrub away her weakness and fear. 'Why are you so frickin weak? This is Cassie you're talking about. Your friend,' she said under her breath. Then louder, 'Stupid... stupid... stupid,' her voice rising to a scream, which she muffled by lying face down on her bed.

7

Of the three hill forts, Marcus preferred Cissbury, where energy flowed through the layers of history from as far back as 500BC, making its way through the chalk bedrock and flint seams, radiating from the inner circle.

Back when he was a Reader, Marcus drew no power from the hill forts. His power came from the State. That was before his encounter with Jay. She drained him, reduced him, then disappeared into the Interland.

Jay's attack reversed the process of transformation to a Reader that he underwent when he was a young student, the process that took his Given power and elevated him to a Level 8 Reader. Now, once again, he drew power from the environment, as did the rest of the Given. The mark on his wrist was now a smudge.

Since that day, when he clashed with Jay, Marcus had opted out. He could no longer exist in normal society. He was neither a Reader, nor accepted as one of the Given. In a world where wielding the powers of the Given had become a greater crime than any other, Marcus chose anonymity and isolation.

And slowly, on his own, the little power he did have grew as he spent time soaking up the energy of the Downs.

On the north side of the Ring, two hundred feet down the slope from the summit, Marcus woke to the sound of birds. Morning light barely penetrated the undergrowth to his den, his home for the most part of twelve months. He shuffled to ease himself out of his cocoon, the tangle of branches, rock and soft woodland materials he had used to fashion a bed, and sat up. He stroked the side of his face, the skin tingling where the two scars extended from his temple down the side of his face, like parallel train tracks curving under as they reached his chin. The first was old, inflicted during his original transformation from the Given to a Reader. It had turned white over the years and hard to the touch. The second was inflicted by the girl, Jay. It was no more than a year old, still red, angry, softer to the touch and sometimes painful – a frequent reminder.

He stood, remaining under cover of bushes and trees in the deep trench that had become his home. It had been built during the War to protect the summit from attack, an anti-tank initiative that now provided Marcus with his own kind of protection. It was somewhere to lose himself, to be alone. He replenished his fire with the driest of the wood from his store, smoke rising almost as soon as the sticks hit the ashes, still hot from the previous night.

A sound caught his attention. He opened up a little, something he avoided for the most part, preferring to remain undetectable, and not least because channelling the power seemed to become more painful as the months passed. A whistle. A man walking his dog on the north face of the hill, closer to Marcus's camp than most ever came. Marcus sensed the man as he continued past with his dog and away to the west. His heart slowed once more to a normal rate, and the experience, the anxiety, put the girl back into his mind – Jay.

He pushed her away and sat by the fire, feeding it with wood and rubbing his hands together to revive feeling in his fingers. The grey monochrome sky was heavy, like a blanket. It was not yet light enough for him to head out on his daily foraging. He preferred not to use his power to hunt, the pain not worth the meagre rewards.

A stag beetle caught his eye, stumbling blindly across the dirt floor towards his boots, the flicker of the flames reflected in the gloss-black shell on its back. He leaned over and moved a stick from its path so that it had a direct passage to his left boot, where it stopped. Its feelers scanned Marcus's scraggy shoe before it mounted and climbed up to settle on his laces, where it decided to rest awhile. Marcus caught himself smiling, an unfamiliar sensation that evaporated as soon as he was conscious of it. He looked into the flames and felt something, like a crack in the curtain of confusion in his mind – there was a fresh wave of activity somewhere, change was coming in on the breeze.

8

Jay lay on her back beneath her blankets, the room pitch black and her eyes wide open.

When the first light peeked through the crevice in the rocks above her head, Jay pulled back her covers and climbed, fully clothed, from her bed. She paced the room, muttering to herself. 'I can feel it,' she said. There was an undeniable pull to the source, the epicentre of the Interland. It promised answers, guidance. With the energy would come clarity. 'No,' she shouted, stopping still in her room and staring at the rock wall. *There are no answers in the source*, she said to herself. *The source has done nothing for me.*

Jay had avoided the depths of the Interland since the last time she was there, when she had been overcome by the power. Zadie Lawrence didn't like Jay being there too much. More frequent visits, Zadie said, could push her too far into the energy. It could be dangerous if she was not ready. She needed to take it a step at a time, to try to learn the language in the whispers from the land, the sea, and the earth.

But of course, she didn't listen. The last time, when she and Stitch connected with the source, the power was like an electric bolt. Stitch was thrown clear, but Jay remained connected. It transported her *into* the energy with such force that eventually she passed out. Her memory of the ordeal was weak. It had taken her days just to recover enough to leave her bed.

Now, she needed the source. She descended the six levels into the heart of the underground. Cool air washed over her as she reached the lowest level. She fumbled in the dark for the candle in an alcove at the entrance. Her fingers found the matches, light flickering into the rock-walled room. She lit more candles, set into alcoves in the wall, then turned to the central pillar where water trickled down from above.

Three separate streams – from the Arun, the Rother, and the unnamed river – combined at the centre of a naturally formed column and out in a single flow into the rocks below. Jay reached out her hand and allowed the water of the unnamed river to flow through her fingers, where it seemed to sparkle in the light before merging with the other streams. Her heart pounded. Images of Readers floated through her mind. The energy was strong. In the heart of the Interland she was joined with her history, her grandmother, Sasha Colden.

She felt a familiar energy. Stitch appeared, looking as if he'd just woken up. 'I knew you were down here,' he said. 'I always know when you are in this place.' He looked around the room, his eyes red in the light from the candles, dark rings around them. 'What are you doing?'

'Looking for inspiration,' said Jay. 'I can feel something.'

Stitch held out a hand to Jay.

'Not now,' she said.

'Just for a moment,' said Stitch, motioning towards the source.

Jay took his extended hand. They locked eyes for a moment, then turned to the source. Together, they pushed their free hands into the pool of water formed from the three separate streams. Jay immediately connected. The whispers came, slow and incoherent at first, great swooping waves of white noise. Then faster, with a familiar urgency. Jay looked to Stitch. His eyes were closed. She turned back to look into the water and began to filter the sounds in her head, to order and interpret them. Shapes and colours emerged from the whispers, shapes bound by feelings and intuition. She sensed a fear within the noise, Cassie's fear, but behind it a greater fear, a fear that threatened them all.

Jay broke the chain, stumbled backwards towards the wall of the cave and crouched on her haunches. Stitch gulped in air. 'Did you feel that?' he said. She staggered towards the entrance to the cave and crawled up the first few steps on her hands and knees as she regained her balance. Stitch called after her, but all she could think of was to get out of the room, to get away from the power of the source, to somewhere she could breathe again.

* * *

BACK IN STITCH'S ROOM, Jay watched as Stitch gathered supplies together in a rucksack. 'What are you doing?' she asked.

Stitch shrugged. 'Whether you like it or not, Zadie is coming for you in a couple of hours with Davey. Better we go now, on our terms.'

'We're leaving?' Jay's heart pounded with fear at the thought of it.

Stitch stared at her. 'You *know* we have to leave.'

'You're coming?'

'Can't let you go without all your weapons,' Stitch said,

puffing himself up. 'You need your full power, and you won't get that from Davey.'

Jay helped Stitch squeeze his supplies into his bag – a change of clothes, some food, all protected in plastic bags to keep them dry and protected from the water they would have to negotiate on their way out.

'Are we doing the right thing?' said Jay, her fears lingering.

'Something's happening, and Cassie is in trouble, so we need to go.' Light filled Stitch's room from above. His room was nearer the surface than Jay's, and the routes through to the open air were much bigger, so it was colder, but also much lighter during the day. Stitch finished packing and slung his rucksack onto his back. Jay stood, and together they stopped by Jay's room for her to gather her things, then pushed on to the main hall. Jay's nerves tingled at the prospect of leaving the Interland and once again stepping outside.

The main hall was empty, as they had expected. They continued through to the entry passage, through the waterfall and on to the place where the boulder covered the entrance. Stitch picked up the heavy branch intended as a lever and put his weight on it, shifting the boulder a few feet, enough for Jay to squeeze through the gap and hold it in place for Stitch. When Stitch was through, Jay allowed the boulder to roll back, blocking the light from the Interland and sealing them on the outside.

9

Davey followed Zadie closely through the passageways of the residential section, towards Jay's room. He had been waiting for this. If Davey wanted to fulfil his potential in the Interland, this mission with Jay to find the Readers was his chance. He could prove himself by showing his loyalty to Zadie and to the cause.

Zadie whipped the covers off Jay's bed in exasperation, then turned to scan the room as if Jay could hide in plain sight.

'Where is she?' asked Davey.

Zadie stormed from the room, picking up pace as she headed back into the warren of rock tunnel passageways. She strode into Stitch's room, letting out a groan before sitting down on his bed, her head in her hands.

'What now?' said Davey.

Zadie was silent for a moment, then sprung from the bed. 'You can track, can't you?'

Davey nodded. He was one of the best trackers amongst the Runners. He had a skill for locking on to a single source of energy. 'Those two will be easy to track. Probably the strongest signal of anyone in here. But what do I do when I get to them?'

'You won't get to them. Keep your distance. When you get sight of them, or a sense of them, report back to me like we discussed. I want to know where they are and in what direction they are headed.'

'Where are they going?' Davey asked, sensing that Zadie knew more than she was sharing. He wanted to do the right thing. If she saw his value and abilities, maybe he'd be the one she'd choose to be her right hand when the Given finally broke free of the underground and back into the world. She'd need someone with his skills if they were going to work alongside Jay and Stitch when the time came.

'We don't know where Cassie and Reuben are,' Zadie said. 'If they've been taken, they might be at the prison.'

'The so-called rehabilitation centre?'

'I don't know,' Zadie said. 'Look, don't get hung up on this. We don't know what's happened and we don't know where they are. We all have different senses, but none of us knows for sure. That's why Jay is out there looking. She should have been with you, and I need you to do as I have asked. Track, watch, and report back. Nothing more.'

'OK. That seems simple.'

'It's not. We can't afford to get this wrong. We need to know what side she's on.'

'What?' Davey interrupted.

Zadie didn't answer. She was edgy. This was not the time to push her.

'Do you understand your mission and do you have everything you need?' Zadie motioned towards the rucksack on his back.

'Yes and yes.' Davey nodded.

'Go.' Zadie nodded towards the doorway and Davey turned on his heels.

* * *

SAT on the edge of Stitch's bed, Zadie tried to get a sense of him. He was out there somewhere, with Jay, moving through the land. Together they were a formidable power, although Zadie couldn't help but think they'd not lived up to their potential. She'd had high hopes for Jay when she entered the Interland. She was supposed to be the one to define a clear path to emancipation of the Given – their victorious return to the world above, and the ultimate defeat of the Readers. How things had changed. The Given were extinct, but for the few remaining in hiding in their underground world. The Interland had become a virtual prison. She put a hand to the scar on the side of her face, and thought of Hinton.

When Zadie was first taken captive after the protest, she was held in the prison built for the Given. They interrogated her, but apart from Marcus, their most powerful Reader, their efforts to infiltrate her mind and take what they wanted were largely ineffective. Marcus had some power over her, but there was such energy when Marcus and Zadie were in the same place that their reality became somehow fractured and unstable. Time seemed to stutter and jerk. Marcus mostly left her alone after that, but then came Hinton – a far more terrifying individual than any Reader she'd come across.

Hinton was immune to her power, and she couldn't read him, couldn't influence him. He had a level of control over her that she couldn't fight or understand. He spoke softly to Zadie at first, as if he cared for her. He wanted her to come on side, to join him. The details of his mission were hazy back then, but the essence was clear: His desire was for her to stand with him so that they could together assume overall power. She didn't trust him, and she resisted.

Hinton was patient, but after Zadie had been in captivity for about a month, he grew weary. He turned and revealed his true self. He approached one morning without a word, entering Zadie's cell flanked by a group of five or six Readers. Then he dug into Zadie's consciousness. She tried to resist, but however hard she focused, she had little impact on the infiltration. The longer Hinton persisted, the weaker she became, until there was nothing but blackness.

She lost time. She woke days later in an unfamiliar wing of the rehabilitation unit. Her mind was scattered, her body weak. They wired her up to monitoring systems she was told could determine the level of any residual power. But she didn't need the machines to tell her what she knew deep down – that her power was gone. On her wrist was the merest of dark smudges where before there had been the number eight. On the side of her face was a scar from temple to chin. She didn't see Hinton again before she was released back into the community, no longer deemed a threat to the establishment, but she felt his presence. His face was in her head. The smell of his freshly pressed suit was in her nose. For weeks afterwards, it was as if, wherever she turned, he was with her – watching, reading, influencing.

The sense of powerlessness hurt Zadie far more than Hinton's act of reducing her. He had allowed her to live, but left her nothing to live for. She was weak and vulnerable to the growing presence of the Readers in society. It even crossed her mind back then that an alliance with Hinton might have been preferable to her gradual deterioration and eventual anonymous death.

Zadie was drawn to the hill forts, where the energy of the land was at its strongest. It was there she felt a spark of power, a seed that would grow with time. It took months to rebuild her strength, and her confidence. She'd regained much of her power by the time she got to the Interland, and with the concentrated energy of the source, she once more became the most powerful of the Given. That was until Jay and her connection to Stitch.

Zadie came across Hinton once more, a few months back. She had been out on a mission with two trainee Runners. She became separated from them as she followed her senses in search of one of the Given. Intelligence received at the Interland told that this person was in hiding in the suburbs in the south of the City. Zadie encouraged her trainees to follow their instincts – learn to read their senses and trust their feelings. They would learn to tune in to the energy of the Given.

Hinton drew her in. He somehow managed to confuse the signal of the power that she sensed, so that the energy of the Given that she thought she was tracking led her into an unfamiliar part of the City, away from the sanctuary of the hills. By the time she sensed the darkness, she was already in the heart of an area teeming with Readers. She could feel them.

She blindly followed her senses, walking past a row of disused houses. A pub on the corner was empty despite the enticing, warm glow emanating from its windows – the smell of hops drifted across her path. Continuing on her trail, she found herself in a dead-end alleyway around the back of the houses. The sense she had of the Given dissolved into the darkness to be replaced by the distinctive energy of the Readers. Zadie turned, and Hinton emerged from the shadows. The sight of him froze Zadie to the spot. Her heart raced as her eyes searched for an escape route. Readers lurked out of sight. Hinton was smartly dressed, as was his way, his immaculate presentation allowing him to hide his evil in plain sight. Without words, he guided her to the pub on the corner.

The proprietor placed two glasses of iced water on the table in front of Zadie and Hinton. Zadie looked at the man and immediately saw that he was a Reader, acting under the guidance of Hinton. He gave a smirk as he turned back to the bar, scuffing his feet as he went. She stared at the water for a moment, her throat parched. Condensation dripped down the side of the glass and the water seemed to fizz with an enticing glow.

'It's perfectly safe,' Hinton said, picking up his own glass, then placing it back down and taking Zadie's glass instead. He took a gulp of the water. Zadie immediately thought of the potential for a double bluff, but her thirst got the better of her and she took the remaining glass and drank. 'There,' Hinton said. 'Better?'

'What do you want?' Zadie asked, looking around and taking note of the location of the exits: two in the main bar, probably one in the saloon bar and then, if she was desperate, a potential for a window exit through the back.

'I thought we should talk. Like the two opposing Generals, meeting in no-man's-land to negotiate a truce.'

'A truce? Is that what this is?' Zadie instinctively tried to read him, despite knowing the futility of the effort. She searched her own mind for why he might be prepared for a truce. It was clear that outside the Interland, the control and dominance of the Readers was absolute. There were few remaining Given to offer any resistance, and the Readers had so infiltrated the heart of the State that the cause of the Readers and of Government were now synonymous.

'It could be. I see no reason to prolong the conflict.'

'That sounds more like a negotiation for our surrender,' Zadie said. She looked around the room once more, seeing that a number of Readers had entered, sitting at tables like any normal customer. Hinton undoubtedly had the upper hand. If Zadie was to get out of this situation, it would be if Hinton allowed it.

'Look.' Hinton leaned forward, his elbows on the table and hands together as if in prayer. 'In essence, we want the same thing. I believe there can be a world in which the Given stand alongside the Readers – a world in which you stand *with* me, not against me.'

'You've already shown how you treat the Given. Look at this place,' she nodded towards the window. 'It's been run into the ground. The Given are in hiding, or dead.'

'I'm not saying it couldn't have gone better. God knows I didn't wish for it to be like this. But we need to look ahead. We cannot even think about rebuilding society while this conflict remains – this impasse.'

'What do you propose?' Zadie said, finishing her water and leaning back to cross her arms over her chest.

'Like I said. A joint leadership. You and me, the faces of the Readers and of the Given. United.' Zadie shook her head in disbelief but her mind was already clasping on to the threads of the proposal as a viable route to the re-emergence of the Given – a route to consolidate her own power and control.

Zadie sighed, feeling a pinch in her chest as if her lungs were constricted. The weight of the energy of the Readers was becoming too much. 'Equal status? Readers and Given?'

'Of course,' said Hinton.

'What about the State?' asked Zadie. The rules of the State still said that the Given were illegal. Not just the *use* of their powers, but their very being.

'We *are* the State,' he said, a smile creeping over his lips.

Zadie saw little option at this point, and the possibility of a leadership position in driving the change required to establish the Given as equal partners was tantalising. But she was in no doubt that this man was not someone who could be blindly trusted. She would need some guarantees. 'How do I know you'll stand by your word?'

He smiled. 'I could have killed you back in that alleyway. In fact, I could have killed you before, when you were my guest in rehabilitation.'

'Guest?' Zadie scoffed. 'You reduced me. You took my power, my life force.'

'Dampened it. I didn't *take* it. Although I could have. It's returned to its full strength now?' Hinton seemed to smirk, as if he'd known that she would regain her power.

'You planned...' Zadie stumbled over her words. He had let her live. He'd reduced her to nothing, but he'd expected her to regain her strength. Why?

'I thought you'd come back, yes. I think we can be better together. With your influence over the Given, and my control of the State.'

'How? What's your plan?'

Hinton sat back, gathering his thoughts and his energy. 'With Jay and Stitch present at the Interland, we cannot integrate. Their connected power repels. It's divisive. We need to get Jay away from there. Only then can we open up the Interland to Reader and Given alike, and free the Given back to the world above. *Then* we can start.'

'The Given won't leave the Interland.'

'I thought you were their leader?' Hinton said. Zadie shuffled in her seat and looked away from him. 'There will be some who will resist,' he continued. 'You will have to be strong and show leadership. Are you strong enough? Are you the one?'

'You know I am,' Zadie said.

He smiled. 'You are a born leader. But great leaders are made in the moment of choice under great stress.'

Zadie's initial anger at being manipulated soon dissipated as she saw a possible route to freedom in Hinton's plans. 'I'll consider it,' she said, standing to leave. Three of the Readers immediately stood, but Hinton signalled for them to stand down. Zadie made for the door without looking back.

PART II

10

In the shadow beneath the bridge abutment, Jay pulled herself from the water. Stitch followed. Jay stood dripping onto the bank, staring off into the distance.

'What's up?' said Stitch, peeling off his wet shirt and replacing it with a dry one from his bag.

'Memories,' said Jay. The last time she'd been here, she'd narrowly escaped an attack from the Reader, Marcus. She pulled off her wet clothes with no self-consciousness. Stitch turned his back. He packed his own wet clothes away and scrambled up the bank to the village green. Jay followed, stepping onto the green and taking a deep breath, trying to settle her racing heartbeat. A conflict raged inside of her. The air smelled fresh outside of the underground, and the sun on her face warmed her cheeks, but an acute sense of anxiety rose in her chest. She felt vulnerable away from the source. She was detectable. And she was weaker. She held her breath for a moment to slow things down, to gain some control.

'Breathe,' said Stitch, placing a hand on her back.

'Sorry,' said Jay as she released the breath. 'Let's move.'

'Where to?' said Stitch.

'We need to get to Sidwell, to pick up the car.' Jay pulled a set of keys from her pocket, jangling them in front of Stitch.

'We're going in the Beast?'

'It's the only way to travel. But it's a good few hours' walk from here, so we need something to help us on our way.'

Stitch stepped into the road and held out his thumb as a car sped by without stopping. 'It's north, right?' Jay nodded.

They risked being picked up by a Reader, or someone unsympathetic to the cause of the Given. Jay had to make a choice. She decided that she'd feel the danger if it was significant, so set off along the road, her back to the oncoming traffic and her thumb out.

The anxiety they both felt about being exposed was diluted by the sense of freedom and beauty in the wide open space around them – the wind in the trees, and the fresh scent of the woodland. Jay had to squint in the light of day, her eyes used to darkness underground.

They walked for less than ten minutes before an old yellow Mini pulled in to the side of the road. Stitch jumped into the passenger seat, talking to the driver as Jay squeezed into the back.

'Sidwell?' the driver said. Jay gave some rough directions, and the man said that he'd be able to take them some of the way if not right into the village. He tucked a strand of his long, lank hair behind his ear and pushed a button on his car stereo to eject the cassette tape. He turned it over. 'You two alright with AC/DC?'

Stitch smiled, 'As long as we're heading north, we're alright with anything.'

Jay shuffled out of her rucksack and placed it on the back seat next to her, then lay with her head up against the door. She wound down the window, so the air flowed over her.

Stitch and the man talked about music, the relative skills of various guitarists. Jay closed her eyes.

* * *

WHEN JAY WOKE, the car had stopped. Stitch and the driver were outside, sitting on the bonnet and sharing a cigarette. She gathered her things and pushed open the door. 'We here?' she asked.

Stitch turned and slid elegantly off the bonnet. 'Near as damnit,' he nodded in the direction of an overgrown pathway. Jay recognised it from when Cassie squeezed the car up the narrow track before it narrowed so much that it wasn't possible to get any further. Somewhere up there would be the Beast, her dad's old Ford. What were the chances of her being able to get it started after a year parked in an overgrown lane? 'Let's move,' said Jay.

Stitch held out a hand to their driver. 'Thanks, man.' He handed Stitch the cigarette and gave a brief wave to Jay before jumping back into the little yellow car and taking off.

'What's all the "Hey, Man" business?' asked Jay.

'What's with the attitude?' Stitch said. 'He was a champ, bringing us all the way here while you slept like a baby.' Jay gave Stitch a punch on the arm and they slung their bags on their backs and started off up the pathway.

They walked for just a few minutes before Jay recognised the opening to the field. The undergrowth had flourished, and on first glance Jay thought the car had gone. Looking again, it was clear that the bushes had grown over and around the car, hiding it from all directions.

'Crap.' Jay spat the word and kicked the front tyre. 'Now what?'

Stitch dumped his bag and began to clear the twisted

branches and leaves away from the car door. 'Here,' he said, opening the door for Jay. She took out the keys and slipped into the driver's seat. She held her breath as she turned the key in the ignition.

Nothing. Not even a minor whir and turn of the starter motor. She caught Stitch's eye through the windscreen as he lowered his gaze and his shoulders slumped. Jay climbed out and looked up ahead of the car where the field fell away into a valley.

'Help me clear this stuff away and we'll bump it,' said Jay.

With most of the bush cleared from in front of the car and the wheel arches, Jay shoved at the back to get it rocking. It rolled a few feet. Jay pushed from the driver's side with the door open and Stitch assumed a similar position on the passenger side. The car rolled towards the top of the slope and began to gather speed. Its soft tyres made a grinding sound in the dirt. Jay jumped in first, followed by Stitch. Halfway down the slope into the valley, as the car reached nearly twenty miles per hour freewheeling, Jay looked at Stitch and put it into gear. The engine jolted. They lurched forward in their seats. The engine turned. Cylinders fired. Stitch gave a victory cheer as Jay revved the engine; black smoke poured from the exhaust. She smiled at Stitch and slammed it back into second gear, taking off down the slope towards the gate at the bottom of the field, through which their journey would begin.

At the foot of Highdown, Jay and Stitch stood by the car, contemplating the climb. Jay was convinced this was where Cassie and Reuben had hit trouble, though the nature of the trouble evaded her. A dark feeling filtered through her.

'We need to climb,' Stitch said, intuitively understanding. Jay nodded, and they moved off together. 'Inside the ring of trees. That's where I can connect.'

At the halfway point, with Highdown directly in front of them, Jay climbed to a ledge to get a view to the other hill forts to the north and east at Cissbury and Chanctonbury. With sight of all three, the energy of the land was palpable. It flowed through her.

'It's strong here,' said Stitch.

Jay too felt the power coursing as strong as it did underground.

'Shall we try it?' said Stitch. 'Like back at the Interland. See if we can channel?' Usually their channelling was through the roots, the ground, the land, but the last time they had tried, Jay felt a human connection at the other end of their energy.

'Connect to the Interland?' said Jay.

'To whatever there is, let's see what happens.'

They both took a seat at the base of a large beech. Stitch took a deep breath. Jay looked up towards the summit of Highdown before taking Stitch's left hand in hers, holding him by his lower arm so that their wrists touched. Their sleeves were pulled back so that Jay's "8C" and Stitch's "C" physically connected. She closed her eyes and opened to the rush of energy.

A jolt of power and they opened their eyes, broke the connection. Both reeling.

'Again,' said Jay. Stitch took her arm and again they closed their eyes. This time Jay was ready for the flow. She channelled it and held tight to Stitch. She felt the power flowing and multiplying through Stitch's connection, as they had felt back at the Interland. Just as Jay felt her head might explode with the pressure and the heat that came from the energy, the power stabilised and took them down into the earth.

Jay moved through the roots of the great beech tree, into the ground through the fractured chalk. She moved through the subsurface aquifer, the groundwater that flowed to the edge of the dipping slope into the valley where it emerged as a river. Together, they entered the roots of the trees on the far slopes, climbing through the trunks and up into the branches, the leaves. Then down into the inner circle at the summit of Highdown, where there was a boy.

Stitch released his grip and fell back, away from Jay. Jay opened her eyes and gasped for breath, her chest burning with heat. She coughed, gagging. Stitch went to her, an arm around her shoulders. 'Breathe, slowly, breathe, Jay.'

Jay composed herself and looked up at Stitch, her eyes stinging. 'What the...?'

'I know,' said Stitch. 'Just slow down, breathe.' He went to his rucksack and pulled out a bottle of water, handed it to Jay and then picked out a packet of biscuits. 'Did you see him?'

'Was that real?'

'Felt like it,' said Stitch. 'A Reader?'

Jay shook her head. 'The colours. They weren't *Reader* colours. But he knows things. Could be one of the Given?'

'We need to get up there,' said Stitch, taking the water from Jay.

'Careful. He has power.'

'But not the darkness?'

'Maybe not,' said Jay. She smiled at Stitch, surprised at what they'd just achieved with their combined connection. 'That was pretty awesome.'

Stitch laughed, 'Did we just channel our consciousness through the environment?'

'There's something in the Sasha Colden history that hints at this kind of power,' said Jay.

'The biography?'

'Yes, but not in the words, in the subtext, like I was telling you. There are messages in there I can't explain. Can't describe how they come through. My grandmother, Sasha Colden, she did this, with her connection, whoever that was, she communicated through the earth.'

'You never said,' Stitch said, readying to head off, his rucksack tight over his shoulders.

'Not sure I knew until just now,' said Jay.

* * *

DARKNESS APPROACHED as Jay and Stitch climbed the final few metres towards the inner circle of trees atop Highdown. As the summit came into view, Jay immediately sensed the presence of Cassie and Reuben, and the taste of something deathly. Someone had died on the hilltop.

She glanced at Stitch. He felt it, too. They reached the edge of the inner circle and Stitch fell to his knees. 'Oh my god. They're dead.'

'Not Cassie,' said Jay. 'But Reuben...' Jay walked to the east edge of the trees. Stitch pulled himself up from the ground and scuffed through the grass after her. 'He died here.' She nodded at the ground where she felt that Reuben's life had slipped away into the earth. Her heart sank in her chest. She and Reuben were not close, but he was a good guy, a role model for the younger people in the Interland, and he was Cassie's first love.

'How do you know?' a voice from behind the trees startled Jay, and she instinctively stepped away, opening, scanning, ready to defend, or attack.

'Who are you?' called Stitch.

'My name is Otis,' the voice replied.

'The vision was real,' said Stitch. 'That's him.'

Jay couldn't deny that the boy they'd seen through the earth from across the valley was standing before them. His frizzy afro-hair, his scruffy clothes and over-sized jumper, his stubble, almost a full beard making him look older than the underlying truth that was a boy of no more than seventeen or eighteen years.

'I'm Stitch.'

Jay scowled at Stitch, not sure that they should engage with this boy. They knew nothing about him. And here he was in the location where Reuben had been killed and their best friend had been taken, and may also be dead by now. Jay couldn't read him. His shield was strong, but she dug, chipped away until she opened a crack, or he allowed her a look. He projected no hostility.

She saw he had buried Reuben's body.

Otis motioned for Jay and Stitch to follow him back into the inner circle of trees, entering the copse through a particular opening, an opening that Jay saw as reflecting the entrance to the ancient iron age settlement beneath their feet. He took a seat on a log beside a smouldering fire in the centre of the copse, waiting for Jay and Stitch to join him.

'I saw it happen,' Otis said as Jay took a seat on the opposite side of the fire, choosing to keep her distance.

'Saw what?' asked Stitch.

'Did you know them?' Otis asked. 'The boy, and the girl. They were up here the other night when the Readers came.'

'How?' Jay said. 'How did you manage to be here to see them when there were Readers up here? Unless you're working with them, of course?'

Otis smiled, a thin smile.

'What happened?' said Stitch. 'Tell us what happened to our friends.'

Otis looked at Jay as if for permission. Jay nodded, and he began: 'This is my place,' he said. 'I've been up here for months, a camp over the ledge there,' he nodded to the north. 'The only place I can get any peace, somewhere they leave me alone and I can see them coming a mile off. I get the occasional Reader up here, I can deal with that.' He looked at Stitch, then to Jay. 'I can shield, you see. Better than most, as you've probably figured yourself. I can tell you've got power. More than I've felt from any Reader.' Otis held Jay's eye, but she said nothing. 'I get power up here. I can keep my shield strong. I'm always topped up, so to speak.' Jay knew the benefits of Highdown for the powers. Her own energy levels were high.

'There was a Reader here?' said Stitch.

Otis nodded, 'Oh yes. There were loads of them that night. It was like a Reader gathering. Maybe twenty?'

'Why?' said Jay. 'What were they doing up here?'

'I think they were here for your friends. They arrived a couple of hours before and waited. I was up there.' He nodded proudly up into one of the largest trees that formed the inner ring. 'Biggest test for my shield. Not one of them sniffed me out. Weird thing was, the one in charge had no power. He was all suited-up like a banker or a politician or something. Shirt and jacket and all that, but no power. He had the lot of them in his pocket, though. Barely said anything and they followed him around doing his bidding without a word. Like the pied piper.'

Jay stood and walked around the fire, trying to gather her thoughts. 'How do you know they were here for our friends?'

'Because they moved in as soon as your friends turned up and came into the circle.' Otis relayed to Jay and Stitch the subsequent events. How Reuben was shown no mercy, and Cassie debilitated by the concentrated attack from at least three of the Readers, probably more.

'Why didn't you help them?' asked Stitch, standing, pacing.

'There'd be more than one dead if I'd tried anything.'

'They knew,' said Jay. Stitch frowned at her. 'Somehow, they knew that Cassie and Reuben would be up here, and they took the opportunity to take down two of the strongest of the Given.'

'Strongest?' said Otis.

'Both level seven,' said Stitch, his eyes lingering on Otis to see if he understood. The expression on Otis's face told Jay that he knew all about the power levels.

Jay looked around the perimeter of the trees, half expecting that they were being watched as they sat in the middle of the copse, in plain view. Stitch stood and followed Jay's gaze around the trees.

'There's no one here,' said Otis.

'You don't know that,' said Jay. 'If they can ambush Cassie and Reuben, then they can ambush anyone.'

'I've been up here for long enough to be able to read even the smallest changes in the signals. That night, when your friend was killed, I'd sensed those Readers way before they got here. Sensed your friends, too.'

He paused, frowning.

'What's wrong?' said Stitch.

'You two kind of confused me a bit. You were coming from all directions at once. Thought you were coming at me from the ground, or through the sky at one stage. Thought I was losing it.'

'Where do you think they took Cassie?' Stitch said to Jay.

Jay opened her mouth to respond, but Otis got there first. 'To rehab,' he said. 'The central rehabilitation unit. That's where they take all the Given.'

'Where my dad was,' said Jay.

Otis looked up, his eyes wide. 'You're Jay?' he said, looking from Jay to Stitch and back again. 'Your dad was in the stage one of rehabilitation when he broke out. You're Jay. The level eight with the "C". Can I see it?' He looked towards her wrist.

Jay kept her wrist covered. 'How do you know who I am?'

'Everyone knows. He's Stitch. Well, there are rumours. You two are a legend for those of us still up here. The level eight and the connected. You give hope.' Otis stared at Jay. 'Or at least *used* to.'

'Stop talking,' said Jay.

'People say you went to the Interland. Is it true? You've been there?'

Jay and Stitch exchanged a glance, and Stitch said, 'It's not...'

'Don't say any more,' Jay interrupted.

'So it is true. I knew it was. And is Zadie Lawrence there too? She disappeared. Not a whisper. All the Given stuck out here, left behind to be picked off by Readers. No room in the Ark I guess?'

'It's not like that,' said Stitch, ignoring Jay's glare. 'It's not a place to inhabit. It's a place to regroup and make a plan.'

'Plan for what?'

'How to fight back,' said Stitch. 'To stand up against the oppression, the Readers.'

'What's the plan?' said Otis, a cynicism entering his voice.

Stitch looked into the fire. 'The plan is survival for now.'

Jay said, 'You said something about all the Given stuck out here? How many?'

Otis shook his head. 'Who knows? We all stay deep under-cover. Most prefer to be alone. Less likely someone's going to turn you in for whatever benefits are on offer from the Readers.'

'We need to stick together,' said Stitch.

'Easy for you to say, from the comfort of your sanctuary.'

'But there's a network, right?' said Jay. 'Links between you all on the outside. You can communicate?'

Otis looked up into the trees. 'Kind of. You need someone with more power than me to communicate wide. Not that we'd want to connect any more. Too dangerous, and what's the point?'

Jay scratched her head in frustration, standing up and wandering towards the edge of the circle of trees. At the time Jay had entered the Interland, she knew almost nothing about the extent of the oppression of the Given. Even without their leader, Marcus, there was little to stop the Readers and the

State squeezing out any of the Given who they couldn't *reha-bilitate.*

'What level are you?' asked Stitch.

Otis pulled back his sleeve and showed the number five on his wrist. 'Five?' Stitch said, his mouth remaining open. 'I thought there weren't any level fives?'

'Clearly,' said Otis.

'Alfred said...' Stitch looked to Jay for support.

'Alf's not always right,' said Jay. To Otis: 'So you can shield, we've seen that. What else does a level five have that we don't?'

Otis shrugged. 'Nothing I've figured out.'

'Or nothing you're prepared to share?' said Jay. Her trust in Otis was thin and getting thinner the more time she spent with him. He was hiding something.

'I could come with you?' said Otis. 'Help you find your friend, then go back to the Interland with you?'

Jay shook her head. 'No. We don't know what we're up against yet. And we don't know anything about *you.*' She stood and motioned for Stitch to stand with her.

Otis said: 'There's something coming if my senses are serving me.'

'Like what?' said Stitch.

Otis remained silent. He stroked his beard.

'Look after yourself,' said Stitch, stealing a glance at Jay as if suggesting they take Otis with them. Jay walked away with no acknowledgement of his look.

Otis stood and looked at Stitch, then turned to head back into the trees. 'Good luck.'

12

Jay gazed into the fire but it held no answers. She looked at Stitch, a deep frown etched his forehead, but she couldn't read what was troubling him.

'What's wrong? I feel you're worried about more than the gang of Readers Otis mentioned,' said Jay.

Stitch stirred from his thoughts. 'It's my dad. Something's wrong.' He stood and looked towards the coast. 'I need to see him.' Stitch had been close with his dad at one time, before they drifted. Their connection remained strong, and Stitch often felt his dad's emotions from a distance.

'We can't,' Jay said. 'You know this. If the Readers can pre-empt Cassie and Reuben like they did, we're next.'

Stitch avoided Jay's eyes. He'd already decided. He punished himself for abandoning his dad back when they left the first time. He would not ignore this call for help. 'I'll come with you,' Jay said. 'I'll go see Mum. One hour. No more.'

'What about him?' Stitch nodded towards where Otis had run off into the trees.

'He's hiding something. I don't trust him. The Readers might already be on their way here for us.'

'I don't think so,' said Stitch.

* * *

As Jay manoeuvred the Beast around the corner onto Stitch's street, she turned off the lights and drifted to a stop a few houses short of Stitch's house. All was quiet. A ginger cat crossed the road in front of the car and leapt onto a shallow wall.

'Henry,' said Stitch, his tone soft.

'Henry the cat?'

'Old bugger. Soppy as anything.'

The neighbour's house was dark, but Stitch's dad's place had a light on upstairs. Jay said, 'Looks like he's up?'

'That's the bathroom light. He always leaves it on at night. He's scared of the dark.' Stitch looked up and down the street. 'Look at this place,' he said. 'Half the houses are boarded.' He pointed across the road. 'That's Phil and Sarah's place. It's empty.'

'Things have got bad,' said Jay.

'I thought it was just the cities.'

'So what are you gonna do?' asked Jay. 'It's midnight. Are you going to wake him up for a chat?'

Stitch opened the passenger door. 'I'll see.'

'Let me know when you're done.' Jay tapped the side of her head. 'If I don't hear anything, I'll be back here at 1am sharp. Be ready.'

Stitch closed the door and gave a salute before silently sloping away towards the house. Jay watched him retrieve a key from under a plant pot and open the door.

Outside her mum's house, Jay sat in the car looking at the kitchen window. The houses here were in a similar state to Stitch's. Almost half looked empty, neglected, some of them with chipboard covering the windows. The economy had deteriorated far more than they'd realised from the shelter of the Interland.

The kitchen light was off, but through the kitchen window, Jay saw blue light, could make out flashes of images from the TV in the lounge.

With a sigh, Jay stepped out of the car and gently clicked the door closed. She bypassed the front of the house, choosing instead to take the pathway around to the back. She shinned up the tree and onto the roof outside of her old bedroom window. The Velux was closed; she had to prise it open with her fingers. It swung on its centre hinge. She climbed in, breathing in the familiar scent of her room. Her bedroom was tidy, not like the Readers had left it after turning it inside out to find her dad's notebook. Now, there was nothing out of place. Her bed had been made, the duvet carefully turned back. She sat, running her hand over her soft pillowcase, its freshly washed scent taking Jay back to how it was before. She recalled the closeness with her dad and Sammy, her mum's distaste at everything she did, everything that Sammy did. The old bitter feelings came back.

Floorboards squeaked downstairs. Her mum must be heading to bed. It was a quarter past midnight, forty-five minutes to go until she needed to be back at Stitch's house. If she kept quiet for a moment, gathered a few of her things – a book, a notepad – then she could sneak back out to the roof until it was time. The thought of seeing her Mum made her feel uneasy, a task to be avoided.

Instead, Jay crept out onto the landing. She leaned over the railing to glimpse her mum as she made her way from the bathroom to her bedroom. She had curlers in her hair. She looked older. She'd lost weight in the year since she'd last seen her, and her hair had greyed. The bitterness faded. Jay felt sorry for her mum. She was alone.

She stepped out from the shadows and Sonia let out a little scream, stepping back into the wall and bringing her hand to her mouth. As she recognised her daughter, her expression softened and her hand returned to her side. From a distance, Jay could see that her mum's eyes had welled with tears. 'Hi, Mum.'

'Jay,' she breathed Jay's name as if in awe.

'How are you?' said Jay.

'Ten years off me, you scaring me like that.' Her voice slurred a little, she'd been drinking.

Jay forced a half smile. 'Sorry,' she said.

'Come down, we can have tea?'

Jay hesitated. Only when her mum moved away towards the top of the first floor stairway did Jay move down the loft stairs, as if she needed to keep a steady distance between them.

Jay followed the noise of the kettle into the kitchen where her mum stood up against the work surface, wiping a tear from her eye with the back of her hand. She turned away from Jay, taking two mugs from the cupboard and scrabbling with an unopened box of tea bags. Jay was surprised at the emotion in her mum's face. Sonia Macfarlane, the mum she'd always known, was as hard as a rock, emotionless, spiteful. This woman seemed broken.

'I knew you'd leave,' Sonia said. 'Can't say I blame you.' Jay pulled herself up to sit on the worktop, legs dangling. Sonia continued, 'Where are you living?'

'I'm safe.' There were things she needed to keep secret for her mum's sake.

'Thought as much. You don't just vanish off the face of the

earth. The police were no use. They got all excited for a bit, even put officers outside the house. I reckon they thought I'd buried you all under the patio.' The kettle clicked and the sound of the boiling water subsided. Sonia remained still, staring at the mugs. Then she poured, her hand a little shaky as she held the kettle. Jay struggled for words. This was not the woman Jay remembered.

'The others? Your dad, Sammy? Are they OK?'

'They're fine. Look, Mum, we had to leave. It wasn't you. It's complicated. There were people looking for us.'

'Your dad,' Sonia snapped. 'People were looking for *him*, not you and Sammy. Your dad's the criminal, breaking out of that place. He's the one they wanted. Why'd he have to take you and Sammy?' She turned away from Jay, stifling tears. She opened a drawer and pulled out a teaspoon. Jay reached for the fridge and retrieved the milk, handing it over as her mum avoided eye contact.

'The Readers,' said Jay. 'It was the Readers. That's why we had to go.' Jay read her mum for the first time since entering the house. She'd been trying to avoid it, to keep things on an even level. Her mum did not know that Jay had power, that she was one of the Given, like her dad. She saw her mum's thoughts race around Jay's words: the *Readers*. Her mum knew all about the Readers. Jay wanted to ask about Marcus, how Sonia had got mixed up with him.

'I know about Marcus,' said Jay.

Sonia looked Jay in the eye and revealed everything in her thoughts. The man with the scar, the Reader who tried to wipe Jay off the face of the planet. Marcus. Her mum still had feelings for him. He was Sammy's biological father, there was no doubt about that, although her dad and Sammy never talked about it. But the man in her mum's thoughts was a quiet, unassuming gentleman - not the ruthless Reader who Jay had battled with.

Sonia lowered her gaze. 'He was kind back then,' she said. 'He worked for the State. Probably still does.'

'He was a Reader,' said Jay.

Sonia shook her head. 'Not back then. Well, at least they weren't called Readers back then, more like civil servants,' she smiled. 'He was a government official if you like. He had a good job, he was making a difference, and he was heading for the top of his profession...' Her words trailed off. 'Not like your dad,' she said under her breath.

He got to the top alright, Jay thought to herself.

'I kind of hoped Sammy might get some of his drive, you know. Not your dad's fantasy thinking,' she said, a bitterness returning to her voice.

'And not like me, I guess?'

'No,' her mum said. 'I didn't mean that. You don't know what it was like with your dad.' She stirred the tea, adding sugar to her own mug. 'You still have sugar?' she asked.

'No.'

Her mum squeezed the tea bags on the side of the mugs and dropped them into the bin under the counter. Handing Jay her tea, she said, 'So, has he? Sammy. Has he any of the power like Marcus?'

Jay didn't want to gratify her mum with the knowledge that Marcus's precious genes might have got through to Sammy. 'The powers aren't passed on through genes.' Jay sipped her tea. 'Genes might be a factor, but not the major factor. In truth, it's possible that a lot of it is environmental. People don't know for sure. And anyway, he's not 18 yet, so we wouldn't know.'

'He'd know by now.' Sonia deflated a little.

Jay shook her head, instinctively looking up and out of the window for any signs of movement, aggressors, Readers. She could see the car up against the kerb outside. No sign of any life. 'So how have you been?' Jay asked. 'The streets are empty. Half the houses are boarded.'

'It's this recession. That's what you get from all the protests, the unrest. It does nothing for the economy. When will people realise we need to work together to get through these times? We need to support the State, all push in the same direction.'

'Whatever that direction is?'

'You sound like your dad,' Sonia said, turning to head out of the room. 'Shall we sit down?'

Jay followed and took a seat on the sofa. 'I'm sorry, Mum. I should have been in touch.'

Sonia put her tea down and stepped towards Jay, her arms outstretched. Jay stood for a moment and accepted her mum's embrace. She could smell chardonnay and menthol cigarettes. She hugged her mum for the first time in as long as she could remember. It felt like a dam might burst inside her body, emotions coming crashing through. She felt her mum tremble in her arms, stifling a sob. They stepped apart and sat at opposite ends of the sofa. Jay looked out the back window into the darkness and relaxed a little, sinking back into her seat, cradling her tea.

'They told me to contact them if you came back, if I heard from any of you,' said Sonia.

'Who told you?'

'The authorities. After I had the police out looking for you three, I got a visit from the suits. They were here for the best part of an hour. I felt washed out by the time they left, had to spend a day in bed.'

Jay imagined the work the Readers would have done on her mum, scraping her thoughts, asking questions and pulling information from her head without her knowing. 'What did you say to them?'

'I told them I'd let them know if I heard from you.'

'And will you?' Jay said.

Her mum shook her head. 'There's no way I'd have shopped you then, and I won't now. I've not done everything the way I'd have liked, I'll give you that, but I wouldn't want those lot getting hold of you and Sammy. They said they'd be in touch, that they'd keep a look out for you all.'

'They looked out for us alright,' Jay said.

'What?' Sonia asked.

Jay shook her head and smiled at her mum, seeing the humour in the way she looked with curlers in her hair. She laughed. 'Loving the curlers, Mum.'

Sonia raised her hand to touch her hair like she'd forgotten she had them in. 'Oh my life, sorry, I must look a state.' She laughed.

Jay smiled to herself. Her mum was different. The *house* felt different, as if released from the tension of her childhood. She sipped her tea and talked to her mum about Sammy, about how he'd met a girl who might be good for him. She told her about Cassie and Stitch, how the three of them had become closer than ever. As they talked, Jay relaxed further, and thoughts of the Readers dissolved into the darkness outside. She felt safe again, in her own home.

13

Jay slipped into the alleyway that led to Stitch's house. She'd left her mum's house in a hurry after waking from an unplanned snooze. Sonia had looked hurt at Jay's rapid departure, but she had no choice.

She broke into a run. She could sense power and her blood pumped hard. She crouched to get a look at the house and saw Readers, six or seven of them. They were paired, organised, each group with a fixed position, military-style. Jay stepped back into the cover of darkness to gather her thoughts. Everywhere ran a strong, dark presence of Readers.

Jay and Stitch had often used the hatch as a route into the basement, an old chute for coal that doubled as a perfect access and escape, out of sight of nosy parents. It was never locked when they were kids. It was locked now.

She caught sight of a gardening trowel and rammed it between the patio and the hatch, levering it up. The lock gave way with a loud crack and Jay ducked, sure someone must have heard the noise. All quiet, she swung the hatch open and slid down the chute and onto the concrete floor as the hatch clunked closed behind her.

It was so dark Jay couldn't see her hand in front of her face. She found the stairs, the sliver of light creeping through the door at the top enough for her to see to climb. She took it slowly. In the silence of the basement, each creak of the wooden steps was a thousand times louder in her head. She paused at the top, listening. Voices drifted through from upstairs, but she couldn't make out the words. There was no one in the kitchen, at least no one with power.

The kitchen was empty. Voices came from the front of the house, the front door where Readers moved in and out, passing information, preparing to take Stitch away. 'What about the girl?' a voice said.

'Orders are to finish the boy and head back to base.'

'Leave the girl?'

'A unit is on its way to her mother's house.'

Jay strained to hear the response. A loud crack, the sound of a gun, reverberated through the house, followed by shouting from upstairs. Readers bolted up the stairs. Jay slipped from the safety of the basement, through the kitchen and to the foot of the stairs. She followed a few feet behind, then stepped into a doorway, out of sight. She heard Stitch's dad shouting in Arabic and Stitch, trying to calm him down.

A violent shove from behind and Jay almost lost her footing, spilling onto the landing and slamming into the banisters. A Reader's hand reached for her; she ducked away and opened her mind in readiness to attack. Before she could infiltrate, a heavy thump on the back of her head sent her to the floor. Hands pulled her to stand and shoved her into one of the bedrooms.

'Jay?' Stitch's voice.

She touched the side of her face where she'd knocked it on the floor. A little blood. Nothing serious. A Reader pushed Jay and Stitch back against the window, next to Stitch's dad, Samir.

'Well, what a lucky day,' said one of the Readers.

Jay tried to see the number on his wrist. She sensed he was a six. A group of sixes would be too strong for her and Stitch unless they could get some time to channel their power. But these Readers knew that. They were poised to attack, to knock them down at any sign of power.

They were all crammed into Stitch's bedroom, a room in which Jay had spent a big part of her childhood. It still smelled of his deodorant. Over her shoulder, Jay sensed a white glow coming from the back garden and she turned.

'Eyes on me,' the Reader shouted at Jay, but his shouts trailed off as he caught sight of the glow.

A man crossed the grass, a magical white glow all around him. Jay looked at Stitch, and then to Samir. Both were transfixed. The Reader stepped towards the window, pushing Jay and Stitch aside.

'What is it?' Stitch whispered to Jay. Jay shrugged. Three more Readers entered the room, one of them shouting to the leader to move out with Stitch and Jay. But he too trailed off at the sight of the white light now pouring over the back of the house and in through Stitch's bedroom window.

The Readers were transfixed by the vision. They stared for a moment and then edged backwards, away from the window. The light intensified and seemed to shimmer around the Readers in the room, forcing them back and out through the door. Jay watched as they left. She looked back to the garden, where Stitch and Samir continued to stare. The glow subsided, leaving Jay's eyes struggling to focus. With the retreat of the glow, the figure of the man was gone.

'What was that...' Stitch said.

'*Madha? 'ana la 'afham*,' breathed Samir.

The Readers had retreated to the ground floor. Voices from downstairs grew louder in argument. Jay nudged into Stitch. 'We need to go. How do we get out?' Stitch looked towards the stairs. 'Not that way,' said Jay.

'There's a balcony on Dad's room, we can jump. Follow me.' Stitch bolted.

Samir followed with Jay close behind. She heard heavy footsteps rushing up the stairs. The three of them slipped into Samir's bedroom as the Readers piled back into Stitch's room, now empty. There were shouts, orders to find them. Stitch edged out onto the balcony.

"*ana kabir fi alsini ldhlk*,' Samir said, stepping out onto the ledge with his son, then he jumped, a clean landing turning into a forward roll. Stitch smiled at Jay, shrugged, then jumped, following his dad into the darkness. As Stitch scrambled to his feet on the grass below, the door of the bedroom slammed against the wall. Two Readers fell into the room and caught sight of Jay. Jay turned and threw herself off the balcony, landing heavily and sprawling onto the grass. She scrambled to her feet and ran towards the back fence where Samir was already up and over, Stitch close behind him. Jay sat astride the top of the fence just as the first Reader landed in the back garden and another three came into view, running around the side of the house from the front. She slid down the fence, catching and grazing her shin on the shiplap. She cried out. Stitch turned and Jay waved him on. 'End of the alleyway, go,' she shouted. She bit her lip and swallowed the pain, taking off after Stitch.

'Keys,' said Stitch, holding out his hands as Jay turned the corner. She pulled them from her back pocket and threw them. He fumbled at the passenger door as Samir doubled over, catching his breath. Jay ran around to the driver's door, looking back down the alleyway as she slammed into the car.

'Stitch,' she said, seeing three Readers powering down the alley towards them. 'We need to leave. Like... now.'

Stitch got the door open, jumped in and leaned over to open Jay's door and then into the back to unlock the door for Samir. The three escapees each locked their doors from the inside as Readers descended on the car, pulling at the handles. Jay fumbled with the keys. The Reader at the back of the car stopped pulling at the door and Jay saw out of the corner of her eye that he was trying to dig into Samir, influencing. Samir turned towards the Reader, his expression neutral.

'Jay...' Stitch said.

'I know,' said Jay, at last getting hold of the ignition key.

'Jay...' Stitch repeated, watching his dad as he stared at the Reader. Samir's hand moved towards the door lock as if he were about to open it.

'Jay!' Stitch screamed, launching himself towards the back door to stop his dad unlocking it.

'I know,' Jay shouted, the engine catching just as Samir had switched the door catch. Two of the Readers pulled at the handle, the car already moving. The door swung open and one of the Readers managed to get a hold on Samir's top, holding tight as the car gathered speed. Stitch grabbed at the Reader's hand, prising his fingers from Samir. Jay put her foot down, the front wheels of the old Ford turning in the gravel until they gained traction and the car lurched forward. The Reader's hand was yanked away, strands of Samir's top remaining in his fingernails. The car swung around, and the door slammed shut, Samir slumping back into his seat and Stitch lying prone halfway between the front and back of the car.

14

The heavy door swung slowly inwards with a clunk, startling Cassie. Hinton peered inside before ushering one of his Readers to a position in the corner of the room.

'What's he for?' said Cassie, remaining seated.

'Wouldn't want you getting any ideas about roughing me up, would we? I hear you have some skills in that department?'

Cassie had already thought about it, but she was so weak she could barely stand. 'What do you want with me?'

'Nothing,' he smiled. 'You're our guest. Think of this as your weekend away, your countryside break from a life underground.' The Reader laughed, and Cassie lowered her gaze. She would avoid meaningful conversation, focussing simply on regaining strength. 'Seriously though, Cassie. You're here to help entice your friend Jay for a visit.' He gestured around the room. 'You think she'll like it here?'

'She won't come here.'

'How can she resist? You're giving off a distress signal as we speak. The wonderful thing about my little invention here, is its functionality in re-radiating the energy. Inside here, the metal *reflects*. Not only will she sense you, but that signal is amplified.' He laughed. 'Even Jay won't be able to resist, however scared she is. She'll smell you out like you're a skunk on overdrive. What do you think?'

'I think Jay and Stitch will take your head off.'

'Stitch? He won't be troubling us anymore.'

Cassie looked at Hinton, dismissing any attempt to read him. Stitch can't have been taken prisoner. She'd have felt it. If he'd been killed, she'd have sensed it for sure. Still, doubt crept into her mind. She was sitting in a steel box, after all. 'Why are you doing this?'

Hinton paced the room, a half smile on his face.

She could feel his desire to brag, to boast about his wonderful plans, but he hesitated.

'You've got nothing,' Cassie said. 'This is just your personal little crusade. You're weak. No power, no plan.'

'Hush,' he whispered. 'You're just bait. Jay's the one we need in here, and now that Stitch has gone, there's nothing to get in our way.'

'Then what?' said Cassie.

'Then it's a little journey to the Interland, to the source, to see if we can put an end to the powers. For good.'

'Your lot need the source as much as the Given...'

'Not true,' Hinton interrupted. He smiled, unable to contain himself. 'Readers draw power from somewhere else,' he said, almost a whisper. 'So, you see, once the source has been destroyed, there's nothing else to threaten the leadership, and the only thing between us and the source is already on her way here, thanks to you.'

15

Jay pulled the car into the car park at Highdown, while Stitch and Samir slept. No one had spoken since they left Stitch's house just an hour before. They were in a daze, exhausted and confused. Jay was naturally drawn back to Highdown, her thinking space, but she felt no pull to climb to the summit. She wound her seat back, closed her eyes and fell asleep almost immediately.

It was light when Jay woke. She rubbed the sleep from her eyes and peered through the windscreen. Stitch was sat on a bench at the edge of the car park smoking a cigarette. Samir snored in the back seat. Jay closed her car door gently so as not to wake him; the sweet sound of birdsong reminded her of Sammy. Toyah called him the *sparrow whisperer*.

Stitch nodded as she took a seat next to him on the bench.

'What happened back there? What was that thing? It was like a ghost or something?'

They remained silent for a minute, looking up into the trees that peppered the slope in front of them. Jay shook her head slowly. 'More like a mirage, or a projection. Did you feel it?'

'Saved our arses.'

'I think that was the point,' said Jay. 'We have a guardian angel.'

'Who?'

Jay shrugged, 'Search me. Not from the Interland. Zadie doesn't have that kind of power.'

'No one has power like that,' said Stitch, flicking his cigarette end into the grass. 'It was weird. I can't get it straight in my head, but it was like the ground opened up and we were on the edge of something.'

'I felt that too. A wider connection. Whatever it is, it's helping us. It pushed those Readers away.'

'What about *him*?' Stitch said, nodding up at the slope. 'Otis. You think he came to our rescue?'

Jay shook her head, but Stitch pressed, 'He's a level five. If Alf's right, they have a different sort of power.'

'No way. That boy's a loner.'

Stitch looked sideways at Jay. 'I don't think we should disregard him. He could help.'

'I'm not sure we can trust him.' Jay shook her head again, and spoke firmly. 'Someone knew where we were going last night.'

Stitch remained quiet for a minute. 'Something is twisted in the energy of this place, but it's not him,' he said.

'What do you mean?'

'I don't know. Just a feeling. Twisted, dark, bitter. A feeling, a taste.' Stitch looked at Jay. 'You know what I mean,' he said, impatience in his voice.

Jay had felt it too, but it made no sense. What she felt was *Marcus.*

She took a breath and searched inside herself, her connection to the ground beneath her feet, the life that stretched through the earth. In her bones, she knew that Stitch was right.

Jay pushed Marcus from her mind and looked back at the car. 'What are we going to do with your dad?'

'We talked last night, before the chaos. It was good. He even spoke English for most of it. He reverts to Arabic when he's under pressure. I don't even think he realises he's doing it.'

'Instinctive,' said Jay.

'Against my better judgement,' Stitch said. 'We will need the old man if we're going to get through all the Readers at the prison.' He smiled, affection in his expression.

'Why?'

'Mum worked on that development. She knew the layout, and they talked about it. There might be a way in without attracting undue attention.'

'Good work, boys,' Jay said, feeling like it was about time they had a piece of good fortune. She stood to make her way back to the car. 'I'll grab a map. We can make a plan.'

16

Davey pulled off his crash helmet, careful to remain out of sight of Jay and Stitch. He leaned the motorbike onto its stand and stepped off. A man slept on the back seat and Davey recognised Stitch's dad. He'd been watching last night but hadn't intervened. He'd been under strict orders from Zadie to keep his distance. Observe and report.

He placed his crash helmet on the forest floor and pulled off his jacket. He took a seat on a log, a vantage point from which to watch over Jay and Stitch, still sat on the bench at the edge of the hill.

It was just three minutes until the pre-arranged time for his next communication with Zadie. He trusted Zadie with his life. She'd saved him. She took him in, trained him, supported him. If Zadie didn't trust Jay to do the job of finding Cassie, then she had good reason.

He looked again at his watch. It was time.

Clearing his mind, Davey connected to the source and to Zadie's consciousness. Without moving his lips, he described the events of the raid at Stitch's house, the white glow, their escape, and the scene in front of him now.

Tentatively, Davey asked Zadie what was going on. Should he join with Jay and Stitch, to support their mission to find Cassie and protect them from the sudden influx of Readers? The message he received was unequivocal. Keep to the plan. Observe, report back. The communication ended.

17

Sammy's head torch played beams of light and shadow against the rock walls of the tunnel. He was tempted to pull himself up through the roof opening into the Free Cave for some peace, see if he could get a little further along the uncharted passageways beyond the high ledge. But not without Toyah, he thought to himself.

The walk from his room in the residential section to the main cavern where food was served was only ten minutes. On the way, he passed the opening that led down to the source and felt its gentle pull. No one was allowed into the source rooms without the knowledge and supervision of a level eight which meant Zadie, now that Jay was out on a mission.

Zadie had become difficult to read. Sammy felt she was shielding. But why? He'd seen her in snatched, whispered conversations with some of her closest companions. If Jay were here, she'd quickly get to the heart of the situation by reading it, not allowing her imagination to do the talking the way Sammy did. The bottom line was Zadie Lawrence made Sammy nervous.

'Stuffing your face as usual?' Sammy said, taking a seat beside his friend Pinto.

'You want some?' Pinto said, pushing his plate towards Sammy.

Sammy shook his head. 'Where's Toyah?'

Pinto shrugged. He finished his food, using his bread to scrape up the last of the stew. 'You want to play?'

Sammy looked around. No sign of Toyah. Then back to Pinto. 'Chess?'

Pinto shook his head. 'Let's fly,' he said with a grin.

Despite neither of them having a marking yet, with Pinto, Sammy could connect and then project a common vision from a position away from their bodies. It was like generating a communal out-of-body experience. He'd tried it with Toyah, but it didn't seem to work with anyone but Pinto.

Sammy held out his hands. Pinto took them and they both closed their eyes. They had this process to connection well-honed. Sammy felt Pinto's energy matching his own as their bodies connected. A warmth filled Sammy's body. He allowed the energy to flow. Pinto had power, as much as his sister Toyah, if not more. Pinto's grip tightened on Sammy's hands and he could feel the warmth lifting him, elevate them both in mind.

Sammy saw himself from above, locked together with Pinto. He could see the tops of their heads, the smile on Pinto's face. Their connected mind's eye rose to the roof of the cavern and drifted further up towards the opening in the rocks. With Pinto's pushing and shoving, Sammy saw into the trees beyond the cavern. Like a bird, Sammy pushed down with a force that projected their vision further up into the rocks. He glimpsed the sun, felt a breeze on his face from the outside.

Back in the cavern, he opened his eyes and saw the grin

still plastered on Pinto's face before he too opened his eyes. 'We could have gone higher,' said Pinto, releasing Sammy's hands and looking into the roof of the cave.

Sammy jumped to his feet. 'Hey, I'm hungry, follow me,' he said. He led Pinto through a narrow opening and into a side cavern that had been converted into a cooking area, with a series of open fire pits with makeshift chimneys in the roof. There were three people with their backs to Sammy and Pinto, preparing food for the evening meal. He turned to Pinto and put a finger to his lips as they crept through the room and continued to another opening. This next room was stocked with shelves full of food. There were tins, packets and all the things you'd expect to see in a supermarket in the outside world, collected by Runners. Then there were crates of vegetables and fruit, some home-grown in the allotments on the east side of the Interland, and some foraged from the outside world.

Sammy waved for Pinto to keep up as he made his way to the far end of the stores and knelt beside the sacks of rice. He shifted one of the sacks to the side to reveal a small opening, just big enough for someone to crawl through. Pinto peered inside, mouth open. 'Where does it go?'

'This passage connects up with the passages that lead to the Free Cave. I've used this passage to move between my room and the stores.'

Pinto shoved Sammy. 'No, you haven't. Why?'

'Midnight food run,' Sammy grinned, pulling a torch from his pocket and shining it into the opening. He was about to look away when he caught sight of something inside he'd not seen before. A stash of crates lined up against the wall of the tunnel.

'What is it?' asked Pinto.

Sammy moved further into the tunnel to see if he could read the writing on the side of the crates. 'Fertiliser,' he said.

Seeing crates of fertiliser wasn't necessarily strange given that they might use it for the allotments, but next to the crates were boxes with electronics, and a stash of batteries. Sammy knew well enough from the TV shows he used to watch in the outside world. This stuff was for making bombs.

'Hey.' A voice from behind them made Sammy jump and Pinto fall backwards. Sammy knocked his head on the ceiling of the tunnel as he tried to edge backwards in a rush.

It was Toyah. Sammy stood and smiled, a warm blush sweeping his face.

She put her hands on her hips and looked at her little brother. 'I've been looking all over for you, Pinto. You and me are on kitchen duty.'

'Look no further, I'm here. I was here before you,' Pinto said, storming out of the storeroom and into the kitchen where he plucked an apron from a hook on the wall. Sammy could smell chopped onions frying.

'What are you two up to?' said Toyah as Sammy shoved the rice sack back into place over the entrance to the tunnel.

'Nothing, just playing,' said Sammy. 'You want to do something?'

She motioned towards the kitchen. 'I'm on rota.'

'I'll help then,' said Sammy.

'Don't be stupid. Go and do something. It'll be your turn soon enough.'

Sammy shrugged. 'Later then?'

Toyah nodded and went to join Pinto as Sammy made for the exit.

* * *

ON HIS WAY back to his room, Sammy saw Zadie emerge from the passageway that led down to the source. He ducked into an alcove in the wall so that she wouldn't see him. She stepped out from the passageway and headed in the direction of the main hall. As she disappeared around a corner, Sammy made his way down towards the source, an urge to head into the heart of the Interland.

Zadie had questioned Sammy, along with his dad, the morning Jay and Stitch had slipped out of the Interland. She had convinced Ben that sending Davey was the only way to keep Jay safe. His dad seemed to buy the story, but Sammy hadn't been convinced.

He followed the steps down to the lowest point of the Interland. He lit two of the candles and approached the three streams of water that bubbled as they came together and flowed away into the rocks below. There was something magical in the shimmering water: hints of colours and sparkles that gave a sense of the power within.

He placed his hand in the pool.

A shimmer of light filled the cave. He felt energy flow through him more than ever before. Whatever power he had was edging closer to the surface as he approached his 18th birthday. Sammy breathed in to the energy, accepted its connection. The light intensified, and he shielded his eyes. When his eyes finally adjusted to the light, he saw he was no longer inside the cave but soaring high above the trees on the outside of the Interland. He had the eyes of a bird.

His vision blurred. The trees below, the hills, and the wider landscape came at him in colours, like through a thermal lens. The trees shone yellow, the hills red, as he swept towards the coast. He recognised the River Arun, its meandering form shining orange, and swooped to follow its path towards the sea, moving faster than he could ever have imagined. Within seconds, he was above the estuary and turning to the east, along the coast. As he looked to the north, he saw the striking energy in the colours of the hills.

Then a dull ache filled his head as a shadow passed before his vision. The water and trees were tainted with an inky-black stain that lurked in the valleys between the hill forts on the downs, and spread in all directions, edging towards the hills, the coast, the Interland.

The piercing bright light returned. The hills, valleys and the landscape disappeared once more. Feeling came back to Sammy's legs just as they gave way and he slumped to the floor of the cave. The candles had been extinguished and the only sound was the trickle of the three streams of water meeting in the centre of the pillar. Sammy reached out his hands to feel for the wall, edging himself to stand. He felt his way to the foot of the stairwell, his mind still with the eye of the bird, soaring above the surface of the earth. He struggled to find meaning in the darkness of the valleys, the swirling black mist that threatened the Interland.

At the foot of the stairs, a chink of light penetrated from above, allowing him to balance himself. With a hand on the wall, and a pounding in his head, Sammy crept back up the steps.

* * *

IT WASN'T until the next day that Sammy finally tracked Toyah down to the reading room. The experience at the source had shaken him. He had lain awake most of the night, pushing thoughts and theories around his head. The darkness he saw hinted at a shift in the power. Without Jay, he had no way to decipher it. All he knew was that there was a growing sense that he needed to get away from the Interland. He needed to find Jay.

Sammy closed the book he'd been pretending to read and glanced at Toyah. 'Hey, do you think...'

Toyah interrupted him with a finger to her lips. She nodded towards the woman on the other side of the reading room with her head in a hardback. Sammy shrugged and Toyah again put her finger to her lips. He caught a slight smile on her face as she returned to her book. Her smooth, dark complexion was like her brother's, if a little darker. Her hair used to hang below her shoulders, but she'd cropped it a couple of weeks back, close to her head so that it was shorter than Sammy's own hair. Pinto had laughed when she'd had it cut, but Sammy had gasped. With nothing to hide her face, Sammy saw her genuine beauty. She was way too good for him. Two years older and a long way out of his league.

The woman on the other side of the room closed her book and returned it to the shelf before leaving. 'We have to go,' Sammy said.

Toyah looked at him quizzically. 'What? Go where?'

'Away from here,' Sammy said. 'I'm worried about Jay. I need your help.'

'You're kidding, right?' said Toyah, concern in her eyes. 'We're lucky to have found the safety of this place.'

Sammy sighed. He couldn't explain his feeling, he just knew. They were all in danger. 'Look,' he said. 'I think we should leave. We can get Pinto, and Dad...'

'Pinto and me are going nowhere.' She closed her book. 'Do you know what we went through to get here?' Sammy lowered his head, thinking that he *would* know if she'd trusted him enough to tell him. 'We spent half of Pinto's life finding this place,' she said. 'We're not leaving.'

Sammy could see it was no use arguing with her. He

thought he might speak to his dad. Ben always knew what to do. But the distance that had opened up between them in the Interland made it difficult. Ben was not the father he'd grown up with. He needed to convince Toyah himself. He needed more proof.

18

The car cantered between the villages of the Downs, Jay making their way east to the prison. Samir had insisted on sitting in the front, relegating Stitch to the back seat. He asked question after question, trying to make sense of what Jay and Stitch were doing. Who were these Readers? Why were they pursuing his son?

'Why do they have your friend? What do they want with her?' Samir said.

'You've not spoken this much English since mum died,' Stitch said from the back of the car.

Samir said nothing, turning to the window. Jay looked at Stitch in the rear-view mirror. He shrugged.

Samir said, 'I'm sorry. It's been hard for you.'

'It's OK,' Stitch interrupted, placing a hand on his dad's shoulder.

Without shifting his gaze from the fields beyond his window, Samir reached to place his own hand over that of his son.

'We think they took her because she has power – simply because she is one of the Given,' said Jay.

'And then they killed her friend?' said Samir.

'Reuben,' Stitch said. 'Yes.'

A dark shadow moved at the side of the road. Before Jay could fully take it in, the car veered sharply, as if pulled into the verge by a magnetic force. She threw her weight into the steering wheel to keep it straight and the car on the road.

'What's wrong?' said Stitch.

'The car,' Jay gasped, 'I can't... hold... it.' Samir leaned across to help Jay hold the wheel. Jay slammed her foot on the brake pedal, but as soon as she did, the car pulled more dramatically to the left, overcoming both Jay and Samir. They ploughed through a fence, a hedge, and launched over a shallow ledge into a lake. Jay's last memory before everything turned white was of the tranquillity of the vast, still surface of the water and the silence inside the car. Samir slid back into his seat and Stitch slammed into his side door as the car twisted in the air.

There was no jolt as they hit the water. There was no sound.

* * *

JAY LAY face down on a hard, dusty-dry surface, stones digging into her torso and legs. She lifted her head and spat grime from her mouth. Stitch lay beside her. White light poured from the sky, bleaching everything so that Jay could see nothing more than a few feet around her, the rest of the land-scape hidden inside the blinding light, a white glow like they had seen in Stitch's back garden. She shielded her eyes as the landscape took form.

They were on an island in the lake, no more than twenty feet across, surrounded by water. 'Dad?' called Stitch, his voice croaky and his legs unstable as he tried to get to his feet. He too shielded his eyes from the bright light. Stood together, the two friends gazed out across the lake, a surreal sense that they were not in the same world they'd left just a moment before.

There was no sign of Samir.

'Where's the car?' said Jay.

Stitch limped towards the shore. He scanned the perfectly smooth surface of the water. 'Where's the road?' All around them was nothing but water. No sign of an end to the lake, a road, hedge line, nothing. The landscape was the same in all directions.

'There,' Jay said, pointing to the distance, 'there's the shore.'

'That's another island,' said Stitch.

'And there,' said Jay, shielding her eyes in the light to see another small island, and another. 'There's a circle of them.' They stood on a small island in the middle of an apparently endless expanse of water, other small islands forming a circle around them, each island perhaps a hundred feet away from the next. On each island there stood a single tree, reaching from its centre into the sky. Nothing else but yellow dust and stones.

Stitch looked at Jay. 'Are we dead?'

Jay wobbled on her feet, and Stitch steadied her with a hand. 'Can you feel anything?' asked Jay. 'I mean power, energy?'

Stitch shook his head. 'Nothing.' He looked out across the endless lake. 'Dad!' he shouted.

'He's not here,' said Jay

'He must be! We have to find him.'

'I mean he's not *here*, in this place, or time, or whatever this is.'

Stitch looked distraught. 'What is *happening?*'

'This is *not* the place we just left.'

Stitch studied his shoes for a moment, then stroked his jumper as if trying to find out whether it was real, whether he was physically present. 'Maybe it's like up at Highdown? Like when we connected and travelled through the environment to that boy, Otis? This is like that?'

'I don't know,' Jay said, pacing the perimeter of the little island and looking up at the tree.

'There! Look!' said Stitch. Jay followed his gaze towards the island nearest to them. A white glow emanated from the foot of the tree and then fizzled and died. A figure stepped out from the shadow of the tree. It was a man, tall, skinny.

The man held a hand aloft in greeting. 'Jay? Stitch?'

Jay and Stitch looked at each other and then back to the man, coming into view as he approached the shore of his little island. Jay could see that he was a little older than them, perhaps late twenties or early thirties, with dark skin. 'Who are you?' said Jay. 'Where are we?'

'Sorry for the drama,' he said. 'I wasn't sure if this would be possible.' He scanned the lake and other islands. He had an accent Jay couldn't place – possibly South African. 'Can you see the source, on your island?' Jay and Stitch looked behind them, seeing only the tree. They looked back to the man, confused. 'At the foot of the tree, are there three streams of water coming from the centre of the trunk and down into the ground?'

Jay stepped closer to the tree and crouched. She dug with her hands until she felt dampness in the soil. She dug further until she exposed three streams of water, combining amongst the tangle of tree roots and soaking away as a single flow into the ground. 'Stitch, look,' she said.

Stitch joined her. 'Like at the Interland,' he said.

Jay stood and turned towards the man. 'What...? Where are we?'

'Is the source there?' the man asked.

'Yes, but...'

'Good,' he said. 'We can be thankful for that at least.' He pointed then, towards the islands on the other side of the circle, the ones furthest away. 'See there? Without the source, the island dies, like those three.'

Jay looked closer. Three of the islands in the distance were blackened as if scorched by fire. Their trees without leaves, trunks charred. 'What happened?'

The man waded towards Jay and Stitch until the water level reached his knees, and he stopped. 'Do you know where we are, Jay?' he called across the water.

Jay shook her head but then found herself saying, 'Yes.' She searched her mind for a name but again felt lost.

'It's not easy to explain in words. In fact, I think you might know better than me where we are. Personally, I think of it as a kind of inner space, where the energy of the environment combines with that of the people, but that's just the way my brain interprets it.'

'Why are we here?'

'Because I brought you here,' the man smiled.

'What for?' asked Stitch.

The man pulled back the sleeve of his left arm, showing Jay and Stitch the marking "8C". Jay stepped back. 'Same as me...'

'You thought you were the only one?' he said. Jay nodded, lost for words. 'Almost right. There are not many. Well, there are eight, exactly, and eight connecting partners like Stitch here.'

Stitch and Jay exchanged confused glances, the information slowly seeping into Jay's understanding, connecting the pieces of the jigsaw that had been there all along, just without coherence. Eight islands, eight sources, and eight people at level 8C. The man nodded at Jay as if reading her understanding. 'This is the first time I've been able to do this, to connect with another 8C in this physical way. You are the first one that's been strong enough, receptive enough.' He smiled, and Jay sensed his joy and excitement.

'I still don't understand why we are here?' Jay said, desperate to untangle her confusion.

He nodded towards the tree behind them. 'To stop your island from going the same way as those over there, so to speak. Which is what will happen if we don't stop what's coming.'

The blackened islands were charred and dead, shadowed in darkness.

The man sat down in the water so it came level with his chest and the tops of his knees. Stitch shot Jay a look that questioned the man's sanity. 'This place,' the man said, 'if it can be called a *place*, is a representation. I'm not sure if it's a construct of my head, my energy and power, or yours, or a combination. It doesn't matter, it comes from deep within, not from our conscious selves. The important thing is what it shows us.' Jay and Stitch remained silent, Jay looking around the lake at the other seven islands in turn, Stitch unable to drag his gaze from the man. 'See there?' The man pointed towards the water. A swirling stream of black water flowed between the two islands. The man stood, water dripping from his trousers. He stepped backwards until his feet returned to dry land. He continued to point at the sinister-looking black swirls, like black paint, or an oil slick drifting and swirling with the currents in the water.

'What is it?' asked Stitch.

'Three of the islands are black already. Five remain, but the darkness is expanding. It's like a hunger.' The man kept his eyes trained on the swirling black streams in the water that flowed between their islands. 'It's not just in your country that the Given exist, you know that?' Stitch and Jay looked at each other and nodded. They knew of the power beyond their own country's shores, despite the State restricting information. And, through the source, they'd sensed a communication that went further. 'And, where you have the Given, you have Readers, if you have a manipulator.'

'A what?' said Stitch.

'Someone who controls them. A manipulator. Someone who transcends the power of the Given and of the Readers. Your manipulator has the power to reduce the Given, and control the Readers,' the man said. Jay thought about Marcus. His scar, originally generated by a reduction and a transformation that created a level eight Reader. Someone had transformed Marcus – the manipulator.

Zadie too had a scar to show that she had been reduced. But she was not transformed. She remained strong, rebuilt her power as one of the Given.

Jay looked at Stitch and saw the same question in his eyes. Had Marcus survived the attack at the Interland gateway?

'So a manipulator has Cassie?' asked Stitch.

'I think that's likely. But you need to see the bigger picture. Look around you. This darkness will soon consume all our islands, and all of our lands will be lost. Your land needs your *connection*.'

'Connection?' repeated Jay.

'And Stitch needs your connection. Without you, Jay, your friend is vulnerable. The same as my counterpart – my level "C".'

Jay stole a glance at Stitch as he stared at the man, like he was trying to absorb the information. She turned back to the man. 'Why does the manipulator want Cassie?' said Jay.

'He wants *you*, Jay. Cassie is the bait. You are the 8C. Once he has you, the source and your Interland will be unprotected.'

The three fell silent, watching the ripples carve across the lake. The thought that she could be the target of the Readers and this manipulator sent fear running through Jay's veins once more.

The man spoke. 'There are three dead islands. Once the manipulator has you, Jay, your island will be the fourth.'

Dark clouds gathered above their heads, over the islands, reflecting the swirling blackness in the lake. 'But our Interland is safe,' said Jay. 'It's protected. There's Zadie, and all the level six and sevens.'

'What level is this manipulator, anyway?' asked Stitch.

'The manipulators no longer have levels. They were once part of the Given, but they rejected the power. The act of rejection generates a polar opposite reaction, a response in the energy that becomes as powerful – *more* powerful. The manipulator in this land, your land, we think, was a particularly powerful member of the Given before he rejected the power.'

Jay shook her head. 'Who is he? How did he reject his power?'

'We don't know. But a true and complete rejection of what is given brings the greatest of the reactive power – a darker power.'

Stitch crouched by the water, watching as the black swirls moved past the island. He reached out to touch the water. 'No,' screamed the man from the other side of the water.

But it was too late. Stitch had dipped his hand in the inky blackness. Steam rose from the water as Stitch screamed and withdrew his hand. The water bubbled, and the blackness intensified. Stitch rolled back onto the shore, his legs on the edge of the water, his foot dangling dangerously close to the expanding blackness. Jay lurched at him, pulling his leg away from the water. Stitch held his own wrist, his fingers burning, sizzling, the skin peeling back like the layers of an onion. He doubled over, retreating into a foetal position, holding on to his hand as if trying to stop it from disintegrating.

'What do I do?' Jay shouted over the water to the man, but he was gone. The white light came once more, and the islands dissolved into the fog. Stitch's whimpers turned to screams that reached such a volume Jay could do nothing but hold her ears.

Jay placed a hand on Stitch as he curled tighter. She felt hopeless and alone. The black swirls expanded and circled the island. Her heart raced, a thumping pain in her head distorting her vision. She closed her eyes and slowed her breathing. Elements of her world had slotted into place – releasing some of the tangles in her mind. The power, the source, and the connections with the environment went far beyond the boundaries of Jay's world. There was a bigger picture, a greater cause than personal freedom. The threat from the Readers was a threat to the very existence of the Given and the environment as they knew it.

Stitch lay motionless. Jay looked into the water at her own reflection in the gloss-black surface. She was alone. The girl in front of her looked spent and weak. Without Stitch, and without a connection between Nature and all the Given, she saw no hope for the resistance to the Readers, and the master manipulator lurking in the shadows.

PART III

19

Jay woke in the front seat of the car, her hands on the steering wheel. Samir was slumped in the passenger seat, eyes closed. Stitch leaned up against the back door, his cheek flattened against the window. The car's front end was submerged in the water of the lake. Jay leaned forward to look for islands, but there was nothing but water for as far as she could see, a light mist drifting across the lake's surface in the far distance.

She opened the door, lifting her feet to avoid the water gushing in to fill the driver's side footwell. Stitch stirred in the back, sitting to peer through to the front of the car.

'Your hand OK?' Jay asked.

'Feels weird.' Stitch and Jay exchanged a look. The skin on his hand was red, but seemed to cause Stitch no pain or discomfort. Without words, they acknowledged their shared experience. Stitch nudged his dad on the shoulder. 'Hey, wake up.'

Samir jolted awake, his eyes wide, streams of Arabic flowing from his lips. 'Dad,' Stitch tried to calm him, 'it's OK, we're OK.'

'What happened?' Samir said in English.

Jay and Stitch silently agreed to keep their experience to themselves for the time being. 'It's an old car, must have been a problem with the steering,' said Stitch.

Samir pushed open his door then recoiled at the sight of water flowing in, covering his feet. He grunted, speaking again in Arabic before stepping out into the water and wading the few feet to the shore. Jay and Stitch followed, the three of them standing on the shore looking at the car.

'If what we just experienced was real, then we need to get back to the Interland,' said Stitch. 'We can't protect the source from here.'

'Not before we get Cassie,' said Jay.

'You heard that man,' said Stitch, leaning close to Jay, fear in his eyes.

'What man?' said Samir.

Ignoring Samir, Jay said, 'We find Cassie first. Then we head back.' Jay turned back to the car and waded around to the driver's door.

'There'll be nothing to go back to if we don't leave now,' Stitch called after her. 'If he's right, the reason they have Cassie is to bait you, and me probably.'

'What man?' Samir repeated, his tone more urgent.

'I'm not leaving her there,' said Jay. Despite her fear, she knew in her heart that she wouldn't leave her friend.

Samir looked from Jay to his son and back again. 'What are you two talking about? Stitch?'

'Nothing,' said Jay. 'Stick to the plan.' She positioned herself to push the car up the shallow slope and onto the shore. 'You two going to help me get this car back on the road?'

Stitch splashed around to the front and Samir to the passenger door. With effort, they managed to roll the car backwards out of the lake, water pouring from the engine bay. Jay lifted the bonnet. 'See if she'll start,' she called to Stitch. He jumped into the driver's seat and turned the key. The starter motor whirred, and the engine turned but didn't start.

'There'll be water in the fuel,' said Samir, joining Jay at the front of the car. Jay leaned in and pumped the fuel supply hose a few times, then asked Stitch to try again. This time the engine caught and Stitch stepped on the accelerator to keep it ticking over.

20

Sammy barely touched his food. Instead, he watched as Zadie ate and spoke with her colleagues, their heads bowed, eyes furtive. Sammy's lack of trust for Zadie was matched only by his disdain for the two at her side. Both Simon and Jared were climbers, looking for attention and power. They'd do anything to get up into the realms of Zadie's world. As far as Sammy could remember, they were both at level six. Powerful enough, but always wanting more.

Pinto and Toyah sat with Sammy, listening intently to Alfred. He was their oracle, a mine of wisdom from his years as a bookseller and a double agent. There were few that knew more than Alfred about the inner workings of the State and the motives of the Readers.

'She looks harmless,' said Pinto, nodding towards the portrait of Sasha Colden on the wall above Zadie's head.

'Zadie?' said Alfred, knowing well enough that Pinto meant Sasha. Pinto laughed and Sammy saw the joy in Alfred's eyes at messing with Pinto. Alfred clearly adored Pinto, they had a special bond, and Alfred had said before he felt certain that Pinto had something strong developing, something unusual, a level-five. Toyah, at nineteen, had a clear number six on her wrist. Alfred always expressed surprise that her number wasn't higher, given the strength of the energy he could feel from her – but then, Alfred often exaggerated.

'She was far from harmless if you were a Reader,' Alfred said. 'Sasha Colden was lethal. Nothing touched her when she had her connected companion with her.'

'Who was her companion?' asked Pinto.

'Like Stitch, the level "C". We don't know who Sasha's level-C was, but we know they died, and Sasha lost something of her power too.'

Toyah pulled her sleeve back and scratched gently at her number six. Sammy watched as she studied it, turning away when she caught him looking. He shielded his thoughts. His shielding power was not strong, but enough to confuse. He looked again to see that Toyah had returned her attention to her wrist, a smile on her face and a hint of a blush on her face. For him? Sammy barely dared hope.

'You think I'll be a level eight, like Sasha, and Zadie, and like Jay?' asked Pinto.

Alfred slung an arm around his shoulder and pulled him close. 'My boy, I think it's possible. But, remember, it's not just the level eights that make this community tick. We need people at all levels to do the work if we are ever going to break free of the Readers.'

Sammy sighed, 'And I'm not convinced that Zadie is your best role model, Pinto.'

Alfred caught Sammy's eye, reading him. Sammy opened up, no longer wanting to hide his feelings about Zadie – her sneaking around, the sense that she was planning something, and her apparent mistrust of Jay and Stitch. None of it quite added up for Sammy, and he needed someone to know, either to tell him to stop being paranoid, or to confirm his suspicions.

'She's under lot of pressure,' Alfred said, looking over towards Zadie. 'Much rests on her decisions in here.' Alfred's tone was not convincing. 'I must admit I preferred it when your sister was here,' he said. 'She certainly brought a sense of perspective and calm, gave Zadie someone to converse with about the powers, the strategy. Can't help but feel Zadie's a little less grounded here on her own.'

Sammy shuffled a little closer to Alfred. 'It's more than that. Can't you feel it?' he said, keeping his voice low. Toyah and Pinto looked over at Zadie, as if trying to see what Sammy was seeing. 'Don't stare,' said Sammy.

'What are you saying?' said Alfred, leaning forward, his arms resting on his knees. Sammy shrugged. He didn't know what he was saying. He had no evidence of anything to show that Zadie's intentions were anything but in support of the Given, and the protection of the Interland.

'It's just a feeling,' Sammy said. 'Maybe I'm wrong.'

Toyah huffed, 'If she's not on our side, we'd have been screwed a long time ago. She's the one that reaches out to the Given, brings them in. Me and Pinto wouldn't be here if it weren't for her.'

Sammy lowered his head. 'I found fertiliser and batteries in the store? What's all that for if not building bombs? What's she planning?'

'Have you communicated with Jay?' Alfred asked.

Sammy shook his head. 'I tried, at the source, but I couldn't get anything.' He was concerned for his sister. She wasn't confident when she left the Interland, and he knew that her vulnerability lay in her lack of self-belief. He sighed, recalling his last visit to the source that took him on a flight above the Interland – the Downs, the hill forts, and the darkness swirling through the valleys.

'You're not supposed to go down there, no one is,' said Pinto.

'*She* goes down there,' Sammy said, nodding towards Zadie, who was in deep conversation with Jared at her left-hand side. Zadie looked over towards Sammy, as if she could hear their conversation. He shielded. 'I saw her come up from there the other day,' he whispered.

'She's allowed. She's a level eight,' said Toyah.

As they watched, Zadie stood. Jared joined her and they motioned for Simon to follow. The three of them left the main cavern, heading out towards the exit, towards the waterfall beyond which was the one and only entrance to the caves. 'Where are they going?' asked Sammy.

Alfred watched after them. 'Secret liaison,' he said. Sammy exchanged a look with Alfred, only for Alfred to shake his head. 'Don't play with fire, Sammy.'

* * *

WITH SIMON AND JARED, Zadie stood just the other side of the waterfall that partitioned the underground – between the entrance zone, and the main caves and caverns of the Interland. Sammy crept as close to the waterfall as he dare, the three leaders talking in secret on the other side. He could hear nothing of their conversation for the noise of the water pouring from the rocks in the ceiling and away through the crevices in the floor.

After a few minutes, the three appeared through the waterfall. Sammy ducked out of sight, leaning back into an alcove in the rocks, hidden by the darkness. They passed him without hesitation. Zadie nodded at Jared and said, 'Collect your team. I'll see you back in the main cavern. Anyone who wants to join us, we welcome.'

'And if they don't come?'

'Then they're against the cause. We don't have time for opposition.' Sammy watched as Zadie locked eyes with Jared, communicating her instructions. Jared put a hand to his jacket pocket and his fingers closed over a gun. 'Like we discussed,' said Zadie. Jared nodded and slid the gun out of sight once more. Zadie looked at Simon. 'You come with me.'

Sammy remained still, not daring to move from the shadows, then jolted to attention at the sound of voices coming from the main cavern. Zadie was calling people together. He stumbled forward, picking his way through the darkness and into the light of the main cavern, now rammed with people. Mutterings of confusion grew louder as more squeezed into the room. Sammy raised himself up on tiptoes to see if he could locate the others. He caught sight of Toyah and pushed towards her. As he ducked between people, a shot rang out from deep in the caves, then another.

'Jared,' Sammy said under his breath, then refocused on moving quickly towards Toyah.

'Hush,' came the voice of Zadie Lawrence, perched on a rock so that she could see over the crowd that filled the room. Simon was by her side, and Sammy saw that he had a rifle in his hands. Back towards the entrance, Sammy noticed that Jared had reappeared, stood with three others, each with rifles. Looking to the waterfall, the route to the exit from the Interland, Sammy could see more of Zadie's soldiers, armed and fixed in position.

'Calm down, hear me out,' said Zadie, shouting above the background noise.

'Why are you holding us like this?' a man shouted.

'Who said I was holding you?' said Zadie, her powerful

voice cutting through the noise. She pointed over to the main exit to the caves, where Sammy could see the waterfall in the distance. 'There is the exit. You are free to leave whenever you wish.' As she said the words, her soldiers at the exit to the cavern stepped aside to show that the exit was open. Sammy looked at their rifles, and the expressions on their faces. He wasn't convinced that they were preparing to let people do as they wished.

'We are entering a new phase of the work we have been doing down here, the work that was started by Sasha Colden herself,' she said. Sammy bristled at the sense that Zadie was using his grandmother to justify her plans. He moved a little further through the crowd towards his friends. Zadie continued, 'We have spent long enough hiding in the bowels of the earth. It's time we re-emerged into the world, to join those with power, not separate ourselves from them.'

Someone called out, 'We *are* together. The Given are mostly all here, safe from the Readers.'

Zadie hushed the crowd again as the noise level rose. 'We need to remove the threat, so that *all* those with power can unite. The Given, the Readers...' Noises of confusion and disagreement increased. 'Wait,' Zadie shouted. 'Think about it. What is it that tips the balance of power and sets people against each other? Reader against Given?' Sammy caught sight of Toyah and pushed through the final few metres of the crowd that separated them.

'Sammy,' she said, pulling him towards her and Pinto. Alfred stood at their side. He looked at Sammy and shook his head, his thoughts coming through loud and clear. Zadie was turning things around. She had a plan that he didn't yet understand.

Zadie stood tall now, shouting across the crowd. 'We need to re-establish the balance of power if we are to reach a steady state, without conflict, and without turning this into a full scale war that will destroy everything we are trying to protect. There's already been so much deterioration out there, even in the last twelve months. There are great parts of the country now run-down. Houses are empty. The economy is on its knees.'

'She's talking about joining with the Readers,' said Alfred.

'It's the segregation,' said Zadie. 'The imbalance that isolates the Interland from others with power – Given *and* Reader.'

'She wants to get rid of Jay,' said Sammy. He knew that the only thing that kept the Readers from being able to enter the Interland was its protection by the power of the 8C, and the connection – Jay and Stitch.

'Why?' asked Toyah.

It had crystallised for Sammy. 'Without Jay and Stitch, Zadie is the most powerful, and can allow access to the Interland to anyone she chooses, including the Readers.'

The background noise grew louder once more. 'Quiet!' Zadie shouted, then nodded towards Jared who pointed his gun back down the passageway and let off a round, the sharp noise echoing through the caves and silencing the crowd. 'Listen to me,' insisted Zadie. More shots rang out from the tunnels.

A fearful voice of a man called out from the crowd, 'What have you done? Where are the others? What have you done with the others?'

Sammy and Alfred exchanged a glance and then looked back to Zadie, her expression neutral, her stance resolute. Sammy stretched to see over the heads of the crowd. 'Where's Dad?' he asked. Alfred shook his head.

The man shouted again, 'She'll destroy us.' He turned to the crowd. 'Can't you see?' A shot echoed through the cavern, fired at the wall by Zadie's other henchman, Simon. The dissenter froze. People screamed. Another shot at the floor near the man's feet this time. Then silence.

'I'm not asking for a consensus.' Zadie spoke slowly and deliberately. Someone interrupted but quickly quietened down as Simon raised his rifle once more and it was clear that Zadie had had enough discussion. 'These plans have been a long time in the making. We need to organise ourselves for the authorities. In a matter of hours, they will be here to help us repatriate the Given above ground.'

Noise grew once more until one of the crowd spoke in Zadie's defence. 'Listen to her. Has she not been here for us for all these months, years? Has she not looked after our interests for all this time? Don't you want to reintegrate above ground? We all have family up there, friends we left behind. We can't stay down here forever. This could be our opportunity for peace. Embrace it.' Zadie nodded, and the crowd quietened.

'We need to leave,' said Alfred, looking at each of the exits to the cavern.

'No chance. Too many of them,' said Toyah.

Pinto's voice shook as he said, 'They'll shoot us.'

Toyah put a hand on his shoulder. 'It won't come to that, we're getting out of here. Sammy, what about back through there?' She nodded towards the main exit, the waterfall.

'Too many of them,' said Sammy. He looked over his shoulder at the opening in the cavern that led through to the stores. Pinto caught his eye and Sammy nodded. 'The cold store has a connection through to the other passageways.'

'How do you know that?' said Toyah.

Sammy ignored Toyah's question and craned his neck to look for his dad. Still no sign of him. He edged backwards towards the unguarded entrance to the store. Alfred nodded at Toyah and Pinto to follow. 'I'll sit tight for a minute, make sure the coast is clear.' Sammy looked at Alfred, communicating his insistence that Alfred follow. Alfred nodded, and Sammy ducked into the storeroom.

The room was empty. As Toyah and Pinto followed him in, Sammy squeezed through the gap that led to the cool zone, the walls damp and noticeably cooler. He moved a sack of rice from the opening and waved Toyah and Pinto into the passageway. Alfred entered the room, his face etched with fear.

A guard held a rifle to Alfred's back. 'Move away,' he ordered.

As Sammy stepped aside, the man saw the opening. He moved towards it, rifle pointed towards Sammy. At the entrance, he ducked down and Alfred dropped an industrial tin of beans on the back of his head. The man went down, letting off a round from his rifle, the bullet pinging through the entrance to the passageway.

Alfred grabbed the motionless body of the guard and slid him away from the entrance to the tunnel, showing a strength that surprised Sammy. He waved Sammy through and followed him as they heard people approaching from the main cavern.

* * *

ZADIE PACED THE SMALL, rectangular room. She was buzzing still from the events in the main cavern. Her guards had retained control, and all but a few dissenters were on board – no longer resisting if not enthusiastically supporting. She had tried to get a message to Hinton that he would find the Interland as they had planned, with no resistance, so he needn't bring his entire army.

One of her guards, Simon, entered the room. 'No sign of them but those passageways go nowhere but down.'

'So they're out, they got out?'

'There is no way through to the outside, chances are they fell through to one of the shafts, and if that's the case they won't make it. They'll be at the bottom of a long drop to nothing but rock.'

'If Jay's brother is dead, then she'll know about it,' said Zadie, suddenly conscious that if Jay sensed it, she might change her strategy and return, instead of rescuing Cassie.

'What does it matter? She's not coming back here.'

'What about the father, Ben?'

'No sign. There are a number still unaccounted for. In the residential section.'

Zadie had assured Hinton the Interland would be clean by the time the Readers arrived. The Given would be out, and the Interland no longer a hidden base for conflict, but a place of peace, somewhere to be visited as a source of inspiration. The main connection into the underground would be sealed, leaving only the source accessible from the outside, nothing else. The source would become a place of pilgrimage for the Given, and a symbol of peace and progression for the Given and Readers alike.

'We can't set the fuse if there are people the other side of the wall,' said Simon.

'We follow the plan. We blow the connection tunnels when it's time.'

'They'll be locked in.'

'Just make sure that all those who are *with* us prepare to leave.' She waved the guard away, following him out of her room. She turned off the main path towards the passageway to the source.

Zadie lit three of the candles in the sub-level, taking a

moment to admire the beauty of the flowing water, and the energy she felt emanating through the cave. With a hand in the source, the pool at the confluence of the three streams, Zadie sensed a presence.

'Davey?' she said aloud.

'I lost them on the road,' Davey replied. 'All three of them.'

'Three?'

'Jay, Stitch, and Stitch's father. Something happened at Stitch's house. The Readers closed in, but there was something else there, or someone, I don't know. The three of them got away from the Readers. I would have helped Jay and Stitch but it was all over so quickly. I followed them through to the main road up to the prison but their car ran off the road.'

'How?' Zadie asked.

'I don't know, it just veered off into the side, through the bushes. I parked up and searched, but there was no sign of them. The lake swallowed them up. Disappeared. But not dead. I can still feel them.'

'Where are you now?'

'Highdown. To see if I can get a sense of them. I have something. I think they're still on their way to the prison.'

'Things have changed here, Davey. We've lost some people. We need to abandon the Interland.'

'What? That makes no sense.'

'Not much here is making sense, but we have intelligence that Jay and Stitch might be behind the events here.'

'What events?'

'Readers.'

'Why...'

'No time to go through it all now. We can't let Jay go free and put the Interland at risk.'

'Shall I make contact?'

'No,' said Zadie. 'She's too powerful and we can't trust that she won't infiltrate and manipulate you. You need to stop her, you still have the rifle?'

Davey hesitated. 'It's on the bike.'

'Use it. Start with Jay. We can't afford to lose more ground.'

'But...'

'Then come back in, but not before it's done. If she gets to the Readers, we can't be sure what she'll do.' Zadie pulled her hand from the pool and took a breath. The communication with Davey ended.

Soon, with the support of the Readers, she would have control of the Interland. With no more of the Given at level 8C, it would be for her to drive change, a controlled reintegration of the Given back into society.

21

The car pulled into the parking area at the motorway services. The Little Chef restaurant was virtually empty.

'You take a seat, Dad. Me and Jay will order food.'

Samir found a table at the back, overlooking a patch of grass that led down to a wooded area away from the motorway. Jay and Stitch studied the laminated menu at the counter as the uniformed assistant waited just out of earshot.

'What happened back there?' Stitch said. 'Feels like it was all a dream.'

'It was real enough,' said Jay. She glanced at Stitch's hand. 'Looks sore.'

'More like a tingling sensation. It feels numb. Do you think the Interland could be taken? What about Sammy, and the others?'

'I can feel Sammy. Something's happening back there, but he's OK.' Sammy was almost always present in Jay's senses. Mostly he was the merest of feelings – a tingle in her temple. But sometimes his emotion came through in a rush, as clear as if he were in the same room.

'We need to get back...'

'Stitch,' Jay interrupted. 'We're not leaving without Cassie.'

Stitch shook his head. 'This whole thing is bigger than just us, just this.' He motioned around them.

'What do you mean?' asked Jay.

'The man said there are other Interlands, in other countries. They're choked, dying. Readers are closing in.'

'But...' Jay started.

'I know,' Stitch interrupted. 'I'm with you. We can't leave Cassie. I know that.' He paused for a moment, staring at the menu. 'But don't you think we're heading into a trap?' he said, looking up at Jay.

Jay nodded. 'Yes, I do. But if your dad knows a way in...'

The restaurant assistant appeared at the counter. She took their order of three cooked breakfasts, which Stitch paid for in cash.

Handing him his change, the woman said, 'You two Givens?'

Jay and Stitch exchanged a glance. As Jay was about to respond, Stitch got there first. 'No,' he said, his voice stiff.

'Thought I heard you sayin' so that's all.'

'Sorry, you must be mistaken,' repeated Stitch.

'We've had trouble before is all.'

'Trouble?' asked Jay.

'People had enough. Nothing but protesting and fighting. They think they're special. Think they're better than the rest of us. My husband, Jack, says we should've rounded 'em all up way back.' She lowered her voice. 'Now, I'm not so extreme as him, but he's got a point if you get my meaning?'

'What meaning?' asked Jay, bristling.

'Well, I ain't prejudiced or nothing like that, but this country was doin' just fine before, and now it's gone to shit.

Used to be teeming with customers in here. Not anymore. No one got any money now.'

Stitch put the change into the tip-jar and pulled Jay away from the counter. 'We're with you on that,' Stitch said, giving Jay a look that told her to keep quiet. He shoved her into the booth next to Samir. 'Don't say anything,' he said. 'In case you haven't figured it out yet, the Given aren't so popular.'

'You're surprised?' Samir said, drawing quizzical looks from Jay and Stitch. 'You haven't been here, in the real world. The Given weren't popular even before you left. They're seen as the enemy now, by almost everyone.'

'Why?' said Stitch.

'People are scared. They believe what they read and see on TV...' Samir gesticulated wildly with his hands. 'They just want everything to get back to normal.' He sighed and looked out the window. 'Whatever *normal* is.'

The restaurant assistant approached with three plates, placing them on the table and sliding one across to Samir. She reached to the table next to them for cutlery and tomato sauce, asked if everything was alright, turned and left.

'Service with a smile,' said Stitch.

Jay picked at her fries. 'We met someone up at Highdown yesterday,' she said to Samir. 'He told us that the Given have been driven underground.'

Samir choked a laugh. 'What's left of them. Most have been taken through rehab. Washed clean of their power, so they say on the television. The rest, if there are any who aren't holed up wherever you kids were, might be in hiding, or...' He trailed off, looking again out the window.

'Or what?' said Stitch.

'Or dead,' he said, not taking his eyes off the horizon.

22

Through the windscreen of the old Ford, the valleys stretched miles into the distance between the rolling hills of the Downs – occasionally punctuated with farms and villages that seemed to Jay untouched – something pure in the growing darkness of state oppression.

The landscape transformed as they crossed into the urban outskirts of Northtown, a once-affluent suburb of London. Its only distinguishing feature now was the ever-expanding prison, the rehabilitation centre that occupied more than half of the Northtown suburb.

Jay slowed as they entered the town. The day's light seemed to fade as they crossed the boundary. A fine rain hung like mist. The prison rose in the distance, austere and forbidding, the lights on its entrance pillars highlighting their rise. The car rolled to a stop next to the kerb.

'What?' said Stitch from the back of the car. Samir stirred in the front seat next to Jay, rubbing his eyes and then stroking his beard.

'It's too late to go in tonight,' said Jay. 'We need to find somewhere to stay.'

'They'll be looking out for us in town,' said Stitch. 'We can't just check in to a hotel.'

Samir sat up straight, peering through the gloom. 'Head to the east side, by the river.' Samir nodded towards a side road. 'There. Take that road down to the riverside and head east.'

'You know somewhere, Dad?' asked Stitch.

Samir sighed, looking out through the side window as Jay pulled the car back onto the road and indicated to turn right. 'Me and your mother lived over that side. When we first came over from Tripoli.' To Jay: 'Take a left here.'

Jay turned the car into a residential street, the Victorian townhouses neglected to the point of dilapidation. Windows on every other house were boarded, roofs of some collapsed and open to the elements.

'You lived here?' asked Stitch.

Samir shook his head. 'This was once the posh part of town.'

'Not anymore,' said Stitch.

'No one lives here now. I thought these houses might be intact enough for us to squat down for a night.'

There were no lights in any of the houses. The only cars parked in the street were blocked up on bricks, their wheels missing, windows smashed.

A shadow flashed across their path. Jay screeched to a halt. Stitch lurched forward, banging his head against the back of Samir's seat. Samir said something in Arabic, breathing rapidly. Stitch gathered himself in the back of the car. 'What was that?' he said.

'An animal, it's OK. A cat, probably,' said Jay.

'I don't like it here,' said Stitch, his voice thin and quiet.

'Look.' Samir pointed at one of the town houses. 'That one looks intact. Park the car and we can have a look.'

Jay parked between an old Transit van with its back door

hanging off its hinges and a small white VW car that looked untouched. They collected their bags, making as little noise as possible so as not to alert anyone to their presence. A flash of light filled Jay's head, and she faltered, placing a hand on the car to steady herself. Another flash. A communication from someone using the power to reach her over distance. Sammy.

'You alright?' asked Stitch.

Jay nodded. 'Sammy's been trying to get a message to me. Let's get inside.' To Samir: 'Which house?'

Samir pointed. 'That one looks good.'

Jay and Stitch followed Samir through the alleyway at the side of the house and around to the back garden. The grass on the lawn was long. The shrubs around the perimeter had encroached on the neighbouring gardens, but Jay figured it hadn't been long deserted, a matter of weeks, not months.

Samir cupped his hands around his face and peered through the glass of the back door. 'Looks tidy,' he said. He tried the door handle. Locked. He looked under the doormat. Nothing.

'There's a cat-flap,' said Stitch.

Samir waved at Stitch to look. Stitch leaned down to thread his arm through the cat-flap to see if he could reach the lock from the inside. He squirmed and wriggled until eventually giving up and stepping away. He rifled through the bushes and came back with a stick. He tried again through the cat-flap. Jay heard a click and Stitch smiled, pulling his arm out and opening the door.

A waft of stale, damp air passed through the door as Jay stood in the threshold, Samir and Stitch behind her. She stepped into the kitchen, her ears hyper-sensitive to the slightest sound in the near silence that surrounded the house. If the Readers were looking out for them, or if they were following them, then this place would be the perfect location for an ambush. Out in the open, amongst the energy of the Downs, the sea and the environment, she could get a fix on the readers from some distance. It was different in the City.

'Go on then,' said Stitch.

Jay stepped over the threshold and into the house. A wave in the energy, a small fluctuation passed over Jay. Someone with power was nearby. She stopped and held up her hand to signal to Samir and Stitch to wait. The sense passed. Jay strained her eyes to see through the darkness in the kitchen and thought she saw a glimmer of light reflecting through the house from a distant room. The dark quiet was shattered when a scream pierced the silence.

A blunt object slammed the back of Jay's head. The pain was intense, but the blow was not so hard to knock her down. Before Samir and Stitch could get through the door, Jay turned to see the pale features of a man, arms raised. His eyes were wide, reflecting the light of the night sky, crazed and fearful. He gripped a baseball bat in his hands. Jay held up her hands in defence, but the man hesitated. In that split-second, Stitch launched himself through the door.

'Wait,' said Jay.

Stitch had the man's arms pinned to the lino floor of the kitchen, sitting on his chest to immobilise him and knocking the bat from his hand. 'Stitch,' Jay put a hand on his shoulder, 'ease off, please.'

Stitch relaxed his grip and edged himself away from the man so that the three of them stood over the prone figure, his eyes flitting from side to side as if seeking an escape route. 'Hey,' Jay said to get his attention. 'You have power, I can feel it.'

'You're not Readers,' the man said.

Jay shook her head.

The man sat up and Jay took a step towards him, crouching next to him.

'Jay,' said Stitch, urging caution.

'Are you alone in here?' Jay asked, looking around the gloom of the kitchen.

He nodded, struggling to his feet as Jay stepped back to allow him space. He moved to a wall cupboard and collected a bunch of candles, which he placed on the kitchen worktop before taking out a box of matches. In the light of the candles, Jay glimpsed his marking, a number one on his wrist. She could see that he was in his fifties or sixties. He'd not bothered to shave or cut his hair in a while. The bags under his eyes darkened in the shadows and the flicker of light from the candles.

'Sorry I hit you,' he said.

Jay rubbed the back of her head. 'I'd have hit me too, under the circumstances.'

He smiled and his face cracked, his eyes lighting up to reveal the younger version of the man underneath the weathered exterior. 'Why are you here? If you're not here for me, then what?'

'We're passing through,' said Stitch. 'We need somewhere to rest for the night.'

'Of all the empty houses you chose mine?'

'It was the only one with a full roof,' said Stitch.

Jay could see the man wasn't a threat. 'This is Stitch and his dad, Samir. And, I'm Jay.'

'My name is Sebastian.'

'Why are you here?' asked Jay.

Sebastian picked up one of the candles and blew out the others. 'Follow me,' he said. He led them to the middle room on the ground floor which had no windows looking over the street, or the back, just one that opened into the alleyway at the side. This room was Sebastian's home, with a bed along one side, and two sofas taking up much of the remaining space.

'What are you hiding from?' said Jay.

Sebastian sat on his bed and motioned towards the sofa. He pulled back his sleeve to show his marking. 'They're taking all of us now.' He nodded towards Jay's wrist. She edged back her sleeve.

'Oh no.' Sebastian sucked in air, staring at Jay's marking. 'Power that strong will be noticed. They'll detect you.' He stood, paced the room for a moment, and then sat back down on his bed. 'Why are you here? They'll sense you. You're the one they want. The rest of us are just a sideshow.'

'They won't sense me. I can shield.' Jay leaned forward in her seat. 'What do you mean they're taking all of us?'

'The last six months it's been a clean sweep. There are barely any Given left, and any that remain hide on the Downs, or they hole up somewhere like this.'

'Like Otis,' Stitch said.

'You can't stay here. They'll come.'

'One night,' said Stitch. 'We'll shield.'

Sebastian continued to pace, eyes moving rapidly from Jay to Stitch, then to Samir. 'One night. No more. You shield. If you get any sense of Readers, then you leave before you draw them in. You can use the upstairs. This is my space.'

Samir stood and turned to head upstairs. Stitch made to stand, but his dad held up a hand. 'I'll go.'

'Thanks,' said Jay to Sebastian. 'We'll be gone in the morning.' Jay felt another flash behind her eyes, like a migraine piercing her vision. 'Excuse me,' she said, and left the room.

Back in the darkness of the kitchen, Jay sat at the small table and cradled her head in her hands. The message was from Sammy. She allowed her mind to settle and decipher the signal. There was something happening back at the Interland, and someone was looking for Jay and Stitch, someone other than the Readers.

'What is it?' said Stitch, appearing in the doorway.

'Message from Sammy. Something's happened back there, and someone's tracking us.'

'Who?'

'That's all I got.' Jay shook her head.

Back in the middle room, Jay quizzed Sebastian about the events of the past few months outside of the Interland. Sebastian described how the tactics of the authorities had shifted from covert operations to all-out war against the Given. The public were being encouraged and when that didn't work, threatened to speak out if they know of anyone hiding from the State. People who sheltered the Given faced prison. The pretence of rehabilitation had been dropped. The fate of the Given was *reduction*, long-term imprisonment, or death.

'Someone told us there is a network,' said Jay. 'Links between the Given that remain on the outside?'

Sebastian snorted, 'Used to be. Not anymore. Like there used to be places we could meet without fear for our lives. If there are any others not yet reduced or killed, then it's news to me.'

'When's the last time you saw another of the Given?' said Jay.

'You're the first humans I've seen this close for nearly six months. That's the only reason I'm alive, and if you don't mind, I'd like to keep it that way. It'll be best for me if you're not here when I wake up tomorrow.' Sebastian pulled his bedcover over himself and turned away from Jay and Stitch. Stitch stood to leave, and Jay followed him up the stairs.

* * *

Samir had arranged the beds so that he and Stitch could share the room. Jay glanced around the room for where to dump her bag. Samir caught Jay's eye and nodded towards the second set of stairs from the landing. 'Thought you'd be OK up in the loft. It looks comfortable up there. Make sure you close the curtains if you light any candles, we don't want to draw any attention.'

'Oh, OK. Thanks,' said Jay, deflated to be kicked out. 'So you were saying about the route into the prison complex? Via the sewer outfall?'

'When we lived here in Northtown,' Samir said. 'It was when they built the rehab centre. I mean, the prison. Most of the local community was people helping with construction.'

'Did you work on it? Or just Mum?' asked Stitch.

Samir shook his head. 'Your mother. I have no skills, you know this.' He smiled. 'Your mother was section project manager. She oversaw construction of the *education* wing.'

'I didn't know she did that,' said Stitch.

'She was a brilliant manager. Great with people. Brain like a big house, that woman. But the job made her sick. Asbestos. Silica. That place killed her and the State never took responsibility.' He paused a moment to gather himself. 'She knew a lot about how the place was built, how it was configured. There's something she told me that sticks in my mind which could be our way in.'

Stitch and Jay exchanged a look. 'Go on,' Jay said.

'Like I was saying in the car, the storm-water outfall from the whole of this area was built at the same time as the prison...'

'The what?' asked Stitch.

'The overflow tunnels that take storm water away and discharge it to the Thames. They only come into use during a major flood, like a once-in-a-hundred-year rainfall. The rest of the time they are mostly empty. And they are taking water from the prison camp.'

He continued, 'I think I know where we can find the connection outfall at the River. Then we just need to work our way back through the tunnels and into the prison complex. There will be surface water connections that we can use to get into the *education* wing.'

'How big are these tunnels? You can't go traipsing through sewers, Dad.'

'Could be two metres in diameter, big enough for walking, no problem.'

'Sounds perfect,' said Jay. 'But *you* need to stay here.'

'What-' said Samir.

'We need someone to see to the car and make sure it's ready for when we get back with Cassie.'

Samir looked at Stitch. 'What about you?'

'Jay will need me.'

'But what about...'

'Dad.' Stitch interrupted. 'Trust me. I'll be fine.'

Samir wore an expression of concern for his son. He shook his head and let out a sigh. 'I suppose I'm the only one who can get that car in shape. It needs a good flushing through of the fuel system since that dip in the lake.'

'Not here though,' said Jay.

Samir and Stitch looked at her. 'Where then?' said Stitch.

'There are some garages in the next street. I say we put the car in one of those. If someone comes for us, then you need to be somewhere out of sight.'

'What about Sebastian?'

'If we're not here, drawing them in, there's no reason to think the Readers will find him. Now, we rest. If we leave just before light, we can enter the storm-water tunnel while it's still dark?'

Stitch nodded, then looked at his dad. 'How far is it from here?'

'Twenty minutes' walk. I can make you a map. I don't know how many connections there will be at the river. One or two for sure, but maybe more. I suggest you take the first one and head north.'

Stitch looked at Jay. 'What do we do when we get into the prison?'

'We keep it simple. We go in quickly, pick up Cassie and straight back here, then back to the Interland. No messing around. I can sense Cassie from here, so when we get close, we'll know where she is.'

'Simple,' said Stitch.

* * *

JAY COULDN'T SLEEP. She was exhausted. Overtired and flushed with adrenaline. She stood and pulled back the curtain in the dormer window, looking over the streets of Northtown. It was not yet ten o'clock and she could see cars moving along the roads not far away. Some streets nearby remained occupied. She saw the lights of a pub just a few streets away and with her window open a little; she heard the waves of music coming over the rooftops on the wind. For a moment she craved the normality of an evening in a bar, a Guinness and some music – some time with friends without worrying about leaking her powers and attracting attention. She couldn't go to a pub, but she could at least get some fresh air.

She laced up her shoes and crept down the stairs, stopping for a moment at the door to Stitch and Samir's room where they slept in silence. She continued to the ground floor and leaned up against the open doorway to Sebastian's room. He looked up from his book. 'You leaving?'

'Just to get some air. Be back in a while.'

'Stick to the smaller streets. If the Readers are out patrolling, they'll be mainly on the central routes.'

'You should leave here, when we've gone,' said Jay.

Sebastian shook his head. 'I'm not moving again. This is it for me. If they catch up with me here, then it's meant to be. I can't keep moving, not at my age.'

Jay laughed. 'You're not old.'

'Feel it. Comes a point when you have to stop running.'

'I'm beginning to see that,' said Jay, turning to head for the back door. She paused. 'Thanks,' she said. 'For putting us up.'

'Whatever it is you're doing tomorrow, I hope you succeed. And I hope that this situation can be brought to an end sometime soon.' They locked eyes for a moment and Jay sensed that Sebastian was urging her on, to take action beyond that for herself and her friends. The whole of the Given were little more than a residual underclass hiding out in city squats and rural camps, waiting for their time to come at the hands of the Readers.

A fine rain dampened her face, and she dabbed her eyes with her sleeve. She pulled up her hood and headed out to the street. In her solitude, in the open air, a sense of freedom ran thorough her veins like she hadn't felt since she first entered the Interland.

A motorbike roared in the distance, getting closer. She turned down an alleyway and picked up speed, turning another corner before she heard the motorbike pass by out of sight. Her heart slowed once more, and she kicked herself for straying too far, for not being careful for Cassie's sake as much as her own.

At the end of the alley, the grey-black surface of the river was ruffled by a blustery wind. She crossed the road and leaned over the railing, looking down at the river wall to see if she could locate the storm-water outfall Samir had spoken of. It was too dark. She could see nothing but the blackness of the river wall in shadow. As she lifted her head, the wind caught her hood and blew it back onto her shoulders, exposing her ears. A loud crack made her jump, its echo bouncing off a building in the distance. She pulled up her hood and tilted her head to listen. Nothing but the wind.

23

D avey opened up the throttle of his motorbike and screamed along the river road and into position. He wore his rifle strapped across his back. He'd seen Jay go into the alleyway by the river. She only had one possible destination. If he could get to the river first, he'd be able to find a spot out of sight. He'd be close enough for his rifle in the wind and poor visibility, and far enough away that he could escape without being seen.

Zadie's instructions echoed in his head. It made no sense to Davey. Why kill the most powerful of the Given? There could be no reason for Jay to succumb to the powers of the Readers. She prevailed in the face of great power from Readers before, surely she would not be so easily overcome. But Zadie would have intelligence that he was not party to, so who was he to question?

He stopped by the river and pushed his bike out of sight behind a disused block of garages. Taking shelter from the misty rain under a lean-to, he took the rifle out of its bag. He wiped the rain from his face and strained to see through blurred vision to load four bullets into the barrel. He clicked it shut and wiped the moisture from it before lifting it to his shoulder to take aim. He focused the crosshairs at space at the end of the alleyway where he expected Jay to appear at any moment. Satisfied that he was close enough for a clean shot, he lowered the gun and waited.

As he waited, he daydreamed. With Jay dead, Zadie would consider him worthy of higher-level duties. He would have demonstrated his loyalty, and his effectiveness. She would surely choose him to lead with her when the Given emerge from the Interland.

Jay appeared at the end of the alleyway, as Davey had predicted. His nerves tingled as he raised the rifle to his shoulder, his cheek against the cold metal. He held Jay in the crosshairs as she walked across the road, her hood down and hair blowing in the wind. He watched as she wiped the rain from her face and leaned up against the railing, peering over at the water. In the telescopic sights, he could see her expression, the searching look in her eye.

He removed the safety and maintained his aim. Jay leaned further over the railing and continued to scan the water's edge, her hood now falling so that it covered her head once more. Davey had the most powerful of the Given in his sights, the one for whom the whole of the Interland had been waiting for so long. The one who had the potential to raise the chances of the Given to match the power of the State.

His finger pressed on the trigger.

He inhaled slowly and held his breath.

The wind died.

He couldn't do it.

Something heavy hit him from the side and he thought he'd been hit by a car, the force was so great. His rifle released a shot as he went down, the bullet pinging harmlessly off the concrete of the garage and into the darkness behind him. Its noise swept away with the wind. He scraped his face along the asphalt floor, pain swallowing him and obscuring his vision. His face was slammed into a puddle on the floor so that his mouth and nose were under water. He tried to scream, tried to shift the sudden, heavy weight from his back. The thing had his head in a solid grip. With one final push, Davey turned his body and dislodged his assailant from his back, sending him to the ground. He was a small man, and Davey was surprised at how much force he'd been able to muster in taking Davey out. They both stood, Davey wobbly on his feet like a newborn lamb, a mix of rainwater and blood stinging his eyes and blurring his vision.

His assailant kept his distance. He was a good foot shorter than Davey, stocky with a beard and straggly hair. In the blink of Davey's eye, his attacker had covered the distance between them and again powered into him at waist level, taking Davey to the floor. Davey hit the ground hard, landing on his back, winded. The long-haired man sat astride him and let loose a shower of punches. This man was quick, but he was no fighter. Davey fought back, bucking the man off his chest and back onto the floor. They both scrambled to their feet, but Davey was ready this time. He assumed a boxing stance and kept a distance. Twice the man ran at him, and twice he dodged and landed blows to the back of his head as he passed.

Keeping his arms up to protect himself, Davey led with his left and landed a powerful right, then a left to the chin. He stumbled but kept upright, running at Davey once more, this time making contact so that they both went down.

They rolled and scrabbled on the ground, the hairy man having more success from close quarters until Davey pushed him away and released two powerful blows. He came again, his energy relentless, landing his own blows with his fists to Davey's jaw, cheek, eye.

Davey was exhausted, in agony, and seeing double. Both men bled from cuts on their faces, above their eyes, their lips. He landed a good punch on the man's nose, rocking him back on his heels, then took a punch himself on his left eye, which already gushed blood.

'What do you want?' screamed Davey through the noise of the pouring rain and the pounding of his pulse in his ears. 'Why are you doing this?' he trailed off as he gasped for breath, his arms heavy at his sides.

The hairy man stepped back and leaned up against the wall. Davey was relieved that he seemed just as exhausted, and just as willing to stop, at least for a moment. The man nodded towards the rifle on the floor. 'That's why.'

'You're a Reader?' Davey said, knowing that this man was no Reader. If he was, then Davey could tell for sure. He could sense power, but not that of a Reader.

The man shook his head. 'Why would I stop you killing a Given if I were a Reader?' He paused, holding his ribs and struggling to get air into his lungs.

'I wasn't going to shoot,' said Davey. The man snorted a laugh and Davey said, 'I changed my mind.'

'Why are you here, tracking and holding a gun at Jay Macfarlane?'

Davey remained silent for a moment, contemplating the sense in telling this stranger why he was pointing a gun at Jay. Although he'd changed his mind, for good reason, he retained a loyalty to Zadie, and to the cause.

'You changed your mind, so I assume you've come around and seen sense?'

'Orders,' said Davey.

'Whose?' asked the man.

'Doesn't matter. I changed my mind, like I said. What do you care?'

'There aren't many of us left. It's up to all of us to care if we want to survive the Readers, and people like you.'

Davey straightened, finally breathing normally again. 'Look, I was told that she was turning to the side of the Readers...'

'You're crazy.' The man picked up the rifle and emptied it of bullets before throwing it into the river.

'Maybe.' Davey looked across the road where light emitted from the ground-floor windows of a pub. 'What do you say we get dry?' He nodded towards the pub.

The man hesitated a moment, looking Davey up and down. 'OK,' he said. 'Let's drink.'

Davey collected his motorbike and pushed it behind the man, picking up speed to catch him. 'I'm Davey,' he said.

The man looked back at Davey, choosing not to reply.

* * *

THE BARMAN PLACED two pints on the table. The men had edged as close as they could bear to the open fire, steam rising from their wet clothes. He said his name was Otis. In the light of the pub, Davey could see that he was younger than he'd thought, perhaps as young as him. They remained silent as they peeled off their outer layers and draped them over chairs by the fire.

The landlady of the pub approached with a first aid kit from behind the bar. 'You boys had some trouble?' she said.

Otis nodded. 'We saw them off.'

She took a seat next to Otis and inspected his wounds. 'Nothing permanent by the looks of it.' She used a sterile wipe to clean him up and applied two steri-strips to the gash above his eye before turning to Davey.

'Thanks, you don't have to...' said Davey.

'We look after our own,' she said, pulling back her sleeve to show Davey a number-three in a deep black marking. She nodded toward his wrist, where his own number was hidden by his sleeve. Otis looked startled. Davey simply nodded and sat back to allow her to clean him up. He presented a more difficult task than Otis by virtue of the gravel-graze up the whole of one side of his face.

'I'm Otis. This is Davey,' Otis said as the landlady patched up Davey's cuts and scrapes. 'How did you know?'

'Sandy,' said the landlady. 'And that there behind the bar is Bill. Power can sense power.'

'I didn't sense any power in here before we came in,' said Otis.

Sandy glanced at him. 'Why do you think we're still here? You won't see many of the Given in plain sight unless they're particularly skilled at shielding, like me and Bill are.'

'That explains it,' said Otis.

Otis lifted his sleeve to show the number five. Davey hadn't seen a level five before. There were none inside the Interland. Plenty of fours, and a fair few at level six. Then there were all the Runners at level seven, like him. He guessed Otis might have something of the power he'd not seen before.

The barman, Bill, dimmed the lights and locked the doors as the other lone customer in the place walked out.

'You closing up?' asked Otis.

'Not to you,' said Sandy. 'You rest up, get dry. Bill will get you something to eat.'

Sandy left them to their drinks, and Otis eyed Davey. 'What?' said Davey.

'You were going to tell me why you were taking aim at the one chance the Given have of standing up to the Readers.' Davey looked away, took a drink from his pint. Otis continued:

'I'd feel a lot more comfortable if you handed over your weapons.'

Davey reached for his bag and pushed it over towards Otis. He considered for a moment how he must appear to Otis. Otis wouldn't know that Davey could never have taken that shot. As much as he supported Zadie Lawrence, her cause, the fight for the re-integration of the Given, he was sure that killing Jay was not the way to do it. 'How did you know I was there?'

'I've been tracking them since Highdown,' said Otis. 'Saw you up there too, spying on them.'

'You have wheels? A car?'

'Little moped. Enough to keep up.' Otis looked almost embarrassed. 'I kept back a bit, to see what you were up to. Good job I did.'

Davey sighed, 'I told you, I changed my mind, I wouldn't have taken the shot.'

'So you say.'

'Why are *you* following them?' asked Davey. 'Why aren't you *with* them?'

Otis leaned forward in his seat, grimacing at pain emanating from somewhere in his body. He warmed his hands on the fire. 'We met, but she doesn't trust me yet.'

'Why not?'

'Just cautious. Quite right too, given what you just tried to do.' He paused, trying to catch Davey's eye. 'I can help them. They just don't know they need it.' Otis stood with his empty glass. 'Another?'

Bill placed two bulging plates of pie and chips on the table. 'On the house,' he said, walking away before Davey had a chance to thank him.

Otis placed the drinks down and snatched up his plate of food. 'You were going to tell me about your apparent assassination instructions?' He spoke through a mouthful of chips.

'Zadie Lawrence,' said Davey, picking up his own plate of food and resting back in his armchair.

Otis stopped mid-chew. '*She* issued the order to kill Jay?' Davey nodded. 'What for?' said Otis.

Davey shrugged. 'Like I said. Jay's under suspicion.'

Otis shook his head as he ate. 'No. Something's gone wrong. I could feel it, but didn't for a minute think it was Zadie Lawrence. That puts a different complexion on things.'

'What things?' said Davey. He was curious that Otis knew of Zadie Lawrence.

'Everything has been deteriorating for the Given over the last six months. The State has stepped up its campaign, forcing us into hiding. The Interland seemed more and more of a myth. With no one coming out of there to support the Given, people assumed it was a fabrication.'

'And you?' said Davey.

'I have a stronger sense for the Given and the powers than most. I could feel it. But the other connections between those on the outside have weakened so much that the Given might as well not exist out here. Then I saw those Runners.'

'Cassie and Reuben,' said Davey.

'The Readers closed in on them,' Otis continued, 'and flushed out Jay, the last of the big powers of the Given.'

'You think this was planned by the Readers?'

'With Jay under their control, there's nothing to stop the Readers putting an end to the Interland, and to the Given.'

'Except Zadie Lawrence and all the rest of the Given back at the Interland. She's a level-eight, remember.'

'Zadie Lawrence?'

'Yes,' said Davey

'The one who issued the order to take out Jay?'

'What benefit can she possibly get from destroying her own kind?'

Otis took a slug of his drink and shook his head. 'That's what we still have to find out. We need to get to Jay and Stitch, to convince them that there's something going on back at the Interland, persuade them to return.' Otis paused. 'That is, if you're with us, and not against us?'

Davey held Otis's eye. He was as sure as he'd ever been of what side he was on. Zadie had used him for her own twisted plans. He just didn't know why. Jay and Stitch were heading to save their friend, and walking right in to a trap. 'I'm with you,' Davey said, and they chinked their glasses together.

24

Sammy froze as an explosion shook the surrounding ground. A few stones fell from the roof of the tunnel. In the light from his torch, Sammy watched as the colour drained from Alfred's face.

Pinto held on to Toyah's arm, squeezing tight as they waited. 'What was that?' asked Toyah.

Sammy shone his torch into the blackness ahead of them. 'They were using fertiliser to make explosives. They're bringing the place down.'

'Why?' asked Pinto.

Alfred sighed, and the others looked at him. 'She's blocking off connection with the deep Interland.'

'But why?' Pinto said again.

'Control,' said Sammy. 'She's all about control and power. I can feel it now.'

Alfred turned on his own torch and pointed it up ahead through the gloom. 'Where does this lead, Sammy?'

'To the connection.' He explained how the opening in the roof of the tunnel near his room led to a series of passageways that eventually led back to where they were.

'So we can get to this place from here, the Free Cave?' said Alfred.

Toyah shuffled closer to Alfred. 'But then what? We can't get back to the main cavern and out through the waterfall. If we are going to get out of here, we need to get back to the exit. That way.' She nodded back towards the store, back the way they had come.

'We can't go back that way,' said Pinto, his voice quivering a little.

'Pinto's right...' Sammy started before he was interrupted by another explosion. This time the noise came from behind them, back through the tunnel.

'That settles it,' said Alf. 'They've blown the entrance. Only way is forward.'

Sammy looked at Toyah. 'The ledge,' he said.

She nodded.

'Follow me,' said Sammy, and he surged ahead.

* * *

AT THE CONNECTION, Pinto automatically took the right branch before Sammy called him back. 'Left,' said Sammy.

'It's always right,' said Pinto, turning back towards Sammy.

'Not from this direction, look.' He pointed his torch down the left branch to show Pinto the familiar tunnel bending around towards where they'd find the slope down into the Free Cave. Pinto recognised it and led the way. At the top of the slope, Sammy and Pinto turned to Alfred. 'It's not as bad as it looks,' said Sammy.

'This isn't for an old man,' said Alfred, a pained expression.

'We can go together,' said Toyah, stepping forward and linking her arm with Alfred. He smiled at her and she showed him how to position himself, then edged him forward alongside her and they slid down together.

'Me next,' said Pinto. Sammy followed.

At the cave, Toyah and Alfred were already heading for the rock face that led up to the high ledge. Sammy knew that this was their best hope of a route out of the underground. When he and Toyah explored the ledge before, he could see that the tunnel led down and away from the caves. If it continued in that direction, it might lead all the way through to the south edge of the Interland.

Or it might lead to a sheer drop, broken bones and a bottomless pit from which they'd never escape. They knew nothing about the nature of the caves and openings in the rocks between the Free Cave and the outside. They didn't even know if there was a route to the outside. They could be trapped forever. But they could do nothing else but try. Sammy thought of his dad, hoping he'd got himself on the cavern side of the blockage.

Alfred and Toyah were the first to make it up onto the ledge, each helping the other along the way. Pinto wasn't far behind. Sammy eventually pulled himself up. Sammy edged the group forwards through the tunnels. Water seeped through the walls and roof. In some places it poured through cracks and flowed through the tunnel under their feet. In these sections, the air was cool and fresh. In other sections the tunnels were dry, and the air stale.

There could come a time when the air would run out and they'd be walking into their grave, gradually overcome by carbon dioxide and slipping into unconsciousness.

As the cave widened a little, Pinto caught up with Sammy to walk alongside him. 'What about the others?' he said.

Sammy pushed away the thought that his dad might have been caught the wrong side of Zadie's explosion. He and his dad had drifted apart a little since being on the inside. As much as Sammy refused to accept that it had anything to do with the revelation that Ben wasn't his biological father, he knew that was part of it. Ben was the only father he'd ever known. His biological father, Marcus, was nothing to him – a Reader destroyed by Jay. Ben was a good man in Sammy's eyes, even if the connection between them had become strained.

The cave narrowed. Toyah and Alfred separated as they negotiated tight opening after tight opening. Alfred slipped sideways through a gap, followed by Toyah, then Pinto and Sammy. On the other side, the cave opened in two separate directions. The simplest, widest path was to the right, but Sammy sensed the left branch was the one. It was the left path through which the water flowed. The water must know which way to go to get out. 'This way,' he said.

Toyah snorted, 'You're kidding?'

'He's right,' said Alfred, moving in to take the lead. He lay down to squeeze beneath the wedge of rock that formed their ceiling and scraped himself through. Toyah followed, and Sammy next – Pinto last. The other side, the cave narrowed further and Sammy couldn't move his arms. He squeezed along the thin passage by shuffling his back and arm muscles like a worm. Alfred and Toyah were quicker than Sammy, putting a distance between them. Pinto stayed with Sammy, nudging up against him. Sammy's thoughts swam darkly around his head. No one would ever find them in this dark place, hundreds of feet below the surface, if one of them were stuck or crushed.

Alfred called back, 'Big drop coming up. It's tight, you need to go through sideways.'

Sammy hesitated, looking back past Pinto in the direction they'd come. 'What's the matter?' said Pinto, looking around.

'Nothing,' said Sammy. Fear pulsated through every cell in

his body. He'd never felt claustrophobic before, hardly batted an eyelid at the caving that he'd done since being in the Interland, but now the walls were closing in. Turning back wasn't an option. They were winding deeper underground, in pitch darkness, possibly trapping themselves. They had no choice but to press on and hope.

Alfred shouted through the gaps in the rocks up ahead. Alfred's voice. Sammy's skin prickled and his heart raced. He strained to see in the complete blackness beyond the torchlight. Push forward. His body swelled in his panic, filling the space between the rocks so that he became wedged. He talked himself down in his head, told himself to relax, breathe, move slowly. Another shout from Alfred, this time a noticeable hint of pain in his voice.

'My hands are slipping,' Alfred called. Sammy could move again. He could see Toyah now, leaning and reaching through the rock towards an opening in the floor, then adjusting her position and pushing herself further through.

'Toyah!' called Sammy.

'What is it?' Pinto's voice was taught.

Alfred shouted again, 'I'm slipping.'

'Nearly there,' Toyah said, but as Sammy reached her he saw over the ledge that Toyah was nowhere near him. Alfred hung on to a ledge more than fifteen feet below them. If his hands slipped, the drop was at least another twenty feet.

'I can jump,' Toyah said.

'You're joking,' said Sammy as he pushed himself over the ledge to reach for Alfred. 'You'll break your legs jumping that far.'

'If he falls, he'll die.'

'Let *me* go,' said Sammy. But, as Sammy readied himself to climb down to reach Alfred, one of Alfred's hands slipped off the ledge and he swung wildly out into the opening. Before

Sammy could react, Toyah flew past him and landed on the ledge, reaching out for Alfred.

Toyah landed hard on the rocks, her arm outstretched to Alfred, a lifeline for him to pull himself up to safety. 'Toyah!' Sammy called, seeing that she'd knocked the back of her head. There was desperation in his voice as he repeated her name and scrambled down the rest of the well they'd found themselves in.

Sammy pulled Toyah's now unresponsive body back further onto the ledge as Alfred climbed back up with Pinto's help. Sammy laid Toyah on her back, feeling around her head for any obvious wounds. His hand came away bloodied. He called her name, trying not to let panic come through in his voice. Alfred sat back against the rocks, breathing heavily. 'I'm sorry,' he said.

Pinto moved towards his sister, his eyes glazed over. Sammy shook Toyah a little more vigorously.

Pinto leaned over her. 'She's dead,' he said.

'No,' said Sammy. 'She's unconscious, but she's alive.'

'She's dead,' Pinto repeated, hysteria building.

Sammy took Pinto by the shoulders and looked into his eyes. 'She's OK.'

Pinto seemed to come around. He calmed down. He leaned over his sister to confirm her breathing. Sammy felt useless. Responsible. This was his idea. He was the one who directed them through the caves. He could have led them out of the Interland with Zadie, and with everyone else. This was all his fault. He thought of Jay, and of his dad. What would they do?

Sammy watched in awe as eight-year-old Pinto deployed his training received in the medical centre. He was calm, as if in autopilot. He made sure that Toyah was comfortable, laying his jacket over her, then turned to Alfred. 'You OK?'

'My ankle,' said Alfred, his breathing in shallow bursts as he tried to control the pain.

'Could be broken,' Pinto said. 'When we move again, we'll have to help him keep the weight off it.'

'*Move* again?' Sammy said. 'Are you kidding? We're not going anywhere like this.'

'Sammy.' Alfred raised his voice and Sammy sat back against the rocks. He watched as Toyah's chest moved up and down with her breathing. He willed her eyes to open and for her to sit up, rub the back of her head and make some stupid comment. But moment after moment passed, and she didn't wake.

25

Sunlight poured into Jay's room. For a moment she thought she was back in the loft bedroom of her childhood home on Beach Lane. It was just over a year since she had last woken in that room, but it felt like a lifetime. She was a different person, and it was a different world.

She'd slept well past their planned departure. She dressed quickly, her clothes still damp from the previous night. Stitch and Samir were awake, readying themselves to leave. 'Hurry,' said Jay, continuing down the stairs, past Sebastian's closed door and into the kitchen. She checked the cupboards. Mostly tinned food. She found a box of cereal and poured some into a bowl, eating the dry wheat flakes with her fingers.

Stitch entered the kitchen and picked a bowl from the cupboard, following Jay's lead with the dry cereal. 'You look like shit,' he said.

'Couldn't sleep for the snoring coming from your room.'

Stitch rolled his eyes. 'Look,' he said, showing Jay his hand, flexing his fingers. The redness had gone.

'Looks better.'

'I did some work on it last night,' said Stitch.

'Your healing trick?'

Stitch smiled, pride pouring from him. 'It's not a trick. I'm getting better at it. There's something in the way I align my thoughts and channel the energy. It's difficult to explain.'

'I'm impressed. Your dad OK?'

'It's been weirdly good to spend some time with him,' said Stitch. 'He's been talking about Mum this morning. First time he's spoken about her like this since she died. It's like he's finally getting his head above the water and seeing that there's a world out there.'

'Ironic,' said Jay.

Stitch nodded. 'Seems everywhere we go there are people squeezed by the State, living in deprivation and terrified of Readers. The only Given still out here are the ones who have learned to shield and avoid detection,' he said. 'And everyone else seems to have had enough, happy to see the end of the Given if that means peace.'

'The State are weeding the Given out of society. They're blaming them for the unrest and the economic downturn. So then the State becomes more powerful. People must realise what's happening,' said Jay.

'How many of the Given do you think have been lost in these purges?'

Jay shrugged and shook her head as she pushed the cereal around her bowl with her finger. She'd not yet allowed herself to think about it in terms of numbers. Her dad, Ben, had told her before that around one in a thousand people had some level of power, though the higher power levels were rare. That would make around sixty thousand Given in the UK alone. There was no way of knowing how many of those were in hiding, and how many had been taken through rehabilitation.

Some would have passed through rehab and would now be powerless. Others would have died in the process, either through becoming reduced too far to sustain life, or through their own resistance to the reduction – and the rest would now be Readers.

'What's that?' said Stitch, taking Jay's hand and examining a graze she'd got back at Samir's house. His hands were warm, his touch gentle.

'Just a scratch,' said Jay, allowing Stitch to cradle her hand for a moment.

Samir entered the kitchen, and Jay yanked her hand back. Stitch turned to his dad, who was munching on a pastry. Stitch looked from his bowl of dry cereal to his dad. 'Where did you get that?'

'Sebastian gave it to me. He's got a whole load in there.'

Stitch snorted and pushed his bowl away.

'Let's go,' said Jay. To Samir: 'I'll show you the garages on the way out, then you can get the car?'

Sebastian came into the kitchen, holding out a torch, which Jay took with a nod of thanks. 'God speed,' he said.

* * *

THE TIDE WAS OUT, revealing a strip of mucky sand and gravel at the water's edge from which Jay looked up at the circular opening in the river wall. Water dribbled from its rim and down the wall, a stain only visible from the riverside. The opening was at least twenty feet above their heads, and there was nothing to indicate whether it would lead them to the prison. A column of step-irons led up to the grill fixed to the opening.

Stitch had to jump to reach the first step-iron. He missed

and fell back down. At the second attempt he got a grip and with his foot found a ledge from which to push himself up to the next hand-hold. He looked over his shoulder and nodded for Jay to follow.

Stitch reached the opening as Jay was still halfway up the wall. As she reached the level of Stitch's feet, she heard a scrape and a crack as he pulled the grill free, holding on to it for long enough to launch it beyond Jay and down to the shore. Water and sludge spurted out of the hole, and Jay leaned away to avoid the spatter. Stitch pulled himself up and into the hole, standing without the need to duck his head. Jay climbed the final few metres and joined him, rejecting his offer of a hand and pulling herself up next to him. They looked out over the river for a moment before turning to head into the darkness.

Jay used the torch to illuminate the invert of the tunnel, dry but for a trickle of water, and mostly clean. She had a sense of the direction to the prison. The further they walked, the stronger Jay's sense of pull towards Cassie, and towards a body of power that was the collective energy of the Given incarcerated at the prison. Without having to articulate it, she knew that Stitch also sensed they were heading in the right direction. Only twice did Jay have to pause for more than a moment at an intersection between tunnels, where the signal was ambiguous. On both occasions, Stitch knew which way to go.

A loud clank echoed through the tunnels from behind them, as if someone had dropped a hammer. Jay looked at Stitch and they peered into the darkness. They held their breath, something scuttled from somewhere to their left. 'Rats,' said Stitch.

'Rats don't make that kind of clunking noise.'

'Let's go.'

After about an hour of walking, they came to the base of a circular concrete-lined shaft that stretched above their heads for thirty feet to the open air through a steel mesh. Water dripped from above, both from the mesh at the top and from several connections to the shaft from smaller pipes at different levels. Jay could see that there was a metal hatch in the mesh that would allow them to get through and out to the surface. Step-irons ran all the way up from where they stood. Jay took the lead this time, steadily climbing towards the hatch at the top, the air growing cooler and fresher as she climbed.

At the surface, Jay edged up the hatch with her head and scanned the yard for signs of guards. Nothing. They rolled out onto the grass and without a word; they made a dash to the cover of the main building, stopping and crouching by a wall. 'She's close,' said Jay, her voice barely a whisper. 'Follow me.'

'Wait!' Stitch said, nodding towards a building on the other side of the yard. Three men walked around the corner of the building and made their way towards the front entrance. 'Readers?'

'Feels like it,' said Jay as the men disappeared into the building.

Stitch followed as Jay stalked between the low-rise buildings towards the main prison block. As they edged around the last of the low-rise, the vast expanse of the back wall of the prison façade came into view. A short dash across the yard and they'd be at the doors in the centre of the block. No sign of any guards, but the building façade was littered with windows from which they might easily be seen. Stitch followed Jay's eyes and scanned the windows for signs of life. 'Can't see anyone.'

They made a run for the doors. They rested a moment in

the doorway as Jay looked back over the yard, eyes alert to any movement. Nothing. 'Weirdly quiet,' she said to Stitch. 'This is too easy.'

'Don't knock it,' Stitch said as he turned and pushed the door which swung open to the corridor beyond. It reminded Jay of a school corridor, running almost as far as she could see, doors off to each side. Deserted. Stitch pressed on and Jay told him to slow down so that she could get her bearings. Her senses told her that Cassie was on the ground floor, on the other side of the building.

From a side corridor, two figures appeared. They stopped in front of Jay and Stitch, in a stunned silence.

Jay knew immediately that the two men were Readers.

She sensed their confusion at Jay and Stitch's presence. She took advantage of their hesitation. She and Stitch connected and combined their power to attack the Readers simultaneously.

Jay felt a wave of energy from them, an attack of their own, but it was quickly overcome by the far stronger combined power of Jay and Stitch. Both Readers fell to their knees, each with his hands raised to the sides of his head. Jay continued to push her energy into their minds, reducing them until they flopped to the floor.

Stitch crouched next to the nearest Reader. He was unconscious, a scar forming on the side of his face.

'More?' Jay tensed, ready to continue the attack, to be sure that they wouldn't come back at them.

Stitch raised a hand to signal for Jay to stop. 'Enough. They're out.'

Jay relaxed. She breathed again. 'Let's move before more of them arrive.'

As they reached halfway along the corridor, the space opened out into a circular, double-height atrium, ringed by a series of steel doorways. They backed up against the wall and looked up into the higher levels, scanning for movement. They communicated without talking.

No sign of any more Readers.

A sense of Cassie.

An uneasy feeling.

Stay alert. Be quick.

Jay remained still. Energy flowed at her in waves from beneath her feet - a dark energy that left a bitter taste in her mouth. The power of the Given was weak within the circle, and Jay felt vulnerable. She itched to get out as quickly as possible. Stitch walked away from her, circling the perimeter, his hand brushing the surface of each door as if trying to feel for Cassie. Jay was certain that their friend was behind one of these doors. She approached the nearest door, a heavy, steel structure. A panel next to the door was open. She peered inside to see a control board with a series of buttons, and a blank screen.

Jay caught sight of something across the room. She turned to see that a man had appeared beside Stitch. Her heart raced. Her feet frozen to the spot.

Stitch turned to the man, then took a step back, looking up into his face. Jay sensed that this man was not a Reader. He had no power.

She wrenched her feet from the floor and made around the perimeter towards them. She tried to read him but got nothing. She pushed her influence into his mind but faced a resistance she'd not experienced before. She stumbled in the sheer strength of the power in the building. It came at her, relentlessly, through the floor. She was dizzy.

Stitch appeared frozen. Jay followed the man's gaze as he looked up into the higher levels. There were Readers there, concealed. Jay felt their presence. The man stepped in front of

Stitch and turned to the control panel. He spoke, but Jay couldn't hear what he said. She scuffed along the floor, edging closer. The energy from the floor and something coming from this man slowed her progress. She was still twenty feet away when the door next to Stitch swung open, controlled from the panel in front of the man. Then he shoved Stitch into the room before pressing another button to close the door behind him, sealing her friend in the cell.

The man turned to Jay, and she saw his name – *Hinton* – not from him, but from the minds of the Readers above them. He channelled their power somehow, and there were too many of them for Jay to resist. She closed her eyes and tried to summon as much of the energy of the Given as she could. She held up a barrier to the Readers, but it was weak. Hinton moved slowly towards her, an unsettling half-smile on his face. He was confident, felt no threat from Jay. Jay was weak. She needed the trees, the water and the earth to realise her full strength.

'Jay Macfarlane,' Hinton said. He emanated darkness, but not power. 'I want to show you something.' He turned to the nearest door and opened its control panel. The door swung open and before she could retreat, he reached out and took hold of her top, pulling her towards him like she was a rag doll. He flung her onto the floor of the room. The door clunked closed behind her.

Jay picked herself up and looked around the room, frantically searching for a means of escape. *Stupid*, she thought to herself as it sunk in how easily they'd been caught.

Nothing but steel walls, floor, ceiling. She could see that the chair too was made of metal. Within a few seconds, the door opened and Hinton entered. She tried her power on him. She was angry. She pushed into his mind.

A spike of pain pierced her chest and forced its way into

her head. Her vision faltered, and she flopped to the floor, clutching her temples. This man's power was nothing she recognised. The pain intensified. Her world went black.

She came back to consciousness sometime later, her head throbbing. The room was empty. She was nauseous, confused. She struggled to her feet, using the wall to steady herself. Once again, the door swung open and Hinton entered. Jay could barely focus on him, her vision swimming and her body pulsating with waves of pain.

'She's ready,' Hinton said. Another figure appeared and led Jay to the chair in the middle of the room. He fastened her hands to the arms of the chair and removed her shoes and socks. He strapped her ankles to the chair legs before he and Hinton left the room. The door clunked closed.

Jay thought of the Interland, and of Zadie. She pictured Sasha Colden, her grandmother and the beginning of the power of the Given. As the image of Sasha floated in front of her eyes, she rested her head back to look at the ceiling.

Then it began.

The light in the room faded. Shadow edged towards her. Her own inner colours seeped from her body, the wisps of colour like gas leaking into the room, taking away the essence of her power. She closed her eyes and her head spun – faster and faster until there was nothing.

* * *

OTIS SHOVED Davey into the side of the tunnel, the concrete rings wet from the water leaking through from the outside. He'd had enough of his random choices of direction whenever they reached a junction. He spoke like he knew which way Jay and Stitch had gone, like he was some kind of expert tracker.

But each time Otis listened to him, they ended up further away from the centre of the prison.

'Look,' said Davey. Let's just continue on this branch and take the next opening to the surface. If we're far from the centre, then we just work our way in, right?'

Otis released Davey's top and pushed himself away with a huff. He stormed off down the tunnel.

Earlier, Davey had spotted Jay from the window of the first floor of the pub that had been their resting place for the night. He gathered Otis, and they tracked Jay and Stitch, figuring that they'd need some help in their mission to free Cassie. Now, with Davey's poor tracking skills, they were probably a good way behind, and likely wouldn't catch them up in time to be of any use. Otis was determined to show Jay that he was on their side, the side of the Given, and that he could be an asset to the cause.

'Here,' called Davey. Otis stopped and turned back. In his fit of anger, he'd walked straight underneath a narrow shaft to the surface.

He backtracked to where Davey stood and looked up. 'Let's do it,' he said.

As soon as they emerged from the tunnel into the open, Otis felt the power of the Readers. It was concentrated on a building south of their location. Davey seemed to register what Otis was thinking. He nodded at Otis and then stood, moving towards the source of the power. Davey broke into a run, his long strides taking him to the cover of the low-rise buildings in no time. Otis reached him seconds later, puffing.

Otis sensed Readers, although no noise came from the building. He also felt the presence of the Given. 'Jay is here,' he said. Davey made to move into the building, but Otis held him back. 'Wait. Her power is weak. Tell me what you sense?'

Davey thought for a moment. He closed his eyes. 'Jay and

Stitch are here. Cassie too. Not much power. They could be shielded.'

'Can you feel the darkness?'

Davey nodded. 'Readers, for sure.'

'We go in covert. You shield for both of us. Let me see if I can get a fix on them.'

They stalked up the corridor. Otis felt the increasing energy of the darkness as they approached the central core of the building, a circular atrium. They stopped short, hidden behind the wall. Otis brushed his shaggy fringe from his eyes and scanned the room. Davey shielded with all of his level-7 power.

'Stitch is in there,' Otis said, motioning towards one of the steel doors. 'And Jay is in that one. I don't sense Cassie.'

Davey pulled Otis back as a man appeared on the other side of the room, heading towards the room that Otis sensed was occupied by Jay. Three others followed close behind the man, like guards protecting their General. The leader opened the control panel next to the door and pushed a button. The door swung open, and the men peered inside.

'Keep shielding,' whispered Otis to Davey.

As they watched, the leader waved away the other men, who retreated down the corridor. Then the man entered the room.

'Let's go. We get Stitch on the way through, then we take him out and get out of here. Grab that fire extinguisher.'

Davey pulled the red extinguisher from its housing and immediately struggled with its weight, almost dropping it. Otis focused his energy on the door behind which he knew Stitch was locked. As they approached, there was a clunk and a click as the door swung open.

'How...what -?' Davey started.

Otis interrupted, 'Stitch!' he shouted as Stitch launched himself at Otis and Davey.

Stitch took a moment to realise that it was Otis and Davey. His attack turned into a greeting as the three turned towards Jay's cell. As they did so, the man they'd seen from across the room emerged from the room and closed the door behind him. He turned to them.

The look of surprise on the man's face lasted just a second before Davey shoved the fire extinguisher into his face, knocking him to the floor.

* * *

SHOUTING from outside the door drew Jay in and out of consciousness. She opened her eyes a crack. All was dark but for a glow of light around the door. Then it was gone. She tried to move her arms, but her fingers wouldn't work. She slipped into darkness.

The door flew open, the noise and sudden light bursting into the room. Jay opened her eyes, seeing nothing but the light of the doorway and shadows moving through it.

'Jay, can you hear me?' a familiar voice.

'We'll have to carry her.' Jay now recognised Stitch's voice – frantic, pained. 'Davey, you and Otis help Jay up, I'm going to find Cassie.'

Jay felt her hands and legs as they were freed, a stinging pain on the inside of her left wrist. Someone on each side of her helped her to stand.

Someone touched the side of her face. 'Shit,' said Stitch. 'She has the scar.'

* * *

THE BOY SUPPORTING HER, Otis, pulled her across the yard towards the storm-water shaft. In front of them, someone else was shouldering Cassie. Stitch led the way. Feeling was coming back to her legs, and she moved them to help Otis. Stitch was the first to reach the opening to the shaft, followed by Davey and Cassie. Stitch flung open the metal hatch.

'Cassie?' said Jay.

Cassie flung her arms around Jay's neck. 'I knew you'd come, you idiot.' Cassie touched Jay on the side of her face. 'You have a scar. They reduced you.'

Jay's heart sank. She felt no power within her. She looked for a similar scar on Cassie's face. 'And you?' asked Jay.

Cassie shook her head. 'No.'

'Move,' shouted Stitch, motioning towards the steps down to the tunnel. 'Talk later.'

Jay looked over her shoulder, back to the building. No sign of any movement. 'What happened to Hinton?'

Stitch followed Jay's eyes. 'Otis and Davey happened to him. Slugged him a good one. He raised the alarm though, so the Readers will be on their way here from all over the unit. Won't take them long to figure out where we've gone.'

Davey put a hand on Jay's arm. 'You next,' he said. Jay looked him in the eye but couldn't read him. Her powers were weak. She felt nothing.

Stitch was the last to enter the shaft. Halfway down, Readers pulled at the hatch. 'Go,' Stitch shouted, pointing at the southern opening. Otis and Davey led the way, with Cassie and Jay following. Stitch hit the base of the shaft and launched himself after Cassie and Jay. More sets of feet land in the puddles at the base of the shaft. One, two, then three people. Then more. Reader after Reader. Stitch was at her back, a hand on her arm to urge her on. Cassie was up ahead with Davey and Otis. Jay's body ached, her head still pounding and throbbing like it had been emptied by whatever happened in that metal room. 'We need to pick it up,' Stitch shouted. 'They're gaining.'

At the second intersection, the Readers took the wrong turn. When Jay and Stitch reached the opening in the river wall, Otis, Cassie and Davey were standing at the precipice, looking out over the river, but the tide had risen, concealing the shore and blocking their path back to the steps to the road. There would be no way they'd be able to swim upstream against the flow, no way of knowing how far the next set of steps would be.

Stitch looked at Jay, then turned back into the tunnel. 'We can't go that way. We won't make it through the currents in the Thames. Who knows how far we'd need to swim.'

The sound of footsteps echoed through the tunnels. Getting closer. As the Readers emerged around the corner and scrabbled to a stop just a few feet from them, Otis linked arms with Jay. Davey did the same with Stitch, and Cassie joined. They turned, and together, they jumped.

The moment she hit the surface, the chain of arms broke. The cold water froze Jay's body and mind. Darkness blinded her. For what felt like minutes, Jay turned and tumbled in the water before crashing through the surface, gasping for air. She went under once more but returned to the surface quickly to take another breath. She was numb. Fear was the only thing keeping her blood pumping. She kept her head above the surface and stopped fighting against the water, instead summoning the power, the tendons of energy to take her to safety. She got nothing. No whispers from the water, no supporting energy, nothing. She felt empty – abandoned.

Jay struggled to keep her nose above the water, the currents pulling and jostling her. She scraped her arm on the river wall as she twisted and turned in the water. Voices. Up ahead, shouting. Stitch's voice. She strained to see. Two figures up ahead, out of the water and leaning out towards her. Stitch and Cassie.

Cassie held on to a railing on the steps as Stitch leaned out over the water, his hand stretched out. 'Take my hand,' Stitch shouted above the noise of the swirling water. But Jay was moving fast. Cassie leaned further out and Stitch stretched as far as he could. Jay thrust her legs down and projected herself up, hand outstretched for Stitch. He grabbed her wrist and clamped his fingers around her hand as she did the same. She jolted, pulling Stitch so that he almost followed her into the river. Cassie held firm, and Stitch's grip was sure. She drifted towards the river wall as Stitch and Cassie pulled her in. She scrambled up onto the concrete steps, bashing both knees as she desperately pulled herself from the water and collapsed on the steps.

'No time to rest,' said Stitch. 'The Readers will be coming. We need to find Samir.'

'Where's Otis, and Davey?'

'Gone to get to their motorbikes. We'll catch up with them later. We need to go.' Stitch dragged Jay to her feet; Cassie took her other arm and helped her up the steps. Back on the road, the wind felt like ice forming on Jay's skin.

Stitch looked up and down the road, trying to get his bearings. He pointed across the street towards an alleyway. 'There,' he said. 'Let's get off the road.' He grabbed Jay's arm.

'I'm OK,' said Jay. 'You go. I'm right behind you.'

Cassie and Stitch ran across the road as Jay caught a breath. As she stepped off the kerb, a Land Rover turned the corner and bore down on her. 'Jay,' shouted Stitch, turning as if to come back for her. Jay froze. The Land Rover stopped directly in front of her, close enough that she could see the look in the eyes of the Readers in the front seats. They stared at her, as if daring her to run. Before they could open their doors, Jay turned and ran as fast as she could towards Stitch and the alleyway, pursued by the sound of feet hitting the tarmac. Jay and Stitch followed Cassie into the warren of alleyways, taking random turns at every intersection. Still the Readers followed Jay.

Stitch took the lead. 'This way.' They poured out of the end of an alleyway into a yard area with a row of garages. 'Here,' said Stitch, running towards the garage at the end where he'd left Samir with the car. They slammed into the wall of the garage, its doors open.

Empty.

The car had gone.

No sign of Samir.

'No,' shouted Stitch, doubling over, his face in his hands. Jay turned just as three men ran from the alleyway, looking in both directions. They spotted Jay. Just fifty feet between them. Jay could not run any further. If this was her fate, to be taken by the Readers, then so be it.

The Readers closed the distance between them like they were in no hurry. Stitch slumped to the floor.

A roar of an engine from the side street. Lights. A car screamed around the corner and slid to a halt next to them. The Readers froze for a moment, then ran. Samir screamed something in Arabic before Stitch opened the passenger door and jumped in. Cassie reached for the back door and flung herself across to the other side, leaving space for Jay. Like a rabbit in headlights, Jay froze, her feet stuck to the floor. She stumbled, banged her knee on the car as Samir pulled away. A Reader was on her, his hand on her arm. Cassie's hands on Jay's other arm. Samir picked up speed, Stitch screaming into his face to put his foot down. Jay squeezed herself away from the Reader's grasp. She tried to summon her powers but got nothing. The Reader looked into her, then turned to look at Cassie before clutching the sides of his head, squirming in pain. Cassie and Stitch both stared down the Reader, digging into him, disabling him. He stumbled and fell as the car picked up speed. With Cassie's help, Jay threw herself into the back of the car and Samir swerved around the corner and onto the main road.

26

Hinton looked out over the tops of the prison buildings towards the hills in the south. The midday sun had burned through the morning clouds and he could feel the warmth on his skin. He dabbed his fingers on the back of his head where his hair was matted with dried blood. The two boys that attacked him had approached shielded. He felt humiliated but undefeated. The outcome would be the same. Jay had already been reduced, and without Jay, the Interland was unprotected.

He pulled back his left sleeve and itched his stub where it attached to the prosthetic. The wound was long healed, but sometimes he still felt his hand, his wrist, his phantom number. Cutting off his own arm at nineteen years old was a small price to pay. Hinton rejected the power, rejected the membership of a club he never asked to join.

The path of the Given, the path that his parents both took, was not for him. The energy of the Given had brought him physical pain no one understood. With the physical pain came a psychological deterioration, a depression that infected every cell of his body.

The day came when he couldn't stand it anymore. His pain and depression had already affected his family, split their lives in two. His mother left not long after his nineteenth birthday, and his father remained distraught for months after. That day, in his father's workshop, with the band saw his father used for the logs sawn from fallen branches, he cut the Given out of his body.

If his father had been another five minutes, he would have bled out on the workshop floor, and if he'd got there two minutes earlier, they said, his arm might have been saved.

The false limb was his reminder of the power he once held, and his connection to the Given. Over the weeks and months that followed his discharge from hospital, as he learned to use the prosthetic arm, a new power grew within him. It was nothing like the painful energy that had been the power of the Given. This new power was in harmony with his body, was something that completed him, and it was unique. With his extreme action in rejection of the power of the Given and all its energy of natural sources, came something else – a power that couldn't be detected by the Given, a power with an unknown source that even Hinton didn't understand. What he sensed was that his power came from deep within the earth. Not from the land, the sea, and all living things, like the Given, but from the core, the heavy metals, the ore. He needed no Interland to exercise power.

'Sir?' A Reader approached Hinton on the roof. 'We lost them in the City. They split up into two groups and got away in vehicles.'

Hinton continued to inspect his prosthetic arm. 'When did you transform? Become a Reader?'

The Reader stumbled over his words. 'Me... Sir? I... Six years ago now, Sir.'

'And what level Given were you before you transformed?'

'Level three. Now a level six Reader.'

'There's a level of commitment that comes with the honour of being a Reader, you know that?' The Reader nodded. 'And with that commitment, from all of us, we control the Given, yes?'

'Yes, Sir.'

'So whose lack of commitment caused the failure today? Whose commitment so failed that we allowed two outsiders to walk through open doors to get to our most valuable prisoners and walk out unopposed?'

'I don't think it was...'

'You know,' the man interrupted. 'That I can reduce any Reader at the touch of a button?' The Reader nodded and lowered his gaze. Hinton pulled his sleeve down to cover his false limb. 'Anyway. The 8C has been reduced, so the Interland is unprotected. We can progress.'

'The Readers are ready to move out on your instruction, Sir.'

'We leave in the morning,' he said, thinking about his wife, and his little girl, Megan. 'We bring all Readers above level six.'

'That could be thirty Readers. Do we need that many?'

'We rendezvous at the Gateway, make sure everyone has the co-ordinates.' The Reader hesitated as if wanting to say something more. Hinton looked at him. 'What?'

'What do we expect to find when we get there?'

'Not your concern. Just get everyone ready. Without an 8C at the gates, the Interland is mine for the taking.'

'But sir. What about Zadie Lawrence?'

Hinton nodded. 'She'll see the higher purpose, particularly when she realises how powerful she can be as a Reader.' Hinton clapped the Reader before him on the back. 'Don't worry! I'm sure you'll get used to answering to her command.'

* * *

IN THE BACK of the car, Jay drifted in and out of sleep as Samir drove them to the agreed meeting place with Otis and Davey, where they could rest and take stock.

Jay's conscious moments were filled with anxiety and sadness. She felt no power. Her mind was deathly silent. No whispers, no feelings. She turned over her hand to look at her wrist. Her skin from the base of her hand almost to her elbow was a fiery, angry red. Through the red wounding, like a burn, there was no decipherable number. The 8C was no longer there, or at least no longer visible.

Cassie leaned over to Jay in the back seat and examined Jay's wrist. 'Looks sore,' she said.

Jay nodded. 'You?' she asked.

Cassie shook her head and revealed her own wrist, which showed her level seven marking, untouched by her experience in the sink-room. 'They wanted my power to remain with me so that I'd attract you. It was a trap. Right from the start, they took me and...' Cassie trailed off, her voice choked. 'They took me and killed Reuben. But what they wanted was you. It's my fault, we should have known...'

Jay silenced Cassie with a hand on her arm. Stitch leaned into the back from the passenger seat. 'We're meeting at High-down. Samir knows a route up the west slope that we can take the car closer to the summit. Not sure you've got much walking in you, Jay?'

Jay shook her head.

Cassie said, 'I thought that route was impassable.'

'Me too,' said Stitch.

'Not if you know it like I do,' said Samir from the driver's seat. 'You kids don't know everything, you know. Wisdom comes with age.'

Jay rested her head on Cassie's shoulder. She had only enough energy to open her eyes and communicate for a few minutes before needing to rest again. She would be no use to them now, to the Given, or to the Interland. One more encounter with a Reader would kill her.

PART IV

27

As soon as Stitch and Cassie set Jay on the ground at the summit of Highdown, she curled up and drifted back to sleep. Stitch had defeat in his eyes. He placed a jumper under Jay's head as a pillow. 'Do you have something we can cover her with?' Cassie rummaged in her bag and dragged one of her own jumpers over Jay.

Stitch turned away. 'I'll get wood,' he said. Samir followed him into the trees.

Cassie put a hand on Jay's head, lightly touching the scar on her face. It looked identical to the wound that killed Reuben. Cassie left Jay to sleep and approached Otis and Davey, deep in discussion. 'What do you think?' asked Otis.

'About what?' replied Cassie.

'I say we get moving. Let's get to the Interland before these Readers can regroup and get there themselves. If we wait, the Interland will be taken.'

Cassie admired his spirit. Otis was small, but he was full of energy and fight. Davey didn't look so sure, looking past Cassie to where Stitch and Samir had melted into the trees. 'You might be right,' Cassie said. 'But without Jay...' She looked back at where Jay lay motionless. 'What chance do we have against the Readers?'

'Exactly,' said Davey.

Otis shifted on his feet. 'That's all I'd expect from you,' he said to Davey. 'There's more to this than survival. What are *you* going to do? Hide out and hope it all blows over?'

'Like you've been doing, you mean?' Davey hit back. 'Living up here in the hills, away from reality.'

'I had no choice. I had no idea about the Interland until I met Jay and Stitch.'

'Hey,' Cassie said, raising a hand between Otis and Davey. She felt conflicted. She owed the Interland nothing. Yet...

'I'm with Otis,' Cassie said. 'We have to do something. For the sake of the rest of the Given still back at the Interland. But it's Jay we need to get into the Interland. It needs the 8C and the C to protect it from the Readers.' Cassie thought of Jay's little brother, Sammy. She cared for him deeply, like she cared for Reuben. And now Reuben was dead. She couldn't face another loss.

Stitch and Samir arrived back at the camp, arms laden with firewood. Cassie helped Samir construct a fire while Stitch went to Jay. Samir broke up the smaller sticks for kindling, carefully placing the wood, and re-placing anything that Cassie contributed. She laughed and sat back, allowing Samir to finish the arrangement. 'Stitch,' Cassie called. 'Lighter?' Stitch threw over his lighter and Cassie handed it to Samir. 'Do the honours,' she smiled.

Samir lit the fire and Cassie sat back. She looked over at Stitch and back to Samir, trying to see the family resemblance. 'What?' said Samir.

Cassie shook her head. 'You two talking again. It's good.'

'Yes,' said Samir. 'I did a lot of thinking over the months

Stitch was away from me. His mother left us some years ago, and I was suddenly alone.'

'You and Stitch both,' said Cassie.

Samir looked Cassie in the eye, his dark irises reflecting the flicker of the flame from the fire. 'I know that now,' he said. 'My son and I were together, but alone. His letter made it very clear, but then he was gone. Disappeared into thin air with you and Jay. Like they say, you don't know the value of something until it is gone.'

'True enough,' said Cassie, looking around at the trees stretching up above the ledge on the summit of Highdown, where Reuben had fallen. She'd once taken freedom for granted. Not now, not when it was so fragile. It seemed inevitable that it would soon slip away from them for good.

'Then Allah brought him back to me,' he smiled. 'And this time I'll not let him go. This time we will stick together.' He turned back to the fire to load more sticks.

Cassie looked over at Stitch. He had his hand on Jay's head and his eyes closed as if he were trying to read her. 'Hey? What's up?'

Stitch opened his eyes and turned to Cassie. He pulled his hand away from Jay, frustrated. 'Nothing,' he said.

'Tell me,' said Cassie.

Stitch stepped over to sit with Cassie by the fire. 'You know I've been trying to develop the other side of my powers, the stuff that's not connected with Jay?' Cassie shook her head, a quizzical look on her face. Stitch rarely confided in her. There had always been an invisible barrier between them that prevented a deeper connection. 'Like with Sammy,' Stitch continued. 'That day we arrived at the Interland and Sammy was injured, you know?'

Cassie nodded. 'I remember.'

'I helped him.'

Cassie held Stitch's eye for a moment. 'You're talking about *healing*?'

Stitch nodded. 'Nothing miraculous, like mending bones or anything like that, but I'm pretty sure my focus dispersed the infection in him. I felt it.'

'What about Jay?' said Cassie, suspending her disbelief for a moment.

Stitch shook his head. 'Not getting anything. With Sammy, I had the time. I sat with him for hours in that place. We connected properly.' He lifted his sleeve for a moment, inspecting the black letter "C". 'I thought with my natural connection to Jay, I might be able to tune into her physiology like I did with Sammy.'

'Nothing?'

'I need her to fight. Why won't she fight?' said Stitch.

'She *is* fighting, she fought for me. She's the reason I got out of that place,' Cassie said.

Stitch said, 'That was more down to those two,' he nodded towards Otis and Davey. 'What I mean is why won't she fight for the power? She's been more scared of the source with every week that passed in there. It's like she won't trust herself to connect.'

Cassie looked at Jay, breathing steadily, her eyes closed. 'She's been through a lot. The fight against the Readers last time took a lot out of her. I'm not sure she ever really recovered.'

'Have you seen her wrist?' said Stitch. 'Her marking isn't there. Just a messy red mark, like a wound from a burn. She's been properly reduced.'

'Then we're screwed,' said Cassie. She nodded towards Otis and Davey. 'Otis is all up for storming over to the Interland, putting up a fight. I think Davey would rather curl up and hide up here. Without Jay's power... I don't know.'

'All we need to do is get her there, to the Interland and the source.'

'But what do you think she is afraid of?' said Cassie.

Stitch jumped to his feet. 'I've got an idea.' He called over Davey and Otis.

28

‘In theory,’ said Stitch. ‘Jay can rebuild her power.’

‘How?’ said Cassie.

‘If the folklore holds true, then the power can be rebuilt through the hill forts. I think that’s what Zadie Lawrence did after she was reduced. After the hill forts, a return to the power of the Interland might be enough.’ He paused, and the others remained silent. ‘From what I read in the notebooks back at the Interland, if I’m interpreting it right, if Jay connects with all three hill forts, she’ll be ready, like *primed*, to re-establish her powers at the Interland. Enough to repel the Readers.’

Davey huffed. ‘You mean the Interland where the Readers are heading, with the source of power they’re planning to destroy? The one Zadie Lawrence is opening up for the Readers? That’s a fantastic idea, Stitch.’ Davey stood and paced.

‘And,’ said Otis, ‘how is she supposed to connect to the hill forts when she can barely open her eyes?’

Cassie groaned, scratching her head in frustration. ‘By the time we get to the Interland, the Readers will already be there, and the source might already be gone. Which means that all this would be for nothing. None of us will have power.'

'Exactly,' said Davey. 'So what's the sense in going anywhere near that place. It would be suicide. We should move as quickly as we can in the opposite direction to the Interland. We need to hole up somewhere they'll not find us.'

Otis shook his head and kicked out at a stick by the fire. 'I've been holing up for long enough. I can't do it anymore, not after what we saw down there at the prison.'

'I'm with Otis,' said Stitch. 'We have to try before every Given ends up in a place like that. If we run, that's the end of the Given...'

'It's the end *anyway*,' said Davey.

'What would Jay do?' said Stitch, silencing the bickering.

Cassie thought about it for a moment. She wasn't convinced that Jay would run towards the Interland right now. She'd be more cautious than that. She'd be thinking of how to keep all of her friends and family safe. The only way they'd all survive this would be to get as far from the Readers as possible. But then there was Sammy. And Jay's dad, Ben. And the rest of the Given trapped at the Interland, held by Zadie Lawrence, if they were still alive.

'She'd go,' said Cassie. 'To the Interland. She'd do whatever she could to free the rest of the Given, by protecting the source. If there was even a chance of a future with at least a sliver of freedom, then she'd try.'

Stitch nodded. Samir nodded too in agreement. Davey sighed and sat back down. 'She would,' he said. 'The idiot. She would.'

* * *

THEY SHARED what food they had left and allowed Jay to sleep. After some time, Jay woke of her own accord and sleepily shuffled over to sit by the fire, pulling her jacket tight around her shoulders.

'Hey,' said Stitch as Jay squeezed to sit between him and Cassie.

Jay rubbed her eyes. 'How long have I been out?'

'Three days,' said Cassie with a smile.

Jay laughed, and Samir handed her a hunk of bread and a bottle of water. 'I feel better,' she said, taking a deep breath and looking up into the trees.

'Recharging?' said Stitch. He reached for Jay's hand and she allowed him to turn it over to have a look at her wrist. The redness had eased, and there was a smudge of a marking, a far cry from a distinguishable number, but something at least. 'It looks better,' said Stitch, looking to Cassie for confirmation.

Cassie nodded. 'You might be right.'

Jay looked between her two friends. 'Right about what?'

Cassie explained Stitch's plan for Jay to connect with each of the three hill forts before heading to the Interland and the source to complete her recharge, the re-establishment of her power.

'Connect? How?' asked Jay.

'Think about it,' Stitch said, an angry edge to his voice.

Jay startled at Stitch's tone. 'What's wrong?'

'This is serious. You need to look at yourself...'

'Stitch, ease up,' said Cassie.

'Ease up? No. I won't ease up. This is it, Jay. You need to decide where you are in this fight. Because if you don't wake up and see what's happening, then that's it for all of us. All the Given.'

'I...' Jay stammered. 'I don't know what you're asking me.

Tell me what I'm supposed to do and I'll do it. You saw the control that man had over us, all of us.'

Stitch held Jay's hands in his, pulling her around to face him. He spoke slowly. 'You need to dig deep,' he said. 'You *know* that you have a much deeper connection with the power. Your grandmother had it. You had it when you fought off Marcus. With me, your connection,' he squeezed her hands, 'you have the tools to control the energy. You can channel the source.'

'I can't,' Jay said.

'Are you scared to let it in? Scared of being unable to control it?'

'I can't untangle it,' Jay said, pulling her hands away. 'You've seen me. Every time we've tried to read the power down there it's knocked me down, and it's taken me days to recover.'

Stitch sighed, looking into the fire. 'It might be enough just to be there, in the Interland. That might be enough to keep the Readers out.'

'But, what-'

'We *have* to try, Jay.' Stitch's tone was firm. 'There is no other choice.'

Jay slumped, looking around at her friends. Cassie forced a smile. Otis nodded and Davey averted his eyes. Samir held Jay's eye for a moment, giving a gentle nod of encouragement.

'What's the plan then, Stitch?' She put a hand on his.

'I think you have to go there. To Cissbury and Chanctonbury,' said Stitch.

'Do we have time?' asked Cassie. 'We need to get to the Interland before the Readers get there. If they reach the source, and Zadie has opened the way, then there will be no power to replenish.'

'Exactly,' said Davey from the other side of the fire. 'It's too late.'

'Shut up, Davey,' said Otis, standing and approaching Jay. He knelt beside her. 'Look,' he said. 'We realise that this is a long shot. But, if we stand any chance at all, then it will be with your power, and your connection with Stitch here. And of course, our help.'

'I can't believe Zadie is helping them,' said Jay. 'Traitor.'

She stared into the fire and Cassie followed her gaze, watching the flames dance as if spinning the roulette wheel on their future.

Jay took a deep breath. 'OK. Let's do it.'

Otis cleared his throat. 'Great. I have an idea.' The others looked to him to continue. 'How about Jay do the tour of the hill forts and the rest of us head to the gateway place that Stitch was talking about, outside the Interland. We can pave the way, do a bit of recon, so that when Jay catches up, we're ready to go.'

'How will we get into the gateway, to the caverns?' asked Davey.

Cassie looked at Stitch. 'We can't hike through the Wilds again?'

'There must be a better way,' said Stitch.

Jay said, 'You can take the River Arun route. Stitch? It will be quicker, not so far to walk?'

'We don't know that route,' said Stitch.

'I do. From my dad's stories. I can give you directions to the Black Rabbit pub, then you follow the river.'

'What about you?' said Stitch. 'Shouldn't we stick together?'

'Like Otis said. I'll catch you up. I'll meet you in the main cavern. Don't go into the Interland before I get there.'

'I don't like the idea of leaving you on your own. I can help you.'

'You take the car. I'll use Davey's bike?' She looked at Davey and he nodded his agreement.

'I'll go with you,' said Cassie. 'You can ride on the back. There's no way I'm letting you ride Davey's motorbike. I saw how you handled that Vespa.'

'Stitch?' Jay said, as if asking permission.

He looked at Cassie, then back to Jay. 'Do it quickly,' he said. 'Head straight to Chanctonbury, then Cissbury. Then back to the Interland, right?'

Jay nodded. Cassie looked serious. 'Let's do it.'

29

M arcus turned the squirrel on the fire. He had grown thin over the past months, the food available in the surrounding woods insufficient to sustain his bulky frame. He would soon have to venture into a nearby town or farm if he were to survive.

He looked again at his wrist, an action he'd repeated more frequently in recent days as his sense of power strengthened. Since Cissbury. The energy of the land seeped into him as one of the Given, an ex-Reader – a Reader reduced to what he once was in the beginning. His marking was becoming more clear at every inspection, now undoubtedly a level six, a formidable power, though not his previous level eight as a Reader. Despite his weakened body, he felt the strongest he had since the conflict with Jay.

With his recuperation, Marcus felt changes in the air, something different in the movement of the trees in the wind, the clouds in the sky and even the way the rain scattered across the woodland floor. Since the Given had been forced to hide, no one was free outside of the Interland, except those like him acting the charade of freedom in a society led by

Readers against the Given. In all this, Marcus had no identity. Worse than the Given in hiding, he was a Reader in his soul, with reduced power and diminished loyalty to the State. He was nothing. A man in limbo.

He finished his food. The fire burned down to embers, lulling Marcus into a sleepy daze. He cast his eyes up towards the other hill forts at Highdown and Chanctonbury. Highdown was dark. A light flickered at Chanctonbury at its highest point. Periodically, the light vanished, then reappeared as if intermittently obscured by someone, or something in the wind. As he watched, he felt something familiar, something he'd not felt in a while, a signature in the energy he felt coming over the Downs. He closed his eyes and listened. It was Jay.

There was someone else with her, someone with power. He wondered if it was Jay's brother, Sammy, the boy with Marcus's blood. The son he'd never known.

Jay was close, but her power was not as he remembered. She was weak. He felt an unfamiliar tingle of opportunity in his bones at the thought of Jay at less than full strength. Jay Macfarlane, the fabled level "8C", was vulnerable. The desire to settle the score between the most powerful of the Given and the most powerful Reader was strong. She was as vulnerable as she'd ever been since coming of age, and she was coming to Cissbury.

30

The last steps to the summit of Chanctonbury, the second of the three hill forts, sapped Jay's strength. Her vision blurred; she longed to lie down. She and Cassie, both gasping for breath, entered the ring of trees. A group of teenagers drank cans of beer around a fire. Jay entered the inner circle and sat down on a log at the edge of the group. She was barely noticed. As soon as she sat, she felt an explosion of energy from the hill, the trees and from the sea on the horizon. It almost knocked her from her seat. Cassie stood next to her, eyeing the party-goers with suspicion, like a bodyguard. Jay looked up at Cassie.

'What?' said Cassie.

'Did you feel any of that?'

'A little...' Cassie said.

Jay stood. 'It was immense. Like a shot of adrenaline in the arm, like diving from a thousand feet into an ice-cold pool.'

'Nice,' said Cassie.

Jay spread her arms wide and took a deep breath. 'Let's go!' She took Cassie by the arm and marched her back towards the bike.

* * *

BY THE TIME Cassie pulled the bike to a stop at Cissbury Ring, the energy had settled into Jay. She felt reinforced. They pulled off their crash helmets, and Cassie took a moment to look Jay in the eye by the light of the half-moon. 'Someone slip you something back on Chanctonbury?' she said.

'The energy took me by surprise.' Jay nodded to the summit of Cissbury. 'Let's go get more.'

A few hundred metres up the steep track, Jay experienced a different wave of energy, dark and foreboding. 'Cassie,' she called. 'Something's wrong. This could be a trap.'

'How? No one knows we're here. Even the Readers wouldn't be able to track us that quickly. We'll go carefully, approach from the north slope, not the main pathway, OK?'

They continued to the top and skirted around the north slope before pressing on towards the ring of trees. Cassie stepped over the final ledge but Jay stopped in her tracks, looking towards the east where beside makeshift camp and a smouldering fire, a man in dirty black clothes stood facing her. Jay knew immediately who it was, and her legs buckled. Marcus.

A scream came from over the hill, a piercing, determined shriek of fear just before Cassie flung herself over the ridge and into Marcus. They tumbled and Marcus landed heavily. Jay watched, still trying to catch her breath as Cassie took a fighting stance. Marcus struggled to his feet and Cassie kicked out at him, landing several blows before he stepped away from her to summon his power.

His *power*. Jay thought to herself. What power could he have? He would have been reduced by their encounter. Cassie moved to kick out at him again, but he blocked and influenced her so that she slipped and fell back onto the woodland floor.

She seemed to knock her head on something – a rock, or a tree root. She remained still as Marcus leaned down and checked on her before turning to Jay.

He walked slowly towards her. Jay's feet were rooted to the floor. She couldn't help but feel afraid in his presence. Her legs trembled as Marcus came close. His features were as she remembered – a little more gaunt, his body stringy and the bones in his face sharper. He stopped a few feet from her, and Jay could sense his weakened state. But she was weakened, too. She looked to the summit of the hill. Perhaps if she could reach the inner circle of trees, she'd stand a chance. She looked past Marcus to where Cassie lay motionless.

'She's OK,' Marcus said, his voice gravelly like he hadn't used it in a while. He cleared his throat. 'She knocked her head, she'll come around.' His face caught the light of the moon and his eyes revealed a new vulnerability. He raised his arm in front of him and pulled back his sleeve, showing Jay the black number six on his wrist. 'Thanks to you,' he said. 'No longer a level eight. No longer a Reader.'

Jay's mind raced.

'I suppose I ought to thank you,' Marcus said.

Cassie stirred in the background, pulling herself up to her knees and looking over to where Jay and Marcus faced each other under the canopy of the outer ring of trees. She jumped to her feet and started towards them.

Jay put up her hand. 'Wait, Cassie,' she said. 'Say that again,' she said to Marcus.

'I said I ought to thank you, for setting me back to neutral in the cavern that day. At the Interland. What you did,' he raised his hand to the two parallel scars on his face, 'brought me here. I've had some time to rebuild my strength, and my mind.'

Cassie gestured behind Marcus's back that she could take

him out, now, from behind. Jay shook her head, her eyes back on Marcus. 'And what about your loyalties? Have they reset, too?' asked Jay.

Marcus gave a half smile and nodded up to the summit. 'Judging by your scar someone has attempted to reset you, too. Shall we head up, so you can soak up some energy?'

31

Jay placed a hand gently on Cassie's arm to reassure her that walking beside Marcus was safe. Jay's sense of Marcus told her he was a different man to the one she'd faced at the Interland. He was strong, for sure, but the source of his power, and motivation, had shifted.

Marcus sat on a log beside the remains of a fire in the middle of a circle of trees. Jay and Cassie sat opposite him and Jay immediately felt the energy seeping into her body – not like the hit of power she received at Chanctonbury, this time more of a steady, trickling recharge.

Cassie wasn't prepared to make amends so quickly with the man who'd recently hunted and attacked them all. 'This is the man that nearly killed Sammy. If it weren't for Stitch, your brother would be dead.'

'That was a different...'

'She's right,' Marcus interrupted Jay's defence. 'I was more than just one of the Readers. I led them. And I meant to do you harm.'

'We can't trust him...' Cassie said, standing.

'But I'm not that man anymore. However, the man who

created the transformation process, he's still hard at work. His goals haven't changed.'

'Hinton?' asked Jay. Cassie returned to her seat next to Jay.

Marcus's head snapped up. 'You've met him?'

'That's one way of putting it,' Cassie said.

Marcus nodded. 'That explains your weakened state. He used to be one of the Given.'

'But he has no power,' said Jay.

'His power is different. He rejected the power of the Given and became something darker even than the Readers. He will be the end of the Given. There's nothing anyone can do about that. He will destroy the source sooner or later.'

'Not if we stop him,' said Jay. She scrutinised Marcus, trying to read him. He presented no shield and she could see he truly believed that Hinton and the Readers would destroy the source, and that the power of the Given, including Marcus's own power, would be neutralised.

He smiled a humourless smile. 'You don't look like you've been doing so well in that battle so far? You can't beat him on your own. Where's the boy? Stitch?'

'Heading back to the Interland,' said Jay.

'You'll need him.' Colours flowed from Marcus, not the familiar dark swirls that he emanated before, but streams of blue and orange that showed compassion. Jay looked to Cassie and could tell that she too could see them.

'You know there are other Interlands?' Marcus said.

Cassie met Jay's eye before they both turned back to Marcus. 'What do you mean?' asked Cassie. Jay thought back to the incident at the lake. What had happened with the man that sucked Jay and Stitch into the place with the dying islands, trees, and the multiple sources of energy no longer felt real.

'Our State, the authorities that run the Readers, is just one of eight worldwide superstates. Only those eight superstates have people with powers – a source, and some kind of *Interland*.'

'There are others?' Cassie breathed the words. Jay nodded at her friend. 'You knew?' Cassie blurted.

'And the Readers,' said Jay. 'They infect all of these states.'

Marcus lowered his gaze. 'I think so,' he said. 'The technology of the *transformation* started here, with Hinton, but other states have their own methods. There's a darkness that creeps into every pocket of light – a poisoned gas that is sucked into every vacuum. You can't stop it. It's inevitable.'

Cassie shook her head. 'I don't believe in fate,' she said.

Marcus laughed. 'It's not about *fate*,' he said, with a familiar venom. 'You can't reach a simple, stable balance in a world like this.' He gestured around himself. 'We have an innate sense of personal survival – a drive that comes before all else – which means we fight until the other side is neutralised. There's no other way.'

Jay recalled the withered islands that she and Stitch had been shown, where the darkness had enveloped their energy, squeezed their life away. 'If the Given are reduced, the Readers will command the ultimate power,' Jay said.

'Yes, and with the dominance of the Readers comes a more powerful darkness. A critical mass brings a flashover of power. A darker place than even I can imagine or understand.'

Cassie shifted in her seat. 'So this regime spreads like a virus, across all eight States?'

'And beyond,' said Marcus.

Cassie stood again. 'We've done enough sitting around talking, let's go.' She pulled at Jay's arm.

Jay resisted. 'Marcus,' she said. 'Show us that your allegiance has shifted. Prove yourself by coming with us.'

Cassie looked at Jay, incredulous.

Marcus shook his head. 'This is not my fight.'

'It's yours as much as it is ours,' said Jay. 'If the source is destroyed it takes your power too.'

Marcus raised his hand to touch the scars on the side of his face. 'I'm done. You're on your own. It would be a suicide mission for me. I can't take another transformation.' He shook his head. 'No, I'll live out my days here. The end will come whether I chase it or not.'

'There are others,' Jay said. 'Others with power that are hiding out across the country. Not all the Given have been taken in for rehabilitation.' Marcus looked up at Jay but said nothing. He stood and Jay stood with him. 'You are the Given now, Marcus. Show it. Connect with the rest of the Given on the outside.'

'Don't you remember?' Marcus said.

Jay gave him a quizzical look.

'How you did this?' He pointed to the scar on his face. 'If you want to fight this battle, you have to use your advantage. It's all you've got.'

'Hinton is different,' Jay said.

'Then *you* need to be different...'

'Jay,' urged Cassie, tugging at her arm. 'We need to go.'

'Help us,' said Jay. 'Link to the others on the outside. Bring them. Join us?'

'I don't have the reach, and even if I did...'

'Figure it out...' Jay said.

'Jay!' Cassie insisted.

When Jay turned back to Marcus, he had slipped away into the trees. She could take off after him, hunt him down and try to persuade him, or she could get back to the others before it was too late. She followed Cassie down the hill, back to the bike.

32

S amir sulked in the passenger seat. He'd wanted to drive, but Stitch insisted he rest. He hadn't stopped talking since they left Highdown, first complaining about Stitch's driving, then asking relentless questions about the Interland and the route they needed to take.

'Rest, Dad, please. We have a long walk once we get parked up.'

'How far is the walk? Will we be OK in this footwear? We should have come prepared. I have some walking boots at the house. Where are the walking shoes I bought you?'

Stitch ignored his dad. In the backseat, Otis and Davey spoke quietly, and Stitch couldn't catch what they were saying. They laughed, and Davey turned to look out his side window, a smile lingering on his face. A connection was growing between them. Stitch thought of Jay, sensed she was OK, was growing in strength, but he felt disconnected without her. He felt alone.

'I'm not going on any river. If you think I'm getting on a raft made of logs then you...'

'Dad, please,' Stitch sighed. 'You want me to drop you home?'

Samir let out a resigned sigh. 'What will you do without me, eh? How will you navigate through the Downs?' Stitch smiled at his dad. 'So tell me about these stories that Jay's dad used to tell you. I don't know why you needed someone else to tell you stories, you never wanted to listen to my stories when you were little.'

'I did...' Stitch started, then thought better of it. 'He told us about a route to the Interland. It was something he'd got from a Runner back before the protest and the crackdown. Then he made it his own, you know, exaggerated it, embellished it with his own imagination, but the basic facts are there.'

Stitch looked in his mirror to see Davey and Otis leaning forward to hear Stitch's explanation. 'Back before the darkness...' Stitch used his exaggerated story-voice. 'When I was a young and handsome adventurer...' Samir laughed but motioned for Stitch to continue. Stitch told of the route to the Interland, much as Ben had told it. 'When we get to the river, we need to make a raft, and float through to the gateway.'

'Can we swim through?' said Otis. Out of the corner of his eye, Stitch saw Samir raise his eyebrows at the suggestion.

'Maybe,' said Stitch. 'But if we can float downstream, it might be easier.'

'Then what?' said Davey from the back seat.

'We wait for the others,' said Stitch.

Otis said, 'Me and Davey can do some recon.'

'We need to stay out of sight,' said Davey. 'No point in going in until Jay gets there.'

'Just a bit of recon. See how the land lies,' said Otis.

Stitch pulled the car into the car park of the Black Rabbit, facing the still moving water of the river. Its surface was a swirl and tangle of currents.

Samir spoke up from the backseat. 'This pub's been closed for months. Economy is in free fall.'

A sense of inertia prevented Stitch from moving. If he could just stay in the car. Opening the door would be the first move along a path that would see the Readers test them more than they'd been seen before. And all while Jay struggled to regain her stripped power. If Jay could not tap into the source of her power, then Stitch would be no use to anyone. His power and influence was contingent on the strength of Jay's power. And even then, who knew what they'd be up against.

He looked around the car – his dad, Otis, Davey. 'Let's go,' he said, sighed, and opened the car door.

* * *

CASSIE OPENED up the throttle and she and Jay raced through the hills of the Downs on Davey's bike. Jay's crash helmet had no visor, so the wind battered her face every time she dared to peek out from behind her friend. Tears dried on her cheeks in the wind, her skin becoming cracked and sore.

'Slow down,' she shouted in Cassie's ear. Jay had avoided trying to read Cassie, for fear of failing. She knew that her power had replenished to a degree, the developing mark on her wrist was evidence of that, but it was far from complete. The flow of energy through the earth, the environment, felt restricted. It was as if the channels were blocked, clogged, and she'd not yet figured out how to free them.

She watched the blur of the trees go by. These hills had become her home, literally, as the Interland was where she lived, and what she considered her spiritual base. She'd always felt connected to the environment in a way that was still only slowly becoming clearer to her. Since she was a small child, she'd spent time out on the roof of her childhood home, building and developing a connection, an understanding with the energy of the land. The sea was her friend, the hills, her adventure, her challenge.

———

33

The trek through the thicket alongside the Arun was easy passage, the banks dotted with reeds and wild-flowers. When the river opened out into the flood-plain the beauty of the scene gave Stitch pause. He recalled Ben's stories. Here, the river flowed to a standstill, spreading out across the fields as if flopping down to rest after an exhausting journey. At the outlet from the floodplain, the Arun flowed west over a small weir and on towards a dark hill that reached high above its neighbours.

'That must be the hill,' said Stitch.

Davey and Samir slipped off their rucksacks to ease the load on their shoulders. Samir sat down and wiped his brow with a handkerchief. He looked up past Stitch towards the imposing hill in the distance. 'So that's the Interland?'

'Not really,' said Davey. 'The Interland itself is under-ground, deep below that hill.'

'But the hillside there,' said Stitch, 'is our way in. There's an opening that will take us into the gateway.'

Otis wandered off. His rucksack lay on the ground next to Stitch. A moment later he returned. 'No boats,' he said.

'Anything we can use as a raft?' said Stitch.

'Logs? Wood?' said Otis.

'Why can't we walk along the edge of the river?' said Samir.

'It'll take too long,' replied Stitch.

Samir huffed, 'You lot swim or float or whatever, I'll keep my feet on solid ground.'

Stitch rolled his eyes. He nodded for Otis to follow him into the trees. They returned with a single log. Davey laughed. 'Is that it?' he said.

'Come on,' said Stitch. 'There's more.'

It took them an hour to gather materials and lash together a makeshift raft using straps from their backpacks. The four of them stood over the creation, studying it. Davey's frown deepened. 'Really?' he said.

They dragged the raft into the water and it dipped under before bobbing reluctantly to the surface. 'There's no chance that will hold all of us,' said Davey.

Otis huffed at Davey's pessimism and took the lead by throwing his rucksack onto the raft. Stitch did the same and then grabbed Samir's bag and placed it next to his on the raft. Samir looked worried but said nothing. Davey sighed and threw his own bag on before Stitch and Otis climbed aboard. The raft wobbled and lowered in the water. Stitch held out a hand for his dad and helped him into position in the middle of the raft, surrounded by the rucksacks. Davey climbed on last and positioned himself at the back of the raft.

'How do we steer?' said Davey.

'Just push us into the flow,' said Otis.

Davey pushed at the river bank until the raft caught the undercurrent and drifted slowly downstream. With the weight of all four, and the bags, the surface of the raft was barely above the water. Stitch could already feel his trousers getting wet as the water seeped up through the logs. 'Don't move around,' said Otis as the raft bobbed and the front edge dipped below the water.

After a minute or two the raft picked up a little speed and moved out into the middle of the river, heading for the weir. 'Shit,' said Otis. 'We didn't plan on going over this thing.'

'It's fine,' said Stitch. 'Just a little speed bump.'

The front of the raft slipped over the weir and Otis's legs were immediately below the water. As he tried to right himself, he went in, splashing like a drowning boy as he grasped for the edge of the raft. Stitch reached for him, which made the raft tip precariously, sending Stitch overboard. The cold took his breath away for a moment and when his head finally broke the surface, he gasped for breath and grabbed for the raft. Samir shuffled close to the middle of the raft, hugging the bags into him as Davey struggled to remain upright at the back which had now dipped into the water with the imbalance of weight. Davey screamed as he slipped into the water and came up for air a few seconds later.

'Shit,' said Stitch. He tried to climb back on to the raft as it picked up speed in the narrowing section of the river. Each time he tried, the raft listed and threatened to tip Samir into the water.

'Leave it,' said Otis. 'Hold on and we can drift down like this.'

'It's freezing,' shouted Davey from the back.

Stitch held on and kicked his legs to direct the raft as well as to try to keep warm.

They drifted. As they approached the hillside, the cave Stitch had heard about so many times in Ben's stories came into view. It emanated a foreboding darkness, and a deafening noise as they breached the opening. Through the hill, all four looked around themselves in fear and wonder, the darkness hiding the details of the rock face. Stitch's fear turned to excitement and anticipation as the light of the pool, the gateway, grew in the distance. He kicked his legs. Finally, they slipped into the pool. The journey was over.

* * *

CASSIE TOOK control of the boat from the back, digging the oars deep into the water, and guiding them downstream on the unnamed river. Despite the explosion of undergrowth since they'd last been here, the connection to the unnamed river had been easy to find. As the boat slipped through the caves and rock tunnels, Jay felt a familiar sense of magic. She felt at home.

Cassie stopped rowing, allowing the boat to drift. Ahead of them, the tunnel opened out into a cavern. The space opened up, its ceiling hundreds of feet above their heads, light penetrating to cast shards over the water.

The energy of the cavern caught Jay's breath, silencing her. She choked, dragging air into her lungs. Her head fell back, opening her airway, and her breath flowed full and open as she stared into the roof. The light intensified; energy coalesced into shapes. White light pulsated in front of her eyes, blinding her to the stone walls. A shadow appeared in her periphery. 'Stitch?' she breathed. No response. The only sound was the thumping of her own blood pumping through her veins.

The light poured down on Jay from above like an endless waterfall, pounding her face and her body. The shadow passed once more and settled in front of her – a figure, featureless but familiar. Without words, the shadow of energy settled with Jay.

'I don't know how,' Jay said into the light, the response to a silent question about why she would not open to the energy, a question only she could hear.

Whispers came at Jay, clear and decipherable. 'You are closed. Resisting.'

Jay shook her head. 'No.'

'You are closed,' the whispers repeated, over and over.

Jay shook her head and put her hands to her ears. All around her, the light began to recede, revealing the surface of the water, the boat, the walls of the cavern. She looked over her shoulder, expecting to see Cassie. She was nowhere in sight. She looked back into the roof of the cave and the whispers came once more. 'You are closed,' came the message.

34

Sammy crawled through a gap little wider than his chest. He had to twist his shoulders and scrape them through before popping out the other side. The others remained at the drop where Toyah lay, unconscious. Sammy was conscious of the need to be quick. He'd left them just over fifteen minutes ago. Deep in the underground, he had never felt so lonely. He thought of Cassie and tried to channel her confidence and determination. Then he thought of Toyah, and how he'd led her into such danger with no certainty that there was anything at the end.

He stood straight for the first time in hours, the space finally big enough. He shone his torch left and right through the tunnel he'd landed in, then back up to the crevice he'd crawled through, incredulous that he got his body through such a small space. The sound of trickling water washed a sense of hope through his body. It echoed, as if flowing into an open space. A welcome relief from the deadened sound of the tight spaces he'd been in for what seemed like hours.

Pinto and Alfred had insisted Sammy press ahead. He was

their only chance of finding a route out. He would find it, then he would head back to them and lead them out. Pinto had taken Sammy's hands. To help with the first few steps into the darkness, Pinto suggested they fly over the ledge and see around the first corner, just to be sure. Together, Sammy and Pinto had connected, left their bodies with Toyah and Alfred, and passed through the narrow opening and into the wider cavern. The view was enough to give Sammy the confidence he needed.

Sammy leaned down and picked up a lump of limestone. He used it to mark a line on the black wall at the location of the opening in the roof through which he'd emerged. He finished his artwork with an arrow pointing up, and a smiley face that was more a hope than a reflection of his feelings. He moved toward the welcoming sound of flowing water.

Just a few minutes passed before Sammy turned a corner and hit a dead end. 'No...' he breathed into the darkness, the light from his torch barely effective in the gloom. There was no longer a sound of running water. He retraced his steps, moving slowly this time, feeling his way through the black hole, his hand dragging along the rocks as if he were reading in braille.

'Here.' Sammy spoke to himself aloud, to convince himself he wasn't alone. He stopped. He shone his torch and moved to the edge of the tunnel where it opened into a wider section. At the far edge, at the floor, a sliver of light showed through a discontinuity in the rock. He could hear the distant sound of running water. A waft of fresh air blew over his face and he closed his eyes. He clambered over the edge of the opening in the rocks and slid sideways through the gap.

Just a few minutes of squeezing through narrow passage-ways and Sammy dropped into another open section, a cave with no obvious entry or exit but for the gap he'd crawled through and a wide hole in the floor into which water gushed. He shone his torch into the abyss and saw nothing but blackness. He could hear that the hole was full of water, from around ten feet down, although he could barely see its surface. He sat, exhausted. Hope, so tentatively grasped, seeped from him. He wasn't even sure he'd be able to climb back through those caves to the others if he had no good news for them. He rubbed his fists into his eyes, fighting tears, then caught a twinkle of light through a hole about halfway up the cave wall. Was he imagining it?

It took a moment before he could focus. He blinked away the stinging sensation and looked again. He gasped at the sight of the chalk cliffs around the turquoise water of the deep pool. He recognised it immediately as the gateway, the hole through which he, Jay, Cassie and Stitch had fallen all those months before. He was somewhere halfway up the cliff. Above the location where the River Rother discharged into the pool. He looked back into the cave and allowed his eyes a moment to adjust to the darkness. 'The Rother,' he said to himself aloud. 'This is the Rother.'

The pool at Sammy's feet was a deep well of water, only ten feet across but likely fifty feet deep. This was the head of pressure that Stitch had explained to them when they were back at the gateway. The pressure would build to a point that it became too much for the blockage, and then it would push itself out into the pool outside. All he needed to do was wait for it to blow.

* * *

IT TOOK Sammy less than half an hour to get back to the others. His sense of relief was overwhelming as he climbed the final few feet to the ledge and saw that Toyah was awake. She lay on the rocks with her head on Pinto's lap, but her eyes were open and she strained to give Sammy a smile as he emerged from the deep. 'Toyah,' he said, placing his hand gently on her shoulder as if he might break her.

'Find us a way out?' she asked.

'Of course,' said Sammy.

'Really?' said Pinto. Toyah sat up, then leaned back onto the rock as if dizzy.

'Steady,' said Alfred. 'You've had a nasty knock. I'm not sure you should move anywhere. How far is it, Sammy?'

'Not far. She can't stay here. I'll help her through.' He looked at Toyah. 'If you think you can do it?'

'I can do it,' she said.

'And how are you?' Sammy asked Alfred.

He moved his foot in a tight circle, wincing. 'It's not broken, but it hurts like hell.'

'I'll help you,' said Pinto.

Alfred smiled and put a hand on Pinto's head. 'You will, young man. I'm relying on you to get this old man out.'

* * *

TOYAH AND ALFRED rested at the top of the well that was full of the River Rother as Sammy explained the mechanism for the blowout. Pinto looked up at Sammy. 'You're kidding?'

Sammy shook his head, 'Trust me,' he said, trying to keep a positive tone to his voice. The level of the pool was almost at their feet, at the lip of the hole. Sammy thought for a moment that the water might rise through the rest of the cave before the pressure was enough to blow, but looking around the floor of the space, he could see that it was permeable. When the water flowed over the edge, the pressure would be at its highest. 'Get ready,' he said.

'What for?' said Alfred.

'When it blows, I'm not sure how long we will have to get ourselves down this well and out through the connection. Might just be a few minutes.'

'How do you know it will not be just a few seconds?' asked Pinto.

Sammy didn't answer.

A deep gurgling emanated from the depths of the pool. Sammy looked at Toyah, her face a picture of fear. Alfred too looked worried. The gurgling subsided and there was a movement in the ground beneath them. A rumbling. Then an almighty noise – rock, water, debris moving through the caves. The water in the pool bubbled for just a fraction of a second and then disappeared in an instant as it flushed through the hole and into the outside world. As it disappeared, light flooded the cave from below.

Pinto screamed with delight and even Alfred stretched to a smile. Sammy leaned over the hole and saw that there was a passable route to climb down. 'Let's move,' he said. But Toyah was already on her feet.

'I'll go first,' said Sammy. 'You follow. Go slowly. I'll guide you.'

At the bottom of the well, they entered a horizontal passage that led to the outside. Sammy could finally see the open air. An almost circular oasis of light at the end of the passage. Water flowed at their feet as the Rother passed freely down the well and along the tunnel to discharge into the pool. Behind them, in the rock passageway, Sammy could see that the surrounding ground mass, a mix of rock and clay soil, had already moved part way to re-block the passage of the Rother.

It would be just a matter of minutes before the passage would be blocked once more and the well would fill again. 'Let's go,' he said. But Pinto was already running full speed towards the opening, to the outside, beyond the protection, and imprisonment, of the Interland.

35

It was dark by the time Stitch had the fire going in the main cavern, their clothes hanging on rocks to dry. Otis paced the cavern as if reading its history in the walls. He ran his hand along the uneven rock as he walked towards one of the openings, a connection to one of the multitude of inter-connected limestone caves.

'Don't get lost through there,' said Stitch.

Otis turned and made his way back to the fire. 'We can dry off a bit and then see what we can find, eh Davey?' he said.

Davey nodded, but Stitch disagreed. 'We should wait for Jay. The Readers could be in there already.'

'No,' said Otis. 'If they were here, the source would be destroyed and there'd be no power. I can feel we still have power.' Otis felt invincible, aching to explore his power. He knew he had something different as a level five, the ability to affect solid objects, to move things, but had never used it with any conviction. 'We need to go in. It's too risky to wait. If Jay gets here after the Readers, then there will be no more of the Given to fight. We can at least find out what's going on, so that when she gets here, we can make a plan.'

'He's right,' said Davey, a reluctant smile in Otis's direction. 'As much as I'd rather snuggle up by this fire, we need to go in. We're here now. If we wait, like Otis says, it could be too late.'

Stitch sat next to Samir. 'If you two go, I'll stay with my dad, wait for Jay.'

'You go,' said Samir. 'I'll be OK.'

Davey shook his head. 'Stay with Samir. We don't need to be leaving people on their own right now, we stay in twos.'

Samir agreed. Stitch headed over to what remained of a set of shelves on the wall of the cave. He found a scrap of paper and took a pencil from his bag before sitting back down. 'I'll draw you a sketch of the layout up there,' he said to Otis.

* * *

THE LEVEL of the unnamed river was low enough that Otis and Davey could easily wade upstream to the connection. They might have missed the opening in the roof had Otis not sensed it. Otis helped Davey up so that he could pull himself through the hole and give a hand for Otis to follow.

They edged towards the inner caves of the Interland, stopping at the waterfall pouring from the roof, masking their way like a giant, shimmering curtain. Otis peered through a gap in the flow, and, seeing that there was no one on the other side, slipped through, wiped water from his eyes and backed up against the rocks out of sight. Tense, raised voices came from the main cavern. Davey leaned out from the rocks to see into the cavern, but Otis pulled him back.

Otis nodded towards a darkened alcove on the other side of the passageway that would make a better, more hidden vantage point.

Davey went first, Otis followed, hesitating at the sight of a woman sitting at the long dining table in the cavern, flanked by armed men in tense conversation.

Davey said, 'That's Zadie Lawrence in the middle.'

Otis took her in. She was not the giant of a woman that he had in his mind – the dominating presence and formidable power who led the infamous protest and commanded the respect and loyalty of the Given. This woman was small, unthreatening. But as Otis watched, she seemed to grow in stature. People stopped to ask her questions, and she gave directions with authority. Her control over those around her was impressive. They lowered their heads when she spoke, as if nervous of revealing their minds, and scared to appear to contradict.

'The two men beside her are Simon and Jared.'

Otis looked around the cavern. He could see a picture on the wall behind Zadie, hanging at an angle like it had been knocked. Davey nodded towards the far end of the cavern. 'Look.'

'What?'

'The opening in the roof. The whole of the upper part of the cavern has been blown away. It's opened up, and the passageway is blocked.'

It looked like there had been a landslide. A pile of rocks and stone rested along one side of the cavern. Daylight pierced the underground gloom where trees and branches slipped into the cavern. Water dripped through and a rope ladder, with wooden rungs, led from the cavern floor up into the trees beyond.

Otis motioned towards the pile of rocks that blocked the main passageway into the depths of the Interland. He saw a passageway off to the side. 'What's through there?' he said.

'That leads down to the source.'

Otis ached to see the source, touch it, feel its power. He

looked back at Zadie and her companions. He put a finger to his lips to quieten Davey so that they could listen to them for a minute.

One of the men spoke. 'Use the source. Can't that tell you when they'll be here?'

Zadie shook her head. 'I don't need the source. I already know Hinton is on his way, with numbers.' Zadie lowered her head and Otis felt a wave of regret wash across the cave.

'There are Given trapped in there,' Otis said to Davey. 'What's she doing?'

'She doesn't know,' said Davey.

'Know what?'

'She doesn't know that the Readers intend to destroy the source. She thinks it's a peaceful union, but the Readers have other ideas. If they destroy the source, she loses her powers the same as the rest of the Given.'

'Then we can tell her,' said Otis, edging forward.

'Wait,' said Davey. Zadie had risen from her chair and was heading towards them.

'What is it?' said one of the other women.

Zadie stopped. 'If Jay and Stitch are alive, there's a risk that this all fails.'

'But she's been reduced. You know that?'

Zadie nodded. 'I know what they said. And I can feel that her power is not what it was. But she is strong. She has been underestimated before, and I won't do the same.'

'What about Davey?' said one of the men. Davey stiffened at Otis's side, holding his breath as he listened. 'Use the source to connect with him and find out what's going on.'

'He's no longer with us.'

'Dead?'

'No. He tried to mislead us. He said that Jay was dead. I can't trust him.'

'If she is reduced,' said the man, 'then she won't come here, she's no longer a concern.'

Zadie stepped towards the man and grabbed him by his shirt. 'Look at this.' She spat her words as she tilted her head to show the man her scar. 'I was reduced. Do I seem like I have no power to you?' The man shook his head. 'Power can be replenished. And if she comes here, and can get access to the source, then she could regain her power. Maybe not immediately, and maybe not back to what she had before, but we can't take the risk.'

Zadie looked to the entrance to the source, then back to her companions. 'How much explosive do we have left?'

'It's in the store. What are you thinking?' said Jared, a tall, spindly man with greasy black hair.

'We block off the access to the source. For good. Do it right.'

Davey and Otis looked at each other in horror. 'We can't let them destroy the route to the source,' said Otis. 'If these rocks come down they'll never be opened again.'

'What can we do?' said Davey. 'They're armed. And there's no way we can face up to Zadie's power.'

Otis needed to make use of his power, his unique nature of the level five. He closed his eyes and relaxed his muscles, connecting with his inner energy. The power came quickly. His proximity to the source was obvious in the way the energy flowed through to his arms, legs, his fingertips. He opened his eyes to see that Davey was staring at him.

'What are you doing?' said Davey. Otis revealed the number five on his wrist. 'I know,' said Davey, 'but what does that mean, what can you do?'

Otis smiled. 'Watch.' Three mugs and a pile of plates wobbled at the far end of the table and then slid sideways with a force that took them smashing into the wall of the cavern.

Zadie and the others physically jumped and then recoiled from the disturbance.

Zadie stood and marched to where the plates lay smashed on the floor. She picked up a piece of broken crockery and stood, studying it. After a moment she looked up and around the cavern as if looking for someone. 'Shield,' said Otis as Zadie's energy felt its way through the cavern.

Otis began to shake from his feet through his body to his head. He'd never moved objects to this extent before. The reaction pulsed through his body. He felt wired. His face flushed, and he glowed. The trembling grew worse, and he throbbed with energy. Stones from the floor of the cave rose as Davey and Otis watched. They hovered in the air a few feet from the ground across the width of the tunnel. If Zadie or one of her men looked in their direction, they'd surely see. Davey shoved Otis, but it made no difference. Otis was no longer in control.

Zadie and the group split, three of them heading out towards the source and three, including Zadie, heading towards the passageway where Otis and Davey hid. Otis closed his eyes again, connecting with the energy.

'We need to go,' said Davey.

'Shh...' said Otis as he opened his eyes and felt the energy surround him. The stones dropped to the floor, and he turned his attention to the gun in the hand of the man who stood with Zadie. He moved it, twisting it out of the man's hands and dropping it to the floor.

'Careful,' said Zadie, glaring at the man. He leaned down to pick it up, confusion on his face. As he reached for the gun, Otis flung it across the floor of the cave and out of reach. Zadie looked after it, a glimmer of understanding in her face. 'We have a level five in our midst.'

'Otis,' Davey whispered. 'We can still make a run for it.'

Otis shook his head. 'It's time.' As he said these words, he stepped out into the open. Without guns, Zadie and her two colleagues stepped back as Otis stepped forward.

'Who are you?' asked Zadie, raising her arm to prevent her two colleagues from advancing on Otis.

'We're on your side,' said Otis. The other three returned to join Zadie's group. Two of them were armed. Jared raised his gun. Otis used his power to push it back down. Zadie watched, impressed.

'You're a level five,' she said. Otis nodded. 'How did you find this place?'

'We know what you're doing, and you're making a mistake.'

'How's that?'

'The Readers are coming here to destroy the source.'

'This is about integration. No more fighting,' said Zadie. Jared leaned in to whisper something that Otis didn't hear but sensed. Jared wanted to end the discussion and was planning to use his gun. Zadie held out a hand once more to calm her friend. 'Who are you with?'

'It's just me,' said Otis, but he could read that Zadie already suspected that he was there with Jay and Stitch, and she was nervous. 'If you let them in here, and they destroy the source, then that will be the end of the power for all the Given.'

'What do *you* suggest?' Zadie remained calm.

'If you allow Jay and Stitch back in here, they can ensure the protection of the Interland. With you, with your power, and Jay's connection, the Readers won't be able to enter. This can be the sanctuary it was meant to be.'

'Bit late for that.' Zadie motioned towards the gaping hole in the roof and the blocked passageways. 'There's no reason for the Readers to destroy the source. This is the root of all power. Without it, the Readers are nothing.'

Otis drew a breath. 'You don't know.'

'What?' said Zadie, frustration leaking into her tone.

'The Readers, Hinton, whatever he is, they don't draw their power from the source. Not anymore.'

Zadie laughed, a humourless smile on her face, a glimmer of uncertainty. 'Everything with power draws from the source.'

Otis shook his head. He sensed that Zadie had some level of belief in Otis's claim, but was burying it. She wasn't able to connect with the truth. Hinton had some level of control and influence over her.

'So what's your plan?' asked Zadie. Otis said nothing. 'And Jay? Where is she?'

'Why are you so scared of her?' asked Otis.

Zadie took a step towards him. 'I'm afraid of no one. You see all this,' she said. 'This was supposed to be mine. I am the one who rallied the support, led the way here when Sasha Colden passed. The Given were nothing when I took over this place. There was no one else out there taking the fight to the State. Then comes Jay with her marking, and Stitch. Who'd have known that there could be another like Colden?' Zadie lowered her gaze.

'She came to *join* you, not fight against you,' said Otis.

Zadie had anger in her eyes. 'Jay's not here. I'd be able to feel her. She's gone, hasn't she? That's why you're here, to talk me out of this?' Otis shook his head, but Zadie continued, stepping closer. Jared retrieved his gun from the side of the cavern, and Simon now also had his hand on his gun. The power flowing through from Zadie rose, and Otis felt his own energy under attack. Jared raised his gun and Otis pushed Jared's arm down. Simon pointed his own gun at Otis and could not deflect both of them.

'Do it,' said Zadie, her expression one of sheer determination, her teeth clenched.

As the sound of the shot rang out, Otis felt Davey pull him from behind into the alcove. He bashed his head against the rock with the force of Davey's shove. The distraction took Otis's power away from its target, releasing Zadie's gunmen. Otis heard three more shots but felt nothing.

Davey slid to the floor behind him, lifeless.

'No!' Otis screamed.

Zadie moved fast, staring at Davey on the floor, a quizzical look on her face. She knelt near, recognising him. 'Davey,' she whispered. She checked his pulse and looked up at Jared. She shook her head. Otis ran from the confinement of the alcove, towards the waterfall. His only thought was that if he could make it before Jared lifted his gun, then the water would conceal him and he stood a chance of escape.

A warning shot. Otis froze steps from the waterfall, raised his hands and turned around to see Jared pointing his gun at him. He looked down to see Davey, his face turned towards Otis, eyes open but lifeless. 'Sorry,' Otis said under his breath. Davey's death was down to him. It was his idea to come into the Interland. His idea to confront Zadie, to think he could persuade her to protect the source. His fault. As Zadie and the others took a further step, Otis turned and slipped through the waterfall. Shots rang out behind him but failed to connect. He ran towards the opening, knowing that the boulder would prevent him from passing through to the unnamed river, but with no other plan, he kept going.

Footsteps behind him pushed him on. He stopped at the boulder. He leaned his weight into it but only moved it a few inches, enough to make a gap but not enough to slip through. Footsteps. Otis darted across the cave, into the darkness of the dead-end in the passageway just as Jared and Simon turned the corner and piled into the space in front of the boulder.

'He's through,' one of them said.

Jared pushed the boulder out of its position so that Simon could look through. 'He's gone,' said Simon. 'Do we follow?'

'No,' said Jared. 'He's no threat out there. Step out of the way.' As Simon moved aside, Jared allowed the boulder to roll back into place, sealing the outside once more. Otis breathed relief as Simon and Jared made their way back into the Interland. He remained there in the dark corner of the cave for some time before he gathered the strength and will to leave Davey behind and push his way back out behind the boulder, back to the gateway.

36

Otis and Davey had been gone for over an hour. Samir noticed his son's discomfort and tried to distract him. 'So this is where you've been all this time?' he said.

'Not here,' said Stitch. This is just the gateway where we fought their head Reader, Marcus. Where Jay destroyed him.'

Debris still scattered the floor like the scene of an ancient battle. 'You could have got in touch,' said Samir.

Stitch looked at his dad. 'We talked about this. I left you a note,' he said.

'I read it many times,' Samir said. 'I didn't know if you were alive or dead.'

'I've already apologised,' said Stitch. 'But it's not like you even noticed if I were alive or dead before I left.'

Samir shifted in his seat. 'I know. I'm sorry for that. *Kunt fi hidad ealaa wafat walidatik...*'

'Speak English, Dad.'

'I was mourning the death of your mother. My mind was in the sky, my heart beneath the ground.'

'I was mourning too. You had your faith. What did I have?'

Samir looked at Stitch as if only realising for the first time how alone he'd been. 'I'm sorry, son.' He made to move, but his ankle was weak and he stumbled, dropping back in his seat. Stitch stood and went to him. His dad held out a hand and Stitch took it in his own. Samir leaned to kiss Stitch on both cheeks, holding him tightly by the hand. Stitch put his arms around his dad's neck and drew him into a hug. When they released, Stitch could see the glisten in Samir's eyes and felt a prickle in the corner of his own eyes, a lump in his throat.

Stitch's ears pricked. There was a second thud from behind. He released his dad's hand. There, in the opening to the passageway that carried the River Arun into the pool, was Sammy.

'Sammy,' he called out.

Stitch ran to Sammy. It felt like weeks since he'd seen him. They embraced, with Stitch's head in his chest as Sammy stood a foot taller than him. Beyond Sammy, Stitch saw Pinto helping his sister shuffle into the cave, and behind them was Alfred – *the bookseller*, as Stitch still thought of him. He noticed Alfred was struggling and moved to help him.

'Stitch,' said Alfred. 'So good to see you.' He looked past Stitch to scan the cavern for Jay. Stitch helped Alfred lower himself to sit next to Samir, who introduced himself. 'Pleased to meet you. You're Stitch's father, I've heard all about you.'

'Really?' said Samir, looking over at Stitch.

Stitch headed back to help Pinto and Toyah. 'What happened?' he asked Toyah.

'Took a bang on the head. I'll be OK.' Stitch studied Toyah's wound on the back of her head. The damage looked minor, but she was unsteady on her feet. He told Pinto to set her down to rest.

Sammy stood with Stitch as the others settled by the fire. 'What happened?' asked Stitch.

'Zadie's destroyed the place. There were explosions. Some passageways have caved in. I don't know what she's doing but most have gone except for the few of us trapped the wrong side of the blockages.'

'How did you get out?' said Stitch.

'The Free Cave. I knew it led to the outside, just never had the guts to test it, until we had to. Wasn't sure we were going to make it to be honest. Nearly didn't.' He nodded towards Toyah and Alfred.

'How bad are they?' Stitch asked.

'Alfred's ankle I think is just a sprain. Toyah... I'm not sure. She took a heavy blow to the head and was unconscious for a while.'

'Come and rest,' said Stitch, slinging his arm around Sammy and guiding him towards the fire.

They rested as they waited for Otis and Davey. Stitch explained how Otis had insisted they go on a reconnaissance mission to get the lie of the land, figure out what they would be facing. Sammy told them that there could be others trapped in the warren of passages behind the blocked exits. He thought his dad might be in there somewhere. 'Can we break through the blocked passages?' asked Stitch.

'Those explosions brought down whole roof sections. You'd need a JCB to get through there.' Sammy thought for a moment, then added, 'I can make my way back in through the caves and bring them out.'

'No,' said Toyah from across the room. 'You're not going back in there, Sammy. It's too dangerous. There are too many side passages and crevices for you to get lost in. It all looks the same.'

'I'm not leaving my dad.'

'He might not be in there,' said Stitch. 'He might have got out with the others.'

Sammy shook his head, and Stitch knew he felt his dad's whereabouts. If anyone would know, Sammy would.

'I think Jay is close,' said Sammy. 'I can feel her. But she's weak. Is she hurt?'

Stitch shook his head. 'She's been through it, the reduction. She has a scar to show for it.' Stitch motioned the shape of Jay's scar with his finger on the side of his face. 'But she's not hurt. Same old Jay. Determined to get here to the source and put things right.'

'She thinks the source will replenish her power?'

'We all do,' said Stitch. 'It's in the legend. We just need to get her in there before the Readers get here and destroy it.'

* * *

CASSIE GUIDED the boat through the final length of tunnel, beneath the connection to the Interland, invisible above her head as they shot through and into the pool.

Jay lay back in the boat, her eyelids flickering in the twilight beneath the darkening sky. The white cliffs of the gateway looked grey in the fading light, the squawk of birds in the cliff face a reminder to Cassie of the phoenix. She believed her friend would rise, more powerful than ever. Yet she was afraid.

She stroked the side of Jay's face, turning her head so that she could look into her eyes. 'Jay? Can you hear me? What happened back there?' Cassie said, but Jay gave no sign that she heard.

Cassie pulled the boat into the side of the pool and jammed the oar into the rock, wedging the boat so that it stayed still while she dragged Jay to stand. The boat wobbled.

'Help me out here,' Cassie pleaded. Jay finally allowed some weight to be carried in her own legs, shooting Cassie a sideways glance of recognition of their predicament. Cassie got them both out of the boat and onto the rocks, where they shuffled together towards the opening to the cave that carried the Arun. Cassie hoped the others had beaten them to the gateway cavern so she could get some help with Jay. There was little chance Jay could get to the source if she couldn't stand.

'Cassie,' came the shout from Stitch as Cassie and Jay edged into the cave. Cassie breathed a sigh of relief at the sight of her friends around the fire. The relief flooded into her legs and they gave way, taking her and Jay to the floor. Sammy and Stitch reached them and propped them up, helping them over to the fire where Pinto too came and held on to Jay's hand.

'What happened?' said Sammy, taking his sister's face in his hands.

Cassie explained what had happened in the cavern on the unnamed river, and how Jay seemed to zone out, like her brain couldn't cope with the energy, or the flow of information from the environment.

'This happened before,' said Stitch. 'In the cave with the source. She seemed to pass out from the source's power.' He'd felt the strength of power himself but it channelled directly to Jay and it was as if her mind could not cope and blacked out, rebooted, and she woke a while later. Stitch said that afterwards, Jay needed complete rest. Silence and darkness. She seemed super-sensitive to stimuli. 'Let's get her out into one of those caves, keep it quiet.'

* * *

CASSIE'S HEAD ACHED, and she wondered if she was still feeling the effects of the reflection of power she experienced back at the prison. Hinton had power that she'd not experienced. It was beyond that of the Given or of the Readers. She did not know what might happen if, or when, he arrived at the Interland, what force he would bring and how they would deal with him. She was especially concerned about their ability to fight back when Jay was obviously so weak. Jay's reaction when they got to the cavern had shaken Cassie, disturbed her understanding of the nature of the powers.

She looked up as Sammy approached. He nodded to the space next to Cassie as if to ask if he could sit. 'Since when did you need permission to talk to me?' asked Cassie.

'Sorry. Wasn't sure if you wanted time alone.'

Cassie shrugged. 'It's been a hell of a few days.'

'I'm sorry about Reuben,' said Sammy. 'He was a good guy.'

'How is she?' Cassie said, nodding towards Toyah.

'I think she'll be OK.'

Just then, Otis staggered into the cavern like he was drunk. His head was lowered and his face flushed. 'Otis,' said Cassie.

'Who's Otis?' said Sammy.

'We met him on the outside, he's OK.' Cassie stood to help Otis as he stumbled towards them.

Stitch came back into the cave. 'Where's Davey?' he asked. Otis looked up at Stitch and said nothing, but he shook his head. Stitch leaned up against the wall to steady himself. 'What happened?'

Cassie helped Otis take a seat by the fire. He rubbed his temples. 'I screwed up,' he said. 'I tried to reason with her. I tried to explain that if the Readers destroy the source then...'

'What happened to Davey?' said Stitch, impatient.

'They shot him. He pulled me out of the way and took three bullets.'

Stitch turned away and slumped to the floor.

Cassie went to him, but his eyes were far away and he looked to Cassie like he'd had enough. 'Stitch?' Cassie said.

'It's over,' said Stitch. 'Jay is out of it. What if she doesn't come around? Zadie Lawrence is out of control.' He looked at Otis and thought of Davey. 'The Readers are coming.'

PART V

37

───────

It was over an hour later when Jay emerged from the connecting cave. Cassie and Stitch were arguing while Samir tried to calm them down. Alfred had his head lowered as he stretched his leg and cradled his swollen ankle. Cassie stood tall in Stitch's face, insisting that he needed to snap out of it, that they had to go in, whether or not Jay was with them. Sammy, Toyah and Pinto stood a few steps away from the heat of the argument.

Pinto was the first to see Jay. He leapt to his feet. 'Are you feeling better?' Pinto said, looking up at Jay with pleading eyes.

Jay nodded, smiled and looked back to the argument. 'What's going on?'

Pinto shrugged. 'They're scared. Without you, we all are.'

When Sammy saw his sister, he looked relieved and exasperated at the same time. Jay's appearance had put an end to the argument. Cassie joined them. 'Good sleep?'

'Better, thanks,' said Jay.

'Then we can stop wasting time and get up there before *they* get here.'

'They will take some time to get through the thicket. But you're right, we need to move quickly.'

Cassie turned away. Sammy put a hand on Jay's arm. 'What's the plan?'

Jay nodded towards the fire. 'Let's go through it together.'

* * *

JAY STILL HAD a wisp of hope that the Readers wouldn't make it to the Interland, and that they could persuade Zadie to end the conflict without an all-out fight. Jay still felt weak. Her power had peaked when they passed through the cavern on the unnamed river, but it had subsided. She needed to get nearer the source, and to do that, she'd have to face Zadie and the other Given that stood in her way.

Cassie led the way through to the unnamed river, Otis following close behind. Stitch nudged Jay. 'Can you freeze the river?'

Jay took a breath and closed her eyes, leaning up against the rock opening to the cave. She reached inside of herself for the buried inner energy. She shook her head. 'I'm sorry.'

Cassie put a hand on Jay's shoulder. Stitch pressed on, wading upstream, followed by Jay. At the connection, Cassie helped Otis up into the opening and one by one the five of them positioned themselves behind the main entrance, closed off by the boulder.

Jay let out a sigh. 'We ready? We do it like we said?'

Cassie nodded and leaned her shoulder into the rock. Otis helped and the boulder rolled away from the opening. On the inside, they crouched in the shadows, moving along the wall towards the water curtain ahead of them. 'The Readers aren't here. I'd feel them by now,' said Jay.

'That's good,' said Stitch. 'Let's move.'

Behind the waterfall, Zadie's presence became impossible to ignore. Jay nodded to her left and right and they walked through the water together. Wiping their eyes clear on the other side, Jay caught sight of Zadie just as she looked up. Jared and Simon reached for their weapons but Otis did as they'd planned and used his full strength to push the guns away and across the floor of the cave, out of reach. Jay and Stitch stood close to each other, their hands touching as they connected their power as best they could. Jay felt Zadie's own power rise and sensed that Stitch felt it too. He squeezed her hand and together they resisted Zadie, pushed back at her rising energy.

'Wait,' Zadie shouted, holding up her hand.

Zadie approached, four of her companions behind her. Jay noticed Jared glance over to where his gun lay across the floor. 'Jay,' said Zadie, stepping up to her. 'Good to see you again.'

'Strange way to welcome us home, Zadie,' said Jay. 'You sent me and Stitch out to get taken by the Readers. You got Reuben killed.'

Zadie shook her head. 'You kids don't get it.'

Cassie lunged for Zadie but Zadie resisted. Cassie doubled up, holding her head. She collapsed onto her knees and Jay's attempts to shield her faltered.

'We need to talk!' said Jay.

Zadie relented.

Cassie gasped for breath and Sammy helped her up.

'Why are you doing this?' said Jay.

'Oh, come on. Your little friend and I have already been through this.' She nodded at Otis. 'The Readers and the Given are united. It's no longer up to you.'

'Then you won't mind if Stitch and I head through to the source.'

Simon lunged for one of the guns. Otis reacted, moving a

chair into his path. Simon tripped, landing heavily. Otis staggered, twitching and trembling. The rock walls around them began to crumble. Stones trickled down the walls to the floor, some hanging in the air as if weightless. Otis shook harder, seeming to glow from the inside.

'Otis?' said Jay. But he couldn't respond. In the confusion, Jared moved, reaching his gun and turning back on them. Jay screamed for them to move but the shot rang out before her words reached her friends. Otis went down. He looked to Jay as his legs buckled, continuing to tremble and shake as he slid towards the floor. Cassie caught him on his way down, holding him up. Another shot pinged off the cave wall next to Jay and Jared pushed forward, his gun out in front of him.

'Stop,' Zadie shouted, holding her hands up. Another shot, this time from Simon's gun. The bullet flew between Jay and Stitch. Jay flung herself to the floor where she came face to face with Otis. His eyes were closed, his breathing shallow.

'Stop.' Zadie's voice again. Silence.

Rough hands grabbed Jay by the arms, dragging her around and marching her in towards the main cavern. Simon had a gun held to Sammy and Stitch, while two others pushed Cassie behind the others.

Jay looked back at Otis. He didn't move. Zadie stood over his body, nudging his shoulder with her foot.

Jay's power seemed to fluctuate, like it was out of control, unfocused. She sensed that Otis was still alive, but the experience in the cavern of the unnamed river had shaken her confidence. It was as if the environment no longer trusted her, and it had decided to withhold the power that she needed to flow through her.

Pushed into the store room adjacent to the main cavern, Jay, Stitch, Sammy and Cassie were placed under the guard of two of Zadie's men, both armed, and both with the protection of power. Others of the Given gathered in the main cavern, some catching Jay's eye and quickly looking away. Stitch shot Jay a challenging look. She nodded. She knew what she had to do. There was only one hope left.

Jay felt a presence. Not the power of a Reader, but something more, a power signal not yet unscrambled. Hinton.

There were Readers with him, the strength of energy indicated enough to fill the gateway. She caught Stitch's eye once more. He felt it too.

38

One by one, the black boots of the Readers filed down the rope ladder and into the main cavern. One by one the Readers greeted Zadie and her companions before taking a place on a rock at the edges, waiting.

'How many are there?' Stitch said, his jaw dropping open.

Cassie paced the small space that was their temporary prison, a caged tiger ready for a fight, no matter the stacked odds. As Jay watched, she saw that the last person to descend the steps of the ladder was the only man in a suit, Hinton. In no hurry, he joined what must have been a crowd of thirty Readers edging their way around the cavern for space to stand or perch on a rock. Hinton approached Zadie, and they exchanged words that Jay couldn't hear above the background noise of marching boots. It was obvious to Jay that it wasn't the first time he and Zadie had met as they greeted each other warmly, like old friends.

'They're solid,' said Cassie, watching the interaction of Zadie and Hinton.

'All part of their plan,' Jay said, thinking back to the beginning. Before Zadie had entered the Interland, she'd been taken by the State, held in captivity for months before escaping to the Interland. 'They got to Zadie when she was inside, in rehabilitation.'

'But she's not a Reader. Her power comes from the source,' said Stitch. 'She's one of the Given.'

'She has the scar,' said Cassie. 'Maybe she *is* a Reader?'

'No,' said Jay. 'She's just forgotten how to be. She's been twisted by this man.' Jay looked at her wrist. Her marking was no more than an indecipherable smudge, little more than had appeared back at the hill forts. Jay looked over at Stitch and saw him check his own wrist, the dark letter "C" still as it had always been, now waiting for Jay's connection that was proving evasive.

'The fact that the Readers could get in here,' said Stitch, 'tells us that me and Jay are not properly connected. It's not enough that we're here in the Interland, we need to get to the source. We need to connect if we stand any chance. They can't remain here if the eight-C and the C are connected.'

'We need to get through the cavern, past them,' said Jay. She turned to Sammy. 'Dad must be through there,' she said, nodding towards the blockage of the rock tunnel, but they had no way to get through to reach Ben, Matchstick, or anyone else that might be trapped behind the blockages and could help.

A shout came up over the sound of the crowd of Readers. Zadie called for quiet and the faces of the Given and Readers together turned to look towards Zadie and Hinton, elevated on Zadie's platform she used for all her speeches in the Interland.

'We are finally united,' she said. A muffled cheer emanated from the Readers and the Given that stood at Zadie's feet. 'We must now safeguard the source for future generations of the Given and Readers. Together!' The crowd remained quiet, some looks of confusion between the Readers. Jay watched their faces and realised that, as she had known, the Readers had no intention of protecting the source. Zadie continued, 'We must secure the sanctity of the source as a place of pilgrimage.'

Stitch looked at Jay. 'She has no idea,' he said.

Zadie brimmed with energy, building to a punchline. 'We will ensure that the magic of the Interland is protected, not as a subterranean prison that hides the Given from society, but as a place to visit, an epicentre and symbol of peace.' She thrust her fist into the air to an unenthusiastic mumbling in the crowd.

'Thank you,' said Hinton, taking a place on the podium next to Zadie. 'And listen,' he said, silencing the crowd. 'Zadie here will be our first in command, as a Reader, she will be the State's leader of all Readers.'

'You misunderstand,' said Zadie to Hinton, just loud enough that Jay could hear. 'I am part of the Given. *We* are the Given.' She cast her arm across the crowd. 'We will remain the Given, and we will work together for the benefit of society. We can rebuild this country as an integrated force, Given and Reader together.'

Hinton smiled and placed an arm around Zadie. He turned to the crowd. 'You think the Given can remain in a new society?' People muttered. 'The time of the Given has run its course.' He turned back to Zadie, his arm remaining around her neck and his smile broadening. 'Thanks to Zadie, we have access to the source. There is no connected power to repel the Readers from this place.' He looked directly to where Jay and the others stood under guard at the back. 'And we cannot let that power become re-established. This is our window of opportunity to end this battle.'

Jay felt the tension rising in the great cavern, but the odds were stacked against any resistance that Zadie and the Given might present. The Readers were too powerful and there were too many of them. Zadie stood virtually alone against the full power of the Readers, unprotected by the 8C. She had delivered Hinton his plan with absolutely no resistance.

A white glow twinkled in the distance. It was almost unnoticeable, a slight mist with a sparkle as it drew nearer.

In the cavern, Zadie seemed to shrink in stature up on the podium. But her expression, and the energy that Jay felt coming from her, showed no signs that she was about to give up her power, or allow the source to be destroyed by the Readers. A shot rang out through the cavern and Jared jumped up next to Zadie.

Zadie lashed out at Hinton, shoving him and sending him into the crowd. A scuffle at Zadie's feet sent Jared back into the crowd. He dropped his gun. Hinton drifted towards the back of the cave, away from the fighting, a smile fixed on his face as if his job was done. The Given were outnumbered, but they fought hard, Zadie using her power to gain any advantage.

Cassie jiggled on her feet, pacing the store room, occasionally stopping to see what was happening in the fight. Jay peered through the entrance to the cavern as a wave of energy seemed to flow above the heads of the Readers. A swirling dust gathered. 'Otis?' said Stitch.

Jay shook her head. 'No. If he's alive, he's not strong enough.' As they watched, more dust gathered, with stones and other debris as if controlled by a level 5. 'It's Pinto,' she said. 'I can feel him. He's working the energy from the Gateway.'

'Alf was right,' said Cassie. 'He's like Otis.' The dust and stones swirled around the heads of the Readers, creating confusion and balancing the odds a little.

The guards outside the storeroom had been distracted by the chaos. Cassie took the opportunity and launched herself into an attack on the two guards. They both hit the floor, and Cassie threw herself into the throng. Jay watched, wide-eyed, as Cassie used her well-honed martial arts skills to take down Reader after Reader. Jay turned to see that the white glow at the passageway had intensified, a white mist reaching towards the entrance to the storeroom in which she was held. Sammy put a hand on Jay's shoulder. 'Go,' he said, nodding towards the mist. 'Just hurry.' He turned and piled into the crowd behind Cassie.

Stitch grabbed Jay's arm, and they stepped out of the store cavern concealed by the white mist that was now leaking through to the main cavern. They picked up speed, striding in the direction of the source. Before they left the main cavern, someone stepped out to block their path. Hinton stood before them. 'That's not going to happen,' he said. Stitch lifted a hand to push him aside but was stopped by the force of the Readers, not coming from this suited man but channelled from the surrounding Readers.

'Stop,' Jay said, and Hinton released Stitch from his agony. Jay turned to see that Cassie and Sammy were stood with Jared and Simon, the men that had killed Otis, and probably Davey. Cassie fought hard. Sammy was knocked to the floor as Jay looked on. 'That's enough,' said Jay.

She looked at the man, and his gaze drifted from Jay to something behind her in the distance. She turned. Someone was coming down the ladder through the opening in the roof. Then another, a stream of people. The fighting below seemed to freeze as they all looked up into the roof. 'It's Marcus,' whispered Jay as Stitch dragged himself back to stand.

'Marcus?' said Hinton. Streams of people came down from the surface and Marcus approached Jay, Stitch and Hinton. The Readers turned to observe the interaction, unsure of the intentions of the new crowd as reinforcements or the enemy.

'Marcus,' said Hinton. 'It's been some time.' Hinton looked at Jay, 'Marcus was my first,' he said, pride in his voice. 'I thought you were dead.'

Marcus turned his head so that Hinton could see his two parallel scars. 'A battle scar thanks to this young lady, I gather?' said Hinton. Marcus nodded. 'So you've come to witness the end of the source? To join in our finest hour as Readers?'

Marcus nodded again and turned to Jay. He winked, then turned round and knocked Hinton off his feet. No sooner had the man hit the floor, Marcus went down in pain as Hinton brought the power of the Readers down on him. The fighting in the cavern resumed. 'Go,' Marcus said between gritted teeth as he forced himself to his feet again. Marcus had rallied hidden Given in support of his mission to help Jay, to save the source and the Interland, and now they all joined the fray.

Stitch grabbed Jay as she stared at Marcus, the Given and the throng of people fighting, this time with more balanced sides. Hinton raised himself from the floor and Marcus lashed out at him again, grimacing at the pain in his own head but managing to get the better of the man. Jay allowed Stitch to pull her down the passageway through an intensifying glow of white mist. 'What is this?' said Jay as she ran alongside Stitch.

'I think we know what this is,' Stitch shouted with excitement. 'This is the other Interlands connecting.'

Jay recalled the man, the islands, and the black tendrils of darkness surrounding them, suffocating the land. As they reached the connection to the source, they stopped. The white glow was at its most intense, at the blocked connection to the rest of the Interland. The rock mass seemed to liquify inside the mist, flowing like water. 'What...' said Jay, staring.

'No time,' said Stitch, pressing on down into the cavern of the source.

* * *

HINTON TURNED TO MARCUS, tired of his attempts to keep him down. He drew on the power of the Readers in the cavern, over thirty of them with a combined energy level that could not be deflected by any of the Given, however many tried to combine. He pierced Marcus's mind with the full force of the Readers' power. Marcus crumpled before him, his face in the dust at the man's feet. He pushed harder, relentlessly digging into Marcus's weak mind, his already damaged defences. Marcus was weaker than he'd thought. The reduction and transformation back to the Given had taken him from one of the strongest that Hinton had ever created, to a Given with little means of defence. He pushed harder.

Another of the Given approached, but immediately fell to the floor under Hinton's energy. Marcus's breathing wheezed as he was crushed into the floor as if by a heavy rockfall. Hinton crouched, not letting up the channelling of power for a second but increasing the digging as Marcus's defences crumpled. Until Marcus stopped breathing. He turned over to lie on his back as he released his final breath. The marking on his wrist was a mass of blood, steaming as if it had been burned off. The two scars on the side of his face had merged to a mass of red. His eyes, still open, communicated a defiance with no substance.

Marcus was dead. Hinton stood and turned towards the passageway to the source where Jay and Stitch had disappeared in the hope of protecting it. 'You're too late,' Hinton said aloud as he moved into the mist.

39

Cassie looked over the heads of the crowd to see Hinton slip away through the passageway after Jay and Stitch, a gaggle of Readers following him like a cloak flowing in his slipstream. She took a blow to the head, and as she felt the blood dripping down her face, she wondered how much more she could take. She swept the legs away from the Reader in front of her, then disabled him with a single punch to the underside of his nose. She looked around for Sammy. She'd had no sight of him for some minutes.

With Marcus's reinforcements, there were as many of the Given as there were Readers, but Cassie could see that the Readers remained stronger, both in their power and their physical strength. They used their power to confuse and disorientate, then their fighting ability to take the Given down. Many had fallen unconscious or worse. Cassie continued to fight like it was the last fight on earth. None of these Readers would get the better of her.

She moved towards the exit, closer to where Jay would need her help. Two Readers stepped in front of her and she wasn't sure if she could lift her arms to fight, she was so exhausted. She steadied herself and kicked out, taking one of them down with a kick to the face, then the other with a leg-sweep. Two more appeared, one landing a heavy blow to Cassie's head. She wobbled, spinning, but she didn't go down, not until a third Reader clumped her on the head from behind. The last thing she saw was the black boot of a Reader in the dust in front of her eyes. Then it moved, swung backwards and came rushing towards her face.

40

Jay stumbled down the rock steps towards the source, her head pounding with pain and confusion. She couldn't get a handle on her power. The energy inside her felt bigger than her. She was not worthy of it, had no sense of control over it. She was afraid of it.

Footsteps behind them. 'Readers,' said Stitch.

Jay sensed it was not just Readers, but also Hinton. She communicated this to Stitch without words. They picked up their pace, but Jay already felt the influence of the man behind them. He was pushing, prodding and delving into Jay's mind. Her head spun and Stitch turned to look at her, instinctively taking her arm and guiding her down the final few steps into the darkness of the lowest level of the Interland. Jay could do nothing but slump onto the floor as Stitch moved to light a candle to provide just enough light to get to the three streams of water – the source.

He leaned to help Jay up, dragging her by the elbow. 'Come on,' he shouted above the noise coming from above. 'It's time. You can do this. You *have* to do this.'

Jay stood and nodded. They faced each other and locked

eyes and braced for what they knew was coming. Then came the energy of the Readers, like a tsunami of dark power flooding down the stairs. Stitch went down, floored by the power of the Readers channelled by Hinton. Jay stood firm, the power growing in her. Hinton appeared and pushed her off her feet without a single touch.

He ignored Stitch and bore down on Jay. 'No more, Jay. This is it. This is enough. Let it go.' He pierced her mind, pushing and digging. Jay could feel his determination, the hate and anger inside him. She could feel her own mind giving way, moving as if controlled by him. Out of the corner of her eye she saw Readers behind him, entering the cavern one by one. As each crossed the threshold, she felt the pain sharpen, a more powerful infiltration. They kept coming. Jay closed her eyes, unable to see for the darkness surrounding her. She concentrated her effort on shielding the attack, biding her time.

Jay was barely conscious when Hinton stopped. Her eyelids were too heavy to open. She heard their words as they talked of the source. 'Is this it?' came the unimpressed voice of one of the Readers. Jay opened an eye to see the man and two of the Readers leaning over the source above Jay's head.

The man put his fingers into the water and Jay wondered whether this would connect him with the power. 'Nothing,' he said. Jay's mind continued to spin. She was unable to open her other eye for fear of falling into the earth. Hinton grunted with derision as he sloshed his fingers around in the water. He cupped his hands and drank, smacking his lips and laughing with the Readers. 'Nothing,' Hinton said again, then swished some water around in his mouth before spitting it out into the flow from above.

Stitch moved, catching Jay's eye. He was a few feet from her, his movement slow and painful. Hinton splashed in the source once more and water fell to the ground between Jay and Stitch. Stitch leaned to touch the water, wetting his fingers and rubbing the water into their tips.

He reached for Jay and she opened out her hand to receive his. He wet her fingers with his own and a spark passed between them, up into Jay's mind, settling her racing thoughts, the pounding in her head subsiding.

She opened her other eye and looked directly at Stitch. She felt his heartbeat. It was weak. He closed his eyes.

Jay reached for the spilled water from the source, took it onto her fingers, and reached out to Stitch. Gently, she brushed the water from the source onto Stitch's lips. She felt the tingle as her connection with Stitch and with the source pushed energy through their bodies.

Again, Jay dipped her fingers into the pool beside her as Hinton and the Readers laughed above their heads. She brushed more onto Stitch's lips and this time he opened his eyes and they sparkled with light.

Jay clenched her teeth in determination, opening her mind and body to the flow of energy, no longer a thought for the danger the power of the connection might bring.

This time, she reciprocated the power. She channelled the energy through her body and back to Stitch.

Her sleeve was pushed up her arm, and she looked down at it, the number eight clear and full, the letter "C" discernible once more. She turned her arm to show Stitch. He smiled and shifted his weight on his shoulder so that he could rest on his hand. He cast his eyes up to the Readers and nodded to Jay.

Jay saw that Hinton had stepped back from the edge of the pool where the three streams of water flowed. Stitch stood and immediately the Readers turned on him. Jay jumped up to stand with him and together they thrust their hands into the water.

Hinton turned, fear and surprise on his face. Their power was evident, and he knew immediately this was his last chance. He threw everything he had at Jay and Stitch. As they reached for each other to make the connection, their bodies were thrown apart. Their hands remained connected to the pool of the source, but they couldn't reach each other to connect the circle.

Hinton pushed with all the power of the Readers in the room. Jay and Stitch swayed and bucked as they held their hands in the water and reached for each other.

A swirling mist, a white glow, seeped towards them from the passageway.

Jay looked over to Stitch, whose face was contorted in pain. She willed him to look at her and he slowly turned his eyes towards her. Mist swirled between them and Jay blocked out the vision of Hinton, the anger and determination in his face to end her and Stitch. She focused only on Stitch, and on opening to the energy of the source. As his eyes drifted away from her, she screamed his name, pulling him back.

The mist thickened and Jay reached out her hand, but Stitch was too far away.

The mist swirled around Stitch's arm and seemed to help him fight against the power of the Readers and raise his arm towards Jay. Their fingers now just inches apart, the white energy passed between them, the mist wrapping its tendrils around each of their wrists and pulling their hands together.

They touched.

The white glow intensified and exploded throughout the room. The Readers who filled the room writhed in pain as their energy soaked into the walls and their bodies became entwined in the stretching roots, vines and wisps of the mist in the cavern.

Hinton laughed. 'This power does nothing to me, I am immune.'

As the words drifted from him, the connection that Stitch and Jay had made with the earth, and the piercing white glow combined, pushing energy out through every cell in Jay's body.

As she shook with the power, the floor vibrated and Jay's vision blurred once more as a figure appeared in the mist – the man from the lake. A white glow emanated from him, drifting so that its epicentre floated between Jay and Stitch, surrounding them and joining with the source.

The power of the Interland exploded through the room. Hinton released a guttural scream as his physical form dissolved into the mist, his body melting into the rocks of the cavern and seeping into the walls like crude oil slipping away through the cracks.

The man from the lake disappeared but the white light remained, growing in its intensity then shooting out through the opening and up the steps towards the main cavern, destroying every Reader in its path. The connection of the level 8C and her connected C became whole.

The Interland was once again protected.

* * *

JAY OPENED HER EYES, spitting out the dust in her mouth and pushing herself up to sit. Stitch woke and sat up, rubbing his head. The white light that surrounded them began to dissipate and Jay recognised where they were. Water lapped the shore near her feet, and behind Stitch was the tree that stretched high into the sky in the middle of the island.

They were back on the island in the lake. The mist cleared. Jay saw the outline of the man, the other 8C, come into view.

He had waded into the water up to his waist and he waved her and Stitch to come join him. Jay looked down into the water, where the black swirls of darkness had before wrapped around Stitch, burning his skin. The water was clear. The swirls in the water carried fish and reeds. Jay led the way and Stitch followed. They got to the man when the water had reached their waists. He held out a hand to each of Jay and Stitch. 'Thank you,' he said.

Jay smiled. 'We couldn't have done it without you.'

'I wasn't there. Not as such. Only in your mind. In your connected power I was there.'

Jay turned to Stitch. Tears leaked down his face, and Jay put a hand on his shoulder. 'It's over, Stitch.'

The man turned his gaze to the other islands, far across the lake. Jay and Stitch followed the direction of his gaze. The blackened islands seemed darker, not lighter from what Jay could see. 'Why...' Jay started.

'The Readers,' said the man. 'Not your Readers, other Readers. When I saw you last, there were three islands down and two under threat, yours being one of those under threat. Now there are four islands down, but thanks to your work, this island,' he nodded behind Jay and Stitch, 'has been released.'

Jay looked on. Swirls of darkness touched at the edges of a fifth island, the island that was closest to this man's. 'The darkness is drawing closer?'

He nodded. 'Yes. And to fight it, we'll need your help.'

'How?'

'I'll show you. There is time, not much, but some. And you both need to rest.' Jay looked over to where the islands appeared to be darkening by the minute. Stitch looked to Jay, and they knew that they would have no choice.

They had a mission.

41

As Jay and Stitch clambered back up the steps from the deep cavern that held the source, Jay felt the energy flowing through her bones. Sparks filled the air between her and Stitch, like static electricity. She felt as strong as she'd ever been.

'Jay,' came a shout from the darkness in the tunnel at the top of the steps. Jay recognised the voice of her father. He came into the light, Matchstick by his side, and she allowed herself to melt into her dad's embrace, the sparks of her power surrounding them both. Beyond him and Matchstick, a group of the Given emerged from behind a mass of rocks and stones that had previously blocked the passageway.

'What happened?' said Jay, releasing her dad and nodding towards the opening in the rockfall.

'A flow of water, mist or something came from through the rocks and washed out the blockage. We've been trapped in there for days. There's no other way out.' Jay smiled at the knowledge that Sammy had found a way through and then led Alfred, Toyah and Pinto to freedom.

Ben looked beyond Jay to see Stitch leaning up against the

rocks. 'What happened to you? Where's Sammy?'

Jay turned towards the main cavern, momentarily concerned for Cassie and Sammy. She sensed they were safe. The Readers had gone.

The main cavern looked like it had been hit by an earthquake. Debris lay all around – bits of the dining table, chairs. The picture of Sasha Colden had been knocked from the wall and lay on the floor. Cassie and Sammy leaned up against the rocks at the edge of the cave. Their eyes were closed as they rested, and Cassie had her head on Sammy's shoulder. Jay breathed a sigh of relief.

Some of the Given hadn't made it. Jay saw at least three dead, and others sporting wounds being patched by others. A movement in the distance, up near the waterfall, caught Jay's eye, and she strained to see four figures emerge through the water and head towards them.

Alfred and Samir came into view first, Samir gaping. His first impression of the Interland was one of total devastation. Toyah and Pinto followed. Pinto ran ahead, overtaking Alfred and Samir to shoot through to the cavern. 'Jay,' he shouted.

Jay met him halfway, and he jumped up to embrace her. 'We were worried. The noises were so loud, we thought the whole place had been destroyed. Are the Readers gone?'

Jay nodded, lowering Pinto to the floor. 'They've gone.' Jay crouched down with Pinto. 'Was that you? Earlier? Did you use power?'

Pinto nodded, a grin widening. 'Did it work?'

Jay smiled at him. 'You bet it did. You helped distract the guards that held us. It was chaos in here. I reckon Alf here was right about you.'

'Is Otis OK?' Pinto asked, looking past Jay. Cassie had moved over to tend to Otis, his shirt covered in blood from a wound in his shoulder.

Jay and Pinto rushed over to them, and Jay crouched. 'Hey, crazy man,' she said. 'What happened? You totally spun out.'

Otis looked up and smiled. 'Something in the power sent me a little mad for a while back there. I lost control. Then I froze.'

'Are you OK?'

'I'll live,' he said.

Toyah joined them. Jay placed a hand on her arm. 'How's your head?'

'I'll live,' she replied, then looked beyond Jay to see Sammy as he rose from the floor. He and Toyah met, and he pulled her into a hug. Jay watched as Toyah held her brother tight, closing her eyes. Sammy looked at Jay over Toyah's shoulder, then over to Cassie who stood to greet Alfred and Samir. Jay leaned to pick up the picture of Sasha Colden. She pushed the wooden frame back into place and offered it up to the wall. It hung on a protruding piece of rock and Jay straightened it. She turned away and saw her dad pulling a cover over Zadie Lawrence. She glimpsed her lifeless eyes, staring up at Ben.

One by one, they climbed out of the Interland through the opening in the roof. Jay climbed the rope ladder behind Alfred, helping to guide his feet into the right places as he climbed. Cassie helped Otis as he struggled with his shoulder.

At the surface, with few words, they climbed to the crest of the hill, the peak that could be seen from where the river Arun flowed into the floodplain. Jay stood at the high point and looked down through the trees where she saw the river. Stitch joined her. 'The Arun?' he said.

'Yes,' said Jay. 'And see there,' she pointed. 'That's the Rother coming in. Can't see the unnamed river from here.'

'That one doesn't surface until its way beyond those hills.' Stitch nodded into the distance. They looked over at Cassie, stood alone on a rock, her braids sticking out at angles they'd not seen before. She kicked at the dirt, sending dust into the wind. She hugged her arms.

Jay imagined Reuben standing next to her. 'She's been through it these last few days. She's going to need some looking after,' she said.

Stitch nodded towards Sammy and Toyah as they looked out over the north ridge, holding hands. They watched as Sammy glanced over to Cassie and it seemed for a moment that he'd head over to join her, but then changed his mind. Ben was with Otis. They wandered up to join Sammy and Toyah, Ben pulling his son away from Toyah for a moment as he slung an arm around his shoulder.

Alfred and Samir had found a rock to rest on at the front of the ridge, looking over the hills of the Downs. Pinto ran to them and Toyah called for him to be careful. Pinto planted himself between Alfred and Samir, pointing them towards the north and across the fields. Jay heard him describe the route that he and Toyah had taken to get to the Interland.

'How do you remember back that far?' said Alfred, ruffling Pinto's hair.

'I'll never forget,' Pinto said in a serious tone, holding Alfred's gaze for a moment.

Alfred pulled him in to hug. 'I know, little one. I know.'

Jay looked further into the distance and imagined the other Interlands, under attack, in danger of being overtaken by the darkness. She felt Stitch's hand drift close to hers and without looking at him she twined her fingers through his. He clutched her hand tightly, and together they stared out across the hills and river valley, towards the distant sea.

End of Book #2

THE DARK

INTERLAND SERIES BOOK #3

For Ash

PART I

1

The faded-blue front cover of the hardback depicted a diagram of a female human body, but instead of being labelled with body parts, it was illustrated with flowing lines of white light around the girl's head. Jay rubbed her hand across the title. *The Physiology of Power*. She crouched in the bookshop's narrow aisle and slotted the text back into its space. Sunlight streamed through the south-facing windows, catching the steel edging along the rows of shelves. The sight of the once banned collection of books sparkling in the sunlight brought a smile to Jay's lips. Those gifted with power - the *Given* - were no longer consigned to the underground. Her feeling of pride sent a tingle of energy rippling through her body.

A handful of customers browsed. The top floor was Jay's domain, *her* responsibility. When Alf, the shop owner, had offered Jay the chance to curate the growing collection of literature on the Given and their powers, she'd jumped at the chance. The top floor now stretched across three town houses. It doubled as a library, and it thrived.

Returning to her desk, she pulled the master index from

the filing cabinet, a thick, loose-bound stack of pages she used for recording everything related to the Given that came into the shop. She flicked through and changed one of the entries, then returned it to the cabinet.

'Excuse me,' said a girl. Jay turned to see a child of only nine or ten years stood at the desk. Her skin was a russet reddish brown, and she had big hair that reminded Jay of her best friend, Cassie. Jay smiled, and the girl averted her eyes, then said, 'Can you help me?'

'Of course,' said Jay, sensing a flutter of energy from the girl. Power was rare, and for it to be detectable in someone so young was almost unheard of, but she sensed something. 'What are you looking for?'

'I don't know.'

Jay waited, allowing the girl some space to gather her thoughts. 'I want to read about the Given,' she said, eventually.

'Come with me.' Jay led the girl through the aisles to a section dedicated to books on the Given for young readers. She was used to children coming into the shop to see the collection and ask questions. She encouraged it, although very few of them had power. She'd been to all the local schools to talk about the powers and sell books into the school libraries. Jay was determined to see truth outweigh the speculation and fear-mongering. 'How much do you know about the Given?'

'Not much. My mum thinks it's silly.'

'Do *you* think it's silly?' The girl looked up, and a smile slipped out before she turned away again. 'What's your name?'

The girl paused and turned to look at Jay, as if deciding whether to reveal her name. 'Angie,' she said.

'I'm Jay.'

'I know,' said Angie.

Jay caught a definite wisp of power then. She rocked back

in her seat. Her colours were neutral, reserved, naïve. 'And do you feel a connection with the power?'

Angie shrugged. Jay ran her finger along the shelves. She pulled out a book: *The Powers and Me* – something by a writer who Jay once met when she came to the shop, a woman with a remarkable inner clarity and understanding of the power. She had written three books, but this one was specifically for kids trying to understand their own powers, their origins, and how they present before the marking appears.

Jay led Angie to a table. 'You want me to tell you about it, or shall I leave you to read for a while?'

'Can I ask you something?' Angie said, looking out of the window towards the hills of the Downs.

'Anything.' Jay sat and followed her gaze. The afternoon sun cast a glow over Highdown Hill, from which energy flowed freely. The combined energy of the three local hill forts was something that never failed to humble her.

She smiled, ready to impart her wisdom on an enquiring mind.

'Can I see your wrist?'

Jay smiled. It was common knowledge that the marking of the Given appeared naturally on the inside of the wrist like a tattoo - branding those with power as something different. She leaned closer and pulled back her sleeve to reveal the dark figure 8 and its accompanying letter "C". Angie pulled her own sleeve back and rubbed at the skin, searching for signs of a marking. 'Be patient,' said Jay. 'It'll come.'

Angie let her sleeve roll back down and turned her attention to the book. 'How will I know what level I am?'

'Only when the number appears. But you might have a sense of it before then.'

'Did you know, before?'

Jay remembered knowing she had power, but she had no

idea she'd be a level eight, let alone 8C. 'I knew I'd be strong. I felt strong. Tell me what *you* feel.'

Angie looked away, as if still unsure whether to speak freely. Eventually, she said, 'I see colours, and sometimes words, too.'

'Wow, that's good at your age. You'll have strength for sure. Can you open up to the energy?'

'What do you mean?'

Jay thought for a moment. For her, to open up to the power, she had to trust in it, allow herself to be moved by the energy so that it became part of her. 'It's hard to explain. Have you ever jumped off a really high diving board into a pool? Or from a rock into the sea?'

Angie nodded. 'At Lulworth Cove I jumped off the big arch into the sea.'

Jay laughed. 'You know that feeling when you've just let go of the safety of the ledge, or the rock, but before you start falling, and you have to go with it, take a leap of faith?'

Angie frowned. Jay scratched her head. 'Well, it's a bit like that. You kind of have to let yourself go.'

Angie looked confused. She motioned to ask more, but then seemed to change her mind. 'Tell me about the different levels, what they mean, what power comes with what level?'

'It's not as straightforward as that,' said Jay. 'Not all people of the same level have exactly the same power. It depends on other things, like how you connect with it, and how you use it. And there are some unusual levels.'

'Like what?'

'Level five is special. Level 5 Given have the power of telekinesis. Do you know what that is?'

Angie nodded. 'Just level five? Not six or seven? You don't have telekinesis then?'

Jay shook her head. 'Not strictly. But with my 8C, I have

something a little special too, especially when I have my partner with me.'

'Stitch?'

Jay laughed. Perhaps it shouldn't surprise her that those with an interest in the power knew of Stitch. He was her best friend, and he was her *connection*. His marking was unique. He had no number, just the letter "C". In each of the centres of the power of the Given, the most powerful was the 8C, like Jay. But each 8C was paired with someone who brought their power to its full strength, the "C", and for Jay, this was Stitch. 'You seem to know a lot already?' Jay said.

Angie let leak a sly smile. 'Tell me all the levels.'

'So,' said Jay, 'people at level *one* or *two* have not much more than a strong sense of intuition. Most at that level just seem to know things, like what someone had for dinner, or what music they like, but without really understanding how they know it.'

'Might be handy,' Angie said.

'My dad is a level two, and he can receive my thoughts sometimes, or used to, when we were better connected. It does vary between different people.'

'I don't think I'd want my dad to read me,' Angie said. 'What about level three?'

'Three and four are mostly just extensions of the telepathy you get at levels one and two. Stronger. At level four, you get a deeper connection with people.' Jay paused for a moment. Angie frowned. 'I know a level four who can focus his power into his hands and create heat. He can even make sparks,' said Jay. Angie opened and closed her hands before her.

Jay opened the book on the table between them and flicked through to the centre pages, pointing to a colourfully annotated scale that illustrated the power levels from one to eight. At the top was a picture of a woman in a superhero cape.

'Is that you?' asked Angie.

Jay laughed. 'Kind of. I don't have a cape though. You think it looks like me?'

Angie nodded and grinned. 'Do you know what everyone is thinking? All the time?'

Jay shook her head. 'No. I have to open up to the energy. It's an active process. It's not like I'm hearing everyone's thoughts all the time. That would be a living chaos. And people can shield too.'

'Shield?'

'With practice, the Given can shield their thoughts from other Given.'

'And from Readers?'

Jay nodded. Hearing someone so young even mention the *Readers* made her wince. The collective name for those who drew their energy from a darker source was enough to make Jay feel uneasy. She pushed the dark feelings away. 'And some people are better at shielding than others. My friend Alf...' She looked up as if to point him out. 'He is the best at shielding. If he doesn't want me to know what he's thinking, then I've got no chance, and he's only a level four.'

Angie reminded Jay of herself as a kid. She could read that Angie was impatient for her own powers to come, but scared at the same time. At her age, Jay's powers had felt like a curse. There was so much danger associated with revealing yourself in those days. She saw Angie's confusion too about the mechanism of deploying power. 'Don't over-think it,' said Jay. 'Try to be open to it; let it come to you.'

Angie frowned. 'How?'

'The strength in the energy comes from inside you. The power flows from the environment around us - the earth, the sea, and all living things. If you open to it, let it connect and become like it's part of you. That's how its true strength will come out.'

Angie's frown deepened, and Jay feared she was doing a poor job of explaining. 'Have a read,' she said, motioning to the book. 'And come back and talk to me whenever you like. Remember, there's no rush with this stuff.'

'As long as the Readers don't come,' Angie said, holding eye contact with Jay.

Jay pressed back into her seat, deflected by another mention of Readers from someone who shouldn't have to worry about the darkness. 'They're not coming back,' Jay said. Angie raised her eyebrows with a look that challenged her certainty. 'I won't let them. They have no home here, no means to channel their power. We made sure of that back in the Interland.'

Jay looked up and out the window as thoughts of those they'd lost came into her mind: Reuben, Davey, and even Zadie Lawrence. Their absence weighed heavily on her chest, and their sacrifice was one she vowed to honour.

'I won't let it happen again,' said Jay.

* * *

ON HER WAY back to her desk, Jay caught sight of Alf emerging from the stairwell. He nodded a greeting from across the room, holding up a couple of books for her. He was light on his feet, almost skipping the final stride as he reached Jay's desk, paying no respect to the fact he was well past retirement age.

She loved his enthusiasm. He'd rediscovered his youth since their emergence from the Interland and re-integration with society. Without the threat of Readers, and with the growing prosperity of the country, people had developed a new optimism. They looked after themselves. Alf still took a run every day on the beach with his dog, Buster, and was up and down the three flights of stairs in the shop a dozen times a day. He was as fit as Jay, for sure. But, like all the Given who lived through the battle for the Interland, Alf was wary of the powers of darkness. When he extended the shop, he included a safe-room connected to his apartment, constructed in the basement. It was his protection should the Readers ever rise again. He vowed they would never again take him from his own bookshop, his own home.

Buster scampered up the stairs behind Alf, almost knocking him over as he slid through his legs and bounded across the shop towards Jay. She crouched to greet him, leaning away as he lapped at her face. 'That dog will be the death of me,' Alf grumbled.

'Hey, old man,' Jay said.

Alf scowled at her, handing over the books. Buster explored the top floor, tail wagging. 'These are for you. Where's Cassie? I thought she was coming in to work with you today?'

'She didn't turn up again.' Jay took the books and linked her arm with Alf's, turning him around. 'Come, I want to show you something.' She led him to a new arrangement of the shelves and cabinets on the back wall, presenting them with pride.

Alf said nothing but opened the cabinets one at a time and flicked through the papers. He looked at the picture Jay had hung on the wall, the picture of Sasha Colden that used to hang in the main hall of the Interland. This arrangement of material was the culmination of weeks of work by Jay, cataloguing and filing the historical documents on the Given, the powers and the myths. There were maps, old notebooks, and other documents that had come in to the shop from all over the country.

'These are from the Interland,' Jay said, motioning to the shelves packed with literature previously stored at the Interland, as well as the old notebooks and maps from the Gateway that survived. She'd systematically worked through them, ordering and referencing. In front of the cabinets was a long desk with chairs where people could study the materials.

'This must have taken you weeks. You kept this a secret?'

Jay nodded, trying to suppress a beaming grin. 'I wanted to surprise you.'

'This is amazing,' he said, looking across the cabinets, the desk and the wealth of organised material that Jay had obviously worked so hard to get in order. 'I should promote you to head librarian,' he said.

'Pay rise?' asked Jay. 'Look, there's a gold mine of information here.' She'd read a lot of it over the weeks and months of collecting and cataloguing. Not all of it was in English, and even some that was in her native language was unreadable, or in a dialect that took some interpretation. She opened the last of the cabinets and pulled out an old hard-backed notebook and carefully opened it on the desk.

'I recognise this from back at the Interland,' said Alf. 'It was originally in the British Library before they flagged it for early references to the power.'

'I've read some of it,' said Jay. 'It's hard going.'

Jay had picked up bits of information from what she'd read in the ageing pages. The old English language was hard to interpret. The notebook spoke of a darkness coming to the land in the seventeenth century, long before Sasha Colden, Jay's grandmother, who Jay had previously thought was one of the first of those with power.

'It's not clear, if I remember correctly,' said Alf. 'But I can see in your thoughts that you've found something interesting?'

Jay nodded for Alf to continue.

'It talks of a dark power, if I recall,' he said, 'before the power of the Given. But it reads like a fairy tale.'

Jay pulled the book towards her and flicked to a particular page. 'See here,' she said, pointing to a line with the name *Atta*.

Alf nodded. 'I remember reading this.' His tone was solemn.

Jay reached and opened another cabinet, rifling through loose-leaf papers until she found what she was looking for, a single sheet of paper, A2 size. She unfolded it and placed it on the table next to the book. 'Here,' she said. 'Read that.'

Alf strained his eyes, then pulled his glasses down off his head and onto his nose. Jay reached for the magnifying glass attached to a piece of string next to the desk and handed it to Alf. '*Blindnes néahlæcaþ*... I've seen these words before. I think *néahlæcaþ* means *approaches*, or something like that. It's talking of a blindness coming, or a darkness.'

'Keep reading,' said Jay.

Alf scanned across the page, running his fingers over the words as if trying to find some that he recognised. He stopped in the place that Jay had wanted him to. '*Atta*,' he said, the letters sticking on his tongue as if he were reluctant to let them out. '*Atta... becíeseþ... Maram.*' He sat back as if worn out. 'I've read the name *Atta* many times, in association with the power of the darkness. *Becíeseþ* is old English for *fight*. This passage is about a battle between the dark and the light, between Atta and Maram. Now, where have I heard Maram before?'

Jay turned to the shelves behind them and picked out a book – the Sasha Colden biography that she'd read countless times and still returned to as a kind of therapy. She flicked through to a page near the back and handed it to Alf.

He read from where Jay pointed. 'Sasha *Maram* Colden...' He looked up. '*Maram* was Sasha's middle name?'

Jay nodded. 'But this document,' she pointed to the notes on the desk, 'is way older than Sasha Colden. So it can't be referring to my Sasha, my grandmother. It's referring to something older, after which they then named my grandmother.'

'We'd need to get a proper translation, but the implication is that there was power back in the sixteen hundreds, way before Sasha, and before the Given were formally identified.'

'Except everyone believes powers didn't exist before the twentieth century.'

'You'll be writing an academic paper on all this at some stage.' He stood and his knees creaked. 'I need to cash up.'

* * *

Buster followed Alf back down the stairs. The only remaining customer was the little girl, Angie, still reading. She was a good third of the way through the book. She jumped when she sensed Jay, then snapped the book closed.

'Hey,' said Jay. 'It's OK.'

'Sorry,' the girl said, standing. 'I have to go.'

'Look,' said Jay, picking up the book from the desk. 'Do you want to take this on loan? Bring it back when you've read it and I'll exchange it for another one?'

'No,' Angie snapped. She sighed. 'I can't take it home.'

'That's OK,' said Jay, tapping the front of the book. She considered pressing a little more about what was going on with Angie at home, but she sensed it wasn't the right time. 'Come back whenever you want. Just help yourself. After school. Whenever you like.'

'Thanks,' she said, turning to leave.

'And, Angie...'

'What?'

'You're safe here. You don't need to be afraid of Readers, not anymore. I promise.'

Angie opened her mouth, but then closed it before disappearing around the corner. Jay returned the book, but left it poking out a little from the other books, easier for Angie to find on her own if she came back.

Something moved. She looked towards the stairs. 'Angie?' she said, although she knew Angie was already out of the shop and likely into the street. A minor adrenaline spike sent her powers into readiness. The shop was quiet.

She scanned the rest of the room, down each aisle, before looking back towards the stairs. A feeling bubbled in her stomach, the feeling she knew so well from when the Readers were in control, and it was the Given doing the hiding. The first time she'd seen a Reader, she'd been standing much like she was now, on the top floor of Alf's bookshop, locking eyes for that split second with Marcus. The Head Reader's scar had glinted in the light, evil laced his face, an evil that Jay eventually destroyed in battle. The memory ran a shiver up her spine as she recalled the oppression, the fear, and the lack of basic freedoms. She scanned the room once more, opening her senses and allowing her power to expand and fill every corner of the room.

Nothing.

She made for the stairs, switching the light off as she left.

* * *

DOWNSTAIRS, Alf finished with the cash register and waited for Jay. 'Come on, get yourself home. Your dad will curse me for keeping you so late.'

Jay stepped down from the last stair and flung her rucksack over her shoulder. It was too light. She'd forgotten The Sasha Colden biography, her comfort blanket. 'Forgot something.'

'Go on, I can wait.'

'You go, I'll let myself out.' She jangled her set of keys.

'As you like. I'm heading out back.'

Alf sighed, and the light from above cast a shadow over his face that made him look old and vulnerable for a moment. Jay never thought of Alf as anything but invincible. 'Have a lie-in tomorrow if you like,' she said. 'I'll come and open up in the morning.'

Alf smirked, knowing Jay would never get to the shop early enough to open up before him. He turned to leave, ducking under the low doorway and out to the back door that led to his apartment.

The Colden book was still on the table where she'd left it. The warm glow of the streetlights bathed the room. Outside, a figure in a shop doorway on the other side of the street caught her eye. He stood facing the bookshop, but the shadows hid his features. She stepped back from the window, out of view, then leaned to turn off the light in the stairwell. She opened up to see if she could sense him, read his intentions, but when she turned back to the window, he was gone. The street was empty. *It's nothing*, she told herself. *Someone sheltering for a minute before heading home. Nothing.* Sometimes, what felt like her powers tingling was just leftover memories.

Outside, darkness settled in and a salty breeze blew off the sea. She slung her bag over her shoulder and headed for home.

Turning off the main high street towards the Beach Lane estate, the noise of Saturday night entertainment dissolved into the background, replaced by the sounds of crashing waves over stones. The tide must be in, she thought. Five minutes more and she turned into Beach Lane.

In the quiet, away from the beach and the town, her lonely footsteps echoed off the houses. Shadows danced between the streetlamps. She stepped up the pace a little, looking over her shoulder. The pulsing heartbeat in her ears muted the sound of her footsteps.

A noise?

Nothing.

She ran.

The bag on her back slammed into her with every stride as she powered home, not daring to look back, her eyes focused only on the pavement ahead. She hit her front door and gulped in air. This wasn't paranoia. Someone was behind her, someone who must have kept pace, someone about to drag her back into the alleyway.

A hand on her shoulder.

She screamed.

'Jay, it's me, Sammy.'

Jay's younger brother stared back at her and she screamed again before he gave her a gentle shake, a hand on each shoulder. 'Sis. It's me. What is it?'

Jay grabbed Sammy and hugged him tight, looking past him into the street beyond. Nothing but darkness. Streetlamps. Front gates and low hedges.

2

The sea turned dark under a dusk sky. Waves raced towards the girl sitting on the stones under the pier, reaching for her outstretched feet as if to take her away, only to swirl around and then retreat. The girl waited for dark. Then it would be time.

The last she remembered being by the sea, the proper sea, not the inter-dimensional shores of the *Islands*, was way back. Before her life became one long conflict. She had craved a moment like this, time alone, with just the sounds and smells of the seaside and her memories.

She ran a finger along the outline of the figure 7 on the inside of her wrist. Sometimes it still startled her. She still expected to see the number 3, the number she was born to display, before she became a Reader and her power increased. With that power came the protection of the Dark. It was like joining the most established and powerful club in the world where nothing and no-one could touch you. She had simply done what her parents would not do, a choice for which they made the ultimate sacrifice. She would never take their path.

They were gone, but she wasn't alone. The *Dark* was her protector.

The girl picked up a handful of stones, throwing one at a time into the water as it rushed up the beach. Whispers came from the sea, and she thought she must be imagining it, confusing the mark of a Given energy with the sound of sea on sand and stone. Her transformation to a Reader should have silenced them. But still they came. She dropped the stones and put her hands to her ears. Still they came, circling the inside of her head as if scolding her. Whispers turned to screams - like the cries of pain of the Given, those with power who had fallen at the hands of the darkness.

The tide retreated and the screams abated. The breeze dropped. She was alone once more. She looked down at the figure 7 on her wrist and clenched her fist. On the post in front of her, two names were carved in the grain: *JAY* and *STITCH*. Her fingers filtered through the stones, looking for one with a sharp edge to it, discarding three. The fourth, a piece of flint as yet unsmoothed by the ebb and flow of the tide, had the edge she needed.

Under the name of *JAY*, she carefully scraped her own name into the wood.

FLICK.

* * *

FLICK MOVED with purpose along the promenade. She imagined the echoes of the day's seaside tourists rising from the black surface as she walked, mixing with a lingering smell of hotdogs and sweet roasted nuts. An image of her parents. A pang of nostalgia quickly brushed away.

A salty breeze buffeted her as she walked. Despite having no desperate need to hide herself, it was in the pools of darkness between the streetlamps where she breathed easier. Under each light, she pulled her hood tight against her head and sped up a little as she moved through the glare.

She crossed the wide seafront road and hopped onto the opposite pavement, ducking into an alcove. She crouched in the darkness next to a discarded bag of rubbish, pulled her hood back down over her eyes and watched the bookshop.

It was nearly half an hour before the lights went out. Another five minutes and the shop door opened with the clang of a bell. Jay had her back to the high street as she turned the key in the lock and pulled the door to make sure it was secure. Flick stepped back into the darkness and Jay turned. Flick sensed her glance in her direction before she made off up the high street.

Spooked that Jay had clocked her, Flick waited a minute in the shop doorway before daring to emerge onto the high street. She needed to confront Jay on her own terms, and not in the middle of the high street. When she finally stepped out, Jay was already out of sight.

Tomorrow will be OK, she thought. But she could feel her strength of power was weakening. She was too far from the source of Reader energy on Island 7, and she would have to make a move soon, before it was too late.

3

Sammy slid a pawn forward one square. Jay was enjoying watching her brother squirm. His streak was down; his mum had beaten him twice in the last few days. She leaned over the chessboard and sucked in air through her teeth as Sammy stared in silence at the pieces. 'The pupil becomes the master,' Jay said.

Ben called Jay from the kitchen, and Jay jumped up from the sofa. 'What's up, Dad?'

'Don't wind your brother up,' he said, continuing to stir the pan - the smell of onion and garlic filling the room. Jay pulled herself up to sit on the worktop. Ben added chicken to the pan. He stirred and lowered the heat. 'How's work? Alf behaving himself?'

'I finished the archiving yesterday. Alf was impressed. There's a lot of information there. You should come and have a look. When's the last time...'

'Slow down,' Ben said as he stirred the food. 'I just meant in general, how is it?'

Jay sighed inwardly at her dad cutting her off when she got enthusiastic about the shop. 'I enjoy working there.'

'Long term?'

Jay ignored her dad's baiting question. In his mind, she should think about university. Her attention was elsewhere.

She was thinking about the names Atta and Maram, wanting to ask her dad about them. He gave mixed messages on the world of the powers. One minute he'd be heading out to his old group to talk about the resistance to the Readers, and the next it was as if to talk of the power was to invite trouble.

'There's something in the older literature on the Given that has me confused,' she said. Ben said nothing, apparently distracted by the challenge of measuring the correct amount of rice for four people.

'What?' he said, eventually.

She paused, thinking of the Legend. The power of the Given was centred at the confluence of three rivers - the Interland. Legend said that this location became a big sinkhole, disappearing underground and taking one of three sisters with it. 'You know the Legend we talked about before, of the sink-hole lake and the three sisters and all that...'

'Yes.'

'Was there another story? An older Legend that spoke of the powers in terms of the *Darkness,* or the *Dark*?'

'You mean the Readers? Not really, because the Readers came later and...'

'No,' Jay interrupted. 'Not the Readers. Before them, before all that. Something else. A darkness of some form that allowed the Readers to exist. Something that came before the Given.'

'The Given came first. The Readers are a twisted version of the Given. You taught *me* that.' Ben placed a lid over the pan and turned to face Jay.

She scratched her head, trying to connect the dots in her mind. While the power of the Given came from the source at the Interland, the power of the Readers emanated from a different place, somewhere deep below the surface. 'Readers get their power from the core, right?'

'Right.'

'And the *sink-room*, the place we destroyed at the prison, was their means of channelling that power.' She paused, recalling the combined efforts of her and her friends in taking apart what the Readers left behind - the building where they imprisoned the Given. It housed their sink-room, their means of routing the dark power from the earth's core. 'But before the sink-rooms, the power was still there, it was just that it was chaotic.'

'I guess...' Ben mused.

'There's a reference to someone called *Atta*, but it's like he's a mythical being, or something. He's a physical manifestation of the darkness that comes from the core.'

'*Atta*?' Ben repeated the name. 'I've heard that before somewhere.'

'What about *Maram*?' asked Jay, watching her dad for his reaction.

'That was my mother's middle name. Sasha *Maram* Colden.'

'I thought so,' said Jay. She jumped down off the kitchen top. 'But the weird thing is, in the older literature, from the seventeenth century, there's mention of Maram as the power who opposed Atta. But this *Maram* was decades before Sasha.'

Ben thought for a moment. 'Sasha could have been named after this myth?'

'Do you remember anyone talking about it?'

'I hardly knew her, remember?' Ben's mother, Jay's grandmother, left without a trace when Ben was just three years old. It wasn't until the past year, in the discovery of the Interland,

and long after her death, it came clear that Sasha Colden was Ben's estranged mother.

'I know, but did anyone in the family talk about it?'

Ben stirred the rice and checked the bubbling curry. 'I think you're getting too deep with this stuff. The Readers have gone. Look out there,' he nodded to the window. The sun had dipped in the sky and the clouds reflected a deep orange colour. Houses in Jay's street previously abandoned and boarded up were once again occupied. The lawns were cut, flowers emerging.

Jay sighed. She knew her dad wanted her to stop obsessing about Readers and get on with life, but she couldn't let it go. She needed him to engage, to help her like he used to. There was no puzzle that she and her dad together couldn't solve. She leaned to look out the window. 'Maybe I'll head to the Island. Talk to the other 8C. He might know something.'

Jay and Stitch had been to the Island, the inter-dimensional space between lands, twice since they first left the Interland. 'Last time we went, there was no sign of the other 8C. His island looked OK, but we didn't cross to it.'

'Why do you need to go there?'

'Research,' said Jay, thinking of the bookshop. 'I might be able to transport there without Stitch. My power is strong enough. With the source, I could probably...'

'Don't be stupid,' said Ben. 'Stitch is your connection. That connection keeps you safe.'

Jay didn't answer. She knew her dad didn't want her to be at risk. But she had others to think about, a responsibility to protect more than just herself. She contemplated how her powers had failed to prevent the damage by the Readers before, and the lives they took. She thought of Davey and Reuben and her heart ached. Nothing she could do would ever bring them back.

'If you like, I can ask my group tonight about the history of those names: Atta, and Maram.'

It was a Tuesday, and Ben would head to the pub basement for his regular meeting with his friends - the *resistance*. It was more of a social club than anything else, but people there knew about the powers, not as much as Alf, but it could be useful. Ben used to ask Jay to join him. He joked that she'd be like a celebrity making a special guest appearance. Anyone with interest in the powers knew about Jay, what she and her friends had accomplished, and the strength in her abilities. But she'd never accompanied him, and eventually he gave up asking.

She surprised them both when she asked, 'Can I come with you?'

* * *

ON THE WAY to The Smugglers, Ben filled Jay in on the activities of the *New Resistance*. Jay had to conceal a smirk behind her hand on hearing the group's updated name. There was very little that was *new* about the well-meaning bunch she was about to meet. The pub basement had been the venue for their meetings for as long as the group had existed, back from when the Readers posed a genuine threat, and the group's numbers swelled to nearly twenty.

'Evening, Ben,' the landlord greeted them, his eyes on Jay. Ben nodded hello and Jay gave a wave of her hand. 'Usual?' he said to Ben. 'And for the lady?' Jay resisted a roll of her eyes and asked the landlord for a Coke. 'I'll send 'em down.'

They squeezed through a narrow door and onto a cast iron spiral staircase. The basement was dimly lit, with a scent of competing aftershaves and the sound of hushed conversation. Plastic chairs with rusty steel legs were arranged around a central table. The six men in the room, all standing, talking with pints of beer in their hands, stopped their conversations and turned to look as Ben and Jay stepped off the foot of the staircase. Matchstick, Ben's closest friend and fellow ex-inmate of the prison for the Given, held out his arms to Jay for a hug. 'The old man drag you down here at last?'

'Something like that,' said Jay.

'Samir is here too,' Matchstick said, turning just as Stitch's dad, Samir, approached. She'd not seen him for a few weeks. He occasionally came into the bookshop. She used to see him when Jay and Stitch would hang out at Stitch's house, but that was rare these days.

'As-Salam-u-Alaikum,' Jay said, remembering Samir's greeting and nodding respectfully.

'Wa-Alaikumussalam wa-Rahmatulla,' said Samir. 'Where is that boy of mine? Never home helping his old father like he should be.'

'I'm sure he's studying hard, looking to make you proud,' Jay said with a smirk.

Samir laughed and turned to show off Jay to the others. 'Here she is,' he said, and the other four men greeted Jay enthusiastically, reaching to shake hands and saying how much they'd heard about her.

A chime rang out, like the single strike of a grandfather clock. Ben opened a hatch in the wall, revealing an old service shaft. A pint of beer and a Coke sat on a tray. Ben took the drinks and rang the bell. The tray disappeared once more, ascending smoothly on a hoist. Ben handed Jay her drink. 'You can't beat old-school service,' he said. 'Let's sit.'

Matchstick and Samir took seats on either side of Jay. The group descended into individual conversations for a while until a man raised his hand as if in a school classroom. It was the man who had introduced himself to Jay as Colson. He had rich black skin, and an unassuming demeanour, a warm smile. As the others quietened, Colson asked Jay from across the table, 'What brings you here tonight?'

Colson had a level of power – the only other one in the room with power but for her dad and Matchstick. Colson had something greater than Ben's level two, and she could read that he was a kind man, his colours warm and open. 'In your work,' said Jay, 'have you come across the names *Atta* and *Maram*?'

Murmurs rippled through the basement room with no-one voicing any recognition of the names. Jay kept her eyes on Colson, whom she was sure had immediately recognised the names. 'Atta and Maram represent the very essence of the fight between the dark and the light.' Colson's voice was soft, paced slow and measured. Despite his outward calm, his colours changed when he spoke of Atta and Maram. Those words meant something profound to Colson, and they clearly raised his levels of anxiety.

'Who were they?' asked Jay.

Colson reached for his tobacco in the inside pocket of his jacket on the back of his chair. He pulled a cigarette-rolling contraption from the other pocket and thumbed tobacco into it, on top of a Rizla. 'The legends are vague. The stories have been written, translated, re-written and re-interpreted to the point where the truth is indistinguishable from a fairytale. The principles of good and evil are presented as physical enti-ties.' He licked his cigarette paper and completed rolling, lighting it with a match. 'Whether any higher power ever existed in a physical form is doubtful.' He exhaled a puff of smoke that rose in the cool air of the basement and hung like a cloud above the table.

Matchstick spoke up, 'Well, this is news to me. I've read nothing about these older powers. I always thought that the power of the Given only came into existence in the last century.'

'Not true,' said Colson. 'We've talked about it before.' He looked at Ben.

Ben nodded. 'Before your time here with the group.' Then back to Colson, 'But it was just speculation. We had no hard evidence, nothing unequivocal.'

Jay straightened in her seat. 'We do now,' she said. 'The work that Alf has done...' Two men snorted at the mention of Alf. Like her dad, others in the group continued to distrust Alf, despite it being clear that his allegiance was to the Given. 'He's probably the most knowledgeable living person on the powers,' Jay said defensively, her back stiffening with anger.

'Why doesn't he join us then?' said one of the men.

'Hey,' said Ben, raising a hand. 'Let's not go there.'

Jay continued, 'The work Alf has done, with others at the Interland, has helped us pull together a load of information on the powers. There's a lot of contemporary writing, but also some of the older literature, from as far back as the seventeenth century.'

'And what does it tell us?' asked Colson, puffing on his cigarette.

'Talk of the *darkness*. Atta. Maram. But, we also know that Maram was Sasha Colden's middle name.'

Colson shook his head and looked at Ben for confirmation. 'Are you sure? If that's true, then...'

Ben nodded.

'Then what?' said Jay.

'I don't know,' said Colson, scratching the grey stubble on his chin that stretched up into his sideburns to join with the hair on his head. 'Sasha Colden was your family, your blood, right?' Ben nodded and Jay confirmed. 'I'm afraid I can't shed any light, but I'd like to come and see what you have at the bookshop.'

* * *

THE FOLLOWING SATURDAY, Colson trawled through the literature. He was like a kid in a sweet shop, hungrily devouring the information Jay had curated. 'It's ambiguous,' Colson said. 'Open to interpretation.' He placed the old notebook back on the shelf.

Jay sighed. 'There's something in it though, right? Maram is more than a myth. She's the original who drew power from nature. And Atta is the original who drew the power of the Dark?'

'I may need to consult the London branch,' said Colson. 'There are people in the London office of the resistance who have other material. They have their own research agenda, but we compare notes from time to time. They may be interested.'

Alf appeared at the end of the aisle, heading towards them, Buster at his feet. Colson looked up, pushed his glasses to the top of his head, and leaned back in his chair. It took a moment for Alf to recognise Colson, but when he did, his pace slowed and he looked like he might turn around and head back the other way.

'Alfred,' Colson said, a coolness to his tone.

'Colson,' Alf returned the greeting. 'I didn't expect to see you in here. Find anything useful to inform the *New Resistance*?' A mocking tone.

'Sit down,' Jay said with a sigh.

'I've got work to do...'

'Please,' she interrupted. Alf relented, taking a seat at the end of the desk, the seat furthest from Colson. Jay sat between them, bridging the gap. Colson reached out a hand to stroke

Buster but pulled it back as Buster's top lip curled and he released a low rumbling growl.

'Look, Alfred,' Colson began, 'Jay's dad is a friend of mine, and you two here seem to be getting on just fine, so we must have some common ground we can work on?'

'It wasn't me who started this whole thing if I remember right.'

'Alf,' snapped Jay. 'Let's be grownups, shall we?'

Alf rolled his eyes and crossed his arms, leaning back in his chair. He said, 'Tell Jay what you did. She deserves to know.'

Jay waited patiently as Colson shook his head. 'What Alf is referring to was a misunderstanding, a mistake.'

'He sold me out to the Readers,' Alf said. 'Back when this place was taken, and I was cast aside. If it wasn't for a bit of luck, and contact from the Runners, I'd have been in that place, the prison, and reduced to nothing. All thanks to Colson here.' Alf sat back in his chair.

'Why?' asked Jay, attempting to delve into Colson's mind. She saw his sorrow. He had screwed up. He'd misunderstood Alf's position. Alf was probably the best shielder Jay had ever met. He led the Readers to thinking that he was helping them, informing on the Given who used the bookshop to learn about the powers, so that the State could keep records of persons of interest. The reality was that Alf used his position to gather intelligence on the Readers, and feed information through to the Interland for the benefit of the Given – work he progressed further when he made it to the Interland himself. Colson had misinterpreted this as Alf working against the Given.

'I didn't know,' said Colson. 'I thought... we *all* thought, including your father, Jay. We thought Alf was on the side of the Readers. After all, that's the front he presented. For God's sake, you can't blame us for thinking that.'

'My dad didn't think that,' said Jay. 'Or he'd never have let me come here.'

'He had his suspicions. He didn't like you talking to Alfred.'

'Well, you were all wrong,' said Jay.

Colson nodded. 'I know, and I've apologised for the part I may have played in revealing your allegiance to the Given. Truly, I didn't know.'

Alf turned to Jay. 'It didn't take the Readers long to hit the shop. I've never felt such pain.' He paused, staring at Colson.

Colson refused to meet his gaze. Under his breath, he said, 'We got it wrong. I'm sorry.'

4

As Jay walked home, the high street seemed darker and quieter than usual. The pub on the corner had just one man outside smoking a cigarette. Thoughts of being followed drifted into her mind, and she brushed them away.

As she turned into Beach Lane estate, she couldn't shake the sense that she wasn't alone. She altered her route, heading into the alleyways around the side of the housing estate that she knew like the back of her hand. She picked up speed and turned onto a path lit at the entrance by an orange glow from a streetlight half buried in the trees. Ahead, the alley was dark. The next streetlight was beyond the corner. With a quick glance over her shoulder, Jay ran to the corner and ducked into a hedge. She waited. From the shadows she could see back to the entrance, and in the other direction she could see the streetlights stretching to the next corner. Her heart pounded in her chest, pulsing through to her eardrums. The twigs and leaves of the bush dug into her side.

A hooded figure appeared at the entrance to the alleyway. Jay's stomach clenched. If she ran now, she could probably outrun them. She hesitated. Seconds passed. The figure stepped into the alleyway. As they passed, she sensed power, dark power, not the power of the Given. This was a Reader, Jay was certain, but Readers had no means of drawing power with no source, and the source, sink-room, had been destroyed. Who was this person?

The Reader stopped and Jay sensed that their power, although of great potential, was weak. She climbed out of the hedge and stood in the alleyway. Slowly the person turned, head down, face in shadow.

'Who are you?' Jay said, stepping forward.

The Reader pulled aside the hood. Jay stepped back in surprise from the woman standing before her. Of all the Readers she'd fought, not one had been a woman, all were men. Instinctively, she attacked.

Power of the Given raised through fear and anger was often the most deadly, and the least controlled. As Jay channelled the power of the earth beneath her feet, the energy of the sea to the south and the hills to the north, and directed them into the Reader, she felt her power grow. The ease with which Jay could raise the power of the environment spurred her on. Energy pumped through her veins, attacking the Reader like a powerful scatter-gun. The girl had no defence against this show of strength.

'Stop!' the Reader shouted, as she fell to her knees, her hands to the sides of her head. 'I just want to talk.' She looked up at Jay, her eyes pleading. Messages came through to Jay, begging.

Jay was confused, both at how this Reader had got to her, and how she seemed different to other Readers. She felt little threat from this woman.

She stopped, but just for a moment, poised to resume.

The Reader flopped to the floor, then slowly raised

herself to her knees, then to her feet, holding out both of her hands as if in a truce. 'I came here to warn you. Don't kill me.'

'Who are you? What do you want?' asked Jay.

'My name is Flick,' she said.

'Why are you here?' Jay saw a faint scar on the side of the woman's face.

Flick raised her hand to the scar, the characteristic marking that came after an attack with power. 'This is old. It wasn't you. Look, can we talk somewhere? I think I need to sit before I fall.'

'Why don't I just take you in? You know what the State will do to you, right?'

'You could,' Flick said. 'I can't say in your position that I wouldn't, but I think you'll want to hear what I have to say.'

Flick wobbled again, and Jay held out a hand to stop her from falling. As their hands touched, a stream of information passed to Jay. She saw Readers, scores of them, working at the construction of a complex of buildings... darkness, swirls of darkness... the Islands blackened. Jay dragged away her hand. 'What was that?'

'The reason I'm here,' said Flick. 'Where can we talk?'

* * *

Jay pushed open the door of the bookshop, careful not to let the bell above the door ring for fear of alerting Alf. She let Flick in and locked the door behind and, without turning on the light, she led Flick up the stairs to the top floor. She switched on a lamp at a reading table and motioned for Flick to sit. She headed to the kitchen out the back and returned with two mugs of tea.

'Thanks,' Flick said as Jay sat opposite her.

'You're a Reader. How are you able to keep your power? There is no source, no connection to the core.'

'There *is* a source. You might have destroyed the sink-room, but the connection to the core remains. I came here from Island 7. Readers can move through Islands in the same way as the Given, you know that.'

Jay nodded.

'But I can't keep power here for long. I'm risking everything to come here, and you nearly killed me.'

Jay tapped her finger against the rim of her mug, waiting for Flick to continue.

'I've been looking for you,' said Flick, taking a sip of tea. 'Yes, I'm a Reader. I transformed a few months ago. Not that I had much choice. I was one of the first from the new facility.'

'Facility?' Jay said.

'The one I just showed you when you touched my hand. It's on Island 7.'

Jay saw the images in her mind again, the buildings, a room with dozens of Readers at work.

'A sink-room,' said Flick. 'A big one. Much bigger than the ones on the other islands, and much bigger than the one you destroyed on this island. That's why I can retain power here, from a source on Island 7. But not for long. My power is weaker here, and with time it will diminish, until I go back.'

Jay's mind raced with questions. If Island 7 had a new sink-room facility, what had happened to the 8C, their companion? Flick seemed to read Jay's thoughts and shook her head. 'You need to forget about Island 7 and start thinking about your own homeland.'

'Why are you telling me this?'

'I was never a willing subject for transformation. I was forced. I did it to stay alive.'

'What's changed? They'll kill you for reaching out to the Given.'

'They'll never know. I shield well.'

'Why should I believe...'

Flick sighed. 'I risked my life, don't you get it? They messed with my mind and body without my consent. If you can't believe me, then I don't know what to tell you, believe whatever you want. Just be ready for a darkness you couldn't even imagine.' She looked out of the window.

Jay studied the scar on the side of Flick's face. 'You've been reduced in the past? But you still have the power of a Reader?'

'It's a long story.'

'What level are you?'

Flick turned over her arm to show the black number 7. Jay wasn't surprised that she had a high level of power. She'd felt her potential - the sharp nip of her energy searching and exploring. 'What were you before the transformation?'

'Level three,' said Flick. 'That shows the strength of these new facilities, these mega sink-rooms.'

'There's more than one?'

Flick nodded.

'What's in this for you?'

Flick sighed. 'If it carries on the way it's going, there won't be anything left. The Readers are coming here next, to this place, *your* land.' She looked around her. 'None of this will survive. The Given cannot exist in a world controlled by Readers. The very existence of Readers depends on the conversion of the Given.'

'They can't come here,' Jay said.

'They can, and they will. Unless you act.' Flick leaned back in her chair and spoke slowly, 'You know what happens when the Readers reach a certain number?'

Jay had read in the literature about the theory of the

balance of power. If the Readers' numbers reached a certain level, then legend said that a darker power would emerge, one that assured their ascendency. She nodded. 'I know the myths.'

'Not myths,' said Flick. 'It's happened before, way back.'

'If that's true, then how are the Given still here?'

'The presence of the deeper darkness does not stop more of the Given being born, but it enables the Readers to control them, convert them to their own cause before they can become a threat. The balance must have tipped back between now and the last reign of the Dark. But now it's tipping again. The Dark is working its way through the islands.'

'I won't let Readers come here,' Jay said, looking Flick in the eye.

Flick shook her head. 'You're not hearing me. Not just Readers. The *Dark*. It's more than just Readers. It's the balance, like I said. They're creating a connection, a channel for the power that will enable the Dark to move between Island 7 and here. It's just a matter of time. The power of the Given won't be enough to stop it. You need to do more.'

'What do you mean by more?'

Flick leaned towards Jay again. 'Connect with The Dark. Use it before they can.'

5

Otis used a stick to lift the lid of the pan and check his soup. Steam billowed. The broth made a pleasant simmer, the smell wafted over him and his stomach rumbled.

One thing about living outside was food was more satisfying, but took forever to prepare. With a different stick, he flattened the embers a little to lower the heat. He looked up into the trees on the south side of Highdown. This was his favourite time of day, when the light had faded to grey, but he could still see enough to go about his business - food nearly ready, tiredness creeping in, no people to mess with him.

Otis startled, the skin on the back of his neck tingling. He sensed a presence. For one with significant power at level 5, Otis's key skills weren't in sensing others - the energy of his abilities was concentrated almost entirely on his telekinesis. So when he sensed someone, it usually meant that they were close.

He stood, scanning the slopes of the hill up towards the ring of trees at the summit. He held his breath, his eardrums throbbing in the silence. A flutter of birds took flight. Something in the bushes moved and his eyes stretched wide to take in as much of the remaining light as he could.

Nothing.

A rustle in the bush up on Highdown was not something to be afraid of. He'd lived with the scurrying sounds of the animals, the wind in the trees, and the groaning of the woods for years. He must be overreacting. He sat back on his log and collected his stick, rubbing his thumb against the rough bark.

He scraped the last of the soup from the bottom of the pan. He didn't mind the burnt taste, liked it even.

Footsteps. Clear this time, not his imagination. Closer. Too dark to see.

He picked up a thick branch as a weapon and readied himself.

'Cassie?'

'Hey,' Cassie said as she came into view, eying the branch in Otis's hand. 'Ready for a fight?'

'You scared me. You could've told me you were coming tonight.' It was unusual for Cassie to turn up on the Hill unannounced. She'd normally get a message to Otis using her powers, something to let him know to expect her. He didn't always hear the message clearly, but he always knew.

'I tried to. You've not been receptive today. Something on your mind?' Cassie took a seat near the fire.

'I thought I felt something just now. It spooked me. Probably a deer.' Otis rubbed at his mop of curly hair.

'Hey.' Cassie reached over and touched his arm, her tone soft. He opened his arms for a hug and Cassie pulled him close.

'Don't know what's wrong with me today,' said Otis as they pulled apart.

Cassie stared into the fire and Otis sensed that she too was not feeling right. She'd been withdrawn more often than usual in the past few weeks. As things had settled in their post-Reader world, the pain and hurt of what had happened to Cassie seemed to bubble to the surface, pushing down on her energy, stifling her passion for life. She hardly spoke of Reuben's death, her childhood friend, or the time she spent incarcerated by the Readers, but Otis knew it wasn't something that she'd easily forget.

'Tell me what you felt. The deer, or whatever it was?' said Cassie.

'Why?'

'Just tell me. What did it feel like?' Her voice was intense.

'I don't know...' He stumbled, thinking. 'Like I said, probably an animal, but...'

'Different?' Cassie prompted. 'Darker?'

Otis nodded. 'It wouldn't normally spook me like that. You know what I'm like. My senses are rubbish at the best of times, but my anxiety levels are sky high lately.'

Cassie stood and scanned the side of the hill. Nothing visible for as far as they could see. 'I felt something on the way up here.' She paused for a moment. 'Actually, it was weird. I sensed nothing, but I saw something. I thought it was you at first, except it was taller than you. And quicker.'

'That doesn't narrow it down by much,' Otis said.

'We need to get away from this place.' Cassie sighed, sitting back down by the fire.

We, thought Otis. He allowed himself to feel warmth before it was taken over again by his and Cassie's unease. 'Are you having those nightmares again?'

She shrugged. 'It's claustrophobic, don't you feel it? I feel like we're just waiting around for something.'

'We need to stick together,' said Otis.

'Me and you?'

'Yes, but... all of us,' he said.

Cassie huffed and turned away from him. 'I don't want this anymore.' She stepped towards the trees.

'Wait. Stay up here with me tonight. We can talk.' Otis hated it when Cassie was like this. What did she mean by not wanting *this* anymore?

'I can't,' Cassie said, striding into the trees and disappearing into the darkness.

Otis called after her, but she was gone.

6

Jay leaned back on the roof tiles and looked up from her book to the hills on the horizon. Turning her eyes back to her book, she re-read the first paragraph of the chapter entitled *The Origins of Power*, then closed her eyes and opened her mind to the energy of the hills and of the sea. Her home on Beach Lane, positioned as it was between the great sources of energy in the land mass and the vast seas, brought comfort.

Within seconds, whispers flowed from the sea, bouncing excitedly around her head like a child eager to play. Her skin tingled, and with her eyes firmly shut, the colours of the whispers swirled and connected with her own colours, and with those sweeping down from the hills. Her chest filled with the warmth from the environment. Her ears bubbled with the pressure of the pulsing energy and her cheeks flushed hot.

A noise distracted her from the connection. Someone approaching from the alleyway around the back. The colours swirled away into the distance as Jay's vision returned and she squinted in the light to see a figure approaching from the other side of the roof.

'Stitch?' she said as his big, round, smiling face came into view.

'The one and only,' he said, sliding down the roof tiles to take a seat next to Jay. He took out his tobacco. 'You mind?' he asked, holding it up.

Jay looked away, back up to the hills. 'You want to kill yourself, be my guest.' He sighed and returned the tobacco to his inside pocket and leaned back on the tiles, the sun on his face.

He'd matured over the past year, since the Interland. He looked older, his features sharper, his face weathered. The experience at the Interland had taken its toll on all of them. But Stitch, more than anyone, seemed to feel the effects of the power of the Readers. It was like their darkness infiltrated his core, messed with his mind.

'I saw your dad the other night, at the group,' Jay said

'The *New Resistance*?' Stitch laughed. 'Why were you there?'

'Has your dad ever mentioned a bloke called *Colson*?'

Stitch shook his head. 'Who's he?'

Jay shrugged. 'I think there's a history to the power that goes back further than everyone thinks. Like, way back. Seventeenth century.'

Stitch turned on to his side and rested his head on his hand. 'We always said the powers probably went back further. There are many stories in the folklore, the myths and legends and all that. We've talked about this before.'

'There was a central force of darkness back then called *Atta*. Have you heard of it... him?'

Stitch shook his head again, then lay back on the tiles, closing his eyes. They heard someone climbing up the back wall from the alleyway and Jay guessed it was Cassie before her head popped up above the roof tiles.

She stepped over Stitch and settled next to Jay. 'Where's Sammy?'

'With Toyah somewhere,' said Jay. Toyah and Sammy had been spending a lot of time together since the Interland.

'How are his powers progressing?' Cassie asked.

Sammy's marking had come through a few months ago, Level 3, but his powers were unusual. He couldn't read minds like most low-level powers, not even a little, not even when the person whose mind he was reading actively opened to him. But he had something different.

'He took another flight this week,' Jay replied. 'With a flock of seagulls. He saw half the coastline. It sounded magnificent, he said it felt like he was really flying.'

'Amazing,' said Cassie. 'And now he's off with Toyah, huh? That one's odd.'

Stitch laughed. 'No more odd than the rest of us. I think we forget what it's like talking to people without power. *That's* normal.' He looked up at the horizon, towards Highdown. 'How's Otis? Has he come in from the wilderness yet?'

Cassie ignored Stitch, not taking the bait.

'When are you coming to help me in the shop?' Jay had been asking her for a while, figured it might give her a little focus.

'I will,' Cassie said with a shrug. 'Soon.'

'Anyone seen Pinto recently?' Jay asked. 'He used to come around. Not seen him for a few weeks.' Toyah's little brother Pinto was not yet a teenager, but he and Jay had a connection. She sensed his developing level 5 power. The only other level 5 she'd ever sensed after Otis.

Stitch said, 'Last time I saw Toyah, she told me that Pinto was struggling to settle in at school. The kids know he has power, and everyone wants a piece of him.'

Jay felt a pang of sadness and anger at the thought of Pinto having trouble at school. She knew that feeling of isolation, but she was lucky. She had Stitch. She looked up towards Highdown and for a moment thought she saw a wisp of darkness flow around its peak. She stood, moving as close to the hills as the short section of the roof allowed.

'What?' said Cassie. She and Stitch stood to join Jay at the edge of the roof.

'Probably nothing,' said Jay, staring at the crest of the hill for a moment. She screwed up her eyes, blinking. 'I've had a weird couple of days. My mind is playing tricks.'

* * *

TOYAH CLIMBED out of Jay's window - past Jay, Stitch, and Cassie - her orange hair tied back but spilling over her face, and made for the route down to the alleyway without a word. 'Hey,' called Jay, exchanging glances with Stitch and Cassie. 'What's up? Where's Sammy?'

'I need to get home,' Toyah called over her shoulder as she slipped down onto the wall and landed with a thump on the pathway below and out of sight.

Sammy appeared at the window. 'Toyah!' he called after her, but she was gone.

'What is it?' Jay asked as Sammy climbed out and took a seat next to Stitch on the roof.

Sammy shrugged and said nothing, leaning back against the tiles. Stitch said, 'We hear she's been struggling with her little brother recently.'

'It's not Pinto,' said Sammy. 'It's the situation. With their parents out of the picture, I think Toyah takes on the role.'

'But they're in the unit. There's support there?' said Jay.

'Of a kind,' Sammy said. 'But she still feels a responsibility. And she's not even supposed to be there. The unit is for kids.

They let Toyah stay there because Pinto is there, but she doesn't really belong. She doesn't really belong anywhere. That's the problem.'

'She belongs with us,' said Jay.

'I think she's pissed with me too, but she won't admit it,' said Sammy. 'I can't get in her head.'

'They've been through a lot,' Jay said, thinking of the journey that Toyah and Pinto made together to reach the Interland after their parents had been killed. The day they lost their parents was the day Toyah's life changed - from kid to parent. She had to be strong for Pinto.

'Like I don't know that,' Sammy snapped at his sister. 'Whatever I do makes no difference. She's just pissed off with the world and everything in it, including me.'

* * *

CASSIE LEANED FORWARD and looked at Jay, scrunching up her eyes. 'Spill the beans,' she said.

'What?' said Jay.

'There's something on your mind. I can see it, we all can.'

Stitch nodded his agreement.

Jay sighed. She'd not been shielding. Perhaps she needed her friends to know. It was muddled. 'A Reader tracked me down yesterday,' she said.

Stitch and Cassie both stared. 'Why didn't you turn him in?' said Stitch.

'I needed to hear what she had to say.'

'She?' said Cassie. Jay nodded and Cassie balked. 'There's a first.'

'She said she came to warn me,' said Jay. 'There's something happening on Island 7.'

'Warn you about what?' said Stitch. 'How do you know we can trust her? She's a *Reader*.'

Jay shrugged. 'I saw her thoughts for myself. She told me that the Dark will come here.'

'The *Dark*? You mean the Readers?'

'No, more like their source. A tip in the energy's balance towards the Dark. She told me I need to connect not just with the power of the Given, but with the darkness too, if we are to protect our homeland.'

'Connect with The Dark? That's not possible,' said Stitch.

'We don't know that. The powers come from a different source, but they are of the same essence. They manifest in similar ways. Like two sides to the same coin. There's a logic there. If I can tap into it, then perhaps I can reach a greater power.'

'If there is such a thing,' said Stitch. He stood, pacing the roof. 'Anything else? Any more revelations? Why would you even *think* about connecting with the darkness? We used to be a team. We used to work this stuff out together.' Stitch's voice was getting louder. Cassie sank further into the roof tiles.

'Stitch?' Jay tried to catch his eye, but he wouldn't look at her.

'Why are you even listening to a Reader over us?' Stitch said, continuing to pace.

'Leave me out of this,' said Cassie, standing and pushing past Stitch to head back down to the alleyway and away.

Jay recalled how scared she'd been, back when she first came across the Readers. When faced with Marcus, she had no idea how they would get away, or if the Interland even existed. The feeling she had now was different. She was scared, yes, but not for her own safety. She could handle the Readers. She was fearful for the safety of her friends and her family. Cassie was at the end of her rope. She clearly wanted no more of this fight, a fight they all thought was over. And Stitch. She looked over at him, his head down, inspecting his hands. She loved Stitch, probably more than anyone. He was like family. And more.

Sammy nudged into her. 'What are you going to do?'

Jay shrugged. 'I can't risk the darkness coming here, not again. I need to know that Island 7 is OK. I don't have a choice.'

7

The next day, Jay reached the bookshop just before closing. She pushed through the door to the sound of the bell. No sign of Alf or Buster. She took the stairs to the top floor and saw Alf hanging out of the window with a cigarette in his mouth.

'Hey,' said Jay. 'You said you gave that up years ago?'

Alf jumped, like a kid rumbled by his parents. 'You scared me. I *have* given up. This is an illusion.' He took a final drag and flicked the cigarette away, then pulled the window shut. 'What are you doing here on your day off?'

'I wanted to ask you something.'

'Your little friend was in earlier, reading that book again.'

'Angie?'

Alf nodded. 'She asked for you. I said you'd be in tomorrow. Is Cassie ever going to take you up on your request for some help in the shop?'

'Doesn't look like it.'

Alf motioned for Jay to follow him to sit at the table. 'What's up then?'

'Someone came to see me.'

'Who?' Alf remained calm.

'Her name is Flick. She's a Reader, and she came with a warning.' Jay explained to Alf how she'd faced up to Flick, and how they'd talked there at the bookshop. 'She took a big risk to come here and meet me,' Jay said.

'Do you think it could be a trap?' Alf asked.

'No,' Jay said, no room for doubt in her tone. 'When I touched her I saw it, the new sink-room, the hundreds of Readers. It's all true.'

'We need to be careful,' said Alf, his voice low and controlled. 'Why are you so sure that Flick is for real?'

'Why else would she risk her life? What has she to gain?'

'There is still so much we don't know about the powers. What we read the other day raises more questions than it answers, and if this *Flick* is genuine, then something's happening and we need to be on our guard. And if she's not...' He stood, turning to head over to Jay's display section on the old literature on the powers. Jay followed. He pulled one of his old prized books from the humidity-controlled cabinet, a heavy tome. He carefully flicked through the pages. He said, 'There's something in here I read before...'

Jay leaned around to watch as the pages drifted by under Alf's gentle touch. There were no pictures, chapters, or even breaks in the text. It seemed to be just page after page of small text cramming all the available space. 'How old is it?'

'Early seventeen hundreds. I studied it on and off for years. It's essentially a book of old stories. It's stories like these that fuel a lot of the folklore. If my memory serves me, there are sections in here that talk of the superstition and witchery of the seventeenth century. Something you said just now jogged a memory.' He continued to leaf through the book, his noises of frustration growing louder as he failed to find what he was looking for. He stroked the book shut. 'It'll have to wait. Come on, we need to lock up the shop.'

'What's the rush?'

'I have something I need to do,' said Alf.

'I'm intrigued,' Jay said with a smile. 'Who is she?'

Alf sighed, frustrated in his inability to keep anything from Jay. 'Her name's Judith. And it's not like that.'

'Where did she spring from?'

'Say nothing to your dad. He knows her. She does some work with the resistance team based up in London. We're just catching up. Don't say anything. Promise?'

Jay smiled and looked at Alf's book on the table in front of them. 'Can I stay a while?' she asked, reaching to re-open the book. 'I'll be careful with it, and I'll return it to the cabinet. And it will help me not to talk to Dad about the London resistance.'

Alf rolled his eyes. He agreed and turned to head for the stairs. 'Do you have your keys?' he asked. Jay nodded. 'I'll lock you in. You can see yourself out. Don't stay too late, you're on shift tomorrow.'

'I know,' Jay said. 'Where's Buster?'

'He's in the flat.'

'OK. Have fun.'

Alf grunted something in reply, but her attention was already on the pages in front of her.

* * *

JAY WOKE with a gentle hand on her shoulder. 'Jay.' Alf's voice. She prised her eyes open, closing them again to keep the light from penetrating her brain. She groaned. Alf encouraged her head off the desk so that he could extract the book. He closed it and pushed it aside.

'Sorry,' said Jay. 'I fell asleep.'

'I gathered,' said Alf as he tidied the papers on the desk and collected his book to return it to the cabinet.

He returned with coffee and sat next to Jay as she stretched and yawned. 'What time is it?' she asked.

'Half hour until opening. Drink that and then get yourself home. I can manage this morning.'

'No,' insisted Jay. 'I'm fine.' She cradled her mug. Her hair stuck up at the side where she'd been laying her head on the desk. There was a line on her cheek where she'd rested her face on the edge of the book. 'How was your evening?'

'Judith never made it, caught up in London.'

'Sorry about that,' Jay yawned again.

Alf frowned at her dishevelled look. 'Come back tomorrow when you've had some sleep. You're no good to me in this state.'

'Sorry,' Jay said again, taking a longer drink from her mug.

Alf forced a smile. 'I need to open up the shop. Go home and clear your head.'

Jay headed home and went straight to bed. Later that afternoon, she woke to the sound of Sammy coming into her room. He sat on the edge of her bed and started talking as if continuing a previous conversation with no preamble. She pulled her head under her cover to muffle the noise.

'Jay? It's three o'clock in the afternoon.'

'Go away,' said Jay, her voice croaky. Sammy stood to open the window, allowing the blind to roll itself up and the remains of the day to pour into the room. Then he put on a James Taylor record and sat back down on the edge of the bed. Jay groaned. 'What do you want?'

He pulled back the cover so he could see his sister. 'I was just saying that I don't know what's up with Toyah at the moment and wondered if she'd said anything to you?'

Jay sat up in bed. 'You could at least have brought me a cup of tea.'

'Has she said anything?' Jay rolled her eyes, then shook her head.

'She's been cold,' Sammy said.

'Talk to her. See her.'

'She told me she's busy today.'

'Give her a bit of space, then. She'll come around.'

'Space? You mean like a break?'

Jay sighed inwardly. 'No, I just mean...'

'You think she needs space from me.'

'Sammy!' Jay snapped. 'Relax. Don't blow this up.'

'I think I'll see if she's down at the pier. She goes there sometimes.'

'If she needs a bit of breathing space, then...'

'I'll go find her,' Sammy interrupted. He stood. Jay slumped back against the wall, watching her brother as the thoughts whirled around in his head. 'Yes, I'll see if she's there and we can talk about it. Thanks,' he said, flashing Jay a smile as he left the room. Jay lay back and pulled the covers over her head.

* * *

'I THOUGHT YOU WERE AT WORK?' Ben said as Jay walked into the kitchen. Sonia glanced up briefly from the washing up.

'Day off,' she said as she opened the fridge and pulled out a carton of milk.

'What happened to you last night? I didn't hear you come in?'

'It was late. I got engrossed in some papers Alf had for me.'

'Sammy was looking for you earlier,' her mum said.

'He found me. Woke me up. Talked *at* me for a bit, then disappeared again.'

Ben put the kettle on and said, 'Colson was asking after you at the club last night.'

Jay poured milk onto her cereal. 'What did he want? He came into the shop earlier in the week. He and Alf finally made up.'

'I heard,' said Ben. 'He asked me to give you this.' Ben passed Jay a book from the kitchen counter. 'He didn't say what for, just said you'd need it back.'

Jay spooned cereal into her mouth, then placed her bowl down so she could take the book from her dad. It was the Sasha Colden biography, the copy from the bookshop, Jay could tell by the condition, and the turned down pages and her own bookmark. 'He took it from the shop? Cheeky...'

'He told me to say that it proves the point. Whatever point that is?'

'The point about the old power,' Jay said absently, then looked up at Sonia and Ben, who both stared back at her. 'What?'

'What's going on?' asked Sonia.

'Nothing, Mum. It's just research.' Jay contemplated opening the discussion with her mum and dad about Flick and the fear that Alf had voiced about something changing. But decided against it. 'You making tea, Dad?'

* * *

BACK IN HER LOFT ROOM, the sight of Toyah climbing in through her window made Jay jump, spilling her tea. 'For ff...' Jay said.

'Sorry,' Toyah said as she slipped in through the window and sat down on Jay's desk chair.

'Sammy's not in,' said Jay, wiping spilled tea from her hand and sitting on her bed. 'He's out looking for you.'

Toyah swung from left to right in Jay's desk chair for a moment and then said, 'I know. I wanted to have a quick word with you, if that's OK?'

Jay's heart sank a little at the thought of having to be the go-between for Toyah and her little brother. 'Sure, I guess.'

'Don't worry, I just want to know if Sammy has said anything?'

'About what?'

'He's been closing in a bit recently. Stifling, you know? I mean, he's great, but things have been hard recently and he's...' She trailed off.

'*Talk* to him. Tell him things are tough and you need a bit of space.'

Toyah nodded. She looked around Jay's room. 'Sorry for just dropping in.'

'It's fine.' Jay smiled. 'What's going on?'

'I just need a bit of breathing space.'

Jay waited.

'Everything seems like hard work, you know? Pinto's struggling, which is hard on me.'

'How?'

'He's only just moved up to secondary school, and he's already having a hard time. It's not full-on bullying, it's more insidious than that. Bullying by stealth. Little things. He gets left out, ostracised, and things get said. His powers are growing, so sometimes they don't even have to speak to bully him. He can see what's in their heads.'

'Poor Pinto,' Jay said, a lump in her throat. She had a genuine fondness for Toyah's little brother. He was like a little version of her own brother, and he played a large part in their victory over the Readers at the Interland. 'Anyone we need to rough up a bit?' she said, a semi-serious expression on her face.

'Maybe,' said Toyah. 'I'm kinda hoping he'll be able to sort it out himself. We can't be there every day for him. And what happened to you last night?' Toyah asked. 'You were supposed to meet us at the pub.'

Jay recalled promising Stitch she'd meet them in the Beach Arms. 'I lost track of time at the shop. Then I fell asleep with my head on the desk.'

Toyah laughed. 'What? All night?' Jay nodded and joined in Toyah's laughter.

* * *

JAY STOOD outside Pinto's school and checked her watch. The students were due out any minute. She just wanted to see him, see that he was OK.

Pinto appeared in a crowd of kids who all seemed to be a good foot taller than him. He was on his own, head down. She read him and she saw immediately that he was avoiding making eye contact with a group of boys just to his left and a little behind him. All his focus was on trying to make himself invisible to them.

One boy threw a stick over the heads of other kids, which then hit Pinto on the back. He was jolted from his concentration, stopping to look at the boys in an instinctive reflex. The boys reached Pinto and laughed, jostling him. One of them put his arm around Pinto's shoulder and, for a moment, Jay thought she saw a smile on Pinto's face, like they were all mucking around. But his inner thoughts betrayed him to Jay. He was scared. He was losing sight of where he fit into this world.

Around twenty feet behind Pinto, Jay sensed someone else

with power. She scanned the faces until she pin-pointed the energy in a girl, much the same age as Pinto, and taking a similar approach of keeping herself out of the limelight – head down, shields up.

At the main gate, Jay called Pinto's name. He looked up and, seeing Jay, his colours brightened, his oranges and greens flowed like a dam had burst.

The boys looked over at Jay and then moved on, heading away from the school in the opposite direction. Jay and Pinto embraced. 'It's been ages,' he said.

'Too long, my friend. I've missed you.'

'What are you doing here?'

'Let's walk.' Jay nodded toward Pinto's foster home.

'You going this way?'

'Who's that?' Jay asked, nodding towards the girl she'd seen walking behind Pinto.

Pinto looked up at Jay and smiled. 'You can sense her power? I can too. Her name's Sasha.'

'Sasha?' repeated Jay. 'As in Sasha Colden?'

Pinto laughed, 'Yes. But her name is Sasha Jenkins, not Colden. I can tell she has something, some level of power developing.'

'You should talk to her.'

'She's not exactly inviting people in,' Pinto said, his expression a little sad.

'Bit like you then?' said Jay.

Pinto shrugged, and they stopped at the crossroads where Sasha's route diverged from their own. They watched as she walked alone into the distance. After a minute, they continued into Pinto's street. 'Thanks,' Pinto said, turning to head up the pathway to the front door of what looked like a big manor house set back from the road in the trees. 'You want to come in?'

'No,' Jay said, smiling. 'I need to go, but next time I see you, you can tell me what Sasha's like?'

'I don't know what she's like,' Pinto called from his front door.

'Find out,' Jay shouted as she turned to head home.

8

In her room that evening, Jay was distracted from her book by the sounds of the wind whipping over the rooftops, rattling her window. For almost an hour, it was as if the world outside had been trying to get her attention. She looked up, then back to her book, trying her best to shut out the noise. Dusk crept up on her. She leaned over to switch on her bedside lamp, its orange glow warming the room. She heard the front door slam and figured Sammy was heading out to see Toyah, or her dad, heading to the pub.

Speaking as if directly to the wind and rain battering her window, she said, 'What do you want?' Persistent gusts squealed and swirled, shaking the roof tiles. She pulled on her hoodie and opened the Velux, the wind immediately rushing through her room as if searching for something. She climbed out onto the tiles and closed the window behind her. The wind pushed at her hood and she had to hold it to keep it from exposing her ears to the pounding cold. She crouched and sat back against the tiles, the wet seeping through her jeans. 'What am I doing?' she said, breathing the words into the wind so that they disappeared before they could reach her ears.

With a final gust from the south, a parting reminder of its power, the petulant wind died suddenly, and the silence was deafening. Jay looked around her. The sense of sudden calm was unnatural. A gentle breeze caught her hair, brushing it from her eyes.

The sun had dipped behind the crest of Highdown Hill in the distance so that the only light remaining cast a mono-chrome greyness over the Beach Lane estate. With the parting of the wind, the twilight felt warm. Jay pulled down her hood and leaned back against the tiles. She closed her eyes, reaching out to the power, the energy of the land.

The whispers came first. It was always the whispers first, and always urgent, like there was something desperate they needed from Jay.

Before the Given emerged from the Interland, the domi-nance of the Readers and their darkness had impacted the land, the environment, and the very existence of the Given. Cities were run down, the natural environment degraded. Even without their ill-fated plan to destroy the source, the Readers had been edging further into power, and the natural world retreating all the time. Now, Jay's world, Island 8, thrived. The eco-systems had re-balanced, and humans, both with and without power, lived in a more free, reciprocal rela-tionship with nature. If Flick was right, then the threat to the new stability was unimaginable.

The whispers turned to white noise, and a smile crept across Jay's face as the messages came. Warm colours flowed through Jay's mind, from the hills, the ground beneath the Beach Lane Estate, and from the sea. The colours seeped into Jay's skin, into her veins and the marrow of her bone. She tingled with energy; fizzed with power.

Tentatively, she thought of the Dark, and Flick's ambiguous challenge. If she could connect with the Dark core, as well as with the source of the Given, she might be able to see into the Dark energy, to see its truth, and the reality of any threat that it might cause. She hesitated to open up to it, searching her mind for the consequences but unable to shake the feeling this was the right thing - a chance for a deeper power, greater control, and a more permanent means to protect her homeland. She focused on the darkness – on her memories of Hinton, the myth of Atta, the power of the Readers. She breathed deeply of the energy that flowed through her chest.

An unusual taste nagged at the back of Jay's throat. It had a bitter metallic tinge. She swallowed and a cool liquid re-emerged at the roof of her mouth, bringing more of the bitterness. She tried to open her eyes, but she couldn't move. She swallowed again, and the bitterness intensified. Fear bubbled under her skin. Her heart raced as she lay frozen against the tiles, heavy like lead.

As frequently as she could swallow the bitterness, it would return, forcing her to swallow once more to keep from choking. She struggled for breath, nauseous with the vile taste. She forced her eyes open. As she did, she sank harder into the tiles, as if in a centrifuge. She was sure the roof would give way beneath her.

She looked to the hills. Black tentacles reached over the crest of Highdown and down into the valley towards Beach Lane, like an infection radiating from a wound. A black mist circled the air, creeping towards her. Jay gasped, and the blackness entered her body through her open mouth. Her head tipped back, opening to the Dark which poured into her body, pushing her own colours out through her skin.

The bitter taste spread.

It was cold. It froze her from the inside out, spreading further to her limbs as if searching her for a place to reside. Her breathing became shallow, and she slumped to her side, her body so cold she had no energy or will. The Dark seeped through her, down into her legs, her arms.

'Jay,' a shout from Stitch, coming from Jay's room. A spark of electricity ran through Jay's head and the Dark retreated a little. 'Jay?' Stitch again, close this time, leaning out of the window. 'Jay!' His voice urgent now. The sound as he clambered out of the window. His touch. He rocked back as if he'd touched a live electric cable, but he returned. He reached for Jay once more. The energy in his touch was so powerful it forced air into Jay's lungs, warmth to her skin and energy back into her bones. She gasped for air and sat up straight, her eyes snapping open. Stitch crouched in front of her, his hands holding hers, his eyes full of fear. The energy flowed through Jay like warm water. She reached for Stitch and he held her as she thawed and slowly returned to herself.

Stitch held her hands for a moment longer before disappearing back into the house, returning a few minutes later, drink in hand.

'What *was* that?' asked Stitch, climbing back out onto the roof and handing Jay the drink.

'I opened to The Dark.'

'You did what?' he said, his tone accusing.

She nodded. 'I've done it before, but not like this.'

Stitch lit a cigarette. 'I thought that was just a feeling, like a sense of the presence of Readers, not *connecting* with it as such?'

'Same thing, really. It's just a sliding scale. This time I got a bit close to the end of the scale, that's all.'

'So, what did you see?'

'It felt like when I was reduced, in the sink-room. But...'

'What?'

'I don't know. It was more like a dream. I don't feel any effects now. I feel fine.' She decided not to reveal to Stitch that she felt weirdly euphoric. With the euphoria came a nagging guilt, like she'd been unfaithful. The feelings were confusing.

'I wish you wouldn't mess with it,' said Stitch.

'What if he's trying to *use* me...' Jay's words trailed off.

'Who's *he*?'

Jay snapped out of her thoughts. 'I don't know.'

Stitch flicked his cigarette over the hedge at the end of the roof and stood. 'I need to get back to Dad. Are you going to be OK?'

Jay nodded, but her smile was forced.

'I need you to promise me not to do that again, OK?' Stitch leaned down and kissed Jay on the top of her head. She smiled up at him, but he'd already turned to leave.

9

Stitch lay back on his bed, his thoughts bashing around on the inside of his skull like a swarm of bees. He turned onto his side and forced his eyes closed. 'Empty your mind,' he said to himself, breathing steadily. 'Count sheep.' Every time he got close to settling and calming himself, the bees returned and his head filled with questions.

He couldn't shake it. He harboured a dark, nagging thought that today was the end of the world. He stomped over to his bedroom window, unlatched it and threw it open in one swift move, leaning out over the threshold and taking a deep breath of cool night air. Breathing out some of the tension, he looked up towards the hills of the Downs, mostly concealed behind the trees at the bottom of his garden, but the peak of Highdown just visible. The hills brought energy and calm. He could just about hear the sounds of the sea in the distance - more of a continuous hiss than any distinctive breaking of waves. He shivered in the cold, his bare torso goose-pimpled. He brushed his fringe from his eyes and was about to turn back to his bed when something caught his eye.

He stopped, looking down the length of his back garden. Nothing but darkness. He recalled the vision of the figure he'd seen before in his garden, the white glow that had helped them get away from the Readers many months ago, and he looked towards that spot in the garden, straining his eyes to see.

The darkness at the foot of the trees at the end of his garden spread. Stitch rubbed his eyes. It spread across the grass towards the house, like an oil slick. He blinked and leaned further out of his window. It approached the house like a wave of thick tar, steady, relentless. His heart rate increased by the second. Darkness engulfed the whole of the back garden and reached the foot of the wall beneath Stitch's window.

He needed to move, to run, to find his father, Samir, and get out. His feet stuck to his bedroom carpet as the black wave climbed the wall of the house towards his window. Wisps of black smoke seemed to drift off the surface of the wave and fizzle away into the night.

As the black wave of darkness reached his windowsill, a pungent smell hit Stitch's nose, and a bitter taste filled his mouth. His head spun so fast that his legs could not hold him. He slipped to the floor and his world plunged into the blackness.

* * *

HE WOKE WITH A JOLT, lying face down on his bed, his covers on the floor.

Light poured through his bedroom window; sunlight streaked across his carpet. He shot out of bed and to his window, which was open and swinging gently in the breeze.

The lawn shone in the sunlight. The trees at the foot of the garden bristled in the wind, the smell of pollen in the air.

He turned back into his room, scratched his head, and looked over at his clock. It was past ten o'clock in the morning. He'd been asleep for hours. 'A dream?' he said aloud to himself, then shook his head and looked back out over the garden. Deep down, something told him it was no dream. Something was coming.

He closed his window and pulled on some clothes. He needed to get to the bookshop, to Jay.

* * *

JAY HANDED Angie another pile of books to return to the shelves. 'See the number printed inside?' she explained. 'Match that with the shelf reference and there should be a gap. Easy, eh?'

Angie staggered off with her arms full of books. She had been waiting at the shop doors when Jay arrived to open up. Her guarded nature had evaporated, and she insisted on helping Jay with the books, following her around the shop like a sheep until Jay gave her something to do. Her thirst for knowledge was growing. Every opportunity she quizzed Jay on the powers, the Readers, and how she should expect her own abilities to surface. Angie's power was evolving and growing almost by the minute.

Jay took the weight off her feet and slumped down on a chair by the windows, allowing the early sun to warm her face. She looked towards the cabinets of literature on the powers, then beyond the window to the sea in the distance. Clouds spread across the sky like chalk on blue canvas. She opened the window an inch and breathed the salty air.

A gust of wind blew the window open further. The handle

slipped from her hand and the frame slammed against the wall. Book covers blew open and pages rustled on the shelves. Angie looked back over her shoulder at Jay in surprise as she battled with the window to secure it on its latch.

As Jay scanned the horizon, white clouds darkened and cast a shadow over the seafront. Jay walked to the back of the shop, and the door that led to the top of the fire escape. She leaned on the push-bar and spilled out onto the steel landing from where she could see Highdown.

The sky was black above the hills and it took Jay's breath. She looked back to the hills as a shadow poured down the slopes towards the town. This was not like the tentacles she had experienced the night before, the stretching black roots that had entered her head when she connected with the darkness. This was different. This was a slow, creeping encroachment of darkness over the land. She squinted to see more clearly, to convince herself that this wasn't an illusion.

Angie walked up behind her and Jay said, 'Do you see that?'

'What is it?' Angie replied. 'I feel like I'm hallucinating.'

The approaching black sea brought with it a palpable wave of energy. It buffeted Jay, and dragged on her body as Angie pulled her back towards the door, pleading with her to go back inside.

The weight of the darkness was too much. Jay sank to the floor, crouching on the landing of the fire escape with Angie tugging at her arm.

The wind howled around the buildings. Jay's breathing became shallow. As the darkness reached overhead, and Angie had all but given up trying to get Jay back inside, Jay heard a familiar voice. 'Jay! Move!'

She looked up to see Stitch in the doorway. He lifted Angie and helped her inside, returning for Jay. He took her hand and dragged her arm over his shoulder so that he could lift her. The door slammed behind them, silencing the screaming wind.

The top floor of the shop was pitch black.

The Dark smothered the building like a blanket. There was a pressure in the air. A blinding pain shot through Jay's head. She slipped again to the floor and looked up at Angie and Stitch, their features melding into the darkness. As she felt she would surely pass out, confused and scared, the darkness intensified and a high pitch scream filled the bookshop. A moment passed before all the windows of the top floor imploded, shattered glass spreading through the room ahead of a wave of blackness so deep it swallowed everything.

Stitch fell. Angie turned towards the Dark and it passed through her, entering her body through her eyes, her mouth, and ears.

It was quiet then. The pain in her head was crippling. She dragged herself onto all fours and squeezed her eyes tight, waiting for the ringing and shooting pain to subside. When she opened her eyes, she saw a thin cloud of dust in the air, shimmering in the sunlight. The darkness had gone. Debris covered the entire top floor. She frantically scanned the chaos for Angie and Stitch.

Angie lay on her back, serene, seemingly untouched by the dust and debris. Her chest rose and fell with shallow breaths. She was alive. She looked more asleep than injured. There was no blood on her. No visible marks. Not a cut, bruise or scratch. Jay took her hand. It was cold. She used her power to delve into Angie, but came up against barriers. She couldn't read her. She turned to see Stitch stumbling in their direction. 'Help her,' she said, pleading with her eyes for Stitch to affect healing. He had done it before.

'I can't,' he said, his face barely concealing his rising panic. He put his hands on Angie's head and closed his eyes.

'Please,' said Jay. 'Try again.' She placed a hand on Stitch to reinforce his power of healing, the power that seemed to have slipped away from him in recent weeks.

Stitch looked at Jay in despair. 'I've got nothing,' he said.

10

J ay pulled the old Ford into the overflow car park at the back of the Black Rabbit pub, where she knew it would sit unnoticed. She switched off the engine, her eyes fixed on the rear-view mirror. The car park was empty. She was alone.

Since the incident in the bookshop, Jay could think of nothing but to get to Island 7 to see for herself what was happening. There was a threat coming, and she needed to understand it. Angie felt like Jay's responsibility, and she had let her down.

Angie hadn't yet regained consciousness. In the hospital they said that she was stable, but that they'd keep her under for a few days as a precautionary measure while they investigated the extent of any brain damage. Jay had to sneak in to see her outside of visiting hours. Angie's parents had refused to allow anyone else permission to see her. They blamed the powers.

The sight of Angie shocked her. She was pale and cold. She wanted to take her out of there, take her up to one of the hill forts to allow the Given energy to flow through her again.

The medical profession was still learning about the effects of the powers. They would not understand how to deal with someone like Angie, suffering the effects of an attack from the Dark. Their standard response was a medically induced coma to reduce stress on the brain and allow the body to stabilise.

First, Jay had reached out through the powers to see if she could sense Flick, but she couldn't locate her. She figured Flick would be able to help her understand what was happening. But she seemed to have vanished as suddenly as she had appeared.

Jay hadn't wanted to tell Stitch about her plan to head to Island 7 because she knew he'd try to persuade her against it. But he read her intentions without her saying a word. 'What good can come of it?' he'd said. 'We'd be better to work out a defence from here. Plan for it. If it's coming, then you heading to Island 7 won't stop it.'

'I need to know,' Jay said. 'I need to be sure that there's nothing coming. That Island 7 is OK, and we won't be under attack.'

In the pub car park, the only sound was of the gush and flow of the water around the wooden posts of the river wall. Jay opened her car door. She'd travelled this route to the Interland three times in the past year. Each time she'd taken the route via the Arun, the quickest and easiest way in. She pulled her small rucksack onto her back and stepped into the trees.

As she walked, the usual sense of calm and safety she got from her connection with the environment was tainted by the darkness from the bookshop, leaving her with a nagging anxiety. She pushed through the bushes, cursing the brambles that cut into her skin.

When she stepped out into the clearing on the riverside, the river level was high, the water stretching out towards her at the tree line. She dropped her rucksack to the floor and rested on a log. She pulled out her orange lifejacket and blew through the valve to inflate it. She had no intention of making a raft; she would drift with the currents through to the gateway. Tugging off her shoes, she deposited them in her rucksack before sealing everything inside a plastic bag. She placed her lifejacket over her head and fastened the straps.

At the edge of the shallow section, Jay leaned into the water and allowed herself to sink up to her chest. She kicked her legs, and after a minute calmed her breathing and relaxed into the flow, allowing herself to drift.

As she turned the first corner, a piercing scream rose from the riverside, back where she'd entered the water. She twisted to look in the direction of the scream, then was shaken by a second call, louder this time and more desperate. Scrambling to reach for the reeds at the side of the river to slow her progress, she got a hold and twisted her hand so that she swung into the bank.

From the riverbank, she looked back towards the tree line. There was someone in the water. A girl had fallen, or been dragged in, and was struggling for air. She ran back along the bank, closing the distance between her and the girl in just a few seconds.

It was Toyah, bobbing in the water as she floated downstream, struggling to keep her head above the surface.

Jay stood on the bank, closed her eyes and opened to the power of the environment. She saw Toyah in her mind's eye, tugged and pulled at by the streams and currents. Reeds and wisps of the dark pulled at her legs, her torso, her neck. Jay squeezed her eyes tighter and connected with the energy of the river, an energy that seemed to Jay more subdued than normal, stifled. She prised the dark tendrils from Toyah's body, freeing her legs just as she was about to give up and sink to the riverbed. Jay continued to guide and support the energy of the river to push Toyah to the surface, where she gasped for air.

Toyah drifted, coughing. Jay ran along the bank to keep up, then get ahead of her. She slid down to the water's edge and grasped for her outstretched hand, finally making contact and clamping her fingers around her wrist. She immediately felt Toyah's fear flash through her body through the connection.

Laid out on the riverbank, Toyah trembled. Jay held her hand to reassure her. 'What are you doing here?' she said, at the same time reading her intentions. She'd wanted to join Jay at the Interland. 'Why didn't you just ask?' said Jay.

'You'd have told me not to come,' said Toyah, still panting. She was right.

'We need to move,' said Jay. 'We can rest and dry out when we get to the Interland. We'll need to drift. It's not much further. Can you do this?'

Toyah stood and nodded. Jay pushed her lifejacket over Toyah's head and led her down to the water's edge. They re-entered the river and held on to each other as they continued downstream, using Jay's bag and Toyah's lifejacket for buoyancy.

* * *

JAY BUILT a fire and fed it with scraps of wood as she and Toyah dried themselves.

There was a space on the wall where the picture of Sasha Colden once hung. Jay had taken it on their last visit. Toyah pulled her top back on over her head, now dry from hanging by the fire. She sat with a blanket around her shoulders and stared into the dancing flames. Jay found a few tins of food that had survived in the side cave that used to be the storeroom of the Interland. She pulled out her penknife and used the can-opener to start work on the tins.

'That was pretty stupid,' Jay said to Toyah. 'You could have drowned in there. What happened?'

'Sorry,' Toyah said, running her fingers through her wet hair. 'I meant to catch you up before you got to the river, but it was harder going than I thought.'

Jay looked at Toyah. She was athletically built, more than capable of trekking through that terrain. Sammy had said how fit she was, stronger than him. 'When I got to the river, you'd already gone.'

'Did you follow my car on your moped?' asked Jay.

Toyah nodded.

'I thought I saw you,' Jay said.

'Then in the trees, it was so dark. The clouds seemed to close in. I couldn't see three feet in front of me.'

'The *Dark*,' said Jay. Toyah looked at her for more. 'Something I've been feeling for a few days now. Then the thing at the bookshop. Something's going on.'

'Is she OK? The little girl?'

Jay shrugged. 'We don't know yet. I told her I'd keep her safe...'

'You're not responsible for her.'

Jay's throat clenched. She felt entirely responsible. 'I'm not sure that's true. I didn't intend to, but I might have opened a channel for The Dark.'

'What?' said Toyah with a deep frown.

'You're a level 6, have you felt it?'

Toyah shook her head, but her eyes and her thoughts told Jay otherwise. Toyah turned back to the fire. She pulled the blanket tighter around her shoulders.

Jay continued: 'Since I connected, there's been this taste in the air and a presence of Readers. Then the Dark hit, yesterday at the shop.'

Toyah stood, looking up into the roof of the cavern where the last of the day's light leaked through the opening. 'Is that what you're doing here?'

'Yes. I need to make sure everything's OK on Island 7, and see for myself if what Flick said is coming true.'

'You're heading through the source?'

Jay nodded. 'Yes. Alone. You can pick up a taxi to your moped.'

'There's nothing back there for me right now.' She looked away from Jay once more.

'What do you mean?' Jay threw another branch onto the fire. Sparks rose with the hot smoke and fizzled into the darkness.

'I just need some space for myself for a while. I need some air, you know?'

Jay shook her head. 'You can't come with me.'

Toyah snorted a laugh. 'Stitch travelled with you.'

'He's my connection. With you, I don't even know if it's possible. It's too risky.'

They were quiet for a minute.

'Has something happened with Sammy?' asked Jay.

Toyah shook her head. 'It's not him.'

'What is it then?'

Toyah sighed and threw a stone across the room, a piece of rock that had crumbled from the wall. 'I just need to do something useful. More than sitting around waiting for stuff to happen: for Pinto to do something stupid, or for me to get moved on from the foster home. They won't keep letting me stay there.'

'They love you there,' said Jay. 'Why wouldn't they let you stay?'

They were quiet as the fire died down. Jay decided that she'd sleep, then slip off to the source before Toyah woke. That way, she wouldn't have to continue this debate. If she was to move quickly through Island 7, she had to be alone, with no-one to slow her down.

* * *

Jay woke at first light, Toyah still asleep by the fire's remains. She stepped fully clothed from her sleeping bag and rolled it tight to squeeze it into its bag. She packed her rucksack in silence, pausing only to drag her fingers across the well-thumbed Sasha Colden book in her bag. She opened it at random, somewhere near the middle. In the light grey dawn light, she absorbed the words. Almost immediately, her mind settled as she connected with the energy of her ancestors, drew strength from the weight of the past.

She returned the book to her bag and glanced at Toyah, her nose poking out the top of her sleeping bag. She sighed, wishing for a moment that Stitch was with her. He injected a strength in Jay that no-one else came close to. But she had to do this alone. She wasn't about to put any of her friends at risk.

She pulled her hoodie over her head and crept towards the exit from the main cavern to the passageway that led to the source. The steps down to the depths of the Interland seemed narrower than Jay remembered, the walls and roof closer. Cool air washed over her face, a light breeze drifting up from the deep. The only sound was the trickling of water. She pulled a box of matches from her pocket and lit the candles in each of the alcoves in the rock.

The three streams of water from the rivers on the surface were as strong as ever, purposefully combining and generating the energy of the Given - a natural turbine. Jay took a deep breath of the moist, fresh air. She dipped her fingers into the pool where the three flows combined and light flashed behind her eyes.

She opened to the energy. The whispers in the power were confused. She focused on filtering the noise. The light faltered and dimmed. Jay stepped back from the water, rubbed her hands together and then wiped the fresh water over her face, blinking away the remains of sleep from her eyes.

The source felt strong. She took a deep breath and plunged her hands back into the pool. The power of the connection nearly knocked her off her feet. She strained to keep her hands in the water, drawing the energy. The white light behind her eyes intensified.

She sensed a presence. Someone with her. Toyah was there, her hands in the water, connected. Jay kept focus, channelling the power until the blinding white light filled her head and there was nothing.

11

Jay prised her face from the floor and spat grit from her mouth. She wiped away the sand and dust and blinked in the white light pouring from the sky. Toyah groaned nearby.

She stood, brushing down her clothes, white dust billowing. The act of transporting through the source was never elegant. Her eyes slowly adjusted and the blinding light receded. But what she then saw made her wish the blindness would return.

Island 7 was black from the shores to the top of the withered oak at its centre. The entire island was charred, dead. Between the islands, the water flowed black. The dark had closed in so that the wisps and swirls of black that Jay and Stitch had seen before had thickened to a homogenous darkness.

Toyah appeared at Jay's side, looking but saying nothing. Her eyes darted between the blackened features of the island and the water that separated them. 'What the...' Toyah studied her own hands as if she were not real, then looked around at the island on which they'd landed. A smile flickered across her face, only to fade when she saw Jay's pained expression. She put a hand on Jay's arm. 'What is it?'

Jay turned on Toyah. 'I told you not to come. We don't know what's over there. Look at this place!'

'What?' Toyah said, but she wouldn't know what it looked like before. Jay peered into the light to see if the other islands were visible. Gradually, the mist-like white light dissipated. The islands in the distance, from Island one, all the way through to Island 6, there was nothing but blackness. Jay's heart filled with dread.

Toyah followed her gaze, taking in the sight of each island. 'What does it mean?'

Jay gathered herself, thinking of how to explain the little she understood. She should take Toyah back to the Interland and leave her there, continue alone on the journey she'd intended. 'As I understand it, this place,' she said, eventually, 'is here because of the Given power, the energy of the land. Each Island represents one of the eight sources of power in eight different locations around the world.'

'What's happening to them?' asked Toyah, looking over at Island 7.

'The Dark.'

'It looks dead.'

'I don't know,' said Jay. 'This is a representation, but someone brought me a warning and it's beginning to look like the truth.'

'So what can we do?' asked Toyah.

Jay strode towards the shore and shivered at the sight of the black gloopy sea of danger between her and her destination on Island 7. She recalled Stitch writhing in agony when he'd touched just a thin wisp of the darkness in the water.

In the streams were intermittent patches of clear water and soon a pattern revealed itself.

'Look,' Jay said, pointing into the water. 'We can't walk through this darkness. It burns. But these clear sections come around with every cycle of the flow.' Toyah moved to the edge, poised to step through. 'Not yet,' said Jay, pulling her back. 'We need more space.'

A moment passed. 'Now!' Jay pushed herself into the water, wading deep into the section of clear water in the channel between the islands and then walking with it as it moved. She scanned for the connecting patch of safety that she hoped would materialise before she became enclosed by darkness. Toyah stepped into the next wave of clear water behind Jay, pushing through the waist-deep water as she looked over her shoulder at the approaching dark.

The black shore-line of Island 7 shone in the light like freshly cleaved seams of coal. Toyah should have been close behind, instead she was hesitating to step through to the next clear zone. 'Toyah!' Jay yelled, then looked to the water. The dark swirls encroached on the gaps. The route through the channel, Toyah's window of opportunity, narrowed.

Jay stepped back into the water, beckoning Toyah to hurry, reaching out a hand although she was still ten feet away. Toyah lunged for Jay, but the tendrils of blackness had marked a line between them. She stepped to the side and lifted a leg out of the water so that she could step over the dark swirls and closer to Jay. She held Jay's hand as she teetered and stumbled safely to the blackened shore. Jay followed Toyah, but something caught her foot.

A piercing pain shot through Jay's foot, and she stumbled. She went down, swirls of black around her foot. The water hissed. Her left foot burned, and she screamed as Toyah dragged her from the water. The pain was intense. Jay held her ankle, watching as the skin on her foot purged steam and smoke as if on fire. Her head swam and just as she thought she'd pass out, Toyah's action of cupping and pouring cold, clear water onto her foot eased the pain. She returned to the water, finding clear sections and depositing the cool, soothing liquid onto Jay's foot, over and over, until the pain subsided. She lay back on the black sand and dirt, breathing heavily. Her foot throbbed from the ankle downwards. She couldn't feel her toes.

'It's OK now,' Jay said in response to Toyah's expression of concern.

'What now?' said Toyah, looking around the blackened island.

'Is the source there?' said Jay, motioning for Toyah to look at the base of the tree, then returning her attention to her throbbing foot.

'You can't go anywhere on that foot,' Toyah said as she stepped towards the tree.

'I'm not sure,' Jay said. 'When this happened to Stitch, passing back through the source seemed to neutralise the injury, like the injury is only real when we're here.'

'The source is here,' said Toyah, surprised. 'There are three streams, weak, but they are here.'

'Let's do it,' Jay said, dragging herself off the floor and limping towards the base of the tree. 'Come,' she said with more urgency to Toyah. She dug her hand into the area at the base of the tree and reached for Toyah's hand. Toyah placed her other hand into the source and connected the ring.

The white light came like a slowly descending mist, intensifying as it drifted to ground level and becoming blinding. Then there was nothing.

* * *

IT WAS DINGY, but light enough to see. They were lying in a basement somewhere. The floor on one side was under an inch of water, three of the walls wet with streams of water leaking from above. The air was warm. Jay pushed herself to sit as Toyah stirred and cleared her throat, her voice croaky. 'How's the foot?'

'Still there,' said Jay. 'I mean, the pain is still there. It's weird. This water soothes it a little.'

'What is this place?' Toyah said, standing and looking around the room. 'It's hot,' she added, wafting her hand to cool her face. The room was only ten feet across in both directions. The ceiling had fallen in, leaving exposed wires, ducts, and concrete beams to hold up the debris from above. Chunks of concrete lay around them on the floor, and the only exit appeared to be a single door in the far wall. There were no windows, but natural light sneaked through from somewhere above their heads. The warm air was thick with dust.

Toyah was already at the door, pulling at it, to no avail. 'Locked,' she said, turning and looking up into the ceiling.

On the only remaining shelves on the near wall, Jay sifted through some old papers, water damaged and barely decipherable. 'Maps?' asked Toyah.

Jay shook her head. 'Building information. I think we're in this building.' She pointed to a drawing of a high-rise tower. 'Or at least what's left of it.'

'So this is the source. The building must have protected it. You think they levelled the building to destroy the source?' asked Toyah.

Jay put her hand up against the wall where water flowed from above. She looked at her hand to see the sparkling within the water, a blue tinge to it. The feel on her hands was immediately energising. Toyah reached to touch the water.

'Like the unnamed river. You think this water is formed from the three streams?'

'There's one way to find out,' said Jay. She scanned the room for the point at which the water from above converged to a single body. 'There,' she said, pointing. She strode over to the part of the basement floor that was under water and crouched down. 'The three streams converge here.' She pushed her hand into the water and immediately there came a white light behind her eyes, and the urgent whispers of the environment. The noise was confused; the whispers were pained.

'They've destroyed the building, but the energy is here. We at least have a route back.'

'We're not going back,' said Toyah. 'We're here now. Let's do it.' She looked up into the roof, searching for the source of the light that filtered through the floors. 'There must be a way through.' She climbed up the only dry wall in the room, using lumps of concrete and fallen sections of the roof as a ladder to the top of the wall. 'Here,' she called. 'There's a route through here.'

Jay looked up to where Toyah waited. The route up to the hole in the ceiling was no accident. It had been used before. She shuffled her weight onto her good foot. 'Can you walk?' Toyah called. Jay nodded and climbed up the wall to where Toyah had disappeared into a hole through to the floor above.

They crawled through layer after layer of debris, heading towards the light. They emerged in the middle of a vast crater, full of bits of the demolished building. Jay could sense no power – either Reader or Given, nothing. The sounds of the City emanated from the ridge at the top of the crater. Car horns, a jack-hammer. The sun pounded its energy down onto their skin through a gap in the clouds.

They picked their way across the bomb-site and out to the

periphery where they stopped to catch a breath. Jay looked back over the expanse of demolished building, probably three hundred feet across. Concrete slabs with protruding steel bars scattered the area like the remnants of an earthquake. Furniture littered the surface, much of it smashed into pieces, stripped, scavenged, and pilfered for anything useful. A thick layer of white concrete dust covered everything so that they were both caked by the time they reached the edge.

'Up there,' Toyah said, pointing up to the rim of the crater. 'We can see from there.'

They climbed the dirt bank, reaching a fence-line with barbed wire. Toyah held up the wire fence for Jay to crawl under.

Signs attached to the fence line at intervals around the perimeter read "Radioactive". Toyah stared. 'Surely not?'

'I don't think so. It's a deterrent,' Jay said. In all directions, a thin smog hung over the City. They stood at the edge of a main street with cars passing nose to tail. Energy from the environment was weak and intermittent. A scent of the sea comforted her, brought a little of home to this unfamiliar land.

Toyah crossed the road between two yellow taxis. A derelict-looking building on the other side of the street with a collapsed front wall exposed its kitchen. She stopped at the remains of a kitchen sink and turned on one of the taps. Nothing. She tried the other, and it spluttered into life, spraying cold water all over the floor. She rubbed her hands together and splashed water over her face. She drank from the tap. 'Water's good.'

Jay looked up at the façade of the building, which must once have been a block of apartments. It stretched higher than most of its neighbours. She followed Toyah's lead and went to the tap. As soon as the cool liquid touched her lips, she realised how thirsty she was and drank greedily. She cupped her hands and poured water over her head, rubbing away the dust and heat that had penetrated her skin.

'Let's get to the roof,' said Toyah. 'We might see through this mist, so we can see what we're dealing with.' She led the way, pushing through the line of orange tape that cordoned off the main staircase. Jay followed, limping on her injured foot.

Every one of the six floors was long-deserted and littered with debris. On the roof, the smog was thinner and they could see over the top of the nearby buildings and into the distance across the City.

Toyah gasped. The City fell away into a bowl in front of them, stretching far into the distance and bounded by the sea – a grey-blue expanse of water as far as they could see. The collapsed building over the source marked the northern edge of the City. A layer of dust and smog hung over the buildings, which looked to be in a poor state – a collapsed wall, missing roof, smoke rising from its depths. Other high-rise buildings looked abandoned. People filled the streets, baking in the heat of the sun.

'What now?' said Toyah. Jay thought about the Island's 8C. Her feeling was that he was alive, despite the obvious absence of any sense of Given power. In hiding, perhaps.

'Look,' Toyah said, pointing to the east. Outside the eastern boundary of the City stood a series of smaller, low-rise dwellings. Smoke rose from discrete locations from within the settlement. A road protruded from the edge, heading out east, through to the mountains barely visible in the mist. There was a checkpoint on the road. Men with guns checked vehicles coming in and out of the City.

'Readers,' said Jay, a little fear prickling her skin.

Toyah looked to the hills in the east. 'What's out there that they need to control access to?'

'That's what we need to find out if we are to know one way or the other.'

'Know what? It's obvious this place is owned by Readers.'

'Atta,' said Jay. 'We need to know if what Flick said is true. If he exists. We need to know what we're up against.'

* * *

DESPITE THE DRAW that Jay felt to head into the City, they chose instead to head north-east into woodland and navigate their way around to the eastern hills while all the time remaining outside the City boundary, avoiding the checkpoint they'd seen from the top of the building.

They travelled for nearly two hours before reaching the foothills of the mountains. The pain in Jay's foot seemed to ease a little and a numbness set in. The eastern pathway meandered through the hills, and the further they got, the stronger Jay's sense of dark energy, and the greater her concern for Island Seven's 8C. 'We're close,' she said, looking up at a steep slope blocking their path, filled with a sense of foreboding. Whatever was beyond this ridge, she had to see with her own eyes. Toyah staggered a little on her feet. She exchanged a look with Jay and she knew that Toyah too felt the energy of the Readers and their darkness.

The climb – an hour of hard graft - took them to a ledge overlooking what appeared to be an old, disused and long since drained reservoir. Jay was the first to reach the lip of the depression and the scale of the operation knocked her back. The reservoir crater must have been over a kilometre in diameter. Down in the vast cavern, a depth of almost half its width, was a hive of activity. Mechanical excavators moved across the northern section, expanding what appeared to be an already vast warehouse-like structure. Groups of people moved between the buildings.

'They're building a City down there.'

'Sink-room. A big one.' Jay thought back again to what Flick had told her. She'd spoken of a *mega sink-room*, but Jay never pictured something as vast as this. 'We need to see what's in those buildings.'

'That's an entire community of darkness,' said Toyah. 'You sure about this?'

'They're not all Readers,' said Jay. Those with power had a certain aura that was visible to Jay. 'Look at them. Regular people under the control of the Readers.'

'Atta?' said Toyah.

'Maybe,' Jay said. 'There's Given power down there too. I can feel it.'

'The 8C?'

Jay pointed into the depths of the crater to a small, single-storey building at the south end. 'That one is guarded.'

'Readers,' said Toyah.

Jay agreed. 'If there are Given down there, that must be where they're holding them. But why here? And why keep them alive?'

'Transformation?' said Toyah.

Toyah was right. What they were looking at was a production line for the creation of Readers, which needed a supply of those with power, the Given. 'Stay here,' Jay said. 'I'll head down and see what's going on. I just need to know for sure, then I'll come back and we can leave.'

'If you go, then I go,' said Toyah, standing.

'No!' Jay said, pulling Toyah to crouch again. 'I can't protect you down there. I won't let anyone else be hurt.'

Toyah simply rolled her eyes and stood, leading the way down the slope towards the buildings.

12

___

A scuttle of stones knocked into the metal structure and made a noise that raised Jay's heartbeat. They froze, and Jay put a finger to her lips. Toyah continued down the slope and stood with her back up against the grey corrugated façade. She waved Jay to join her, then held up a hand for her to wait as she pressed her face against the building and peered through a crack. From the building came a deep humming sound.

'What is it?' asked Jay, edging to get a look through the crack.

Toyah moved out of her way so they could both look. 'I think it's a power plant?'

Around the edge, on the inside of the warehouse, was a concrete walkway about three feet wide. Beyond that, a hole opened up in the earth, stretching down as far as Jay could see. The hum they could hear was coming from the hole. 'I can't see anyone,' Jay said.

'There,' Toyah said, nodding towards the other side of the building. Several people worked on a piece of equipment, while two more with guns patrolled. 'And there.' Toyah pointed up at a platform constructed above the hole. Two guards paced the length of the walkway, both carrying guns.

'Just two,' said Jay. She stepped away from the crack to see that Toyah had already wandered off. She was looking up at a metal staircase that led to a door halfway up the side of the building. She waved for Jay to join her as she began climbing the steps.

At the top, the door led to the walkway that the two guards were using to watch over the facility. 'Guards,' said Toyah. 'They're not Readers.'

Jay nodded. 'Are we ready?'

Toyah flung open the door and strode directly towards the two guards. Jay had no choice; she followed. The guards turned and raised their guns, but Toyah's energy was already powering towards them. Jay put a hand on Toyah's shoulder, the touch helping her to amplify Toyah's attack. Together, they entered the minds of the two guards. Jay read their fear and confusion as they fought to raise their guns.

The guns clattered to the floor, and both guards put their hands to the sides of their heads. Jay broke off her energy, leaving Toyah to manage the guards, who offered no resistance.

Jay looked down over the elevated platform. So far, they were undetected. The deep humming sound pulsed in waves, creating vibrations in the air. The hole was black, as if the light itself was being pulled in and swallowed up. The strength of power in the building was palpable. This was the sink-room, far more powerful than the sink-room the Readers had used in her homeland.

Her head pounding and heart racing, Jay looked back at Toyah, transfixed on the two men writhing on the floor at her feet. She was in a trance, focused on digging into the minds of the guards as their life force seeped away.

'Toyah!' Jay shouted, while sending a disruption to Toyah's energy flow, enough to break her concentration. She turned to Jay, allowing her to pull her away from the two guards.

'They're not Readers!' Jay said. 'And look. Something's moving down there.' Beneath them, a machine rotated like a fairground ride, sending waves of power and glimmers of light with each rotation.

'Is that a control panel?' Toyah pointed to a panel on the wall of the building at the other end of the walkway. Behind the panel door, a switchboard stared back at her with a series of buttons and levers. Toyah skimmed a finger over the labels on each control and then pulled down a lever with a clunk. Lights powered on around the crater below them. The rotating machine came into view. It was like a giant waltzer. Three arms with grey chunks of metal at the end rotated at speed. With each rotation, a spark emitted from its centre and a wave of vibrations expanded through the air.

Jay's skin turned cold. A bitter, metallic taste seeped into the back of her mouth. With each pulse of energy, her eyes lost focus, as if the whole of the earth vibrated for a moment. *This is their mega sink-room or whatever they call it*, she thought to herself. 'This is their source,' she said aloud.

Toyah came back to her side.

'It's like a tap into the core. Like the one we destroyed back home, but bigger.' Jay was no longer sure that they'd destroyed the source of dark power in her homeland. Yes, they destroyed the buildings that housed the sink-room, but if the power came from a connection to the core, then it was possible that the connection remained. The strength of the dark power that emanated from the hole below them was undeniable. This was a force of power they'd not encountered before.

The pulsing energy churned Jay's stomach. Her legs wobbled. 'We need to get out of here,' she said, staggering back towards the door at the end of the walkway. She felt Readers. The darkness closed around her from all sides. Readers whispering inside her head. The pulsing energy from the core made the walls of the building quiver like a hologram, an illusion. She dropped to her knees, no longer able to hold herself up against the weight of the darkness, and slid to the floor, the cold metal grating hard against her face.

Toyah's touch energised her. She opened her eyes and dragged herself to a sitting position. 'I'm OK.'

'What happened?' asked Toyah.

'Just keep a hold on my hands for a minute,' Jay said, looking into Toyah's eyes and trying to understand what was happening to her. She returned her gaze and took both of her hands, squeezing tight and allowing their energy to combine.

Jay opened to the energy and allowed Toyah to help her to stand. She rubbed her eyes and shook her head to clear the fog in her mind.

'I can feel Readers,' she said. 'Not like just a few, but hundreds, thousands.'

'That's not possible,' said Toyah.

'I know.' Jay looked down at the machine, the channel to the darkness. 'Atta,' Jay said, locking eyes with Toyah. 'This power of the Dark. It must be Atta.'

Before her eyes, Toyah seemed to quiver in the energy from below. A dark stream of mist swirled around Toyah's head and the walkway beneath their feet shifted. They stumbled, breaking their grip on each other and reaching for the handrail. The sound in the warehouse changed, as if they'd been submerged in a thick liquid. As Toyah reached for the railing, it moved away from her, down into the depths below, Toyah following it, a muffled scream escaping her lips as she went.

Jay remained standing on the edge of a broken walkway,

reaching out as her friend slipped further away and into free fall. The section of walkway that had held Toyah plummeted towards the hole in the ground. She watched helplessly as Toyah faded into the darkness at the edge of the hole. She landed heavily in the dirt, unmoving. Jay's heart pounded in her ears. She screamed Toyah's name and stepped towards the edge of the broken walkway.

'Not sensible,' said a deep, smooth voice. A man stood a few feet away, a vision in black clothing with pale features and white hair, like a ghost. Jay was paralysed in his presence. He exuded immense power, an aura that flowed with the energy of the darkness, as if Readers floated from him, surrounded him, were part of him.

'Help her,' Jay said, looking over the railing into the hole below, the only words she could formulate. The man glanced over the edge as if he didn't know what Jay was talking about.

'I'd like to thank you,' he said, his voice authoritative, tone silky. Jay kept her eyes on him but her senses reached for Toyah. She found her. She was still alive.

The man stepped closer, peering into Jay.

'Who are you?' asked Jay.

'You know who I am. I can see that you know. I knew you'd come. We are connected now. Thank you for that.'

'Atta...' Jay said under her breath. 'What do you mean?' She edged away from him, feeling his energy, her heels edging over the end of the broken walkway.

'You opened the channel. I knew you would. You are so very predictable. We connected, and now it is just a matter of time.'

'You have no power over my homeland.'

Atta laughed. 'We will see.' He motioned towards the hole beneath them. 'We have the means to open the earth to the core. *This* brings power in a way you wouldn't understand.'

Jay turned to look into the abyss, scanning for signs of Toyah.

'There's someone I want you to meet,' Atta said, and without another word, turned back to the door.

Jay followed without conscious thought. She was drawn to him as if connected with a length of rope. He passed through the door and down the steps to the outside of the building. The sound of the rotating power machine and its pulsating waves of energy at last dampened behind the closed door as Jay reached the ground.

He led her to the building on the periphery of the abandoned reservoir crater – the building guarded by Readers who parted like curtains as Atta approached, allowing him a wide berth as he flowed into the building, Jay close behind.

Atta's presence dominated as he entered the room, the power of the darkness pushing others back against the walls.

There was a woman, her face drawn, smooth brown skin scratched and bruised, her eyes with a look of someone lost. She felt no power flow from her, only a life-force weakened to the point of extinction. As she looked up at Jay, she saw the red, angry scar on the side of her face, the characteristic marking, like a tick mark from beneath the chin up to the temple – a confirmation of her reduction.

As their eyes met, the woman seemed to deflate further, as if her only hope had finally been extinguished. 'You shouldn't be here,' she said, struggling to release the words. She lowered her eyes.

Jay looked at Atta, a smile on his face. 'Here we are,' he said to the woman. 'This is the best of the best,' he motioned at Jay. 'The ultimate power of the Given, right here in this room.' He laughed. Jay's fear turned to anger, and she took a deep breath, searching for her inner power to deflect the control of Atta. She felt a momentary release, like she'd shaken herself from his grip. She searched for life in the ground to connect and strengthen her power. She scanned for Toyah to reinforce her strength. Then a wave of darkness slammed her into the wall and she slumped to the floor, Atta's energy gripping her around the throat and squeezing life from her.

He stood above her, a few feet away, his eyes flitting between her and the woman behind the bars of the cell. Jay's lungs emptied and she gasped for breath. The woman shrank to the floor as Atta turned his attention to her from Jay.

'Leave her,' pleaded Jay. The woman's arm flopped to her side and Jay saw the inside of her wrist. She was the Island's level "C".

The woman grew smaller by the second. Jay tried to scream, to push out at Atta's control over her body. The more she tried, the heavier her limbs became. The C made no sound as she disintegrated into the soil, her body becoming nothing but a pile of ashes, blackened by the energy flowing from Atta.

Jay felt Atta's grip loosen, and she flopped further to the floor, as if his power had been physically holding her up. She tried to open her eyes but couldn't prise open her eyelids.

Nearby, the woman was dead.

She felt Atta's presence as he approached and crouched next to her. She felt his breath on her face, warm with bitterness. He whispered in her ear. 'Who do you think you are, Jay?'

A sound distracted Atta for a moment. Readers entered the room, only to rock back on their heels when faced with Atta's energy. Atta stood. 'What is it?'

'The electro source has stopped turning. We're investigating.'

Atta marched towards the door. 'Watch her. If she stirs, kill her.'

Toyah, thought Jay, desperately hoping that Toyah was already safely away. She turned to look at her guards, considering whether she'd be able to draw enough power to get away from them.

* * *

TOYAH WATCHED the rotating machine slow and grind to a halt. The third boulder she'd pushed from the lip of the crater had wedged in the central core, breaking in two and settling to jam the mechanism.

She turned and scanned the inside of the vast warehouse for signs of movement. Nothing yet, but she guessed there'd be Readers all over her soon enough. Moving towards the back wall, she ducked behind a spoil heap, out of the line of sight from the remains of the walkways above.

She could feel the power of Atta, but had no sense of where Jay had gone. Atta's energy was everywhere, as if he were part of everything around her – the walls of the warehouse, the sink-room machine, the earth, and the very air that she breathed. She had to concentrate on shielding from him. He was looking for her.

Toyah was not easily shaken by Readers. She'd seen worse. Since her epic journey to the Interland with her little brother, Pinto, back when she was just a kid, she'd developed a resilience to the paralysing effects of fear. The responsibility for someone else, someone more vulnerable than yourself, has some kind of transformational effect on your ability to shrug off a threat to your own safety. She looked around the vast building, the roof hundreds of feet above her. The place nipped at the ankles of her confidence like nothing had since before the Interland. The pull of the darkness was draining.

She leaned up against the wall of the warehouse. People, only some of them Readers, moved above her head on the walkway, entering the building from the staircases at either end and then exiting once more when they saw that the route was blocked – the walkway collapsed over its central section. Over the far side of the building, more people entered at ground level, edging towards the sink machine, guns raised. A flash of an image passed inside her head and she knew Atta was coming for her. *I need to get out*, she thought to herself. *Jay will find me.*

Readers pored over the sink-machine. A loud clunk vibrated the ground. Another, and the machine kicked into life, the three arms spinning once again. Toyah immediately felt the strengthening waves of darkness.

She turned to the wall of the warehouse and dug her fingers behind a loose piece of corrugated metalwork. She prised open the metal panel, grunting as she gave a final push, creating a gap big enough to squeeze through.

Outside, the southern slope rose at a steep gradient. She took a last look along the side of the warehouse. No one in sight. She began the climb.

* * *

ATTA HAD LEFT THE ROOM, but his presence remained. He was a source of energy for the rest of them. The two Readers left to guard her seemed more powerful than others. They guarded knowing that Atta was there with power to draw upon.

A pain shot through Jay's temples like a stab of a knife, then withdrew. 'Don't even think it,' the nearest Reader said, his eyes piercing.

Jay put up her shield, the version that appeared invisible to others who might attempt to read her. She gave herself a little space to think.

Angie came into her head, her smiling face a vision of light amongst the darkness of her captivity. *What are you doing here?* Jay said without speaking. Angie's smile broadened. *I don't know*, she replied. With her presence came a confidence and energy. Angie seemed to be able to enter her mind and work with her, provide avenues of thought and energy that weren't available to her alone.

'Together,' Jay muttered under her breath. The Readers turned to her, but she had already launched her energy at them. She attacked with all her power, plus Angie's support. The Readers went down, both of them working hard to raise their inner shields. But Jay was too quick for them. She stood, drew more power from beneath her feet and the weight of the hills. The Readers squirmed. She stepped back towards the door, continuing her attack until they lay unmoving.

She breathed heavily, taking a moment to recharge a little. She focused her energy on Toyah and found her, making her escape to the hills. Jay breathed easier. She put up her shield with all her remaining energy, flung open the door and ran, the adrenaline masking the pain in her foot.

At the crest of the hill, she spotted Toyah, crouched amongst the rocks. 'You're a sight,' Toyah said as Jay approached. 'What happened?'

'Later,' Jay said. 'Let's get some distance between us and this place.' She pointed to the south, not to the pathway on which they'd come, but to the hills. 'That way.'

Toyah nodded.

'Shield,' said Jay, looking back down towards the buildings, immediately sensing Atta. 'As much as you can. We need to get a clean break.'

PART II

13

On the edge of a barren slope, worn out from what felt like hours walking through the difficult terrain of the southern hills, Jay flopped to the floor in exhaustion, her foot aching. Toyah sank down next to her. 'There,' she said, pointing towards a string of farm buildings in the valley before them. 'We can rest there.'

'What about the people who live there?' Jay pulled off her shoe and peeled back her sock to inspect her bad foot.

Toyah scanned the valley. 'No Readers,' she said.

Jay couldn't scan. The energy from Atta's lair, although weakened with distance, confused the signals she felt from her own energy, and shook her confidence in reading the signs.

'No people either, by the looks of it,' said Toyah, 'and we have to rest somewhere.'

There was a nip in the air. The sun had dipped in the sky. The alternative to risking the farmhouse was camping in the hills. They'd be up higher and able to see all the incoming routes.

Toyah stood, stretching out her shoulders. 'You OK?'

'Fine,' Jay said. 'Let's do it.' Her desperate thirst clinched the deal. She pulled her shoe back on and stood, tentatively putting weight back on her foot. Toyah steadied her, but Jay refused the hand. Toyah seemed older suddenly. In control. Jay turned to the pathway.

At the foot of the slope, Jay led Toyah around the back of the farmhouse, along the fence line, careful to remain out of sight of the windows of the building. The bushes and shrubs in the yard had taken over every available space. Dust clung to the glass in the windows. The house had been empty for weeks, but not months. The back door was ajar, hanging from a single hinge. Jay looked up at the old building and felt for its owners, driven out of their beautiful home nestled in the valley between the hills, now stuck between the City and the rats' nest of the Readers' lair.

Inside, the house was tidy, as if someone had been careful to leave it ready for their return. The ground floor was open-plan, criss-crossed wooden beams holding up an imperfect ceiling, sagging from years of structural effort. In the kitchen, a layer of dust covered the surfaces. Jay held her breath and turned on the tap. Cold water flowed immediately, and she breathed again before leaning down to drink until she had to gasp for breath, then took some more. She wiped her mouth and moved aside for Toyah to fill a glass from the tap.

She opened each of the kitchen cupboards. 'Well stocked,' she said. There were tins, pasta, rice. She checked a loaf of bread on the worktop, knocking it against the side to show how stale it was. A turn of the dial on the hob proved that they had gas. She pushed the ignitor switch and smiled at the sound of the rush, hiss and whoosh as the gas caught and the girls knew they'd be able to eat well that evening.

* * *

THEY SETTLED IN THE LOUNGE, spread across the two sofas with bedding brought from upstairs. With no electricity, their only light came from the few candles that Toyah had retrieved from the drawers in the dining room. The silent television on the wall hung like a blacked-out window.

Full from their meal, Jay sank deep into the sofa, her mind taunted by images of Atta. She couldn't get a hold of what he was, or how they would deal with him.

'I can read that expression,' Toyah said. 'Don't tell me, *we're gonna need a bigger boat...*'

Jay nodded. Toyah was too close to the truth for Jay to laugh. The words of Atta nagged in the back of her head: *Who do you think you are...?* It was as if he couldn't believe that she'd even have the gall to confront him.

'He said something to me,' Jay said. 'He said I'd opened a channel. Like I opened the gate to our land, Island 8.'

'What *gate*?' asked Toyah. 'They can't cross over to Island 8. There's no sink-room.'

Jay rubbed her temples, searching her mind for the snippets she'd read in the bookshop – the history of the powers, and the myth of Atta. She wished Alf was there to help her piece it together. She tried to picture Atta. He had a kind of glow about him, like a dark aura. And he seemed to be fluid, his outline continually changing, like a trick of the light.

'What is he?' asked Toyah, reading Jay's thoughts. 'A Reader?'

'No,' said Jay. 'It's difficult to explain. I think he's a kind of manifestation of the energy of the Readers. But he only comes to being when a critical mass occurs.'

'Critical mass?' Toyah repeated, looking confused.

'When the numbers of Readers gets to a point, the energy balance tips in the darkness's favour...' Jay trailed off, unsure of her own words. 'My understanding of this is vague in the extreme. This imbalance hasn't happened before as far as we can tell, and for it to happen so quickly is unlikely.'

'We dealt with Hinton, and we can deal with him,' said Toyah.

Toyah's words comforted Jay, but she missed the calming presence of Stitch and the fearless confidence of Cassie. When the three of them were together, it was like they had an impenetrable shield, like they could do anything. The darkness of Atta was deeper, more profound than the anomaly that was Hinton. 'We need to get back to the source so we can head home. We need to regroup and tell the others.'

* * *

JAY TURNED over on the sofa and looked at her watch - nearly an hour since Toyah had dropped off and still she couldn't sleep. Three out of the four candles continued to burn, casting ominous, moving shadows across the walls and ceiling. Electricity fizzed inside her head.

She turned onto her back and stared up at the ceiling. The flowing shadows above her head moved and merged, continually changing shape. The darkness formed waves that flowed between the walls, receding for a moment, then raging as the candles flickered. Her mind played with the shapes, creating images from their outlines, stories from their movement.

She thought of Angie, probably lying just like her, on her back, motionless. She closed her eyes and tried to empty her mind. Her breathing steadied and as soon as she had relaxed, whispers came.

These whispers were of a different tone and feeling to those back home. They whirled around her head, more subdued, less urgent. The sense they brought was one of defeat. Inside the whispers, Angie came back to her. It was her voice that came through, her colours that shimmered behind Jay's eyes. Her oranges and red hues were among the warmest Jay had ever seen. Angie's presence took Jay deeper into the power, further into her subconscious. She was connected.

A flash of white light.

Jay was on the shore of Island 7. Darkness pervaded. The water was thick with swirls of black, the tree charred, the sand mottled with black grains. She looked over to Island 8 , her homeland, to see Angie standing on the shore, her body rigid as she gazed over the water towards Jay.

'I'm here too,' Angie called, excitement in her tone.

Jay staggered towards the shore, her head pounding. She squinted in the light. 'What's happening?'

Angie shrugged. 'This is the place you told me about. You brought me here.'

'I don't know how...'

'It doesn't matter,' said Angie. 'This is amazing.'

'Where are you really?' Jay asked.

'I don't know,' said Angie, thinking. 'In hospital. Still under. They're bringing me around tomorrow, I think. I don't know how I know that.'

'You're OK?' asked Jay.

'I reckon,' Angie smiled. 'Where are *you*?'

Jay looked around her. 'In some farmhouse, on our way back home.'

'Toyah is with you,' Angie said, a statement, not a question.

Jay nodded. The white light intensified and Jay sensed they had no time. Whether it was Jay's subconscious or Angie's, she couldn't tell, but either way, they were about to be thrust back into their physical worlds.

'Hurry home,' said Angie.

'We're coming,' said Jay, her words swallowed as the light pierced the Island world and all turned white.

14

When Jay woke again, it was pitch black, and it took a moment for her to remember where she was. The candles had burned themselves out and the smell of hot wax tickled her nose. Toyah snored lightly.

A noise. A thump from outside, like the closing of a gate on its sprung hinge. Jay's eyes widened; she didn't dare to move in the dark, there wasn't even a glint of light to dilute the madness that comes with pitch black.

As her eyes adjusted, she could just about make out the lighter shade of black that was the blind at the window. She slipped off the sofa, nudging into Toyah's legs as she sloped onto the floor, arresting her snoring for just a moment. She crawled around to the window and pulled herself up to a crouching position. She edged the blind back to see over the yard.

People.

Jay fell back into the room, then lifted herself once more to look through the blind. By the light of the moon, there were six people stalking through the yard towards the house, military-style, dressed in black. Every one of them carrying a rifle.

'Hey!' Jay shook Toyah.

She grunted, unmoving for a moment, before launching into action. Jay turned on a torch and frantically packed her rucksack.

'Readers?' asked Toyah.

'Yes,' Jay whispered. Toyah remained calm, systematically packing her things away and pulling on her shoes like there was no need to hurry. As Jay slung her bag onto her back, Toyah motioned for her to follow as she led the way to the internal door that connected through to the garage.

'How did you know...' Jay started, but Toyah put a finger to her lips and motioned towards the two vehicles – one a Land Rover, the other an open-back truck.

Jay moved towards the Land Rover, jumping into the front seat. Toyah went to the truck. Jay searched for keys but found nothing in the ignition, nothing above the sun visor.

She turned to look for Toyah, but the truck was empty. A moment later, Toyah appeared in the open doorway to the house. She stepped down onto the garage floor and closed the door behind her. A finger to her lips, she flung her bag into the open-back truck and held up a set of keys, then jumped back into the front seat.

Jay stepped out of the Land Rover and unclipped the garage door, opening it a crack and quickly closing it again. She shook her head and climbed into the truck next to Toyah. 'We'll have to make a run for it.'

Jay sensed Readers at the door between the house and the garage. She reached out and held onto Toyah's arm to strengthen her connection with the power, then pushed into the minds of the Readers behind the door to confuse and delay them. Toyah started the engine. It spluttered for a moment and kicked into life. Black smoke belched from the exhaust. The door flung open. Toyah slammed the truck into gear and launched the truck at the garage door, slamming it back on its hinges.

Out front, three vehicles stood in the yard, Readers on guard. Toyah slid the truck past the vehicles and onto the main road that led up into the hills. Jay looked into the eyes of the first Reader through the door of the garage as he ran towards the truck. In the wing mirror, she saw the strength of his power in his eyes, felt it seep into her consciousness as he tried to infiltrate her. He reached for her, but was not quick enough. Toyah accelerated away as the Readers rallied around their vehicles and Jay knew they would catch them up before long.

'You feel that?' Jay said to Toyah, still looking back towards the Reader who chased them. 'He was strong.'

'Evil, I'd say,' said Toyah, sliding the truck around a sharp bend in the dirt roadway.

'I haven't felt a Reader that strong since...'

'Hinton?' said Toyah.

'Hinton wasn't a Reader. Marcus.' Marcus had been the strongest of the Readers, the only level eight Jay had come across.

'Level eight,' said Toyah, a sideways glance at Jay.

* * *

JAY LEANED back in the truck's cab, watching in the wing mirror through the dust and the darkness for any signs of Readers. The disappearing road glinted in the moonlight. She rubbed her eyes. They must have had little more than a couple of hours' sleep.

The road narrowed as they stretched deeper into the hills.

Toyah slowed to negotiate the bends and avoid the steepening drop on both sides. Jay looked out over the edge and shuffled closer to the middle of the truck as if to keep the centre of gravity away from the steep drop. They passed over a wooden bridge and Jay felt the supports flex. 'Stop!' She shook Toyah's arm, and she slammed on the brakes. The truck screeched to a halt just past the bridge. Jay jumped out. 'Come!' she shouted.

Toyah followed her back to the wooden bridge where she had already side-stepped down the embankment and was pushing her body weight into one of the wooden bridge piers. 'Help me out here!'

Toyah joined her, and the wooden strut moved under their weight. A few more shoves and the strut moved again, its joint with the bridge slipping. 'It's moving,' said Toyah.

In the distance, headlights approached. Three vehicles. 'Keep going. One more,' said Jay.

With a last shove, the bridge pier creaked and gave way, its base sliding down the slope and into the valley. The bridge deck remained suspended. 'It's not falling,' said Toyah.

'But it won't hold their weight,' said Jay.

They returned to the truck just as the Readers' vehicles came into view around the corner.

Toyah slammed the truck into gear.

'Wait,' said Jay, looking out of her open window as the Readers' Land Rovers approached.

As they watched, the truck engine idling, the front Land Rover stopped just the other side of the bridge. 'Shield,' said Jay. 'Don't let them read you.' A moment later, the convoy continued onto the bridge.

The first vehicle was almost halfway across, with no obvious movement of the deck. Jay and Toyah remained calm. As the second vehicle rolled onto the bridge deck, the road surface twisted violently, then dropped three feet. Both vehicles remained upright on the deck. Both stopped. The front Land Rover then continued, picking up speed, but the bridge deck disappeared from beneath its wheels and it plummeted the short drop to the slope of the valley. Jay craned her neck to see as the Land Rover slid down the bank and onto its side. The second Land Rover had reversed off the bridge. 'One down,' said Jay.

'And the other two are not getting through here,' added Toyah.

Jay looked over at Toyah and they smiled. She put the truck into gear and they pushed on deeper into the hills.

Sunrise crept up through the valleys, the light breaking the darkness and bringing a little optimism after their minor victory.

Through the hills, they skirted the southern edge of the City for a few miles before they dared turn towards the centre. The peace and safety of the hills was difficult to give up for what would surely be a hard journey through the City and back to the source.

As soon as the truck crossed the boundary into the City, Jay felt it. A sense of the power of the Given, not of the source, but of someone with strong Given power. The Island Seven 8C was close.

15

'Take a left here,' Jay said. Toyah frowned, but maybe for the first time since the Interland, did what Jay asked.

'Where are we going? The source is on the north side.'

'Head that way.' Jay pointed in the direction of the energy.

Toyah parked the truck on the side of a street. Across the road, a row of townhouses stretched several storeys above street level. 'Can you feel it?' Jay asked Toyah.

'Nothing,' said Toyah, to Jay's surprise. 'I'm getting no power from this place.'

But Jay needed to know more. They stepped out of the truck and the cool, early morning breeze felt good on her face. They stood shaded from the sun beneath the branches of a chestnut tree, its pink blossom scattered over the ground across the street from the townhouse. The black door with the number 42 had a small window in the top section. A note pinned to the glass on the inside said something in a language Jay couldn't translate. Meanwhile, their presence was already attracting attention from passers-by. 'Let's check it out,' said Jay.

'Wait,' said Toyah, looking uncharacteristically nervous. She looked up into the branches of the tree above their heads and drew a deep breath. 'Are you sure?'

Jay nodded. 'I feel powerful energy here.'

'It's too dangerous. And we don't even know how much power we have, how well the source is functioning here,' said Toyah.

Jay moved around to the rear of the tree, out of the main path of pedestrians, and placed her hand on its trunk. She held out a hand to Toyah. In their connected energy, they travelled into the earth's crust, through the tree and into the parched topsoil and deeper, searching, exploring. They hit groundwater. Within it, life thrived, hundreds of feet below the surface. Jay felt its energy. It fed her power, and she glowed with it. She and Toyah opened their eyes, and the whispers swirled around their heads as they leaned against the tree. The power flowed between her and Jay through their joined hands. Jay's energy reciprocated that of Toyah, combining with the energy from below.

The girls blinked in surprise. 'There *is* power here,' Jay said. 'But it's a long way down and we'll have to dig deep if we are to use its full force.'

Together they turned to face the street and stepped out into the road towards the black door.

* * *

THE CURTAIN in the window twitched, and Jay knocked again.

Without warning, the door swung open, and a gun was thrust into Jay's face. A hand on her shoulder pulled her into the house. 'Get in here,' the man said, without lowering his gun. He slammed the door shut behind them. Jay recognised him immediately as the man they'd met before - the 8C.

'It's me,' said Jay.

The man lowered his gun, but kept it pointed in their direction as he scrutinised Jay, recognition in his expression. She peered into him but he was closed down tight. 'Jay?' he said.

Jay nodded.

'How did you find me? What are you doing here?' He lowered his gun.

'Through the source.'

The 8C shook his head and moved to the door, peering through the spyhole to check for anyone who might have followed. He muttered to himself - something about sensing her presence but not believing she'd be so stupid as to come here.

'How long's it been like this? Readers in control?' asked Jay.

'Months. What planet you from?'

'You know where we are from,' Jay said, keeping her tone friendly, reassuring.

The 8C continued to hold his gun. Jay sensed his confusion, his fear, and desperation. At last, his defences lowered a little and Jay reached into his mind and saw his name, *Tiago*. 'You're Tiago?'

Tiago nodded. He lowered his gun and clicked on the safety.

'You shouldn't be here,' he said to Jay. Then, with a little reluctance, he ushered them through and into a wide, open-plan ground floor room that formed a kitchen-dining area. Jay heard a noise and looked towards the stairs, sensing others in the house.

'Come,' he shouted to his family. 'It's safe.' He turned to Jay, 'Sit, here,' motioning towards a chair at the table.

'It's OK...' Jay started, but Tiago cut her off.

'Sit. I bring you water. You need food. You must eat.'

'We just...' Jay tried again, but Tiago interrupted once more.

'Sit!' he blurted, then raised his hands in apology. 'Please.' Jay and Toyah stole a glance and then took a seat. Toyah edged back from the table, looking over her shoulder as if planning her exit.

Two little feet appeared on the stairs, followed by the rest of a little girl, hand in hand with a woman Jay assumed was her mother. The mother held another girl in her arms. All three stared at the travellers, nervous of their intentions. 'Come,' said Tiago, ushering them into the room. 'This is my wife, Thabisa. And my children, Enzo, and Faith. My name is Tiago, but you know that already. We are happy that you are here. Sorry for the gun.' His words were welcoming, but he remained guarded.

Jay looked over at the two little girls. 'I'm Jay, and this is Toyah.' The older of the two girls smiled, the younger turned her head into her mother's shoulder.

'Can I see?' Tiago said as he placed two glasses of water on the table for Jay and Toyah. He looked at Jay's wrist. He turned his arm to show his "8C". Jay drew back her sleeve and smiled. Tiago sighed, as if relieved. To Toyah, 'But you are not the connection, no? The "C"?' Toyah shook her head.

'Stitch is back home,' said Jay.

'I would have liked to meet him. He has some healer in him, no?'

Jay nodded, surprised that Tiago knew this. 'Like my wife, Thabisa here.' Thabisa looked away, embarrassed.

'Where are we?' said Jay. 'I mean, what *country* are we in?'

Tiago reached for Jay's hand and led her to the window. 'See there?' He pointed into the distance where the low-lying mist had cleared and the outline of the mountain range was visible. Jay recognised the distinctive shape. The central section was flat, as if the peak had been sliced away. The wide expanse was flanked by narrower peaks on either side, like sentries watching over her. The slopes were a dark red colour in the sun's glare through the mist. 'This is *Kaapstown*,' Tiago said. 'You are in South Africa.'

* * *

THEY GATHERED around the table to eat, squeezed up against each other as Tiago and Thabisa prepared the food. Enzo was eight years old, and Faith just three. The two girls sat quietly, nudging each other and occasionally conversing in Afrikaans, giggling.

Jay and Toyah had hardly spoken since they walked through the door of Tiago's family home. Jay was a little shell-shocked at the fact they'd travelled through the source in the South Downs of England, through to the source of Island 7, in South Africa. She needed to focus, to straighten her thoughts.

'Tell me,' said Tiago, placing a bowl of stew in the middle of the table. The smell of the spiced, cooked food filled the room. 'I thought the source was destroyed, so how did you move?'

Jay shook her head. 'The power is still there. As long as the three sources combine, then the power will come.' Jay reached down to rub her foot. She'd pushed the pain to the back of her consciousness, but now they were resting properly, the pain was again intense. 'I caught my foot in the swirls of darkness between the shores. It's still painful.'

'Let me look at it later.' Tiago smiled, dishing out the food. He exchanged a glance with Thabisa.

'Thank you,' said Jay.

'I have not felt safe to visit the destroyed building where

the power resided,' said Tiago. 'We dare not leave this house. Atta's people are everywhere, not just his Readers, but his informants. The entire City works for Atta.'

'But you are so close to the source here,' said Toyah.

'It's dangerous. The source is in the City's heart. My level "C" was taken months ago. No-one has seen her. She is probably a Reader by now.'

'They can't force transformation,' said Toyah, more a question than a statement.

'They are strong persuaders,' said Tiago.

'I saw her,' said Jay, lowering her gaze but opening her mind. Tiago stopped eating and turned to glance at his wife.

Tiago put down his knife and fork. 'She is gone?'

Jay nodded.

'Atta?'

Jay nodded again. 'He killed her in front of me. I couldn't help her, I'm so sorry...'

Tiago raised a hand to stop Jay from continuing. 'I knew this. I felt her loss just yesterday. She has grown weaker over the months. Some weeks ago, I thought she had died, as I no longer felt her pain. I was relieved that she was no longer suffering. But she was still alive?'

'Until yesterday,' Jay said.

'I should have done more.'

'What could you do?' Thabisa spat the words. 'What good is it to die for nothing. What help would you be to the Given?'

Tiago stood and walked from the room, returning a moment later with a bottle of something that looked like a dark wine, or port. He filled four shot glasses and raised one to make a toast. 'To my connection. To Annika.'

Tiago swallowed his drink in one. Jay and Toyah followed Tiago's lead. 'To Annika,' said Jay.

'To Annika,' said Thabisa.

* * *

TOYAH AND ENZO made faces at each other across the table. Enzo giggled. 'You look older than eight. You're so tall,' said Toyah.

Enzo smiled coyly. 'I am nearly nine,' she said.

'You speak English well,' said Toyah. Enzo nodded.

'English is the strongest second language here,' said Tiago. 'They learn at school. Enzo is top of her class, right Enzo?' She nodded again, pride brimming over at her dad's words.

Faith had curled in Thabisa's lap, silently observing their guests with a thumb in her mouth. Jay sensed a twinkle of power in the little one. Thabisa's expression was stern, reserved. She was uncomfortable having strangers in her house, especially strangers who might bring trouble. She had been through enough conflict, and had no appetite for more. Her focus was on her daughters and their survival. The Readers would have torn through the City without compassion. After they had eaten, Jay turned to Tiago: 'What happened here?'

Tiago's expression darkened. He caught Thabisa's eye, and they silently agreed that she'd take the children upstairs.

Tiago began, speaking slowly at first. 'There were always Readers, we knew that. They had a sink-room east of the City, and there were fights. But the Given were strong here. The source was at the centre of the Mother City. The connections between the heart of our great City and the surrounding environment were strong – the strongest. The Readers were small in number and small in power compared to the Given.'

Toyah said, 'Why did the Given not destroy the sink-room?'

'We did,' said Tiago. 'But as we only learned later, you

cannot destroy the link to the core. You can take away what is on the surface, but underneath remains.'

Toyah and Jay exchanged a look that flickered with fear.

'We should have been in control, but we made mistakes,' Tiago said. 'You saw the mountains. The energy in these living mountains was unparalleled. Then there is the ocean. Our City is in an epicentre of energy between mountains and ocean. The Given should have been impenetrable here.' He shook his head, his eyes on his shoes, a pair of faded trainers.

Tiago pointed through the window towards the hills. 'Look.' Jay searched the horizon. The mountains, although shaded by dark clouds, seemed to shine. They were a dark red, almost black. Tiago shook his hand at the window, urging his guests to see what he saw. 'The flora is depleted. The trees are wilting. The shrub-land, the fynbos, are grey.'

'But you survived,' Jay said.

Tiago looked up. 'Some of us remain. But only because we know how to evade their scanners. They search for us, but we have become good at hiding. There are materials in these walls that help us to shield.'

Jay looked at the walls and frowned. 'But I was drawn here,' she said.

Tiago nodded. 'I'm hoping that it is because we are the same. A particular connection?' He brushed his hand over the marking on his wrist.

'You can fight back. Connect with the Given who remain?'

'There are too many Readers, and there is Atta.' Tiago shifted in his seat, agitated. 'It's not a fair fight anymore. We've already lost...' His words trailed off. Jay waited. 'We have a resistance. It is small, but it could grow.' He looked again at Jay and she saw a glint in his eye, a determination. 'Give me your hand.'

Jay eyed his outstretched hand, understanding that he

intended to impart information, to show Jay what they'd been through. 'You too,' Tiago said, looking at Toyah. Jay reached to hold on to Toyah's hand and the three of them connected in a ring.

Flashes of images embedded in their subconscious. The Readers had come in night purges, taking Given or suspected Given without warning and without confirmation of powers. None had returned.

Jay broke the chain and rocked back in her seat. Toyah slipped off her chair and onto the floor in a daze. Tiago went to her, helping her up. Jay reeled as the information percolated through her conscious mind. The darkness had come over the hills to the mountain peaks and then down into the City. In its wake, the Given were rounded up. Women and children dragged from their houses in the middle of the night and taken to camps to the east. Readers walked freely through the City. Those without power were left alone, unless they resisted or harboured the Given - then they were killed. As the number of Given taken grew, so did the number of Readers.

Toyah stirred. Tiago helped her back on to her seat and poured her some water. She looked at Jay, wide eyed and scared.

'How did Atta come here?' asked Jay.

'We don't know if he came into power once the balance tipped, or if he found a way to move here from Island 6.'

'How many in the resistance?' Jay asked.

Tiago shook his head. 'Not enough. With each purge, we become weaker. Some have left the City to settle in the hills, seeking places away from where the Readers patrol.'

'We saw a checkpoint on the eastern side?'

Tiago nodded. 'Readers control the access into and out of the City from the hills. The eastern road is the only one remaining. It connects the City with the rest of the province.

Nothing comes in and out of here except through the eastern checkpoint.' He rested back in his chair and sighed. 'The resistance is on its last legs. The City is no longer safe.'

'We've been to the hills,' croaked Toyah, regaining her composure.

'Atta is there,' added Jay. 'The sink-room is bigger than you can imagine, and the power is immense.'

Tiago lowered his head. 'We thought so. It is now just a matter of time.'

'Come back with us,' said Jay.

Tiago laughed. 'This is my land. These are my people. We are all they have left, the only thing between them and the Readers. We are weakened but not yet defeated. We need help, not asylum.' Tiago shook his head and pulled a packet of cigarettes from his back pocket. He stood, motioning for the others to follow him out back. They stepped out into a small back garden. 'So what's your plan?' he asked Jay.

Jay glanced at Toyah. They had no plan. 'We need to get back home,' she said.

Tiago leaned back against the house. 'Rest here tonight. We will top up your supplies. Get you as strong as we can.'

* * *

TOYAH SLEPT, but Jay was restless, the pain in her foot distracting. Out on the landing, she saw light and heard talking coming from downstairs. She limped down to find Tiago and Thabisa at the dining room table, smoking. Tiago quickly stubbed out his cigarette. 'Ah, I thought you were one of the kids,' he said. 'I need to quit this.'

Thabisa smiled at Jay and nodded to a chair. Jay stumbled and sat, taking the weight off her foot. Tiago looked concerned. 'It's bad?'

'It comes and goes.'

Thabisa turned to Jay. 'You want me to try something?' She showed the figure "3" on her wrist. 'I've had mixed results, but your power might help me.'

Stitch's healing power, too, had been unreliable. Since he helped to release Sammy from the spreading infection in his leg back at the Interland, he'd had little success, although he understood the mechanisms well, and the rest, Jay was sure, was about self-confidence and belief.

'Let me try,' said Thabisa.

Jay lifted her leg and rested her foot on the chair in front of Thabisa. 'That's nasty,' said Tiago. The skin over the toes and up to the ankle was an angry red colour, like a severe burn. 'How can you walk on that?'

'Close your eyes and relax a moment,' said Thabisa as she placed her cool hands on either side of Jay's foot. The cold brought a little relief, and Jay relaxed. She breathed deeply. Thabisa's hands slowly warmed, as if taking the heat from Jay's foot. She opened her eyes, half expecting to see a glowing light emanating from Thabisa, but there was nothing. Her eyes were closed and head bowed as she focused on Jay's injury. Tiago watched in silence. Thabisa's hands continued to absorb heat so that Jay's foot became cold. She moved her hands to another position and Jay saw that the redness on her skin beneath Thabisa's fingers had faded. Her foot was stiff, as if frozen. She moved her hands once more before finishing and sitting back in her chair, her eyes remaining closed.

Jay leaned forward to inspect her foot. The redness had almost entirely gone. She rolled her foot around, stretching the ankle. Tiago smiled, pride in his eyes. Jay lifted herself carefully from her chair, naturally avoiding putting weight on her foot. Tentatively, she shifted weight to her vulnerable side. It felt strong. No pain. She looked to Thabisa as she opened her eyes, snapping out of her trance. 'That felt like it went well,' Thabisa said. 'The energy was strong. How is it?'

Jay laughed. 'It's good!'

Tiago laughed too. 'This is progress.'

Jay paced the room, testing her foot. 'It's good,' she said, again. 'Thank you.'

* * *

TOYAH NAVIGATED the truck through the City without urgency, deciding that inconspicuous was preferable to quick. She chose the back roads to stay out of sight of any Readers who might be patrolling. It was early morning, and the streets were already bustling. People hopeful for fresh bread formed long queues through the buildings. There were more mopeds and motorbikes than cars, weaving in and out of each other, their exhausts spewing smoke.

The warmth and humidity already rose from the streets. It wouldn't be long before the hot South African sun burned through the clouds and scorched their skin. She stretched out her foot, testing for signs of any residual pain, and felt nothing. Thabisa had done a good job.

Toyah sped up around a corner and passed by a police Land Rover. Jay instinctively sank down in the passenger seat of the truck as Toyah maintained speed. The police Land Rover turned off into a side street and Jay breathed again. Toyah eased off the accelerator and took a sequence of turns so they were deep in the back streets of the City centre. They were out of sight, and once again edging slowly towards the demolition site that was once the source of power for the Given in this land.

A little under half an hour later, they parked alongside the perimeter fence that marked the edge of the crater. A thin layer of dust hung in the air above the mangled concrete and steel that was once a high rise building. In the heat hung a smell like the construction site near Jay's home, when they doubled the size of the housing estate in less than six months. Scanning the perimeter, Jay noticed something she'd not seen when they had emerged from the source. There were two huts, one on each side of the site. They were small, just big enough for one or two people to shade from the sun.

'Security?' said Toyah. A man emerged from a hut, leaned up against the security fence, then returned to the shade.

'And there,' Jay said, and pointed towards the other hut.

'They weren't there before,' Toyah said.

A Land Rover pulled up by the one on the south side. Half a dozen people spilled out from the vehicle. 'Readers,' said Toyah. 'Can you feel it?'

Jay nodded, not daring to take her eyes off the group of Readers, one of whom approached the security guard. 'That's him,' said Jay. 'That's the one from back at the farm. He's a level 8.'

'We need to continue to shield,' said Toyah, already moving towards the fence. As Toyah manipulated the fence so they could squeeze through, a second Land Rover appeared on the north side, screeching to a halt at the other security hut. A new group of Readers emerged.

'They're looking for us,' said Toyah, before following Jay through the fence. Their strategy would have to be speed. They scampered down the slope and into the concrete labyrinth.

Toyah led the way as Jay concentrated on shielding as best she could, hoping that the tangle of concrete and metal around them would help to at least confuse any signal to the Readers.

They picked their way through the concrete jungle,

following the route back that took them past a vending machine, emptied of its chocolate bars, and the row of cabinets spewing files.

Toyah reached the hole that led down to the basement where the three watercourses converged and was about to lower herself through when they heard a bang.

Readers moved across the concrete beams above their heads. Jay made a signal for Toyah to press on, and she disappeared into the hole. A scatter of dust and debris fell on Jay's head and she shielded, but felt the Readers tapping away at her defences. Their leader, the level 8, was directly above her, his heartbeat, his anger beat in Jay's veins.

She draped her feet over the hole, not taking her eyes off the figures silhouetted against the sky above her head. If they looked down, they might not see her, but would sense her. As these thoughts passed through her mind, the level 8 Reader looked straight at her, catching her eye through the gaps in the tangle of rubble between them. He read her immediately, his blue-eyed gaze penetrating her mind. In a moment, he knew where both she and Toyah were – and how close they were to the source.

Jay slipped through the hole and began running. She was moving too fast, her foot slid on a wet surface and she bashed her knee, crying out. She caught up with Toyah just as she manoeuvred herself to hang and then drop to the floor of the basement. 'Get ready,' Jay called.

A shot rang out behind them – the bullet ricocheting off the concrete. A speculative effort by the Readers. Jay landed on the floor of the basement as Toyah rested one hand in the water and held out the other for Jay to connect.

Debris tumbled through the hole in the basement's ceiling.

White light radiated from the middle of the connection between Jay and Toyah.

The black boots of a Reader emerged from above. His legs, then his torso. He dropped to the ground, launched himself at Jay.

White light filled the basement. The Reader fell, and Jay saw his physical form dissolve into the light, his face a picture of agony.

* * *

JAY WOKE WITH A START, recoiling from the image in her mind of the Reader in the basement – his piercing blue eyes dissolving into nothing as the energy of the source overcame him.

She brushed the sand from the side of her face and sat up. The tree to her side was blackened. A coil of darkness stretched up its trunk into the canopy above, where it had already strangled and suffocated the life from its branches. Across the water, Island 8, her home, remained a shining light amongst the darkness of the rest of the Islands.

She took a deep breath and pushed herself to her feet.

Toyah woke.

In the water between the Islands, there was a clear pathway avoiding the swirls of darkness. The two friends exchanged a glance. 'Let's get home,' Jay said, and stepped into the water.

16

The blinding white light that characterised the passage through the source rapidly dissipated as Jay plunged into the water of the Interland pool.

The aftereffects of moving through the source messed with her senses. Disorientated, she struggled in the water, unable to discern which way was up. Her lungs burned. She exhaled forcefully to ease the pressure and pain and saw the surface of the water, an impossible distance away. She kicked her legs and began to rise.

As she neared the light, debris rained down on the pool, the rocks shooting past Jay as she powered toward the surface. As she drew closer, the muffled noises became louder and clearer.

Shouting.

Explosions.

Her head burst through the water and as she gasped for air, a piece of rock glanced off the side of her head, cutting a gash down her cheek. Blood diffused into the water. She cried out, gasping. Her head swam with pain, the water stung her wound. She kicked hard to get back to the surface, her focus on nothing else but getting to the edge of the pool before another rock stopped her for good.

Another explosion.

This time, Jay ducked under the surface as the rocks rained down, dodging the full force of the debris.

She pulled herself into the shallows and finally looked up at the devastation before her. The caves of the Interland had been all but destroyed. There were people, Readers, busying across her field of vision, unaware of her presence. They continued to position explosives. 'Clear!' came a shout from the rock face, then an almighty explosion and a further downpour of rocks.

'Toyah?' Jay whispered under her breath.

A scream rang out from the other side of the pool where Toyah tussled with two Readers. They knocked her to the floor, but she recovered, kicking out as the men approached her once more, this time subduing her. Jay watched, too far away to help. She and Toyah had landed in a completely different world to the one they'd left.

Toyah screamed again. Jay thought about running the perimeter of the pool but knew that too many Readers would see her. She wouldn't be able to fight them all, not injured and alone. Instead, she tucked herself tight to the wall and focused on the two Readers who had Toyah by the arms and were dragging her away. Jay's heart pounded, pumping the anger through her body.

Jay easily entered their minds and began to dig. She closed her eyes, pinpointing her focus. The two men fell to their knees, their hands to the sides of their heads, and Toyah ran, heading for Jay. Jay continued digging into the Readers until she was sure they wouldn't get up again.

The Interland pool was fast becoming a lake as the caves

continued to disintegrate and the ground beneath their feet shook.

Jay felt the power of darkness nipping at her consciousness and turned to see Readers on the side of the lake, facing them. They were joining their power together to infiltrate the minds of Jay and Toyah.

Jay and Toyah stood facing their attackers across the water. They held hands. Jay grit her teeth and together they focused their energy. It was like a torrent through Jay, channelled from the power of the Interland.

The three Readers nearest them took their full force and stumbled back against the rock face. Jay pushed, drawing energy from the ground, and from the water of the lake, the hills, and the source. Vines and tree roots broke free of the rock face and entwined the three Readers, pulling them into the cliff, deeper as Jay opened to the power flowing through her. Their physical forms squeezed into the side of the hill until they were no longer visible.

Jay moved on to the second group of Readers, pushing until they each dropped to their knees in the shallows of the lake. They sank deeper as Jay summoned the full power of the environment. Soon they were up to their chests in the soft bed of the lake. As Jay pushed harder, they fought back. Their combined power strong given their distance from the nearest sink-room and source of dark energy. But Jay's power, with Toyah, was at its peak. She gave one final push and the heads of the three submerged Readers disappeared below the surface of the lake.

With the remaining Readers scattered into the caves, Jay and Toyah picked their way back across the rocks to an alcove in the cliff wall.

Toyah looked around in disbelief. 'The Interland…'

'Gone,' said Jay, feeling a deep sadness.

'Like Island 7,' said Toyah.

The landscape around the lake was unrecognisable. They stood at the base of a pit, like a quarry, the sides steeply rising to woodland above. It was as if the entire area of caves had imploded, bringing the surface into the hole, and disturbing the natural flow of the three rivers. The mass of rock that formed the underground cave network had been levelled, leaving a barren slope of boulders and rubble down to the shore of the lake. What was once a deep pool some hundred feet across at the most was now a wide lake spread over an area that, before, was underground. Jay couldn't tell where the original source would have been - somewhere below the surface of the lake. Three rivers continued to feed the lake. The sparkle of the unnamed river was clear as it meandered through to the eastern side.

Sun warmed Jay's face. A light breeze played with her hair, bringing the scent of the woodland. 'The power is still here,' said Jay. 'Same as on Island 7. The power comes from the convergence of these three watercourses.' Jay dipped her hand in the shallow edge of the lake. The energy flowed into her body as she expected. 'Try it,' she said to Toyah.

Toyah did the same, turning to Jay with a smile to acknowledge that she felt it too. Her expression darkened. 'It's been a long time since I've seen that many Readers here.'

'They weren't strong,' said Jay. 'They offered almost no resistance. Maybe they were using the power of the source on Island 7. Like Flick.'

'How do they come here?' asked Toyah.

'Through their source, the power from the core that exists at the old prison.'

Footsteps sounded on the stones and Jay turned to see a figure approach. Toyah peered into the shadows at the base of the rock slope as the figure emerged and walked towards them.

'Flick?' said Jay.

Toyah looked at Jay, then at Flick. 'The Reader? She's the one. She led them here. She did this?' Toyah reached for Flick as she approached, knocking her to the floor as soon as she was within reach. Before Jay could intervene, Toyah was astride Flick and grappling to hold her down, the anger glowing red in her face. Flick resisted without a word, protecting her face from a glancing blow from Toyah.

Jay grabbed Toyah by the arms, dragging her away. 'It's not her,' she said.

Flick stood and brushed herself down while Toyah seethed. Jay put a hand on Flick's arm and felt that her energy was weak. She'd been away from the source of power on Island 7 for too long. She'd had enough of the battling, the fear of the Given, and the fear of Atta. She was exhausted and had nowhere to go.

'What happened here?' asked Jay.

Flick held Jay's eye. 'I don't know.'

'Why are you here?' Toyah blurted.

Jay answered, 'She came to find us.' Flick's shoulders slumped. Her face was drawn, and she swayed as she struggled to remain upright. Jay pulled Flick's arm around her shoulders. 'Let's get out of here,' she said.

17

Jay dropped Toyah at home, then drove Flick to the bookshop. Alf set up the spare room in his apartment out the back of the shop so that Flick could rest. She was asleep before Jay and Alf even left the room.

'Maybe we should let her know about the panic room, just in case?' Jay said, knowing that Alf would never agree but testing his response.

Alf gave a single, emphatic shake of his head. He wouldn't entertain any notion of revealing its existence to anyone but Jay and Stitch. Even Cassie didn't know, and there was no way that he would allow a Reader to know about it, whatever her allegiances.

'You trust her?' Alf said, as they headed back into the shop.

Jay nodded. 'What she told me I've now seen for myself, it's all true. She's coming back to the Given. Isn't that what we hope for all Readers, eventually?'

Alf gave a gentle nod, and Jay motioned for them to head upstairs.

'See your family,' Alf said.

'Later,' said Jay, heading for the stairs.

On the top floor, Jay talked Alf through every step of her journey with Toyah. Alf rested back in his chair, taking it in. Buster curled up under the table. Alf didn't seem surprised at the extent of deterioration of Island 7 that Jay described. 'Colson has called on help from the London branch of your dad's *new resistance*,' Alf said.

'How will they help?' Jay asked, watching as Alf mumbled to himself, searching through papers. 'There was *something* back at the Interland about the...' He spread more papers over the table, next to the books already piled two feet high. 'There's something more in here about the source of the dark energy.'

'The London branch,' Jay said. 'What do they have that we don't?'

'Judith. I told you about her.' Jay nodded. 'And Hannah. Friend of Judith. They have a lot of knowledge. Your dad's gang has worked with them before.'

Jay looked at the mass of papers and picked up a single sheet from the table but could decipher less than 10% of the words, the rest either too faint or in a language she couldn't understand. She placed the soft, yellowing piece of paper carefully back on the table. 'We have to help them on Island 7.'

'First, we need to make sure we can protect ourselves,' Alf said, his expression grave.

'Their power comes from the core, channelled and controlled by their new sink-room. We need to destroy it.'

Alf shook his head. 'We've been here before,' he said. 'This time, we have to interrupt the flow of their power from the core permanently. Destroying the buildings clearly does nothing.'

Jay knew Alf was right. She could think of no means to stop the source of dark power. 'It might be impossible? Our

Interland has been destroyed beyond all recognition, yet our power is just as strong.'

'I feel it too,' said Alf, resting back in his chair. 'It's not the source itself. The physical arrangement of the caves and rocks at the source is not important. We know that now. The rivers are still there, so the power comes.'

'What if it's the same for the energy from the core? What if there's no way of stopping the flow of darkness?'

Alf looked at the overwhelming pile of indecipherable papers on the table. 'There's a way,' he said, his tone unconvincing.

'What if I face him?'

Alf's expression hardened. 'From what you described to me about your recent encounter, that is the worst idea that's come out of you, my girl. Your suicide will not help the cause.'

'Not on Island 7, but *here*, where my power is the strongest?'

A noise from the stairs. Buster's ears pricked up, his eyes fixed on the top of the stairwell. Jay and Alf turned to see Colson stepping up the final stair and onto the top floor. Buster gave a single bark then settled as Alf raised a hand to reassure him. Colson was breathless, resting a moment, his hand on the door frame and two heavy books cradled in his other arm. 'I think it's you,' he said to Jay.

'What...?' Alf started.

'Maram,' said Colson, pausing again for breath. He moved closer and sat next to Alf. Buster growled, and Jay placed a reassuring hand on the dog's head.

Colson edged a little away from Alf. 'It's like we said. I've spoken to Judith. You remember her?' Alf nodded and stole a glance at Jay. 'And I've been reading this one.' Colson plonked one of the big old notebooks on the table. 'We thought Maram was simply a symbol, someone to give the true power of the

Given a physical form. The ultimate 8C if you like. An 8C-plus.' He smiled.

'What are you talking about?' said Alf.

'A symbol. Like Atta is the symbol to represent the dark, Maram is the symbol to represent the power of the Given.'

'We know that but...'

'But,' Colson interrupted. 'What if Maram and Atta are not just fairytales? I cross-referenced the story in here,' he tapped the cover of the old notebook, 'with recorded historical events of the time, and I found something.' He sat back as if waiting for applause.

'What?' said Jay.

'Here,' Colson said, opening the second book, a contemporary encyclopaedia, its gloss cover in stark contrast to the other references on the table. 'The *Shamakhi* earthquake of 1667.' He paused again. Alf and Jay waited for explanation. 'I scanned current maps, and look here... At the recorded epicentre, there's a village. See what it's called?' He pointed to the full-page map in the encyclopaedia.

'Maramatta?' repeated Jay. 'As in, *Maram – Atta*?'

Colson nodded.

Alf leaned to get a closer look. 'What does it mean?'

'Over 1,000 people killed,' said Colson. 'They *say* it was an earthquake, but of course the records are sketchy, and much of the narrative around the event hints at a post-event desolation that sounds very much like what you get in a world of Readers – a withering environment, wide scale destruction of animal and plant life, deprivation, and famine.'

'So, what are you saying?' said Alf.

'I think this was the last clash of Maram and Atta, in whatever form they took at that time.' They were quiet for a minute as Alf and Jay took in the information. The words in the old notebook were barely decipherable. Interpretation was subjective. But the name of the village in the contemporary reference was clear. 'So,' Colson said, 'this confirms, in my mind...'

Alf finished Colson's sentence. 'The existence of the powers back as far as the 1600s.'

'Yes. And the power of the conflict between the Given – Maram – and the Dark, Atta.' Colson continued, 'The most recent incarnation of Maram was probably Sasha Colden. But, during her reign, the Readers were contained. And, thanks to Jay, were contained again. But now...'

'What?' said Jay.

'I think that the current incarnation of Maram is you,' Colson said. 'And Atta has returned. He has reached a point where the power of the core is sufficient to sustain him once more.'

'Oh no, it can't be...' started Alf, shaking his head.

'The earthquake,' said Jay, 'That was the ground-zero for the confrontation?'

Colson nodded. 'That's what Judith and Hannah think.'

'And Atta came out on top?' said Jay.

'We don't know. But the fact that it was contained to that single event, and no further spread of the darkness materialised, makes me think Atta was contained. Or destroyed.'

No one agreed or disagreed with Colson. They all just looked worried.

* * *

JAY NEEDED SPACE TO BREATHE. Back at her desk on the top floor, she tidied the papers and books into piles. She sat down and flicked through a book she'd already catalogued. She'd read it twice over the past few months, in shifts. It was one of the more progressive titles, delving under the surface of attitudes towards the powers, the already developing gender stereotypes, and the presentation of a vision for equality that could be written into the DNA of society, through education and policy, *before* the tendencies to prejudice surfaced and become embedded. It received little attention.

On the back cover was a picture of the author, a woman Jay's age. How could someone so young write a book of such authority? "The Three Pillars: A New Approach to Power". She pushed the words around inside her mind and allowed them to spill onto her tongue: 'Three pillars,' she whispered. Things always seemed to come in threes. Something clicked in Jay's memory, something she'd read, or something Colson had said.

She sprang from her chair and rejoined Alf and Colson. 'The darkness has been threatening,' she said, drawing their attention. 'But it hasn't arrived as such. It can't actually *come* here. Atta cannot venture into our land. We know that, because of the three conditions.'

Alf frowned and looked at Colson. Colson nodded thoughtfully. 'Yes,' Colson said. 'But how confident can we be that the conditions won't be met?'

'What conditions?' Alf straightened in his chair, looking mildly annoyed.

'Something Jay and I discussed before. You were there, Alf, don't look so surprised.' Alf slumped in his chair.

'Tell us again,' Jay said to Colson.

'We should take these words seriously. There is evidence of their validity. But we need to remember the darkness cannot prevail where there is no firm connection to their source of power. And to create such a connection, as we have established, they need to be embedded here. So it's a chicken-and-egg situation.'

Alf shifted in his seat, impatient. 'The *conditions*?'

'Yes. Without their connection, as the legend goes, and this has been confirmed by Judith and Hannah.'

'Do they have power?' asked Jay.

Colson shook his head. 'Not that I am aware of. You don't need to *have* power to study and understand its history.'

'Carry on,' Jay encouraged.

'To move between lands, one must fulfil the three conditions, after which they are free to create their permanent connection with their power.' Colson sat back in his seat, making himself comfortable. 'So we need to make sure those conditions cannot be met.'

'And the conditions are...' Alf pushed.

'The first condition is that there must be a channel opened between the two lands, a channel that connects the darkness with the power of the Given.'

'What's that supposed to mean?' Alf asked.

'Your guess is as good as mine,' Colson said, becoming annoyed with Alf's impatience. 'That's as much as we can glean from the words. It's up to us to figure out what it means.'

'What do Judith and Hannah say?' Alf asked, a hint of mockery in his tone.

Colson ignored the baiting question.

'And the second?' asked Jay.

'The second condition is a little clearer. It says that there needs to be an *invitation* from the Given to the Dark.'

'Well, that will never happen,' said Jay.

'You'd think not, but the Dark is devious,' said Colson with a shrug. 'The third is more sinister. This one is right out of the witches' playbook. It says that for the last condition to be met, there needs to be a sacrifice.'

Jay sat up straight. 'Seriously? A sacrifice. At the altar or something?'

'The spill of blood in the land sacred to the Given.'

'The Interland?' said Jay.

Alf shook his head and leaned forward, placing his head in his hands. 'It's not clear.'

'It's pretty clear to me,' Jay said. 'We have a solid barrier. He can toy at the edges, but he can't come here. We just need to keep it that way.'

* * *

FLICK APPEARED in the doorway and fear spread across Colson's face. He slammed his books shut. 'Who's this?'

Jay introduced Flick, but Colson interrupted. 'A Reader,' he said. 'You shouldn't be here.'

'It's OK,' said Jay. This is Flick. She's been helping us.' Colson continued to back away from Flick, his two books clutched tight to his chest. He eventually stopped when he had placed Jay between himself and Flick.

'Hi,' said Flick, her voice little more than a whisper. 'Yes, I am a Reader.' She turned to Jay. 'I need you to *reduce* me.'

Jay looked into Flick and saw only pain.

Flick gasped, 'If you don't reduce me, I will die. I can't sustain myself here, and I won't go back to them. I want to be reduced.'

Jay and Alf exchanged a glance, and Jay turned to Flick. 'Tomorrow,' she said. 'We will do it tomorrow.'

18

As Jay made her way to the hospital, she felt a message coming through the energy from her dad. She pushed a message back to say that she was OK, but before she could head home, she needed to see Angie. The sense she got on her way up to the sixth floor confirmed that Angie was awake. On the ward, there was no sign of her. A nurse approached. 'Who are you looking for?'

'The little girl, Angie?'

'She woke about ten minutes ago.' The nurse smiled at the good news. 'She's gone for some tests. Her parents are through here...' She motioned for Jay to follow.

'It's OK,' Jay said. I don't want to get in the way of family. I just wanted to see that she was OK.'

The nurse looked disappointed for a moment, then went back to her duties. 'Shall I tell her you were here?'

'Thanks. Just say that Jay was here.'

'Anything else?'

'No. Just say I was here.' She turned and headed back to the car park.

By the time Jay arrived home that night, the house was

asleep. She crept through the alleyway at the back and up onto her roof, slipping through the window and into bed.

She woke mid-morning, still half-clothed, to the sound of a bird squawking outside her window. Turning onto her back, she listened for the sounds of her family. They'd be worried about her. The muffled, low frequency of her dad's voice filtered through the floor. A faint smell of coffee.

She showered and made her way downstairs. Sonia startled at the sight of Jay entering the kitchen. Ben immediately held her, saying nothing. When her dad finally released Jay from the hug, she caught her mum wiping a tear from her face. Sonia turned her head away. 'We didn't know if you were dead or alive,' she said, and her voice turned stern. 'You should have told us where you were.'

'Hey,' said Ben. 'I told you she was OK.' Ben had a connection with Jay that prevailed when they were apart. 'I knew she was fine.'

'I'm OK, Mum,' said Jay, reaching for Sonia's arm.

Jay told them about her excursion to Island 7, about Flick, and about the possibility that the Readers were hunting for a route onto Island 8.

'So where is Flick?' asked Ben.

'With Alf at the shop,' said Jay, switching on the kettle to make tea.

'And what's she going to do? She's a Reader?'

'A reluctant Reader. She wants to be reduced, so that she can develop again as one of the Given.'

'Can she do that?' asked Sonia.

'Marcus did,' said Jay. The mention of Marcus's name brought a silence to the kitchen. The kettle clicked off. 'Where's Sammy?'

'In bed,' Ben said.

'I'll go see him.'

With tea in hand, she headed up the stairs to Sammy's room. Voices came through from the other side of his door. She recognised Toyah's voice and sensed tension. She knocked and walked in without waiting for a reply. 'Hey.' Jay smiled at her brother and Toyah, sitting upright, squeezed together in a single bed. An air of conflict between them. 'Look at you two, lovebirds.' She put a hand briefly on her brother's head before sitting on the end of the bed.

'I've been hearing about Island 7,' said Sammy. 'What are we going to do?'

'Not sure yet.' She sipped her tea.

Sammy's bedroom door swung open and Cassie appeared in the opening. 'Do about what?' She pushed the door closed behind her and took a seat on Sammy's bed, next to Jay.

'Seriously?' Sammy said, his pitch rising. 'This room is barely big enough for me.' Toyah slipped down against the wall to make herself small. Cassie nudged Sammy's and Toyah's legs out of the way so that she could sit and lean back against the wall.

Toyah edged out of Cassie's way. 'How's Otis?' she asked. 'Did you see him last night?'

Cassie answered, without looking at Toyah. 'He's upstairs actually, with Pinto.'

'In my room?' asked Jay.

Cassie nodded. 'On the roof.'

Sammy put a hand on Toyah's arm, but she refused to look at him. Whatever their disagreement, it hung in the air like a weight. Sammy looked at Jay and widened his eyes when he said, 'Why don't you guys go up and see Otis and Pinto? We'll come up in a minute.'

Cassie jumped off the bed and headed up without another word. Jay followed, giving her brother a wink as she left his room.

Otis and Pinto were sitting together on the roof outside Jay's room. Jay climbed out to join them. Cassie peered through the window, leaning on the ledge. 'Hey,' she said. 'You want coffee?'

Otis nodded, and Pinto opted for tea. 'Hi Pinto,' Jay said, pulling him into a side-by-side hug as Cassie disappeared.

'We missed you,' he said.

'Heard you had an adventure,' Otis added.

'Something like that,' said Jay. 'Could have used you two, with your skills.'

Pinto smiled. 'Otis has been teaching me. Shall we show you?'

Jay nodded, and Pinto sat up, readying himself. 'There are some movements that are easier than others. If there's organic matter, carbon-based material, and it's light, then that's easy.' He looked at Otis for an encouraging nod. 'So those leaves, for example.' Pinto was quiet for a moment as he focused on transmitting his energy through the scattering of green leaves on the roof, fallen from the overhead sycamore. Within a few seconds, the leaves moved, then with a whoosh, they flew off the roof as if blown by a sudden gust of wind.

'Impressive,' said Jay.

'What about something a little more challenging?' said Otis.

'The same is true for bigger things, of organic constituents. Like the tree. It's bigger, but relatively easy compared to something smaller that's inorganic – like a wall, concrete or metal.' Pinto focused on the great sycamore rooted in the garden next door and towering above Jay's roof. The branches swayed for a moment before the entire trunk of the tree tilted to the side so that its leaves brushed the roof of Jay's house. He released his focus, and the tree sprang back into place, its leaves rustling and birds scattering.

'That's brilliant, Pinto. You've been practising. So what about other stuff that's not living. That's more difficult?'

'Takes more focus,' said Otis. 'But I'm getting the hang of it.'

Cassie appeared at the window, handing mugs of hot drinks out to Otis and Pinto. 'You controlled those guns back at the Interland,' she said to Otis.

'The energy of the other people there made a difference, especially as it was life or death.'

'It might have been the person you controlled,' said Pinto. 'Not the metal gun?'

'Maybe. The natural energy inside all of us, including the Readers, and those without power, makes it easier to manipulate people than objects.'

Jay sensed Pinto was trying something. His influence tugged at her. She smiled, avoiding looking at him. A pull on her legs made her slip a little on the tiles. A stronger pull, and she slipped onto her back with a squeal as Pinto erupted in laughter. The others laughed too as Jay righted herself. Otis gave Pinto a high-five.

19

Later that afternoon, Jay arrived at the bookshop to find it locked up. She knocked on the door. Alf opened up from the inside. 'I heard Colson found something,' said Jay.

Alf raised a hand in a gesture, asking for patience, then closed the door behind Jay. He opened the blinds to allow just enough light into the dark bookshop for them to navigate to the stairs. 'Don't want anyone thinking we're open for business today,' he said.

'Where's Flick?' asked Jay.

'Out back. She was asleep. I'll check on her then we can head upstairs.'

As Alf left the room, Colson burst through the front door in a bluster, tripping over the threshold. 'Sorry,' he said, closing and bolting the door behind him. 'I found something. Where's Alf? Let's go up.' Without another word, he took the stairs two at a time. Alf returned, indicating that Flick was asleep, and that she was OK. They followed Colson, swept up the stairs in the wake of his enthusiasm.

The three sat at the table with the literature of the Given

spread out in front of them. Colson remained standing, and like a conductor, he began. 'So, what do we know?' Alf made to respond, but Colson held up a finger. 'We know that the balance has tipped, and Atta is here.'

'Well...' Alf began, his tone unsure.

'Yes,' said Jay emphatically.

'Good,' said Colson. 'And we know that whatever he is, he is powerful, and he channels the power of the Readers. He's like a super-Reader? Yes?'

Jay nodded. 'He's part of the dark power. He doesn't channel the power of the Readers, he has his own power, and it's on a scale like nothing else.'

'He's seeking a route through to our land here. We are the last stop on his railroad to complete power. He's looking to establish a base on each of the eight Islands, a link to the core in each energy centre, do you agree?' asked Colson.

'Yes,' said Jay. 'Ours might be the last remaining freedom for the Given.'

'We also know that we can't simply destroy the buildings and the infrastructure around the sink-room. It's the connection to the core that channels the power. The rest of it is just window dressing.'

'And they need electromagnets...' began Jay.

'Only to allow the Readers to remain *charged*,' interrupted Colson. 'But like the source at the Interland, the power is the power. It's there, as long as there is an environment, living things, to enable the power of the Given. And the Readers' power is there as long as there is a deep connection with the core.'

'Makes sense,' said Alf. Jay agreed.

'So the *only* way we win, the *only* way we can survive in the longer term, is by severing the connection with the core.'

'Agreed,' said Alf.

'Or we defend this place from the Readers,' said Jay. 'If they can't come here, if Atta can't come here, then they'll never overpower us.'

'Yes,' said Colson. 'In the short term, perhaps. But longer term, the risk is too great that they find a way through to fulfil the three conditions. Back in 1667, the so-called earthquake came *after* a period of hardship, not before. So it was the event of 1667 that *ended* the period of depravation, famine, and drought, not started it.'

Alf thought for a moment, then said, 'You think the period before this last earthquake was the period of Atta's control?'

Colson nodded.

Jay said, 'So the event, whatever it was, the earthquake, put an end to the Reader control, and an end to the desolation? What happened?'

'I don't know, but I *think* the Shamakhi earthquake in 1667 occurred at the location of the original connection to the core, and the place where the Readers drew their energy.'

'Is it on one of the Islands?' said Jay.

Colson nodded. 'And maybe this location is now free of the dark power, because they found a way to sever the connection between the core and the surface.'

Jay thought back to the vision of the Islands, connected in a circle of eight, all enveloped in darkness. 'But all the other seven islands are blackened. We saw them.'

'Are you sure? Absolutely? If I am right, then one of those Islands is free. Probably Island *One*.'

Jay shook her head. 'Island One is dark, if that's the other closest to our Island 8. Both seven and one are dark.'

Colson sat down. 'What about the others?'

'All dark as far as we could see...' Jay thought for a moment. 'I'm not sure. There could be one on the far side that's not dark.'

'There must be. I don't know whether it's Island One or Four or whatever, but I *think* this place, Shamakhi, is the first to be free of Atta. The first to have severed the connection. So there is a way.'

* * *

COLSON AND ALF continued to debate the merits of Colson's theory as Jay sought solace back at her desk. She couldn't help but be drawn to her usual comfort that was the Sasha Colden book, her means to connect most deeply with the true power of the Given. If any of Colson's theories had merit, then surely she would have seen something in the Sasha Colden book, or felt something when the book took her to a higher plane. She was sure that this book held the answers to Colson's questions.

She returned to Alf and Colson, making a show of placing the book on the table between them before taking her seat.

'The biography?' asked Colson.

'Autobiography. It was penned by Sasha's hand. It contains her very essence, her energy. It's at the heart of everything I know to be true about the powers. You said it could be the key?'

Colson nodded. 'But you've read it all,' said Alf. 'More than once. There's nothing more in there that you don't already know.'

Jay agreed. She'd read it probably a hundred times, and each time had deepened her inner understanding of her world, and of the Given, in ways she couldn't articulate. She expected to read it another hundred times.

'There are elements that make no literal sense to me yet,' she said, thinking particularly of the last pages where the text deteriorated into a mix of languages. Jay had never worried too much about the literal meaning of those sections because the inner meaning came through in her subconscious. There was no reason for her to study the detail of the words. That wasn't the point as far as she could feel.

'What do you mean?' said Alf. 'You never said…'

'If there's an answer in here, then that's where it's hidden.'

Alf put a hand on the cover of the Sasha Colden book as if trying to feel its answers. Colson opened one of the old notebooks and pointed to the full-page map. 'See here,' he said.

'The village?' Alf said. 'Maramatta?'

'Yes, but look here,' he pointed to what looked like a reflection of the village outline in the space next to it. In very faint letters, the name of the village was repeated, but this time spelled backwards.

'*Attamaram*,' said Jay. 'Atta is a palindrome, and so is Maram.'

'So what? What does it mean?' said Alf.

Colson frowned, a bead of perspiration forming on his forehead as Jay watched him scour his mind for answers. She picked up the Sasha Colden book and flicked directly to the end section, where the words scattered more like a waterfall than the logical flow of a river. She studied the words and letters systematically for the first time, casting her eyes over their sequence, using logic instead of intuition for once.

'Turn it over,' said Alf. Jay looked at him quizzically. 'Turn the book over and read the words backwards.'

Colson peered over Jay's shoulder. 'These words mean little enough in the forward direction.'

'The palindrome,' said Alf. 'It might be the key. Try it upside down and backwards.'

Jay did as Alf suggested. She sat back and allowed her eyes to flow over the words, following their path backwards from the top of the upside-down page until the patterns emerged.

'Source... Stone,' Jay said, picking the letters from the sea of words on the upside-down page.

'What?' said Alf, leaning to get a look at what Jay was reading. 'Where?'

Jay tilted the book towards Alf but he simply frowned and shook his head, and Jay wasn't sure whether the letters she just picked out were actually on the page, or if they were in her head.

'What's the source stone?' asked Jay.

'Was there something at the source? A key-stone, or a central structure?' Colson asked.

Jay shook her head.

'There must have been something?'

Jay pictured the damp cave that was the confluence of the three streams of water at the Interland. The flows emerged from the rock and converged at a central pillar, into a bowl-like rock scoured from decades of flow from the three rivers, then out into the cracks in the rock floor. 'The bowl,' she said.

Alf and Colson waited for Jay to elaborate.

'The point at which the three streams converge.' She looked at Alf. He'd seen it. 'You remember?'

'I can't think what it's like down there. I was only there the one time.'

'It must be the *bowl*. It's a stone that's been battered by the magic of the unnamed river for decades.'

'We need to find it,' said Alf.

'We can't,' said Jay. 'The entire Interland has been destroyed. There's nothing left.'

'It will still be there, somewhere,' said Colson.

'I told you, everything's gone. The whole of the cave system is under water. There is no source.' As Jay said the words, a tingle of energy flowed over the surface of her skin. She faltered and rested her head in her hands. There was a chance that she'd sense the power of the source stone if it was near.

Colson seemed to read the energy in Jay. 'I think we can find it. We can go together and...'

'I'll go alone,' said Jay.

Colson looked disappointed. Alf shifted in his seat. 'Take Stitch, and Cassie, at least. You might need some help if you run into Readers.'

'No, I need the space to connect.'

'Then take Stitch...'

'I have to connect alone. With no interference.' She thought of Stitch. If he could hear her, he'd be annoyed. They'd drifted a little, and she couldn't figure if she should allow him space to find his own pathway, or if she should try to re-connect.

Colson and Alf looked at each other. Colson gave a slight nod, and Alf sighed in resignation. Jay felt a powerful need to be at the Interland without distraction. She would connect once more with the source on her own terms, with no compromise. She would connect with her roots, and if the source stone had survived, she'd find it.

20

Jay locked the door behind Colson and, as she turned to head back up to Alf on the top floor, she caught sight of Flick standing in the shadows. 'You scared me, standing there like a ghost.'

'Are you going somewhere?' asked Flick.

Jay hesitated. 'Not sure yet. How are you feeling?'

Flick sighed. 'Tired.'

'Come up. We can sit with Alf.' Jay held out a hand to Flick, who instead took the banister. They ascended slowly, Flick taking regular rests.

'You need to do it now,' Flick said. 'I can't go on like this much longer.'

'Cassie and Otis are on their way,' said Jay. 'Alf and I will reduce you, then you can go with Otis to Highdown to re-build.' Highdown was one of the strongest sources of energy for the Given, along with the hilltops at Chanctonbury and Cissbury.

As Flick and Jay stepped up to the top floor, Alf saw them and moved to help Flick.

There was a bang on the door downstairs.

'That'll be Cassie,' said Jay, leaving Flick to Alf as she bounded back down the stairs. She swung open the shop door and caught Cassie and Otis in each other's arms. 'Sorry to interrupt,' she said with a smile. Cassie rolled her eyes and pushed past Jay into the shop. Otis, her unlikely partner, shorter and more upbeat than Cassie, followed.

Jay felt a momentary pang of sadness. She'd always assumed that *Sammy* and Cassie would be together one day. It was written in the stars. A year on from when Otis almost died at the battle for the Interland, and now he and Cassie were tight. And they were good together. Life was full of surprises.

Upstairs, Flick sat on a chair with her back to the window facing Alf. Cassie and Otis stood, waiting for Jay. 'If we work this together,' said Jay, 'we can control it better. We need to go easy. Too much infiltration and we'll do damage.' She turned to Flick. 'Are you sure?'

Flick nodded. 'Just be careful.'

Jay held Flick's hand, then reached for Cassie, motioning for Otis and Alf to complete the circle. 'Follow my lead,' she said, 'and go slowly.'

Flick closed her eyes and leaned back in her chair. Faint wisps of grey emanated from Flick, the remains of the darkness leaking from inside her. Cassie's energy flowed in support. Otis and Alf too, contributing, edging up the pressure as the last of Flick's power flowed from her body and into the room. *Slow down*, Jay said without speaking. The energy from the others eased off in response and Jay could bring Flick to a neutral state in a controlled manner. Flick slumped as Jay released her hand, then moved to support her to stop her from slipping onto the floor.

'Did it work?' asked Otis.

Jay nodded, placing her hand on the scar forming on the side of Flick's face. It wasn't the first scar that had marked

Flick's cheek. An older scar was clear, running alongside the new. Jay frowned as she studied the scars. It looked like there was a third scar, faded but visible. The poor girl had been reduced several times.

Flick twitched to consciousness and pulled her head away from Jay. They exchanged a glance and Jay read that Flick was uncomfortable with Jay studying her face.

Flick's eyes darted from Jay to the others and back to Jay. 'What happened?'

'You're safe. We reduced your power, the dark is now gone.'

Flick seemed to remember where she was and the process she'd been through. She puffed out her cheeks and leaned over with her hands on her knees. 'That was painful,' she said, staggering then leaning on the back of the chair.

'Slowly,' said Alf. 'There's no rush.'

'I need to get up to Highdown.'

As if this were his cue, Otis stood. Cassie asked if Otis wanted her to go too, but he shook his head. 'You need to go home, and there's only room for one on the back of the bike. Come up to see us tomorrow.' Otis put a hand on Cassie's shoulder and she placed her own hand on top of his.

Otis led Flick to the stairs to begin their journey to Highdown, where Flick would at last be able to leave behind the life of a Reader, and once again welcome the power of the Given.

* * *

AT HOME, Jay packed a small rucksack with some basic supplies – a change of clothes, waterproofs, and some cash. In the kitchen, she filled the pockets of the bag with food from the cupboard – bananas, chocolate and cereal bars.

As she slung the rucksack onto her back, Sammy walked in. 'You're leaving again?'

'Not for long. I'm not leaving the Island.'

Sammy looked visibly relieved that his sister wasn't planning on heading back into the lair of the Readers. He pushed his hair out of his eyes. 'Where, then?'

Jay contemplated what would be the short version of the story. 'I've been working with Alf and Colson on...'

'Colson?'

'Dad's friend at the club. We have a theory. I need to check it out.'

'You're heading to the Interland?' Jay nodded, and Sammy said, 'I thought it had been destroyed? There's nothing there?'

'It's still the source of the power. We think there's a *source stone*, something with the power to sever the Readers' connection to their own source, the connection to the core.'

Sammy frowned. Jay turned away from him, not wanting to be influenced by any of Sammy's scepticism. Not now. She needed to be focused. Sammy's frown broke, and he smiled. 'You need help?'

Jay relaxed. 'No, I need to do this on my own. If this thing is there, I'll find it.'

Sammy flung his long arms around Jay, and she allowed his gangly body to swallow her up for a moment.

'Tell Mum and Dad I'm fine,' said Jay. 'I'll be back in a day or so.'

'They're in there.' He motioned towards the lounge, where Jay could hear the muffled sound of the TV. 'Tell them yourself.'

Jay shook her head. 'Please? They'll start up again. I don't need to debate this right now. And can you speak to Stitch?'

'Why can't *you* speak to Stitch?'

'I need to go. Tell him not to worry. I'll be back before he knows it.'

Sammy agreed. 'You taking the Beast?' Jay nodded and checked her pocket for the car keys. Sonia shouted for Sammy to come into the lounge. He smiled, and Jay turned and headed out, quickly dissolving into the darkness as she broke into a run.

21

___

Up on Highdown Hill, Flick and Otis rested on a log by the fire inside the ring of trees. Flick already felt the energy of the Given flowing through the ground and into her body. Despite having experienced it before, it was a strange sensation. The tingle over her skin was different to that which came from the power of the Readers. Dark power from the core seemed to penetrate her bones. The power of the Given was superficial, flowing only over the surface of her body.

'You feel anything?' Otis asked.

'It's coming.'

Otis put a hand on Flick's shoulder, and she sensed his trust and affection. He was loyal to the Given. He *belonged*. These people were his family. She felt compassion, a sense of belonging to Otis's circle, and it caught her off-guard. She leaned away from him so that his hand slipped from her shoulder. The tightness of the community of the Given repelled her. She had experienced the power from both sides, and it was the power of the Given that most unsettled her. The power of the Readers was more direct, simple, and unambiguous. It came from the centre of the earth and radiated without discrimination. The power of the Given was selective. It chose its subjects, anointed the few.

She shook herself from contemplation and reminded herself of her mission. The triangle of conditions would soon be met. The pathway for Atta could be completed.

* * *

OTIS'S EXPRESSION WAS GRAVE. He sensed something shifting in Flick. She looked up into the trees, the grey sky visible between the branches, and the wind creating a chorus of rustling leaves. As Otis followed her gaze, she pulled her knife from its sheath strapped around her ankle. She leaned down and dragged the knife across the back of Otis's left heel, slicing deep across his Achilles tendon.

A second passed before the pain registered, and in that time, he leaned down and pulled up the leg of his trousers to see blood seeping from the cut. His face was twisted with pain and confusion.

He screamed and pushed himself away from Flick, but when he tried to stand, his leg gave way. He landed headfirst in the leaves on the woodland floor. As he struggled, Flick approached him once more and sliced his other Achilles. He screamed again before he began whimpering.

'Shh,' Flick said. 'Be still.' She tore a strip of cloth from her own shirt and tied it around his bleeding cut. Then another, tying both of his wounds in makeshift bandages to slow the bleeding.

'What...? Why?' Otis stammered.

'Atta will decide your fate now.' She again looked up into the trees. There was a whoosh and rustle of the wind in the branches and leaves. A wisp of darkness circled, the grey sky darkening by the second.

'Atta...' Flick said to herself.

Otis panted and groaned in pain. 'What's happening?'

'This is the final stage,' Flick said, brightening as she felt her master. Atta was close now. 'This is the last remaining Island. The ultimate destination.'

Otis turned over and pulled his knees to his chest. He reached down to feel for the wounds on his heels. Flick looked at him with some sympathy. She cleaned her knife on her shirt and slipped it back into its sheath. 'It won't be long now.'

The swirl of wind picked up again, collecting the leaves scattered over the floor inside the ring of trees and flinging them into the surrounding air.

Flick raised her hands, feeling the power of Atta in the air.

The wind seemed to take a physical form. The darkness mixed and merged with the scattered leaves. A swirl of energy. A shape appeared.

Atta.

The wind dropped.

Silence enveloped them like a heavy blanket.

As the leaves drifted to the floor, the figure of Atta stood in the forest like a ghost – the serenity belying the evil. He looked up and around himself, taking a deep breath, taking no notice of Flick or Otis.

After a moment, his gaze settled on Flick and he smiled. Without looking at the shivering Otis, curled up on the floor, he stepped up to Flick and put a hand on her shoulder. She immediately felt the weight of his power. The air caught in her throat and it was as if she were breathing thick treacle.

As he released her from his spell, she breathed again, stepping back from his great presence.

'You've done well,' he said, now looking down at Otis. 'For the third time, you don't disappoint.'

The first time Flick had facilitated Atta's movement between Islands was from Island 5 to Island 6. Then on to 7 and now, finally, to 8. How he had moved across all the Islands that were now dark, Flick did not know. She would surely hold a position of power in the new world. She would receive her thanks for the three scars on the side of her face – the sacrifice she had made in three times losing the power of the Readers, only to re-energise as the Given to facilitate Atta's movement between Islands. The three conditions had once more been met, thanks to Flick's manipulation of Jay and her friends.

'What now?' asked Flick, knowing that their destination was to be the prison, to finish the job the Readers had started. They would commission the final electro-magnets and begin the process that would ensure the balance towards Reader power would be maintained on Island 8. Then Atta could remain, and move freely between all the Islands. His power and his control would be unopposed.

'We leave,' said Atta, his words seeped from him - slow but controlled.

'The sink-room? The prison?'

'First, we have to head south. The bookshop.'

Flick looked down at Otis.

Atta said, 'Take off those bandages. We will leave him to the mercy of his environment that he so loves. He will see how it cannot protect him.'

Atta stepped away towards the outer ring of trees as Flick leaned down to release the makeshift bandages tied around Otis's ankles. The blood flowed as soon as she loosened the knots.

'Please...' said Otis, trying to make eye contact with Flick.

She shielded him, sensing that he was trying to get inside her head. 'Don't leave me here to die.'

Flick blocked out his words, standing with the blood-soaked bandages staining her fingers red. Fate would play a part in whether Otis lived or died. If he was meant to live, then he would find a way to those bandages, a way to stem the bleeding. But if it was not meant to be, then his end would come inside the inner circle. She threw the bloodied bandages into the bushes, and looked back just once, seeing that Otis had not moved from his foetal position on the floor, and she judged that his fate was decided.

22

Jay pulled open the garage door and secured it on its latch before climbing in to the old Ford, taking a breath of its familiar musty interior. It started first time, and she pushed it into gear, hesitating a moment as she thought about Stitch and Cassie, before releasing the clutch.

As the car edged forward, a figure appeared at the end of the bonnet. She slammed on the brakes and rocked back in her seat, straining her eyes to see who it was. 'Stitch?' She said under her breath.

He moved around and climbed in to the passenger side of the car, a small rucksack on his back. 'Ready?' he said.

Jay switched off the engine. 'What are you doing?'

'Coming with you.'

'How did you know?'

Stitch pulled back his sleeve to remind Jay of his marking, of their connection. 'And Alf told me.'

Jay huffed and looked away. 'I didn't want...'

'What is it, Jay?' Stitch interrupted. 'Why are you freezing me out? You think you're the only one who can do this, and you have to do it all on your own? What are you trying to prove?'

'I'm not...'

'And who are you trying to impress?'

'Come on, Stitch. I just don't want anyone else to get hurt. We don't yet know what this new darkness is capable of. We don't know how long we can remain safe here. I need to figure this out.'

'Not *you*, Jay. *We* need to figure this out.' He yanked back his sleeve once more and shoved his wrist forward. 'Connected.'

'Fine,' Jay said tersely, and started the engine. The car jolted forward and out into the streetlamp-lit side streets.

It was almost ten minutes of aching silence before either spoke. Some of the tension had leaked from Jay's body and she looked over at her friend, his head up against the side window and his eyes flickering with the passing trees on the side of the road. She glanced down at her exposed wrist and studied the 8C for a moment before returning her eyes to the road. She wondered what it meant - the 8C and the C. Were she and Stitch *meant* to be together, both in their connected power, and in every other way? Or was the opposite true? Perhaps their relationship should be focused entirely on the development of the power for the safety of their homeland.

Stitch seemed to sense her muddled thoughts and looked at her. 'Look,' he said. 'Can we be honest with each other?'

Jay tensed once more, bracing herself for an argument. 'Always,' she said.

'I just need to know what this is,' he motioned between them. 'Me and you.'

'I love you, Stitch. You know that.' Jay kept her eyes on the road and her shield raised. She didn't want Stitch to read the confusion in her mind over her feelings for him. There was love, for sure. The confusion came with how those feelings twisted and turned as she tried to pin them down, understand them. What kind of love? Was it love driven by the connection, or despite it?

Stitch let out a deep, frustrated sigh and turned back to the window. A minute passed. 'I know,' he said. 'I love you too.'

'That's all that matters right now,' said Jay. 'We can figure the rest out later.' She turned into River Road and headed for the village to the south of the Interland. The road narrowed and Jay sensed a change in the energy in the air. The atmosphere near the Interland was charged. She felt the static on her skin. This was her spiritual home.

She looked at Stitch and knew that he felt it too. He smiled and straightened in his seat. 'We're close,' he said.

They pulled into a small car park by the river. Jay stepped out of the car, slammed and locked the door. Across the green, a row of Vespa mopeds lined up outside the cafe. Stitch looked over and smiled. 'Is that where Cassie *borrowed* that moped from?'

Jay nodded, recalling how Cassie had turned up to save her, collecting her in the woods where she'd fallen. She was sure that they'd never have been able to defeat Marcus if it weren't for Cassie's determination to get to Jay. That all seemed so long ago, and so much had changed. They turned away from the village centre and slid down the river bank to the tow-path.

'Are you sure we can get through this way?' asked Stitch.

'As sure as I can be.' The new Interland was no longer characterised by hidden caves, secret routes through to deep underground. The caves were gone. When she and Toyah left there a few days before, it more closely resembled a flooded quarry than a magical centre of power. There was a bonus, however: an easier route in. There was no longer a need to trek through the undergrowth to approach from the north or the east. The route in from the south, along the River Arun, would take them to the lake, where they'd find whatever was left of the source.

They were quiet as they pressed forward along the river bank. Jay caught the occasional wave of thoughts through the air from Stitch, but nothing she could get a hold on. She sensed that he too was keeping his thoughts hidden.

'You know the other day?' Stitch said. 'When the darkness, or whatever it was, attacked the shop?' Jay nodded for him to continue. 'I got nothing. No energy when I tried to heal Angie. Not even a bit.' His expression was pained.

'It'll come,' said Jay.

'It's gone. It came and went. I don't know what's happened.'

'Hey,' Jay said. 'Calm down. You know how it works. You don't control the power through sheer determination. You control it through here.' She pointed to her chest. 'Through your emotions.'

'I know, but whenever I focus in on it...'

'Don't *focus* in on anything,' Jay interrupted.

'But that's how we used to build up the strength, by channelling the energy.'

'Not with your mind.' Jay stopped on the footpath and turned to face Stitch. She held out both of her hands. 'Close your eyes.'

Stitch did as he was asked. Jay opened to the power of the Interland, allowing the energy to flow through her and connect her with Stitch. She too closed her eyes and couldn't help but smile at the sensation - the intensity of the power so close to the source. Stitch gulped a breath, as if coming up for air. He swayed a little. 'Relax,' said Jay, keeping her voice low.

'Just *feel* it for a moment, in your body, not in your mind. Don't try to do anything with it.'

Jay opened her eyes and watched Stitch as he opened to the flow of the energy. He swayed and twitched as it passed through Jay and into him. Gradually, his movements became more steady, more cyclical as he tuned into the waves of power. His shoulders relaxed and Jay could feel the energy flowing back into her from him. At last he was connected. Still holding his hands, she turned her arms slightly so that she could see the markings on their wrists. She let go of his hands for a moment and brought her left hand to his so their markings became physically connected.

She closed her eyes once more.

Together, in their minds, they sank into the ground beneath their feet, into the banks of the river, below the deep river channel and raced through the tangle of tree roots stretching deep into the earth. Stitch's strength of power matched Jay's own energy as they flowed through the land, expanding thorough the soil and integrating with their environment until there was nothing between Jay and Stitch and their surroundings.

As they snapped out of their trance, Stitch stumbled backwards, falling into the long grass before Jay could reach for him. He came to and stood, laughing, brushing himself down. 'Wow,' he said. 'Haven't felt that level of connection for a while.'

'Me neither to be honest.' Jay turned to continue along the pathway. 'Come on. Before it gets dark.'

Twenty minutes later, the pathway petered out to nothing. They fought their way through thick undergrowth. Jay stumbled. Something washed over her like a wave of dark energy. She glanced at Stitch, then up to the hills. Wisps of black cloud circled above the Interland, then away. She steadied herself. Her breathing regulated once more, and they pressed on.

A further twenty minutes and still no sign of the sunken lake. The energy of the Interland was waning, and she considered for a moment that they could be walking in the wrong direction. She craned to see over the tops of the wild undergrowth. 'Can you see the river?'

Stitch jumped up to see. 'No.'

'I think we're lost,' said Jay.

Stitch turned full circle as if taking in the energy around them. 'Do you feel anything?'

'I'm getting mixed signals,' said Jay. 'I can't home in on the location.'

'Something moving,' said Stitch, his eyes closed.

Jay looked up into the air. A bird came into view. It looked like the falcon from the Interland. Before she could say anything, Stitch opened his eyes and said, 'There. Our guide. The *phoenix*.' The bird that had taken to Cassie, flown to her. The same bird that had flown to Cassie's grandad years before. Jay was sure of it. The markings on the wings. It circled once, twice, three times before heading away towards the hills in the distance.

Jay laughed. 'I thought birds were Sammy's special talent?'

'I'm feeling a little more connected,' Stitch said as he linked arms with Jay and they adjusted their course and moved off in the falcon's direction. Within a few minutes, the falcon re-appeared to guide them once more. It swooped down to just twenty feet above their heads and off again.

The sky had darkened as they stepped out of the woodland and onto the lake shore. Stitch looked around, open mouthed. He'd not before seen the changed landscape. 'Looks different, eh?' said Jay.

'I'll say.'

Jay flopped onto the stones at the water's edge and pulled off her shoes. She stretched out her legs and dipped her feet in the water, the cold immediately relieving the aches and pains.

'How's that foot?' Stitch said.

Jay looked down and squeezed her foot where it had been burned in the darkness of the water between the islands. It was a little red. 'It's a funny colour, but it doesn't hurt.' She leaned to take some water in her hands, letting it flow away through her fingers. She felt its energy. Closing her eyes, white light entered her head, warming her body.

The lake was the point of confluence of the three sources – the three rivers. But the location of the river entry points was not clear. There was nothing obvious above the ground, and it was likely that the three sources connected below the surface of the lake. It was the unnamed river that brought the power, the magic they would need to tap into to find the source stone. If indeed the stone existed.

'Where do we start?' asked Stitch.

Jay shrugged. She stood and squeezed on her shoes. Together, they walked along the shore of the lake, taking some minutes to travel a short section of its circumference. The light faded further and little was visible beyond the immediate shore. Jay hugged her arms to her chest, feeling the chill that came with the dark. 'I think we need to do this at first light. We have no hope of seeing anything tonight.'

'Over there,' said Stitch, pointing to an alcove in the cliff face. 'We can shelter in there.'

There was enough wood scattered across the shore of the lake for a hundred fires. Much of the woodland that sat above the caves had been deposited on the lakeside by the explosions. Stars appeared in the sky. The fire warmed Jay's cheeks and the darting orange flames intermittently illuminated the surface of the lake just twenty feet away.

Feeling the cold on her back, Jay pulled on a hoodie and edged a little closer to the fire as Stitch fed it with wood. Without sleeping bags, they would have to make do with limestone beds and their rucksacks for pillows.

'Thanks,' said Stitch.

Jay looked up. 'What for?'

'I needed that re-connection.'

'Me too.' Jay smiled into the darkness.

* * *

A RELENTLESS STREAM of light pierced Jay's mind, bringing haphazard images and feelings from her subconscious. Tiago was there, but he looked different. Each time she moved to look him in the face, he turned away. Then he fell, with darkness circling him and the space where his face should have been, a blank, faceless mask. She asked his name. 'Maram,' he said, as the darkness entwined his neck. But that wasn't his name. It squeezed. 'Maram,' he gasped. It squeezed tighter, flowing around Tiago and then in through his nose, his ears, his mouth. Then came a wail of pure fear, like a scream of a baby caught on the wind.

Jay woke to the call of the falcon, a whistle in the distance bringing her out of her dreams. The fire had all but died, the last wisps of smoke carried in her direction by a morning breeze coming off the lake. She coughed as smoke caught in her throat. Stitch was still asleep.

She tried to get a hold of her dream, to remember it, but it slipped away like water through her fingers. The morning air was fresh, not too cold, but her toes were frozen numb.

Up on the distant cliff face, the falcon preened its feathers, all the while closely watching Jay and Stitch. Energy fizzed through Jay's body, giving her a sense of invincibility. Her fingers tingled, and she looked at her palms, expecting to see them sparkle.

In the lake, currents rippled the surface, moving in tidy sequence. Leaving Stitch to sleep, she stepped into the shallows up to her shins to get a better look. The green sparkle of the unnamed river was clear in the three converging colours. She was drawn to it, the tingling in her body intensifying, and the surface of her skin becoming warm.

Finding the stone in the vast space left by the destruction of the Interland felt like an impossible task. Where would they start? She turned to look at the cliff face, her eyes hunting for a clue, something out of place, an energy signal that she might lock on to. Stones crumbled and fell from the cliff face as if to wave her away.

Nausea hit her stomach, and, in a beat, Angie was with her. She straightened, her eyes half closed as Angie's smiling face came into focus in her mind. Before Jay could speak, her image faded and disappeared, leaving Jay confused and light-headed.

The falcon swooped. It flew past just a few feet from Jay, then circled to pass again. Jay looked over to see if Stitch was watching. He stirred and sat up. The bird touched the surface of the lake. Jay expected its claws to emerge clutching a fish, but there was nothing but the spray of water as the falcon rose and circled again. Stitch stood, stepping closer to the edge of the lake. The falcon whistled as it powered back towards Jay like a bomber, turning at the last and diving into the lake.

This time, the falcon had something clutched in both claws. Its wings beat the water as it struggled to free itself, the force of the surface tension holding it back for just a moment, as if it were frozen in time. The falcon broke free of the water and turned immediately towards Jay, releasing its boon as it passed overhead. Jay caught the rock in both hands and turned, grinning, to Stitch. They watched after the falcon as it returned to its perch on the cliff face where it rested and dipped its head as if to say *there you go*.

Jay looked at the stone. 'Thanks,' she said, smiling up at the bird and thinking of Angie. The stone was smooth, the shape of a large bowl. Into its hollow, the three river sources deposited their flow deep in the underground cave of the Interland. She stroked the smooth surface and turned it over in her hands. It was heavy given its size, like it was made of something denser than rock. She felt the energy in her hands, like this piece of stone had for years absorbed the energy and power of the Given.

'Thank you,' she said again, to the falcon.

23

Atta towered over Flick, an expressionless sculpture. He looked up at the bookshop's façade and then stepped towards the door. Flick felt power ripple from his body before the door gave way. He entered ahead of her. His presence sent chills through Flick. Her fear of him was stronger than any sense of allegiance. His power was stronger than ever before, growing with every Island conquest. When Island 8 was his, his power would be absolute. No one could challenge him again.

With a wave of his hand, the books along the back wall of the shop flew from the shelves and scattered across the floor. Flick stepped through the book debris towards the stairs. 'What you want is upstairs.'

Without looking back at Atta, Flick headed to the top floor. She heard the sounds of scattering books, smashing of shelves on the ground floor, and then the middle floor, as Atta destroyed all in his path.

As she stepped up to the top floor, Alf was nowhere to be seen, and Flick felt relief. She'd rather not look Alf in the eye and acknowledge her betrayal before his death. It was Alf's work, with Jay at the bookshop that had made the passageway to Island 8 more challenging for Atta. The power of the Given on Island 8 was greater than on any of the other Islands, and the bookshop was no small part of that. It provided structure for the Given, a means for them to learn and develop. The destruction of the bookshop was Atta's priority on entering Island 8, a greater priority even than the destruction of the Interland, and the completion of the sink-room.

'He's here,' Atta said. 'I feel him.' He walked the length of the top floor, running his fingers along the books as he went, as if he were taking in their contents, identifying those that he would mark for destruction.

He reached the fire escape at the far end and pushed open the door, stepping out onto the landing for a moment and breathing in the air, like a dog searching for a scent. Flick watched as he returned and made his way to the back wall. She followed. As she turned the corner of the bookshelves, Atta stood still, gazing at a wall of books. He flung open cabinet doors to see more books on the Given. His anger bubbled to the surface, and the books fell. Book after book slipped from the shelves, the cupboards and onto the floor.

Atta groaned as if in pain. The energy of the Given enveloped and supported the top floor of the bookshop, created conflict with the opposing power of the darkness that flowed from Atta.

Flick sensed Alf; he was nearby. Knowing how good he was at shielding, that she sensed something of him let her know he was close. For reasons she couldn't untangle, she didn't mention his apartment to Atta.

'Where is he?' Atta growled.

For reasons she couldn't figure, Flick kept silent.

Atta's speed increased as he made his way along the wall of books. Wisps of smoke rose from the books piled onto the floor, as if the friction between Dark and Given generated sufficient heat to burn.

Flick stepped aside as flames flickered on the shelves and on the floor. Atta shouted as he pulled the last rows of books onto the floor and into the growing flames.

'Let's go,' said Flick, backing towards the fire escape.

Atta stared at her. She was still one of the Given. She had not yet been reduced and returned to the tribe of the Readers. She felt the power of the Given within her, fighting against the energy of the darkness, against Atta's destruction of their history.

The flames rose and licked the walls and ceiling. He stepped towards Flick, and past her to the fire escape. Without words, he flung open the fire escape door and out onto the steps.

* * *

STITCH CRADLED the source stone as Jay steered the Ford through the streets towards Cassie's house. Jay was jittery. She felt darkness all around as if there were Readers on every corner. With no response to Jay honking the horn, Stitch went in to find Cassie. By the time they returned, Jay was beside herself.

'Hurry,' Jay said, a tightness in her voice. The darkness had infiltrated, and the energy of the Given was threatened.

'What's the matter?' Cassie said as she slid into the back seat and leaned through to the front.

Stich fell into the car as Jay pulled away. 'Something's wrong. We need to get to Alf,' she said.

In the short journey to the bookshop, Jay described her fears to Cassie. She told them both about Colson's theory, and the three conditions. And she told them she was determined to ensure the darkness would never take their homeland again. What she didn't tell them was what she felt deep down in her bones - that the darkness had already arrived.

They saw the smoke rising from more than a mile away, and when the car screeched to a stop outside the bookshop, there was already a fire engine in the street, its hoses trained on the windows of the top floor. Flames licked the window frames. The glass in one of the windows shattered, raining shards down onto the street below.

They leaped from the car. 'Alf?' Cassie said.

Jay sensed Alf. Their connection had strengthened over their time working together. She felt his fear, his uneasiness. He was afraid, but not in immediate danger. 'He's alive. He's here. Panic room,' she shouted above the background noise. Alf's panic room in his apartment was built into the refurbishment of the bookshop to protect from attack. Alf was determined that his first experience of being taken by Readers wouldn't be repeated.

Without explaining further, Jay took off around the side of the building to the back entrance, with Cassie and Stitch following close behind. She kicked open the door of the outhouse in the rear car port and lifted the floor hatch that led down to the back entrance to Alf's panic room.

She pounded on the steel door at the bottom of the steps. Cassie and Stitch perched on the steps above her. 'Alf!'

A clunk and a click came from the door and it swung slowly inward. Alf's face appeared, Buster at his feet, agitated. Jay almost broke down with the relief. 'Thank God,' she said.

Alf took Jay into a hug. 'I thought you were them,' he said. 'Readers. They were here. Their power was strong. I was sure they'd sense me down here.'

'We need to leave. The top floor is on fire.'

Alf's eyes filled with dread. 'The books. *Your* books?'

Jay nodded.

A second fire engine arrived and doubled the flow of water aimed at the top floor. Jay begged to be allowed in but the fire department formed a barricade and pushed them back. There was nothing they could do but watch. With a sigh of sadness, Alf beckoned Jay, Cassie and Stitch to the pub opposite.

* * *

THEY FOUND a seat by the window from which they could see the bookshop. Cassie and Stitch placed drinks on the table and they sat in silence, watching the streams of water blast into the shop's top floor. Beneath the table, Buster whined.

The smell of cigarette smoke and beer turned Jay's stomach. She sipped her iced water and looked out at the burning building. A firefighter trained a powerful hose on one of the top floor windows. He was joined by another, who shouted something in his ear and took a turn with the hose. Jay imagined the valuable, irreplaceable material on the top floor being destroyed, either by the fire or by the water. She instinctively looked towards her bag, thankful at least that she'd kept the Sasha Colden book with her.

Alf stared at the spectacle beyond the window. A reflection of the orange flames danced in his eyes.

'I'm sorry,' said Jay, breaking the silence.

'What for?' said Stitch, not averting his gaze from the burning building.

'It's my fault,' she said.

Cassie shook her head. 'It makes no sense. If this is the work of Atta, like you said in the car, then how has he gained access? You said that there were conditions?'

Alf and Jay exchanged a glance. They had both felt the power of the dark energy.

Jay thought back to what Colson had said about the conditions for the opening of the channel to the darkness. She'd connected with the darkness herself, up on the roof outside her bedroom window.

'It could have been me,' Jay said, pushing the thoughts around her head. 'That time on the roof.' She looked at Stitch. 'Condition 1. Maybe I opened the door?'

'How?' asked Cassie.

'Something Flick said.' Jay paused. 'I have to protect this place. If I can't do it then who…'

'What are you saying?' Cassie interrupted.

'If I stand any chance of keeping the darkness out, then I need to control it. The power of the Given is just half the story. True power will only come from the integration, the joining of the light and the dark. Maybe that's the answer.' Jay's confidence in her own words waned. She looked defeated.

'What have you done?' Cassie stood, her mind searching, links connecting.

Alf held up a hand. 'Hold on,' he said. 'You never *invited* Atta through. The second condition requires an invitation from the Given to the darkness to use the channel.'

Cassie shuffled on her feet, unable to sit back down. 'Well, something's going on,' she spat, accusatory.

'Even if Condition 2 has been met somehow,' said Stitch. 'Then the sacrifice, the spilling of Given blood? No way.'

'He's found a way,' said Jay, looking at Alf. He knew Jay was right. 'Colson might not have it right.'

'Where is Flick now?' said Stitch.

Alf, his voice low, 'We reduced her.'

Cassie paced up and down. A noise from outside drew Jay's attention. A piece of the roof of the bookshop had dislodged and fallen onto the pavement below. Firefighters stepped back, then re-positioned to direct their water into the hole in the roof.

'She's re-building as the Given,' said Cassie. 'She's with Otis.' Cassie stopped her pacing and looked at Jay.

'So Flick is one of the Given...' Jay said.

Alf leaned forward in his chair. 'What have we done?'

'Otis,' Cassie said and bolted for the door.

'Wait. I'll come with you,' Jay stood.

'You've done enough,' Cassie shouted before she stormed out.

PART III

24

———

At the sight of the bookshop's top floor, Jay's heart sank. More than half of the books were burnt and charred, those that survived the fire were sodden pulpy lumps. Irreplaceable books –gone forever.

Fire had ravaged Jay's special collection on the top floor. Wet, black soot and ash clung to everything. The smell fizzed in her nose like a chemical burn with every breath. Three out of the four cupboards of papers and notebooks had fallen off the wall, their contents unsalvageable.

The fourth wall cupboard remained hanging from its supports. The cupboard door was blackened, but it remained closed and relatively intact. She held the side of the cupboard to support it as she carefully pulled open the door. Inside, the papers were virtually untouched. She allowed herself a half smile as she ran her fingers over the spines of the notebooks. Then she opened her backpack. The source stone rested at the bottom, next to the Sasha Colden book. She placed the rucksack on the floor and ran her hand over the smooth surface of the source stone. The bowl, worn down by the action of the three river sources, was so soft it felt like soap-stone. She pushed it to the side in her bag and began slotting in the books from the shelves.

Alf knelt by the shelf of books on the Given that looked least touched by flame. He carefully packed his own rucksack, then turned to Jay and opened his arms. 'Load me up,' he said. 'We can take as much as we can carry, then come back later.'

'Where to?'

'I was thinking about your dad's pub. The basement. Will you call him?'

'Of course. We can get a taxi,' she said, feeling the weight of the books and the source stone on her back.

* * *

JAY AND ALF edged down the steps into the basement of the pub, their arms laden and backpacks full. The room was empty but for her dad standing at the foot of the steps, and Colson at the table. When Ben saw them, he rushed to help Jay with the books, taking an armful and stacking them on the far side of the basement. 'Are you hurt?' he asked.

'Not physically,' said Jay. 'Atta has destroyed most of the books.' She unloaded her backpack, leaving the source stone and Sasha Colden book in the bag.

Alf stacked his books next to Jay's and turned to an expectant looking Colson. 'The conditions have been met,' Alf said, sitting heavily in a chair at the end of the table.

'How?' asked Colson, pausing from his tobacco rolling and leaning forward.

'We think it was Flick.'

Jay's legs wobbled as she staggered to sit, her dad's hand guiding her. She felt light-headed, as if dehydrated. She was sick to her stomach for allowing this to happen. 'It was my fault,' she said.

'Don't,' said Alf. 'This is no-one's fault.' Alf explained to Ben and Colson what had happened at the shop, and their theory about Flick.

'What happened to Otis?' said Colson.

'Cassie's gone to Highdown to find him.'

'Alone?' asked Ben, looking fearful.

'Stitch is following,' said Jay. 'I'll know if they hit trouble.' She lowered her gaze, trying to hide her shame. She was responsible for Flick's betrayal. Cassie had barely looked at Jay.

Colson moved to open the hatch from the bar above, bringing back four steaming bowls. Jay's stomach turned at the meaty smell and she pushed her bowl away. Alf had already tucked in, reaching to rip a hunk of bread from the loaf that Colson placed in the middle of the table. Colson returned to the hatch and brought back four glasses of water.

Ben handed a drink to Jay, along with a spoon. 'You need to eat,' he said.

Colson couldn't eat either. He was distracted. He grabbed himself a crust of bread and stood. He paced the floor of the basement. 'Even if the conditions were met, Atta…' He paused, rubbing his temples. 'I can't believe I'm saying his name. He has been nothing but a myth and now he's here, in our world.'

'He exists. I've met him,' said Jay. 'And he has power like I've never felt before. He controlled me.'

Colson nodded. 'But he can't sustain power without the energy of the core, the sink-room.'

'They will build a new sink-room here,' said Jay. 'We destroyed the building, but not the connection to the core. We saw the construction on Island 7. They've built over the core, created some kind of power station, a means to amplify the power coming from below.'

'What was it like?' asked Colson.

'A huge warehouse over the top of a massive crater, like an alien landing site or something. In the hole were three rotating electromagnets, connected into the central column. The power was obvious. I felt it. They'll plan to replicate that here.'

'We don't know that...' started Ben.

'What else would they be here for?' Jay snapped.

'Well, it's not the first thing they did, is it? They took out the shop,' said Ben. 'It's the centre of all things relating to the Given. They've hit the central knowledge source.'

'So now they'll just leave it at that? Conquer all the other Islands and leave this one? Be serious, Dad.'

'And they've destroyed the Interland,' Ben added.

'Surprised they haven't taken out the new resistance,' Jay said, losing patience. She immediately felt bad for belittling her dad's group. If it weren't for the basement of the pub, and for Ben and Colson's help, things would be even worse.

'I'm sorry,' she continued. 'The caves have gone, but not the power. The Given power is still strong. Taking out the Interland, and the shop was just a message, a sign, something for them to let us know that they're strong, and that they can come in and destroy what's dear to us. He won't stop there. He's just warming up.'

'Then we have to stop him,' said Alf. 'Tell us about what you found at the Interland.'

Jay retrieved her rucksack from the floor, feeling the weight of the source stone. She unzipped the top and reached inside, lifting out the lump of stone with both hands.

Colson gasped at the sight of it, holding out his hands to take the bowl from Jay. He held it in both hands.

'What is it?' asked Ben, looking at his daughter.

'The stone at the centre of the source, in the underground, from the Interland.'

'How did you find it? I thought the place had sunk into the earth.'

'A little bird helped me.' Jay smiled.

'This is it,' Colson said, his eyes wide. 'I can feel it.'

'Maybe you should put it down?' said Alf, getting jittery as Colson's hands shook.

Colson seemed not to hear Alf. 'Was this in the location of the confluence? Where the three sources joined?' Without waiting for an answer, he placed the bowl on the table and took two books from his own bag. Looking at the big notebooks that Colson placed on the table, Jay was momentarily annoyed he'd taken them from the bookshop, then immediately thankful he'd saved them from the fire.

'What now?' Ben asked, looking at Colson.

'That's what we need to work out,' Colson said, taking another mouthful of bread before opening the cover of the notebook.

25

O tis had been lying beneath the circle of trees for what felt like forever. He was exhausted from moving the bandages telekinetically towards his outstretched hands before tying them around his still seeping ankles. The ground around him was soaked with his blood. Above, a breeze gently rustled the leaves in the trees.

He sent out messages of desperation to Cassie and to Jay, but his energy levels were so low he was sure they would never hear.

The darkness overhead was oppressive. There were no stars in the sky, as if Atta had wiped them away.

He floated in and out of consciousness, shivering one moment, burning with heat the next. Nausea drifted from his stomach through to his chest and into his throat. He wasn't sure if he'd have the energy to survive throwing up.

Otis wished for the end. When he heard footsteps approach, he didn't lift a hand to defend himself. If it were to end his pain, then the re-emergence of Atta and Flick was welcome.

The crack of sticks, the rustle of leaves as two people approached. Otis closed his eyes.

'Otis!'

He recognised Cassie's voice and his body stopped fighting to survive. He slipped into unconsciousness.

* * *

CASSIE REMAINED CALM, slipping into autopilot. As soon as she crouched beside Otis she felt her hands sink into his warm blood. 'His ankles,' Stitch said. 'They're cut.'

Without a word, Cassie inspected the bandages. She used the bottom of her t-shirt to wipe away some of the blood so that she could see how bad he was. Blood seeped from deep wounds to both heels. 'How could she do this?' She re-arranged the bandages and pulled them tighter. 'We need to get him down to the car park.'

'I can carry him,' said Stitch.

'I'll do it,' insisted Cassie. 'You run down to the phone box in the car park. Call an ambulance.' The nearer of the two car parks was only a fifteen-minute walk. Cassie wiped blood from her hands onto her t-shirt and reached for Otis's arms. Stitch helped her drag his body diagonally over her shoulder, careful as he manoeuvred his legs into position.

* * *

AFTER SOME TIME, Colson looked up from the notebook. He had a sparkle in his eyes. He picked up the Sasha Colden book once more, flicking to the back pages where Jay had read the coded message about the source stone. He placed the Colden book gently on the table and picked up the source stone itself, turning it over in his hands, inspecting every inch of its surface as if looking for something.

'What is it?' asked Jay.

'This is it,' said Colson. 'This little packet of power is what will break the flow of dark energy.'

'How?' asked Alf, straightening in his seat.

'We simply need to position it within the channel.'

'*Simply*...' scoffed Ben. 'You're talking about getting that stone into the hole beneath the sink-room, if it's even possible to get to it?'

Alf reached for Jay's hand. 'If Atta is on our Island, then won't he be there, waiting? You can't just walk in there and throw this into the hole.'

'That's exactly what I can do.'

'What if the hole isn't there?' said Ben.

Colson placed the source stone down on the table with enough of a thump to draw attention. 'It must be,' he said. 'We've already agreed that Atta and the Readers cannot be here without a source of power. It's wishful thinking to believe that he's here because of the power on Island 7. We need to get real. He's here, there is a channel to the core, and they're probably building one of those big sink-rooms like Jay saw on Island 7.'

'I'll go,' Jay said. She looked at her dad, and then at Alf. 'I can do this. He might be strong on Island 7, but this is *my* home.'

'This isn't Marcus,' said Alf. 'Or even Hinton. This is a whole new level.'

Colson reached for the source stone and pulled it towards him. He nodded. He stood and placed a hand on Jay's shoulder. 'We know nothing for sure,' he said. 'But if you can get that thing deep into the core, then I think there'll be no coming back for the darkness in this land.'

'How deep?' asked Alf.

Colson shrugged. 'As deep as it goes.'

'What happens then?' said Alf.

Colson looked at Jay. 'You run.'

* * *

BEN LEFT WITH COLSON, and a few minutes later, Stitch appeared in the stairwell. He edged down the last steps and slumped down opposite Jay.

Jay startled at the sight of him. 'Where's Cassie? Otis?'

'Hospital. He's alive. Lost a lot of blood, but he's alive.'

'What happened?'

'Flick. That's what happened.'

Alf stood and paced. 'Otis was the third condition. The sacrifice.'

Stitch nodded.

'The spilling of blood wasn't at the Interland then? It was at Highdown.'

Jay said, 'The legend said it needed to be at a sacred place of the Given, which could have been any of the hill forts, or the Interland.'

'I couldn't do anything. Couldn't help him,' said Stitch, looking at his open hands and then wringing them together as if trying to scrape off the surface of the skin. '*Fricking* useless.'

'You tried to heal?' Asked Alf.

Stitch nodded. 'I've been working on it. A lot. So much for all that.'

'It's coming, Stitch,' said Jay. 'Earlier, your power was strong. Keep going.' She leaned towards Stitch across the table and rested her hand on his. He pulled it away, and Jay thought she could see tears in the corners of his eyes. They were quiet for a moment.

Stitch turned back to the table and the source stone drew his focus. He reached for it, touching it gently with the tips of the fingers on one hand. He seemed to get a spark of energy from the contact and drew his hand away.

'Colson worked it out,' said Jay. 'I need to get it into the channel to the core.'

Stitch shook his head but said nothing.

'Hey,' said Alf, drawing Stitch's attention. 'We need you on this.'

'No,' said Jay, before Stitch could respond. 'This is my responsibility. I won't have anyone else getting hurt.'

Stitch was silent, staring at the source stone. Jay knew that his confidence had taken a hit, and his faith in the power was waning.

'Stitch,' Alf continued, ignoring Jay. 'There's a reason you're branded a "C". You're Jay's connection. Together, you two...'

'Leave it, Alf,' said Jay. 'This is not up for discussion. This is just something I need to do. No casualties on this one.'

'Except you?' Alf snapped. 'What makes you so invincible?'

'Look,' she said. 'There are too many unknowns. What if we go in there together and it's a war? We face an almighty battle and none of us survives? I go alone, under the radar, see the lie of the land and get the stone into position. No-one gets hurt. I come back.'

Alf sighed. 'You remember when we first met?' Jay shook her head, trying to recall the first time she saw Alf in the book-shop, back when she was only six or seven years old. 'Well, I remember it well. You came in with your dad, and I felt the energy. I'd seen your dad before and I knew he had a little something, but that day the energy flowed into the shop like something else.'

'Not when I was *that* little?' said Jay.

Alf nodded emphatically. 'For sure. I knew. Probably before you did, or your dad. I knew you'd be something special.'

'Took a while before I really felt it...'

'But that was nothing,' Alf interrupted. 'Compared to what happened when you made the connection.' He looked at Stitch. He reached for Jay's arm, taking her by the hand and pushing her sleeve back to see her marking. 'This is a gift. And a responsibility.'

'I know,' snapped Jay, pulling her hand away. 'I'll *take* that responsibility. I've caused enough pain already; it's time now for me to finish this.' She picked up the source stone and fed it back into her bag with the Sasha Colden book. She slung the bag onto her back and left without looking back.

* * *

JAY LEFT her house by the back alley, avoiding Sammy and her dad, to head to the hospital. She needed to see Otis. The Beast, the old Ford, was there for her as always. It had become like an old, reliable friend. She turned the key, and it kicked in first time.

The lift doors at the hospital opened. There was a smell from the toilets in the lift lobby mixed with that of bleach to give it a sweet, corrosive flavour. She resisted the urge to pull her top up to cover her nose and stepped into the corridor.

She crossed the reception area and headed for the ward, seeing Cassie as soon as she entered. Jay moved slowly towards the bed. This would be the second person in this hospital with serious injuries resulting from Jay's own failure to protect them. Angie was clear of danger, out of the medically induced coma but still poorly. And now here lay Otis.

As she drew closer, she saw Cassie had Otis's hand in hers. She glanced at Jay.

'She sliced both of his heels. He lost a lot of blood.' Cassie nodded towards the machine at Otis's side with a drip and blood supply. 'He was in the ICU but he's stable now, so they brought him out here.' Cassie looked around the empty ward. 'It's like a morgue.'

Otis lay asleep in a hospital gown like a straitjacket, bandages covering both of his ankles. 'I'm sorry...' Jay said under her breath. It was she who insisted they trust Flick. It was she who swallowed Flick's story about the reduction and re-building as one of the Given. She hadn't even questioned the third scar. She had allowed the most powerful agent of the darkness a path straight into their world. 'I'll make it right,' Jay said. 'I promise.'

Otis's eyelids flickered and Cassie lifted herself in her chair to see into his face. 'Otis?' she said. He opened his eyes and smiled at Cassie, then looked at Jay, his smile remaining fixed.

'Thought I was a goner,' he croaked.

'Shh,' said Cassie, holding a finger to her lips. 'Take it easy. The nurse said you need to go slow.'

He looked over at Jay. 'That friend of yours...' He took a breath. 'She's quite something.'

'I'm sorry, Otis. She took us for a ride...'

'Took *you* for a ride,' Cassie said. Jay nodded solemnly, looking away from Cassie and Otis.

'Hey,' said Otis, turning back to Cassie. 'Don't blame Jay for this. None of us saw through her. How was Jay to know she was a psychopath?'

Cassie shrugged. 'If there's one person on this planet who

should have known exactly who she was and what she was planning...' She turned to Jay, her eyes stony.

Jay avoided Cassie's eye and looked back at Otis. 'I'm going to put this right.' She turned to leave. No one called her to come back.

* * *

As Jay turned the corner into the lift lobby, her mind shifted to little Angie. She had been in this same hospital and last she knew was still here. She looked at the hospital map on the wall next to the lifts and searched for Angie's ward. 'Sixth floor,' she said to herself and slapped the button to call the lift.

With both lifts stopped on the ground floor, Jay turned and pushed the door into the stairwell. She took the two flights of stairs two steps at a time and spilled out into the corridor on level six. Following signs to the wards, she picked up speed, breaking into a run as she felt a genuine sense of urgency to see Angie.

Turning a corner, she narrowly avoided a head on collision with a nurse. 'Hey! Slow down.'

She caught the door before it snapped shut and strode through Angie's ward, looking left and right at each bed as she passed. In the middle of the ward on the left-hand side, there was a couple sat at Angie's bed, one on each side. Angie's parents looked too young, but when they turned to look at Jay, she saw that pain and worry had etched years into their faces.

'Jay!' Angie shouted, waving her over.

'Hey, little one...'

'Who's this, Angie?' her father asked.

'This is the most powerful of the Given... ever,' said Angie, a smile from ear to ear.

'Oh, I see now,' the man said, his expression hardening.

Angie's mum stood and held out a hand. 'She hasn't stopped talking about you,' she said.

'How is she?' Jay asked.

'She's had a bit of a scare. We think it was a shock more than anything else. The coma was a precaution, to enable them to do some tests without fear of damage. She's strong.'

'She's a determined soul,' said Jay. 'I'm sorry,' she said again.

'Bit late for that,' Angie's dad said, standing but not looking at Jay. 'I don't know what you allowed to get to our little girl, but whatever it was, it nearly killed her.'

'Dad...' Angie's face dropped. 'It wasn't Jay, it was Readers.'

'I don't care what...'

'Phillip!' Angie's mum cut him off. 'Take a minute.' She motioned for him to leave. He turned and made for the door without resistance.

'He's just scared. We both are. We don't understand all this...' She trailed off as she waved her hand about. 'We are helpless here. Maybe you can tell us what is going on?'

Jay sat in the seat vacated by Angie's dad. Angie reached for her hand and gave her a warm smile. 'We don't know everything,' Jay said. 'Not yet.'

'It was Readers though,' said Angie, as if she were excited by it. 'Readers attacked, and we fought them off.'

Jay smiled, enjoying Angie's version of events. Her smile faded. 'But I promised I'd keep you safe. And I failed.'

'It wasn't your fault. If it wasn't for you, the Readers would be in charge already.'

'I won't let it happen again,' said Jay.

'Well, it's not all up to you, is it?' said Angie. 'It takes all of us.'

'I hear you,' Jay said softly.

'Do you, Jay?' said Angie. 'You know, it's a sign of strength to ask for help.'

Jay nodded, her eyes downcast as she took in the words.

'You taught me what makes the Given different from the dark power,' Angie continued. 'It's all of us. Together. You, and Stitch. And me.' She smiled and looked over at her mum. Her mum nodded. 'And Alf, and everyone Given. Like when I found you and helped with the phoenix.' Angie smiled.

'Yes, you're right...' Jay started.

'Not just that though,' said Angie. 'Remember you said the most important thing you taught me is the *total* connection. The animals. The sea, and the hills.'

Jay shook her head with a smile. For someone so little, Angie had deep wisdom. She had soaked up so much information on the Given in so little time in the bookshop. Every time Jay saw her, she was full of questions that she'd stored up through her reading time. And her thoughts were always insightful. Angie had great potential.

Angie was right about her needing to connect. She'd never felt so distant from her closest allies, Stitch and Cassie. Jay pictured Otis, his face pale, his body so weak. It was Otis who had been closest to Davey, before Davey met his end in the crossfire in the fight between the darkness and the Given. And Reuben, who was Cassie's first love, killed by Readers. Seeing Otis in that hospital bed, so close to death himself, and Angie, so little, just reinforced the resolve in Jay to put things right while endangering no one else.

'So you need to step up, Jay,' Angie said with a grin. 'Get everyone together for a big fight.'

Jay nodded again but her face was set. She wasn't listening anymore.

26

When Jay arrived home, the atmosphere was frosty. Her mum and dad had been arguing. The tension hung in the air and there was no sign of Sammy. She hooked her jacket on the end of the banister, and out of the corner of her eye, she spotted her dad in the kitchen. He was deep in thought, gazing into a bubbling pan on the stove.

Ben looked up as if nudged by Jay's intrusion into his thoughts. He smiled. 'Hey,' Jay said, stepping off the stairs and entering the spicy, humid kitchen.

'You look tired,' Ben said. Jay rubbed her forehead. She dumped her rucksack in the hallway and lifted herself up to sit on the kitchen worktop. Ben looked at her bag. 'Is the stone in there?'

Jay nodded. 'It pulses. Can you feel it?' He shook his head and turned back to the stove. His eyes glazed over as he stared into the broth. 'Everything OK?' asked Jay.

Her dad smiled and straightened, as if to pull himself out of his ruminations. 'Sorry if I've been difficult recently,' he said, taking Jay by surprise. It was true he'd been a little more insistent that Jay be careful, but she wouldn't have called him *difficult*. 'It's been a weird time.' He looked up. 'With your mum and all that. Getting through and coming to terms with what's happened. Figuring out our future. You know?'

Jay nodded. 'You've been doing really well. None of this is easy.' Her mum's affair with the Reader Marcus, an affair that created Sammy, had only come to light last year, even though Jay suspected her dad had known about it. He'd raised Sammy. The biology of a child ceases to be important when the baby arrives. How could anyone resent an act that produced something so perfect? Her parents' decision to make a go of their complex relationship when Ben returned from the Interland would never make for a smooth ride.

'You remember the stories? Back when you two were little?'

Jay smiled. 'Always. Those stories are in my DNA.'

'Who'd have known how it would turn out?' He glanced towards Jay's wrist where her marking seemed so dark as to absorb the light from around it.

'We wouldn't be here if it wasn't for you, Dad. It was your insight that got us to the Interland, got us to where we built what we have now.'

Ben laughed. 'I pointed the way, but you took the lead in that journey, my love.' He put a hand on Jay's arm for a moment, then turned to lean against the kitchen side. He looked at the chessboard on the fridge, its magnetic pieces arranged in a battle not yet played out to a conclusion. 'Is this our game?'

'Me and Sammy's. He's getting the better of me this time. It's been a while. I don't even know whose move it is.'

'You used to let him win,' Ben said with a smile.

'Wish I had that option now,' said Jay.

They were silent for a minute and the only sounds were

the distant noise of the television in the lounge and the bubbling stew on the stove. The windows in the kitchen had steamed up and the orange glow from the streetlamp outside sparkled in the moisture on the glass.

'I get a sense that something bad is coming,' Ben said. 'Whatever happens, I want you to know that I'm proud of you. Proud of what you've achieved, for sure, but mostly I'm proud of how you've done it.' He leaned back and took in a deep breath before letting it out slowly, as if trying to calm his nerves. 'Back when the Given were forming as a collective, at the Interland, people gravitated to your way of doing things. You have a way about you that garners a consensus. Looking back, I didn't always do things right. And I'm sorry for that.'

Jay made to interrupt, but Ben raised a hand for her to allow him to finish. 'Whatever happens with this...' He looked up at the ceiling. 'With this resurgence of the Dark, or Atta, or whatever it is, I want you to know that I love you. I'm proud of you, and I've got your back. Whatever you need, I'm here.'

'That means so much, Dad,' Jay said. They hugged.

Her dad pulled away and turned off the stove, removing the pan and placing it on the side. 'You want some?'

'No thanks,' Jay said.

Sammy spilled into the room from the bottom of the stairs. 'What is it?' he asked.

Ben smiled at Jay. 'He only comes when he smells food.'

'Not true,' said Sammy, taking a bowl from the cupboard and ladling stew into it.

'Dish some out for me and your mum,' said Ben. Sammy did as he was asked and Ben took two bowls out to the dining room where he'd eat with Sonia. Sammy pulled himself up to sit on the kitchen top opposite Jay, spooning food into his mouth.

'Good?' asked Jay.

'Not bad for Dad.'

Jay looked at the chess set stuck to the fridge. 'Whose go is it?'

'Yours,' Sammy said between mouthfuls. 'It's been your go for weeks. Anyone would think I scared you off.' Jay studied the board with little recollection of the game. 'You're black,' Sammy said. They were down to a few remaining pieces and with Sammy's queen already gone, Jay was in a commanding position.

She moved her rook into attack. 'Check,' she said.

'Give me a couple of weeks and I'll get back to you,' Sammy teased.

Jay picked up the empty pan from the stove and put it in the kitchen basin, filling it with water to soak. 'Where's Toyah?'

'No idea. She's like a ghost. I thought you'd know better than me. You've spent more time with her than I have recently.'

'I'm not sure we would have got away so cleanly from the Readers if it wasn't for her,' said Jay.

'Yes, she told me about it,' Sammy said, finishing his food and handing Jay the bowl to put in the sink. 'What's going on with that? She says we are safe here, is that true?'

'Yes,' Jay said. 'As long as we take measures.'

'What measures?'

'We're working it out. But don't worry.'

'You could let me in, you know?'

Jay turned to her brother with a frown.

'Come on,' said Sammy. 'This is *me* you're talking to. I know you. And you should know that I'm on your side. You shouldn't need convincing.' He jumped down off the kitchen surface. On the fridge, he moved his king out of reach of Jay's rook and headed for the door. 'I know you'll do it right, Sis. I'm here if you need me.'

Jay looked at the chessboard as Sammy disappeared into the lounge. 'Stalemate,' she said under her breath, seeing that Sammy had manoeuvred into a no-win position for both of them.

* * *

BACK IN HER ROOM, Jay pulled open the Velux and climbed out onto the tiles, only to startle at the sight of Toyah walking away across the roof towards the back alleyway. 'Hey!' she called.

Toyah turned, looking disappointed to be seen.

'What are you doing up here?' Jay asked.

'Just leaving.' Toyah turned again to continue away from Jay.

'Hey!' Jay repeated. 'You can't just...'

Toyah edged back over to Jay and sat down on the tiles, nodding for Jay to join her. 'I sit up here sometimes.'

Jay smiled, trying to draw Toyah's eye. 'On your own? When I'm not here?'

'Sometimes.'

Jay laughed. 'Well, I'm glad to provide a facility for you.'

Toyah remained silent and Jay asked: 'Are you OK? I've hardly seen you since we got back.'

'I've been keeping out of the way.' She nodded back towards the house.

'Sammy?'

Toyah nodded. 'It's complicated. It's nothing to do with *him.*'

'It's not him, it's you? Heard that one before.'

'I need to sort my head out. It's not fair on him until I do.'

'So why are you here?'

Toyah let out a humourless laugh. 'Ask my psychologist. I don't know, to be honest. I'm drawn here, to you as much as to Sammy.'

'I'm flattered.'

'More a draw to the *place*, I think.' Toyah laughed to herself. 'Sorry. I know I'm not making sense.'

'Sammy's downstairs.'

'I guessed as much. I saw him yesterday.'

'Why don't you...'

'Can we leave it?' Toyah said, a tone of pleading in her voice.

Jay left it. 'How's Pinto?'

'Still struggling at school. He told me you went to see him. He appreciated it. Thanks.'

'He's strong. He needs to see those boys off. He's too nice.' Jay pictured the boys throwing things at Pinto at the school gate. She remembered that feeling of isolation, and her heart ached for Pinto. She resolved to see him again, and this time she wouldn't stick to the sidelines. This time, she'd make sure the bullies knew what they were dealing with. 'And what about you? Is home OK?'

'That place has never been my home. Not sure I know where my home is, maybe that's the problem.' Toyah looked out and up to the hills. The dark clouds that had gathered over the past few days lingered, ominous.

'I think you need to do something for *you*. For your future. Pinto will work things out.'

Toyah dragged her focus from the horizon to look at Jay like she'd suggested something crazy. Emotions flickered across her face, intrigue, even hope. 'Maybe,' she said, returning her gaze to the hills. 'So what's going on? What does the oracle say about this darkness?'

'Alf?'

'And the other one, what was his name?'

'Colson. We think there's a way to protect Island 8. For good.'

Toyah nodded, like she knew Jay would already have a solid plan. Her confidence energised Jay. Cassie and Stitch had offered little in the way of support and solidarity in recent weeks, so Toyah's positive energy had become important.

'Thanks,' said Jay.

'What for?'

'Lots of things. Thanks for getting us out of that place, Island 7. At one stage I wasn't convinced we'd make it back.'

'Never in doubt.' Toyah smiled. 'Can't help worry about Tiago and his family. You think the Readers will get to him in the end?'

'He's made it this far. He has some means of shielding they haven't cracked yet.'

'You cracked it.'

'I'm Given. It's different.'

Toyah shrugged. 'I guess. You'd know.' She stood to leave. 'Let me know if you need anything. Whatever your plan is.'

'I will.' As much as she valued Toyah's ingenuity, she had no intention of dragging her into her journey to the source. This one was meant for her alone. 'And don't worry. You'll work it out.'

Darkness hung like a cloak over Highdown. The hilltop seemed to emit tiny sparks of light, like a thundercloud. With each spark, a picture came to Jay's mind. 'The channel,' she said to herself, her words drifting on the light breeze off the sea.

It was Flick's deception that tricked Jay into opening the first channel to the darkness. What she now saw was a consequence of Flick's attack on Otis. The pathway for Atta was wide open. There was no way of telling how much time she had. Atta could already be at the sink-room, building, preparing to take the final Island, the last remaining stronghold of the Given.

Looking into the darkness, Jay felt the power of the Given flow through her body. The sea whispered. The power was as strong as ever. Jay was as strong as she'd ever been. A spark pierced the darkness and shot through the distance between the house and the hills in a fraction of a second. This time, Jay opened and saw a vision of Atta. She sensed his weakness, that his eagerness to get to her would be his downfall. She was far more powerful.

She stood, opening to the waves of dark energy, matching their force with her own Given energy. She felt no fear. The sparks became a stream of white light, a pathway between Jay and the dark. The light expanded to encompass the whole of the grey sky so that nothing was visible but for a figure in the distance, heading towards Jay as if crossing a bridge. Jay beckoned. This was Atta, yet, still, she felt no fear.

The physical form of Atta came into view as the white light cleared. Jay stood on the shore of Island 8, looking over the water to Atta, on the shore of Island 7. Neither moved.

'Very brave,' Atta said, his voice low, steady, and calm. 'Bringing me here like this.'

Jay's energy outweighed her fear. While she hadn't intended to summon Atta, she was surprised at how easy it had been. She sensed she would have the upper hand if they were to fight. Could he be defeated here, in interdimensional space?

She wasted no time. Jay attacked with all the power she could summon. Atta rocked back, stumbling into the trunk of the tree in the centre of Island 7.

She reached deeper into the Given lake of power, directing

a growing stream of attack. Then she paused. Atta recovered, slowly standing tall again. He niggled at the edges of her defences, but she chased away his infiltrations like batting insects buzzing around her head.

Jay took a deep breath and opened fully to the energy in the environment, the tree at the centre of her Island, the ground beneath her feet, and the three streams of water from the rivers flowing into the foot of the tree. She dug deep into Atta's mind, pushing his consciousness around as easily as if she were sweeping leaves. He lost his footing for a moment and fell to the floor on all fours.

The full power of the Given flowed through Jay. She sensed the energy of the source stone and made one decisive attack on Atta as he struggled to get to his feet.

The energy knocked Atta flat. White light filled the sky and descended once more on the Islands. Jay kept up the flow of her attack, determined to finish Atta here, now. He seemed to shrivel under the weight of the white glare of the light from the sky. Then everything went white and Jay stopped, crouching to rest. She breathed heavily for a minute, peering into the light to see what remained of Atta.

As the light eased, like a clearing mist, she saw the prone figure of Atta on the shore of Island 7. She sensed no dark energy from him, and for a moment she dared to hope that he could be dead, or at least reduced. Then his leg moved.

She drew a deep breath once more. He was weak. She would finish him. She thrust her power into his mind. He squirmed, turning over on the shore. He seemed to gather whatever remaining power he could and fired dark pulses of energy at Jay, but it was a distraction more than a concern.

Atta raised himself to his knees and looked into the sky. The white mist intensified, swirled around the Islands mixed with black smoke-like swirls of darkness. The light intensified until Atta was nothing more than a dim outline across the water. He turned then, away from Jay, and the light filled her head until there was nothing else.

Jay woke face down on her bed, with no memory of how she'd got from outside on the roof to her room. She shook her head clear and sat up.

She'd taken on Atta and got the better of him. His attacks had been feeble. His attempts to fight her off ineffective.

But he was alive. She felt him still.

So now she knew she couldn't defeat him on the Islands. She would need to finish him in the physical world. But any vestige of fear was now gone. Jay knew her power was enough.

27

At first light, Jay climbed in to the front seat of the car to head to the prison. She threw her rucksack with the source stone onto the passenger seat. Before she turned the key in the ignition, she paused, sensing something. She looked over her shoulder and jumped when she saw Stitch laid out on the back seat, his legs folded over one another and a coat over his body for warmth. He stirred.

'Sorry to wake you,' Jay said, sarcasm in her tone.

Stitch croaked a reply. 'Ah, you're here. I figured you'd slope off early.'

'You could have come in to the house?'

'Didn't want you to talk me out of it. I'm coming with you.'

Jay stifled a laugh at Stitch's bedraggled look. She was relieved to have him with her. She needed him. As much as she tried to push the fear from her mind, she was scared for sure, and she didn't yet know how much resistance she would get from Atta and his Readers. With Stitch, she was stronger. She knew that now. He clambered into the front seat, knocking Jay's bag onto the floor.

'Careful,' Jay said. 'That's only the most valuable and powerful piece of rock you'll ever come across.'

'Sorry,' Stitch said, pulling his seatbelt on. 'Let's hit the road.'

Jay drove with her window rolled down and sea breeze blowing through the car. She glanced over at the bag on Stitch's lap, the source stone safe inside. With their combined strength of power, they'd get the stone into the channel to the core. Where uncertainty fluttered at the edges of her mind, she pushed it away. There was no time for second thoughts.

She shifted the car down into second and turned into Northtown, taking the route along the river. She pulled over, pausing for a moment on the river road. It was here they'd scaled the river wall and entered the storm water system to free Cassie from Hinton. 'This time we take the front entrance,' she said.

'Go in fighting,' said Stitch.

She looked up towards the alleyway between the houses and wondered about Sebastian, the guardian of the house that was their overnight resting place before moving in for their rescue of Cassie. Sebastian had been twitchy, nervous of their presence, fearful of capture by Readers. The estate had improved since then. More of the houses were occupied. There were people on the streets – families heading home, teenagers on their way out. She looked through the windscreen towards the prison.

'What are you thinking?' asked Stitch.

'That we see if Sebastian is there, check he's OK?'

'You sense something?'

'No,' said Jay. 'That's the thing. I don't feel him.' She turned the car around and headed for Sebastian's place.

The windows of Sebastian's house remained boarded, much as they were before, but now the windows on each side showed life. Jay pulled on the handbrake and they slipped out of the car, the rucksack with the source stone over her shoulder. They hopped over the low front wall and around to the side alley, which led to the back door of the house. Jay cupped her hands on the glass to look for any signs of movement. Sebastian should be less reclusive now that the Given were accepted in society.

She knocked, waited, then tried the handle. The door clicked open and Jay pushed it far enough that they could squeeze through. Stitch closed it behind them. The kitchen was dingy. The smell in the air was of a house left empty - no scent of human activity. She opened the fridge, which stayed dark and held nothing but a half-empty container of milk, solid at the bottom. She exchanged a look with Stitch. Her heart sank at the thought that Sebastian had been taken by Readers, and that it could have been payback for sheltering her and Stitch.

In the middle room, Sebastian's belongings were scattered all over the floor. She feared the worst for him, but retained hope that he'd moved on, and not fallen to the mercies of the Readers.

Stitch sat on the bed as Jay sifted through his scattered belongings, organising them into piles as she tidied. A drawer full of papers had been upended onto the floor – correspondence, bills, old bank statements, and a few personal effects. She stacked them neatly back in the drawer and returned the drawer to its cabinet.

Opening a photo album, she recognised Sebastian as a younger man, standing with a woman Jay figured was his partner, and two children, girls both under five.

'What's that?' asked Stitch.

'His family.' One of the little girls hung onto his arm, pulling him towards the floor. She was crying in the photo.

Sebastian looked young, maybe not much over twenty. 'I wonder what happened to them.'

Stitch stood. 'We should go.'

Jay felt an urgent need to find out what had happened to Sebastian, but she knew Stitch was right. She closed the photo album and pushed it onto the table beside Sebastian's bed, knocking something onto the floor as she did so.

'What's that?' asked Stitch.

Jay leaned down to pick it up. 'His old staff pass for the prison. He used to work there.'

'Any use?'

'No. It's more than two years out of date and, anyway, the prison's been closed for months. But this...'

'What?'

'The pass is for a staff entrance on Southdown Road. I didn't know there was a staff entrance. That will be a better route in than the main entrance.'

* * *

JAY KEPT THE ENGINE RUNNING. The guard's box was occupied, just like the one at the main gates which they had passed by on their way through. It made no sense for security to be in place if the prison had long been abandoned.

She pulled up to the lowered gate and shielded. A Reader stepped out of the security hut and approached the driver's side, pulling his hood up against the gathering wind and spotting rain. Jay looked at Stitch, then wound the window down halfway.

'The prison is closed,' said the man, speaking slowly, his voice low and his breath steaming the outside of the window. Jay felt his power and immediately directed more energy into her shield. He scrutinised her, then Stitch, his grey-blue eyes reflecting the colour of the sky. His expression was neutral - not suspicious, not interested.

He was a level seven, strong, but still no match for Jay and Stitch. She looked over his shoulder at the other guard in the security hut. His level was lower, perhaps a four or five. The Reader at her window would be the one to focus on. 'Ready?' she said. Stitch nodded.

Working together, they entered the Reader's mind. They twisted the level seven's thoughts. His expression turned from neutral to confused. He straightened, staggered a little and then leaned with his back into Jay's window. Jay doubled her effort, and the Reader shook his head as if trying to rid himself of their influence.

The other Reader called out, 'Hey?'

Jay and Stitch turned their attention to the Reader in the booth. He went down with little resistance. Without taking her eyes off the level seven, Jay reduced the weaker Reader to the point of unconsciousness. The level seven saw what was happening and turned to run. Jay and Stitch entered his head, digging, manipulating. He stumbled, then fell over his own legs, hitting the ground with force where he remained prone, unmoving.

Both Readers incapacitated, Jay stepped carefully from the car to the booth and opened the gates, looking towards the prison complex for any movement.

Jay followed her intuition, guiding the car through the old prison access roads, her senses tuned to the presence of more Readers. It was eerily quiet.

There were few buildings remaining from the old prison complex. Most of the area had returned to its natural state, with grass and foliage weaving through the rubble. In the distance, she saw one of the few structures still standing, the main building, which sat above the old sink-room.

28

The tarmac surface of the old staff car park had deteriorated over time, making way for weeds and grass impatiently pushing up from below. They could see the remains of the sink-room building they had destroyed, the building where the Given were led to have their powers ripped from them by Readers.

'You feel that?' Jay said. She sensed dark power emanating from the building and knew that the connection with the core was active. The strength of the power shocked her, given that the electromagnets, like she'd seen on Island 7, couldn't yet be operational. It crossed her mind to turn around and head as far from the facility as possible.

'I can feel something,' said Stitch.

Forcing the fear from her mind, Jay pushed open the car door. They strode across the car park to the outside of the part-demolished building. The hum of the facility grew louder as they approached, reminding Jay of the noise that came from the sink-room on Island 7. The closer they got, the surer she became the electromagnets were more advanced than she'd expected. Jay shuddered, thinking how Flick had played her. Atta was closer to taking control than she'd let on.

Not one door to the main building was intact. The rehabilitation of the sink-room by the Readers hadn't included repairs to the superstructure. This was a functional repair, no time for the aesthetics. They passed through an opening and into the building. As they turned a corner, they were faced by a lone Reader.

'What are you doing here?' he said. 'How did you get in?'

Before Jay or Stitch answered, the Reader seemed to recognise who they were, and he reacted. A sharp pain entered Jay's head, knocking her off balance. She staggered against the wall of the corridor, her bag dropping to the floor by her feet. She shielded, resisting his influence. Stitch reacted, launching a counterattack on the Reader. The Reader intensified his digging, piercing Jay's mind and disorientating her. Stitch struggled to penetrate the Reader's mind. As Jay wobbled on her feet, he came at her. His switch to physical attack took his concentration and Jay was momentarily released from his grip. She ducked, and he stumbled past her into the wall. When he turned, Jay and Stitch were ready.

He hit the ground with the force of their combined attack. On the floor of the corridor in front of them, he writhed in pain, holding the sides of his head. Jay saw through the darkness to the fear in the level eight Reader. He'd not experienced the Given with the connected strength of Jay and Stitch's power before. She preyed on that fear, used it as a door to the deeper parts of his mind until she dug into his subconscious.

He let out a defeated gasp of air and his arms dropped from the sides of his head as he slipped over onto his back, unmoving, unconscious.

With her foot, Jay pushed back the Reader's sleeve to confirm her sense that he was a high level. The black figure of

8 stared back at her, a marking she'd seen only a few times, including her own. She looked at Stitch and his jaw dropped open. 'This is bad,' he said.

Jay picked up her rucksack and pressed on towards the source of the hum, her confidence growing with each step. The level 8 Reader had caught them off guard, but proved little resistance in the end. She would find the opening to the core and free this place from Atta's darkness.

They turned the last corner into an atrium. A deep tomb opened in the ground, not as wide as the hole on Island 7, but deeper. It fell away into darkness as Jay neared the edge.

The hum emanated from the depths. As she came closer, a glint of light emerged where the three heads of the electro-magnet rotated around a central core.

It's complete, Jay thought with shock. The system was already fully functional, much like the system on Island 7. She looked around, her eyes darting between glints of light in the depths of the hole, looking for Atta.

'What is this?' Stitch said, staring into the darkness.

'Like I saw on Island 7. This is the sink-room.'

Atta was close. Jay could sense him. He was already channelling the power from the core. Feeling the dark energy, Jay knew that this facility was powerful, more so than that on Island 7.

Jay's heart raced as she scanned the room. Near the far shadows, a figure moved.

Flick.

Jay stood rooted to the spot as Flick approached. 'Traitor,' Jay said, off guard at the sight of the girl she had considered a friend.

'You two can't do anything here,' Flick said. Her expression was almost of concern for Jay. 'It's too late.'

'We'll see.' Stitch stood alongside Jay as she pulled her rucksack off her back. 'I trusted you,' she said.

'We *helped* you,' Stitch said.

'It's too late, Jay. I'm sorry.'

Jay ignored Flick and opened the zip of the rucksack. 'You have to find the Given to feed into your machine before this will have any impact.'

Flick sighed in resignation. 'The power we get from the core on this Island does more than transform the Given. We can transform any member of the population.'

Jay remained silent. She looked at Stitch, and he nodded encouragement for her to get on with it.

'We can also use it for the *refinement* of Readers. With the energy of these new sink-rooms, we can increase the strength of power of existing Readers.' Flick looked frustrated as Jay continued to ignore her. 'Don't you see?' Flick said. 'There will soon be great numbers of level *eight* Readers, and of course diminishing numbers of the Given as we work through your population.'

Jay shook her head, no longer willing to discuss Flick's dark plans. She pulled the source stone from her bag and allowed the bag to fall to the ground. She held it in front of her with both hands, expecting Flick to react. Flick simply looked at the floor as if disappointed in Jay.

Atta appeared first as a shadow, barely more than a wisp of smoke. Then his physical form materialised much like it had the first time Jay faced him. Stitch stepped backwards at the sight of him. Jay felt his extraordinary energy once more.

'Thank you,' he said to Jay, his voice gravelly. 'For bringing the stone.'

Jay looked at the stone and stepped closer to the edge of the hole that stretched down into the core.

'I enjoyed our little game on the Islands yesterday,' Atta said.

'When I took you down, you mean?'

Atta laughed. 'That's not the real world, you know that.'

Jay readied herself. 'Your weakness felt real enough to me.' She looked from Atta to Flick. Flick averted her gaze.

Jay gathered her Given power from within, opening to the energy of her surroundings, both the dark and the light - building her strength. She drew closer to Stitch so that their arms touched and their energy flowed together.

'How sweet,' Atta said, smiling.

The anger Jay should have felt for Flick's betrayal was strangely absent. Her only emotion towards her was pity. Flick continued to avoid eye contact, choosing instead to slip behind Atta as he stepped towards Jay and Stitch. His physical form consolidated, he was a man of little more than thirty, athletically built. Jay focused her and Stitch's energy on their shielding, anticipating his first attack and preparing to throw the stone. But something held her back.

'Why did you come here?' Atta said, genuine confusion in his tone and in his mind.

'To finish the job I started on the Islands,' Jay said.

Atta turned to Flick and smiled briefly. 'And you two came alone?'

Atta's power came at Jay and Stitch in waves, as if he was struggling to keep it back.

Jay moved quickly. She threw the source stone as far across the hole as she could so that it plummeted towards the centre. Then, with Stitch, she turned to Atta, and they shielded them- selves and the trajectory of the source stone with all the power they could muster. He looked at them, then at the stone, and raised a hand. Jay and Stitch fell back, stumbling and slamming against the floor. They watched helplessly as Atta turned to the hole and halted the stone in mid-air.

The stone landed gently in his outstretched hand. 'You thought it would be that easy? Have you lost your minds?' He took the stone in both hands and released Jay and Stitch from his control. He turned his nose up at the source stone, as if it were a lump of dirt. As he placed it upright, he seemed to flinch as its energy pulsed. 'You can't just throw this in there. It's not a football,' he laughed. 'This facility is the most concentrated source of dark energy on all the eight Islands. You think this little stone would simply drift into the core?'

Jay slumped back to the floor. That was exactly what she had thought. She desperately weighed options, furious with herself for her naivety.

'We need to leave,' said Stitch under his breath.

Digging into her fury, Jay attacked, channelling all her energy and desire to survive into Atta, its lightness circling him and piercing his mind. Stitch reached out and touched Jay's arm, channelling his own power through her. The source stone dropped to the floor with a loud crack. Atta staggered. Jay rocked back on her heels as his resistance came hard, deflecting their attack and powering back with a darkness that penetrated to her very bones. Stitch seemed to glow in the energy and crumpled to the floor. Jay's legs trembled and gave way as she dropped to her knees.

The darkness swirled around her head and into her body – through her nose, mouth and ears. It filled her as Flick looked on and the source stone rested, inert, up against Flick's foot.

She had misjudged Atta, misread the strength of his power – or completely over-estimated her own ability to control the power of the Given in her own land, even with Stitch. Her head swam, and she felt Atta's sense of victory.

He crouched beside her. 'Not yet,' he said, breathing in her face. 'I still need you.' Jay looked over at Stitch, his body still.

Atta stood, keeping his dark grip on Jay and turning to speak to Flick. Jay couldn't hear the words, but Flick picked up the source stone and turned to leave as Atta returned to Jay's side, tightening his grip. Jay struggled to keep her eyes from closing. The blurred images merged into one. She sensed that if she closed her eyes, then that would be the end.

'Let me in,' Atta said. Jay felt his energy pushing at the edges of her deep subconscious, and she resisted. He seemed to lose patience and stood, grabbing Jay by the collar of her top and dragging her towards the edge of the room, flinging her against the wall then pulling her into an upright sitting position. She slumped to the side. He grabbed her by the hair and forced her upright once more.

He stood before Jay. He raised his head and closed his eyes. Through her blurred vision, the edges of his body seemed fluid, with wisps of dark smoke escaping his form every few seconds. His eyes closed. Jay felt his attack once more, and she was helpless to resist. She screamed as his energy opened her up and she saw what he was trying to do.

Atta's eyes sprang open, and a smile crept across his face as he gained control of Jay. Images flashed through her mind of her friends, of Alf, her dad. 'What are you doing?' she mumbled through pain and weakness as her head lolled. Alf's image came to the front of her mind, his face grey and his expression grave. Jay's eyelids drooped.

'Don't resist,' Atta said.

'Stop...'

'You are my channel to the old man.'

'Alf...' Jay mumbled. A spike of adrenaline forced her eyes open. 'Don't hurt him.'

'He evades me, always. Not anymore. Thanks to you, he will no longer be a threat.'

The image of Alf in her mind was squeezed and distorted, his face a picture of pain and hurt. 'Leave him,' Jay said, pushing back at Atta's power. She refused to be his conduit to attack Alf. Pain shot through her head and into her chest. It felt like her heart had stopped. She couldn't breathe.

Jay slumped to the floor. She felt her friend's presence. Alf was with her. But the strength of his energy slipped away and after a few seconds, he was gone.

Atta took a deep breath, then sighed with a sense of satisfaction. 'Thank you. That's been a long time coming. You feel it?'

If you could feel the absence of something, then, yes, she could feel it.

* * *

ALF HAD BEEN a big part of what Atta saw as the defence of Island 8. He had dealt with him, and now he would deal with the last remaining threat. He would finish Jay. Without her and Alf, he would be free to complete what he'd started here on Island 8.

Atta faced Jay. The pain in her head doubled. She could no longer focus on shielding and the pain ramped up in waves. She thought of Stitch.

Then there was nothing.

Everything stopped.

She fell onto her side. The darkness receded from her eyes and she saw Flick standing over her with Stitch. Flick leaned down and shook Jay by the shoulders. 'Get up! You need to go. Now!'

Jay staggered to her feet and pushed Flick away from her. Stitch held Jay's arm. 'We need to go,' he said.

Flick handed Stitch Jay's rucksack and she could see that the source stone was inside. She looked at Flick, whose eyes bore into her, pleading with her to leave before it was too late.

Jay could do little more than be guided by Stitch towards the exit. Flick hurried them up as she looked back over her shoulder. The dark wisps of smoke came once more. They circled, and a warm breeze flowed into the building from the outside as if sucked into a vacuum. Flick turned to face Atta as he re-formed in front of her. 'Leave,' she said to Jay and Stitch. 'Don't look back.'

As they fled, the noise of battle grew behind them. At the entrance, Jay glanced backwards. Flick faced Atta. She would stand no chance of resisting his power. Jay took a step back towards Flick and Atta, but Stitch held her back, and a shake of the ground knocked them off their feet. Warm air flushed through the corridors.

Dust and debris flew through the air. Flick screamed as Jay tried to summon some power to help, to resist Atta, but already the noise abated. The fight was over.

Jay and Stitch backed towards the door.

As the dust settled, Atta stood over the still body of Flick. Stitch grabbed Jay by the arm and dragged her towards the exit.

Dark energy buffeted them, pushing them from the building. Now Jay knew the truth: she was no match for Atta, even here in her homeland, with Stitch, with her power at its strongest.

As they reached the car, Stitch pulled at the passenger door and shoved Jay inside, she looked back towards the building. It shook and rattled, the top floors buckling. The remains of the windows and doors imploded, sucking in air so that Jay felt the car being dragged towards the building. Stitch stumbled as he tried to prise himself into the driver's seat. It was as if a black hole had opened up inside the building, consuming all matter within its reach.

The vortex grew stronger, and Stitch had to hold on to the side of the car to prevent from being dragged across the car park. He climbed into the front seat and used all his strength to shut the door. The engine started first time and Jay breathed relief.

A figure appeared at the epicentre of the destruction. Stitch slammed the car into gear and spun it around in the car park. Without looking back, he powered towards the exit. They were out of Atta's reach. In the wing mirror, Atta continued to suck everything within range into his tornado of darkness.

29

___

Dark clouds thickened. Jay asked Stitch to drive to the Hill; she was drawn there, as she often was in times of desperation. Being anywhere else seemed to make no sense, and she needed to recover. The clouds moved in unnatural patterns in the sky and Jay knew that the influence of the Dark was growing.

She wiped the rain from her eyes, and they crossed the boundary into the central ring of trees. The energy of the Given flowed through her on the Hill with a renewed vigour. They both sat on the floor next to the log seats around the fire. Jay stared into the cold, wet ashes as a deep ache of sorrow grew in her chest. Alf. Her dear sweet friend. Had she yet again been responsible for the destruction of one of her friends?

She looked at Stitch. He felt her pain. 'Alf,' Jay said.

'I know,' said Stitch.

She felt nothing of him in the power.

* * *

JAY AND STITCH lay back on the sodden woodland floor and looked skyward. The rain had stopped, but big droplets continued to fall from the trees. A half-moon peeked through the clouds to illuminate the branches. The wet leaves shone, sprinkled with diamonds.

'Alf?' she said aloud, closing her eyes and taking deep breaths of the cool, fresh air. A cool droplet landed on her forehead, the sound exaggerated, echoing through the trees. She allowed herself to be consumed by the power of the land, sinking into the woodland floor and into the network of tree roots, earth fissures and groundwater flows. She submitted to their direction, flowing with the power, searching for Alf.

'Alf?' she said again. 'I'm sorry.'

His image came to Jay. His energy was low. He was weak. Whatever Atta had done, he had succeeded in diminishing Alf, and he'd done it by channelling his dark power through Jay - *she* had provided him access to Alf.

She sank deeper into the power.

Alf appeared as if he was sitting before her, inside the ring of trees at Highdown. He reached out for her hand and she sat up. The woodland floor no longer wet, daylight streaming through the gaps in the branches above their heads. The sky shone blue.

'Alf?' Jay stammered. 'What have I done?'

Alf smiled. 'You've achieved more than anyone else I can think of. In this messed up world, you, my girl, are a shining light, a beacon of hope.'

Jay shook her head and looked up at the sky for inspiration. 'What is this?'

'This is *my* creation. You brought me here, but I created the backdrop, so to speak.' Alf waved his hand to take in the sky and as he did, a rainbow appeared above. 'Look, there's only so much I can do. Everything that Colson said is right.'

Jay looked Alf in the eye and could see his anxiety as clearly as if it were her own. He continued: 'But I have faith in you, my girl.'

'We can do this together. Whatever we need to do, we will beat him.'

'I know,' Alf said with a sad smile. 'I *never* doubted. But now is the time for you to focus.'

'What do we do?'

'That's for you to work out, but you are not alone. You need to remember your roots.' Jay frowned, and Alf leaned closer. 'In here,' he said as he tapped his chest. 'Dig deep, my girl. Trust your instincts, your intuition. I can't do this for you. You are far stronger and more capable than me or anyone else.'

'He's too strong.'

Alf shook his head.

Jay slumped. This test, or whatever it was, was designed for her to fail.

'Remember where all this started?'

Jay thought for a moment. Her powers had come to her at a relatively young age. She was drawn to Alf's bookshop back then. At first it was an inexplicable draw, but after time, as her power became clearer, the draw was clear to Alf, and the community of the Given, although she still didn't understand it back then. 'The bookshop,' said Jay.

'Yes, and your connections. Stitch. And Cassie,' Alf said, taking Jay's hand once more. 'Cassie has lost her way. You need to help her, and she will help *you*.'

'She's so angry with me.'

'She's scared. Of becoming isolated. She's scared for *you*.'

Jay almost laughed at the thought of Cassie being scared, but Alf's expression was serious. She looked up at him and his energy seemed to fade, his complexion becoming paler as she watched. He glanced up at the sky. 'It's time,' he said.

'For what?'

'For you to get to work. Remember what I said.'

'Which bit?'

Alf smiled, his hand still holding onto Jay's, but his grip weakening. 'Whichever bit you think is important.'

The sun seemed to slip behind a cloud and the area inside the ring of trees on Highdown darkened. They both looked up as clouds thickened. The sun made way for a half-moon before that too became obscured by black clouds. 'Alf?' Jay said. His hand slipped from hers and when she turned to him, he was gone.

The rain came.

Jay stood and lifted her face to the sky, the rain bouncing off and splashing into her open mouth. Stitch stirred and stood with her.

There was a missing part to her world now. Alf had gone. Not just gone from her mind, but gone from this world. He was dead.

His words pinged around inside her head, not yet able to find a home where they made any sense. A hole in her gut expanded to swallow her entire body. Her tears mixed with the rain on her face.

The rain stopped abruptly, and the moon reappeared, casting light over the hill.

What they faced now was something *never* seen before, not even Sasha Colden, *Maram,* the first recorded 8C of their homeland, had faced anything like this, and with Alf gone, there was no-one to help.

PART IV

30

Cassie approached from the inner tree-line, like a ghost in the light of the moon. She pulled a towel from her rucksack and threw it at Stitch before sitting down on the log. Jay and Stitch joined her, Stitch rubbing the towel on his head. 'Thanks,' he said.

Cassie's expression was grave. She looked from Stitch to Jay and was about to speak when Jay said, 'I know.'

'Know what?' asked Cassie.

'Alf's gone,' said Jay. 'Atta used me to get to him.' She explained to Cassie what had happened. As she spoke, it was as if she were outside of herself, watching herself explain the death of Alf. He was family. She couldn't stop thinking about what would happen to his dog, Buster.

Cassie nodded and lowered her gaze. 'We thought he was OK. Then he slipped away.'

'I'm sorry, Cass,' said Jay. 'I've been doing this all wrong.' She looked away into the trees. 'I've made everything worse.'

'It's not your fault,' said Stitch.

'Otis is improving,' said Cassie, standing. 'He'll be OK.'

'Thank God,' said Jay.

'What now?' said Stitch, standing with Cassie and helping Jay up.

'We'll work it out, but we need to stick together,' Cassie said. She drew Jay into a hug and immediately recoiled. 'Ugh, you are soaked.'

'I'm all out of plans,' said Jay. 'This hasn't happened before.'

'Not since 1667,' said Stitch.

Jay used Stitch's towel to dry her hair. '1667,' she said. 'We don't know what happened back then. Alf and Colson were guessing.'

Cassie said, 'If anyone knows what happened, then it's those two old guys. Alf knew all there was to know about the origins of the Given, and what Colson doesn't know about the powers isn't worth knowing.'

'What happened at the prison?' asked Cassie.

'Atta was not what I imagined him to be, not what I'd seen on Island 7. He barely had a physical form. It felt like we were grasping at mist in the air. He was impenetrable. His power was like nothing I've experienced from the Readers.' she said.

'What is he?' asked Cassie. 'If he's not human, then what?'

'He looked human to me,' said Stitch. 'Mostly.'

'How did you get away from him?' asked Cassie.

'Flick,' said Stitch. 'She did something. Distracted him. Shielded us. I don't know.'

'Is she dead?' asked Cassie, as if she already knew the answer. Jay nodded. Cassie snorted. 'She deserves whatever she got.'

They were silent for a moment as Cassie's words bounced between them. Neither Stitch nor Jay responded. Cassie felt deeply for Otis, and Flick had attacked him in a way that Jay could barely imagine.

'Look,' Cassie said, 'if Atta can be distracted, like you said, then he's human enough for us to get to him.' A character-istic confidence came through in her voice, despite the obvious imbalance of power, and the uncertainty. This was the Cassie who Jay remembered from before, from the Inter-land. 'Is that the stone?' asked Cassie, pointing at Jay's bag, sodden and scrunched up next to the log. Before waiting for Jay's answer, she grabbed the bag and pulled out the source stone. A breeze seemed to pick up and rifle through the trees as she held it in both hands. 'So how do we get this into the core.'

'We tried that,' said Jay. 'We have to get past *him* first. And however many Readers he's created.'

'Since when have a few Readers scared us off?' said Cassie

'Us?' Jay said, liking the sound of the word.

'You bet,' said Stitch.

* * *

STITCH TRAVELLED with Jay in the old Ford. Cassie travelled alone, using Otis's moped. By the time Jay had parked the car back in the garage at Jay's house and walked to the pub, Cassie was already annoyed. 'Took your time,' she grumbled as Jay and Stitch strode into the pub car park where Cassie had parked the bike.

Jay and Stitch chose not to respond.

'There's a bunch of them already in there,' said Cassie. 'I saw your dad and Colson go in.'

Jay pushed through the pub door towards the basement steps. The landlord caught her eye and nodded for them to head down. The door at the top of the stairs scraped along the concrete floor as Jay pulled it back. She stepped down into a waft of musty basement air tinged with the smell of burned paper from the remains of their library that they'd transported to the basement from the shop. She checked once over her shoulder that Stitch and Cassie were still with her.

Jay dumped her bag on an empty chair. There were three men and two women in the basement, all leaning over the table in the middle of the room. Alf's dog, Buster, ran to her, jumping up and licking her face. 'Oh, Buster, I'm sorry,' said Jay, hugging the dog.

As well as Ben and Colson, Matchstick was there, along with two women Jay had never met. All heads lifted to look at Jay and her friends as they entered. 'What happened?' Ben said to his daughter, appraising her for damage. 'We all felt it.' He motioned towards his colleagues. 'For a moment back then, we thought you were dead. It was only when I felt your power coming back to you we stopped short of heading out to find you. You know Alf is...'

Jay nodded. At her feet sat Buster, looking up into her eyes as if for answers.

'It's not your fault,' said Ben, holding on to Jay's shoulders. The immediate insistence from everyone that Alf's death was not her fault was convincing Jay that her gut was right, and it was no-one else's fault but her own that Atta had found a way through her to get to him.

'I should have...'

'What?' Ben interrupted. 'Alf would be the first to say that you had no way of predicting this.' Ben drew Jay into a tight hug. 'Come. Sit. Tell us what happened.'

Jay described her experience at the prison, sparing no details. She told the gathered resistance gang about Atta's presence, his power, and what was happening at the new sink-room, as well as repeating the story of the blight of Island 7 for the new members around the table.

'Like I told you,' Ben said to the others.

'It's a repeat,' one of the two women said before lowering her eyes to the floor.

She looked deeply sad. Her words stuck in her throat and the other woman had to continue. 'A repeat,' she said. Her beautiful red hair draped over her shoulders, ringlets stretching lower than the level of the table. She reached down to stroke a dog at her feet, smaller than Buster, older.

'This is Hannah,' Ben said to Jay. 'She's come down from the London branch.'

Hannah smiled. 'And this is Benji.' She motioned to the terrier at her feet. 'And Judith.' She nodded to her friend, whose tears now made sense to Jay as she connected the woman to Alf.

Her dad's reference to the resistance groups as different branches would have amused Jay at any other time. Not on this day.

'A repeat of what?' asked Cassie.

Hannah remained silent, as if deep in thought. Ben spoke: 'Tell them what you told us, Hannah.'

She snapped out of her trance and looked around at the expectant faces. Her eyes lingered on Colson as he met her gaze. 'Like Alf, and Colson here,' she said, 'me and Judith have studied the history.'

Judith straightened in her seat, put a hand on Hannah's arm, and took over for her. 'We have some unique literature on the powers in our own personal library.'

'Yes,' said Hannah, her enthusiasm building.

Judith continued: 'Materials we haven't even dared to bring down here before today, before we had the call from Colson. Given what has happened to Alf...' She paused, unable to complete the sentence.

Hannah took over and Jay thought that these two women

were connected like odd twins. 'If what you say is true...' Hannah said.

'Of course it's true,' Stitch snapped.

Jay put a hand on Stitch's arm to calm him. Hannah raised her hands in defence.

Judith leaned forward. 'I know, but we have to be sure. We have to check every detail, tick every box if we are to save our homeland from the same fate as the other six.'

'Six?' said Jay. 'There are seven other Islands.'

Judith and Hannah nodded in unison. 'Yes,' said Judith. 'But there is one other that has successfully resisted. Island 4, we think.' She paused a moment to catch her breath, and Jay thought she looked a little tearful.

'Sorry,' Judith said. 'It's been a long journey to get to this point in our understanding. We always suspected that the events of 1667 occurred at a centre of power, but we couldn't be sure.

'Until now,' Judith and Hannah said in chorus. Hannah's dog Benji struggled to his feet and moved closer to where Buster lay curled at Jay's feet. He sniffed at Buster's nose and curled up next to him.

'So Island 4 is free of the Readers? Like Alf and Colson said?' Jay asked.

'Yes,' said Hannah. 'And free of Atta. In 1667, they severed the Island's connection with the core. The Dark can never penetrate their land, not even if the Readers approach by land. No dark power can prevail on Island 4 without a connection to the core.'

'Can the connection be re-made?' asked Jay.

'Not if the severance has come from the clash of power between the Dark and the Given. The impact is catastrophic and final.'

'And the other Islands?' said Jay.

'The other six Islands are already dark. We have lost contact with all six...'

'Contact?' said Jay. 'You have contacts in the other Islands?'

'Of course. Within the Given, we share knowledge,' said Judith. Jay tried to read her. She sensed only a wisp of power in Judith or Hannah. Their minds were open books, their thoughts pure, and intentions almost entirely altruistic as far as Jay could read. These two women cared about their environment, their society, and all within it. She even sensed pity and compassion for the plight of the Readers.

'But, one by one,' Judith continued, 'our contacts have been silenced, the last being Island 7.'

'Tiago?' Jay said.

'Yes! He is a good man.' Judith fizzed for a moment, then slumped once more. 'We are afraid for him.'

'I met him. The man I met on Island 7 was their 8C, Tiago.'

'He's alive?' Hannah asked. Jay nodded, bringing synchronised smiles to the faces of Judith and Hannah. 'We thought Island 7 would be the one to succeed in its resistance,' Hannah said. 'Tiago is strong. Almost as strong as you.'

Jay turned away at the thought of Tiago on Island 7, trying to stay hidden whilst the Readers ravaged his homeland. Spikes of guilt and sadness ran through her veins, and she did her best to push them away.

Jay looked at Colson. He stared admiringly at the two women. His expression hardened, and he reached for Jay's hand. 'Hannah and Judith, with their London team, filled us in when we reached out for help, when Atta destroyed the shop.'

Through Colson's touch, Jay could feel Alf's energy. It saddened her. She pulled her hand away and turned back to Judith. 'So what do we do? How do we follow those on Island 4?'

Judith looked at Hannah, as if handing her the baton once more. 'The *source stone*,' said Hannah, looking at Jay's bag on the chair. 'The stone is the key.' Jay handed it over the table to Judith, who shifted some papers on the table to set it down like a dinner party centre-piece. 'With Colson, we have shared our knowledge and pieced it together.'

As Judith inspected the stone, Hannah said, 'There is a stone in each of the eight Islands.'

'Are you sure?' asked Stitch. We've been to Island 7 and there was nothing there.'

'It stands to reason,' said Hannah. 'Each of the sources of power of the Given is a confluence of three rivers, right?' Stitch nodded, and Hannah continued, 'And at each of these places, there is a point, a distinct point, where the three rivers meet. It might be inside the rocks, the caves, or above ground, we don't know. But each of these lands will have something at this point that has been the recipient of the power of the Given for centuries. It is the minerals at this point that form what we call the *source stone*.' She nodded towards the stone in the middle of the table, a little awe in her expression. 'And here is ours. Finally, we see it.'

Cassie stared at the stone, then, speaking for the first time since they'd arrived, said, 'Shouldn't it be glowing or something?'

Colson stood and moved closer to the table, leaning heavily on the edge with both hands so that the light hanging from the ceiling provided a glow to his grey hair. He looked at the stone and reached out his hand, stopping short as if not daring to touch it. To Jay: 'This is it.'

Jay nodded.

'*This* is how we sever the connection.'

Jay nodded again.

'We just need to figure out how to get it past Atta,' he said.

31

On the short walk home from the pub, Jay's body temperature plummeted. She was still wet from the rain up on Highdown, and now that the adrenaline had truly subsided, the cold had sunk into her bones. Her teeth chattered as she slotted her key in her front door and pushed her way inside.

The house was warm and smelled of cigarettes. In the hallway by the front door, she pulled off her wet top and replaced it with one of Sammy's hoodies that was hanging on the banister. She hung her bag on a coat hook and made her way through to the lounge.

'Oh...' Her mum startled, stubbing out her cigarette and wafting her hand at the smoke as if to cleanse the air. She jumped up from the sofa and took Jay by the arms, looking her in the eye. 'You're OK?' she said, examining Jay for wounds.

Jay nodded.

'Sit down,' Sonia said, guiding Jay to the sofa. 'I'll make you a hot drink.'

She disappeared into the kitchen, leaving Jay alone on the

sofa. She looked out through the patio doors, barely recognising her reflection in the glass. A minute later, Sonia returned with a cup of tea for Jay and the remains of a bottle of red wine for herself.

Jay warmed her hands and sipped the tea. Far too sweet. 'Thanks.'

'Your dad still at the pub?'

Jay nodded. Then she started to tremble and tears fell from her eyes. Her voice shook as she said, 'I don't know what to do.'

Sonia moved from the chair to sit beside her daughter on the sofa. 'Oh, honey. Once you've had some rest, things will seem less complicated. You shouldn't have this all on your shoulders. I know what that can be like.'

Jay looked sideways at her mum.

'OK, fine. Not the same, I know,' said Sonia. 'But I feel for you. I'm your mum. I feel what you feel. Not like powers, but *mum* power, you know?'

Jay smiled. The thought had crossed her mind that the battle she was soon to instigate could be her last. What she hadn't thought about was how her death would affect her mother or the others she might leave behind. Yet the thought was also strangely calming. It carried no fear. If this was her intended end, then so be it, so long as it secured the long-term survival of the Given in her homeland.

'What is it, love?' Sonia asked.

Jay looked at her mum, and for the first time, felt no animosity. It was the first time she could truly say that to herself. Her mum was human, flawed, like everyone else. Like Jay herself. 'Thanks Mum,' Jay replied. 'For listening. I feel better.' She sipped her tea, the warmth at last reaching her core.

The knock on the front door was so gentle that Jay barely

heard it. She looked at her mum. 'Are you expecting someone?'

Sonia shook her head. 'Probably your dad forgot his key, or Sammy.' She stood.

Jay knew that it wasn't the knock of Ben or Sammy. 'I'll get it,' she said, placing her empty mug on the coffee table and heading for the door.

She recognised Angie's parents immediately and looked down to see Angie standing between them, a broad grin on her face.

'She insisted,' Angie's mum said with a smile.

'She can't stay long,' her dad added, an eyebrow raised as if suspicious. 'She's under doctor's orders.'

Jay stepped aside. 'Come in...' she motioned to Angie's dad.

'No,' he said. 'We'll come back for her.' Angie's mum gave him a searching look, and he added, 'If that's alright with you? If you don't mind our daughter imposing on you for a few minutes?'

Angie's head snapped up to look at her dad. 'We agreed. Half an hour.'

'But that's a long time to impose on...'

'Half an hour is more than fine,' Jay said, leaning to take Angie's hand in hers and feeling an immediate connection, like the closing of an electrical circuit, a warming jolt of energy. Angie flung her arms around Jay.

'Angie, give the girl some room,' her dad said.

'I've been worried about you,' Angie said to Jay.

Angie's mum took her husband's arm. 'We'll come back in a while.'

Jay nodded and beckoned Angie into the house, closing the door as her parents retreated down the pathway to the road.

'Who's this?' Sonia exclaimed as Jay and Angie entered the lounge.

'This is my friend, Angie, the one I told you about.'

'Oh my. Are you feeling better? Jay told me what happened at the bookshop.'

'I'm fine, thank you,' Angie said, taking a seat on the sofa between Jay and her mum. She looked smaller than the last time Jay had seen her, but still as smiley as ever despite an underlying pain Jay felt but couldn't quite decipher.

Jay made eyes for her mum to leave them alone to talk. 'Oh... sorry,' Sonia said, jumping up. 'I'll be in the kitchen if you need me. Would you like a drink of anything, Angie?'

Angie smiled and shook her head.

After Sonia had left the room, Jay said, 'It's good to see you up and about, in the flesh. You've been in my head the whole time. I was worried about you.'

'That's why I'm here,' Angie said, her tone more serious now that they were alone. 'It's like we have a connection, right?'

Jay nodded.

'I don't know what it is, but this connection isn't just *your* power, it's more than that. Something just between us.'

'You think...?'

'I know it. I've been with you these last couple of days. I mean really *with* you.'

'I've felt you there,' said Jay.

'I was inside your head when you went to the prison. I saw you fight that thing with Stitch, the dark man.'

'Atta.'

'Flick saved you. She used her power to distract Atta for long enough for you and Stitch to escape. I saw what she did.'

Angie closed her eyes and reached for Jay's hand. Jay felt

the electrical connection once more, but this time, she felt something more. Angie's image swirled around inside her mind like before. She too closed her eyes and Angie came to life in her head, more real than she'd experienced before. Her entire being seemed to be connected, to be at one with Jay's, as if they were joined in mind and body. Some minutes passed before she snapped her eyes open and withdrew her hand. 'What is that?'

'The powers.'

'But you're too young.'

'Not *my* powers. Your powers. Something in your power is drawing me in.'

'How?'

'I have no idea. But the point is, I *know what's wrong.*'

'Know what?'

'That you need to get a grip.'

Jay almost laughed out loud. Angie was without doubt one of the wisest kids she'd ever met, but she'd not been told to wise up by a pre-teen before. 'Let me see your wrist.'

Angie smiled. 'Too young for that.' She pulled back her sleeve and showed Jay her unmarked skin. 'It's *your* power I am tuning in to. I'm like a radio or something.'

'I told you that you were special.' Jay smiled.

Angie looked at the clock on the wall. 'Fifteen minutes left,' she said.

'And I can tell you still have more to say,' Jay said.

'There's something missing. I can feel it, and I have seen it. Missing from your heart.'

'Angie, what do you mean?'

'Tell me why you feel that this is your mission alone. Your mission to protect the whole of this land with no help from all these people who can and want to help you?'

Jay bristled despite herself. 'Stitch was with me. I only

want to keep more people from getting hurt. There's been enough pain in the people I love.'

Angie didn't answer, just smiled her sad, wise smile.

Jay thought of Alf and marvelled again at Angie's maturity.

'You see what you're doing?' Angie continued. 'By keeping others apart from you, you end up putting them at greater risk.'

Jay stood and moved away from Angie, feeling like she was slowly losing her sense of self. Who was this little girl to erode her confidence, and at such a critical point when she needed to be strong?

'I've felt it. Your power is weakening. The longer you deny your wider connections, the further you will get from your true goal. You can't do this on your own. This thing, the darkness, Atta, he is more than a Reader. You know that. I saw it in him, through your eyes. If you go alone to fight him again, then I don't know what will happen. We will lose you for sure. And if we lose *you*, we lose everything.'

Jay scratched her head as she paced the room. 'How?' she said. 'What am I supposed to do?'

'That's your job to figure out. I'm just telling you what I know. If you shut everyone out you risk us all, and you lose out on the greatest power the Given have. Our connection.'

There was a knock at the door - three assertive knocks. 'My dad,' said Angie, and stood to leave.

32

Jay slipped through the Velux and onto the roof of her house. The moon was obscured by clouds on a night as dark as she'd ever seen over the hills. A wind gusted off the sea in angry bursts. She pulled her hood snug around her head and slid herself down the tiles to sit.

Angie's words fizzed around her mind and under her skin. Try as she might, she couldn't resolve the tension she felt with a decision. Losing Alf hung over her like a cloud as dark as the moonless night. Could she really risk any more of those she loved, or was she risking them already by trying to tackle Atta on her own? The decision of what to do next left her paralysed.

Stitch and Cassie crept up the back wall onto the roof and sat one each side of Jay without so much as a "hi". Together, they looked out towards the hills in silence, each caught up in their own thoughts.

'We need to get the stone into the core,' Jay said eventually. They all knew that disrupting the flow of dark energy would not be simple. This would be their last chance.

'How?' said Stitch.

'We'll all work together.'

'But how? And even if we do, what next? Colson said that it could create a massive explosion.'

'I have an idea,' Jay said. 'But we'll need *everyone* for it to work.'

'Who?'

'Everyone. Toyah, Sammy, Colson.'

'Speak of the Devil,' Cassie said as Sammy climbed out through Jay's window, Toyah close behind, and planted himself next to Stitch. Jay and Toyah exchanged a glance, and Jay sensed that she and Sammy had finally worked some things out. She gave a half smile.

'Don't let us interrupt you,' Toyah said as everyone went quiet.

Sammy leaned forward to peer at the others. 'Anyone would think the world was ending.'

They were quiet for a minute.

'What's the plan then?' asked Stitch.

First, a good night's rest. We're going to need it,' said Jay. 'Tomorrow we meet in the pub to go through the plan.'

* * *

AFTER EVERYONE HAD LEFT, Jay closed her eyes and turned her face into the wind, a light sea spray cooling her face. She felt energised with anticipation for what was to come in the morning. She was no longer afraid. She at last understood what needed to be done.

She drifted into the fog of her thoughts. The energy of the environment was alert, nipping at her consciousness and preventing her from drifting off to sleep.

The whispers came, becoming louder with every hiss and

crash of the sea just over the rooftops to the south. She opened to them, breathing in their energy, their urgency. Whispers turned to white noise that came with colours flowing through her mind. She filtered the white noise as she had become adept at doing and the words became clear.

The power and energy of the Given was with her, connecting the hills and energy sites of Highdown, Cissbury and Chanctonbury, amplifying and growing the force with each connection.

As the colours brightened and the energy flowed, a wisp of darkness crossed her mind, like the passage of a train before her eyes. When it returned in the next breath, it dispersed and diffused into the white light like a puff of smoke. She sensed Atta - his confidence, arrogance. He was letting her know he was ready for her, for whatever she could muster.

33

At the prison, the buildings below the ground now outnumbered those above.

Atta drifted through the corridors, making mental notes of the numbers of people in the rooms approaching the main hall, where the sink-room resided above the connection to the core. It used to be that only those with power could be subject to the process of generating Readers. Now that the power of the system had been optimised during Atta's push through the Islands, the process could be applied to any person.

Many of those in the holding cells had turned into willing participants. They sensed what was coming and the advantage in choosing the right side to support. Many, of course, remained resistant, an exercise in futility. The sink-room could create a level six Reader from anyone, even the hesitant. The Island 8 facility was already creating over twenty Readers per day at level 6 and above.

For the Given, much fewer, but much greater potential. Someone with Given power of any level, even a level 1 or level 2, could be transformed into a level 8 Reader. The process was now so efficient that Atta was almost guaranteed a level 8. It was a similar case for the Readers. Any Reader of any strength would emerge as a level 8.

'Sir?' A Reader raised a hand like a schoolchild to get Atta's attention at the entrance to one of the open holding cells, a room containing members of the public open and willing for the transformation process. 'We have some difficult subjects.'

Atta stepped up to the entrance to the room, a simple concrete box of a structure. No windows, no furniture.

'Some are expecting something more from us in return for their cooperation and support.'

As the Reader said this, three men from the room stepped closer to the door to address Atta. 'Sir,' one of them said, a short man with mousey hair thinning to a bald patch on the top of his head. 'We are looking for someone to put a case for something rather more comfortable than we have here.'

'I'm listening,' said Atta, his tone measured, without emotion.

'We are willing participants here. And we think we can offer great potential. We are physically fit, being part of the community rugby 1sts for some time, and I think you can see,' he turned to draw attention to the rest of the room, 'that we are, relatively speaking, likely to offer you more than most.'

'Do you have power?' Atta asked, knowing full well that no-one in the room had power but for him and the Reader who stood next to him.

'Not power in the sense that you mean, but we have skills that, when combined with the power we will pick up in the transformation process, will put us up there in the management potential.'

Atta turned back to the corridor. 'Follow me.'

The man with the thinning hair turned to the others with

a victorious grin and the three of them filed past the reader to follow Atta.

At the next junction in the maze of connecting corridors, Atta stopped and opened the vision panel in the door in front of him. He opened the door and gestured inside. The room was a little smaller than the one the men had come from, but it was empty of others, and there was at least some furniture - a single chair in the centre of the room.

The three men entered, and Atta could see the metal floor flex a little under their weight. 'Just one chair?' the taller of the three men said.

'You won't need the chair,' said Atta as he closed the door behind them. In the corridor, he opened a control panel next to the door and slammed his palm into the centre button to begin the process. Then he tapped at the keypad.

The three ex-rugby players squirmed and writhed on the floor. Their screams echoed in the close confines of the metal box. As one man fell into his death throes, gasping for a last breath, his leg kicked out, sending the lone chair skittering across the floor and into the wall.

34

Jay, Ben, and Sammy were last to arrive at the pub. The basement room hummed with fear. Judith and Hannah were sitting at the table, Benji at their feet with Buster, watching as Pinto displayed his early telekinesis skills by moving a pen across the table. Toyah and Matchstick were over by the far wall, flicking through some of the Given literature charred at its edges.

Colson was crouched, talking to a little girl. 'Angie!' Jay said, approaching her. 'Why are you here? I thought your mum and dad had whisked you away?'

'I convinced them that this was a matter of life and death.'

Colson stood to greet Jay. 'You look like you have a plan.'

Jay nodded, then turned to the room. 'Let's do this.'

The room fell silent and everyone drew closer to hear what Jay had to say. Colson was the first to break the silence. 'When do we leave for the prison?' He sat down at the table. Others took seats as Jay remained standing, gathering herself.

She drew a deep breath. 'We know that a straight fight will not work.' She nodded at Angie. 'Something this wise little girl said to me last night has given me an idea. We need to get the stone into the core, no doubt about that, right?'

Colson nodded, and others murmured agreement. Stitch raised his head, his voice low and resigned: 'She's planning to plant the stone herself, physically. To *take* it into the core.'

'That's madness,' said Colson.

'It could be the only way,' said Judith. 'The dark energy in that place would never allow the source stone to fall naturally into the core.'

'What about the energy interface?' said Colson, agitated.

'The what?' asked Stitch.

'The inevitable expansion and chain reaction. Explosive *runaway*?'

Blank faces.

'If the source stone, the very focus of Given energy, comes into contact with the deep core, then chances are we'll be seeing a mini black hole develop here on earth. It's one thing to launch the stone into the hole and get clear, it's quite another to follow it in there.'

The room remained quiet as they processed what Colson had said. He continued, 'Everything within a mile radius will be levelled. Everything could be sucked into the cavern that is created, at least in the initial event.'

'There really isn't much point dwelling on possibilities right now when we have certainties,' Jay said. 'It is certain Atta will soon have enough power to obliterate the Given for good. So I don't see where we have a choice.'

Colson refused to concede. 'If you and the core are connected with the source stone, you will die.'

Jay ignored him, pushing the thought away. 'Something came to me yesterday, after talking to Angie, and then connecting with the power. I think we need an opening to the power of the Given at each of the three hill forts as we confront the darkness.'

Silence.

'A connected consciousness will allow us to amplify the energy.'

'How?' asked Toyah, frowning.

Colson scratched his head, thinking.

'Jay's right,' said Stitch, shooting her a supportive glance. 'We've used the hill forts before to help channel the power. We know they are a source of energy. But we will *all* need to connect deeply. Not just Jay.'

Colson nodded. 'It makes sense, but how? What are you thinking, Jay?'

Jay glanced across the faces around the room, all looking to her for the answers. 'Toyah, we will need your strength of power to get things moving. With Cassie, you are the highest level among us.'

Toyah nodded, touching the inside of her wrist instinctively where her number seven was clear, deeply defined, reflecting the clarity of her power. 'Just tell me where you need me, and what I need to do.'

'Colson, Dad, up on the hill forts, you will need to connect with the ground, the roots beneath our feet. Everything is connected. The power in the hills will guide you.'

Ben and Colson nodded as they thought it through.

'We'll need someone here too, at the basement.'

'Why?' asked Cassie. 'What's here?'

Hannah took the question. 'This room has become a centre and focus of the energy since the bookshop was destroyed. The Given literature is that source.'

'That makes no sense,' said Cassie.

'She's right,' said Jay. 'Our collective presence, our shared mindset, and even our documents, carry a focus of energy to this place. The physical locations of energy, like the hill forts and the Interland, are just part of the picture. An equal, and possibly *more* important, element is the essence of those with power - what is in their heads and their hearts, and how they choose to channel the power.

'I think if Dad gets to Highdown Hill and Colson to Cissbury Ring, then Sammy and Toyah can head up to Chanctonbury.'

'I'll take Highdown,' came a familiar voice from the foot of the stairs. Jay looked up to see Otis standing with a walking stick, a grin on his face. Pinto went to him, helping him stand.

Cassie stood. 'What are you doing here?'

Pinto answered for Otis, 'He's here to help. Me and Otis can help. He's a level five, and I'm a five in the making. We can help.'

'You two take Highdown then,' said Jay with a smile for Otis. 'If you think you can do it?'

'With this little power-pack,' he nodded at Pinto, 'we can do anything.'

'I'll come with you,' Cassie said.

'I need you and Stitch with me,' Jay said. 'And here in the basement we need Angie.'

Angie visibly slumped. 'I want to be with you,' she said to Jay.

'You will be,' Jay said, tapping the side of her head. 'In here.' Angie humphed. 'I need you here with Judith and Hannah. You can help them guide me. You will be their eyes, through me, into the darkness.'

Angie gave in. 'OK,' she said, looking up at Hannah and Judith, who both smiled.

'We have one chance,' said Jay. She hoped that her inner fear was well contained and shielded from her friends, and that her doubts about their chances were not leaking through.

The basement emptied, leaving Angie with Hannah and Judith. She felt small, uncertain of how she would play her part in what was to come next. Jay, Stitch and Cassie were the last to leave, heading for Jay's garage to pick up the car and head off to the prison.

Judith and Hannah busied with the papers on the table, sorting and arranging into piles that seemed to have some kind of order that Angie couldn't fathom. 'What are you doing?' asked Angie.

Hannah paused a moment and took a breath. She was fidgety, looking to the door and back to the papers. 'We need to be prepared. They will need us focused.'

'What for?' Angie was confused. Hannah and Judith seemed to know what was coming, and what they needed to do.

Judith sat down, motioning for Angie to do the same. Hannah continued arranging the papers. 'In the past day or so, we've been talking through all the ways that this could play out. Truth be told, we don't know the answer, but there are things we can do to prepare for the worst, then hope for the best.'

'Jay said she needs me to be your eyes. What did she mean?'

Judith looked over at Hannah. 'We may have limited power, but we have a lot of knowledge about the power, and how the energy of the Given and the Dark behave - how they interact and how the darkness might be a threat to Jay. That's what Colson and Alf think...' Judith corrected herself. '*Thought*. That's what Alf thought.'

'But what about me? Why am I here?' Angie pressed.

'You have power,' said Judith.

'Great power,' Hannah added, shifting a pile of documents into the corner of the table. 'If Jay's intuition is right, and I'd guess it is, then you have a new kind of power. For someone so young, your connection with the Given energy is unprecedented.'

'Except for Jay herself, perhaps?' Judith said.

'Perhaps,' said Hannah with a nod.

'So,' Judith continued, 'with your ability, we think you will illuminate the path as Jay moves in on the core. You can be our eyes and senses into the darkness, so that we can best help Jay understand what she's seeing.'

'You can tell her what to do?' said Angie.

Hannah stopped sorting papers for a moment. 'We hope so. At least, we hope we can make some kind of contribution.'

* * *

OTIS POWERED the little moped up the last section of dirt track to his camp on the edge of the summit at Highdown. With Pinto on the back, the bike was heavier, and it had been a struggle to keep from flipping over backwards as he negoti-ated the steepest sections.

'Here,' said Otis, carefully stepping off the bike to protect his heels from pain. Pinto jumped off and positioned himself to help Otis. They staggered together the few feet to Otis's camp, where he sank down onto a log. 'I might need you to do the fire,' he said.

'On it,' said Pinto, turning to look at the remains of their last fire, burned almost to nothing. 'I'll top up the wood stock.'

'We have some time,' said Otis. 'I reckon we have a good half hour before Jay is anywhere near the prison. We should eat.'

Pinto scurried away to collect wood as Otis opened his bivouac and unpacked cans. Pain radiated from both his heels. The hospital had warned him that leaving so soon was not recommended, and that he should rest, keep the weight off his feet for a few more days. If he wasn't careful, an infection was possible, or further tendon damage. The doctor told him that he was lucky. Slightly deeper and his healing process would have been months, not weeks. He didn't feel so lucky. Despite Flick's grievous attack on him, he felt no great malice towards her. He could tell that she was conflicted. She had her reasons, mostly fear, he thought, for following the wishes of Atta.

Behind him, Pinto dumped an armful of wood and arranged it in the fire pit. From his store, made with reclaimed stones from around the perimeter of Highdown, he pulled a loaf of sliced bread, still within its best-before date, and three tins of soup.

'Sit down,' called Pinto as Otis emerged from cover.

Otis dumped the food beside Pinto and slumped back down on the log. 'I feel so useless like this.'

'You will be useless if you don't ease up. Like the nurse said.'

'Yes, boss.'

'And if we are going to be any use to the others, we need to conserve our energy and get focused.'

Within a few minutes, the fire raged, and Pinto suspended a pan from a metal tripod above the flames. He opened the tins with Otis's penknife and poured the contents into the pan, singeing his hair as he did so.

Otis laughed. 'You're supposed to prepare the pan before you light the fire. Or let the fire die down before you hang the pan.'

'No time,' said Pinto.

'Who needs eyebrows anyway, eh?'

Pinto rubbed his eyebrows. Otis laughed again. 'Sit down. You're fine.'

He sat opposite Otis. They exchanged a glance. 'Are you ready?' Otis asked.

Pinto nodded, knowing that Otis wanted to test the strength of their power, to get ready for what was coming later.

Otis took a breath and, with a quick glance at the flames, opened up to the power of the earth. Pinto closed his eyes. Otis let his eyelids droop and channelled his energy into a connection with Pinto. Like they'd done before, and like they would need to do to help Jay, they connected.

* * *

THE WALK up to the summit of Cissbury was steeper than the other two hill forts. Sammy had sensed an easing of Toyah's frustration over the past couple of days, but she seemed distant on their journey to Cissbury. He tried to focus on the job at hand.

'Wait,' Sammy said, stopping to catch his breath, Toyah a

few feet ahead. Three sparrows circled above their heads, coming closer as Sammy watched. His connection with birds was nothing new, but it had grown stronger over recent months. He had tried to cultivate it but it seemed to have a life of its own. He would put all his focus into connecting with the energy of the birds, like he had done back at the Interland, and it seemed random whether it had any effect. Then, when he wasn't trying, the visions would come to him.

'What?' said Toyah, her tone impatient. 'We need to get to the top. Get ourselves organised.'

'There are people up there,' said Sammy.

'How do you know?'

Sammy looked up at the birds. One of the three came close, and he ducked out of its way, sliding to sit on the grass. Toyah watched. As the bird retreated, a familiar curtain of blindness came down over Sammy's eyes and he knew what was coming. The opaque screen before his eyes faded to a transparent blur as he soared with the bird into the sky. His eyes cleared as he rose, travelling with the little sparrow as it skirted the outer ring of trees towards the summit of Cissbury.

'I'm at the summit,' he said to Toyah.

'People there?'

'Some. Our age. Drinking. Smoking.'

'How many?'

'Only a handful.' In Sammy's mind's eye, he circled the ring of trees and peered down on a group of six teenagers around a fire. They would be no threat. There was no power that he could detect. His vision blurred once more and Sammy's sight came back to him. Toyah was watching him with pride.

'Thanks,' Sammy said.

'For what?'

'For having my back. Believing in me.'

'Always,' Toyah said. 'It's easy. OK, let's go.'

At the summit, Toyah strode into the inner circle and told the four girls and two boys to leave without explanation. When one girl squared up to her, Toyah used her power to force the girl to the ground, her hands clutching the sides of her head in pain. She didn't need to ask again.

Sammy lumped another branch onto the fire and sat down on a log. 'How long do we have?' he asked Toyah.

Toyah checked her watch. 'Twenty minutes. We'll hear something from Jay or Stitch when they're close. Keep your senses open for something from your sister.'

Sammy delved into his powers once more, feeling confident after his success with flight. He connected with the energy that flowed freely at the hillfort. Smoke rose in the distance towards the south. He stood and walked to the edge of the treeline for a better look. At Highdown, the smoke rose in a tight plume and mixed into the wind above the trees. 'Otis,' he said under his breath, just loud enough for Toyah to hear. 'Can you connect?' Toyah asked.

'Not yet. You?'

Toyah shook her head.

'I can feel him though,' said Sammy. 'His power is strong, coming over the hills in waves. I've not felt someone's power like this from such a distance.'

'It's the hill forts. The amplification.'

* * *

THE THIRD HILL FORT, Chanctonbury, was the highest of the three, and probably because of this, the least visited by the Given. The energy of the land was spread over a wider area, with less of a focus at the summit. Nevertheless, the flow of

Given energy was significant, and its importance in the full connection of Given power to support Jay's quest undeniable.

Ben called Colson's tiny, apple-red Mazda a 'mid-life crisis' car as they jumped in, Ben pulling his seat forward as far as it would go so Matchstick could scrunch up in the back. 'Better?'

'You need to get yourself a proper car,' Matchstick muttered.

Ben smiled to himself. Matchstick had become his closest friend since their time escaping prison and trekking to the Interland. Matchstick was the most powerful of the three of them. At a level 4, he could connect well with the Given energy. His telepathic ability was modest, but he had a little something more in the heat he generated from the energy. His nickname wasn't unrelated to his ability to create fire from his hands when the energy flowed at its maximum. Ben's own level two power seemed to be enhanced when he was in the presence of Matchstick.

Colson turned onto the straight road that would lead them to the peak at Cissbury. There were two locations for them to set up, and Jay had suggested that the highest peak was the one they should find. It was there she was sure that the power flowed at its greatest. Colson's own power was tangible. Ben could feel its strength in the car alongside that of Matchstick, although his felt more muted, subdued. 'What's your level?' Ben asked Colson.

'Four.' He awkwardly pulled back the sleeve of his left arm whilst holding on to the steering wheel.

'Same as me,' said Matchstick from the back, thrusting his wrist between the two front seats.

'Ten between us then,' said Ben.

'More than a match for any Reader,' said Matchstick with a grin.

'There are level 4 Given and then there are level 4 Given,' said Colson.

'What do you mean?' said Matchstick.

'Alf was a level 4 and he was far stronger than me.'

Ben nodded. Matchstick remained quiet. Ben felt a strange pang of guilt for the way he'd always been towards Alf. They never saw things the same way. It was true. Perhaps he suffered jealousy for how well he and Jay got on in recent times. The closer Jay and Alf became, the more distant Jay seemed to become to Ben. Nothing that Alf had done was ever in confrontation with Ben, yet Ben had never seen fit to communicate with him, to accept him into his world. 'We left him out in the cold for too long,' said Ben.

Colson nodded. 'He was a good man, and a major contributor to the knowledge of the Given. In a different life, we would have been good friends. I will miss him.'

From the car park, the walk took longer than they had thought. Almost twenty minutes and they were only just reaching the high point. Matchstick gathered dry wood, held his hands over the tinder, and in seconds a flame took hold.

'How do you do that?' asked Colson.

'To be honest, I'm not entirely sure. The energy just seems to flow through my hands, and when it's flowing well, the heat is intense and I can concentrate it enough to generate a spark or a flame.'

'Useful,' said Colson.

Matchstick shrugged and looked up into the trees. The sky was grey, fast-moving clouds hiding the sun. 'Come on.' He called Ben over to sit down. 'We need to get ready.'

'Tell us the plan then,' Cassie said, taking a roundabout at speed. The old Ford handled like a minibus, and Cassie enjoyed the challenge of keeping the wheels on the road around the tight corners. Stitch leaned forward between the front seats to catch Jay's answer.

Jay thought for a moment. She knew exactly what she needed to do, but she had to put it in a way that offered up no opportunity for alternatives from Cassie and Stitch. They wouldn't like it, but it was non-negotiable.

She picked the rucksack from the footwell and took out the source stone. Its energy expanded through the car. Jay felt its connection. 'You feel that?' she asked the others. Cassie didn't respond, but Stitch nodded.

'Can't quite make sense of it.' Jay said. 'I can feel it, but it's not like the power from the hill forts, or the Interland itself. In those places, the energy is clearer, like a communication. This thing is radioactive. A little atomic bomb. I need to get this into the core.'

'You mean *we* need to get it into the core,' Cassie corrected.

Jay avoided her glance. 'I'll have to go in with it, *take* it in there, as deep as I can get.'

'I knew that's what you were planning,' Stitch said. 'So what do *we* do whilst your body is becoming vaporised, scattered to all corners of the planet?'

'I might get out, once it's in there, deep enough that we know it will do its job.'

Cassie was incredulous. 'I'm not taking part in your suicide mission.'

'Remember what Colson said? At least a mile radius when this thing goes in. You two need to be a mile back from the opening to the core. This isn't negotiable.' She turned to look out of the window, hugging the source stone to her.

'No way,' Cassie said. 'We find another way.'

'There must be another way,' said Stitch.

'There is no other way,' Jay spat the words, losing patience. 'This is my call. I'm the one who's seen Atta, seen what he can do. We only get one go at this. The others are ready and positioned to channel the power. I need you to play your part. This needs all of us.'

Cassie shook her head, and they were silent for a minute.

'What do we do?' Stitch asked, his head down, resigned. He looked at Jay. 'Tell us what you need.'

Jay forced a smile. 'You know where we went before, in Northtown?'

'Sebastian's?'

'That's a mile or so out from the centre of the prison, so that's around the spot you need to be. Not at his house, at the river. But no closer than that. You'll be no use if you're in the prison. Use the river and the sea, and help me focus the power from the hill forts. We won't be able to get past Atta if we can't draw the full potential of the Given energy.'

Stitch nodded.

Jay continued, 'We're making connections. Otis with Pinto at Highdown, Colson and Dad at Chanctonbury, and Toyah with Sammy at Cissbury. Their connections will draw the power of the land. I need that power here, and I need the power of the sea that we have coming in on the river through Northtown. That's what I need from you.'

'I can't do that without you,' Stitch said.

'I will be with you. I need to be connected to you. I'll help. We just need to connect with the others. Then I will have the full power of the Given and I'll have a chance with Atta.'

'How do you know it will work?'

Jay looked at Stitch. She shrugged.

'What about Angie and the others at the basement?' Cassie asked.

'They are our intelligence. Angie has something I've not come across in any other Given. She is a power in development for sure, but even now she has an extraordinary ability. She seems to connect with me, see what I see and feel my thoughts from a distance.' Jay looked at Stitch. 'A bit like you can. But she's not even a teenager yet, let alone eighteen.'

'You think she'll be a "C"?' asked Cassie.

Jay shook her head. 'She's the next generation of the Given. Today she's the eyes and ears for Judith and Hannah's knowledge.'

Cassie let out a sigh. 'Let me and Stitch come with you. We can help channel the power from inside the mile radius just as well as we can from Northtown. In fact, if we are closer to you, then we stand a better chance of directing it to where you need it.'

'Too risky,' Jay said. 'Do it like I said.'

'What if we can't connect to you from back in Northtown?'

The question put words to Jay's biggest fear. Under the cloak of Atta's darkness, she might not receive the power from the others, and all the efforts of positioning people at the hill forts, and having Stitch and Cassie channel the energy from Northtown, would be a waste of time. There was no way to know for sure. 'We have to try. It's the only way. His energy is too much to fight on my own. He will simply take the stone, preventing it from ever entering the core. If that happens, then it's over.'

* * *

'THIS IS THE PLACE,' said Jay as she pulled the car up to the side of the road at the main river wall of Northtown. The estuary and the sea were just visible in the distance. Rain pounded the metal roof of the car, drowning Jay's words.

'How do you know?' said Cassie. The windscreen wipers struggled to keep up with the snap downpour and Jay switched them off, then turned off the ignition.

'I can feel it,' said Jay, turning to look at Stitch.

'She's right,' said Stitch. 'This is it. See the sea?' He nodded downstream. 'And feel the power of the river?'

Cassie rubbed condensation from the window and peered out. 'This is where we entered the tunnels last time,' she said.

'Bit further up,' said Jay. 'It's not the tunnels we need, it's the power of the ocean. You need to combine the energies.' She looked at Stitch, trying to read if he really understood what was being asked of him and Cassie. He gave a slight nod and Jay continued. 'Connect it with the power from the hill forts. Only you two can do this. Channel it to me. But do it from *here*, keep your distance. I'll know when you have it.'

Stitch nodded again, his thoughts revealing his fear for Jay.

He searched his mind for an escape plan for her, but came up with nothing and looked away, out of the window.

'How do we do it?' Cassie asked.

'Stitch will know. He will just need your power to keep it all under control. Take your lead from Stitch.'

'Whatever you say,' Cassie said. The rain eased and the noise in the car ceased.

Jay opened her door to let out some of the humid air and to take a breath of the fresh, salty breeze. 'Go, now,' she said.

Cassie flung open her door and stepped out into the cool air. She stuck her head through Jay's open door. 'Just make sure you do it right this time,' she said. 'OK?'

Jay nodded.

She turned to Stitch in the back of the car. 'Send a message to the others. Tell them to start.'

He nodded, lingering for a moment. 'Please,' he whispered. 'Get yourself back here in one piece.'

She leaned and placed both hands on the sides of Stitch's face, looking him in the eye. 'We can do this,' she said. 'We have to do this. It's bigger than me, or you, or anyone else.'

'I know.' Stitch lowered his gaze.

'Go!'

Stitch hesitated.

'Go!' Jay repeated and pushed the Ford into gear. Stitch stepped out and Jay pulled away.

37

Jay drove directly to the staff entrance to the prison, her mind clearer and more focused than it had ever been. She screeched to a halt at the gate as two Readers in the security box watched, open-mouthed. From the car, she attacked both Readers simultaneously, reducing them to their knees with little effort. Her power bubbled below the surface, ready at her fingertips. The Readers screamed in pain, their hands to the sides of their heads, then slumped unconscious to the floor. She used her power to push the button to release the gates.

She drove on to the main car park, using the same space she had used the last time, making some point that was lost in her subconscious. She stepped out of the car. Her trainers were scuffed and coming apart at the seams. Her jeans were dirty, one leg riding up over her high-top shoes. She looked at her hands, turning them over to inspect her palms. She had nothing. No weapons. No protection, only the stone. She felt naked suddenly. Scratches, old and new, on the backs of her hands and up her arms, reminded her of what she'd been through already. She turned over her hand to see the "8C" marking on her wrist. *This* is me, she thought. This is my calling, my mission. Her arms by her sides, she clenched her fists and turned towards the main building.

The building structure was barely standing, dilapidated further after the tornado generated by Atta the last time she was there. She walked through what was once a set of double-doors and stood at the top of the steps down to the lower levels. The power of the darkness flowed up from underground like the pulse of air from an underground train. She stepped down, taking the steps slowly as she acclimatised to the energy flow around her. There were no guards, a reminder of Atta's arrogance - his belief that there was no-one on Island 8 to threaten him.

On the first floor down, the building had been expanded and modified. She shrugged her shoulders to feel the reassuring weight of the rucksack on her back. Although she sensed the closeness of the source stone, feeling its weight was reassuring. She wondered if Atta knew already that she was here.

She came to a corridor with rooms off the central route that she'd not seen before. Everything was grey concrete - the floor, wall, ceiling. Only the doors themselves were not concrete, their shiny steel surfaces reflecting the grey of the walls. Her skin prickled with anticipation.

Through the vision panel in the first door, she saw a room crammed full of people. Their fear hung like a grey cloud in the air. They had no power, and they feared for their lives. Using the control panel on the wall, Jay released the lock and pushed the door open. The people inside recoiled, shrinking away from Jay as she entered. She raised her hands to show that she meant no harm. 'What are you...' she began, but needed not finish. She read in their minds the plan that Atta had for them.

Jay's head swam as she tried to take it in. The dark energy could not create Readers from those without power. It wasn't possible. She looked at the faces staring back at her. It was true. He had found a way. 'Go!' Jay said, pointing them back towards the steps to the car park. 'Now!'

They moved. A man edged past her through the door and headed in the wrong direction. 'This way,' Jay said. 'Head for the east exit. You will see it from the car park. The security hut is unmanned. Leave and don't look back.'

He needed no more instruction. He ran to the steps, leading the way for others. A woman stopped as she passed Jay. 'Thank you,' she said, and took the hand of the man next to her, leading him away with the others.

Jay stopped the last man out of the room. 'Hey,' she said. 'Are there more?'

The man nodded and motioned towards the remaining doors along the corridor. 'These are the holding cells for the resistant, like us, those who refused to sign up to their doctrine.'

'There are so many,' Jay said.

'This is just one batch. And we were not the first. Before us, these rooms were full of other people, already turned no doubt.'

The scale of Atta's plans floored Jay. She'd had no idea.

'The next level down, the bigger rooms, are the willing participants,' the man said. 'Those people *want* to become Readers. I don't know if they are deluded or scared, but they have undertaken to be transformed in return for their loyalty.'

Once transformed, Readers could be easily manipulated by whomever has control of the sink-room. Reader power is not innate, it flows from the core via the sink-room. Without the channelling of that energy, Readers can be stripped of their power.

'Then beyond that you have the Given. They are held close to the core. First in line for transformation.'

'Help me open up these rooms?' Jay said to the man. He nodded, and they set to unlock each room off the central corridor from their control panels. There were six, and more than a hundred people. When the last had filed through to the steps, Jay thanked the man and turned towards the steps to the deeper levels.

'You need me to help?'

Jay shook her head and smiled. 'Thanks. You get moving. Make sure those people get clear. They need to be at least a mile out. Don't hang about.'

He nodded. 'Good luck,' he said.

* * *

JAY SENSED the change in the energy's feel on the next level down. The holding rooms were not locked. The atmosphere was one of celebration, like graduation. There were Readers too, patrolling the corridors with guns, keeping the levels of excitement under control as people waited for the call to the sink-room. You people are crazy, she thought.

A Reader carrying a pistol turned in her direction and she ducked behind a column. He seemed to sense something and walked towards her, his gun held at waist level. As he approached, he slowed, treading carefully over the final few paces. She shielded, holding back until the last minute before attacking his mind. Simultaneously, she dragged him around the column and out of sight of the rest of the readers and pulled the gun from his weakened grip. He went down, and she intensified her attack, pushing him physically to the floor before looking back towards the others to check that she'd not been detected. She was safe. The Reader at her feet was out. She kicked the handgun away into a dark corner.

Peering over the edge of the landing, Jay saw that the shaft plummeted into the depths directly below. She could drop the source stone from where she stood without having to head any deeper. It might make it into the core, but the dark energy would be sure to deflect it, and if the source stone were to get into Atta's hands again, there wouldn't be a third chance. She cursed. She would head lower.

The next level down was like the top floor - doors off a central corridor and no sign of Readers. Through the first door vision panel, Jay saw that the room was empty, as was the next room along. The third room contained a single person, sat on the floor, her head in her hands. Jay sensed that this woman had Given power. She pressed the door release, and the woman looked up, her face lighting up as she sensed Jay's Given energy. 'Thank God,' she said, standing.

'Let's go,' Jay said. She saw on the woman's wrist that she was a level 3. 'Are there more Given?'

The woman nodded and moved to the next door in the corridor. She pushed the button in the control panel and ran in, embracing the man stood the other side. 'This is my husband, Ravi. I am Jess.'

'Are there more?'

'There were,' said Jess, moving further down the corridor and looking through the vision panel in each door. 'All empty,' she said, looking at her husband, whose eyes dropped to the floor. 'There were people we knew in these rooms.'

'They will probably be Readers now.'

'But they can be turned back?' Ravi asked Jay.

Jay nodded. 'Only if they can escape the control of the sink-room. Jay felt a wave of dark energy and stumbled, holding on to the handrail to stop from falling.

Jess held her arm. 'Steady,' she said.

'Sorry,' said Jay. 'I need to press on. You head back to the entrance. Be careful on the next floor up, there are Readers, but beyond that it's clear. Head to the exit and...'

'Where are you going?' asked Ravi. He looked at Jay's backpack. 'There's a powerful signal from there.'

Jess looked at Jay with a flicker of recognition. 'You're Jay. The 8C. I've read about you.'

'I need to get down to the lower levels and get this...' she motioned at her backpack, 'into the core. There are others, as we speak, channelling the energy. You need to go. We don't know what will happen when this thing is inserted. This place could be levelled.'

'We're coming,' said Jess. 'You need our help. You don't look well.'

'No,' said Jay, emphatic.

'We're not asking,' said Ravi. 'We were put on this planet for a reason. *This* is the reason.' He looked at his wife and she nodded.

* * *

JAY LED the way down the final set of steps. She stepped onto a steel platform that circled the rim of the crater below. The hum from the electromagnets was loud, releasing a pulse of energy with every rotation.

No Atta. No army of Readers. Jay felt a deep unease. Why was it possible for her to just walk right up to the core of their power with such ease?

The circular landing had three entrances. A control panel was fixed to the wall next to the door. Jay knew what she needed to do.

'What now?' asked Ravi.

'Throw it in?' asked Jess.

'You two can leave. Now,' said Jay. 'I can take it from here.'

Jay looked over the edge and tightened her rucksack over her shoulders. She looked up through the centre of the shaft, past the levels of holding cells and to what she could see of the dilapidated building above. She wished she could see the sky for one last time.

'But...' Jess started.

Ravi continued for his wife, 'But you don't know how deep this is. We can't see the bottom. How are you planning to get out?'

Jay remained silent, and the penny finally dropped for Jess and Ravi. 'No...' said Jess. 'Throw it. Then we leave together.'

Ravi saw the determination on Jay's face and took his wife's arm. 'Come on,' he said.

Across the opening of the crater, darkness descended the corridor opposite. Jay's heart sank into her gut as figures appeared at the entrance from the corridor. 'Readers,' Jay said under her breath. Jess and Ravi turned back, one standing on either side of Jay like bodyguards.

'Good,' said Jess. 'We like a good fight. If we can keep them off you, then you do what you have to do.' Jess held Jay's eye for a moment and they silently agreed the plan. She looked skyward once more, wishing to see a shard of white light, Given power coming in to help, but there was nothing.

Atta appeared in the shaft with a burst of warm air from the corridor. He was as Jay remembered, wisps of darkness floating from him as if his very being was not completely physical. He immediately waved away the Readers approaching the steel platform towards Jay. They fell back behind Atta, and Jay sensed them retreating down the corridor. Jess and Ravi exchanged a look of concern.

'So, here you are again,' said Atta. 'You do surprise me.'

Jay tightened her rucksack and glanced down into the hole. She wouldn't be able to do this with Atta's power resisting. She wasn't sure that Jess and Ravi's power would be enough to pave her way into the core. She needed the others, but she had no sense of them, no feeling for any building of the Given energy. *Where are they?* She looked around the cavern as if for inspiration. 'Ready?' she said to Jess and Ravi. 'We're going to have to do this.'

'Ready,' said Jess.

Jay clenched her fists, gathered her full strength and launching an attack at Atta. He reeled, caught by surprise. She sustained the attack, sensing some success in penetrating his mind. Jess and Ravi backed her up, pressing their own power through with Jay's. Atta stepped back, pushed by their energy.

Atta's form became more fluid and for a moment Jay thought that their attack was succeeding in taking him apart. Then a dark smile crossed his face as if he were enjoying the moment and fear flowed through Jay, interrupting the attack.

Atta raised his arms into the air, deflecting the Given energy with the merest of movements. Jess and Ravi hit the wall of the shaft, slipping to the floor in a daze. Jay crouched to help Jess up as Ravi, too, got to his feet. When she looked again to where Atta had stood, he was gone.

The door to the room off the side of the platform was open, a red light blinking in the control panel on the wall. 'Come on, Stitch,' Jay said under her breath, certain now that she stood no chance of succeeding in her plan without the full power of the Given. She looked back to the steps, contemplating their chances of getting out before Atta pursued them.

Ravi nodded towards the holding cell. 'If he's in there. Will it hold him?'

'If we can close the door. But he won't let that happen,' said Jay.

'He's luring us,' said Jess.

'All we have to do is hit the button,' said Ravi, taking a step around the circular walkway towards the door.

'Wait,' said Jay. 'You two go together. I'll come around from the other way. Give me a minute.'

Jay skirted the perimeter of the shaft on the metal platform until she was opposite Jess and Ravi. Jay had a bad feeling about what Atta was doing in the holding cell. This had to be a trap, but there didn't seem another choice.

Ravi made a dash for the control panel. He reached inside for the button to close the door, but as he did so, he crumpled in pain, withdrawing his hand and holding it to his chest as he fell to the floor. Jess went to him, then quickly stood, looking into the room as Jay arrived next to her. Atta was sitting on a chair alone in the middle of the room. He locked eyes with Jay and the grin returned to his face. Jess reached for the button on the control panel and Atta's eyes flicked to look at her. She fell like Ravi, clutching her hand, groaning with the pain.

Jay looked at the control panel. Atta shook his head. Ravi and Jess had crawled clear of the door and propped themselves up against the wall of the shaft. Ravi recovered a little and helped Jess, inspecting her hand.

'Come in,' Atta said. Jay shook her head, looking once more at the control panel. 'Try it if you like,' he said.

In her peripheral vision, Jay saw Ravi stagger to his feet, extending a hand to Jess. They conversed for a moment, then turned to Jay. Jay read their plan. *Distract Atta*, they told her.

Jay took a step forward into the threshold of the doorway. 'Why do you want me in here?' she said. 'So you can generate a Reader out of me? You'd like that. A Reader from the Given 8C.'

'Why not?' said Atta.

'Maybe I will,' said Jay, as a look of victory dawned on Atta's face.

Ravi and Jess both screamed with determination as they launched themselves at the panel. They hit the button, and the heavy door swung. As Jay stepped out of the path of the closing door, Atta moved. The door thumped closed. Atta banged into it from the inside. He looked at Jay through the vision panel, a familiar smile returning to his lips. He nodded behind her. She turned. The hand rail behind her had fallen, and there was no sign of Ravi or Jess.

She ran to the edge. 'Jess!'

Nothing but darkness.

She turned and looked back at Atta, his grin visible through the vision panel. Without taking her eyes off him, she straightened her rucksack once more and stepped back towards the hole. Atta shook his head, as if advising Jay not to do it. She turned away from him, not willing to risk any further influence of his power. She looked into the hole and hesitated a moment. It reminded of her leap of faith into the hole that landed her in the Interland. She thought of Stitch, Cassie, and of Sammy, and ached to know what had happened, and why their plan had not worked.

Then she jumped.

38

She couldn't jump. She hung as if held back by a harness. The energy from the depths flowed up and out of the hole, preventing her progress. With Atta in control, she could not overcome the resistance.

She stepped to the control panel and from the cell, Atta read her intention and shook his head. 'This facility can't be used against its maker.'

Jay said, 'You can't get out.'

He laughed. 'I can't be contained within these walls. I *am* these walls. You still don't get it. This is why you will never win.'

As Jay watched, the door between them seemed to quiver. Then she felt the heat radiating from it. She stepped back, shielding her face.

Atta continued to talk on the other side of the door, but Jay could no longer make out his words. His anger grew and the thick metal door melted at its edges. Atta's words grew louder. His tone changed, twisting in a flow of dark energy. A language she didn't understand.

The door slipped off its hinges, no longer able to hold its

own weight. Smoke rose from the molten metal and Atta stepped through, looking down on Jay like she was nothing.

Jay pushed at his chest and used the reaction force to throw herself towards the shaft, but Atta's power stopped her. He ripped the rucksack from her back and wrenched it open. With the source stone held aloft in his hands, he continued to speak in indecipherable tongues.

* * *

THE BASEMENT SHOOK like there was a minor earthquake. Angie held on to the side of the table, the motion of the floor making her queasy. 'What was that?' she said, looking at Judith and Hannah for reassurance.

The women looked just as perplexed. 'There was supposed to be a quake back in 1667,' said Judith. 'The last time there was a big confrontation between the Dark and the Given. Can't be a coincidence.'

'This is not the same,' said Hannah.

'It could be the power? From the hill forts,' said Judith.

'We need to try again,' said Angie. She'd been unable to get into Jay's head, despite several attempts. The last time she'd made some progress, and saw Jay fighting with Readers in the lower levels of the prison. 'She's in trouble, we have to try again.'

'Anything from Toyah or Colson?' asked Hannah.

Angie shook her head. There was no power flowing. Angie felt flooded with doubt. Was there any power buried deep inside her? Could she help Jay? She sat down at the head of the table once more and closed her eyes.

Judith and Hannah busied with their papers. They searched for something that Hannah recalled about the clash in 1667 that told of a means to connect the Given when under attack from the Dark. 'Here,' said Judith, pointing Hannah towards a passage of old text.

'Yes,' said Hannah. 'This is what I thought. I remember now. Keep trying to connect, Angie.'

Angie concentrated. 'Jay!' she screamed. 'I have her. She's down. On the floor. She's hurt.'

'Is she alone?' asked Hannah.

'Atta is there.' As Angie took in Jay's surroundings through Jay's own mind, she saw the outline of Atta come closer to Jay. He held the source stone in his hands. Jay struggled to her knees, and he taunted her. 'He's moving in on her again.'

'Can she hear you?' asked Judith.

'Jay?' Angie said, trying to get her attention. Jay seemed to register Angie's voice and opened to the connection. 'She can hear me,' said Angie.

'Tell her not to resist his attack,' Hannah said. Angie looked at her like she was mad, waiting for explanation. 'Only at first. Tell her to flow with his power, like you might do in directing the force of someone's punch. You know?'

'I think so,' said Angie.

'Then she needs to picture it flowing around her, not *into* her. If she can roll with the punches, so to speak, she will direct his strength so that it surrounds but does not penetrate. It will buy her time.'

Angie relayed this strategy to Jay. She pictured the streamlines of darkness flowing towards Jay and then around her, like the flow of a river past a bridge pier. 'It's working,' she said. The smooth boundary layer of darkness in Angie's mind became a harmless stream of energy diverted from its target.

* * *

UP ON HIGHDOWN HILL, Pinto and Otis both stood, the energy flowing through them. Otis felt no pain in his heels as his skin tingled with the power. He looked down at Pinto. He seemed to shake with the strength of the power coming through the ground at the hill fort.

'It hurts,' Pinto called to Otis, his eyes remaining closed. Otis cast his eyes around the ring of trees. Shards of light penetrated from below as if the sun was rising beneath their feet. Pinto became bathed in white light.

'Look,' said Otis.

Pinto opened his eyes. He and Otis watched as their power drew the energy of the land up from below and from the surrounding air. The noise grew louder as more and more shards pierced the woodland floor. Pinto grinned, laughing. Otis was too scared to laugh. He felt as though it needed all his concentration just to keep the energy flowing, that if he lost concentration for a moment, the power would spin away and career off into the atmosphere and be of no use to Jay. He held his nerve, and Pinto calmed down to focus once more.

'What now?' shouted Pinto above the background noise.

Otis didn't know what to do next. But he sensed it didn't matter.

* * *

ATTA CROUCHED NEXT TO JAY, the source stone in his hands. He held it away from her as if tempting her to take it from him.

Her legs wobbled as she tried to stand, deciding instead to lift herself onto her knees.

A flash of white light.

Angie was in her head. Jay almost cried from the flood of relief. Angie's presence gave her strength. Pictures flowed into

Jay's mind as Atta continued to talk. She could no longer hear him. Angie's voice was predominant. She pictured the stream-lines of the low of darkness around her body and she recog-nised Angie communicating resistance tactics. 'Angie,' Jay said aloud into Atta's face.

'Who?' he said as he stood, preparing himself to attack. Jay cleared her mind of everything but Angie's pictures, the streamlines. Atta took a breath. 'We could be so powerful together,' he said.

'No chance,' Jay mumbled back to him.

Atta growled at her rejection and attacked once more, but Jay was ready. She focused not on stopping his power entering her mind, but on its diversion, deflection, and re-direction around her. The strength needed for the re-direction was much lower than for a full defence. The energy flowed and instead of wearing her down; she drew from it, taking a little of the energy into her own reserves to replenish her strength.

'Interesting,' Atta said. 'You have some control over the Dark. From your connection with it.'

'Don't make me sick, I have no connection to your power.' Jay stepped back.

'The combination is powerful,' Atta said, continuing to search inside of Jay. 'You have kept something from that connection. You have a mix of dark and light. Feel it. Breathe it in. It's part of you.'

Jay shook her head, filtering the darkness and gathering her Given power.

'Why would you want to destroy this connection? The core? This is the pathway to your dominance over all the power. You can draw on the darkness and the light of the Given. This hasn't happened for centuries. You can be all powerful. More so than even I could hope for. Embrace it,' Atta said.

* * *

'JUST FOCUS,' said Toyah, irritation in her tone. Sammy had done nothing to help her draw the energy at Cissbury. She sensed he was sulking when he should channel all his efforts to helping his sister. 'If Jay stands any chance of living through this, she needs us.'

Sammy took Toyah's hand. Together they stood inside the ring of trees atop Cissbury. Toyah felt the energy flowing beneath their feet and drew from it. With every passing minute, the power grew, and the ground seemed to warm the soles of her shoes.

'It's coming,' Sammy said.

'Open up,' Toyah said, gripping his hand even tighter.

* * *

AT CHANCTONBURY, Ben, Matchstick and Colson formed a connected circle, their hands clasped tight as they stood around the embers of the fire.

Colson directed. 'Clear your minds,' he said. 'Steady your breathing. In for three, out for five.' The three of them breathed deeply as Colson instructed.

Ben felt little in the way of Given power and was feeling sceptical about the whole thing. 'Perhaps we should just head over there, to the prison. We can help Jay more by fighting with her than we can summoning the spirits up here?'

'Shush,' Colson said. 'It was Jay who defined the plan. We need to see it through. She knows what she is doing.'

'Look,' said Matchstick, nodding towards the hill fort in the distance at Highdown. Streams of white light shot up from the crest of the hill and into the sky like searchlights. 'And there,' he motioned to the other hill fort at Cissbury, where a similar array of lights pierced the tops of the trees and shot up into the sky.

'Stay connected!' Colson shouted as both Ben and Matchstick loosened their grip. 'It's time. Focus!'

The lights in the distance continued to ascend high into the atmosphere, joining above their heads. The ground at Chanctonbury shook. Ben's head vibrated like he was in a dentist's chair. His vision blurred and a shard of light shot through the ground from between the three men. Colson audibly squealed with delight. 'This is totally awesome!'

More lights shot up out of the ground and they looked up into the trees just in time to see the Chanctonbury energy connect with that from Highdown and Cissbury.

* * *

ATTA DROPPED his force of power and came nearer to Jay. He pushed her back against the railings and drew his hand up to her throat, still holding the source stone in his other hand, hugging it to himself. Jay sensed he sought a connection with the Given energy as much as he needed to retain the dark power.

'It doesn't matter to me whether you embrace both elements of the power, or if you die right here. Either way, the outcome is the same.' Atta pushed Jay so that she leaned back over the railing. She glanced down into the hole. She could see the intermittent flashing of the rotating electromagnets and feel the pulsing energy. This was as close as Jay had got to the source of the darkness. The strength of power was clear. It felt different to the Given energy. It had an edge to it, a promise of something transformative.

* * *

STITCH HAD NOWHERE TO GO. All he knew was that he needed to be away from Cassie before she wound him up any tighter. The energy from the hill forts had not come. And there was no contact from any of them. Cassie seemed to think this was Stitch's fault, despite him being the only one of them not to have an actual number on his wrist. The level C had proven useless.

'Hey,' Cassie called, waving him back. He turned, relenting slowly. He took a step and then stopped when Cassie followed up with, 'Don't be such a diva,' at the top of her voice. Stitch turned away from her and walked towards the river.

At the top of the steps down to the riverside, the pavement was suddenly illuminated as if a flare had gone up overhead. He looked skyward, and his jaw dropped.

Streams of light from three locations in the hills thrust into the sky to combine at a point high above them. The white light burned through the low-lying clouds, forcing out all darkness. Stitch continued to stare as Cassie came crashing into him, out of breath. 'This is it. Let's go!'

Stitch followed Cassie to the wooden jetty above the surface of the river. At the end was a circular viewing platform ten feet in diameter, where they stopped and turned to look at the growing ball of white light in the sky. 'They've done it,' said Stitch under his breath. 'All of them. They've done it.'

'Come on,' said Cassie, taking Stitch's hand, then looking up into the sky. 'That's Highdown,' she said, pointing to what looked like the strongest stream of light. 'That's Otis,' she said with pride.

'And Pinto,' said Stitch. He looked to the two streams further north and thought of Sammy and Toyah, and of Jay's dad with Colson and Matchstick.

'Come on!' Cassie repeated, taking Stitch's other hand and dragging his gaze from the sky. 'Concentrate.'

Stitch heard Cassie's words, but he needed to clear his mind and trust in his intuition. Cassie managed the power differently to Stitch, and he'd never been able to figure her out. For Stitch, the power has never been controlled through strength of mind. For him, it is a flow of energy through the body. It takes its course from the essence of the person through which it flows. All he had to do was to be open to it...

Cassie screamed. Stitch knew it was a scream of effort and concentration as the energy from the ocean and the river grew around them. He felt light on his feet, buoyant, as if the level of the river had risen to take them higher. Then it came. The light from the joining of the power of the hill forts shot through the sky and enveloped Cassie and Stitch. The end of the pier lit up like a firework, light scattering over the surface of the river.

Cassie shone in the power of the Given and Stitch opened up like a conduit to her energy. Together, they channelled the flow of energy towards Jay. Light flowed down from Cassie and Stitch like dry ice in a nightclub, flowing over the wooden boards of the pier and down to the surface of the river, where it slowly enveloped everything in its path.

Stitch opened his eyes and saw that the streams of light remained strong, but along the road a crowd gathered. 'Readers,' he said to himself. Then louder, 'Readers!' he shouted to Cassie.

Cassie's eyes snapped open, and she followed Stitch's gaze to see the gathering of Readers, some looking up to the power in the sky, attempting to disrupt it, others making their way towards the pier. 'Keep it flowing,' said Cassie. 'We need to keep the power flowing to Jay for as long as possible.'

'We can relocate,' said Stitch, shouting above the noise generated by the flow of energy.

'No time,' said Cassie.

Stitch looked across at the advancing group of Readers. There must have been over twenty of them filing up the wooden jetty towards them. They had no escape route now, even if they had decided to run.

'Hold it...' Cassie said.

Stitch looked beyond the advancing Readers to see more arriving. They teemed through the side streets, congregating along the river wall. 'We need to relocate,' Stitch said again.

Cassie looked towards the Readers, now just a few feet away and tentatively edging closer, looking a little unsure of how to breach the white light of their power. 'OK,' Cassie said.

Cassie and Stitch broke their connection and opened out their arms. The white light bowled through the Readers, knocking them to the floor, allowing a route along the pier for Cassie and Stitch to escape. As they reached solid ground, the Readers gathered themselves. More Readers appeared from the side streets.

Before they could carve a route to get clear, the Readers closed in around them, their exits cut off. Stitch felt attacks coming in, but he deflected. It wouldn't be long before they'd get it together to attack with multiple Readers at the same time. There would be no chance they could resist a collective attack. A thought flashed before his eyes, and Stitch hoped that there were no Readers attacking the hill forts.

Cassie nodded at the moped behind Stitch, a Honda C50 with an ignition barrel that was even weaker than the one in Jay's car. He could probably turn it with his fingernail. He reached into his back pocket for his swiss army knife, holding it behind him as he opened one of the blades.

'I'll shield,' Cassie whispered, and immediately stood in front of Stitch.

He felt the attacks intensify, but he was quick. He pushed

the bike off its stand and rammed the blade into the ignition, turning it with no resistance. The lights on the round display on the front of the bike lit up, and he flicked the kick-start into position, then thrust his foot down to the warm sound of the engine kicking in first time.

Cassie made a final push of Given energy at the advancing Readers and jumped onto the back of the bike as Stitch picked up speed. Readers reached for her, one of them getting a hold on her top but releasing when Cassie's foot connected with his jaw. She punched and kicked at any Reader who came within range. She almost lost her balance more than once as Stitch twisted and turned the bike through the parting crowd.

Just as Stitch thought they were clear, a stocky Reader got a hold on the handlebars. The bike spun around precariously on the promenade that formed the river wall, then burst through the railing protecting pedestrians from the twenty-foot drop to the shore of the river. Cassie flew off the back of the bike and slid to the edge, toppling but hanging on to the wall, her legs dangling over the shore of the river. The moped slipped from beneath Stitch and slid towards Cassie, narrowly missing her as it toppled over the wall, catching on the railings to stop it from landing in the river. The Reader who had grabbed the handlebars went over the wall and into the water. Stitch held tight to the bike, his hands gripping the handle-bars as he slipped over the edge. The only thing stopping him following the Reader into the water was his vice-like grip on the bike.

He swung with the bike, its front wheel slipping from where it had caught on the railing. One more slip and both Stitch and the bike would end up in the river.

'There!' shouted Cassie, hanging from the river wall and motioning Stitch towards the six foot round opening in the wall. The groundwater outfall that they'd used as a route in to the prison before. Stitch didn't need a second prompt. He swung his legs and got enough movement to catch his feet on the invert of the outfall and slide inside.

'The bike,' Stitch shouted at Cassie, a plan materialising in his head. He grabbed the back wheel of the bike, dangling in front of him. Cassie read his plan and, after a moment of hesitation and a look of incredulity, she edged herself along the wall to where the bike hung snagged on the railing.

Readers appeared at the top of the wall above Cassie. Stitch warned her, but it was too late. A Reader snatched at Cassie, taking her by the arm of her top and pulling her. Another joined him and they both dragged her back towards the top of the wall. Cassie shrieked. Stitch attacked the closest Reader with his powers the best he could, but in the end it was a flying punch from Cassie that wrenched her free of the Readers' grasp.

As Cassie fell, Stitch reached out for her, but it was the bike she got a hold on. She clasped the back wheel and swung into the outfall. Stitch grabbed her and pulled her towards him, but her top was attached to the bike. The force of her fall had dislodged the moped from the top of the wall. Time seemed to slow as Cassie and Stitch realised the bike was free of the wall at the top and that Cassie was still attached to the other end of it.

They braced themselves. Stitch held on to Cassie and with his other hand grabbed a metal step-iron before the bike jolted to a stop, hanging from Cassie - half in the hole and half teetering over the river. Cassie screamed.

'Pull it in,' Stitch shouted as Cassie gathered herself. Together they pulled the bike into the outfall, offloading the weight from Cassie's arm and they both collapsed back on to the floor. It was only then that Stitch realised that the engine of the moped was still turning over- idling, as if nothing had happened.

The sound of Readers from above spurred Cassie and Stitch into action. Stitch pulled the moped upright and revved its engine. The noise echoed through the tunnel. Cassie registered Stitch's plan and jumped on the back of the bike. They sped away into the tunnel, through the earth towards the prison.

* * *

AN IMAGE of Angie came into Jay's mind, and almost immediately, she felt an almighty eruption of Given energy, a powerful enough burst for Atta to release his grip from her throat and reel backwards. The cavern filled with white light. They had done it. Her sense of relief and euphoria exploded to the surface as the energy filled every cell in her body. Now she had the advantage.

Atta stared around the cavern in disbelief. 'I don't understand.'

Jay waited no longer. She drew in the entire power of the Given and attacked. She pushed into Atta's mind and immediately felt his pain. He stumbled for a moment, then straightened, and for a second Jay thought that her attack was being deflected. She opened further to the energy, allowing it to flow through her. It was so intense, the pressure almost hurt. The darkness ignited within her when she opened the channel had already dissipated. There was nothing flowing through Jay but the power of the Given.

Atta recovered once more, the attack appearing to affect him in waves, between which he took the time to shield and regain his strength. But the light continued to stream into the cavern from above, bleaching the walls. Atta weakened. He put a hand to his head and leaned heavily on the railing. He dropped the source stone at his feet and Jay prepared herself for a final push.

Then it stopped.

The light faded and, once again, the cavern was illuminated only by a few electric lamps slung from the walls. Jay looked hopefully into the roof of the cavern and up towards the higher levels. Nothing but darkness. Fear permeated her mind.

Jay made a move for the source stone, but Atta had already righted himself. With a grimace, he straightened and raised a hand, throwing Jay back against the railings like she was nothing. She slipped to the floor. Through half-closed eyes, she saw Atta reach down and take the source stone once more.

* * *

CASSIE AND STITCH entered the main building unopposed. Jay's presence radiated from below them. 'Do it here,' Stitch said to Cassie.

'We're inside the zone, the mile that Jay talked about.'

Stitch shrugged. 'What choice do we have?'

'Can we really do it here? No river carrying the energy of the ocean?'

'We're close enough,' Stitch said, then turned to climb the steps back to the outside. He looked into the sky. The white ball of light hung like an alien craft above the hills and he thought of the others, their resolve in keeping the flow of energy. Of Angie, who he felt was keeping the communication between the groups, keeping them going. He turned to Cassie and took both of her hands in his, then looked up at the sky once more.

* * *

As Jay crumpled under the resurgent power of Atta, Readers came to his aid, flowing down the steps like ants around a discarded piece of fruit.

In her weakened state, she couldn't determine if the picture of Angie in her mind was simply wishful thinking. Angie spoke to her. She said that Stitch was close.

'No,' said Jay. 'Not here. Tell him to leave. It's too dangerous.'

Angie spoke again, this time her little voice clear and defined, 'Throw it in.'

'I can't' Jay whispered aloud, under her breath.

Angie's voice: 'Stitch is coming. He will free you. Throw it in.'

Jay slipped further to the floor, the metal grate of the platform cold against her cheek. Her vision blurred. She could just make out the outline of the source stone smothered in Atta's grasp.

There seemed to be no sound but for her own breathing.

White light exploded into the cavern once more, this time with such a force that it knocked the gathering Readers to the floor. Atta stood, looking up into the shaft, the light blinding him. The energy flowed through Jay once more and she staggered to her feet just as Atta recoiled from the light, shrinking into the wall.

'Throw it in' Angie's voice came.

Then an echo in Stitch's voice, 'Throw it in.'

She threw herself at Atta, pushing him back against the wall. He held tight to the source stone, his smile at last dissolved from his face. The light streamed from above. Readers shrivelled, some appearing to melt into the walls of the cavern with the power of the energy from above.

Atta continued to resist. Jay combined an attack with her Given power with a physical onslaught. She kicked, punched, and pushed him.

He fought back, his elbow catching Jay and momentarily knocking her off balance.

She released him from her physical grip and used her powers once more, opening her heart to the full power of the Given energy.

He reeled from her, stumbling.

She ran at him again, head down, catching him in a kind of rugby tackle. She kicked out, flung her head up, catching him on the chin. Then she stood and punched him, landing a blow to his chin.

He weakened, dropping to one knee but still refusing to release the source stone. She made a grab for it, grappling with Atta like they were challenging for possession of a football. They spun around on the platform. Jay had a firm grip on the source stone, but Atta refused to release. His power was weak, but his body remained locked around the stone.

With a cry of effort, Jay spun Atta around and to the edge of the gaping hole. He looked her in the eye, and for the first time, Jay saw his fear. She made a final push.

Jay and Atta's hands remained firmly locked around the source stone, as Jay launched them both over the edge - diving, falling, deep into the core.

39

I've got one of those feelings, like your brain can't quite click into gear and you don't really know where you are. Well, you know, but you can't quite recall why, or how. Then you just kind of hope something will tick over, a cog will slip into place, and it will all become clear. And it always does. But it hasn't yet.

No pain.

Nothing to see. Only light.

Orange light. Not white, not dark, orange. Smells too. Like the smell you get when you light a match.

Matchstick.

Dad's friend.

The cog is turning.

I did it. I think? I pulled the stone into the core. I took it there.

Now I remember.

Atta was with me, but I don't feel him. He's gone. The energy here is thick, like soup.

Throw it in.

The energy is transparent, clear as day. I can see through to both sides. If I look down, I can see the power of the Given, a phys-

ical entity. And above me is the power of the Dark. Both spheres with solid cores and fluid edges.

I am in the middle. A part of both. In the orange treacle which forms the space between the energy of the Given and of the Dark.

Sasha Maram Colden. My grandmother.

Maram. Atta. Maramatta. Attamaram.

* * *

JAY WOKE on the shore of a lake. Before opening her eyes, she heard the gentle trickle of water from the rocks, and could smell minerals in the air. She knew she was at the Interland.

I'm alive, she thought, opening her eyes to bright sunshine and a cloudless blue sky. She sat up, inspecting her hands as if to check that they were real, and that she had a physical presence. *Cassie and Stitch*, she thought, looking around the perimeter of the Interland lake.

A noise drew her attention. She turned to see Cassie walking towards her over the stones, like a vision obscured by the brightness of the sunshine. She dragged herself to her feet to accept her embrace. 'Thank God,' said Cassie.

Jay looked her friend in the eye, and she knew that Cassie and Stitch had been within the blast zone at the prison. 'You came into the zone?'

'We had no choice.'

Jay smiled. 'Thanks.' She looked over Cassie's shoulder. 'Where's Stitch?'

Cassie shrugged. 'I can feel his annoying presence. He's here somewhere.' She smiled.

Jay turned to see Stitch emerging from the shallows on the other side of the lake. He must have re-materialised in the lake. Water poured from his sodden clothes. Cassie laughed.

They watched as Stitch looked into the sky, then over to where they stood. He headed towards them.

Cassie looked up into the sky. 'Did you see it? The power?' Jay shook her head. She knew what Cassie was talking about, and could see in Cassie's thoughts what she'd seen. 'It was something else. Everyone did their bit. I've never felt anything like it.'

Stitch trudged over the stones towards them. Cassie laughed and Jay couldn't help but smile. Stitch didn't yet see the funny side. 'What happened?' he said.

'What do you remember?' Jay asked, directing her question to both Stitch and Cassie.

Cassie motioned to a space they could sit down. Jay and Stitch followed. 'We were channelling the power when everything went white, like before,' said Cassie. 'Except this time there were no Islands, nothing. Just *white*.'

Jay and Stitch sat down as Cassie collected an armful of wood and built a fire.

'Me too,' said Stitch. 'It was weird. But it wasn't scary. I kind of knew it was OK.'

'And me,' said Jay. 'But my colour was orange.'

'Orange?' said Stitch.

Jay nodded.

'What does that mean?' said Stitch.

'No idea,' said Jay.

Cassie finished building the fire and turned to the others with a smile. 'Anyone bring any matches through the inter-dimension?'

Stitch and Jay laughed, and Jay shuffled closer to the fire. 'Watch,' she said, rubbing her hands together and then presenting them to the fire. She did not know how she could generate the heat in her hands, like Matchstick could do. But somehow she knew. Her hands glowed orange, and sparks emanated, sprinkling through the dry wood and catching the kindling.

'Who needs Matchstick?' said Cassie as Stitch stared open-mouthed.

'Since when?' asked Stitch.

'Since I swam in the orange soup,' said Jay.

* * *

THEY RESTED BY THE FIRE. It grew dark. It was as if they each needed to process what had happened in their own time and in their own way. They talked about the work that the others must have achieved at each of the hill forts. And they talked about Atta.

'Is he gone for good?' asked Cassie.

Jay shook her head. 'He's gone from here. The connection with the core has been destroyed. That's not coming back.'

'So we are like Island 4?' asked Stitch.

'If what Judith and Hannah said is right, then yes. We are free. But Atta remains free to trample wherever he likes in the other six Islands.'

A look of relief came over Stitch's face. They, at least, were free from the darkness. Jay thought of Tiago on Island 7. With Atta banished from their own homeland, Tiago would be in greater danger than before. The focus of the Readers would be on spreading through the dark lands, taking more for their own purposes. It would surely be a matter of time before they got to Tiago and his family.

Cassie seemed to read Jay. She nudged at her foot with her own. 'One step at a time,' she said, and leaned back on the stones.

Jay looked at her two friends. Their colours came to her. They were tired, worn down by the past few days of battle. She also saw the light inside them, and the glow of energy that drove them. She felt warmth for them both, and a deep sense of peace.

40

Jay drifted down the steps to the basement as if she were walking on air.

Since they'd returned from the Interland, something had changed. Her energy levels were higher than she'd ever experienced. She could see deeper into the power, into people, and into the energy - its nature, and its fundamental essence.

In the basement, Buster ran to Jay, with little Benji scampering after him. Colson and Hannah lit candles. Judith placed them around the room so that the place resembled a church mass. They'd agreed to meet to talk about what was to happen next, and to remember those who fell in the *Event,* the day at the prison when the earth quaked. Some of them insisted it was an earthquake, much like the one in 1667, but others were not so sure. The aftermath, Colson said, resembled the aftermath of a nuclear event more than an earthquake, and anyway, how could an earthquake be so localised?

Whatever they wanted to call it, to make sense of it, Jay knew the Event was neither an earthquake nor a nuclear event. It was the head-on collision between the peak of the powers of Dark and Given. It resulted in everything within two miles being razed to the ground.

Angie ran to Jay, wrapping her arms around her. They'd spent much of their time together in the two days since Jay returned with Cassie and Stitch from the Interland.

Ben and Colson busied themselves ferrying plates of food from the hatch in the wall, then sending the mechanical lift back up for more. Otis sat with Pinto and Toyah at one end of the table. Pinto practised his power by passing objects to his sister and to Otis with his telekinesis. Jay waved at him across the room, and he grinned with pride.

'Before we start,' said Judith. 'Can we take a moment to remember?'

Jay took a seat with the others, electing to sit between Stitch and her brother Sammy. Judith continued, 'Jay, would you like to say a few words?'

Jay straightened in her seat. A hush came over the room. 'Two people who you guys never had the chance to meet. Ravi and Jess. I knew them for less than an hour, and in that time they gave their lives to enable my access to the core. They were Given. Their drive was for the greater good. They will have a place in the history of the fight for the cause.' She paused a moment. 'Alf, of course,' she said, her eyes dropping to the floor as she focused on keeping it together. 'I feel a sense of responsibility for Alf.'

'Hey...' started Stitch, but Jay held up a hand for him to let her finish.

'I know he wouldn't want me to blame myself. But the fact will always remain that I facilitated Atta's attack on him. And that was Atta's plan. Alf was the glue that connected all of us. He was the common factor. He affected every person in this room in a way that advanced our cause. He is an enormous loss to the Given. And an even bigger loss to me personally. So,

Alfred Harvey, I'm sorry, and I thank you on behalf of all the Given for what you've achieved. And, I vow to re-build what you created, and what we lost in the fire.'

Colson wiped a tear away and cleared his throat. 'Hear hear,' he said, raising his glass. 'A great man, and a friend.' Buster ambled over to Colson and sat at his feet.

They all drank a toast to Alf, and the silence felt heavy on Jay's shoulders.

'Who else would like to say something?' asked Judith, breaking the spell.

Cassie cleared her throat. 'I want to remember Reuben and my grandad. They've both been gone for a long time now, but it still feels like yesterday. Reuben was taken by Readers. He was my mentor as a Runner. And he was my friend. I will remember him. My grandad was my idol. He knew the powers, and he made sure I connected when we were at the Interland. I miss him.'

'And Davey,' said Otis. 'He gave his life for mine.'

Sammy shifted in his seat next to Jay. 'And Marcus,' he said, looking over at Ben.

Ben returned Sammy's gaze and gave him a reassuring nod. 'Marcus was Sammy's biological father,' Ben said. 'And he was a Reader. But in the end, he fought for our cause. We will remember him.' He caught Sammy's eye and Sammy thanked him.

'We also remember those who died in the final battle,' said Stitch. Northtown had largely escaped the effects of the *Event*, but there were casualties inside the facility. Mostly, it was the public who had volunteered for transformation to readers. They were in the open holding cells when the Event reached its peak, and all were lost, some two or three hundred people Jay estimated, along with an unknown number of Readers.

'Thank you,' said Judith. 'Now we pray for a period of peace. Let's eat.'

* * *

AFTER THEY'D EATEN, and the conversations drifted into analysis of the Event, and the fate of the Readers, Jay slipped away and up onto the roof terrace at the back of the pub where she could be alone.

It was late in the afternoon and the sun had already dipped on the horizon, a cool breeze coming off the sea. She looked up to the hills. They seemed unfamiliar to her now, looking from the roof of the pub, a different perspective perhaps than that from the house. She wasn't sure. Whatever it was, it intrigued her. The effects of the Event had been more than simply the physical destruction of the connection with the core. The collision between Dark and Given, with Jay in the middle of it, had affected her connection with the power in ways she was only beginning to understand.

Stitch appeared at the top of the steps to the roof terrace. He had two pints of Guinness in his hands, spilling the white froth of the head over his knuckles. Jay took one and thanked him. 'Haven't had one of these for a while,' she said.

'Thought as much.'

They were silent for a minute as they drank and looked out over to the hills in the distance.

Stitch spoke first: 'Talk to me,' he said.

Jay turned to him. 'What about?'

'What's on your mind? You've been ruminating since we got back.'

'What do you expect after...'

'Something more,' Stitch interrupted. 'This is me you're talking to. You think I can't read you?'

'Sorry,' Jay said, turning back to look at the horizon. 'There is something. I just don't know what it is yet. Not sure I can find the words.'

'Give it a try,' said Stitch.

Jay took a deep breath and let out a sigh. 'There's something deeper in my power.'

'How do you mean?'

'It's as if I connected deeper into the source. That *Event*, whatever happened, opened me up to greater strength of power.'

'You mean you can do more? Like when you created fire up at the Interland?'

Jay nodded. 'But more than that. The fire was just a simple concentration of the energy. I'm not sure, but I might have been able to do that before. This is more than that, and it comes from different places.' She looked Stitch in the eye to see if he understood what she was saying, what she felt.

He returned her gaze. 'Different places?' Jay nodded. 'Like more than one source?' Jay nodded again. Stitch turned away to think for a moment, then said, 'Do you mean more than one Given source, like one from here and one from Island 7 or something?' Jay shook her head. 'Oh. You mean the Dark,' Stitch concluded.

'I can't be sure about anything. But it's as if the collision of those forces created some kind of combination power inside me.'

'You connected with the Dark before, up on the rooftop of the house. I was there.'

'This is different. This is inside of me.'

Stitch let out a frustrated sigh. 'What does it mean?'

'Search me,' said Jay. 'Maybe I'm turning into some super-Given or something,' she said with a smile.

Stitch laughed.

41

———

Within two short weeks of the *Event*, Jay and her dad had persuaded the pub landlord to allow them to transform the basement into a new centre of literature for the Given, and had begun to fit it out. Ben rediscovered his love of carpentry and had shelved most of the basement walls, as well as fitting out a storage room which used to be a wine cellar.

Jay and Angie worked tirelessly to re-catalogue the remaining works that had survived the fire in the bookshop and were already a good way through re-shelving them. With new lighting and other fittings, the basement had turned from dingy meeting place to an open-plan library-come-bookshop. One thing that remained untouched was the little mechanical lift in the hatch that led to the bar upstairs. Above the hatch were two pictures: the Sasha Coldon portrait that once hung in the main cavern in the Interland, and a picture of Alf that Jay had framed.

Jay and her dad were on their own since Angie's parents had persuaded her to take a day off from the basement. Although it was only the first week of Angie's summer holidays, her dad wasn't keen for her to spend its entirety underground. Jay could think of little she'd rather do than avoid human contact and surround herself with books.

The bell rang, telling Jay that someone was coming through the door from the pub. She turned to look and saw Toyah step down onto the basement floor. Buster ran to her.

'Wow,' she said, stroking Buster. 'You really have transformed this place.'

'In memory of Alf.' Jay nodded towards Alf's picture on the wall.

'He'd be proud. Seriously. He'd be staggered at how you've done this.'

'Much thanks to that man over there.' Jay motioned towards her dad, hammering away at the shelves in the corner.

'What's up?' asked Jay.

Toyah nodded to the table in the middle of the room, the only piece of furniture Jay had insisted on retaining - somewhere for people to sit and read. Somewhere people could simply *be*. They sat, and Toyah took a moment to gather her thoughts. 'I've decided,' she said.

Jay smiled. 'Go on.'

'I'm leaving.'

'Wha...' Jay started.

'It's OK. I'm going to college,' she smiled. 'I've talked to Pinto, and he's good with it. And you're here for him?'

'Of course,' said Jay, thinking how much she'd miss Toyah. 'He's like a brother to me too, you know. Have you spoken to Sammy about it?'

Toyah nodded. 'Wasn't easy, but he understands. We'll be in touch.'

'What are you studying?'

'You'll laugh.'

'Hey,' said Jay. 'Come on.'

'Combined honours degree. Physics, with a focus on earth physics, and Powers.' She smiled. 'You'll be a visiting lecturer on the Powers.'

Jay laughed, and Toyah gave her a friendly shove. 'You said you wouldn't laugh.'

'Sorry,' said Jay, continuing to laugh. 'I'm just pleased for you. I'm happy. This is the best news. You need to do something for you. Pinto will be fine. He's strong. He has a good home, and he has us.'

'Thanks, Jay. Thanks for everything.'

* * *

AT THE GATE to Pinto's school, Jay stood under the cover of the trees, the rain easing now, and most of what was landing on Jay's head came from the accumulation on the leaves. She stepped out into the sun, watching as the kids filed out towards the front gate on their last day of the summer term. Their spirits were high.

She saw Pinto. He walked with a girl next to him and they laughed together. Jay remembered the little girl with power, the only other person in Pinto's year with any level of Given power developing. Jay smiled, watching them together, their genuine laughter.

As they moved up the main pathway to the exit, Jay watched as the girl elbowed Pinto and motioned towards a group of boys sitting on the grass under a tree on the front lawn of the school. Pinto responded by shaking his head and linking his arm with the girl to persuade her away.

She wouldn't be diverted. She dragged her arm away from Pinto and moved under the cover of the trees, where she could observe the boys from a distance. Jay laughed aloud as she tried to guess what the girl was planning. Pinto joined her, dragging his feet.

There were four of them under the tree, older than Pinto. Jay guessed they were likely nearer sixteen years old. One of the boys was rolling a cigarette, or something more illicit, a last-day-of-school rebellion, rolling a joint on the front lawn. Two of the other boys smoked cigarettes as they waited for the joint. Jay looked back at Pinto and his friend, debating her plan in the shadows.

Pinto seemed to agree with something and they both turned to face the group sat on the floor. Jay saw it then. The sprinkler system spread through the grass area of the lawn. It was attached to a valve and standpipe near to where the boys sat. Jay watched the valve handle as it slowly turned under the power of Pinto and his friend. She laughed as the water emerged at pressure from the sprinklers, soaking the four boys. They sprang up, their drug paraphernalia scattering as they ran from the full force of the spray.

Pinto and the girl doubled over with laughter as they made their escape. Pinto turned to see one of the boys running back in to the middle of the spray to salvage his weed. Jay decided she'd add to the game and manipulated the boy's balance so that he slipped onto his back, sliding through the water as Pinto and his friend looked on, doubling over once more.

Jay dissolved away from the school, satisfied that Pinto had it covered.

* * *

BACK AT THE BASEMENT, Jay and Angie shelved the last pile of books received from the London branch. Judith and Hannah had sent through their stock which they hadn't room to display, as well as the stock that would sit better alongside the material that Jay and Alf had retrieved from the Interland, and that which had survived the fire.

Jay looked around the basement. The new sign that Ben had made identified the shop as *Alf's Books*. She was surprised at how much of the wall space was covered by the salvaged material. There was a wealth of information for them to build upon. 'We'll get there, Alf,' she said. 'Thanks to you, we will get there.'

Stitch came up from the lower, connected store room and brushed some dust and cobwebs out of his hair. Jay laughed at him, his hapless, awkward demeanour. 'What?' he said as he approached. 'It's full of spiders in there.'

'There's a duster out the back.'

'Maybe later,' he smiled. 'Anyway, are you done?'

'Almost. Angie's on the last pile of books.' She nodded to where Angie was sitting cross-legged on the floor, brushing the dust from the covers of the books before placing them on the shelves.

'So I'll see you tonight?' Stitch asked.

'A date?'

Stitch stammered and looked away. 'Yeah... I mean, all of us. Cassie too, if you like. We can just hang.'

'I'm kidding,' Jay said, enjoying winding up Stitch. They'd grown close again over the time since the *Event*. It was like before - before they even understood the power. It was fresh, and Jay felt something more developing. She was still petrified of losing what they had, the friendship and the bonds they'd established as best friends for years. But there was something coming that she felt powerless to stop.

'Great. Nice,' said Stitch, turning to head for the steps up to the pub.

'Hey,' Jay said, taking his arm and pulling him back to her. She hugged him, and he froze a moment before relaxing into it and holding her tight. She took his face in her hands as she'd done in the car. His blue eyes sparkled in the lights in the basement.

Angie called from across the room, 'Jay!'

'I'll see you later,' Jay said to Stitch.

'You bet,' he said with a smile, turning to leave.

'What's up, little one?' Jay said as she got to where Angie was about to place the last book on the shelf, with Buster curled up on the floor a few feet away.

'Last one.' Angie held up a hardback book, brushing her hand over the faded-blue front cover with a picture of the human body, lines of white light swirling around the head. 'The Physiology of Power,' Angie read, then placed the book on the bottom shelf. 'Done.'

Jay smiled. 'I have one last book I need you to find a home,' she said, turning and heading back to her desk in the corner. Angie followed, watching as Jay rifled through the drawer of her desk.

She pulled out the Sasha Colden biography and handed it to Angie.

Angie looked from the book to Jay and back again. 'I can't... this is yours.' She held the book like it was made of gold, cradling it.

'I think you're ready,' Jay said. 'And you need to get reading if you're going to help me with Island 7.'

Angie looked at Jay, and her eyes sparkled. She turned her attention back to the book and carefully flipped open the front cover.

End of Book #3

THANK YOU!

I hope you enjoyed the first three books in the Interland series. If you can spare a minute to leave a short review or just a rating on your preferred store, then I'd be very grateful - Thanks!

If you've not joined my Reader Club, where you can keep up to date on forthcoming publications, news and freebies to go with the INTERLAND series - including a free eBook prequel called *The Reader*, an insight to the background of the Readers - then please join by visiting my website - www. garyclarkauthor.co.uk

ABOUT THE AUTHOR

Gary graduated from the University of Surrey in the UK with a degree in Engineering, embarking on a career that has taken him all over the world from the Far East to the Americas. He is a graduate of the Faber Academy and Curtis Brown creative writing programmes. Now a father of three, he has settled with his family close to where he grew up on the edge of the South Downs in Sussex, where he indulges his love of books, and passion for writing.

I'd love to hear from you so feel free to contact me on the email address here - let me know what you thought of the books.

Author email: gary@garyclarkauthor.co.uk

Or visit my website: www.garyclarkauthor.co.uk